D0712141

Page
bottoms.
⑩ 108854

THE POISONER'S RING

THE POISONER'S RING

A Rip Through Time Novel

KELLEY ARMSTRONG

MINOTAUR BOOKS
NEW YORK

First published in the United States by Minotaur Books, an imprint of St. Martin's Publishing Group

THE POISONER'S RING. Copyright © 2023 by KLA Fricke Inc. All rights reserved. Printed in the United States of America. For information, address St. Martin's Publishing Group, 120 Broadway, New York, NY 10271.

www.minotaurbooks.com

Library of Congress Cataloging-in-Publication Data

Names: Armstrong, Kelley, author.
Title: The poisoner's ring / Kelley Armstrong.
Description: First edition. | New York: Minotaur Books, 2023. | Series:
    A rip through time novel; [2]
Identifiers: LCCN 2022057564 | ISBN 9781250820037 (hardcover) |
    ISBN 9781250907325 (Canadian edition) | ISBN 9781250820044 (ebook)
Subjects: LCGFT: Detective and mystery fiction. | Novels.
Classification: LCC PR9199.4.A8777 P65 2023 | DDC 813/.6—dc23/eng/20221212
LC record available at https://lccn.loc.gov/2022057564

Our books may be purchased in bulk for promotional, educational, or business use. Please contact your local bookseller or the Macmillan Corporate and Premium Sales Department at 1-800-221-7945, extension 5442, or by email at MacmillanSpecialMarkets@macmillan.com.

First Minotaur Books Edition: 2023
First International Edition: 2023

10   9   8   7   6   5   4   3   2   1

For Jeff

THE
POISONER'S
RING

ONE

There are many skills I hoped to master in my professional career. Scrubbing chamber pots was not one of them, and yet here we are. Oh, I don't *need* to scrub chamber pots anymore, in recognition of the fact that I'm not a nineteen-year-old Victorian housemaid but a thirty-year-old modern-day Canadian police detective. A detective who found herself, through some inexplicable whim of the universe, stuck—temporarily, I hope—in that maid's body.

Having learned and accepted the truth, my employers have made it clear I don't need to scrub chamber pots or scour coal grates or even polish silver. I still do, at least when I don't have the excuse of being busy acting as an assistant to my undertaker/forensic-scientist boss, Dr. Duncan Gray. Believe me, I am much happier studying wound patterns. But I'm in the body of his maid, living in the house he shares with his older sister, and I'm damned well going to earn my keep. That means perfecting the art of scrubbing a toilet in a world that hasn't discovered the wonders of latex gloves.

"Mallory!" Gray's voice echoes as his boots clomp up the stairs.

Those boots had better be clean. We've had a talk about *some* people walking in from the horseshit-laden streets and expecting other people to clean the floors behind them.

"Mallory! Where the devil are you?"

Before I can answer, Gray rounds the doorway and stops short to glower at me. He's really good at glowering, and will I seem like a swooning Victorian maiden if I admit he looks really good doing it?

Duncan Gray is a year older than me. With wavy dark hair, piercing dark eyes, and strong features, he's about six feet tall, which puts him above most Victorian men, particularly the lower classes. Wide-shouldered with an athletic build, Gray is a far cry from the stereotypical undertaker. His brown skin also makes him, unfortunately, a far cry from most Victorians' idea of a physician with multiple degrees, an upper-class Scottish accent, and a town house in Edinburgh's New Town.

"I thought we agreed you did not need to do that," he says, lowering his voice so the other staff won't hear.

"It's Alice's half day. Who else is going to do it? You?"

To his credit, he pauses at that. Most Victorians would sputter at the idea, at least those wealthy enough to hire a servant, which in this world means anyone middle-class and above. This is what staff are for, and even when that staff person has a half day off, well, chamber pots aren't going to clean themselves, are they? Doing it yourself is a twenty-first-century concept, and when I suggest it, I see the wheels turning in Gray's mind.

"The next time Alice has her half day, I shall empty it when I rise in the morning," he says. "I am not certain it needs to be scrubbed daily, but I can at least empty it myself."

I push the pot back under his bed and rise. "Is there something you needed, Dr. Gray?"

He strides to the door and shuts it. I open my mouth to say that's not a good idea. I don't want Mrs. Wallace hearing the murmured voices of her boss and housemaid behind his closed bedroom door. Gray can be oblivious to such things. He intends nothing untoward, so surely no one would imagine anything untoward.

"Do you have any experience conducting police work in disguise?" he says.

"Pretending to be someone I'm not?" I wave my hands down my maid's dress.

"Yes, but can you do it *well*?"

"Hey!" I say, and there might be a squawk in my voice. "*You* bought the act."

"I am hardly the most perceptive audience."

True. Gray was the only member of the household who didn't question my performance. His maid suffered a head injury that transformed a scheming thief into an industrious young woman with a keen interest in his studies? Huh. Well, the brain is a mysterious thing, and since he was in need of an assistant, he saw no problem with Catriona's transformation.

"You want a Victorian housemaid?" I change my tone to a sweet voice and lower my gaze as I curtsy. "Please, sir, might I know what you had in mind for this police work? I do not think I can help, being only a simple girl, but pray permit me the opportunity to distinguish myself."

I straighten. "Better?"

"If you are playing a maid in a theater melodrama."

I roll my eyes. "Fine. What sort of undercover work are we talking?"

"You'd be visiting a public house with Hugh. It is in the Old Town, and not in one of its best districts. Hugh would be a workingman, and you would be his . . ." He clears his throat. "Companion for the evening."

"His doxy? Please tell me I get to play a doxy?" I hike up the hem of my skirt. "Why, hello, good gentleman. Note that I am exposing a very fine pair of ankles, which can be yours for the small price of a few shillings. Pox included at no additional charge."

Gray shakes his head.

"I'm joking," I say. "With Isla gone, I'm bored and a little giddy."

And it's been weeks since you had any non-maid work for me.

A month ago, Gray learned the truth about me . . . and discovered that I'd told his sister Isla first. I'd withheld it from him even after he tentatively cracked open the door for me as an investigative partner. I might have had good reason, but he still felt the sting of it.

There have been times over the last month where I've glimpsed the real Duncan Gray, passionate about his work, brimming with enthusiasm, relaxed and confident, and as quick with a teasing jab as I am. But those moments are rare, and then he seems to remember himself and shut that door. Not slam it. Just quietly close it and retreat into being my dignified and aloof employer.

"Okay," I say. "So I'm going to a pub with Detective McCreadie as part of an undercover assignment. Is this a new investigation? You haven't worked with him since the raven case."

He hesitates. When that hesitation stretches disappointment slams through me.

"Ah," I say. "You *have* worked cases together." *You just haven't brought me in.*

Gray rubs his mouth. "This one is still in the early stages. It is not entirely Hugh's investigation, and there are . . . complications."

"Complications?"

"Yes. You cannot tell Isla of tonight's adven—assignment. If you join us, I must be assured of your full discretion, particularly when it comes to my sister."

I stare at him. "You're kidding, right?"

He straightens. "Certainly not. Hugh agrees."

"Is Isla a suspect?"

He sputters before saying, "Hardly."

"Then you're putting me in the same position she put me in last month, when she asked me to keep a secret from you. We all saw how well *that* went over."

He pulls at his cravat. "It is not the same."

"No? Look, if it's a gory case, while Isla does have a weak stomach, you need to let her make those decisions herself. Otherwise, you are treating your older sister like a child. I know that's how things are done in this world, but I thought you and Detective McCreadie were better than that."

It's a low blow, one that strikes hard, Gray pulling back, his color rising even as his eyes harden.

"I would not do that," he says, enunciating each word. "I am keeping her out of this investigation because it touches on a delicate subject."

"Sex?"

More sputtering, and his color rises higher.

I lift my hand against his protest. "If it is sex, then *I'll* tell her about it. Otherwise, you really are putting me in a position I won't let myself get into again. Isla asked me to keep my secret for your own good. You didn't see it that way, did you? You saw it as a sign that your new assistant couldn't be trusted."

He glances away, leaving me with a hard profile. When he looks back, his jaw stays set, and he says nothing.

"What if I have a valid reason?" he says. "And if I am only keeping her out of it temporarily."

"Temporarily because she should eventually know? Or temporary because she's bound to find out?"

He doesn't answer.

"I will help you tonight because Isla is away," I say. "However, at the point where taking part in this investigation requires me lying to her, then you have to tell her."

He sighs. "How can I refuse when you are fair and reasonable? Go back to being silly. It is much harder to remain angry when you are in that mood."

"Ah, so you *have* been angry."

"Occupied, not angry. Come along then. I will explain the case on the way."

TWO

I need to change out of my work clothing. When I'd first arrived, I'd thought it was a uniform. I know now that this time period predates standard domestic staff uniforms, so what I wear is simply one of two outfits provided by Isla, which is not so much about appearances as having an excuse to provide us with working clothes rather than expect us to buy our own.

Changing in my time would have taken five minutes. Triple that here, and that's with leaving on my chemise, corset, corset cover, petticoats, stockings, and drawers. We're in the age of cage crinolines, but that doesn't apply to housemaids, and I prefer the layers of petticoats, mostly because it keeps me warm. June in Edinburgh is not exactly my idea of hot summer weather, especially when the wind is blowing, as it often is.

I don't mind the corset as much as I expected to, but it does take some getting used to, especially when I'm accustomed to bending easily. I keep it as loose as I can while still fitting into Catriona's dresses. Tonight, I put on my outdoor boots upstairs. Then I tighten the corset to fit my going-out dress, which is tricky without Alice's help. When I can barely breathe, it's ready for the petticoats.

Finally, I don Catriona's most fetching going-out dress: wine-colored wool satin, brushed to a shine. Even with the fancy—and obviously secondhand—dress, I'm not really dressed for the role of doxy. While Catriona wasn't shy, her middle-class Victorian upbringing kept her from highlighting her assets to an unseemly degree. Or perhaps it wasn't so much her upbringing as her own nature. Flashing her cleavage to distract a man was one thing, but she didn't want him thinking he might be able to buy a few hours—or even minutes—of her time.

Catriona doesn't have any makeup, and I'm not sure whether anyone in the household would. It's not like the modern world, where we're so accustomed to seeing women in makeup that if I go out bare-faced, people tell me how tired I look. Isla doesn't wear any. The other options would be Alice—the twelve-year-old parlormaid—and Mrs. Wallace. I know Alice won't have any, and I'm definitely not snooping around Mrs. Wallace's room.

I don gloves and tweak my dress to be a little more revealing—which mostly just means rearranging the already low neckline. Then I arrange Catriona's honey-blond hair with more dangling tendrils. Mostly, though, it's going to have to be the attitude that sells it.

Gray is already in the coach when I arrive. I stop to greet Simon, the stable hand and coach driver. It'd be more efficient to just wave as I climb in, but waving—as I have learned the hard way—is not a thing yet. So I walk around to the front for a quick hello before hoisting my ankle-length skirts and climbing into the seat across from Gray.

The coach is a business asset. It's not the hearse—I've seen that, which is a carriage enclosed with glass so people can see the corpse within. I'm kidding. It's so they can see the casket, which presumably contains a corpse. This coach serves as a conveyance for grieving relatives, which means it's entirely black, with no metal or other flourishes. Gray would say that using it as his private coach is pure practicality, but it also suits his style, simple and utilitarian.

Once inside, I arrange my skirts on the leather seats. Then I peer out the window as the coach rolls forward. The stable is located in the mews, which is the land behind the row of town houses. It's an interesting setup, similar to ones in big cities where the garages are along a road in back. I imagine that in the modern world these have been converted to houses, probably priced far above my income bracket.

It's late June, and a wonderfully warm evening, still nearly full light, from the northern latitude. It's nearly ten, but looks like a summer's mid-evening, with residents enjoying the gardens and strolling along the roads to visit friends.

Gray lives in the New Town, with its gorgeous town houses and wide roads and gardens in bloom. Oh, there's still shit in the streets, but you can be sure most of it is equine, if that's any consolation, and while the air reeks of coal smoke, it's not the thick blanket that stifles the Old Town.

The Old Town is where we're heading. For centuries, it was the whole of Edinburgh. As the capital of Scotland—with a castle once occupied by a king or queen—the city is a walled one. When the population grew, the wealthy did what they always do: abandon the increasingly crowded and filthy town center to the less fortunate.

In Edinburgh's case, that meant building outside the wall. Thus, the New Town was born. Oh, there are decent parts of the Old Town, where the working class and some middle class make their homes. But there are also tenements with a level of poverty beyond imagining.

As we head up the Mound into the Old Town, I glance at Gray. He's looking out the window, lost in thoughts spinning lightning fast. As much as I hate to interrupt, I know better than to presume he'll snap out of it on his own.

"You said you'd tell me about this case," I say.

It takes a moment for him to mentally transition. Then he nods and says, "There have been two recent poisoning deaths in the city."

"Right. I saw that in the papers." I pause. "Wait. *This* is the case you're not telling Isla about. Your *chemist* sister?"

"I said we are not bringing her in temporarily. We will, of course, as we may need her help. The problem for now is that it is a suspected poison ring."

"Poison ring?" My eyes widen. "Please tell me that's an actual thing. Fancy rings with little compartments of poison for killing off enemies and inconvenient lovers. Also, I want one." I pause. "A poison ring. Not an inconvenient lover."

Gray shakes his head. "There is no such thing."

"As a ring full of poison? Or an inconvenient lover?"

"There is a fashion for rings with a small compartment in which women are said to carry poison. In truth, the small compartments are used to hold pills, perfume, and even mementos. Yes, I am certain some women buy them purely for their air of mystique and whiff of scandal, but that is not the sort of ring I mean."

"Which is . . . ?" I say.

"A ring of women who murder their loved ones with the help of another woman, who provides them with poison."

"Like a book club, but instead of sharing books, they share poison." I waggle my brows. "And murder."

He sighs, but there's a note of indulgence in it. Now that he knows my story, he's becoming accustomed to my modern language and sense of humor.

"Fine," I say. "Murder is never a laughing matter. But given what I've seen of some Victorian husbands, I wouldn't blame their wives for stirring a little arsenic into their tea. The same would go for some Victorian fathers. Possibly even some Victorian brothers." I raise my hands. "Present company excepted. You understand my meaning, though. If women in this time are imprisoned, the ones holding the keys are often their male relations."

"I will not deny that. I would say that the situation is better in Scotland, but I understand that better is relative."

Coverture doesn't apply in Scotland—coverture being the common-law practice that says once a woman marries, control over everything from her money to her basic rights goes to her husband. A married couple is legally one person, and that person is her husband.

I continue, "So a poisoning ring theorizes that women who want to get rid of an inconvenient family member find another woman who'll sell them poison. Once they've offed their husband, another woman says 'Oh, you lucky duck,' and the killer provides the address of the poisoner."

"Correct."

I look out the carriage window, giving myself a moment to think. We're reaching the top of the Mound. Even this late, children scurry about on errands, desperate to make a few coins before the sun drops. I catch a glimpse of a girl in a doorway. She's no more than twelve, and when the carriage passes, she flips up her skirt, an invitation for the wealthy gentleman in such a fine coach.

Tenement buildings soar on both sides of the narrow road. Some reach ten stories, and the higher you go, the worse the living conditions. I've seen enough on lower floors not to be sure I can stomach going higher. What I've witnessed so far makes even me want to duck my head and pretend I don't see it.

I glance over to see Gray gazing out as well. *He* sees it. Even when he'd rather not, he sees it, and he feels it.

He points out the window. "Over there is where the first victim and his suspected killer—his wife—lived," Gray says. "On his death, she received a payment from the burial society."

I don't ask what a burial society is. I've learned a lot about the business of death, Victorian style. For Gray's father, undertaking was only the public face of his business. The real money came by investing in the auxiliary trades. As kirkyards filled, the need for private cemeteries rose, so he'd invested in those. As the cost of funerals increased—largely *because* of undertakers—grassroots organizations known as burial societies sprang up offering burial insurance, and Gray's father invested in those.

There's a good reason the poor are so eager to bury their loved ones: the Anatomy Act of 1832. Intended to stop the trade in cadavers, the act arose partly in response to the case of Hare and Burke, here in Edinburgh, where the two men not only sold corpses, but created them.

Until that point, British doctors could only study the cadavers of executed criminals. The act allowed the medical colleges to obtain cadavers in other ways. Most significantly, they could take unclaimed bodies.

Makes sense, right? Except that unclaimed bodies don't always belong to people without family. Mostly, they belong to people whose families can't afford burial fees, people who used to rely on the church to bury their loved ones. Now those corpses go to the colleges. Worse, it's commonly believed that if the body isn't intact, the soul won't be accepted into heaven. So by not being able to pay for burial, they doom their loved ones to purgatory.

Like so many regulations, the Anatomy Act was created to solve one problem and caused another, and as usual, it's the poor who get screwed.

The partial solution was burial societies, which allow people to pay into an insurance policy that will let them bury their loved ones.

"So the first victim's wife got a burial-society payout," I say. "What difference does that make?"

"She didn't use it."

"Didn't use—? Oh. You mean she allowed her husband's body to be taken to the medical college as a cadaver."

"Yes, and that might never have been discovered, if not for Hugh.

While he isn't in charge of the case—that would be Detective Crichton again—Hugh followed up on an informant's tip."

Detective Crichton is the senior officer who'd been in charge of our last case as well. I open my mouth to ask more, but the coach pulls to the side and Simon calls down. "Here, sir?"

Gray peers out to the darkening street beyond. "Unfortunately, yes. We must walk from here. I would have preferred to walk the entirety of the way, if someone had not delayed our departure with her ethical quandary."

"Ethical? You cannot mean our Catriona, sir." Simon's eyes twinkle as I peek out the window. Then his smile twists into a rueful one as he says, "I mean Mallory."

"Either is fine," I say, returning his smile.

I would have been okay with sticking with Catriona, for simplicity's sake. But Isla had understood that I was already uncomfortable in this world and using my own name would help.

As "Catriona," I had suffered a head injury that supposedly explains my personality change. It was only a short leap, then, to telling the staff that I wished to be called by another name, as I no longer *was* Catriona.

"Mallory is what you wish to be called, and so Mallory is what I will call you," Simon says. "And if you were delayed by an ethical concern, then you truly are not the Catriona I knew."

While he tries to smile, there's a sadness there. Catriona never met a person she couldn't bully or blackmail or betray, but if there was an exception, it was Simon. Or I hope it was. He was her friend, and she better have deserved it.

We alight from the coach. Yes, "alight" is a word I never had cause to use in the twenty-first century, but as the daughter of an English prof, I am in my element here, throwing out all the archaic words I learned in a lifetime of reading. Admittedly, sometimes my enthusiasm gets the better of me. When I first arrived, I decided that to sound like I came from this time period, I should use all my five-dollar words. That would have worked much better if I weren't in the body of a housemaid who at least *claimed* to be illiterate.

Gray sends Simon home with the coach. We'll walk back afterward. I must say that's another thing I love about this time period. Walking. Oh, sure, the roads aren't exactly clean, and the air is definitely not clean. But most every place we could want to go is within a mile or two, and that walk is through an elaborate Victorian-world theme park, filled with wonder.

This entire world is filled with wonder for me. That doesn't mean I want to stay. My parents are at home. My friends and career are there. And when I left, I'd been visiting my grandmother on her deathbed, with only days left before cancer stole her from me.

Is Nan gone now? Do my parents think I disappeared—kidnapped and murdered thousands of miles from home, mere hours before my grandmother died? Or is Catriona in my body? And is that *worse* than thinking I'm gone, because their only child has twisted into a stranger who'll lie and take whatever they'll give her?

Yes, these are the things I try very hard not to dwell on, and that's a whole lot easier on a night like this, when I can drown myself in a Victorian adventure.

When Gray said I'd be playing the role of *McCreadie's* girl, I presumed that was because Gray isn't the detective half of the duo. As we walk, though, I am reminded of the real problem.

This is the sort of neighborhood where people mind their own business. They pay attention to us, though. I'm a pretty blond nineteen-year-old who probably looks like a high-priced sex worker, out of place in this neighborhood. Gray looks even more out of place as an obvious man of means, and maybe that could be ignored—just another highbrow man with lowbrow tastes—if not for his skin color.

People here might not be able to afford curiosity, but they'll make an exception for Gray. In undercover work, one cannot afford to be memorable.

We head downhill on one street and then turn in to a close. In Edinburgh, closes can be narrow lanes into courtyards or they can be equally narrow shortcuts between buildings. This is the latter—an established and official shortcut—but it's shadowed enough that I'd hesitate to enter even in daylight. I worry that going this way is another sign of Gray's obliviousness, but when a footfall squeaks behind us, my boss turns even before I do.

Gray pulls himself straight, his gaze fixed on the shadows behind us.

"May I help you?" he says, his tone clipped and confident with an undercurrent of annoyance.

Silence.

Gray sighs, the sound fluttering along the silent close. "I see you, lad. I am looking directly at you."

A young man steps out. He's about Catriona's age, average height and whip thin, his slight stature only accentuated by an outdated style of men's clothing still worn by some of the poor—oversized jackets and baggy trousers. The most crucial part of his appearance, though? What he holds in his hand.

A truncheon.

I tense, but Gray only drops his gaze to the baton, and the young man slides it down to his side, like a schoolboy caught with a pocketknife.

"May I help you?" Gray says again.

The young man hesitates. To be fair, he's half a head shorter than Gray and maybe fifty pounds lighter, but it's not just the size difference that gives him pause. It's Gray's complete lack of concern as he fixes the young man with a level stare.

"I will ask one last time—"

"I thought you might be lost, sir," the boy says, in the thick Scottish brogue that I've learned to smooth out mentally. "I was going to offer directions."

"I know precisely where I am going, though I appreciate the concern. In lieu of directions . . ." Gray holds up a coin. "Would you be so good as to ensure no one else delays my passage? I am in a bit of a hurry."

The young man's gaze goes from me to Gray. "I know a place you can get a few minutes of privacy, sir."

Gray's brows knit. "Privacy?" He follows the young man's gaze to me. "Certainly not. I am a doctor, attending to a patient, suffering from a—" He clears his throat. "—private ailment. Now, if you have the time and inclination?" He flashes the coin again. "If you are otherwise occupied, I will bid you good evening."

"I'll watch your back for you, sir."

"Most appreciated."

Gray deftly flips the coin. The boy catches it, and we carry on.

Now, as a cop who walked a lot of beats, I know there's a fifty percent chance the kid will *still* try to mug us . . . and a twenty-five percent chance he'll take the money and run. Yet Gray knows that, too, judging by the way he stays on alert as the young man falls in behind us.

We continue on for a quarter mile, approaching a better neighborhood, more working class. There, I spot a figure leaning against a shadowy wall, with his arms crossed. I slow until I recognize him. It's the sideburns that give it away. Detective Hugh McCreadie may be dressed as a workingman—a far cry from his usual sartorial flair—but one look at those luxuriant sideburns and he is instantly recognizable.

"Have a care, Duncan," McCreadie murmurs as we draw near. "You are being followed."

"Yes, I know." Gray turns and calls into the darkness. "Thank you for your services, lad."

The young man steps out and tips his cap. "Pleasure, sir." He eyes McCreadie. "This is your patient? I am sorry for your plight, mister. It's a terrible thing."

Gray flips the young man another coin, and he disappears into the night.

"My plight?" McCreadie says.

"I told him I was meeting a patient with a 'private ailment.' Do not worry. I have brought your mercury pills."

McCreadie sputters.

"Mercury?" I say. "Please tell me that you realize mercury isn't a medically sound treatment for *anything*."

"Yes, it will eventually kill Hugh, but so will the pox, and he'd likely prefer the poison." Gray looks at McCreadie and deadpans. "The pox is a terrible thing."

"Which I do *not* have," McCreadie says.

"Of course." Gray adjusts his glove. "To contract it, one cannot live as a monk, pining for—"

McCreadie clears his throat.

"I have brought Mallory for you," Gray says.

"But not to end your monkish state," I say. "Sorry."

McCreadie sputters again.

Gray shakes his head. "Be careful. Mallory is in a playful mood."

"You make me sound like a kitten," I say.

"More like a small tigress that is temporarily feeling playful, but is also likely at any moment to show her fangs and claws, should we mistake her gamboling for more than a temporary whim."

"*Small* tigress?"

His brows rise. "That is the part to which you object?"

McCreadie clears his throat. "I see you are *both* in a playful mood. Might that have something to do with the prospect of adventure?"

"Yes, I am happy to be here, even if I feel a bit like . . ." I drop in a deep curtsy and look up at them. "Please sir, may I have a bit of respite from my daily cares, if you would be so kind."

"She's been feeling neglected," Gray says. "I have told her that there have not been any serious crimes in which we might enlist her assistance."

"Only common thefts and batteries," McCreadie says. "If you are interested in helping with those—"

"Yes! Oh, yes, please."

A passing woman glances over and then quickly looks away, seeing me half bent in front of two men, uttering exclamations of excitement.

McCreadie gives a soft laugh. As usual, Gray notices nothing and continues, "That is my oversight. I did not wish to bother you with minor crimes. I know better now."

Didn't wish to "bother" me? Or just wasn't ready to work with me after what happened last month?

McCreadie puts out his arm. "Come, my bonny lass. A stout pint awaits us."

I put my arm through his, and we proceed back to the road, leaving Gray in the shadows to wait.

THREE

The public house is, like most things in Victorian Edinburgh, both what I expect and not what I expect. My visual renderings of scenes like this all come from Hollywood, where I'm going to guess that—unless it's a mega-budget movie—there's a standard-issue "Victorian pub" on a soundstage somewhere. Or, at least, the blueprint for such a place exists, and the set designer makes a few adjustments. How much research did the original set designers do? Also, how readily can one even research such a thing? And what is more important for the audience: an authentic Victorian pub or what they expect from one?

If they're set in neighborhoods like this, they're usually dark and dingy, and that is accurate enough. The darkness comes from the inadequacy of the lighting—gas lighting is still too new for a working-class public house. It's all lanterns and candles, which lend both a wavering illumination and a miasma of smoke. The smoke does help cover the smell, which isn't the body odor and bad breath I'd have expected, but lemon and rose and what I've learned is bergamot.

In the modern world, we get the sense that our ancestors didn't notice bodily smells. The truth—at least in this time period—is that they sure as hell noticed and, worse, they recognized it as the smell of the so-called great unwashed. The obvious solution would be soap. That's less obvious in a time when soap is expensive, and hot—or even clean—water isn't easy to come by. While Victorians are much cleaner than I expected, they also use a lot of cover-up scent, and that's what I smell here, with only an undercurrent of actual body odor.

It's a mixed group of patrons. Based on whatever impression has formed in my brain, I expect only a few women, most of whom would be situational sex workers. As Isla has pointed out, the number of full-time sex workers in a neighborhood like this is low. Most are just women willing to do that if it means having money for a doss-house bed . . . or money to feed an addiction . . . or money to feed their children.

While I spot a few women who'd fall into that category, there are overall more women than I expect, and most are just enjoying a drink, sometimes alone, sometimes with friends. Isla could never do that in our neighborhood. Here, the tight corset strings of Victorian morality are relaxed, and women can simply be out for a drink, same as I might at home. There are also children. Some are waiting for their parents, while others just seem to be hanging out, possibly hoping for a job—or hoping to pick the pocket of a patron too drunk to notice.

The place is crowded, I'll give it that much. The crush of humanity would exceed any modern fire code. We only get a table because someone's leaving, and McCreadie shoulders past a man who'd been waiting to snag it.

We settle in and play our roles by flirting. Luckily, McCreadie is very flirt-worthy. Handsome, bright and ambitious, with the progressive attitude that comes from a kind heart and an open mind. If Hugh McCreadie were a fellow detective at a training seminar, I'd have flirted with him for real. This is different.

The fact that I'm comfortable with McCreadie, though, means I have no trouble fake-flirting with him. Plenty of eye contact and smiles and giggles as we talk, but if anyone could hear our conversation, they'd get a very different impression.

"The second victim frequented the present establishment," McCreadie says as he leans forward, his hand on mine.

I pull back and rap his knuckles, and he grins for any audience that's watching.

McCreadie continues, "A few days ago, the man—Andrew Burns—complained of stomach troubles but brushed it off as 'feeling poorly.' Then, the night before last, he was visibly unwell and told his companions his wife had made his favorite pudding."

"Uh-huh." I bat my eyelashes. "Tell me more."

"The pudding was very rich, and he feared he'd been eating too much, which was upsetting his stomach. But he hated to turn it down when she'd gone to all the trouble—and expense—to make his favorite sweet."

"Let me guess. She never had any herself? Insisted it was all for him?"

"He didn't say. As he was drinking, he became violently ill. One of the lads"—he glances around, his gaze lighting on a couple of the children—"was sent to fetch Burns's wife. By the time she arrived, he was in the roadway, nearly passed out from retching."

"And her reaction?"

"Annoyance, according to the witnesses. She said he was going to drink himself to death and she wouldn't make it easier on him. She stalked off. Two men carried him home and put him to bed."

"Did his wife say anything to them?"

"Unfortunately, they were not among those willing to talk to us."

"Is that suspicious?" I say with a flirty giggle as I lean forward. "Or just the state of things around here."

His lips quirk in a half smile. "The state of things around here. Is it the same in your time?"

"I'm sure it's the same in every time. So you're having trouble finding witnesses willing to talk."

"We are."

"And that's why we're here."

"It is."

"What happened after Mrs. Burns left?"

"The two men returned and spoke to others here, but our witnesses didn't overhear what was said. The next day, one of the regular lasses"—his gaze crosses a few at the bar, suggesting he means a situational sex worker—"went by his house with a bottle of stomach bitters. Mrs. Burns ran her off. Created enough of a scene for a neighbor to take an interest, slip into the flat, and check inside the Burnses' apartment."

The first time I heard someone here say "flat," I'd been confused. In modern-day Scotland—like England—that means what I'd call an apartment. In Victorian Edinburgh, a "flat" is a level in a building of units called apartments, which makes more sense. And a "tenement" is simply an apartment building rather than a slum.

I say, "So the neighbor checked in on Burns. How was he?"

"Dead."

"Ah. And the coroner, uh, police surgeon ruled the cause of death was poison?"

McCreadie gives me a look.

"Right," I say. "You have Addington, and the only thing he can reliably be counted upon is to tell whether the victim is actually dead."

"No, he got that wrong once, too. Twice, if you count the time he called Duncan in to remove the body, and there was no one there. We never quite determined whether the 'corpse' was stolen or walked away or only existed in Addington's mind. He did have quite a lot to drink that evening."

"Wait," I say. "I know Addington uses Dr. Gray's funerary parlor to conduct his autopsies, but I haven't seen the victims of these poisonings there."

"Because Addington didn't conduct autopsies."

I blink at him, forgetting our flirting.

"You do realize, Mallory, that when you give me that look, I feel as if you are judging our police system and finding it wholly inadequate."

"It . . . is a work in progress."

He gives a sharp laugh and taps my hand. "You do not need to be so circumspect. I recognize the inadequacies of our system."

"But it really is a work in progress. You only have about fifty years of policing behind you. My world has hundreds, and even then, so much needs overhauling."

He sobers. "So we never do get it right?"

"We will," I say, with more certainty than I usually feel. "But you're saying that no autopsies were conducted because Addington knows it's poison. How?" I pause. "Is it the Marsh test? You have that by now, right, to test for arsenic?"

McCreadie throws up his hands. "There is some sort of test, and presumably Addington conducted it, because he ruled arsenic. That is all I know."

"Can we get Dr. Gray to examine—?"

I'm stopped by a voice over my shoulder. We both freeze, like bloodhounds catching a scent. Instead of a scent, though, it is a word.

Poison.

I wave my hands, as if telling a story, and while my lips move, I say nothing. Instead, we focus on the voice behind me.

"I'm telling you, she poisoned the pudding. Everyone knows it. If the police cared to catch her, they'd have taken it straight from her icebox for ana-lyz-ation."

"Can they do that?"

"Did you not read about that English case last year? Scotland Yard suspected the poison was in the chocolates, and they had them tested, and lo and behold, they were stuffed full of arsenic."

I glance at McCreadie, but he's pulled into himself, gaze emptying as he focuses on listening.

A third person joins in as the two initial conversationalists debate whether the police are inept or simply don't give a damn.

"It had to be the pudding," the newcomer says. "You know why they haven't arrested her, don't you?" He doesn't wait for a response. "They're being canny. Watching her. Waiting for Mrs. Burns to sneak off to whoever gave her the poison. Then they can hang the lot of them."

I glance at McCreadie. This time, he gives me a wry half shrug, one that says it wouldn't be a bad idea . . . if they actually believed there *was* a poison ring.

Could there be? Oh, I understand why Isla would bristle at the idea. "Poisoner" is an easy charge to level at a female chemist. Clearly she is not a "real" scientist and is only producing poison to sell to her fellow deviant women.

But here's the thing: Couldn't the urban legend of poison rings implant the idea of *creating* a poison ring?

The three continue talking. It's simple speculation, no clues embedded in the narrative, and I'm growing frustrated when I catch another conversation, this one coming from behind McCreadie.

It's two women at a table beside ours, their heads together. I can't tell who is saying what. I can barely pick up the conversation at all.

"I heard she got the poison from Queen Mab."

"Who?"

"Queen Mab, over in—" The rest is drowned out.

"Does she sell . . . ?" The woman's voice drops, and I catch part of an unfamiliar word.

"She does. How far along are you?"

"I missed my last monthly. Been poorly in the mornings."

"Go see Queen Mab. She'll set you straight. Tell her I sent you. Better be quick, though, before the police catch up with her."

More whispers, and when I glance at McCreadie, he's listening intently, his brow furrowed. I lean and whisper, "Did you get the directions?" and he shakes his head.

The two women rise from their table. I glance at McCreadie.

"Ready to go, luv?" I say.

He slides an arm around my waist as we follow the women outside. I'm hoping they'll pause to exchange goodbyes, and the one who gave the directions will repeat them. At the very least, I expect some hint as to *which* woman is heading to Queen Mab's. But they walk out and go their separate ways with only a nod of farewell.

The dark-haired woman heads left along the street. The light-haired one turns down a side street across from the public house. McCreadie and I pause, giggling and swaying, as if we consumed far more than a half-pint of ale.

"Split up?" I whisper.

When McCreadie hesitates, I say, "Could you tell who was saying what?"

"No, but . . ."

"If you'd feel better with me to watch your back, just say so."

He gives me a mock stern look. I take out Catriona's switchblade. He rolls his eyes. Then he catches sight of something down the road and relaxes. I glance to see Gray half exposed between two buildings.

"Good," I say. "You and Dr. Gray can follow the dark-haired one. It's not the worst neighborhood, but you should still have backup."

"To be quite honest, I *would* rather have an officer at my side, but as I am currently without one, I will follow the dark-haired lass, who is walking toward a better area of town. You and Duncan shall follow the light-haired one, who seems to be heading into a neighborhood I would fear to tread alone."

I sigh. "Fine. Be all reasonable about it."

"You ought to thank me," he says. "For putting you into a situation I suspect you will quite enjoy, even if you would not admit it."

I follow his gaze to Gray and narrow my eyes. "Situation?"

"Why, an opportunity for danger and adventure, of course," he says. "Whatever did you think I meant?"

He tips his hat and sets out after the dark-haired woman. I head down the darkened street the light-haired woman took. I make it about ten steps before the cobbled lane ends and a narrow alley looms ahead. I slow and let Gray catch up.

"Going in there, are we?" he says.

"Apparently. We're—"

He's already striding down the alley.

We must enter a pitch-black alley at night? All right then. No explanation required.

I shake my head. I'm not the one who will enjoy this "opportunity for danger and adventure."

Okay, I'm not the *only* one who'll enjoy it.

FOUR

I hike my skirts and jog after Gray. As I catch up, he waves me closer without looking back.

"Yes," he says. "Stay near. That's safer."

"Safer for me?" I say. "Or for the guy who marched into this alley without waiting for a reason?"

"I presume there is a reason. I also presume that it is a sound one. While you are rather overfond of courting danger, you are not reckless. Not unduly so."

"Might I suggest, sir, that I take the lead?" I say. "As I possess a knife? And as I would prefer not to be grabbed from behind by someone who thinks I seem a delightful confection?"

"That depends," he says. "Are you going to keep mocking me by calling me 'sir'?"

"It's not mockery. It is acknowledgment that you are my social superior."

"In your guise of Catriona, perhaps. Would I be such in your world?"

"Mmm, hard call. You're better educated, and your family is somewhat wealthier."

"In other words, we would occupy the same general social standing."

"Yes, but I *am* in the guise of Catriona. Calling you 'sir' is a reminder to myself. If it bugs you, I'll stick to Dr. Gray."

"While I call you by your given name? You call Isla by hers in private. Would you not call me Duncan in your world?"

"Our voices are carrying. I'll take the lead."

I pass him as he mutters, "I pity the man who would grab you from behind, mistaking you for a delightful confection."

"I heard that. Also, I am *very* delightful, in my own special way. Now, hush. We're tailing someone."

We've been speaking in low voices, needing only a whisper to be heard in this dark and silent place. We can hear our target's boot clicks, far ahead. She's moving fast, and as we pick up speed, we stop talking and I roll my footsteps.

The close is a disappointment. Being so dark, it'd seem the sort of place where a mugging came guaranteed, like the one where the young man followed us earlier. But this one is too narrow for an attacker to lurk without being tripped over by their target. The young woman we're following obviously knows the area and realizes she faces minimal danger cutting through here.

She reaches the end and turns left. I hurry along and peek out, only to stop short as a man slides from the shadows and sets out after the young woman.

Behind me, Gray gives an irritated grunt, and I glance back to see his narrowed gaze fixed on the woman's newly acquired stalker.

"Two options," I whisper. "We can follow and see if he causes any trouble, or we can make a bit of a scene in hopes of scaring him off."

"The latter."

I smile at him. "Excellent choice."

I loop my arm through Gray's, and we continue along up the hill. The woman and her stalker turn right onto another road, taking them out of our sight. I walk faster, and Gray matches me. When we round the next corner, I let out a yelping giggle and fake a stumble. The woman doesn't notice, but the man glances back.

I lean against Gray. "The road is very uneven. I can scarcely walk upright."

"I do not think it is the road."

I swat at him. "Are you implying I am inebriated, sir?"

"I am not *implying* anything."

The man shoots us a glare of annoyance, and as he does, I recognize him from the pub. He'd been one of the guys talking about the poison ring. Is that a coincidence? Or had he also overheard the women's conversation?

I break from Gray's grasp and prance ahead with my nose in the air. "If that is what you think of me, sir, then I fear you shall lack for company this evening."

Gray grabs me by the waist and swings me up, making me shriek in surprise that's only half faked.

Gray growls a laugh. "I think you are *delightfully* tipsy, my dear. It brings out the roses in your cheeks."

"Put me down, you . . . you . . ." I don't finish the line, mostly because I'm unsure of the period-appropriate term.

Gray continues to walk while holding me outstretched before him. "Are you certain, lass? You seem quite unable to stand on your own. I am helping."

"You are manhandling me."

"Of course. Because I am a man. I cannot handle you in any other way."

I sputter a genuine laugh and turn it into a girlish squeal as I struggle. We have now caught the attention of the young woman. Seeing the man behind her, she stops short. Then she wheels, as if to run, and her stalker charges.

"Goddamn it," I mutter as Gray plunks me down.

He takes off after the two. I bring up the rear, hampered by my skirts as I struggle to hike them higher and only succeed in fumbling the endless layers and almost tripping.

As I pass a building, a figure lunges from the doorway. I spin, about to raise my knife, only to realize that hand is also clutching my damn skirts. I manage to drop the skirts and *not* the knife, but that split-second delay costs me any advantage I gained by seeing my attacker's charge.

Hands grab me. I elbow hard, getting a satisfying gasp in response. Then another pair of hands grab my legs and hoist me into the air.

I snarl, kicking and punching, each twist a fight against my corset, as I curse myself for not spending more time learning how to fight while wearing one. My boot catches a man in the gut, and I pull back to deliver a harder knock in the same spot. He lets out a curse, and I kick again. I find the knife release and press it. The blade flies out. Another slam of my boot, and the man holding my feet loses his grip, and I swing my feet down as I slash with the knife. It makes contact. The other man yowls.

I get my footing and dance back, knife raised. The two men both look at me. Then they look at each other, as if to say *"You* grab her." They're so focused on the knife-wielding doxy that they fail to notice the guy standing right behind them, looming a half foot above their heads.

Gray reaches out, almost casually, and lifts one man by the back of his collar. Then he swings him around and delivers a perfect right hook with that same equanimity. The man flies to the ground, and we both step toward the second man.

I would like to think me brandishing my knife spooks the second man. Or maybe the look in my eyes. But let's be honest—the guy never glances my way. He's too busy staring at the hulking shadow beside me.

The man glances down the street toward where the young woman ran off with the stalker in hot pursuit. A momentary pause. Then he bolts in the other direction.

His companion wobbles up from the ground. Gray grabs him by the shirt and swings him into the wall with a thud that makes me wince.

Gray doesn't say a word. Doesn't even bring his face down to the man's with a menacing glare. He pins him for three seconds, and then tosses him aside and waves for me to help chase the woman's stalker.

This time, Gray motions me into the lead. He glances back at the other man, still picking himself up from the ground.

"They have knives!" the man bellows. "Both of them!"

With that, he scrambles away. Gray and I exchange a look. Okay, so I didn't coincidentally get jumped as we pursued the woman. We were distracted to let her stalker catch her.

"Go on ahead," I say as I run. "I can't go any faster in these damned skirts."

Gray stays behind me, and I resist the urge to snap that I had looked after myself just fine. That isn't the point. If he'd been the one jumped, I'd stick close, too.

We don't need to go far. Down one street and then looping back the way we came before we catch voices in a courtyard. I slow to listen.

"I heard you talking about Queen Mab," the man is saying. "You know where the witch lives."

"I said it before, and I'll say it again, no matter how many times you strike me. The only Queen I know sits on the English throne. Not *my* throne, whatever the law might say. Mine's in the castle yonder."

"I heard you mention Queen—"

"You are mistaken."

"I am not," he says.

"If you're trying to get a free tickle, threatening to turn me in for treason, you'd best walk me down to the police office now, because I don't sell my favor, and I certainly do not give it away to the likes of you."

"I'm talking about Queen *Mab*. The witch. The *poisoner*."

We duck down the close leading to the courtyard. Then I peer around the corner. The woman stares at the man in a show of confusion. As a cop who has interviewed hundreds of witnesses, I can tell she's overdoing it. I'm not sure he can, though.

"You're calling the English queen a poisoner? A witch?" The woman chortles. "It seems I am not the one who needs to worry about paying a visit to Calcraft's toilet."

I glance at Gray and arch a brow. He leans down to my ear.

"William Calcraft. City hangman."

The two continue arguing, the man getting increasingly frustrated. I whisper a plan to Gray, who nods, and I'm about to step out when the man slaps the woman again, the blow hard enough to send me barreling out there faster than I intended.

"What's this?" the man says, his eyes narrowing. He looks past me.

"Your friends are busy with my fellow o' the evening," I say. "Doesn't seem he'll be in any shape to pay my fee, so I was wondering if you were interested."

"What?" His face screws up.

I motion at the young woman. "She does not seem interested, and I am. A half crown for a half hour?" I step toward him. "'Twill be the best half crown you've ever spent."

He stares at me in confusion. I take one more step, tossing my curls, and the young woman shoves him hard. He stumbles, and she punches him square in the stomach. Then she bolts.

That is not what I want—I need to talk to her—and I glance over at Gray. I want him to take the guy while I go after the girl, but before I can say that, someone shouts, "Knife!"

I think it's the guy's companions. After all, one warned him that we both allegedly had knives. It takes a split second for me to realize the voice seems younger than the two men we fought.

I yank back just in time to avoid a knife in the gut. The tip still catches in my dress, and between that and the momentary confusion, I don't have a chance to pull out my own blade. Also, my knife is not in a place where it's easy to pull out, because my damn pockets are big enough to hold a whole freaking picnic lunch, wine included.

Falling back from the attack, I instinctively reach for my knife, and my hand gets lost in the voluminous fabric of my pocket. Before I can get the blade out, the guy is slashing at me again. I stumble out of the way, only to hit a wall. I dodge the next blow, and I have my switchblade then, but he's danced out of reach, intent on a newer and—to him—much more serious threat: Gray.

Gray faces off against my knife-wielding attacker by raising his fists. The guy lets out a snorting laugh. He slashes at Gray, and in a blink, Gray has him by the arm, knife clattering to the ground. As Gray deftly pins the guy to the wall, I resist the urge to clap.

"I'm going after the girl," I say, already jogging off.

Before I get three strides, a shadow moves behind the building where Gray had been hiding—a few feet from where he now stands with his back to the shadow. That same young voice shouts, "Watch out!"

"Duncan!" I shout as I run back.

I'm too far away to intercept, and Gray hears us too late. One of the men who attacked me earlier charges from the shadows, broken bottle in hand. He slashes at Gray. Gray blocks, but the man he'd been pinning wheels and pushes him toward the newcomer. Gray's feet tangle in just enough of a stumble to let the bottle-wielding man slash again.

I stab the newcomer in the side. My blade barely penetrates his damn jacket and waistcoat and shirt and undershirt. It's not just the women here who wear multiple layers of clothing.

Still, the jab is enough to have the man backing off. Gray catches his arm, and I take the bottle and pitch it into a wall, where it smashes to pieces. Gray stomps, like squashing a bug, the first man diving for his knife as Gray steps on it.

Gray releases the second man, and I advance on that one with my switchblade. He looks over at the smashed bottle, as if gauging whether any pieces are big enough for a weapon. Then he sees another figure stepping from the shadows. It's the young man from earlier, the one who'd tried to mug us.

The kid smacks his truncheon into his hand, and the guy decides that's enough. He runs. Before I can even turn back to Gray, his opponent is doing the same, taking off out of the courtyard.

Gray stands there a moment, fists still clenched, as if waiting for something to hit. Then he winces, and I glance down to see bright red blood soaking his white shirt.

FIVE

Doctor!" I say as I sprint to Gray's side. I'd been about to say "Dr. Gray," when I noticed the young man still there and had the sense not to give away Gray's name.

Gray braces one hand against a wall and makes a face, as if in annoyance. He looks down at the bloodied shirtfront, and that annoyance only grows.

"Doctor?" I say. "Sit down. Please."

"I am quite fine."

"Sit down before you fall down."

That look of annoyance aims my way. "I am not going to—" He makes a face, pushing back an obvious stab of pain.

"Then sit down so I may examine you."

"Are you the doctor here?"

"No, but—"

"Go after the young woman," he says. "Take care—"

He winces again, and sweat breaks out on his brow. I catch his arm and forcibly lower him to the ground.

"She's gone," I say. "And you might be, too, if I leave."

"One cannot die of a shallow cut. At least, not unless it becomes infected."

"Which cuts seem to do at an alarming rate when one does not wash one's hands before treating them."

"The only time I do not wash my hands is when I am working with a corpse, the patient being beyond the concern of infection. Also, I am quite certain *your* hands are not clean either."

"Are you?" I pull off my gloves. "Did you think I put on gloves right after cleaning the chamber pot? My hands are clean—scrubbed half raw."

A movement to the side startles me. I'd been so intent on distracting Gray that I forgot we weren't alone. The young man steps forward as I peel back Gray's bloodied shirt.

"Thank you for the warning," I say.

"The gent's crown bought you that much," he says. "It wasn't enough for me to throw myself into a knife fight."

"I wasn't being sarcastic. I appreciated the warning. How long have you been trailing us?"

"That's what you paid for, isn't it?"

I glance over at him. As I do, he moves through a patch of light, and I squint. He's taller than me, thin and wiry, as I noted before, but something in his profile has me doing a second take, especially when paired with his voice, which is notably lower pitched than it had been when he shouted his warning. I'd presumed he was male; I'm no longer as sure. He's presenting as male, certainly, so I shake it off. None of my business.

Gray answers. "I paid you to follow us until we met up with our patient, after which I sent you off."

"Did you?" The young man rocks back on his heels. "Must not have caught that."

"You followed because you were curious," I say. "Wondering what we were up to."

"Partly curious." He smiles. "Partly bored. Can't say I regret the decision."

I examine Gray's wound. It is not a "shallow cut." He's been slashed twice. The first was on his arm, where his jacket protected him. But he'd unbuttoned his jacket earlier to fight, and he'd left it open. The glass caught him above the V of his waistcoat and went deep enough to nick this breastbone.

"How long do I have to live, Doctor?" he says dryly.

I glare at him.

"Not fatal?" he says. "What a surprise."

"Just because it isn't fatal doesn't mean it isn't serious. It's going to need stitches."

"Which you base on how many years of medical education?"

"Which I base on having two working eyes."

The young man snickers. "You make quite the pair. I'm afraid she's right, Dr. Gray. The wound does require mending."

"There," I say. "A second opinion from someone who also possesses two working—" I peer at the kid. "What did you call him?"

He leans back against a closed storefront. "Dr. Gray. The undertaker. He is, isn't he? That's why I followed you. After he said he was a doctor, I remembered a friend talking about an undertaker doctor who looks like . . ."

The young man jerks his chin toward Gray. "No offense, sir, but there aren't many toffs like you, and I don't mean because you're quick with your fists. You lent my friend a quid to buy his father's body from the dead house. You were there on business, with a fellow who called you a doctor. That struck my friend as interesting, what with your . . ." He taps his cheek. "Again, no offense. He just found it interesting and mentioned it to me, mostly so if I saw you, I could find out where he can repay the quid, as you did not give him an address to send it to."

As the young man chatters, I clean Gray's wound as best I can. Gray tells him his friend's debt is repaid, and they speak some more, but I don't catch it. I'm busy taking off one of my petticoats. That part they notice, mostly because I'm sitting on the ground, struggling to get it off, my skirts hiked up.

"Turn away if you don't want to see my drawers," I mutter. "I need a tight bandage for the wound."

"A what?" the young man says.

I wrestle off one of my petticoats. Then I slice it with my switchblade and tear off a strip, which I wrap around the wound.

"Finally," I say, "a use for all those layers."

The young man chuckles. "You're an odd one, aren't you?" He lifts his hands. "Which is no insult. I don't mind people being different. It makes life interesting."

I meet his gaze. "It does, doesn't it?"

He grins and winks, as if he knows what I mean—that he's presenting as male—and isn't the least bit distressed that I figured it out.

I return to tying the binding. "That should hold until we can get you to a doctor."

Gray clears his throat.

"A doctor's *office*," I say. "With the supplies to stitch you up." I glance at the young man. "Is there someone trustworthy nearby? We can pay."

"Oh, I've no doubt you can pay, but no doctor lives in this part of the city unless his real skill is providing Dr. Gray with new clients."

He has a point, and it's not as if there's going to be an after-hours clinic or emergency room nearby.

"I can walk," Gray says. "Which means I can return home and tend to myself." He pushes himself up as he fastens his shirt. Then he pulls his jacket and buttons it, covering the blood. "There."

I point at his sleeve, where the knife earlier tore a slash in it. He twists it, pushing the slash out of sight. Then I point at his collar where blood smeared from below as I'd worked to stanch the bleeding. He grumbles and adjusts his jacket.

"I would not be too concerned, sir," the young man says. "Around here, people will presume you took that fancy shirt and jacket off a dead man in an alley."

"True," I say. "And you're usually walking around with a smear of blood on you somewhere."

"That is ink."

"Also blood. I think you owe the laundress a raise. I don't even want to know what she uses to get your shirts clean."

Gray glowers at me, adjusts his collar again, and looks around. I walk across the street and retrieve his top hat from a doorway. Yes, it's an actual top hat. That's the fashion these days, and I'll admit it doesn't look nearly as ridiculous as I might have thought. At least, it doesn't on Gray. He runs a hand through wavy dark hair, which only succeeds in unsettling it more and smearing blood on his forehead.

I look at the young man and sigh.

"Still a sight better-looking than most toffs we get around here," he murmurs under his breath. "Though that fellow you met up with earlier . . ." A low whistle. "Presuming he doesn't truly have the pox, I'd take an introduction."

"Introduction to whom?" Gray says, apparently catching that last part.

"To a hansom cab," I say. "We ought to get you home as quickly as possible."

"Cab in these parts? At this hour?" The young man shakes his head.

"No," Gray says. "I would trust such a conveyance even less than I would a local physician. Also, we need to tell Hugh that we lost the scent."

"Right," the kid says. "You were following that lass."

I glance a question at Gray, who shrugs, and I say, "We're looking for the same thing those men were looking for. Queen Mab."

His brows rise and his gaze drops to my midriff. "If you need to rid yourself of an unexpected guest, you ought to talk to your man here. A doctor can fix that better than a chemist."

"He's not my man," I say. "He's my employer."

His brows shoot up. "Really?"

"It's complicated. Also, I do not need an abor—to rid myself of anything. We . . ." I consider my options and glance again at Gray, who only shrugs again, which I'll continue to interpret as permission to say what I like.

"We're concerned that locals may consider Queen Mab a person of interest in a recent poisoning," I say. "Dr. Gray works with the police, and we fear locals might take matters into their own hands, which seems even more likely after that encounter a few minutes ago."

"You have an odd manner of speech," the young man says.

Gray clears his throat. "My assistant possesses an extensive and varied vocabulary, including words and turns of phrase more commonly found in her homeland."

The young man frowns at me. "You sound even more Scottish than me."

"I sound like a lot of things," I say. "But no, I'm not from around here. I hear Queen Mab is, though."

He grins. "Nice bringing us back around like that. No, Queen Mab is also not from here. And no, I'm not going to tell you where to find her, but I will pass along your message warning her to be careful."

"It would be better if she spoke to the police," I say.

"Nothing's ever better after speaking to the police."

Gray takes over and tries to convince the young man as I consider my options. This kid isn't giving us Queen Mab, and I really need to get Gray home to tend to his injuries properly.

"Tell Queen Mab that we would like to speak to her," I say. "Dr. Gray lives at 12 Robert Street. She could also speak to Detective Hugh McCreadie, but I wouldn't suggest she go to the police office, in case Detective McCreadie isn't the one she ends up speaking to. If she comes to Robert Street—or sends a message—she could meet Detective McCreadie there. I would also suggest that, before deciding against doing so, she ask after Detective McCreadie's reputation. That may convince her to speak to him."

The young man eyes me, and I don't think it's actually my word choices or speech pattern throwing him off; it's that I don't speak like the young woman I appear to be. I'm not a cop here. I'm a nineteen-year-old girl in a frilly dress. Even if I were twice that age, I wouldn't talk this way, especially when my boss is right here to do the talking for us both.

The young man looks between us, and I resist the urge to defer to Gray. His silence means he approves.

"Does that work?" I ask the young man.

"Warn Queen Mab about possible trouble. Suggest she speak to Detective Hugh McCreadie at Dr. Gray's residence at 12 Robert Street."

"Yes, please. We appreciate you passing along the message."

Gray's hand slides out, a coin between his thumb and forefinger. "We do appreciate it."

The young man waves off the money. "I'll do this to settle my friend's debt. If you have any other business in this neighborhood, you can ask for me at Halton House."

"And who would we be asking for?" Gray says.

"Jack."

"Jack . . ."

"Just Jack."

"Mr. Jack?" I say.

He grins. "That's a rather awkward way to ask the question you want answered. I expected better from you."

"I am not asking any question that is your own private business. I am asking to be sure I use the mode of address you prefer. Mister? Miss? He? She? Something else?"

The grin grows, and he tips his hat. "Now *that* is a very polite question. Thank you. I prefer just plain Jack. As for the rest, I use she, but I do not mind he, as that is what is usually presumed when I am out dressed like this."

"Understood," I say. "Then good night, Jack, and thank you for your help."

SIX

There's no way of easily getting a message to McCreadie. I've always thought communication must have been difficult before the time of cell phones, but it's damn near impossible before the time of cell phones, pagers, regular phones, and every other electronic method of contact. There's a reason the mail here arrives multiple times per day. That doesn't help in a situation like this, though. We must make our way back to the New Town and presume McCreadie will come along when he is able.

I want to talk about the case on the way home. I want one of Gray's forensic-science lectures . . . the ones no one except me seems to appreciate. Tonight, while I'm desperate to understand the current state of toxicology, that discussion must wait. Gray is in worse shape than he let on. His labored breathing has me worried about lung damage from a punch. He assures me that the problem is only his ribs, but if he's having trouble breathing, I shouldn't tempt him into lecturing.

Instead, I'm the one who talks, on a subject that I'm slightly more expert in. Gray didn't fail to miss the implications of my final discussion with Jack. He's curious, especially when I seemed so casual about a matter that's verboten in this world. Still, Jack wouldn't be the first person he's ever met who at least occasionally crosses gender lines.

Every employee in the Gray household has had brushes with the law. That's how they end up there. Isla offers employment to those ready to start a new life, with McCreadie finding the candidates. I don't know all the stories, but I do know Simon's, and Gray would, too, since it was headline news at one time.

Simon is gay, which is legally more acceptable in Scotland—which never made sodomy a capital offense—but if the law is murky, general opinion is not, and being gay is not something one is open about . . . unless one is an eighteen-year-old boy with more courage than common sense. Simon and a friend used to dress up as girls and go out on the town with gay men. It's a subculture here, and I get the impression it was roleplay rather than Simon preferring a female identity.

Simon made the news when he was framed for the murder of his friend and his friend's lover. That was all before I came along.

As for our new friend, Jack apparently identifies as "she," so I'll switch to that pronoun. Is she gender fluid? Or has she just decided it's easier to make her way in the world as a young man? It's none of my business. It just gives me a topic of conversation to keep Gray distracted until we're back at Robert Street.

We enter the town house through the mews. Gray runs his funeral parlor out of the main floor. While there's no sign to indicate a business, the neighbors know it's there and aren't exactly thrilled, even if the situation has been that way since before they moved in. I'd say to hell with them. Gray is more conciliatory, and if he's suffering from multiple wounds and flecked in blood, he's coming in the back way.

As we enter the courtyard, I'm reminded of one of the many things I take for granted in the modern world: lighting. We have an infinite supply of it, right at our fingertips. Are there areas of our homes where we struggle to read or see the contents of a cupboard? That's the fault of poor lighting choices, which can either be remedied or temporarily solved with a cell-phone flashlight.

In 1869 Edinburgh, houses like Gray's have gas lighting. Great, right? So says anyone who has never experienced Victorian-era gaslights. Oh, it's a damn sight better than candles and oil lamps, which are also still in use, but the wavering, harsh illumination of gas means everything is lit wrong, and it's always too much or too little.

The other problem with Victorian lighting is that it's not as cheap, plentiful, and safe as electric. That's a security issue as well as a comfort one. If there are lamps at the rear entrance, they're certainly not left burning all night. The only light comes from the moon, and it's just enough to illuminate a figure standing at the back door.

I presume that figure is McCreadie. He lost his target and arrived here ahead of us. Still, I slow and catch the back of Gray's jacket. Gray keeps striding forward, which tells me it *must* be McCreadie . . . until skirts swish with a rustle of fabric.

A woman steps from the doorway.

"The key, Duncan. Where have you moved the key?"

Even in the dark, I know it's not Isla. Yes, this woman is also tall, and Isla *would* say those words, but with affectionate exasperation. *Where—my dear absentminded genius of a brother—have you put the key this time?* These words are instead clipped with genuine annoyance.

The woman steps into the moonlight. She's older than Isla. Raven haired with a generous figure, a handsome face, and snapping blue eyes. For a split second, I wonder whether it's a lover of Gray's, maybe even the mysterious Lady Inglis.

I'd found a letter from Lady Inglis in my room. Catriona had stolen it for blackmail, the letter being what one might call "correspondence of an intimate nature." Basically, a former lover of Gray's was trying to tempt him back to her bed. She seems to have failed so far, which could explain that snap in her voice.

I can't imagine any woman who knew Gray would show up at his house, though. More than that, when I look closer, there is something in her face that reminds me of both Isla and Gray.

The woman snaps her fingers. "Duncan? Are you even listening to me?" She stops and turns her gaze my way. "Is that your *housemaid*? Are you actually dallying in the stables with a servant? I am not certain whether to be horrified or smug that you have finally toppled off your high horse."

"I am quite certain you can manage to be horrified and smug at the same time, Annis," he says. He turns to me. "Mallory, this is my eldest sister, Annis."

"Half sister," Annis says. "And I have met your little housemaid several times. Now, where is the key, Duncan? If you have moved it, so that I may not access my own family home—"

"I would not do that. If it is not where Isla keeps it, then she has taken it. You need only to ring the front bell, Annis."

"I did, and that gorgon of a housekeeper pretended she did not see me."

Score a point for Mrs. Wallace.

Annis turns to me. "Run along, girl. I have business with your employer."

I glance at Gray.

"What are you looking at him for?" she snaps. "I gave you an order."

"Yes, but *he's* my boss."

Her face darkens. "I am just as much your boss as he is, considering that your wages are earned by cleaning my family home and paid by my family's fortune."

I turn my back to her. "Sir? We really do need to see to that injury you sustained."

"Injury?" Annis peers at him. "So that is fresh blood, and not merely bodily fluids that you forgot to wash away before venturing into public?"

I open my mouth to defend him, but she has a point, so I only say, "Sir?"

"I ought to take care of the injury," he says. "It may require stitching."

"And it definitely requires disinfecting," I say. "Lord knows what was on that bottle."

"You were stabbed with a bottle?" Annis says. "Do I even want to know—? No. I do *not* want to know why you're skulking about with the housemaid. I do *not* want to know why you were stabbed. I do *not* want to know how these two things might be related. As for your injury, Duncan, as you do not seem to be in immediate danger of death, it will need to wait. I am not on your doorstep at midnight for a social visit. I require your assistance."

"He really does need to stitch—" I begin.

"Do you let her talk like that? Interrupt her betters?"

Gray says mildly, "I believe you are the one who interrupted her, Annis. As for being her betters, we were actually debating that earlier. We have decided that, as Mallory comes from a middle-class family, while we may be her employers, we are not her social superiors." He pauses. "That is a terrible way to put it, as if we would be her *superiors* by dint of being born into—"

"Stop," Annis says. "You are starting to sound like Mother and Isla."

"I believe I have always sounded like Mother and Isla on such matters."

"Dr. Gray?" I say. "Please. I am concerned about your injury."

"And I am concerned about my life," Annis snaps. "Which is in danger."

Gray looks over sharply. "Your life is in danger?"

"It will be, when I am arrested for the murder of my husband."

The yard drops to silence. Gray and I glance at one another as if each thinking we've misheard.

"The murder of Gordon?" Gray says.

"He is the only husband I have, thank heavens."

"Gordon is . . . dead?" Gray asks carefully.

"Not yet."

We exchange another look.

"I . . . don't understand," Gray says.

"No, of course you do not. Because while you are brilliant at some things, you can be quite a dunce at everything else."

"Hey!" I say, rocking forward.

Gray lifts a hand to warn me back, and when Annis casts a look my way, he intercepts it with a subtle side step.

"Your husband is not dead," Gray says. "Yet you fear being arrested for his murder. You have come for my advice, which I am happy to provide. If you do not wish to be arrested for his murder, then you ought not to murder him."

He lifts a hand. "No need to thank me. I am quite happy to provide such advice, free of charge, to a family member. Mallory? Come along. We shall leave Annis to her murder-free evening and—"

"That's supposed to be witty, is it?" Annis says.

"I thought it was," I murmur.

"I am not planning to murder my husband, Duncan. He has already been murdered. He merely has not yet succumbed to the notion, stubborn ass that he is."

Gray opens his mouth, but she keeps talking. "I did not come for your advice. I came because I want you to summon that detective friend of yours. I would have done it myself, but I cannot remember his name."

"You have known Hugh since he was in short pants, Annis."

"I am supposed to remember the names of my brother's friends? My coach is down the lane. We shall collect your friend, and together you shall attend my husband. You are a trained doctor, and so it will make sense that I have summoned you to save his life. I would prefer you did not, but if your friend thinks I am indeed liable to be arrested for his death, then you may."

"Save Gordon's life?" Gray says slowly.

"If you must." She looks toward the darkened mews road. "Enough of this chatter or the fool will be dead before we return."

"I really do need to be stitched," Gray says. "Go on ahead, and I will collect Hugh, if I can find—"

Annis flutters her hands and then strides away, as she says, "The one time I come to you for help, and this is what I get."

"Annis," he says, taking a step toward her.

I catch his arm. I don't grab it or hold it. He could continue after his sister if he wanted, but at my light touch, he stops.

"You know where she lives, right?" I say.

He nods.

"We can catch up after we've seen to your wounds."

SEVEN

Gray's wounds have been tended to, and we are in the coach heading to Annis's house. We don't have McCreadie, and without him, she might not even let us in. Gray left a note on our town house door, and that's really all we can do. Well, no, we could see whether McCreadie stopped by his own apartment, but we don't because Annis's request doesn't make sense on that count.

Strike that, Annis's entire story doesn't make sense on *any* count. If her husband *is* dying, then it's logical for her to run to her brother, who has degrees in both medicine and surgery. It does not make sense for her to run to a criminal officer . . . unless she murdered her husband and is hoping a friend of the family can keep her off the gallows.

If my husband were at death's door and I was worried about being charged with murder, would I want a detective I knew there? Yes. Not to "fix things" but to be damned sure they were handled properly. On that score, Annis is behaving logically. Except she's a Victorian lady, with a husband about to die, and she's expected to be on her fainting couch with her lady's maid passing smelling salts under her nose. She isn't, because she's Gray and Isla's sister, intelligent and clearheaded. Also, it seems, she's not that broken up about her husband dying, which is going to help with the clearheadedness. It is not, of course, going to help with avoiding a murder charge.

While Gray and I tended to his wounds, he'd decided he would not go looking for McCreadie. He would leave a note at home and let McCreadie make up his own mind on the matter. Obviously, he didn't dare write a note saying that his sister is about to be accused of murder, so he used a cipher the two had developed as children. Which is very clever, and also totally adorable.

As Annis lives outside the city, Gray had to wake Simon. His apology may have sounded perfunctory, and a few weeks ago, I'd have held that against him. I know better now. There are expectations on both sides, and Simon would be confused and maybe even uncomfortable if his boss profusely apologized for getting him up in the middle of the night. The true apology comes in the extra ten shillings he gives to compensate for the disturbance, which is easier for Simon to accept and definitely more appreciated.

We are in the coach now. As for why I'm there, the answer is simple: Gray presumed I was coming. I helped with his injury, and then he suggested I might want to "fix my toilet" while he changed his shirt. In other words, tidy up my hair and dress and face after playing doxy and going a few rounds with our attackers.

At that point, I could have said I'd rather stay behind. I certainly wasn't doing that. He swept me along in his preparations, and I happily obliged, if only to find out what the hell was going on with Annis Gray.

Annis *Leslie*, I should say. On the ride, Gray tells me that's her married name. Lady Annis Leslie, in fact. His sister married an earl, which makes her a countess. Maybe that should explain why she calls Gray her *half* brother and treats him like shit, but from what I heard, Gray was a source of embarrassment for Annis long before that.

The Gray family has four children. The first three are the "legitimate" offspring, being from both Mr. and Mrs. Gray. Then there's the youngest: Dr. Duncan Gray. One day, Mr. Gray came home with a brown-skinned toddler, said that the child was his son and that the mother was no longer around to raise him and so Mrs. Gray would. Mrs. Gray recognized that the fault here lay with her husband and not the boy, and so Gray was raised as if he were her own.

As for the three others, Annis is the oldest. Then there's a son, Lachlan, who washed his hands of both the business and the responsibility of caring for his female relatives. He tossed that on Gray's lap and waltzed off to . . . Where? What? I have no idea. I just know he isn't around on a regular basis. Neither is their mother.

Despite my presumptions, Mrs. Gray is alive and well and living in Europe. When her husband died, she stayed a couple of years to help steady Gray in his new role and then left to pursue her own interests abroad, which her children—well, Gray and Isla at least—fully support. That's where Isla is now: visiting her mother.

The coach leaves Edinburgh, which doesn't take long at this time of night, the streets empty except for delivery vehicles. We quickly pass into the countryside, and we've gone maybe five miles when we turn in to a lane.

In Victorian times, we're in rural Scotland. In the twenty-first century, I'm sure this is a suburb, the estate long since divided into residential lots. Is the main house still there, perched on a few acres? If so, it'd be worth a fortune.

The Grays have money. The Leslies vault over that. They are the wealthy elite, with both title and money. Annis did very well for herself, despite the "family scandal" of their dad bringing home an illegitimate child for his wife to raise.

It takes at least five minutes to get from the road to the main house. I say "main house" because I spot other buildings, although it's too dark to tell their purpose.

The estate reminds me of ones I've toured with my nan. Is it possible I've toured *this* one? After a while, they blur into one big "Can you imagine living in a place like this?"

Nan always said she could imagine it very well—she could imagine how quickly she'd become one of those Victorian madwomen in the attic, faking insanity just to get a room of her own. I never quite understood what she meant until I came to Victorian Scotland.

As spacious as the Gray town house is, there's no place in it that's truly private for Gray or Isla. The library, the drawing room, even their own bedrooms are subject to invasion at any moment, Alice sliding in to clean a hearth, me rapping at the door to see when they want tea. Don't get me wrong—I would *love* to have someone bring coffee and fresh-baked cookies for my morning snack. I would just prefer it to be dropped off by a delivery service. My condo is my private abode.

The house Simon pulls up to is big enough for an extended family of twenty-five. Even without that, there will be enough work for a staff of that size. To a modern person, a large staff seems like an obscene show of wealth. As I've come to understand, though, it's a way of life. Gray and Isla don't need four full-time employees and one part-time gardener. It's partly to free them up for their private studies, but it's also about offering employment. Even if that's not Annis's motivation, this massive estate still provides employment in a world where the options may be that or the poorhouse.

Gray has Simon drop us off at a side entrance, one I suspect is mostly used for deliveries and staff. I presume he's being discreet, but when a woman in a housekeeper's dark dress and chatelaine answers that door, he says, "Dr. Duncan Gray," and there is no sign on the woman's face that she realizes he's anything other than some random tradesperson. In fact, as her gaze fixes on his face, her eyes narrow.

"A doctor?" she says.

"Yes," Gray says, with the patience of long years of practice.

"A medical doctor?"

"Yes. I was asked to attend by Lady Leslie herself."

The woman stays where she is, blocking the door. Her gaze drops to his medical bag and takes in his suit, but again it returns to his face and stays there, as if the rest cannot negate that part of the equation.

"Are you a foreign doctor?" she says. "You sound Scottish."

I rock forward, ready to end this nonsense, when a voice from down the hall says, "Mabel, please let Dr. Gray in. He is not only a physician but Lady Leslie's brother."

Mabel backs up, looking even more confused. The newcomer is about Annis's age but small and delicate, with finely cut features, chestnut-brown hair, and a perfect Cupid's bow of a mouth. She might be closing in on forty, but she's gorgeous in a doll-like way.

"Duncan!" she says. "How delightful to see you. And it's *Doctor* Gray now. That is wonderful to hear. I always knew that brain of yours would take you far."

"S-Sarah," Gray stumbles on the name. "I did not realize you . . ." He trails off.

Sarah smiles. "You did not realize I was back in Annis's good graces?

Yes, I was surprised at it myself. It only took fifteen years. That must be a record for your sister overcoming a grudge."

Gray shifts and then rolls his shoulders as if to hide his discomfort. "It has been a long time."

"Since the day Annis accepted Lord Leslie's proposal, to be exact. One does not disagree with your sister without risking the consequences. But it truly is good to see you, Duncan. May I still call you that? It was appropriate when you were a schoolboy, but perhaps it is no longer."

"No, of course. You were—are—Annis's dearest friend. Duncan is fine."

I clear my throat, as discreetly as possible.

Gray looks over, starting as if I appeared from nowhere. "Oh, of course. This is Mallory. Mallory Mitchell. My assistant."

"A female medical assistant? Oh, I am glad to hear we are heading in that direction at last. Pleased to meet you, Miss Mitchell."

"And you as well."

"Duncan," a sharp voice sounds down the hall. "Are you actually going to attend to my husband? Or did you come to make eyes at Sarah?"

"He is doing nothing of the sort, Annis. Stop needling him or he will not attend to your husband at all." Sarah arches one perfect brow in her friend's direction. "Unless that is your objective. Drive him out before he can help?"

Annis waves a hand and strides back down the hall.

"We have been summoned," Sarah murmurs. "Ignore it at your peril."

"I heard that," Annis says without turning.

"You were supposed to, dearest."

"Is there any chance we can know what has befallen Lord Leslie?" I say. "In advance of seeing him?"

Annis looks back then, fixing me with the look you give a child who has spoken out of turn.

"Poison," Sarah says. "Lord Leslie has been poisoned."

Annis leads us down enough corridors that I'm beginning to wonder whether she really is trying to stall until her husband dies. We walk down multiple halls lined with dead people. Well, portraits of old and presumably now-dead people. All men, too. Unless the Leslie family mastered the art of self-procreation, there must be women in their family tree, but none warranted a spot in these corridors.

There are a lot of rooms. From my admittedly brief stint as a time traveler, I've concluded that Victorians like their rooms to serve specific functions. Of course, that doesn't apply to the poor, who have three generations living in a room smaller than my tiny Vancouver condo. For the middle class and up, though, room function is important in a way it isn't in my world, where rooms often meld together in open-concept areas or serve multiple functions—office, library, TV room, and sitting area.

Even in this mansion, rooms are small and very distinct. Through open doors, I see a music lounge, a library, a sunroom, and two "sitting" rooms with different decors.

Victorian decor is another thing altogether. It's loud and it's cluttered and it's often themed, even if that theme is as loose as "everything is blood red scarlet." Many items come from other parts of the world—this probably being the first time period where you could easily do that—and in this house, culture is a major theme, with an Egyptian room, an African room, an Indian room. There's even one that I suspect is a Canadian room, complete with dead beavers and the most garish fake totem pole I've ever seen.

Are these all places Lord Leslie has visited and brought souvenirs home from? That's possible, but it also screams "colonial Britain," each room proudly displaying the art and culture and creatures as if they are spoils of war to which Leslie is personally entitled. In that context, the "Canada room" takes on a whole new meaning, as if my country—and its Indigenous peoples—are a trophy.

I think there's a sense that the Victorians were unanimously proud of their empire and blind to the damage it did. That is not the case, as I've learned. Some are uncomfortable with its implications even in this time.

As we walk, Sarah explains Lord Leslie's condition. He began complaining of stomach trouble three days ago. Annis was in London, where she'd been standing in for her husband on a business matter. Why was she doing that? Gray doesn't ask, which means this isn't surprising. Is Lord Leslie in generally ill health? Elderly? The point is that Annis was away, and she was summoned back when her husband came down with this stomach ailment.

The doctor had prescribed what Sarah calls cleansing medicines. From the discreet description, she means emetics and laxatives. In other words, stuff that will clean out your digestive system from both ends. That didn't work, and soon what was coming out was blood. Gray seems unconcerned about this and asks only what was prescribed, leaving me wondering how harsh Victorian laxatives are.

It was the housekeeper—Mabel—who first raised the specter of poison. A package of candied figs had been delivered in Lady Leslie's absence. According to Mabel, they'd been taken directly to Lord Leslie. Sarah—who'd been staying at the house for the past month—was in the room with him, playing cards. She'd asked who sent them, and Lord Leslie made some noises and changed the subject.

"A lover," Annis says curtly. "His response means he believed they came from a lover."

"Are the figs still around?" I ask. "If so, perhaps they can be tested . . ." I cast a questioning glance at Gray.

"Yes," Gray says. "Isla knows methods for detecting poison in food."

"The figs are gone," Annis says.

"Eaten?" I say.

When I get another look from Annis, Gray says, "Please consider Mallory's questions to be for Hugh. She has excellent instincts for detective work."

"Originating from her experience on the wrong side of it?" Annis says sharply. "I know my sister's practices. Bringing convicted criminals into our family home."

"I was never convicted," I say. "Owing to my aptitude for detective work."

Sarah laughs. "Careful with this one, Annis. She is not one of the simpering lasses *you* hire."

"I do not hire them. Gordon did, and simpering is exactly how he liked them."

I clear my throat. "You may not want to refer to your husband in the past tense just yet."

I expect her to snap at me, maybe tell Gray to call me to heel. Instead, I get a very different look. Appraising. Considering. Then she nods and says, to my surprise, "Fair point. All right then, Detective Mallory. When I say the figs are gone, I select my words with care. At first, Lord Leslie refused to produce the box. I presume there was some love note scrawled on the inside. Then, when Sarah convinced him that it was important, he went to produce the box and it was gone. That is when he began accusing me—"

"Lady Leslie," a sharp voice calls from down the hallway. "Your husband is on his deathbed, and you are entertaining guests?"

I peer down the semi-dark hall to see a slight-statured woman with gray-streaked hair and a cane, which she waggles at Annis.

"Come," she says. "Now. He has been calling for you."

The woman turns and stalks off.

"He only wants me in there so she can harangue me," Annis mutters. "Same as that damnable sister of his."

"Language, dearest," Sarah murmurs. "You are a woman of quality."

Annis mutters more under her breath, but she does pick up her pace. Gray matches it as he walks alongside her. I hang back with Sarah.

"I presume that was Lord Leslie's sister?" I whisper.

"Yes," Sarah says. "The Honorable Helen Bannerman."

"She is not fond of Lady Leslie?" I whisper.

Sarah gives me a look, complete with a small smile. "No one is fond of Annis, my dear. Except those she is fond of, and they are exceedingly fond of her in return, though I've never been certain whether that is because it's deserved or because we are flattered."

When I don't respond, she leans in and say, "I am teasing, of course. Annis is not the woman she appears." She purses her lips. "Well, she is, and she is also not, if that makes sense."

"She is exactly as she appears, but to those who know her well, she is more."

Sarah taps my arm with a gloved hand. "Precisely. As for Helen, she is next in line to the title as Annis has no children."

Gray looks back and says to me, "If a peerage has no male heirs, the title may pass to the eldest female to avoid extinction."

Sarah nods. "Helen will inherit the title and the house."

A woman can inherit? Is that because Scotland doesn't practice coverture? If so, how does that explain what happened in Gray's family, the house and business and assets passing from Lachlan to Gray, despite Annis being the oldest and Gray being the youngest?

"Annis does not begrudge Helen the house," Sarah continues. "It is a greedy, devouring monster. What Helen *won't* inherit is the money that keeps it fed. That is Annis's . . . unless she is sent to the gallows for murder."

"Ah."

"Ah, indeed."

"Annis, there you are." A male voice wafts out, one that sounds oddly hollow, as if it is accustomed to booming but can no longer manage that. "Where have you been? Who is that—? What is *he* doing in my house? Damn it, woman, at least wait until I'm dead before you bring that half-breed bastard through my door."

I pick up speed as Annis says she has invited Gray to perform a medical examination.

"Examine me? Speed me on my way more like."

I finally reach the room. It looks like . . . Okay, I have no idea what purpose this room would serve. I'd say it's a sitting room, but we passed two others that also looked like sitting rooms.

This one definitely has a masculine air to it, complete with dead-animal heads on the wall.

Oh, wait, the dead critters aren't only on the walls. There's a meerkat rearing in the corner and a cobra posed midstrike and— Holy shit, is that a tiger? Yep, there's an actual stuffed tiger, snarling. Or I presume it's supposed to be snarling, but the creature seems to be howling in outrage at being turned into a daybed.

A man lies in that daybed. He's big—he'd likely match Gray in height and build if he were standing. Gray-haired and handsome, probably in his midfifties. I'd expected him to be older. Maybe that's a stereotype for a guy who married a woman climbing the social ladder.

Lord Leslie is also dying. I don't need to be a doctor to see that. His breathing is labored, his skin sallow, eyes dull, and he seems to holding on by sheer willpower. Or maybe it's just spite, given the way he's glaring at Annis.

"Duncan," Annis says. "Please examine my husband."

The shadows in the room shift, and I realize there are other people there. It's night, obviously, but the single oil lamp only illuminates Lord Leslie. Also, I may have mistaken the other two people for more dead animals.

One is Helen. The other is a man. In his case, I'd seen only a long shadow in front of a shadowy wall trophy, and I mistook him for an elephant's trunk.

He's not quite that thin, but when he does move into the light, I can't help thinking he exactly matches my mental picture of an undertaker. A thin wraith with white hair and a pale hound-dog face.

"Yes, Dr. Mackay?" Annis snaps. "You wish to register your objection? Feel free, but be sure to offer supporting evidence for whatever claim you are about to make about my brother. Have you heard anything to suggest faulty medical skills?"

The man starts to open his mouth, but Annis cuts him short. "If you are about to say he is not licensed, we acknowledge that. That is why you are present to oversee this examination. Ultimately, you are his physician, which is probably why he is about to die."

Sarah sighs audibly.

Annis continues, "My brother graduated second in his medical class. He would have been first, if the other boy's parents hadn't made a significant contribution to the college."

Gray clears his throat. "That is not exactly true. We were well matched in—"

"You were robbed."

I look from Annis to Gray. Isn't this the woman who called him a "dunce" an hour ago?

"My brother would have made a first-rate physician," Annis says, "if duty did not require him to take over the family business."

"Duty and a small matter of grave robbery," Lord Leslie wheezes.

I look at Gray, whose face is studiously blank.

"It was a misunderstanding," Annis snaps. "A plot perpetrated by those who could not bear to see a brown-skinned man become a proper doctor."

Gray still says nothing, which makes me suspect that's not the entirety of the story.

Annis turns to Dr. Mackay. "Do *you* have a problem acknowledging the medical skills of a man who looks like my brother?"

As Dr. Mackay blusters, I grudgingly award Annis points for manipulation. She's defending Gray because, in this moment, it behooves her to play the proud sister, supporting her maligned brother.

Do you have a problem with his skin color, Dr. Mackay?

This may be a very different time period, but even if Dr. Mackay were a full-blown bigot, he might still not dare *say* he has a problem with it.

"Lord Leslie?" Gray says, his tone even, expression unreadable. "I am going to examine you now. Dr. Mackay is here to confirm that I am doing nothing else."

Gray unbuttons and then removes his frock coat. "As you can see, I conceal nothing."

Do I detect a bit of theatrical mockery as Gray folds back his cuffs and then extends his hands to Dr. Mackay to check them? Oh yeah, Gray knows this is bullshit. He also knows, from his studiously closed expression, that his sister's praise means nothing. And yet, beneath all her mockery, she must think he's a capable doctor or she wouldn't insist he examine her husband.

"Mallory?" Gray says. "Please assist me."

Leslie, his sister, and the doctor all blink at me, as if surely I'll transform into a man at any moment.

"She is his assistant," Annis says.

"His . . ." Dr. Mackay chokes on the next word, unable to get it out.

"My assistant." Gray turns and fixes the doctor with that same unflappable expression. "There *are* women in medicine, particularly in the United States, which is embarrassingly ahead of Scotland in this regard. Are you truly surprised that a doctor who looks, as Annis says, like me might also employ a female assistant?"

Sarah struggles to hide a smile.

"My brother is quite the radical," Annis says. "Now, dear brother, please do what you can to save my husband's life, as little as he deserves it."

Sarah lets out a long-suffering sigh, but no one else seems the least perturbed.

When we move over to Leslie, the dying man glares at Gray. Then I come into the light, and his head whips around fast enough to make him wince with the effort.

"I say," he murmurs. "What have we here?"

"May I introduce Miss Mallory Mitchell," Gray says.

Leslie smirks. "Assistant, indeed. Never thought you had it in you, boy."

"What are his symptoms?" Gray asks Mackay.

"I'm right here," Leslie says. "Ask me. I can't keep anything down, and my bloody hair is falling out in clumps. My feet feel as if they are on hot coals, and if you touch them, I will strike you down with my bare hands, even if I can scarcely draw breath."

"Severe abdominal pain," Mackay says. "Evacuation of the stomach and bowels. Difficulty breathing. Pain in the feet and lower legs, and a sensitivity to touch. Also, unexplained hair loss."

"I said all that, didn't I?" Leslie says.

Gray examines Leslie. As he does, I murmur, "Thallium?"

His brows knit.

"It's presenting like thallium poisoning," I whisper, as low as I can.

"I do not know what that is."

Has it not been discovered yet? "I'll explain later."

When Gray is done with the examination, he motions for Dr. Mackay and Annis to join us in the hall.

"None of that nonsense," Leslie wheezes. "Whatever you have to say, say it in front of me."

Gray glances at Annis, who shrugs.

Gray clears his throat. "I agree that it is acute poisoning. I am not certain I would have prescribed any course of action different from Dr. Mackay's. Clean out the system in an attempt to rid it of the poison. That did not work. While there is always hope, I would personally prescribe morphine, in as heavy a dose as is needed."

"To let me die in peace?" Leslie says.

Gray meets his bother-in-law's gaze. "Yes."

EIGHT

Leslie does not accept the morphine. He insists he isn't in that much pain, despite the fact that he can barely stay upright. More important, he is not letting anyone inject him with anything that might later let his wife's lawyers claim he wasn't in his right mind when he changed his will. He wants his lawyer here with those papers he'd drawn up, and he wants him here now.

Annis wisely doesn't argue. When her husband shoos us all out, she leaves without a word. Mrs. Bannerman waits until the door shuts and then starts in on Annis again.

It might seem that we should stick around to help, but Annis can look after herself, and I don't imagine she'd appreciate a defense from either her little brother or his assistant. She has Sarah, who stays at her side but also stays out of the fight. As we make our retreat, the last thing we hear is Annis telling her sister-in-law that she doesn't give a damn about the will. She'll escort the lawyer in and hold the pages while Leslie signs them.

It's still a long walk to the side exit, which suggests Annis hadn't led us on a roundabout path—the house just really is that big. Several times, I start to speak, only to catch a whisper of motion down the hall. No one is sleeping tonight. The staff are everywhere, silent and listening.

I wait until we're outside in the courtyard. Simon took the coach to the stables to water Folly. I'm not sure how a Victorian man of means summons his coach. It's not as if he can pop off a text to say "I'm ready to go."

Whatever the answer, it doesn't apply to Gray. Why summon the coach when it is a pleasant evening and the stables are only a couple of hundred meters away?

As we cross the courtyard, I want to ask Gray whether he's okay. He might have seemed unaffected by Leslie's insults and insinuations, but I recognize his calm tone and empty expression for what they are: protective walls.

Gray has had a lifetime to test every possible mode of defense against bigotry and bastard-shaming, and at some point, he decided equanimity was the best response. Unruffled and untouched, insults rolling off him.

Would I want a near stranger to express concern when I thought I'd hidden my hurt feelings? I would not. So when we step outside, I just say, "I have a question."

"Only one?"

"It's multipronged, but I'll start with one."

"The answer is yes."

"Yes, you think Leslie's poisoning could be connected to the other two deaths?"

He glances over. "*That* was your question?"

"What did you think I was going to ask?"

"Whether I was actually censured for grave robbing."

"Oh, I'd have gotten to that eventually."

We pass a small rose garden. I inhale. When I don't get the expected perfume, I bend over a bloom to smell nothing. It's a perfectly tended garden of perfectly matching roses, which might as well be plastic.

I glance at Gray. "The answer is yes—you did rob a grave?"

"No, the answer is yes—I was denied my medical license based on an accusation of grave robbing."

"Which was unfounded? Or a misunderstanding?"

His brows rise.

"Misunderstanding would be my guess," I say. "You did something, and they accused you of grave robbing, which is technically inaccurate. There was, however, a grave and a corpse involved. Some youthful misadventure in the pursuit of science."

He slows and then stops as he faces me. "Isla told you?"

"I'm a detective, remember? Sometimes that's about following clues, and sometimes, it's about making educated guesses based on a person's character. So I'm right?"

"Discomfortingly so." He peers at me. "Are you quite certain Isla did not tell you?"

"Is it the sort of thing she *would* tell me? Or is it the sort of thing that makes you uncomfortable—mostly annoyed at how it was handled but, possibly, a little embarrassed at having done such a thing." I consider. "No, not at having *done* it, but at having not been more careful to *conceal* it."

"That is . . ." He stuffs his hands in his pockets and then pulls them out again, starting to cross his arms before stopping himself. "Isla tells me you studied a form of mind reading at university. You were trained as a criminal alienist."

"Ha! No. There *is* a field for that, and I took courses in it, but my degree is in criminology and sociology, which is more about societal factors than psychological ones. Definitely not mind reading, though that'd be cool. What *did* you do that got you into trouble?"

He glances around, as if to be sure no one lurks in the bushes. Then he lowers his voice. "I opened a grave."

"You dug up a dead body."

He seems about to protest and then squares his shoulders. "Yes, but not by choice. That is to say, I chose to dig it up, but that was not my preferred method of action. The man was the victim of murder, and I believed the official cause of death was incorrect. I wanted to check. I applied for permission to see the body before burial, but I made the mistake of being honest and explaining that I thought the cause of death was incorrect."

"Ah, and that didn't go over well, coming from a recent graduate. When they refused, you took matters into your own hands."

"Yes."

"Were you right?"

"Yes. I exhumed the body with the help of . . . a friend."

"Detective McCreadie."

"A friend," he says firmly.

"And you were caught with the body?"

"No, I was caught because I made a second error of hubris."

"You told someone that you were right about the cause of death, which meant you'd dug up the body. They called it grave robbery and denied you your medical license."

He doesn't answer. I think he doesn't want to discuss it further—even if he's the one who brought it up. Then I notice his gaze, narrow eyed and fixed on a stand of trees. He lifts a hand, motioning for me to be careful. It's only then that I spot a figure outlined against one of the trunks.

"It is only me, Duncan," McCreadie says, stepping into the moonlight. "Testing those preternatural senses of yours."

"Dare I ask why you are lurking around my sister's gardens?" Gray says.

"Because it means I might not actually need to speak to her?"

Gray shakes his head.

McCreadie turns to me. "You have now met Lady Leslie. Your thoughts?"

"She's a real piece of work."

"I presume that is an insult."

"The politest I can come up with. To her credit, she is interesting. In the same way as a venomous snake. I am intrigued in spite of myself. Doesn't mean I want to spend more time with her than necessary."

"You obviously received my note," Gray says to McCreadie.

"And Duncan pulls us back on course," McCreadie says. "Yes. I received it, and I agree it's a difficult situation on multiple counts. Did you feel Annis wants me here because I know her? I have always gotten the impression she barely remembers my name."

I glance at Gray.

McCreadie laughs under his breath. "Ah, she did not, which is why she couldn't approach me directly."

I glance toward the house. "She also wanted Dr. Gray to examine her husband."

"I am not certain *why* Annis insists on you being here," Gray says. "So that she would have an ally among the police? Or because she has misinterpreted your good nature."

"Mistaking it for ineptitude?" McCreadie says.

"Perhaps? But more likely she mistakes it for sympathy. You are my friend. She is my sister. You will be horrified that anyone could think she killed her husband."

McCreadie bursts out laughing, the sound spooking an owl into a hoot of reproval.

"If Annis wanted someone to think she isn't capable of murder," I say, "she'd be better off with a cop who hasn't spent a full minute in her actual presence."

Gray sighs. "You are not wrong. I do not think my sister *in*capable of murder. In this particular instance, though, Leslie's death isn't in her best interests, and so I doubt she is responsible."

"Doubt," I murmur. "Hardly a ringing endorsement."

"The question is what we do next. I appreciate that you came all this way, Hugh. I invite you to ride back to the house with me to discuss this—along with what happened earlier this evening—over a glass of whisky."

"Am I included in that invitation?" I ask.

"I fear not," Gray says. "There isn't room in the coach. You must run behind it like a loyal Dalmatian."

I narrow my eyes.

"Are you not always grumbling about the lack of proper exercise options for young women?" he says. "A good run should do the trick."

McCreadie looks at me. "Yes, you're included, Mallory. In the conversation and the whisky. And possibly the coach but—"

"Duncan?" Annis's voice rings out. "Where the devil are you? I can hear you and that girl of yours." She rounds a garden and spots us. "There you are. And you, too."

"Me, too," McCreadie says. "What is my name again, Lady Leslie?"

"If you don't know it, then I certainly cannot help you. You are an officer of the law, and that is all I need of you right now. Come along."

McCreadie salutes.

Annis peers at him. "Have you been drinking?" She doesn't even wait for an answer, just waves again. "I have oil of peppermint inside to disguise the smell on your breath. My husband buys it by the jug."

"Annis?" Gray says. "Hugh is not going inside with you. He met us out-of-doors because we agree that having him here is not in your best interests."

"Why not?"

"Because he's a criminal officer you have summoned to assist in the investigation of your husband's murder," Gray says. "Except your husband is still alive. Which means your foresight, while admirable, may seem somewhat suspicious."

"My husband is already dead. He only needs to stop breathing to make it official. Gordon has accused me of his murder himself, and his sister is waiting to be sure I am arrested the moment Gordon is pronounced dead. I am protecting myself against an inevitable outcome."

"Maybe," I say, as softly as I can. "I agree it is logical, but most people *aren't* logical. Are the newspapers going to commend you for being so prepared? Or are they going to wonder *why* you were so prepared? Wonder why you showed such foresight . . . when you are a woman, supposedly ruled by emotion. If you didn't kill your husband, you should be prostrate at his bedside, wailing in grief. If you are not what they expect . . . ?" I meet her gaze. "I think you already know what happens when we are not what people expect."

Her eyes lock with mine for a beat past comfort. Then she draws back sharply and grinds out, "I take your point. I do not like it, but I take it."

Annis looks at McCreadie. "You ought not to come into the house, but I would appreciate your advice. How do I handle this so that I do not appear guilty? Should I show grief, even if others know I will not grieve? Or will fakery act against my case?"

"I would suggest—"

A scream from the house cuts McCreadie short. The sound echoes through open windows, and we all go still.

"The master!" a young woman shouts.

I brace for the next part. *He is dead.* That is what will come next, and I try to catch Annis's expression, but it's hidden in shadow.

"His door is locked!" the young woman continues. "Someone has locked his door."

Annis exhales in something like relief and then hisses annoyance through her teeth. "This is why one ought not to hire simpering housemaids. That girl hasn't a brain in her head."

Annis starts walking. Then she turns.

"Duncan?" she says.

"Yes?"

"You are coming back inside, are you not?" She sees the answer in his glance toward the stables. "You cannot leave. Gordon is dying, and I am going to be charged with his murder. If I cannot have your friend here, then you must stay."

"I have things to do," Gray says gently. "Lord Leslie is not going to die tonight, and I have business, as well as—"

"My husband is dying. I will be charged with murder. I am surrounded by idiots and jackals."

I need you. That's what she's saying. Words she cannot manage, even as panic touches her voice.

"You have Sarah," Gray says. "I am glad to see you have reunited—"

The young maid screams for help again, and Annis looks at him.

Gray sighs. "All right. Let us go inside and resolve this. Then I am leaving."

I'm tagging along with Gray because he didn't tell me not to. McCreadie hangs back but still follows us inside. He isn't in uniform, and so he must have decided it's safe to join us.

Finally we reach the hall and find Mrs. Bannerman rattling the knob while Sarah tries to calm the panicked maid.

When the maid sees Annis, she hikes her skirts and runs to us.

"Oh, ma'am," she says. "Someone has locked His Lordship in the room, and he is not answering us, and I fear he has been done for."

"Done for?" Annis says, arching her brows.

"Murdered. Someone has murdered him before the lawyer could arrive and . . ." The girl stops, her eyes rounding. "Where were *you*, ma'am? I went looking for you before His Lordship rang."

"Turning detective now, Dolly?" Annis shakes her head. "You are a very silly girl."

"With a very good point," Mrs. Bannerman says.

"I believe," Annis says dryly, "that we ought to ascertain my husband's condition before I am interrogated for his murder. Did you not just say he rang the bell, Dolly?"

"Or someone did. Perhaps it was his killer."

Gray moves to the door. "Can we please consider how distressing it must be for Lord Leslie to hear people shouting murder accusations before he is dead? The door has been locked by some means, and he is a very sick man who has rung his bell for help and now has to listen to everyone argue instead of coming to his aid."

Gray begins to unbutton his jacket. "I shall break open the door."

"You certainly will not," Annis says. "There is a key somewhere."

"It's missing," Dolly says. "Conveniently."

The maid seems about to say more, only to stop and stare at Gray, who has his jacket off and is now rolling up his sleeves. Now, I'll admit he fills out a dress shirt very nicely. I will also admit that I never found men's bare forearms nearly as attractive as I do now, when I rarely see them, and Gray has very nice ones. However, that is not why Dolly is gaping.

"Wh-what is that?" she says, pointing to a red spot on his white shirt.

"Blood," Gray says. "A vital substance that courses through our bodies and, when we are injured, sometimes courses out of it . . . and through both bandages and shirt, apparently."

"What the devil happened to you?" McCreadie says.

"I was attacked," Gray says. "It was most inconvenient, but Mallory . . . What are you doing, Mallory?"

While everyone chatters, I've crouched before the lock with a hairpin. Victorian women get a lot of very handy pins—hairpins, stickpins, hatpins. I give this particular pin another nudge. Then I twist the knob and crack open the door.

"Well done," McCreadie murmurs. "You really must teach me that."

I push open the door . . . and there is Annis's husband, half on the floor, head thrown back, eyes bulging.

It's now official: Lord Leslie has been murdered.

NINE

There is an advantage to having so many people milling about, eager to accuse others of murder. They tend to ignore everyone who isn't their target, which is why I'd been able to get that door open without anyone stopping me. It was also how McCreadie was able to join us without anyone asking who he is. And now it's how McCreadie, Gray, and I can begin our investigation without anyone telling us to get the hell away from the body.

I must also allot some credit to Annis and Sarah. Annis wants her brother and McCreadie to get a look at the scene before Lord Leslie is taken away. She also won't want to give Leslie's sister ammunition by letting her realize Gray is examining the corpse, maybe even tampering with evidence.

Is tampering with evidence a concern yet? For as long as people have been murdered there has been the risk of evidence tampering, but we aren't yet in a world of CSI. Detective novels are a new genre. Hell, *detectives* are new.

I've already learned that there's no such thing as crime-scene containment and there are only the vaguest concerns about contamination. Why would there be, in a world where forensic science is even newer than detective work? If Mrs. Bannerman caught Gray near Leslie's body, she'd probably flip out, but she might not even know *why* she's flipping out. She'd just have a general sense that the lead suspect's brother shouldn't be touching the murder victim.

Annis keeps her sister-in-law's attention off us, letting Mrs. Bannerman rant about how Annis wasn't content to poison Lord Leslie—now she hurried his death along to keep him from changing his will. The maid, Dolly, joins in with her accusations. Sarah calls for someone to fetch Dr. Mackay back and then says they should leave the body until he arrives and scoots them all out of the room . . . with nobody seeming to notice that we're still there.

In fact, except for the maid's bloodcurdling screams on seeing her dead employer, no one has paid *any* attention to Lord Leslie. They'd just continued arguing beside the corpse half slumped on the floor.

I know Annis is hardly a grieving widow, but her sister-in-law has no excuse. The only thing Mrs. Bannerman seems to care about is that Leslie died before he could change his will and pass along his money with the house. Even Dolly's wailing struck me as pure drama. Like a paid mourner, except her payment is theatrical pleasure. And Sarah? Her attention had been on Annis, all her concern there, because Leslie hadn't earned any even from her.

Is *anyone* going to mourn the dead man? That remains to be seen.

The first obvious question is whether Mrs. Bannerman is right. Did someone decide not to wait for the poison to do its job? Was Leslie, in effect, murdered twice?

Gray doesn't tell McCreadie or me to step back. He trusts we won't contaminate evidence, and so we are welcome to not only examine the body but vocalize our findings.

Isla believes Gray has what we'd now call mild ADHD. He might, but she's wrong in thinking he needs to be left alone to focus or he'll get distracted. He gets distracted only when he wants distraction. That is, when whatever is being offered is more interesting than what he's doing. Otherwise, he's able to examine Leslie's body while we do the same and talk to him. He wants to teach, and he's delighted that we're interested in learning.

Still, neither student is eager to interrupt the master, and so McCreadie and I whisper together as we examine Leslie, which is mostly either me passing on my observations or McCreadie asking for my interpretation of *his* observations.

What we see is the ravages of poison. I've sat in on poisoning autopsies—I'm the keener who volunteers—but this is different. This isn't someone who accidentally ingested a toxin and died in a hospital under treatment. Nor is it someone who has been slowly poisoned, the killer trying to hide their tracks. It isn't even fast poison, killing before the victim understands what's happening. This is poison at its ugliest—breaking down a body in a world that has no way to reverse or stop the process. Leslie knew he was dying of poison and that no one could help him, and while he hardly seemed like a man I'd want to know better, I can mourn him for the sheer horror of his fate.

It's hard to tell whether someone hurried the process along with another murderous method. While we don't dare strip off Leslie's clothing, there are no obvious stab wounds. No obvious head wounds. No marks around his neck.

"Conclusions?" Gray says.

"Honestly, I don't know," I say. "If he was murdered, I'd say the most likely cause would be suffocation. One of those throw pillows pressed to his face. His eyes are bloodshot, but they were earlier, too, so there's nothing in an external examination to argue for or against suffocation."

Gray's gaze drops to Leslie's hands.

I curse under my breath. "Right. Look for signs of a struggle." I check Leslie's fingernails. "Two are broken, and I don't know whether there's any way to tell how recently. Poison could weaken the nails."

"The break on his middle finger is still jagged," Gray says. "That could indicate a struggle. However, it might also have happened earlier. Filing it smooth would hardly have been a priority in the past day. Lord Leslie is wide-eyed and his expression is one of shock, which one might see as proof of murder, but it can also be proof of, well, death."

"He knew it was coming, and he didn't think it'd be quite so soon. Also, he was waiting for the lawyer, so if he realized he was going to die before the guy showed up, he'd be horrified."

"Presumably." Gray straightens. "An autopsy will help indicate whether he could have been suffocated or otherwise murdered in a way we cannot see from an external observation of his clothed corpse. Is there anything we can determine from the scene?"

Here's where McCreadie takes over. Yes, I'm a detective, and I certainly *want* to analyze all my modern-day scenes, but if the crime is big enough to warrant that kind of attention, it's also big enough to warrant crime-scene techs.

I've spent years immersing myself in forensic studies, with hope first of becoming a detective and then in hopes of joining major crimes, but it really is, again, just me being a keener. As a detective, I mostly talk to people. Hell, even my detective work isn't searching for clues so much as searching for more people to talk to.

I know the theory of thorough crime-scene investigation—I just haven't put it into practice. McCreadie *does* put it into practice. He may not have learned the importance of crime-scene containment, but he does know the importance of the scene itself.

"The door locks from the inside," McCreadie says, walking over to it. "It only requires the twist of this little thumb turn. That makes it difficult to determine whether Leslie himself could have locked it after we left—if it was a key, we'd expect to find it on him. But if someone else locked it from the inside, they'd need to exit afterward, and these windows don't open."

"Can the door be locked and then pulled shut from the hall?" I ask.

McCreadie smiles. "Excellent question. Let's find out."

He reaches for the door. Gray clears his throat, and McCreadie stops.

"Finger marks," McCreadie says. "We are now being aware of finger marks."

They were already "aware" of them, in the sense that they knew fingerprints were allegedly unique. That's still hard for me to wrap my head around. If you believe fingerprints are unique, why aren't you using them? Several reasons. One, it's a new science that most people aren't aware of, and even some who are, like McCreadie, aren't convinced of its validity. Two, the police lack an easy method of revealing prints on a surface. Three, while they could develop that method, what's the point when the legal system doesn't recognize the validity of it? More important, lacking that official recognition, they cannot compel a suspect to "give up" their fingerprints as exemplars.

Yes, forensic science in 1869 is a lot more complicated than I expected. I presumed that they don't use things like fingerprints because they hadn't "discovered" that science. Not true. There's just a massive gulf between discovery, acceptance, and practice.

"I'm not sure you're going to get a useful print off that tiny thumb turn," I say. "Yes, twist it from the edges, please, but even if we found Leslie or

Annis's prints . . . or the maid's, the doctor's, his sister's, and so on, these are all people who may have had reason to lock it in the past few days."

McCreadie gingerly turns the mechanism to the locked position and then attempts to close the door. It stops at the latch. He gives it a harder push, but that latch stays firm. I walk over and test the latch with my fingers. It doesn't retract until the lock is turned.

I turn to Gray. "What's the chance Leslie could have gotten over here and locked the door himself?"

"I see no sign of a cane or other walking device, which suggests he wasn't able to walk with the pain in his lower extremities."

"He did mention how much his feet hurt. He didn't strike me as the sort who'd stay bedridden if he didn't need to."

"True, to a point. He was quite happy to order others around, but he abhorred weakness. He once fired a groom when the man's leg didn't set properly after a horse kicked it. The dragging leg meant that the groom was not in perfect physical condition, and that was unacceptable. I will confirm my suspicions with Dr. Mackay, of course, but the lack of a cane suggests Lord Leslie could not walk and therefore could not have locked that door."

"Yet it was locked, and there's no other way out. Gentlemen, we have ourselves one of my favorite types of mystery. The locked-room murder."

McCreadie's brows shoot up. "The what?"

"It's a trope in detective fiction. Someone dies in a room and there's no way for their killer to have escaped. Hey, this could be the *first* locked-room murder. The actual basis for the trope. Lord Leslie dies in a locked room and it makes headline news and, boom, the first locked-room mystery."

"Except that he may have died of poison," McCreadie says.

"Ah, but that doesn't explain the locked door."

Gray clears his throat.

I look at him and sigh. "Yes? What rain do *you* wish to dump on my parade?"

"The key."

"What key? The key is . . ." I groan. "Right. There is a key, which is missing, and which could have been used by the killer to lock the door."

"Also . . ." Gray begins.

"Right. I picked the lock. Maybe it can be locked that way, too."

I take out a hairpin and bend at the keyhole. As I'm tinkering, Gray says to McCreadie, "Anything else you observed at the scene, Hugh?"

"No. Go ahead and show me what I missed."

"What the devil are you doing, girl?" a voice says from down the hall.

It's Dr. Mackay, striding my way.

I straighten and turn to Gray. "I could not get it to lock that way, sir, which doesn't mean it's impossible."

"Mean *what* is impossible?" Mackay says.

"That someone killed Lord Leslie, and then locked the door behind them without a key."

"Killed Lord Leslie? The man was poisoned. He died . . ." Mackay trails off as he sees Leslie lying half on the floor. "What the devil did you do to him, Gray? I understand you have something of a reputation for . . . examining the dead, but you cannot go pushing and pulling the poor man around to satisfy your morbid curiosity."

"He was like that when we walked in," McCreadie says. "Everyone—including his sister—can attest to that, which is why we left him in situ."

"In what?"

"In situ. It means—"

"I know what the term means. I don't know why you are using it. Who are you anyway?"

"I am a friend of—"

"You're a policeman, aren't you? One of those detective fellows. I met you a few months ago. I was tending to a young woman who had been—" His gaze shoots to me. "Tampered with, and you were in charge of the case."

"Yes, but I came here to speak to my friend, Dr. Gray, on another matter, and we were outside when—"

Mackay cuts McCreadie off with a wave of his hand. "I do not care how you got to be here. I am only glad that you are. You must arrest Lady Leslie. She poisoned her husband, and I promised Lord Leslie I would see her arrested . . ."

Mackay trails off as his gaze drops to the body. "You said you found him like this?"

"Yes."

"That seems an odd position, if he died of the poison."

"That was our thinking on the matter," Gray says without a drop of sarcasm. "You would agree then, Dr. Mackay?"

"I would agree that this is clearly a case for the police surgeon." He looks at McCreadie. "Yes?"

"It is, sir. I only needed you to confirm that. I will notify Dr. Addington posthaste."

Here's where it gets weird. Okay, yes, it's already weird. A locked-room murder. Gray's sister accused of killing her husband, whom she openly disdained. Her husband himself accusing her of poisoning him. Her husband dying before his lawyer could arrive to write her out of his will. Her husband *poisoned* while the city is aflutter over two other poisoning deaths, with the wives already convicted in the court of public opinion.

Yet the next bit of weirdness is another of those Victorian detective experiences that leave me shuddering. Like watching people tramp through a crime scene. Or leaving Gray with his brother-in-law's body . . . when his sister is the prime suspect.

Admittedly, this new concern is just an extension of one that's been boggling my mind for a while now. There's one police surgeon in Edinburgh. Dr. Addington. The city isn't that big yet and there aren't enough murders—or deaths recognized as murder—to warrant a second position. With that in mind, I have no problem with the idea of a single primary medical examiner. I do have a problem with Addington.

The man is as incompetent as they come, but even here I can't lay claim to the moral high ground on behalf of the twenty-first century, because we have our share of incompetent medical examiners. No, the real mind-boggle is that the guy who *actually* examines the bodies is Gray. Oh, Addington conducts the autopsies, which makes it worse—Gray would do a far better job. But being a lazy ass and a fastidious snob, Addington refuses to autopsy bodies in the local morgues. He likes Gray's funeral parlor.

This is damned convenient for Gray, giving him a chance to study the bodies to further his forensic studies *and* slide his observations into McCreadie's ear for the investigators. Gray has a very sweet setup here, kindly letting Addington use his facilities, keeping them in pristine shape, even making sure he's served tea and biscuits.

So that's weird. Clever as hell, and a boon to the police, but still weird. And tonight it gets weirder still.

McCreadie sends Annis's coach to fetch Addington and let him know that Gray's brother-in-law has died and an autopsy is required. The coachman is instructed to also tell Addington that Gray's sister has been at least unofficially accused of the murder. The coachman is to convey Addington to whichever morgue he wishes to use for the autopsy and then return to bring him the body.

Once the coach is gone, we wait. I'm not sure why, but we do, all of us in a room, drinking tea and not talking. It's a very crowded sitting room, and there's a lot to say, but no one seems eager to talk. We can't discuss the crime in front of Annis and her sister-in-law, and they seem to have said all they wish to say to one another.

Thirty minutes later, the coachman returns. He walks into the room and clears his throat.

"Dr. Addington says we are to convey Lord Leslie's remains to Dr. Gray's house, and he will conduct the autopsy there."

I look at Gray, trying to keep my jaw from dropping.

Gray only sips his tea, and I realize this is why we're hanging around. To receive this answer, and to be clear to everyone concerned that this *is* Addington's answer, as bizarre as it might be.

"You gave him the entire message?" Gray says when he lowers his tea-cup. "He understands that Lord Leslie is my brother-in-law and my sister has been accused of his death."

"Yes, sir, and he wanted to know what difference that made. He seemed most confused."

"I only wished him to be aware of the circumstances."

Gray looks at Leslie's sister and the doctor. "Dr. Addington commonly utilizes my funerary parlor, as a convenient and well-stocked laboratory for his autopsies."

They don't stare at him in shock. They just wait for him to go on.

Gray continues, "If you have no objection, I will have Lord Leslie taken there, where Dr. Addington will meet us and conduct the autopsy."

"In the morning," the coachman says. "Begging your pardon, sir, but Dr. Addington said he is in bed and will do it in the morning."

"The morning then," Gray says. "Is that acceptable?"

"You aren't sending him in *my* coach, are you?" Mrs. Bannerman says.

"No, in one of Lord Leslie's coaches."

"Which are now mine. They're part of the estate. Do you not have some method of conveyance? A police wagon?"

"I hardly think Lord Leslie's remains should be conveyed in a common police wagon."

"Then you have a hearse carriage, do you not? Send for that." Mrs. Bannerman rises. "I am going to bed. I will have a long day tomorrow. Annis? Have Dolly and Dot attend to me at breakfast. I wish to interview the staff tomorrow and determine who will be staying on."

And that's it. No one has the slightest concern about Leslie's body spending the night at the house of his alleged murderer's brother. In fact, he can be taken there in Gray's own hearse.

I have no words. Strike that. I have plenty of words, but I'm sure as hell not going to speak them. This is in Annis's best interests, and so it's in Gray's best interests. It is also, because I fully trust Gray and McCreadie, in the best interests of the justice system.

TEN

Fine, I don't keep quiet. That's fundamentally impossible for me, as has been pointed out on many occasions, by many people. My parents raised me to be an independent thinker unafraid to speak her mind, and I love them for that, but it does get me into situations where I really wish I'd been able to keep quiet.

Once we're outside, I make my case to McCreadie and Gray. That "case" is that I am afraid if the procurator fiscal finds out that Gray had possession of his brother-in-law's body, pre-autopsy, he'll use it against Annis. Alternately, if someone else is charged, the defense could use it in their client's favor, alleging Gray covered up evidence that his sister murdered her husband.

They are both momentarily confused as to what Gray could cover up. A valid point, when there's not much the courts will accept as legitimate forensic evidence. As both men have explained, the evidence Gray finds is mostly used by McCreadie to obtain confessions from suspects frightened by his uncanny knowledge of their crimes.

Still, Gray and McCreadie *do* see my point. It helps that I'm not just throwing out problems for them to handle; I'm also offering a solution, in this case that McCreadie bring in a police constable to escort the body and stand guard over it until Addington arrives. That way, no one can accuse Gray of tampering.

As for Annis, while the lawyer has arrived—finally—and Mrs. Bannerman has called for him to have Annis arrested, that doesn't happen. It's all showmanship, and even Mrs. Bannerman doesn't seem to expect an arrest. Annis isn't some common housemaid. It's going to take more than even her husband's dying accusation to get her dragged to a police office.

Simon drives Gray and me back to the town house. Then he returns with the hearse for Lord Leslie's body, McCreadie, and the constable. Gray and McCreadie may not be sure what kind of tampering I fear, but now that I've raised the possibility, they aren't leaving the body alone in the Leslie house either. McCreadie escorts it to the funeral parlor, where he helps the officer bring it into the laboratory.

Gray and I wait upstairs in the sitting room, kept awake by biscuits alone, our solemn munching the only sound. The clock has rung four, and neither of us has suggested retiring for the night. With everything that's happened, we haven't even had time to tell McCreadie about earlier this evening, our failed chase and our encounter with mysterious Jack.

When McCreadie comes up to the drawing room, he doesn't suggest going home either. He slumps into a chair, and I offer to make tea while opining that the sound of the kettle might wake Mrs. Wallace—sleeping beside the kitchen—and so perhaps we should have a drink instead? They declare that a fine idea. Terribly pragmatic of me. I break out the scotch—*whisky*, I remind myself—and more biscuits, and we settle in.

Gray allows me to tell our side of the night's earlier adventures. I'd be more flattered if he didn't just want first choice of the newly added biscuits.

When I finish, McCreadie tells us about *his* evening, which seems even less productive. My guess is that the young woman we followed was the one who'd told the other about "Queen Mab." That means McCreadie followed the one who'd been told, but while she'd gotten directions, she only headed home, obviously planning to use them another day, if she decided to attempt an abortion at all.

I say "attempt" because I have no idea whether that *can* be done by chemical form. I show great restraint by not jumping in to ask. I've learned that certain subjects make the men very uncomfortable, and while that can be fun, I'm feeling respectful tonight.

As it turns out, I've misjudged. I hedge around the question, and they tell me to speak to Isla, not because they won't discuss it but because they can't. Ultimately, whether "Queen Mab" can provide some kind of abortion powder is hardly the point. What matters is that she is the person others believe is behind any poison ring, which means she is both someone we need to interview and someone we need to warn. Jack will handle the second part. The first? That may be trickier.

We're trying to stay awake until Addington arrives, but once we've hashed out the Queen Mab lead, the cookies and the booze settle in, and I know I have questions—so many questions—but I can't remember any of them. McCreadie falls asleep first, and I glance at Gray, expecting him to suggest I head to my quarters, but he only lifts his empty glass.

"More?" he says. "Or are you ready to retire for the evening?"

In answer, I rise and take the whisky decanter to him.

"I wasn't asking you to fill my glass," Gray says while not making any move to get up. He's reclined on the sofa, his jacket off, cuffs unbuttoned, feet propped on an ottoman. Dark curls have escaped from their hold, spilling over his forehead and making him look very young and very relaxed.

As I add a shot or two to his raised glass, his knuckles brush mine, and I suppress a shiver. That's one thing about this world: the lack of touch. To greet someone with a hug is rare and reserved for close relationships. Casual touches are avoided, especially between men and women, and the accidental brush of Gray's knuckles feels as intimate as if he ran his fingers up my arm.

When I finish pouring and step back, he catches my hand lightly. I look down at him, still relaxed and unguarded after the first glass of whisky.

"I am sorry for the end of the evening," he says. "It was going quite well before Annis arrived."

I sputter a quiet laugh, careful not to wake McCreadie. "You were *stabbed*."

One shoulder lifts in a shrug. "A scratch."

"That required stitches. How is it?"

"Quite fine. You make an excellent seamstress of human flesh."

I choke back a louder laugh. "If you ever need to write a recommendation for me, please don't put that on it."

"If you are seeking other employment, I might very well put that on it."

"Nah, I'm not going anywhere. What other boss would take me out to play a doxy? Pursue a target through midnight streets and alleys, and fight off not one, not two, but *three* ruffians intent on terrorizing an innocent woman. It was quite an evening."

"Agreed."

He lifts his glass, and I toast with my unfinished one. Then I slide back down to my chair.

"So, thallium," he says. "Tell me about thallium."

"It's a heavy metal. I know it was discovered—accidentally, I think—in the nineteenth century, so it hasn't been yet? Not discovered, that is. It exists, obviously. But if it hasn't been identified, I doubt it's being used for poison."

"Unless it is *commonly* used for poison, I would not be aware of it, even if it has been discovered. We will speak to Isla on her return the day after tomorrow. For now, tell me what you can."

"I studied it for a case I was involved in. It's tasteless, odorless, and colorless, which is why it'll come to be known as the poisoner's poison."

"It sounds a beast."

"It is. It presents like a lot of heavy metals. What made me think thallium was the hair loss plus painful legs and his complaint about his feet burning."

"Peripheral neuropathy."

"I guess? You're the doctor. I just recall the symptoms. I also think those can take a while to develop, but every case is different."

"It does seem like a match. I don't recall seeing that particular constellation of symptoms before."

"Have you handled any interesting poisoning cases?"

His lips twitch. "Are you looking for a bedtime story, Mallory?"

"Possibly."

"All right. Let me see. Ah, there was one, when I was still in medical school . . ."

I settle in, close my eyes, and let myself fall under the spell of Gray's voice.

"Mallory!"

I startle awake to find myself staring into the face of a preteen girl. There's a surreal moment where I think I'm a teen myself, shaken awake from a nap by one of my babysitting charges. Yes, I was the world's worst babysitter.

"Mallory," Alice whispers, her dark eyes wide with alarm. "Get up! You've . . . you've . . ."

She can't finish the sentence. Her gaze only darts from side to side, as if that is enough. When it travels the same path again, I follow it to see McCreadie slumped in his chair, mouth open, while Gray has taken the sofa, his long legs over the end of it. Both men have their eyes closed, deep in sleep, though their poses suggest a far more sinister conclusion.

"No," I say quickly. "They're fine. I didn't poison them. I . . ."

I trail off as I see her confusion, and I realize her shock comes from the fact that I am sleeping with them. I will point out that they are ten feet away, and we are all fully dressed, but from Alice's expression, we might as well be naked in Gray's bed—all three of us.

"You need to get out of here," she whispers. "Dr. Addington is coming upstairs. He cannot see you—"

"Sleeping fully dressed in the same room as two men?"

Her glare tells me I am dismissing her very legitimate concern. I grumble under my breath, push myself to my feet, and adjust my bodice. Alice rolls her eyes and motions for me not to bother. Having my breasts half exposed at 8:00 A.M. isn't nearly as scandalous as falling asleep in the same room as my employer.

Victorians.

I head into the hallway. "I shall need to don my work dress and—"

"Oh, please do not bother," a voice says from down the hall. "Not on my account, dear girl."

My expression has Alice sniggering. I straighten and turn to face the newcomer. He's younger than me—well, younger than the real me. Twenty-nine, I'm told, with a lean and lanky build, red hair, and blue eyes that are currently fastened to my half-bared bosom.

"Dr. Addington, sir," I say breathily, as I curtsy to give him an even better view.

Having slipped behind Addington, Alice gives me a clear "What the hell are you doing?" look. Then she grins as she figures it out. She might not yet possess the "assets" for this particular trick, but as a former pickpocket, she is well versed in the art of distraction.

"It is lovely to see you again, sir," I say. "Please, allow me to fetch Dr. Gray, who will be most eager to speak to you about the autopsy."

"No need," Addington says. "I shall send McCreadie a report. I am done and returning home for breakfast, which I delayed, as is wise when performing such an operation. It is most . . ." A nose wrinkle. "Unpleasant."

"I can but imagine. It is so good of you to do such a repulsive task in the name of public service. I must imagine you are quite famished, though. Might I bring you a pot of tea and a platter of breakfast? I believe I smell Mrs. Wallace's oatmeal rolls. I will, of course, deliver it myself, if you do not mind that I am still dressed most inappropriately."

His gaze slides over me. "Most *fetchingly* I must say."

"Oh, Doctor!" I should follow this with a titter, but I'm not sure Catriona's vocal cords have ever uttered such a sound. "Let me show you into the library. You need not worry about Dr. Gray interrupting. He had a long night, and he is still fast asleep."

Addington allows that he would not mind some of Mrs. Wallace's delicious oatmeal rolls, if I do not mind serving him. While I take his coat and cane to the wardrobe, Alice scampers along beside me.

"Would you fetch the tray, please?" I whisper. "And then tell Dr. Gray that I have the wild doctor trapped in the library?"

She grins and scurries off.

ELEVEN

In the Victorian world, I am discovering so many hidden facets of myself. Like the fact that I'm even more fascinated by forensics than I thought. Or that I actually don't mind a full day of manual labor that has me dropping deadweight into bed and waking mentally refreshed. Also, that I know how to flirt.

My friends back home would be shocked. Shocked, I tell you. At home, I show a guy that I like him by making eye contact and giving him my full attention, which either does the trick or has him expecting to be arrested for those shoes he lifted in tenth grade. Of course, that only applies when I'm actually interested in the guy. I sure as hell wouldn't flirt to get something, as I'm now doing with Addington. The former would have baffled me and the latter? That is not the behavior of a modern woman. It is, however, a valid strategy when I need information from an arrogant specimen of Victorian male.

Victorian flirting doesn't require much. Flatter him. Laugh at his jokes. Let him ogle my cleavage. Okay, this probably also works in my own time. Yet it *wouldn't* work on McCreadie or Gray, so I must admit it's probably more about the man than the time period.

I laugh and flatter and flirt until, thankfully, Gray and McCreadie arrive, along with breakfast. While I serve Addington and McCreadie, Gray parks himself in the doorway, casually sipping his coffee. Addington still eyes the space, as if wondering whether he could squeeze past.

This is why I lured Addington into the library and summoned Gray. Because otherwise, Addington would leave before Gray or McCreadie could ask a single word about the autopsy.

I serve breakfast and then take a plate and sit behind the desk. Addington stares at me, until I begin to wonder whether I'm breaking Victorian protocol by eating at a desk. To be fair, I think even eating in a library is against the rules of Victorian living, but I'm the only one Addington is gaping at.

Gray clears his throat. "You may recall, Dr. Addington, that Mallory is my new assistant."

"Mallory?"

Gray nods at me. "After her accident last month, Catriona would like to be known by her middle name. A rebirth, one might say, spurred by a near-death experience. As part of that, she is taking over from James as my assistant, and thus, she joins us for breakfast in that position, rather than the role of housemaid, which she kindly continues to fill until my sister can hire a replacement."

Ah, right. *That's* the problem. The lowly maid is dining with the menfolk. I murmur something suitably demure and sip my coffee.

"Thank you for conducting the autopsy so promptly," Gray says without a hint of sarcasm. "Lady Leslie will appreciate it. May I ask what you found?"

Addington relaxes and smiles. "That Lord Leslie is dead. Definitely, beyond any doubt, dead."

McCreadie gives the obligatory chuckle, and Gray attempts a lip twitch.

"And the manner of death?" Gray asks.

"Poison." Addington takes a bite of bread.

"Any idea what type?" I ask.

"Arsenic," he says.

"You have . . . conducted the proper test?" McCreadie says.

He knows the answer. I'm not even sure Addington knows how to do a Marsh test, but he certainly hasn't had time. Still, McCreadie's tone is hopeful. He wants—needs—Addington to be marginally competent. At least let him have found a valid indication that it could be arsenic.

"No need," Addington says. "He experienced leg pains, which is a clear sign of arsenic."

"You have . . . seen that before," McCreadie says carefully.

"No, but I have read about it."

Here is where Gray perks up. "A medical journal? Or an independently published treatise? I would be very happy to borrow a copy. My sister and I have some difficulty finding toxicology research results."

"Not being an undertaker or a widowed woman, I scarcely have the time for medical journals, Gray. I mean I read it in a novel."

McCreadie chokes.

"More coffee, sir?" I say to Gray as I rise. "You look as if you are about to collapse.

"It has been such a long night," I continue as I take his cup. I fill it and add double the sugar, fortitude for this conversation. Then I take Addington's. "That is a most interesting conclusion, Dr. Addington. I presume you will have Mrs. Ballantyne perform the appropriate tests?"

He stares at me as if I've spoken French. I'm tempted to do exactly that and see if his expression changes.

"While I am certain it *is* arsenic," I say, "it will help the courts if her science can support your theo—your findings."

Behind Addington, McCreadie wildly gestures for me to stop talking.

I continue, "I should very like the opportunity to watch Mrs. Ballantyne conduct her experiment."

Addington pulls at his collar. "I am not certain I find such an interest in poison advisable for two women. You might . . ." He clears his throat. "That is to say, it could lead . . ."

"To proper science that can infallibly detect poison and convict killers?"

"Infallibly?" Addington says.

"Fair point, sir. No science is infallible."

McCreadie laughs under his breath. "I believe it was the word, rather than the usage, that startled the good doctor. Our Mallory has been expanding her vocabulary with extensive reading."

"I see." Addington's expression says he suspects that this, like poison studies, may not be wise for young women. Or any women.

"The point, sir," I say, "is that if science can reliably detect poison in the deceased, and the public knows this, then we will have fewer poisonings, which I believe we can agree is a good thing. When Mrs. Ballantyne returns, we shall analyze tissues for proof of the arsenic, which I am certain we shall find."

Addington opens his mouth, as if to object, but I barrel on. "Now, I have what I am very certain is a silly question, but being a silly girl, I believe I am entitled to ask it, though I beg your forbearance in advance."

Both McCreadie and Gray tense. Gray even takes a step from the doorway, as if prepared to tackle me if I ask . . . Well, god only knows what I might ask, which is the problem, isn't it?

"You said Lord Leslie was poisoned," I say.

Addington smiles and sips his coffee. "Yes, child, I believe we have established that."

"But are we certain that is what killed him?"

At this, poor Gray hesitates, torn between not wanting me to upset Addington—which could endanger their arrangement—and really wanting the answer to this most important of questions. In the end, he has no choice really. He needs this answer, as awkward as it is, and if someone must ask it, better it is the mere housemaid rather than the fellow professional who might be questioning Addington's competence.

"I . . . do not believe I understand the questions, Cat—Mallory," Addington says. He speaks slower. "Arsenic is a deadly poison. It does kill people."

"Yes, but given the circumstances, is it possible Lord Leslie was murdered in another fashion, after being poisoned?"

"Circumstances?"

I think he's questioning my vocabulary again, but Gray says, "I left details in a note, which I believe the officer guarding the body handed to you upon your arrival."

"Oh, that. Yes. Very important, he said. Read this before you begin, he said. Most annoying, Gray. I thought there might be something critical in it, and it was only telling me that you and Dr. Mackay think the death came on unexpectedly. No one expects poison, old chap."

Before Gray can comment—or find words to comment—Addington continues, "I am joking, of course. I understand that you did not expect Lord Leslie to die quite so promptly, which raised concerns, but Mackay is a country physician and you are an undertaker." Addington raises his hands. "I know you are a trained surgeon, but you are not a police surgeon, Gray. You must leave such things to the professionals."

McCreadie clears his throat. "It was me that raised the question in that note, Doctor. I shall need to be quite certain of the cause of death, as it can have a tremendous effect on the investigation."

"How? From what I understand, Lady Leslie killed him. As she was in the house at the time, the manner of death does not matter. It was still her."

"How did you hear that?" I say.

"I inquired, of course. Had my man run out for the latest news. There is a baker down the road that opens early and always has the latest from the police office. I find it is very helpful. How am I supposed to perform an autopsy if I do not know the presumed manner of death?"

Gray moves as fast as a cat, getting between me and Addington and saying something I can't hear over the blood pounding in my ears.

I leave the room. If I stay, I'll make this worse. I don't storm out. I know better than that. I murmur something about getting to my chores, walk down the hall, veer around a corner, and nearly plow down a tall woman in a dove-gray dress.

"Mallory?"

I stop short, looking up with a start. "Isl—Mrs. Ballantyne." I half curtsy. "We were not expecting you until the morrow, ma'am."

She lowers her voice. "Alice is upstairs, and Mrs. Wallace is in the kitchen. You can be yourself."

"At the moment, ma'am, I believe that would be unwise." I cast a look back toward the library.

She starts to speak, and then her chin lifts, as she catches voices. Her mouth sets in a hard line.

"Dr. Addington, I presume," she mutters. "What has he done now?"

When I don't answer, she says, "I know the man is an incompetent booby, Mallory. I doubt anything he's done will shock me, so there is no reason to demur on that account. He is a disgrace to the profession and a blight on our city, and in a just world, the police surgeon would be my brother."

She takes a deep breath. "See the effect the man has even on me? I scarcely blame you for being out of sorts with him. Now, what seems to be going on?"

I hesitate.

"Is it murder?" Her eyes round. "Of course. If Dr. Addington is here at this hour, there has been a murder. Is it a devious one? Oh, I do hope so. We are in need of a puzzle. A dastardly killer who must be brought to justice."

I'd hesitated at first because of the poison angle. Obviously, we can't keep this from Isla any longer, but the situation requires more than a quick explanation. Now, though, I realize the real reason I can't blurt it out.

Because her brother-in-law is dead. And her sister is the prime suspect.

"Mallory?" She takes my arm. "Come sit in the drawing room. You look quite pale. I cannot imagine a murder gruesome enough to have that effect on you, but if it is so, and you are concerned about my stomach, then only tell me the barest of details."

I shake my head. "You need to wait for Dr. Gray."

"My brother is not going to begrudge you the telling of the tale, Mallory."

"I know. It's just—" I shake it off. "How is your mother? Is she well?"

As soon as I say the words, they remind me of what is *about* to be said. That Annis is accused of murder. Their mother will not be well after that, will she?

"Mallory? You really do look ill." She continues steering me into the drawing room as she lowers her voice. "Has something happened to remind you of your situation? An anniversary or a birthday?"

It takes a moment to realize what she means. She thinks I am feeling down because something has reminded me of my real life. My parents' anniversary. A friend's birthday. No. When my father's birthday came last week, I secreted myself away to deal with it in private.

It can't be easy for Isla either, to be constantly reminded that your new friend would rather be somewhere else. Still, she's incredibly considerate and invites me to talk about it whenever I need to. Gray . . .

Well, Gray is different. If anything brings up the fact that I am only here because I cannot get home, he changes the subject. He's even been known to leave the room. I understand that. He needs my full dedication and attention, and he doesn't like the reminders that his assistant could vanish at any moment, leaving him with no aide and returning a liar and thief for a housemaid.

"It isn't that," I say. "But thank you. It's . . . It was a long night. We didn't get to sleep until a few hours ago, and even then, I can't say I did more than drowse so—"

Boot thuds in the hall save me from needing to blather more, stalling until Gray comes out. The men are passing the open doorway when Mc-Creadie seems to sense Isla and turns with a smile that lights up his eyes.

"Isla, you are home early," he says.

Addington reverses course into the drawing room to join us. "Mrs. Ballantyne. You may wish you had not returned home quite so quickly. I fear young Mallory here has volunteered your services for a case of poisoning."

"Poisoning?" Isla turns to me. "Is that what this is about? I am certainly happy—nay, delighted—to help, Dr. Addington."

"Excellent. I will leave you to it." He starts to leave and then pauses. "Oh, and my condolences on the passing of your brother-in-law. I met him once or twice, hunting. An excellent chap. Most excellent. I am sorry, and also for your sister. A nasty situation. Quite nasty."

McCreadie lunges forward to strong-arm Addington down the hall. "Time for you to be off, sir. We do appreciate your efforts. As always, they leave us quite speechless."

Isla turns to Gray, blinking. "Duncan?"

"Come in and sit down, Isla."

"I'll fetch tea," I say, and scurry off.

TWELVE

When I bring a tea tray, McCreadie is hovering in the corner while Gray talks to Isla. I slip in, and I'm ready to leave the tray and go, but Isla motions for me to stay and McCreadie shuts the door. I sink into a chair as Gray explains while Isla sits, stunned, trying to process.

When they finish, Isla says, "I should go to Annis."

McCreadie steps forward. "Of course. We'll take the coach. I will accompany you." He pulls out his pocket watch. "Does half-past give you time for whatever you need to prepare?"

"I need nothing to prepare. I am quite ready to fly to my sister's side now. As for when I will go, that is another matter, and I fear the answer is: when she summons me. Which may be never."

McCreadie frowns. "But if you wish to go to her . . ."

"I want to go. I *need* to go. Yet she will not wish me there."

McCreadie bristles. "You are her sister, running to her side in her time of need."

She smiles softly for him. "I appreciate the defense, Hugh, but if she does not want me there, the only person I would be helping is myself." Isla inhales and rises. "I will ask Simon to take her a message and let her know I am at home and would love to see her. I suspect, if she answers at all, it will be to tell me that if I feel the need to be of assistance, do so with my 'silly beakers and potions.' That is what I shall do. Do I dare ask Dr. Addington's findings?"

"Best not," McCreadie murmurs. "Unless you fancy heavy drinking at eight in the morning."

Isla sighs. "That bad, is it? Please tell me he didn't try to say it was gastroenteritis."

There is the briefest of pauses here, as if everyone is torn between wanting to tell Isla to take a moment to digest the news . . . and knowing that would be the worst possible thing to say. Yes, she's had a shock. Yes, she may be too quick to jump into action. But you can't tell a woman to chill and insist she deal with her emotions before taking action.

Gray nods to me, my cue to explain.

I bring the tray over, and pour her a tea. That lets me give Isla a moment to collect herself.

Once she has her tea, I settle in beside her and tell what Addington said. When I finish, she holds out her cup to McCreadie.

"Brandy, please, sir," she says. "I fear you were quite correct. Heavy drinking is required."

He opens a cupboard and takes out a bottle.

"I was joking," she says.

He lifts the brandy. "So you do not want it?"

She hesitates and then holds out her cup again. "A little, along with more tea."

She takes that and then sits back to sip the fortified brew. When she's done, she says, "I will focus on the poison. Yes, that may not be what killed Gordon, but it would have killed him soon enough. It is almost certainly not arsenic, or at least not arsenic alone."

"Mallory mentioned thallium," Gray says. "I admit I am not even familiar with that."

"It is a new heavy metal. Discovered in 1861. I believe there are efforts under way to study its medicinal properties."

"Ah," I say. "So no one has realized it's poison then."

Her brows shoot up. "Simply because an element has been discovered to be poisonous hardly precludes it being used in readily available products, Mallory. Has that changed in your time?"

"Er, no. Not really. So you know thallium is lethal."

"I do. I can also think of at least one case where it was suspected as the agent in a murder. It is, however, not your typical poison and not something your typical killer would think to use, which is good, because otherwise . . ." She shudders.

"Odorless, colorless, and tasteless," I say. "Nasty stuff. That's my guess for this, mostly on account of the sudden hair loss and burning in the feet."

"It is a valid hypothesis. I cannot test for it specifically, but I can be sure we're dealing with a heavy metal and one that is *not* arsenic." She glances at Gray. "Will I be able to get tissue samples before the family claims Gordon's . . ." She wavers. Then her voice drops as she says, "I suppose the person to grant that would be Annis. As she is his closest family. And also the primary suspect."

"I will provide the samples needed," Gray says. "Annis will not object, and Dr. Addington knows the tests are being done, so there is no need for subterfuge, which I would hesitate to engage in when it could affect Annis's case."

"You think she is guilty?" Isla says.

"I . . ." Gray clears his throat. "I hope the evidence will prove otherwise."

"For her sake," Isla murmurs. "Otherwise, she may carry herself to the gallows on the sheer force of public sentiment. While I do not believe that women should be forced to downplay the stronger aspects of their person-alities, I fear our sister is . . . not an easy woman to like."

"And a *very* easy woman to *dis*like," McCreadie says. "Which is, in this case, far worse."

"It most certainly is." Isla sets down her teacup with a sharp clink. "We must act quickly to answer our questions. Is there anything else I need to know?"

Isla rises, clearly expecting us to say no.

When no one speaks, she looks across our faces. "Yes?"

"This has . . . not been the first poisoning since you have been gone," McCreadie says. "There have been two so far. Along with talk of a, er, that is, a . . ."

She turns on him. "No."

"Yes," Gray says. "The papers talk of a poison ring."

"Well, the papers, as usual, are wrong."

Gray's eyes shift to me.

"Duncan?" she says. When he glances my way again, she says, "Fine. Mallory then. What is my brother not telling me?"

"He's punting the ball my way because it's my observation, and he'd really rather not be the one to suggest a so-called poison ring. While I understand why the accusation would piss you off, it's also kinda fascinating. The idea of passing around poison, like a shared recipe for dealing with abusive husbands—"

"Not an actual thing," she cuts in. "I am sick to death of such nonsense. People act as if women are out there with pocketfuls of poison, victims dying daily." She looks at me. "Did you know there was a move to restrict the sale of arsenic to men only? Based on what? The majority of poisoning deaths are accidental or the tragic taking of one's own life. Poison rings are the product of overworked imaginations and misogynistic paranoias. A mere fiction."

"Until it's not. That's the problem, right?" I settle on the sofa. "Last week, you and I discussed the Lord William Russell case, how the murder was blamed on a novel. Well, a novel that spawned a gazillion hugely popular plays because you guys have a shitty concept of intellectual property. But we have the same argument in my time. Can a fictional representation of crime—in a book, a movie, a video game—give someone the idea for a crime?"

"Dare I ask what a video game is?" McCreadie says.

"A game you play on TVs, cell phones, and computers. I'm especially fond of postapocalyptic zombie first-person shooters."

"I . . . understood none of that."

"Which is why she says it," Gray says. "Having fun at our expense. I presume the point you are making, Mallory, is that it is possible that the unfounded fear of a poison ring has led to that exact thing? In short, that it gave someone an idea."

"Yes."

Isla looks my way. "I almost hate to ask, because I know the answer is yes, but I presume you have evidence of that?"

"Not hard evidence. Just a theory, which I didn't even have until about ten minutes ago. It's your fault."

"Of course it is. What did I say?"

"That thallium is a relatively recent discovery, and while it is known to be poisonous, it is not yet commonly used by poisoners, meaning that if multiple people in Edinburgh died of it in a short period of time that would suggest . . ."

"The poison was supplied by the same person," McCreadie says.

"And the others died in a similar manner?"

"Yes," Gray says.

"Bloody hell," Isla says, and slumps back onto the sofa.

I'm in the laboratory with Gray. When I first saw this room, I presumed it was for embalming. We aren't at that era yet. There's no reason for a funeral parlor to have a place to store the dead at all. That isn't their function. Gray has it for his studies, and what he's studying right now is the body of his brother-in-law.

With Addington having finished his autopsy, there's the familiar Y-shaped incision. I always presumed the cut was that shape for a surgical reason, but Gray has said it's for the undertaking profession. Doctors conducting autopsies used to just slice open the corpse down the middle, and some still do. The problem there is that it leaves an ugly mark, which can be seen on a female corpse once she's in her dress. And so the Y incision was born, allowing the family—and later undertakers—to hide the damage with regular clothing.

As much as I hate to give Addington one speck of credit, he is a decent surgeon. His cuts are precise, as is his handling of the internal examination. Normally, in an autopsy, you'd begin with the external. I don't know how much of that Addington does. Very little, from what I've seen of his reports. That's another thing—the police surgeon's primary function is judicial. He presents his findings at court and, presumably, to the police, being paid by them for that service. That doesn't mean Addington always writes anything up for McCreadie or even seeks him out to deliver an oral report. It's up to the police to corner him, as I did today.

Gray goes through the steps of both an external and an internal examination. He cleans out Lord Leslie's fingernails—especially the broken ones—to look for skin, though he obviously can't use DNA from it. He thoroughly checks for external signs of trauma and sees nothing that wouldn't be explained by the poison.

Here, Gray can do a better job of checking for head injuries than he could at the scene. He's poking and prodding at the scalp when he stops and bends over the right side of Leslie's head. Then he makes a motion, which I am supposed to distinguish from all his other vague and distracted motions to mean he wants a magnifying glass. I get it wrong the first time, which earns me an impatient finger snap, which is apparently easier than just saying "magnifying glass."

I make up for the error by also passing him a comb and bringing over the lantern. He frowns at the lantern until I move in place, illuminating what he's trying to see.

Gray uses the magnifying glass and the comb, and then passes me the glass and takes the light as he holds the comb in place. I bend over Leslie's scalp and peer through to see an abrasion I hadn't noticed before. It's faint, just a reddening of the scalp, the abraded patch maybe the size of a dollar coin.

I step back and consider. Then I pull up an image from memory. I'm getting better at doing that. It's a skill forgotten in the age of the cell phone, when you can capture anything from a sunset to a parking spot number to that certain toothpaste you like but you always grab the wrong one because you forget the exact subtype. Now I'm in a world where we can't even call in a crime-scene photographer. Everything must be memorized.

I consult my memory, and then I walk into the drawing room, where there's a sofa and several chairs—a sitting room for the grieving to comfortably discuss funeral plans. I tuck down my skirts, lie on the sofa, and then hang off of it, with my head on the floor. When I hear footsteps, I resist the urge to leap up.

"Yes, I look ridiculous," I say, head still on the floor.

"You do," he says. "But I am also impressed by your dedication to the science. I was planning to do the same thing when you were not around to see me."

"Meaning I am *more* dedicated to the science than you."

"No, simply meaning that you are less afraid of looking ridiculous than I am."

"Am I in the correct position?"

"Tilt your head slightly to the left."

I do that. Then I put my fingers to the spot where my head touches the carpet, and I pull myself up.

"That is it," he says. "Our presumption was correct."

"The abrasion is only a rug rash from Leslie sliding off his sofa as he died."

When Gray hesitates, I say, "No?"

"Yes in general. I am objecting to the use of 'only.'"

I frown. Then I hitch up my skirts and run back into the laboratory. When Gray arrives, there's a ghost of an indulgent smile on his face. I'm holding up a probe.

"May I use this on the abrasion?" I ask.

"You may."

Here again is a difference between my world and his. A medical examiner might let me prod to get a better look at evidence, but they aren't going to let me do anything that could damage evidence. Yet what would I be damaging here? It's not as if Gray will be taking photos for the procurator fiscal to use in court. He has already made his observations, and even those are only unofficial ones for the police investigation.

I poke the spot for a moment. "Shit."

"You do have the most colorful profanity, Mallory."

"Vulgar, you mean."

"I wasn't going to say it."

"As for what prompted the profanity, there's a soft spot under the scrape. A contusion. Caused by a fatal blow to the temple? Or the force of his fall to the floor?"

"Yes."

I give him a look.

Gray shrugs. "It could be either. That is the problem. To know more, I would need to open up the wound, which I cannot."

I hesitate, then I swear again. "Because it's on his temple, where anyone can see it, leading to questions regarding the incision, which you are not supposed to be making."

"Yes. Now I have checked for other signs of a hard blow to the temple, in his pupil and such, and I do not see it. I also noted potential signs of suffocation, with a soft object, as we speculated at the scene, but even now I cannot say he suffocated any more than I can say he was hit on the head. Ultimately, I am not certain how much it matters whether or not the poison killed him."

"The poisoner still planned to kill him, making it first-degree murder."

Gray arches a brow. "There are multiple degrees?"

"Basically, first is planned, second is unplanned, third—or manslaughter—is accidental."

"With presumably different levels of punishment, depending on the degree of culpability. That makes sense."

"Here, they just toss everyone on the gallows, right?"

He waggles a finger at me. "Not every killer goes to the gallows."

"Yeah, some are transported to Australia."

"Not anymore. The Australians began to object to that practice."

"Shockingly. In my time, Australians *love* that their country was once used as a dumping ground for your most unwanted."

"I shudder to think what it must have become."

"It's actually fine. Nice people. Great beaches. Amazing surfing."

He frowns. "People go to Australia on purpose?"

"Only if they can afford it." I look down at Leslie. "So even if we proved that the poison didn't kill him, it wouldn't matter, because the poisoner *intended* to kill him. The only problem would be that someone could get away with murder, if they hurried it along and left the poisoner to take the blame."

"Unless the same person did both."

"In that case, the finger would point directly at the person who benefited the most, both from his death in general, and his hastier—pre-will-change—demise."

"Annis."

THIRTEEN

Gray is gone. Where? I have no idea. We finished the examination, and he took samples for Isla, and then he left. Here is the problem—one of many, really—with wearing the disguise of a housemaid. Gray can say he recognizes that I'm a police detective. But then we're in the middle of investigating, and he takes off, leaving me with the slap of the front door as I'm trotting down to see him after delivering the samples to Isla's lab.

Is he delivering his findings to McCreadie? Pursuing a lead? Either way, shouldn't I be invited along? Or is it personal business, and therefore none of *my* business? Whatever the answer, it is a reminder that we may have spent the last twelve hours together in the heart of an investigation, but that doesn't mean we are actually investigative partners.

Isla wasn't in her lab when I dropped off the samples, so I go to track her down, only to discover she also stepped out, though at least she left word she'll be back in an hour.

So it's back to playing housemaid. I mop the floors and polish some silver and pretend I am fully engaged in the work and not mentally with the case and all my questions.

I want to know more about the previous poisonings. I want to know what's going to happen with Annis—will she be arrested? I want to know whether the murder will hit the news—along with Leslie's accusation against his wife—and whether that will affect Isla and Gray. There are a dozen other questions, but those three loom largest in my mind . . . until I realize I can answer them *without* Gray's help.

I zip through a half-assed polishing job and then tell Alice I'm stepping out. That's not technically allowed. I can bristle at that, but it's no different from working in a shop where I couldn't just pull off my name badge and pop out whenever I liked.

Now that I'm "Mallory," I have special privileges, which include being able to leave or assign a task to Alice or just tell Mrs. Wallace I'm busy. That's great . . . if I'm willing to work in a household where the rest of the staff justifiably hates me.

Today, I decide to take the risk. Mrs. Wallace and Alice know I've been out all night "working" with Dr. Gray, and so any housecleaning I do is a bonus.

Alice promises to hold down the fort, and I slip out the back door. As I do, I pass Isla's poison garden. That gives me pause. I've been meaning to ask her about this little garden—gated with warning signs. That will come later. Right now, I'm flying along the path, searching the stables for a sign of Simon, fearing that he's gone, taking Gray into the city.

When I see Simon hauling out a pile of manure for compost, I get up-wind and then wave him over.

"I need newspapers," I say.

"Lovely to see you too," he says. "Pleasant day we're having. Looks like the sun will be coming out soon."

"Fine. Yes, isn't it lovely? I do hope for sun. It has been dreadfully dreary. Now, I need newspapers."

He shakes his head. "In some ways, you are nothing like I remember. In others, you are exactly the same."

"In other words, I'm as rude as ever."

"Not rude. Just focused. Very, very focused on the task at hand, which seems to be . . . newspapers?" He pauses. "Ah, you are seeing whether there is any mention of Lord Leslie's death."

"Is it too soon?"

"It is never too soon for the press. If the daily edition had been printed, they would have added a special page. Or put out the evening edition early. Also, by now, I'm sure someone has printed a broadsheet or two. I'm presuming Dr. Gray wants me to gather what I can?"

"He hasn't asked yet, but he'll want them, so I am being proactive."

"Pro . . . ?" He shakes his head and doesn't ask.

I continue, "The problem is that I cannot remember how to do so."

"You cannot remember how to obtain a newspaper?"

I tap my temple, where Catriona had received the blow.

"Ah," he says. "Dr. Gray did warn there would be such holes in your memory, where you might forget commonplace things."

"I have seen the newsstands," I say. "But I do not know which is closest, and how much money to take, and which papers are the most reliable."

He nods. "You wish me to fetch you newspapers, then."

My tone softens. "I would not ask you to do anything I can do myself, Simon."

"Then you truly are not the Catriona I remember."

"Perhaps, but in this case, I should understand how to do it, so that I may do so myself."

"All right then." He sets the wheelbarrow by the stable wall. "Let me change my boots, and we will go together."

"You do not need to do that. I can take instructions."

"I know you can, but Dr. Gray has an account, and as the papers are for him, then you ought not to pay for them."

When I hesitate, he eyes me. "You are definitely not the Catriona I remember."

"Yes, but you have a point. If I can avoid dipping into my savings, I will. I shall wait while you change your boots. Also, you ought to wash your hands."

He looks down at them. "I do not intend to eat."

"Still, as you have been shoveling manure, it is wise for your general health. Trust me on this."

He shakes his head. "You are an odd one."

"I know, I'm not the Catriona you remember."

"Oh, she was odd, too. You are simply your own unique type of odd."

"I take that as a compliment. Wash up, change your boots, and let us be off."

We visit two vendors on Princes Street. One is a corner stand, not unlike what I've seen in New York. The other is a boy shilling his wares. The first has newspapers, both today's and those a few days old, which are marked down in price.

The newspapers average three pence. Cheap, right? It seems so, until I calculate that I'm making about five pence a day—and Gray and Isla pay well above the standard. A daily paper would be over half my wages. While Scotland has higher literacy rates than England, that doesn't mean the average person can afford something the modern world considers a cheap commodity. This explains why there's a market for day-old newspapers. There's also apparently a market for *used* newspapers.

Most shoppers seem to be domestic servants, like Simon, getting them for their employers. Then there's the boy just ahead of us, who has come running from a shop a few blocks over, where he is employed to read the paper to the workers. They chip in to buy a newspaper and pay him a small wage to sit at a table and read aloud while they work. The Victorian version of a radio newscast . . . complete with child labor.

Simon picks out papers from the corner stall, and once we're away, he gives me the ideological rundown on each. Again, it's not much different from my own world. There are ones that lean left and right politically, and those that consider themselves serious purveyors of fact versus those that lean into sensational.

Our next stop is the kid hawking his wares, which consist mostly of broadsheets. Broadsheets are what they sound like—a large single piece of newsprint. According to Isla, they were much more popular a few decades ago, but the tradition carries on, for better or worse. For better if you see them as a source of entertainment. For worse if you expect a newspaper level of reporting.

All the broadsheets I've seen are crime related, though there may be others. The crime ones are certainly the most popular. As for the reporting, they're like those movies that are "based on a true story." Yet not everyone reading broadsheets realizes they aren't accurate reporting, making them the internet news sites of the Victorian era. They're also cheap, at a penny each, so for those who only want the most salacious tidbits, this will be their main source of printed news.

When we approach, the boy holds out a sheet. "Would you like that on your account, Mr. Simon?"

Simon arches his brows. "How do you know which one I'll want?"

"Because it's the best I've got, sir, and a discerning fellow like yourself only wants the best."

"What does 'best' imply, might I ask?" I say.

"Why, the tale least fit for your pretty eyes, miss." His own eyes gleam. "I must ask you not to read it, and if you choose to ignore my advice, then I hope you will remember me when you have need of other unsuitable reading purchases."

I have to laugh at that. *Nicely played.* "Yes, I fear I will ignore your advice. In fact, I will take all the unsuitable sheets you might have on the death of one Lord Leslie. If you do not have any yet, I would ask that you put any you do receive aside for me, and I will pay one and a half pence for those."

"Ooh, I think you will regret that, miss. Let me give you a proper deal, as a new customer. You may have four for three pence, and any others at the same rate."

He holds out the one he'd offered Simon plus three others.

"I only need the ones on the Leslie case," I say.

He sweeps an ink-stained hand over the stack at his feet. "They are *all* on the Leslie murder today, miss. Four already, I expect twice as many by sundown."

I turn to Simon. "So quickly?"

"As fast as they can print them," Simon says.

"And write them."

"Oh, that does not take long at all, if one combines the barest of facts with a proper imagination."

The boy harrumphs. "The barest of facts? These contain the truth of the matter, every one."

Simon holds two side by side. "So the truth is that Lord Leslie was both murdered in his own bed *and* murdered in his mistress's bed?"

"Perhaps he considered his mistress's bed his own," the boy says.

"Quite right," I say. "Truth is a variable thing, subject to interpretation."

"Exactly, miss," the boy says. "I'll use that. It sounds right fancy."

Simon grumbles about me "encouraging the lad" as we take all four broadsheets. When I go to pay, Simon stops me.

"Put them on Dr. Gray's account," he says to the boy. "You shall make more that way."

"I will indeed. Thank you, sir. Should I save the others, as the young lady asked?"

"Yes, and you should also allow her to pick them up for the doctor, who is our mutual employer."

As we step away, I take one of the broadsheets from Simon. Then I stop and turn to the boy.

"May I ask your name?" I say.

"Tommy, miss."

"And I am Mallory. I will be back tomorrow for others. Oh, and Lord Leslie did not die in his bed or his mistress's. He was at home, in his hunting room."

Tommy's face falls. "That is rather disappointing."

"No, because here is the interesting part." I lean in and whisper, "He was alone in the room when he died. In a room where there are no other exits, no windows that opened, and . . . the door was locked."

Tommy's eyes round. Then they narrow. "How would you know that?"

"Because I was there, of course," I say as I walk away.

Stunned silence. Then the boy's laughter follows us as Simon shakes his head.

After I return to the house, I'm about to settle in with the newspapers when Isla returns from wherever she'd been. I hear her come in, and I go to the door to find her tugging off her gloves.

"Mallory," she says. "Just the person I wished to see. I presume Duncan has the samples ready? Do you have time to test them with me?"

"Absolutely."

"Excellent. First, let me go down and get a glass of water. It is rather warm out, and I was walking."

"I'll get that for you. Wait in the library and catch your breath before we get to work."

Her lips quirk. "Yes, Mother."

When I return, Isla is in a library chair, relaxing as best she can into her corset, her head dropped forward, betraying her exhaustion.

"Long day already," I say as I come in. "And it's not yet noon. You must be worn out from travel."

"I will survive. However, I would not object if you mothered me to the point of insisting on loosening my stays, now that I am indoors for a while."

I hand her the glass of water and motion for her to rise. Not having a ladies' maid, Isla normally relies on Alice to tighten the stays. While I'm getting the hang of it, I'm really better at the loosening part.

"How are you doing?" I say as I unfasten the corset strings. "I'm sorry you had to find out about your brother-in-law like that."

"Hmm."

"I'll offer my condolences, though I'm not sure how close you were."

"I despised Gordon. The only good thing he did was make Annis seem positively charming by comparison. He was the worst sort of gentry—the sort that mistakes the luck of birth for an actual accomplishment. As if he chose to be born into money and title and had nothing but contempt for those of us lacking the foresight to do the same." She pauses. "And speaking of contempt, that was rather too far in speaking of the newly dead."

I work on loosening her stays. "Since I'm the only one here, you can be as contemptuous as you want. I only met the man briefly, but I already wasn't blaming anyone for poisoning him. Even on his deathbed, he was nasty to everyone around him."

"Particularly Duncan, I presume."

I accidentally tighten a stay, making her gasp and then laugh softly. "That answers my question. Yes, he was always terrible to Duncan."

"And to you?" I ask.

She stiffens.

"Sorry," I say. "I wasn't trying to pry."

"No, you're trying to be a friend. Gordon was . . . fond of Lawrence."

"Shocking," I mutter. "Absolutely shocking."

Lawrence was Isla's husband, who'd married her for her money and treated her like shit until she agreed to fund his expeditions abroad just to get him out of her life. He died two years ago, and she's still working off his debt.

"We'll drop the subject of dead asshole husbands," I say as I finish loosening her stays.

She smiles over her shoulder at me. "The Gray women are notorious for finding them. I could blame my mother for setting the example, but that would be an unkindness she ill deserves. Nor is it entirely true in Annis's case. Mother and I were too easily wooed by men who accepted our eccentricities. Annis knew exactly what she was getting, which is why I cannot imagine her killing Gordon. Their relationship suited their needs. Also, poison?" She shakes her head as I button her dress back. "That is too sly for Annis. She'd have stabbed him in the heart. Or lower, given that Gordon outdid both Lawrence and my father for philandering."

"But the charge is poison," I say. "Which worries me . . . for your sake."

"Because I'm Annis's sister. And a chemist."

"Yes."

"I do not have thallium or arsenic, and I am quite willing to have my laboratory searched for them, if that helps. First, though, we should head upstairs and see what those tissues tell us."

FOURTEEN

I take Isla's glass downstairs before Mrs. Wallace finds it and gives me shit. Then I head up to her laboratory, which is in the attic along with my bedroom and Alice's. The normally locked door is cracked open, and I enter to see Isla at her laboratory table, wearing a pair of goggles that won't look out of place on early pilots. She motions me over to the table, where she's about to conduct the Marsh test.

Here's where I *do* know a bit of forensic history, because the Marsh test was a milestone development. It allows a scientist to detect even the smallest trace of arsenic in food, tissue, or stomach contents. A chemist named James Marsh was hired by the prosecution in the case of a guy believed to have poisoned his grandfather's coffee. Marsh tested using the old method and found proof of arsenic, but the telltale evidence evaporated before the jury could see it. Upon his acquittal, the accused confessed to killing his grandfather, and Marsh was so pissed off that he developed a new test with more permanent results.

Isla begins by placing a small sample of Leslie's stomach contents in a glass beaker with arsenic-free zinc and sulfuric acid. The zinc and acid will create hydrogen, but if there's arsenic in the sample, it'll also produce arsine gas. The gas rises into a horizontal length of glass tubing, where it is heated with an open flame. The heat will turn the result back into water vapor and arsenic, if it is present. The arsenic should then appear as a silvery-black powder.

Isla conducts the experiment . . . and we don't see so much as a smudge of gray at the end. We have enough sample that she lets me try it. Same result. No arsenic.

Next we use the Reinsch test, and there we get a positive result. What does that mean? Only that Leslie's stomach contents contain one of a subset of six heavy metals. We know it's not arsenic. While it could be mercury, bismuth, antimony, or selenium, there's one other heavy metal on that list. The only one that matches Lord Leslie's symptoms.

Thallium.

I'm in the library with Isla. The newspapers and broadsheets are spread over the desk. I have one of the papers in my hand, and I'm struggling to read the article. It's not the language that's a problem. Even with unfamiliar words, I can fly along as fast as I could with a Dickens novel. The problem is Isla. She wants to talk chemistry, specifically poisons, and any other time, I'd be hanging on her every word. Right now, though, I'm trying to get a better understanding of the previous murders, and without Gray to summarize them for me, I must rely on these damnable newspapers. Also, yes, I'm still annoyed about Gray taking off.

"I do not know how Dr. Addington could see heavy metal poisoning and conclude arsenic without any testing," she says.

"Hmm."

"I suppose, giving him the benefit of the doubt, arsenic is the most common method. And if it is thallium, he would never have heard of it being used in such a way. He might not even be aware of its existence, being a medical doctor and not a chemist. Still, would it hurt him to leave room for doubt? To say that he suspects arsenic but requires analysis to be certain?"

"Hmm."

She sighs. "You are already annoyed with him, and I am not improving the situation by reminding you of his incompetence."

I make another noise and reread a line for the third time.

She continues, "You are correct that I am going to require samples from the other victims. I presume Dr. Addington was the attending surgeon. Did he also insist they were arsenic?"

"I don't know."

There's a long pause. Then she says, as gently as possible, "I know you are trying to read those accounts, Mallory, but this is more important. What can you tell me about the other poisonings?"

"Not much."

Her voice cools. "I hope that is not because my brother forbid it. I may abhor talk of poison rings, but if we might actually have one, then I must be involved in the investigation."

"Agreed."

"Having been out of the country, I know nothing of these deaths. Would you please tell me what *you* know?"

"Like I said, not much. That's why I'm reading these."

She hesitates and then says, "I do not believe I understand correctly. My brother brought you in on the case, did he not?"

"He needed me to go undercover last night, with Hugh in a pub. There wasn't time for more than a quick overview of the cases. I know the second victim may have died of poisoned pudding, but before I could ask Detective McCreadie or Dr. Gray for more, things got busy—chasing down that lead, and then coming back to find Annis here. I planned to ask Dr. Gray after the autopsy, but he must have had pressing business. I figured I'd get the newspapers and see what I can find out, rather than bother him."

"*Bother* him? By asking for more than the barest of details on a case you're working together?"

"We aren't exactly working it together. Or, I guess we are now, but it was kind of accidental."

"Because he needed you to play a role?" Her voice rises a notch. "The role of a bauble on Hugh's arm? You were a theatrical prop? What the bloody hell is Duncan thinking?"

The door opens just as Isla is cursing, and Alice stops short.

Isla sighs. "I am sorry you heard me say that, Alice."

"I have heard it before, ma'am," she says with a small smile. "Is everything all right?"

Alice's gaze slants my way. Catriona bullied the girl, and it's going to be a while before she trusts that I'm not up to something with this new persona.

"Everything is fine, Alice," Isla says. "Mallory was relating a distressing circumstance, and I was expressing outrage on her behalf." She checks the mantel clock. "You ought to be at your lessons by now, yes?"

"Yes, ma'am. I was just finishing up."

I rise from the desk. "Are any of my chores keeping you from your studies?"

"No, I only need to return the mop and empty the bucket."

I start to say I'll do it for her, but Isla waves me back into my seat. "Do that, then, Alice, and then it is upstairs for your lessons." When she's gone, Isla turns to me. "Now, back to my righteous outrage over my brother and Hugh's behavior."

"I don't think it was Detective McCreadie." I pause. "Er, I mean, I do not blame your brother either. Not overly much."

She snorts. "Meaning you are trying very hard not to admit you want to throttle Duncan. I honestly do not know what he was thinking. No, that is incorrect. I know the problem, which is that he was *not* thinking."

"I do hope you aren't speaking about me," Gray says as the door re-opens.

"Who else, dear brother?"

His good humor fades, and his gaze slides between us. "Dare I ask what I have done?"

"Dare you *not* ask and risk doing it again?"

"It's fine," I say quickly. "Isla was asking for details on the other poisonings, and I said that's why I'm reading the papers—because we haven't had time to discuss them."

He frowns. "But we did, did we not? On the way to the public . . . No, later, as you were bandaging . . . No, not then either. Surely, though, at some point . . ." He trails off.

"You gave me the basics. I was going to ask for more today, and then you left. Which is fine. I would, however, appreciate it if, while we are on a case, you let me know what you need me to do, if anything, while you are gone."

"It was personal business."

"I didn't ask where you were going. Or what you were doing."

"Do not make this worse, Duncan," Isla warns. "Mallory is being very gentle in her rebuke."

"It's not a rebuke," I say. "It's negotiating a new professional relationship. If I am your assistant—and not merely a housemaid who helps you now and then—I need more communication."

Isla clearly wants to say more, but another look from me stops her.

"I apologize," Gray says. "I had business to attend to, getting that out of the way so that I might focus on the case, and I ought to have told you that I was leaving. I also ought to have discussed the other cases with you."

He pauses, with a look I have come to know well. It's his expectant look, when he makes what he considers a difficult admission and expects a cookie for it. If I'm in a good mood, I find that look kind of adorable in an exasperating way. I am not in a good mood, and I answer it with a curt nod that has him slumping.

"Moving on," I say. "Isla has news."

"I'm not certain he deserves it," she mutters.

At my look, she says, "Fine. I confirmed it was not arsenic. It is definitely another heavy metal, with a limited list of possibilities that includes thallium."

"The relatively new element," Gray says. "Meaning if thallium is the culprit, that is significant."

I cut in with, "I'm not saying it's definitely thallium. Hair loss is the classic symptom, though like I suggested last night, it can take a couple of weeks to develop. Still, yes, it's presenting as thallium."

"The point," Isla says, "is that whatever killed Gordon is definitely a heavy metal and definitely not arsenic. Now I want to know what Dr. Addington found on the other bodies and whether I can gain access to tissue samples, which is how we came to discuss Mallory's lack of information regarding those subjects. I ought to have been clear on that. She was not complaining about you. She does not do that, even when she should."

"I will see what I can do about the tissue samples," Gray says. "Though the second victim—the public house customer—was buried today."

"Exhumation?" I say. "Tell me we can do a proper Victorian exhumation, in the cemetery at midnight, ravens perched on the nearby gravestones, as the casket is slowly lifted from its grave."

"That put you in a better mood," Gray says. "Next time you are cross with me, I shall not bother with apologies. I will take you to an exhumation."

"Please. Also, I'm pretty sure you didn't actually apologize."

"It was implied. I will see what can be done, though for an exhumation, we'll need the approval of Dr. Addington, which I doubt we will get when we are requesting it because we question his findings."

"Leave that with me," I say. "I can find a way to convince him."

"By flaunting your bosom under his nose?"

"It's currently *my* bosom, meaning I can flaunt it any way I like. This, though, will require more. Maybe a striptease."

Isla shakes her head. Gray turns, slowly, toward me. "Please tell me I am misunderstanding that phrase."

"Probably not. Also, I was kidding. I don't want to see an exhumation badly enough to get naked in front of Dr. Addington. And, yes, I know, that displays a serious lack of dedication to science."

Gray doesn't answer. He doesn't seem to know how.

"What about the first body?" I say. "No, wait. You said it's now a medical cadaver. So we can buy it, right? How much does a dead body go for these days?"

"We are not buying that poor man's corpse." Gray pauses. "Not unless absolutely necessary. But yes, we won't require Addington's permission to get *that* sample."

"Great. Now, can you tell us the backstory on these two poisonings?"

FIFTEEN

Victim number one was James Young. Occupation: gravedigger. This is the one whose wife didn't collect his remains, meaning his corpse would be given to the medical colleges for study, saving her the expense of burying him. She'd apparently collected *twice* the usual burial-society payout, because he'd been paying double into it. As a gravedigger, he must have seen so many bodies unceremoniously dumped into a hole that he wanted to ensure his mortal remains received better treatment.

Yes, his wife took the money and abandoned his corpse, but any horror at that disappears when I remember Gray saying that the couple lived in one of the worst parts of Old Town. Now he says they lived in a single room shared with their three children and two elderly relatives. Grave digging is at the low end of the laborer pay scale, which is saying a lot in this time. Young was known to be an alcoholic who often didn't show up for his shifts, which meant he often went without pay. Can I really blame his wife for keeping the burial payout?

Still, having kept it immediately put her on the suspect list. In fact, she has already been arrested and is in prison, while the police continue their investigation.

The second victim was Andrew Burns. He's the pub regular whose wife made him his favorite pudding and he kept eating it even after his stomach started bothering him. The one whose wife had publicly ignored his symptoms. The police hadn't realized this until McCreadie overheard it last night. That might seem like poor investigative techniques, but it's more a case of witnesses not wanting to speak to the police. When McCreadie relayed that evidence to Detective Crichton—the officer in charge of the case—Crichton had gone to arrest Mrs. Burns, only to find she'd fled.

The Burnses were a step up the social ladder from the Youngs. Lower-middle-class, living in lodgings better than one might expect from his salary, according to McCreadie. Mrs. Burns is also the second to bear that title. Andrew Burns left his first wife and two kids a year ago and married his mistress. He did not pay child support or alimony, this being a world where a "decent" man does that as a matter of course and everyone else just doesn't.

As for the bigamy, it seems there had been no actual first marriage. Oh, his first wife certainly thought so, but he'd paid a friend to play officiant and marry them. Yep, Andrew Burns sounds like a peach of a guy, and I suspect his wives—both of them—aren't the only ones who might want him dead.

If we'd been a little faster, we could have gotten tissue from Burns before he was buried. Addington's verbal report of leg pains, though, suggests thallium poisoning.

"Any chance the pudding is still in the icebox?" I say.

"Wouldn't his wife have thrown it away?" Isla says.

"Not if it isn't the murder weapon," I say. "Also, the fact that she didn't even act worried about him being sick suggests she's not the most devious killer ever. It's worth looking into. I'd like to get access to the home anyway. If all three poisonings were thallium, that definitely suggests a single source."

"Agreed," Gray says. "I will send a message to Hugh and request access."

"Good." I look at the stack of newspapers and broadsheets. "Anyone up for a little reading while we wait?"

Tommy the newsboy was right. The death of Lord Leslie is all over the news. Not all the papers got it out in time, but those that did put it on the front page, and one that missed the print cutoff has already added an overlay sheet—a single page to fold over the original front page.

There is no mention of Gray or Isla in the articles. That will come. I've seen how some—possibly most—of the police treat Gray: like a ghoul who gets off on cutting up corpses. I tell myself they're just confused. The police don't understand what he's doing, and they almost certainly *have* seen people with an unhealthy interest in the dead. Add in the fact that he's also an undertaker, and it's little wonder that they're quick to misread his interest. That's the logical explanation. The emotional one is that I am furious on his behalf.

From that, though, I can extrapolate that it won't only be the police who have a problem with Gray. Does anyone else know what he studies? I suspect local medical academics will, but beyond that? I can't see him giving public lectures or telling clients about his side gig.

From what I understand, Gray conveys his findings to the police through McCreadie and other open-minded officers. He doesn't submit reports. He doesn't testify in court. And he sure as hell doesn't talk to reporters. Is that going to change? He's the brother of a murder suspect, and he's a fascinating subject on his own—a man of color with a scandalous birth story, trained as a surgeon *and* a doctor, now an undertaker and a forensic scientist.

The press will find him. They will find officers more than happy to tell them what he does in his spare time.

Is Gray ready for that? Does he know it's coming? Do I warn him, as I did Isla? *How* do I warn him?

I need to think more on that. For now, the papers are focused on Lord Leslie and his wife. Leslie was well known as a hunter, which explains the trophy room. He was married once before, to a woman who died in childbirth, taking his only offspring with her. A few years later, he wed Annis Gray. While Miss Gray had no title, nor any claim to nobility, she did bring a sizable dowry, courtesy of her father, a wealthy investor who had made his fortune in private cemeteries and burial clubs.

There's no mention of Mr. Gray having been an undertaker. I can't imagine the papers would omit that detail. Undertaking isn't the most respectable of professions—this is the era where they get their reputation as vultures feeding on the grieving. Gray is more funeral director than funeral salesperson, but the profession has used the mourning mania surrounding Prince Albert's death to its full advantage. I'm guessing Annis— and probably Lord Leslie—re-framed that aspect of her past, positioning her father as an upper-class man of leisure investing his family money.

I wonder how the press could make such a basic research error . . . until I remember I'm in the nineteenth century. It's not as if they could pop online and research the Gray family. The fact that papers were able to report on Leslie's death at all suggests they knew he was sick and had either bought off staff or positioned themselves nearby, awaiting the inevitable.

A man of property and title has been murdered by poison . . . when the city is already working itself into a tizzy over a poisoning ring. It's a wonder there weren't journalists thronging Lord Leslie's front gate.

Reporters must have obtained whatever scanty details the staff could provide, with a greater interest in the murder than the background of the lead players. That background will come later. And it will catch Gray in its net.

I read all the articles and then move on to the broadsheets, including a few extras Simon has already brought over. I'm moving faster than Gray and Isla, having gotten an earlier start. The newspapers had largely stuck to the facts, but the broadsheets have no such probity. Being someone who enjoys a lurid tale, I can't help but admire the creativity here. While a few of the broadsheets are utter trash, barely even intelligible, there's one writer who shows serious talent, at least for fiction.

No, that's not entirely fair. This particular writer of broadsheets gets enough of the facts right to suggest they actually do their research. They just don't feel compelled to stick to those facts.

I've read this writer's work before. Their byline proclaims them "Edinburgh's Foremost Reporter of Criminal Activities." There's no name attached, as if no other identifier is needed, and I'm kind of impressed by the chutzpah.

This particular writer has already put out two broadsheets today, which is incredibly fast in a world before even a copy machine. The first focuses solely on the Leslie murder. The new one also recaps the first two murders.

To properly serve its audience, a broadsheet must function as an independent story. When the writer wants to publish new information, they update the original story, condensing the earlier parts to accommodate the new bits.

This update summarizes the earlier poisonings and then adds the Leslie one. The writer notes "a similarity between the cases," with all victims having experienced similar symptoms. That's a scoop on the papers, and I'm about to tell Gray and Isla when I hit the final paragraph.

It is not only the dreadful signs of poison that connect these three tragic cases. This reporter has heard that Lady Leslie's own brother, Dr. Duncan Gray, was seen in the Old Town the night of Lord Leslie's death. Known to assist the police, Dr. Gray seems to have been pursuing the very poison ring his sister, Lady Leslie, now stands accused of joining.

I read the paragraph twice to be sure I'm not misunderstanding. Then I set the broadsheet down.

"Dr. Gray?" I say.

"Hmm?"

"Who knows you were in the Old Town last night investigating the poisoning deaths?"

He frowns and gives another "Hmm?"

I repeat the question, and his expression doesn't change, so I read the paragraph aloud.

"That . . . that is not possible," he says. "Simon took us to the Old Town, but he knew not the purpose and would never speak to a reporter about it. Hugh knew, obviously, but even when he passes along his findings, he does not mention me."

"You stayed in hiding while Detective McCreadie and I were in the pub," I say. "The only people who might have suspected you were chasing the poisoner were the men who attacked us. Yet they didn't know who you were."

"The young woman did," he says. "The one who calls herself Jack."

I wave the broadsheet. "She sold that story to this reporter. But as much as that pisses me off, it's also an opportunity for us. This reporter seems to know more than most. I want to speak to them, and Jack—having rewarded your kindness with betrayal—owes you a favor."

"Is that not . . . ?" Isla takes the broadsheet from my hands. She reads the byline and says, "No one knows who that is. It is one of the city's great mysteries, at least for those of us who follow the crime broadsheets."

"Well, Jack knows. And she's going to tell us."

Isla wants to immediately set off into the Old Town to confront Jack. Just the two of us on an adventure together. I love the sound of that. I really do. But this isn't an adventure—it's an investigation, and I need to prioritize.

Jack isn't going anywhere—we know to ask for her at "Halton House." The more pressing avenue of investigation is the homes of the two victims and suspects. The police have already gone through them, and any remaining evidence is slipping away. Mrs. Young's apartment is still occupied by the elderly relatives, who are caring for the children, and I can picture evidence literally being thrown in the rubbish bin as they tidy their overcrowded lodgings. I mention this to Gray, but he points out that's not how Victorians handle unwanted items. We aren't in the world of cheap manufacturing and landfill sites. Whatever they don't want will be given away or sold to someone else. Still, the concern remains—they will discard what they can't use. Also, the Burnses' apartment might be unoccupied now, but McCreadie worries the landlord won't wait for month's end before finding new tenants.

The answer is clear then. I must postpone my adventure with Isla and go with McCreadie. I tell myself that's fine. It's investigative work . . . even if it's not as interesting as chasing down Jack.

"I will inform Hugh," Gray says, "and ask him to meet us at the Burns residence."

"You're coming?" I say.

There is a shift in his features, one I'm beginning to recognize as the subtle closing of a portcullis. "I believe I ought to, as you are imparting lessons on future police work, and I should take mental notes for Hugh. Is that a problem?"

I want to tell him to stop being so damn prickly. Also to stop making excuses—if he wants to help because he enjoys investigating, then he should say so.

"I'm not sure how much 'training' I'll be doing," I say. "I'm just going along as an extra set of eyes and hands, and if you can do the same, I'm sure Detective McCreadie will appreciate it."

I think I've phrased it well, but his mouth tightens, just a little.

"Duncan?" Isla says, which tells me I didn't imagine that show of annoyance.

Gray rises. "I will send Simon to convey the message to Hugh. You will want your walking boots, Mallory. We shall depart on the hour."

SIXTEEN

If you rank the Old Town neighborhoods on a ten-point scale—from "should be condemned" to "relatively livable"—this one ranks about a six, which is lower than I'd expect, given that McCreadie suggested that the Burnses seemed to be living above their means. I realize my mistake soon enough. It's not the neighborhood; it's the apartment.

It's on what North Americans call the second floor, but here is considered the first floor—my "first" floor being called the ground floor—and I'm trying to adopt that terminology. The first floor—the second level—is where people with money live. The ground level is too open to the streets. The higher floors are tricky to access, with increased fire risk. The Burnses' apartment also has multiple rooms and is twice the size of my Vancouver condo. Around here, that's positively palatial, especially for only two people. I don't want to see where his first wife and kids are living.

There's a police constable posted at the door. McCreadie won't have had a chance to arrive yet, so I expect we'll need to wait.

We do not wait. Gray walks up to the front door, nods to the officer on duty, and walks inside.

"Ah," I murmur once the door has closed behind us. "He knows you."

"Never seen him before in my life."

That gives me pause . . . until I look at Gray, in his fine suit and top hat. The officer didn't stop him because, as a gentleman, Gray is clearly allowed to enter.

When I say as much, Gray shakes his head. "Yes, that helps, but he looked the other way because I passed him a half sovereign. It is a crime scene, one with a small degree of infamy. He will presume I simply want a closer look."

"Crime-scene containment. Say it with me now. *Crime-scene containment.*"

"I am hardly the one you need to convince, Mallory. Nor is Hugh. The problem is that young officer is paid less than a common laborer, and therefore he is open to corruption. In fact, many young men join the constabulary expecting it. Have you resolved that issue in your world? Are your police incorruptible?"

I grumble under my breath. He has a point, of course. I've been offered my share of bribes. At least in my time, it would take a helluva payoff for an officer to let a stranger onto a scene, but only because you'd presume they want to tamper with evidence. Officers have no such concern here, and we are inside, alone, to do what we want.

I head straight for the kitchen and open the icebox. The smell hits me, and my hand flies to my mouth and nose. Right, it's an icebox, not a refrigerator, meaning that with no one to replace the ice, the contents have already spoiled.

Wait. Mrs. Burns only went on the run this morning. That suggests she wasn't the one who usually replaced the ice. Or was her husband's death such a shock that she wasn't eating and never realized the contents had begun to spoil?

I turn to Gray as he walks over behind me. "The icebox is out of ice."

"I am surprised they even have one," he says.

"I'm guessing they aren't in every kitchen yet?"

"Certainly not."

He walks over to examine the appliance, which is more of a small chest, only big enough to hold maybe a dozen cartons of milk.

I've never given much thought to what people did before the advent of refrigeration. At the town house, there's an icebox as big as a fridge. But it's not as if you can stick water in a freezer and get ice. For that you need, well, electricity. There's someone who drops off ice, which can't be cheap.

"I see the problem," Gray says when he rises from examining the icebox. "Substandard construction."

"A used icebox?"

"On the contrary, it seems very new."

I look closer, noting the lack of wear marks on the wood. "So just cheaply made?"

"Yes. An icebox must be well insulated. Otherwise, the ice melts too quickly. You have a wooden exterior, a tin interior, and insulation of sawdust or straw."

The interior of this one is wood. While there's probably some kind of insulation, it's not going to keep the ice from melting for long.

"So they had money to spare and decided to splurge on an icebox," I say. "They bought the cheapest one they could find, not realizing that meant they'd end up spending more on ice in the long run. In summer, that would be even worse."

"Also, the food is improperly arranged. One ought to store uncooked meat on the bottom, cooked food next, and then fruit and vegetables up top."

"Because the ice is at the bottom, so the most perishable items go there."

"Yes, which I know because I was distracted when I took out a bottle of milk at home and replaced it on the top shelf."

"Mrs. Wallace schooled you after you spoiled the milk." I look into the icebox. "Not only is the ice melting faster than expected, but the food would have been spoiling even when there *was* ice. Pudding has milk or cream in it, meaning it would be in the icebox. The fact it's a new icebox would explain why Mrs. Burns made that pudding for her husband—taking advantage of the new appliance to cook what he liked. Was it actually poisoned then? Or did he die of severe food poisoning, like botulism or salmonella."

"Bot . . . ?" Gray begins.

"The world hasn't discovered that yet? Lovely. A little something for me to remember the next time I eat out." I point at the icebox. "Spoiled food develops bacteria, which is what causes food poisoning, both the mild kind—which just means you spend a day in the water closet—and the kind that can kill you."

"Bacteria causes . . . ?"

He trails off, his gaze going distant as his mind races through the implications. And with that, I lose him.

Here is another part of history I'm still struggling to understand. What seems like basic science to me can be revelatory to someone in 1869. It's like having a time traveler come back to the twenty-first century and tell us, quite casually, that house flies cause cancer.

Is there a danger in revealing future discoveries to Gray? No, and this is something else I am learning. It would be like that time traveler telling me about house flies. I could email every top scientist with the news . . . and they'd drop my discovery into their spam folder. The only thing it would mean is that I'd personally avoid contact with flies and make sure my loved ones did, too, and that is what Gray and Isla will do with the information.

Gray continues thinking it through while I check the icebox, holding my breath against the stench. The pudding is there. At least, I presume it's pudding. The British version isn't always what North Americans think of as pudding, and so when I find a sticky dome studded with dried fruit, I pull it out.

"Is this pudding?" I say.

I need to say it twice before Gray startles from his thoughts enough to nod.

"It is."

"What's the chance they'd have had two, and this is the wrong one?"

"This is a sweet pudding, and Hugh said that is what made Mr. Burns ill."

"Right." I open the icebox again and frown. "What goes into making such a pudding?"

His brows rise, as if I'm asking what goes into one of Isla's alchemical concoctions.

I say, "Would that not require cream? I suppose she could have used it all."

"Or she may have lied about making it herself." He takes paper from a jacket pocket. "I will note the ingredients in the icebox, and we shall check with Mrs. Wallace."

I'm removing a slice of the pudding when I realize I brought nothing for carrying evidence. That's complicated in a world without plastic. No baggies or Tupperware. Gray hands me a section of waxed brown paper from his pocket, along with twine. I start to wrap the pudding, and he sighs and waves me aside and then does it himself, creating a waterproof, leakproof packet.

"You are going to need to teach me that," I say.

He's about to respond when a voice sounds at the door. I pop my head out to see McCreadie. He comes in, and I tell him about the pudding and the icebox. Then it's on to searching the rest of the apartment.

We don't find anything particularly noteworthy. But as we're finishing up, I take in the whole of the place and ask, "What did Burns do for a living again?"

"He was a salesman," McCreadie says.

"Selling what?"

"Land, mostly."

"Real estate? I'm surprised he still lived in the Old Town."

"I did not say he was a *good* salesman."

"Ah."

"He seems to have been less than reputable in his dealings," McCreadie continues as he surveys the contents of a dresser drawer. "He was sued—unsuccessfully—on several occasions. The last case was three years ago. Since then, there have been no obvious complaints, but I also struggle to find any recent *sales* transactions."

"Suggesting he's selling something else, something illegal?"

"Possibly."

"Which could have gotten him killed."

"Yes. As could his dealings with his former wife or former mistresses or clients he cheated. With Mr. Burns, there is an endless list of possibilities."

I pace around the small bedroom. Then I bend beside a throw rug. Like the icebox, it's new. I lift the sheets on the bed. The mattress is coarse and rough, probably stuffed with straw, but it's in excellent condition.

"Lots of new furnishings," I say. "How long have they lived here?"

"About six months. Their former apartment was a third the size and on the fourth floor."

"You're right about them seeming to live above their means. Could they have come into some money?"

"His former landlord says Burns quit the place halfway through the month, telling her she could keep the rest of the rent. Burns said a wealthy uncle had passed, and he'd come into an inheritance. I can find no record of such an uncle."

I turn to Gray, who is examining the bed. "Dr. Gray? How old would you say the icebox is?"

He doesn't miss a beat—proving that he *has* been listening. "A month or so?"

"Burns came into money, and then *kept* getting money, using it for luxuries like an icebox. I don't suppose we can pull his banking records?" I catch their looks. "Is there such a thing as banking records?"

"Yes," McCreadie says. "But I rather suspect they look somewhat different a hundred years from now, if they could help in such a case."

"It'd be a record of deposits and withdrawals, which might show a suspicious pattern of activity."

"Such a thing exists, obviously, so that the bank knows what a customer has in their account. However, that supposes that someone like Burns has an account, and that we could find it. I have gone through the few records he keeps here at home, and I do not see a bank listed. He may not use one. Many people do not."

"Ah, right. Because we are in a time before the Great Depression and the advent of deposit insurance? Nothing to scare people away from banks like realizing the place that's supposed to keep your money safe can also lose it."

"This . . . Great Depression," McCreadie says. "Is that happening anytime soon?"

"Nineteen-thirties. Stock market crash. Banks failed. People lost everything. Not sure how bad it was in Scotland, but when you hit retirement age, get your money out of the bank. And the stock exchange."

"Presuming I have money to put in either, I will remember that. As for Burns—"

Gray clears his throat. When we look over, he holds out his hand. There's a sovereign and a small silver ring on the palm.

"I believe I know where the Burnses kept their money," he says.

"And when were you going to tell us?" McCreadie says.

"When you were finished conversing. It would be rude to interrupt."

I look from Gray to the bed, which he'd been examining. "Please don't tell me they kept it under the mattress."

"All right, I won't tell you."

I sigh. "How much is there?"

"Only these, but there are marks on the fabric that suggest there was more. I am presuming Mrs. Burns emptied it out when she fled, and in her haste, she missed these."

I walk over to take a look at the ring. It's just a plain silver one, no inscription or anything obviously useful.

"Okay," I say. "Bag them."

"Bag . . . ?" he begins.

"Wrap them up and take them. Please."

"Any other evidence you have not seen fit to share with us?" McCreadie asks Gray.

"Someone else has searched the room," Gray says.

"That would be the police," McCreadie says. "Detective Crichton searched it after Burns's suspicious death and again this morning after Mrs. Burns disappeared."

"I mean since then. When we came in, there were damp boot prints. I thought it might be from the officer on guard, but they seemed rather small. I'll speak to the guard and see whether he admitted anyone else, perhaps with a bribe, but the footprints indicated entrance through an open window. They proceeded throughout the residence, most concentrated in front of the small desk."

"Suggesting someone came in and searched the desk," I say. "Any chance of a hidden compartment?"

"I failed to find one myself, but you both ought to look, in case I missed it."

"I doubt that's possible," McCreadie grumbles. "Could you please tell us these things earlier, Duncan?"

"I was giving you both a chance to discover it for yourself."

"Thanks," I say.

"You're quite welcome."

SEVENTEEN

We don't find anything else of note at the Burns apartment. From there, it's on to the Youngs' residence. This one is trickier, because the Youngs—at least their children and parents—are still in residence. Also, Mr. Young being dead and Mrs. Young being in prison for his murder really isn't going to help the family feel hospitable toward the police.

Our arrival causes a scene, awkward and uncomfortable, as such scenes always are. If you are the victim of a crime, you're usually fine with the police searching your house for clues. Not so much when you're related to the accused.

The Youngs' oldest child isn't actually a child, being at least sixteen. She meets us at the door with her grandfather, and the older man just stands behind her while she reams McCreadie out. Gray steps away. While I don't blame him, I stay where I am, understanding that McCreadie needs the support, even if it is silent.

McCreadie does the only thing he can do, really. He is calm but firm. The police have the right to search the premises again, and they are only trying to gather evidence. Their job is not to convict the girl's mother— it's to find out who killed her father.

"What's she here for?" the girl says, jerking her chin at me. "She's not the police."

"She is the assistant to my colleague, who is a . . . a consulting detective."

I've teased Gray with that phrase, which is even more fun twenty years before the creation of Sherlock Holmes. Apparently, that is now what we're going with as Gray's job title. I send up a silent apology to Sir Arthur Conan Doyle.

"Consulting detective?" the girl says. "What's that mean?"

"He is an independent professional retained for his detecting skills, and this is his assistant, Miss Mitchell."

She eyes me. "She doesn't look much like a detective's assistant."

"I assure you," I say, "I am fully trained in the art of detection and police work. As Detective McCreadie said, we only want to solve this case. Detective McCreadie was not the officer who arrested your mother, so he has no vested interest in her conviction. In fact, were he to find evidence that another party is responsible, it would be to his advantage by allowing him to solve a case already believed solved."

She wrinkles her nose. "You talk like a schoolmistress."

"Blame my father. He's a university professor."

"That's fancy," she says.

I shrug. "It can be. It can also mean that I was forced to read classical literature when I would much rather have picked up a gothic novel."

She snorts at that, but it does the trick, forging that tiny bit of a connection. She steps back, still grudgingly, her gaze saying if we make one false move, we'll be out on our asses, whether that's her legal right or not.

I walk into the room. The *only* room, as McCreadie had warned. It's no more than two hundred square feet, with makeshift dividers for bedrooms. Otherwise, it's one big open space. The two other children are both boys and much younger than their sister, maybe four and seven. I pass them a smile. The older boy turns away. The younger one just stares at me.

Having so many people in such a small area means any worldly goods are packed tight in crates and old wardrobes. Those are the only things we can search, and it makes it even more awkward, because we are literally pawing through their possessions right in front of them.

McCreadie assigns us crates. I get the boys' box, as I realize when I open it. It contains one extra set of clothing for each child—folded shirts and trousers so old that Goodwill wouldn't accept them. Yet someone has lovingly kept them on life support, with perfect stitches repairing every tear and frayed seam.

As I gently unfold one of the shirts, the youngest boy gasps, as if I've ripped it from the box. The older one scowls, and when I turn to say something, he stomps off. I check the clothing and refold it as carefully as I can. Then it's on to the children's playthings—two tattered books, a few marbles, a stuffed toy worn beyond recognition, and a handcrafted miniature wagon.

"This is beautiful," I say as I take out the toy wagon. "Is it yours?"

The little boy doesn't respond.

"Did your father make it?"

"I made it," the girl snaps from across the room. "If you don't believe me, I'll tell you how."

"My apologies," I say. "That was an inexcusable assumption. It *is* beautifully done."

"No, I made a mistake on the wheels. That's why I gave it to them. It wasn't good enough to sell."

If there's a mistake, I can't see it. That just made a good excuse for passing it on to her brothers.

I examine the wagon. Then I put it aside and continue searching everything. When the box is empty, I peer into it. I reach in and then hold out my clenched hand.

"I think you forgot this," I say.

The boy looks at my hand. I open it, revealing an empty palm. He deflates and shakes his head.

"What?" I say. "Isn't it yours?"

"There's nothing there."

I frown at my hand. "Oh, it must be invisible. Let me try that again." I close my fist, wave it, and then, with an awkward sleight of hand, open it to reveal a penny.

"How'd you do that?" he asks.

"Magic."

He eyes me with suspicion. "What do you want for it?"

My heart sinks a little. The kid is barely old enough to be in school, but he's already realized nothing comes for free in his world.

"Clever lad," I say. "I do want something."

Across the room, his sister tenses.

"If you'd like this penny," I say, "you need to find it. Now, follow the coin."

I flip the coin in the air and then catch it and do a quick bit of fast handwork. When I'm done, I hold out my fists.

"All right," I say. "I'll give you two chances."

The boy rolls his eyes. "That's not a proper game."

"Should I only give you one instead?"

He shakes his head and points to a hand. I open it to reveal nothing. I close that hand, and he points to the other.

"Are you sure?" I ask. "Remember where you saw it last."

He meets my gaze, with the appraising look of a much older boy. Then, slowly, he points back to the hand he picked the first time. I open it reveal the coin.

"Trust yourself," I say. "You knew that you didn't make a mistake."

I hand him the coin. He glances at his sister and then takes it. I put his belongings back into the box, and we talk as I do. When I close it up, I walk to McCreadie.

"I saw that," he murmurs. "Nicely done."

"I loved magic tricks as a kid."

He lowers his voice. "What did the boy tell you?"

"Nothing."

McCreadie's brow furrows. "You were not lowering his guard so that he might talk?"

"No. I just wanted him to know that what's happening isn't as scary as it seems. That we aren't as scary as we seem."

He looks at me a moment and then nods approvingly.

"Are we finding anything?" I ask.

He shakes his head and glances at Gray. I head over and ask him the same question, getting the same response.

"Nothing at all?" I say.

Gray lowers his voice. "From what I have seen, the family is as impoverished as they seem, with no sign of sudden wealth, as we saw with the Burnses. There is a bottle of gin under a floorboard, which I presume belongs to Mr. Young. It suggests his wife knew he had a drinking problem and did not allow spirits in the house. I also found a pawn receipt in his belongings, for what seems to be jewelry. Women's jewelry. He had it very well hidden, which suggests his wife did not realize he had pawned what I presume is hers. In addition, I found a pair of gold cuff links, quite old, perhaps belonging to his father or grandfather."

"So he secretly pawned his wife's treasures, but not his own. Nice."

At a throat clearing behind us, I spin, thinking I spoke louder than I intended. It's the daughter.

She looks at Gray. "I want to speak to her."

"Miss Mitchell? Of course." Gray waves her over and steps away.

"No, I want to speak to her outside."

"Then you must ask her, not me."

McCreadie must overhear, because he steps in our direction.

"Not you," she says to McCreadie. "Only her."

"Let's go outside," I say.

EIGHTEEN

Miss Young and I head out into the crowded and narrow street. She walks quickly, and for a moment I think she's leaving me behind. Then she glances back with an impatient jerk of her chin, and I hurry to catch up.

"Nettie didn't kill my father," she says.

"Nettie?"

"My father's wife."

"Oh, I'm sorry. I didn't realize she wasn't your mother."

"She is two-and-twenty," she says. "That would hardly be possible. My mother died when I was a child. My grandparents raised me until my father remarried. Before you ask, this is not some fairy tale with the wicked stepmother. I like Nettie far better than I liked my father. And she did not kill him. I'd have understood if she did. I'd have done it myself if I had the nerve."

She walks a few more steps and then crosses her arms, as if against the cold, though the June sun beats down. "No, that is a lie. I could not have murdered him. He didn't deserve such a fate. But she deserved better. We *all* deserved better."

"Can you tell me a bit more about your family, so that I might fully understand the situation?"

"What is there to tell that you will not have heard a thousand times, from behind a thousand doors like these?" She meets my gaze, defiant. "Do not think such problems don't exist in your side of the city, either."

"Oh, they do. They're just easier to hide in a big house, with thick walls and staff paid for their loyalty and their silence."

She snorts a quarter laugh. "Yes. It is much easier to hide one's problems when the walls aren't little more than paper. My father lost himself to the bottle after my mother died. Or that is the story, though I do not know if it is true or a kindness my gran tells me so I will imagine some grand love between them. I knew little of him growing up. He only came to see us when he needed a place to sleep. He was handsome, though, and could usually find a woman to provide that. Then he got Nettie with child when she was younger than I am now. He married her, and she wanted us to live all together—her and my father, my grandparents and me." She pauses. "I liked that. Nettie and I get on like sisters."

I nod and continue walking, letting her story come in its own time.

"He never struck us," she says. "Not me or the boys or Nettie. My grandparents wouldn't have let him. Nor would Nettie or I. He wasn't around enough to harm us in that way. He was gone for days on end, drinking in some whore's bed."

"He had mistresses?"

She snorts. "That's a pretty word for it. He had women who would fill his glass and give him a bed. I do not know names, but I can tell you where to ask."

"Thank you."

"My father may never have lifted a hand to Nettie, but that does not mean he treated her well. She is very sweet. A gentle soul." Miss Young makes a face. "That sounds odd to say about one's stepmother, doesn't it?"

"She is naïve?"

A sharp laugh. "Oh, no. Not naïve at all. I said sweet and gentle, not gullible. She is a good woman, who wants nothing but to see her family cared for, a family that includes both me and my mother's parents. My father did not provide for us, and so she did, and that is how I know she did not poison him."

When I don't answer, she looks over. "You are wondering how those two things are connected. Am I saying that she is a good provider and therefore could not have murdered her useless husband? No. That would be part of providing, would it not? Particularly if he stole her money and bought drink with it?" She shakes her head. "I ought not to say that, or it might put ideas in your head."

"It doesn't."

"Nettie couldn't have poisoned him because she was not at home. She was earning a living, in a way that she will not wish to tell the police, and so I am doing it for her, because no shame is worth dying for."

"She sold her favors."

"You do put things prettily."

"Oh, I can put them far less prettily, but I have found that people do not appreciate me asking whether someone was in the sex trade. They turn quite red and begin to stammer."

A sharp laugh. "Then you are speaking to too many people in the New Town. It is different here. Whether Nettie is in the 'sex trade' depends on how you define such a thing. She poses for artists. Without her clothing."

"Pornography?"

Miss Young bristles. "Certainly not. Or, if it is, that is not what she was told. It is for art."

"Ah, she's a nude model." I momentarily wonder why that is so scandalous that she wouldn't use it to save her from the gallows. Then I remember that any sort of nudity would be a scandal.

"And that proves she wasn't the killer because . . . ?" I prompt.

"Because she was in Glasgow, where they had offered her a princely sum. By the time she returned, my father was abed, ill, and he died the next day."

"Do you have any idea how he was poisoned? Is there something in the house he eats that no one else does?"

"Eats, no. Drinks, yes. He has a bottle hidden under a board beneath their bed."

"We found that. Did anyone gift him that bottle?"

"If they did, I know nothing of it. I can give you names of some of his friends, but if they had the money for a bottle, they would keep it themselves."

"Is the bottle we found his usual choice?"

"His usual choice is whatever he can find, including poteen. That is the first time I have seen a bottle of real alcohol there."

"Did he seem to come into any money lately?"

"If he did, we saw none of it. That's why Nettie took the job in Glasgow."

"May I ask more questions?"

"If you're going to ask why Nettie took the money from the friendly society and did not fetch his body, that was my idea. I . . ." She crosses her arms again. "I told her that his body should go to the doctors so that they might discover what makes drink take such hold of a man. I told her they might be able to find a cure."

"Ah."

"It was not a lie. They might, mightn't they? But yes, I was thinking more of the money and that it ought to go to his family, not into the pockets of those who'd bury him. He's dead and gone. Not like he'll care. Not like he'll know."

And on that, I must admit that I agree.

An hour later, I'm in a coffee shop, and no, I didn't magically transport to my own time. If I'd read the words "coffee shop" in a Victorian story, I'd have thought the writer didn't do their research. Which only proves how little I understood this world.

Gray had wanted a tea shop—for the pastries, obviously—and I jokingly asked about a coffee shop . . . and they took me to one.

It's also not quite what I had in mind. Yes, there's coffee, and no, I didn't expect mochas and lattes, but I expected a more . . . bohemian vibe. I realized my mistake once I discovered that my "coffee shop" was in a stately New Town hotel. At least that meant Isla could walk over and join us.

The shop does serve coffee, and it's halfway decent. It also serves baked goods, which are not quite decadent enough for Gray—he eats his slowly and never once eyes my share or McCreadie's. I have oatcakes, which I'm very fond of, and here's where I'll grant Victorian coffee shops a point— they do know how to make a proper oatcake.

I also see the precursors of our coffee shops in the comfortable furnishings and the small groups of people enjoying a leisurely cup of caffeine while chatting. There are even tables set up with chess games.

What's different is the vibe, which seems to be trying for casual and not quite finding it. The atmosphere is a little stiff. A little austere. Almost as if the place is trying to be more of a fancy pub than a tea shop, which seems strange until I realize that's exactly what it's supposed to be—the mocktail of Victorian public houses.

When Isla joins us, she explains that coffee shops like this are a response to two nascent movements: women's suffrage and temperance. In the New Town, women can't frequent public houses or hotel bars, and they want some of that casual vibe, very different from a tea shop. This is a place where they can be comfortable, either with or without male escorts. It's also a place where men can meet to discuss business without alcohol. The temperance movement began in Scotland—and elsewhere—about forty years ago, and taking "the pledge" is an increasing movement within church congregations.

"Yay for suffrage," I say. "Not so keen on temperance."

Isla's brows rise. The two men wisely sip their coffees in silence.

"You do not recognize the evils of drink?" she says.

"Oh, trust me, I saw them on full display today. I knew that suffrage and temperance had some underlying links. Women were tired of men getting drunk on the grocery money and abusing their wives and children. If temperance means *tempering* access to alcohol—while understanding and dealing with addiction—then I'm all for it. But whatever it means now, it will come to mean complete prohibition. The United States will try that in about fifty years. It does not go well."

"What happens?" Gray asks.

"Let me guess," McCreadie says. "People didn't stop drinking. Making it a criminal act simply meant that the only ones who profited were the criminals."

"Bingo. Alcohol continued to be sold, just underground and at exorbitant prices. Also, if it's being sold underground, with no regulation . . ."

Isla shudders. "Poison."

McCreadie frowns. "They poisoned the alcohol?"

"No," Isla says. "But the distillation of alcohol is a precise science, and it is easy to either do it wrong by accident or to do it wrong intentionally to save money."

"Actually . . . the American government did poison alcohol, in a way," I say. "They ensured that industrial alcohol contained toxins, which was supposed to discourage people from drinking it, but of course, it just ended up making things worse."

"That is . . ." Isla says. "I have no words."

"So many deaths," I say. "From all sources. Not to mention blindness and other complications. Alcohol might destroy people and families, but turning off that pipeline destroys even more."

"So what is the answer?" Isla says.

"Hell if I know."

"I feel that the more I discuss the future with you, the more discouraged I become."

"On the upside, at least you know not to advocate for complete alcohol prohibition."

"And not to keep my money in banks," McCreadie says.

Isla cocks a brow at me.

"I'll explain later," I say. "For now, we need to check out Miss Young's alibi for her stepmother. I'd also like to speak to her."

"In prison?" McCreadie says.

"I'd rather do it in this coffee shop, but I doubt that's an option."

"We will visit her in prison," Gray says. "Hugh will arrange it. Isla, I'd like you to analyze the contents of that gin bottle. If it's poisoned, we need to find out where it came from."

"I'd also like to get some idea where Burns's newfound wealth came from," I say.

"Do we see a connection between Lord Leslie, Burns, and Young?" Gray says. "There must be one, if all three died of the same rare poison. Yes, we have not proven that, but their symptoms do suggest it."

"A connection between an alcoholic gravedigger, a shady salesman, and an earl," I say. "The only thing they seem to have in common is that they all cheated on their wives. Miss Young says her father did, and Annis says her husband did, and Burns abandoned his family to marry his mistress."

"It's a possible link," McCreadie says carefully.

"But it might also link half the husbands in Edinburgh?" I say. "Regardless of social class?"

"Yes."

"Which would leave the connection, not with the men themselves, but with the poison. Three poisoners, all procuring a rare substance from the same provider. That would make it a poisoning ring."

McCreadie sneaks a look at Isla. "I'm afraid so."

The gin and pudding are both poisoned. Again, while Isla can't specifically test for thallium, she can tell that they contain one of a limited set of heavy metals, which is not arsenic. Thallium is a fair bet, given the symptoms and the fact that neither man complained of tasting poison. Young drank a quarter of the bottle and Burns only thought the pudding was upsetting his stomach because it was rich.

Once the testing is complete and we've eaten dinner, Isla and I are off to talk to Jack. Gray and McCreadie aren't pleased with this plan, mostly just because we don't invite them. They have other avenues to pursue, and also, Isla and I want to do this ourselves. That concerns them because we're going into the Old Town in the evening chasing a young woman who has already betrayed us. After a brief argument, though, they back down. They have registered their concerns, and that is enough. Or I think it's enough, until we're heading out the back door and find Simon waiting.

"Good evening, ladies," he says. "I have been asked to follow you on your excursion. As I know you spotted me the last time, Mallory, I decided perhaps I ought to ask whether you would prefer I escorted you openly."

Isla curses under her breath.

I look at her. "As frustrating as it is, Dr. Gray does have a point this time. We're going into a dangerous area, and I was already attacked there once."

"Twice," Simon says. "Not that we are keeping track."

"Fine. Twice. Yes, it is dangerous, and yes, if you want to tag along, I agree to it."

Isla gives a slow nod. "I understand that my brother has placed you in an awkward position, Simon, but that is an issue to bring up with him, and I will not put you in the middle by insisting we go alone."

"Thank you," Simon says.

I understand what Gray is doing by telling Simon to shadow us. He's avoiding confrontation with his older sister. Avoiding making her feel that he doesn't think she can take care of herself, when *he* clearly ventures into the Old Town alone at night. Yet it is not the same thing, and he needs to trust that Isla can rise above her annoyance to realize that.

Also, if I'm being honest, I don't think Isla *can* take care of herself in the Old Town at night. That's no reflection on her; it's purely her upbringing. She was raised in an open-minded family, who did their best to encourage her to lead as full a life as her brothers. That meant an education, a career in chemistry, the freedom to choose her own husband and such. It did not mean teaching her how to handle herself in a rough neighborhood at night, because why on earth would she need to do such a thing?

I'm sure no one taught Gray how to handle himself either. He learned to fight defending himself against bigots in school, and that—plus his sex and size—lets him venture confidently across the Mound. Even then, he might overestimate his safety, but as someone who tends to do the same, I can't really blame him.

Isla must learn to defend herself. She must also understand that we are targets in a way her brother is not, as much as it chafes. Gray is doing the right thing. He just needs to do it openly and have this discussion rather than secretly send a bodyguard, which is patronizing as hell.

As we walk, I tell Simon what happened last night—how we were followed and Gray paid our pursuer to "guard" us. That makes him laugh.

"Dr. Gray is a very clever man," he says.

Isla makes a noise at that.

I continue the story. When I reach the end, he says, "So this apparent young man was, as you suspected, a young woman."

"Yes."

"I do not know her, in case you were wondering."

"I wasn't going to ask," I say. "It's not the same thing, and even if it was, I wouldn't presume you'd know her. In Jack's case, she may be assuming a male persona to allow her to pass more easily through the city. It would also allow her to more easily pursue her occupation, which I presume is at least tangentially criminal in nature. Presenting as male would protect her. Or, she may *prefer* to present as male, which is her choice."

"That is an interesting perspective from someone who preferred not to discuss that part of my past."

"I have changed, and I am sorry if I ever suggested it made me uncomfortable."

He shrugs. "It was, as you say, a persona, one I found quite fun. It may be the same for this Jack or, as you say, she may prefer it, which also happens. Either way, while I do not know her, I do have contacts that might."

"Thank you. With any luck, we'll find her tonight. We were told to ask at Halton House."

"Halton House?" He looks over sharply as we cross into the Old Town.

"Is that a problem?" I ask.

"That depends on whether you expect to find her there."

"It's not a rooming house, is it?"

He chokes on a laugh. "No, it is not. It's . . ." He glances over at Isla. "You may wish me to summon a hansom to take you home, Mrs. Ballantyne."

She arches a brow. "Because whatever Halton House is, it is not a place for a lady?"

"Yes."

"Then our evening has become infinitely more exciting. Lead on."

NINETEEN

Simon takes us through the streets of the Old Town until we draw near the neighborhood of Burns's favorite public house. I expect Simon to take us to some seedy dive, but the building we approach is in decent shape, even with several stories of apartments piled above it.

The ground level is Halton House, and it *is* a rooming house. Or that's what the sign insists, along with one that says NO ROOMS TO LET, its distinct layer of dust suggesting there are never rooms to let.

Inside, we find what looks like an inn, complete with a front desk and an older woman writing in a ledger. When we enter, she barely glances up.

"We're full, lad. You'll need to take your friends elsewhere."

There is no sarcastic twist on the word "friends." She thinks Simon is looking for a bed for three, and she places no judgment on that.

The lobby smells of lavender, but under it, cheroot smoke permeates the place. A low rumble sounds from below, one I hadn't noticed until everything went quiet. I pretend not to hear it, even when a thump follows.

"We've been told to ask for Jack," I say.

The desk clerk's head rises at that, and she peers at me, and then puts on a pair of spectacles and peers some more. When she looks at Isla, her frown deepens. I told Isla to "dress down" for this excursion, but that only means she's wearing the dress that she uses in the laboratory. Like all her late-mourning wear, it's a shade of gray, and very simple, with nothing more than a bit of pretty black and silver trim above the cuffs and hem. It's still exquisite workmanship, and in this time period, another woman is going to recognize that.

"You don't belong here, lasses." She turns to Simon. "Take them on back to the New Town. This isn't a stop on Black's walking tour."

"As I said, I was told to ask for Jack," I say, firmer.

"I do not know who you mean."

"If she is around, then please tell her it is Dr. Gray's assistant, Mallory. If she is not, then I would like to leave a message, and I believe she will want to receive it."

Her look changes as soon as I say "she." It's appraising now.

A rustling has me looking over to see Isla opening her purse. I subtly shake my head. Here, too, is where she lacks her brother's experience. Gray knows when and how to offer a bribe, and she only knows that it works when he does it.

"Dr. Gray, you say?" the woman says.

"Yes, of Robert Street. My name is Mallory."

"Bob!" the woman barks, loud enough that we all give a start. She has to call again before a door down the hall opens. Someone whoops in the basement, and a cheer rings out.

The woman glowers at the boy hurrying her way. "Did I not tell you to close the door behind you?" She turns to us. "You will have to excuse the noise, ladies. They are having a game of cards downstairs."

"Cards?" I say. "I'd heard this was a fight club. Oh, right, I forgot the first rule of fight club. Don't talk about fight club."

Simon glances over. "Is there a second rule?"

"Yep. Don't talk about fight club."

"In case one missed the first rule?"

"Exactly." I turn to the woman at the desk. "Any chance we can see the 'card game,' since we already know the first and second rules?"

She eyes me. Then she turns to the boy. "Fetch Jack. These ladies and this young man would like to speak to him."

"Tell him it's Mallory from last night," I add.

The boy glances at the woman, who nods.

As he scampers off, I say, "So I don't get to see the fight club?"

"It is not a place for ladies."

"That's good, because I'm not a lady."

"I am reaching that opinion," she says, in a tone that suggests she doesn't consider it an insult. "However, your friend here most certainly is one."

"True, but she's also a chemist. If you're in need of painkillers—or the gentlemen below are—she's your woman." I glance at Isla. "I know you make them for your brother."

"Far too often," she mutters. "And if you tell Duncan that there is a fighting establishment in this building . . ."

"I can't. That'd violate both rule one and rule two of fight club."

"Is that Miss Mallory I hear?" a voice says as the basement door reopens and Jack walks out.

"A friend of yours?" the woman at the desk says.

Jack cocks her head and studies me. "I'm not yet certain. She seems quite an odd duck."

"Which is why I presumed she was a friend of yours."

Jack flaps a hand at the woman. "Ignore Elspeth. She is completely correct, of course. Being one of my oldest and dearest friends, she knows my taste in them. Now, Miss Mallory, if you have come about that business last night, I have nothing for you. I have spoken to the person in question, and she is considering the matter."

"All right, but that's not actually why we came."

Jack's gaze slides over Isla and Simon. When it stops on Simon, she frowns. "Do I know you?"

He stiffens, though he tries to hide it, and when he speaks, there's a chill in his voice, masquerading as formality. "I do not believe we are acquainted, miss."

"Not acquainted, but I feel I have—" She stops and her eyes widen. "Oh. Yes. I see it now."

He tenses more. Being at the center of a Victorian scandal means you don't need to worry about your photo being plastered all over the news. As notorious as his situation was, he doesn't have a memorable face, and I presume "Simon" isn't his real name. That doesn't mean no one will recognize him—either people he knew from that life or even people who might have seen an artistic rendering of him.

Jack continues, "Well, I am glad to see you landed on your feet, sir. That was a nasty bit of business. Those with money think they can buy their way out of anything and trample anyone who gets in their path."

Simon relaxes a little and murmurs, "Quite."

Jack turns back to me. "What is it you came for then, Miss Mallory?"

"I would prefer to speak in private."

She looks about. "There's no one here except Elspeth, and when dealing with someone I do not know well, I have learned that having a friend around is an advantage."

"All right then." I take out the folded broadsheet and pass it over.

She opens and only glances at it. "Ah."

"You sold information on our encounter last night to this news writer. I don't begrudge you the ability to make a living, even if I did hope you were more fair-minded than that."

"Did you now?"

"I'm an optimist. Naïvely so, sometimes. I made a mistake, but I didn't come to hassle you about selling your story. That's your business. This writer knows things about the death of Lord Leslie that the others did not. I would like to speak to them, whether in person or by message. I can offer information on the case in return for the same."

"Information on the case? From Dr. Gray, I presume, and his friend, Detective McCreadie?"

"Yes."

"You seem to be wanting a lot from me, Miss Mallory," she says, leaning against the front desk. "First contact with that other person and now contact with this person."

"I'm offering both something in return. For the first, protection. For the second, information."

"Mmm, yes, but I have the feeling what you're asking for is worth more to you." She leans a hip against the desk. "Or at least to your employer, Dr. Gray, whose sister . . ." Her gaze turns to Isla. "Ah. Now I understand why you brought your friend. Lady Leslie, I presume?"

"You presume wrong," Isla says flatly.

"She's a chemist," Elspeth says. "Or so she claims."

"Well, then, that would make you the *other* sister, wouldn't it? The widowed one." Jack pauses. "Or I suppose that no longer distinguishes you from Lady Leslie."

Isla says nothing.

"Lady Leslie," Jack muses, "who stands accused of murdering her husband with poison. Lady Leslie, who has a chemist for a sister. I am surprised no one has made that connection yet."

I'm in front of Isla before she can blink, and my shoulder smacks against Simon's, as he moves in just as quickly.

"No," I say. "If that connection is made by your broadsheet writer friend, then I will presume it came from you, and that would be ill-advised."

Her brows shoot up. "Is that a threat?"

"I'd prefer not. Threats are rude, and they set a discussion on an adversarial path. Rather like threatening my employer does."

"I agree with all that," Simon says. "If the connection is made, it had best not be made by that particular writer."

"Nor anything about our groom," Isla says. "And his misfortunes."

Jack raises her hands. "No need to get your knickers in a twist. The connection *will* be made, though. Perhaps it is best for you to make it yourself. Speak to my writer friend for an exclusive interview."

When Isla stiffens, I say, "You do realize you're speaking to the sister of the woman who has been accused of murder. Mrs. Ballantyne's brother-in-law died last night. She is not a witness who happened to see a crime. She is the family of both the deceased and the accused."

"All right. My friend can interview Dr. Gray then."

"How is that different?" I meet her eyes. "Because he is a man and therefore better able to handle such an interview?"

She flaps her hand again. "All right, all right. But I daresay Mrs. Ballantyne here might change her mind when the news does come out. I can promise my friend will conduct a fair and honest interview."

"There is no such thing," I say. "Not when the sharks smell blood in the water."

"Sharks? You have no liking for the fine profession of newspaper reporting, Miss Mallory?"

"I have moderate respect for newspaper reporters who have proven they can be trusted. In my experience, though, the words 'fair and honest' are a lure, tempting those desperate to set the story straight. Rather like police officers promising to be fair and honest with suspects eager to set *their* story straight. I begrudge neither their right to pursue their profession. It doesn't mean I want to chum the waters for them."

"You say what you think, don't you, Miss Mallory? Am I to guess then that you would rather I leave your employers and your fellow servant out of this and deal with you directly? Make my bargain with you?"

"Yes."

"All right then. I will give you what you want in return for a fight." Jack waves toward the basement door. "From what I heard, you know what goes on here."

"Knows?" Elspeth snorts. "She wants to *see* it."

"Well, this is your lucky night, Miss Mallory. You not only get to see it but join in the fun. We've got a boy down there, new to the art of fighting. Take him on in the ring and—win or lose—I will convey your offer to my writerly friend."

"You want . . ." Isla sputters. "You want Mallory to *fight*?"

"Have you seen her, ma'am? She is better at it than I am, which is why I do not offer myself up as an opponent."

"No," I say. "I'm not boxing some boy for the amusement of a crowd, in order to win an offer that may be refused."

"Oh, I doubt my writerly friend will refuse."

"Then go to them and have them pay you to be the go-between. We will pay you as well."

"No," Elspeth says. "If you say the girl can fight, then I want to see her fight. Four shillings for each round you stay on your feet."

"How many rounds are there?" Isla asks.

"Five. That's a guinea in your pocket if you win, lass."

"Then I will give you a guinea if you refuse," Isla says.

Elspeth's eyes narrow. "Six shillings per round."

"Which I will match."

I turn to Elspeth. "Can you bid a guinea a round, please? Not that I'll accept, but if Mrs. Ballantyne is willing to match, it would be a nice bonus on my quarterly earnings." I lift my hands as they both start to speak. "No, I'm not fighting."

"Afraid you'll lose, lass?" Elspeth says.

"If that's supposed to egg me into it, you've picked the wrong tactic. I can fight, and I will if I need to defend myself, but I don't do it for fun. I don't do it for cash. I sure as heck don't do it for an audience."

"Heck?" Jack says.

"It's an American word. The point is that I'm not fighting."

"Then I guess I'm not taking your message to my writerly friend."

I shrug. "Suit yourself. They were first on my list, but I have a meeting with Joseph McBride tomorrow morning, where I'll make the same offer."

McBride is another broadsheet writer, and I have no idea how to contact him—or whether that's his real name—but the look on Jack's face tells me I pulled off the bluff.

"I would rather have dealt with you," I say. "Also I'd rather have dealt with your friend, who seems more likely to make good use of my information and give me some in return. That's why I came to you first, but obviously your friend doesn't need the help. I only hope they won't be too upset when they find out you turned down my offer, because they're *going* to find out."

"You'll make sure of it?" Jack says.

I shrug again. "Your friend seems the better reporter, and so I might want to deal with them on another case. I'll find them another way."

"One that cuts out my payment."

"Can't claim a messenger fee if you aren't delivering a message."

Jack only sighs. "I thought you were fun."

"Fun and gullible are two very different words." I turn to Isla. "Anything else we need?"

"No," she says frostily, her gaze fixed on Jack. "I do believe we have quite wasted our time. That is why I suggested meeting with Mr. McBride directly, rather than trying to approach this nameless scribbler through an intermediary."

"You were right. I was wrong. Won't be the first time or the last."

We start for the door, Simon falling in behind us.

"Wait," Jack says, the word itself a deep sigh. "I'll pass on the message for a crown."

"Make it—" I begin, but Isla cuts me off.

"A crown if the response to our proposal is favorable," she says. "Nothing if it is not."

"Fine," Jack says. "I will have an answer by ten tomorrow. I'll bring it to Robert Street."

"One last offer," Elspeth says as I open the door. "A half sovereign per round with a week's advance notice, so that I may make it a private event."

"I don't fight for money," I say. "And I don't fight for an audience. Good evening to you both."

As the door closes, I turn to Isla. "You know I've already mentally spent that money you offered, right?"

"Dare I ask on what?"

"Dresses with knife-sized pockets. Also, a pistol. A pocket pistol and pockets I won't lose the bloody thing in." I glance over at a pair of students passing around a flask. "One of those, too. Maybe two."

"Young men?" Simon says with a smile.

"Mmm, that'd probably cost me more than I can afford. I want dresses with knife-sized and pistol-sized secret pockets plus a pistol and a flask for whisky."

"You have no idea how much anything costs, do you?" Isla says. "After that hit on the head, I mean."

"I'll settle for smaller pockets on my existing dresses and a pistol. A teeny-tiny, adorable pistol."

She shakes her head, and we continue along the street.

TWENTY

We're back in the house, Simon in the stables, the door closed behind us. Isla peers down the hall and nods at the bottom of the door into the funeral parlor, where light seeps out.

"Duncan is working late," she says.

"He is always working late," I say.

"You should go speak to him."

"About working late? Yeah, that's not my place. Also, I get the impression it's not *over*working. If you're doing things you enjoy, it doesn't seem like work." As I talk, I switch my outdoor boots for my indoor ones, which is not a quick process. "The problem comes when all you do is work. Been there, done that. I don't think Dr. Gray has that problem, does he?"

"No, and I wasn't suggesting you speak to him about that. I meant speak to him about what happened earlier, with Simon."

"Mmm, also not my place."

"Did he not send Simon to watch us both?"

"He sent Simon to watch over you. I just happened to be there."

"I believe that is a misinterpretation of the situation. However, I do think it is your place to discuss it with him when you were included in his subterfuge. I am also . . ."

She pops a peppermint from her tin, her personal sign of stress. "I am also asking you to speak to him, Mallory, because if I do, I will handle it poorly. I will take offense, even if none is intended. I will make him feel bad, when he simply sought to do the right thing. I will fully intend to approach it in a logical manner, and I will not, and thus nothing will be resolved because I will storm out, and he will only be more crafty the next time he sends Simon after me."

When I don't answer, she snaps the last button on her indoor boots. "I am putting you in an uncomfortable position. I apologize. You are correct. I need to handle this myself."

"No, you have a point. I'm just not sure I can make it. You're not the only one Dr. Gray doesn't quite see clearly, despite his best intentions. He knows I'm not 'just the maid,' but that doesn't mean I can speak to him on an equal footing."

"Are you not on equal footing?"

"Oh, *I* think I am."

"Do you? Has he not asked you to call him by his given name? Yet even when I am the only one around, you refer to him as 'Dr. Gray.'"

"It's complicated."

"Then perhaps this is a step toward making it *less* complicated."

"While also solving this problem you'd like me to solve?"

Her lips twitch in a smile. "A single action can have multiple intentions and outcomes. This one simply happens to benefit us both."

"Fine," I grumble. "I'll talk to your brother."

"Duncan."

"Your brother," I say, and head down the hall toward that illuminated door.

I slip into the funerary parlor. Gray is in his office, with the door half shut. I'm tempted to tiptoe in and see how deeply he's immersed in his work, and then retreat if he's busy. However, that sets me up for a charge of "sneaking around" if I'm caught.

Also, it's a cheat. I *want* him to be deeply in his work, so I can skip this conversation. Oh, it needs to be had, and I might even be the right person to do it. I just don't want to piss him off. That's the crux of it. I don't want to do anything to raise his walls again.

But this isn't about me. It's about his sister, and that's the relationship that counts. I'm only a visitor in their world, in their lives. I can repay Isla's kindness by doing this thing for her, even if it damages my wobbly relationship with Gray.

I peek through the door. Gray's already looking up, having heard my footsteps. He's been writing, ink on his forehead from having run his hand through his hair.

"Mallory," he says as he sets down the pen. "All went well tonight, I hope."

"Jack agreed to deliver a message to the broadsheet writer."

He waves me in. "No need to hover in my doorway. I was only making notes on the investigation. I know you do that, and it seems an excellent way to better organize my thoughts. I certainly do it with my own work, but as detection is not *my* work, it seemed an overreach, and . . ."

He trails off as he sees my expression. "Something is amiss, and I am prattling on, and you are waiting most politely for me to finish."

"More like happily listening so I can postpone a discussion I'd rather not have."

I say it with a smile, but his guard shoots up.

"I see," he says. "You have found a way back, I presume."

"Back . . . ?"

"To your own time."

"No, it's nothing like that."

His shoulders relax a fraction. "Come in, then. Would you like a drink?"

"I'd very much like a drink, but it would only give me an excuse to postpone this more." I take a deep breath. "Isla and I know Simon followed us tonight. Or that was his order, presumably from you, but we found him out and asked him to accompany us instead."

"Ah." He picks up the pen again and taps it, as if clearing the ink. "I understand you find my maneuvering objectionable. However—"

"I don't, actually. Find it objectionable, I mean. I *do* find it patronizing to have you agree to let us go and then send Simon. Like agreeing a child is old enough to go to the corner store alone and then following them. That's understandable for a child who needs to experience responsibility without risk. Isla and I aren't children."

The wall solidifies. "I understand that."

"Treating women as children always makes things worse because historically, that's how we've been classed. But I'm not going to lecture you about that. I'm also not going to lecture you about thinking we—as women—need an escort in the Old Town at night because, frankly, I agree."

"You . . . agree?"

"I do." I move into the room and sit in front of his desk. "It has nothing to do with being able to take care of ourselves and everything to do with being targets, on account of our sex and perceived weakness. Maybe I should have realized it myself right away but—like Isla—I'm sensitive about that. Even in the twenty-first century, I know I shouldn't walk down an empty street, alone, in the middle of the night. Hell, that's how I ended up here, right?"

"True . . ."

"Being in danger just because I'm a woman sucks. It really sucks. But just because it *should* be okay doesn't mean I can act as if it is. That'd be like seeing my house on fire and deciding I'm going inside anyway because it shouldn't *be* on fire. Until that fire's out, I can't take that chance, however inconvenient it is, and however much I just want to say I'll be okay, I'll be careful, I won't get burned."

I lean back in the chair. "I'm blathering, aren't I? I'm trying to explain a concept that's still difficult for me to accept—that I can't do everything men do."

"*Because* of men," he says. "Presumably men are the danger in your time as well."

"Yes, but if you say that, you get the rallying cry of 'not all men.' Not all men are dangerous. Not all men are assholes. Not all men are going to mug or assault me."

"I should hope that would be obvious. Saying doctors can harm more than they heal certainly does not mean *all* do."

"Right. It's wise to be wary of doctors who run shady operations . . . just like it's wise for women to be wary in rough Victorian neighborhoods, at night, without a male escort. I needed you to point that out, Dr. Gray. You asked to join us yourself, and I thought you just didn't want to miss an adventure. If you had said you thought it was unsafe, we'd have bristled but agreed. Yet pointing it out puts you in the shitty position of offending us."

"Yes."

"The alternative was to send Simon after us, which puts *him* in a shitty position."

He sets down his pen. "I had not considered that."

"It also risks offending us more than if you'd said it was unsafe. The answer is compromise. I will acknowledge now that venturing there alone at night is unsafe. I can make Isla understand that."

"In return, I shall acknowledge that I not only put Simon in a difficult position but was patronizing to you and my sister."

"And in future you will not send Simon—or anyone else—to watch over us if we refuse the offer of an escort?"

He hesitates.

I lean forward. "We'll discuss Isla in a moment, which is another matter, but I am capable of analyzing a situation and assessing threat. If I make a mistake, then I deal with those consequences. For you to override my decision . . ."

"Is the very definition of patronizing," he says with a sigh.

"Yep. Now, being new to this time, I need help understanding its dangers, but I also need you to let me make that final call. Isla is . . . another matter." I glance toward the door and lower my voice. "May I speak frankly on that, Dr. Gray?"

"Of course."

I explain how I interpret the situation: that Isla can't accurately assess the danger because she's been sheltered from it.

"The answer isn't to continue sheltering her," I say. "Or to make choices for her."

"It is to give her the data and experience she needs to assess the danger, as I will do for you."

"Plus the tools to deal with it. Self-defense lessons. A weapon—and training in how to use that."

When he hesitates, I say, "You're afraid her enthusiasm for adventure will get her into trouble."

He exhales in relief, as if glad he didn't need to say it. "Yes."

"Which is, again, patronizing." I pause for a beat. "Just as the way she sometimes treats you can be patronizing. I don't have siblings, but I can see both the amazing side of it *and* the frustrating side. She sometimes treats you like her little brother, in need of protection from threats like distraction."

His cheek ticks, but I plow on. "She is the older sister who *has* gotten herself into trouble, chasing adventure, blinded to everything else . . . as she did when she married."

"You know about that."

"I know she married an asshole, and you said she was marrying an ass-hole, and she didn't appreciate your warning. That caused friction before she discovered you were right . . . and caused awkwardness afterward. For her, at least."

"For both of us." He rubs his mouth. "I do not wish to burden you with our family troubles, but yes, I did not want to be correct about Lawrence. For obvious reasons. She suffered with him. More than she'll ever let on."

I soften my voice. "I know. But Isla isn't the girl who married Law-rence, and you aren't the boy who needed to be kept from distraction. I will speak to Isla. We'll get her to the place where she knows she can't sneak off to the Old Town at night . . . and get *you* to the place where you know you shouldn't send Simon to follow her."

He's silent for a moment. Then he says, "Would you like that drink now?"

I feign collapsing onto his desk. "*Please.* I know I interrupted your work, so I'll take it to go."

"The work you interrupted was work on the case. I would very much like to get your opinion on my theories and conclusions . . . unless offering to leave me alone was your polite way of saying *you* would like to be alone."

"If I wanted that, I'd say so."

"Good." He rises from the desk. "Whisky or brandy?"

"Unless you have beer, it's always going to be whisky."

TWENTY-ONE

As we go through Gray's notes, I realize how different his brain is from mine. I've been called methodical, which always implies "plodding." I much prefer "organized." I'm very structured and meticulously organized. That extends to my life, too. I am single-minded in my goals, sometimes to the exclusion of everything else, like losing track of my social life in my pursuit of a spot on the major-crimes squad.

Once I realized I wasn't going home soon, my first step was to rearrange Catriona's bedroom. I've had people tease me about being OCD, which pisses me off, but only because it's joking about a serious condition. I like organization. That's how my brain functions best. Seeing a mess makes me wonder how anyone can relax in that room.

As Gray said, I keep case notes. I'm not obsessive about it, but I do like to organize my thoughts. I write everything down, and when I'm considering a theory, I start a new page and rewrite the clues as they support or fail to support that theory.

This is not how Gray's brain operates. I should have realized that. I've watched him madly scribbling. Or it looks like mad scribbling, but when I've seen his handwriting, it's enviably perfect. That, as I've come to realize, is less a personal trait than the product of a Victorian education. In a world without computers, your handwriting must be legible. Mine is average for the twenty-first century, but to him, it's atrocious.

Despite perfect penmanship, his notes are . . . Well, they take a while to decipher, and when I do, I'm both bemused and a little envious. It reminds me of my one and only university math course. The prof would scrawl across an old-fashioned blackboard, all these numbers and equations that my brain struggled to process because it looked more like modern art than mathematics.

Gray has covered the pages in notes, written horizontal, vertical, and diagonal, all of them connected by arrows with more writing on the arrows, some of those lines slashed out. Once I start to read, I see what he's doing. Taking data and making connections between the pieces and speculating on other connections and ruling out some of them as implausible. It's messy but brilliant, and the envy comes from that part of me that stings at being called methodical, the part that feels as if my intelligence is a very ordinary sort, where getting an A means working my ass off, while people like Gray would need to work to *not* get an A.

We discuss his findings, and that makes me feel a little better, because he obviously values my opinion and, in the end, he hasn't found anything that I don't have in my much more mundane notes.

There's no obvious connection between the victims, beyond the fact that they all seem to have been shitty husbands. This, unfortunately, puts us where we don't want to be: with the wives poisoning their husbands, having obtained that poison from the same third party.

Embedded in the concept of a "poisoning ring" is the idea that the women find out about the poisoner from a mutual friend. Like lamenting that your hairdresser is retiring, and a friend tells you about hers.

That would imply that Lady Annis Leslie knew either Mrs. Young or Mrs. Burns. A countess knowing the wife of a gravedigger or the wife of a shady salesman. In the modern world, this wouldn't be implausible, though it would be most likely a service relationship—one of the younger women being Annis's manicurist or cleaning lady. While that concept still works here, there would be a buffer between them. Not a manicurist or a cleaning lady, but a laundress or a seamstress . . . whom Annis would only access through a staff member. Also, from what McCreadie could glean, both Mrs. Young and Mrs. Burns worked at home. Yes, we know Mrs. Young had another occupation, but "nude model" seems unlikely to have brought her into contact with Annis.

We spend two hours—and two glasses of whisky—going over Gray's notes and then theorizing. Soon, under the influence of booze and a lack of sleep, we're no longer in our chairs. I'm not quite sure how it happened, only that by the time we're spitballing theories, we're both on the floor.

On the floor in a perfectly decorous manner, I might add. Decorous by twenty-first-century standards, that is. Gray sits with his back propped against the bookcase, one long leg stretched, the other bent with his whisky glass held on his knee. I'm cross-legged in the other corner.

I'm listening to Gray talk, and watching him talk, his hands gesturing in a way I don't ever see unless he's enrapt in his subject. It's more than just the hands. He's taken off his jacket and loosened his cravat, and his hair tumbles over his forehead, and with his beard shadow, he doesn't look like a Victorian at all. He looks . . . Well, he just looks like a guy. Like a guy who has joined me in escaping a formal event, maybe a family wedding, and we're holed up, drinking and talking.

Gray is less than a year older than me, which can be hard to remember, and not only because I'm in a much younger body. He *seems* so much older. Maybe that's the Victorian in him. But it's also the responsibility of being thrown into the role of patriarch before his thirtieth birthday.

His brother abdicated, and while Mrs. Gray is clearly the matriarch in a family that places her authority above Gray's, to the world, Gray is the guy in charge. In charge of his mother, of Isla, maybe even of Annis, now that her husband is dead. That means he can't afford to be young, but he is here, in this moment, gesticulating and explaining some scientific concept that makes my tipsy brain swim.

When he says, "What's it like?," I have to replay the last few sentences, certain I missed something.

"What is . . . what like?"

"Being . . ." He gestures at me.

"A woman?"

"No, no. Being in another body. I keep thinking about that. It is not your body, and that must be very disorienting."

"Disorienting." I consider. "That is the perfect word for it."

"Because it is not simply seeing another face in the mirror, but moving in a body that is not your own, that would not feel like your own." He pulls his legs in to sit cross-legged as he leans forward. "Is it not exactly like your own, I presume?"

"Not at *all* like my own."

"How is it different?"

"Hmm. Well, I'm a few inches taller, for one thing."

"And . . . ?"

I sip my whisky. "I'm about the same weight, but mine is more muscle than curves. I'm athletic."

"Catriona is not."

"No, but she has a type of strength—from work and daily life—that I'm not used to."

"So you are taller and leaner. And the rest? What is it like to not see your own face in the mirror?"

"Disorienting?" I smile. "It's like wearing a costume. Do people ever wear them here? Outside of the theater?"

"There are masquerade balls, but they aren't truly in fashion."

"Do you have Halloween? I know trick-or-treating is mostly North American, but I'm not sure about Halloween itself. Do you celebrate anything on October thirty-first?"

"There is Samhain, though that is frowned upon."

"Okay, well, in North America, Samhain has turned into Halloween. Kids dress up in costumes. Sometimes it's things like princesses or superheroes, but traditionally it's the creepy stuff. Believe me, I was all about the creepy stuff. Witches. Skeletons. The Grim Reaper."

"A memento mori."

I nod. "The recognition that we all die someday. The holiday has its roots in paganism and the honoring of the dead. Which probably sounds really weird to you—little kids going door-to-door getting treats for dressing up as witches and ghosts."

"Treats?"

"You knock on the door and say 'trick or treat.' You're threatening them with a trick if they don't give you a treat, but there are no tricks. Just candy—confections."

"Confections?"

I grin. "Thought you'd like that part."

"I am not overly fond of actual confections, preferring pastries and biscuits, but I believe I could make an exception for a plate full of treats."

"Plate? Try a *bag* full of them."

"That sounds positively delightful."

"It is." I sip my whisky. "That's what this feels like. As if I'm wearing the mask of a Victorian housemaid. Except I can't take it off. Which is . . ."

"Disorienting."

"Yep."

"And if you could take off the mask? What lies under it?"

"Me."

"Which would be?"

I shrug. "Darker hair. Shorter hair—shoulder length. Green eyes. Leaner face. Straighter teeth—no offense to Catriona."

His head is tilted, eyes narrow, as if trying to imagine it.

"White skin?" he asks.

I make a face. "Sorry, I should have included that. Yes, I'm white. Even in my day, in my part of the world, we tend to default to that—unless otherwise stated, we presume white—which is shitty."

"Is life otherwise better for someone who is not white in a predominantly white country?"

"As a white person, that's hard for me to answer. You're a doctor, which is unusual for you here. We wouldn't think twice about it in Canada. However, you'd still have new patients asking where you came from and expecting you to speak with an accent."

"Nothing new, then."

"The ease of travel means the borders are more fluid, which has been going on long enough that no one should presume a person of color *wasn't* born in Canada, but it's still—"

A loud knock sounds, making us both jump. I go to scramble up, glass in hand, but that's not happening from a sitting-on-the-ground position in this clothing. I set the glass down, and Gray extends his hand to help me up. Another knock, and now it's clearly coming from the front door.

I go to check my watch. I'm so much better about that lately, but my fuzzy brain forgets until I see a wrist that's not my own, and my gaze goes instead to the clock on a shelf.

"It's after two," I say. "Who would be at the door?"

"Someone in costume, looking for a treat while threatening a trick?"

"That's probably the best of options at this hour, isn't it?"

"No," he says, moving past me into the hall. "We do receive the occasional potential client at such hours if a family member passes in the night."

"Should I open it?" I say, straightening my dress as I reach the door. "Being the maid?"

He waves that off and pulls open the door to reveal a teenage boy in a cap, with sharp eyes and skin a little darker than Gray's.

"I have a message for your employer," the boy says with an English accent.

"For Dr. Gray?" Gray says, calmly, no hint of annoyance.

"Yes."

"That would be me."

The boy hesitates. His gaze travels up and down Gray, who simply waits it out, letting the boy take his time analyzing the situation.

"You're Dr. Duncan Gray?" he says finally.

There's no incredulity in his voice. It's a question, maybe a little wary, as if fearing a trick.

"Yes," Gray says. "May I help you?"

"You're to come with me. You and your assistant."

"That would be Miss Mitchell here."

The boy notices me for the first time, and his reaction is equally cautious. I look no more like his idea of a doctor's assistant than Gray looks like his idea of a doctor.

"I presume," Gray says, "that if you are asking for us both, it is a matter related to detection rather than undertaking, and in that, Miss Mitchell is my apprentice and assistant."

"Whatever you say, guv."

I know what the boy's thinking—what most people think when Gray claims to have a pretty teenage girl as his "assistant."

"She is my assistant," Gray says. "To imply otherwise is to suggest she lacks some trait that makes her worthy of such a position. The same as it would be to suggest I lack some trait that makes me worthy of mine."

The boy only purses his lips in thought and then says, "Fair point. All right then. Bring her along."

"Thank you," Gray says dryly. "But neither of us is going anywhere in the middle of the night without more information."

"Why not? From what Jack says, you can take care of yourself."

"Who are we going to see?" I ask.

"You've been granted an audience with the queen," he says. "And I don't mean the one in Bucky Palace."

"Queen Mab," I say.

"The only one that counts in these parts."

Gray nods. "Wait here while we gather our things."

TWENTY-TWO

We don't cross the Mound to the Old Town. That surprises me a little. When I picture a woman who deals in birth control—and possibly poisons—I picture some dingy shop down the darkest of dark alleys. Instead, we stay in the New Town, walking until we reach a row of small town houses close to Princes Street, making it a quick crossover from the Old Town and, perhaps equally important, easily accessed by the women of the New Town.

As we walk up, I'm assessing. Does Queen Mab live in this town house? Or does she rent a floor for business? Maybe the basement? That seems most likely as the boy—who has ducked the question of a name—leads us down the mews to approach from the rear. It seems even more likely when we take stairs down to enter through the basement door.

The inside is dark, which far better fits my image of such a place. There's a low hum coming from behind a closed door down the hall. We head for that door, and the boy opens it, calling, "They're here, ma'am." Then he retreats, letting the door shut behind him. As he walks past, he gives Gray a final, appraising look and then lopes out the way we came.

I glance from Gray to that closed door. He considers. Then he opens the door and walks in. I follow.

We find ourselves in what looks like Gray's town house library. Leather-bound tomes fill floor-to-ceiling bookcases of gleaming wood. A fireplace crackles. Flickering gaslight illuminates an armchair beside the fire. A book rests on the chair. Gray goes straight to that book, but I can tell even from here that it's not in English.

He pauses there for a moment, while I look around and realize something's missing from this room. Queen Mab. I jog back down the hall and wrench the back door. It opens easily.

I hesitate there, and then return to the library, where Gray stands with his head cocked. He's staring at a bookcase, and I soon realize why. That low hum comes from behind it. He steps back and examines the books. When he touches one, I lean in and read the title.

"*Romeo and Juliet*," I say. "The original Queen Mab reference."

He tugs it, and the bookcase moves to reveal an actual hidden door. Ten-year-old Mallory squeals with glee. Okay, even thirty-year-old Mallory might make a tiny noise of delight.

The bookcase opens into another room, this one more brightly lit. I peer inside to see what looks like Isla's laboratory, except with older equipment. Several mortars and pestles rest on a stone table, along with a distilling apparatus. Where Isla has shelves of bottles, here there's an entire wall of ingredients, some in bottles, some in bowls, some just dried roots on a plate. More drying herbs hang from the ceiling.

Behind that table, a woman is hard at work with a pestle. The noise we'd heard is some sort of automated mixing device, endlessly turning a corked vial end over end. When it slows, the woman reaches out to wind it without even stopping her work.

"Queen Mab, I presume," Gray says.

The woman is tiny—no more than four ten—and with an unlined dark-skinned face and dark curls raked back from her face by clips. Gorgeous hair clips, I might add, gold-filigree works of art. Her dress is equally gorgeous, a waterfall of jade silk that is the height of current fashion, with what I've learned is an elliptical crinoline—it sticks out a bit at the front and then sweeps back with a bustle pad.

"Not going to mistake me for Her Ladyship's servant?" the woman says with one arched brow. Like the boy, she has an English accent, but there's more there, hints that Edinburgh is but the latest stop in a lifetime of travel.

"I would not make that presumption," Gray says.

There's no sarcastic twist to Gray's voice. No emphasis on "I." Still, Queen Mab's eyes narrow as she studies him. Then she sighs.

"The boy mistook you for a manservant, didn't he," she says. "I fail to warn him, and he makes the most inexcusable of errors."

"He recovered with aplomb," Gray says. "And I doubt he will make it again."

She puts a dried herb into the mortar bowl. "The infamous Dr. Gray, I presume."

This time he does react, even if it's only the barest tightening of his lips.

"You don't like being infamous?" she says. "I do."

Before he can answer, she continues, "One would think that you would not pursue your particular line of study if you did not expect to be infamous."

"My line of study being?"

"The science of the dead, of course." She eyes the bowl and adds a few more tiny dried leaves. "A man *without* your skin color or scandalous birth would *still* earn his share of sidelong looks and whispers. But you?" She shakes her head.

"Perhaps I am too dedicated to my studies to allow myself to care about that."

"But you do care," she says without looking up from her work. "You need to overcome that peculiar disease, Dr. Gray."

"What disease would that be?"

"Giving a bloody damn what anyone else thinks of you."

Gray elegantly lifts one shoulder and says nothing.

"You're young," she muses, still grinding her pestle. "The world will beat the caring out of you soon enough." She turns to me. "Has it beaten it out of you, child? The pretty girl who takes a job working for the likes of him? The girl who eyes a higher rung on a very unusual ladder?"

"Jack makes some bold assumptions based on a brief acquaintance," I say.

"Is our friend wrong?"

"She is not." I steer the conversation onto the right track with, "So you're the infamous Queen Mab."

"Not what you expected?"

"Honestly? No. You're named after a fairy. I expected more . . ." I gesture. "Theater."

"More theater than a secret passage?"

"That *was* a nice touch."

"As for the title, yes, I am not as flashy as a fairy. But they wanted to call me Queen Sheba, being the only 'queen' they know who looks like me. Better for me to choose my own moniker."

"That of a fairy, able to take any shape she likes."

"Yes."

"Also, if one goes back to Shakespeare's reference, midwife to the fairies. That's really why you chose it. Maybe for help with childbirth, but mostly for help preventing it."

She laughs, a low, musical sound. "Jack is right. You are more clever than you appear. Such disguises serve us well."

"You know why we're here?"

"Of course. The police believe I supplied the poison to kill three men, and you will protect me from them . . . you, who *work* for them."

"You know there's more to it, or you wouldn't have invited us to your home."

"*My* home? This belongs to an elderly couple who never venture into the basement and have no idea there is a very wicked woman working behind a secret passage. A passage which will, once you leave, not reopen, leaving you looking very foolish indeed if you return with the police. Consider my bringing you here an act of trust in the reputation of Dr. Gray as a fair and honest man. Or of his sister, whose work interests me far more."

Mab is playing an intricate game here, one above my pay grade, having dealt with the black market only in a law-enforcement capacity. Bringing us here seems to put *us* in a position of power, but that's an illusion. She's subtly threatening us . . . while making this an act of trust . . . while also letting us know that even if we use this information, it will get us nowhere, which is a show of power in itself.

She's right that we wouldn't tell the police where to find her. We won't even tell McCreadie, mostly because—if I'm judging him correctly—he wouldn't want the information. If he doesn't know where to find Queen Mab, he can't be expected to pass the information on to his superior officers.

"I did not supply that poison," she says. "Which is what you would expect me to say." She purses her lips. "Does anyone ever admit to such a crime?"

"Occasionally," I say. "If they're mentally disturbed. Or if they're proud of it."

Or, if they just want a place to sleep with regular meals. Having experienced Victorian prisons, I find that hard to imagine, though I suppose anything is possible, if one is destitute enough.

"Well, I will take the expected course, as dull as that may be, because it is true. I will admit to many things I should not, but never to things I have not done, including supplying poison."

"Intentionally," Gray says.

She wags a finger at him. "Correct, and being the brother of a chemist, you well know that most remedies can be poisonous if taken wrong. However, I have heard that the poison used here is arsenic, which I do not carry. Nor strychnine nor cyanide. I know only too well how people presume that any woman who deals in herbal or chemical remedies also sells poison."

She waves at the shelves. "You may check for yourselves, though I am not certain how much that would help. It is not as if someone who sells arsenic would have it labeled as such."

Gray still moves to the shelves and begins surveying the jars. When I look his way, he nods, telling me to continue taking the lead in the questioning.

"You sell contraceptives," I say.

Her brow furrows.

"Methods of preventing pregnancy."

"I do." She pauses and meets my gaze. "Is that a concern?"

"Depends on what you're supplying and how effective it is, and how effective your clients *think* it is. However, that's a personal opinion with no bearing on the present investigation."

"Except that a personal opinion may affect a professional one. You are concerned that I might be selling a useless assortment of herbs and misleading women into thinking they are protected. I can assure you that my methods are more effective than . . ."

She trails off and looks at Gray. "Would you prefer to step out for this conversation? I know it can make men uncomfortable."

"I am a doctor, and it is, to me, a medical concern. It is also a societal one, as I do not believe any woman should have a child she is not prepared to raise."

"So you practice methods of protection yourself, I hope."

He blinks, and then his eyes narrow, as he realizes she's baiting him, testing his assertion that he is comfortable with it.

She continues, "Do not tell me that you are unmarried and therefore do not need such things, or I will be offended that you should think me such a stupid woman."

He only looks at her.

"Not coitus interruptus, I hope," she says. "I know anal penetration is fashionable, and perhaps the most effective—"

"Male shields," he says quickly.

"Good ones?"

More eye narrowing. "The best."

"Oh, I can assure you whatever you use is *not* the best. I have the best, which I would happily give you to sample—"

"No, thank you," he says.

She turns back to me. "Whatever I sell, it is better than coitus interruptus, but worse than male shields, which as I said, I also sell, for those women fortunate enough to have lovers as considerate as Dr. Gray. That is the problem, and if you are not yet of an age to have discovered the delights of the bedchamber, Miss Mallory, then I warn you in advance. A man will say he has taken care of it. He may even show you a shield. But they can be true magicians at making such things disappear at the last moment."

"Since I'm the one who'd suffer the consequences, I'm the one who shoulders the responsibility."

"In this and in most things, yes? Do not rely on a man—particularly one caught in the heat of passion—to make the correct choice, not when he may decide he will enjoy it more without a shield on his—"

Gray clears his throat.

"All right, Dr. Gray. I will cease needling you. You have done remarkably well at tolerating this conversation, and I will reward you with a package of my shields when you leave."

"I do not need—"

"Too bad. They are yours."

I draw her attention back to me. "The reason I'm asking about contra—methods of preventing pregnancy is that we have three women who have been accused of poisoning their husbands. Three women who come from very different backgrounds, and so I've been racking my brain to think of how they might be connected. What service might all three use? One that Lady Leslie might prefer to access herself, rather than sending a servant."

"I applaud your thinking, Miss Mallory. I will not deny that my customers come from all parts of the city. However, your theory would mean I provided poison rather than methods of preventing pregnancy, which takes us back to my original denial."

"I'm not saying you gave them the poison. I'm saying that's how they could be connected. Possibly one approached you for such a thing, and you refused her. Possibly someone else overheard and sent her another way."

"One of my employees."

I shrug. "Perhaps more of a contact. One who'd know other purveyors of herbal and chemical remedies."

I expect her to deny it, but she says, "Describe the other two women."

I glance over at Gray, who describes Mrs. Young and Mrs. Burns—information I didn't think to get.

"Anything usual about them?" she presses. "Memorable?"

"Not that I am aware of."

"Then they are very like many of my customers, and I cannot say whether I have served them or not."

"All right," I say. "One final question."

"You wish to know whether Lady Leslie is a customer of mine."

"No, she is. You asked us to describe the other two women only, which means you know Lady Leslie, likely as a customer. My question is about thallium."

She frowns. "Who?"

"Thallium. It's a heavy metal."

"A poison?"

"It can be used as such. What do you know of it?"

"I have never heard of it. Is there another name I might know?"

"It's a recently discovered heavy metal element."

She shakes her head. "It is new to me. When I say that I don't carry arsenic or strychnine, that is not a hardship. I am not a chemist in the way Mrs. Ballantyne is. I am a herbalist, with some knowledge of chemical elements. Treatments such as mercury have their uses, but I do not deal in them."

With that, I have nothing more to ask, except that she let me know if she thinks of anything that could help solve the case . . . especially as that would also help exonerate her as a suspect. When she tries to give Gray a package, he refuses to take it, so I do.

Once we're outside, I give him the package.

"I do not need—" he begins.

"I need them even less, having zero intention of adding that to my Victorian experience."

I shove the package into his pocket and ignore his protests.

"What did you observe?" I say. "I presume that's why you let me lead. So you could observe."

"No, I let you lead because you are the professional in such matters. But, yes, also I prefer to observe. I noted that her claim to carry only herbal medicines seems to be correct, though she may have chemical ones hidden elsewhere. Also, one should not confuse herbal for nonpoisonous, which is a common misunderstanding."

"And one we're still fighting in my time, when people think herbal remedies are always safer than medicine."

"Yes, most medicines can be dangerous if taken incorrectly, and even sometimes if taken correctly. Therefore, I would not expect her shelves to be devoid of any dangerous substances and she did not claim such. I can only say that I did not see anything that might have been thallium, as Isla described it."

I nod, and we turn a corner, taking us back toward the New Town.

He continues, "Also, her story about using the basement of an unwitting elderly couple is false, as you doubtless suspected."

"I'm sure there *is* an elderly couple living upstairs, but there's no way they wouldn't realize Queen Mab was there. They're camouflage. Whether she lives there herself is another matter."

"I believe she does. Or, at the very least, she has lodgings there. She was wearing silk slippers, and I did not see any sign of boots nor an outdoor jacket—not in her laboratory nor the library nor at the door, where there was not a closet."

"Anything else?"

"She is very well educated, as her diction proves. Her accent suggests time spent in both the West Indies and France, as well as England. Also the boy is a relative. They share the same chin and similar eyes. He has likely been raised in close proximity to her, as he emulates many of her gestures."

"Nice."

"And you?" he says. "What did she tell you without meaning to?"

I glance over.

He continues, "I am rather adept at observing and interpreting my surroundings. You do the same with people. She unwittingly revealed that she knows Annis. What else?"

"You're right about the boy. I didn't pick up the chin, but I noticed the eyes and gestures. When she talked about him, her tone was exasperated affection. As for Queen Mab, she's worried. That's why she brought us in. She's concerned enough to take a risk in hopes your reputation is deserved and you can be trusted. She definitely knows Annis. I think she knows one of the other women and fears she also knows the third, possibly under an alias. That puts Queen Mab in a bad spot. She's a woman of color who makes a very good living at a dubious trade. Could she be the link? Yes, but that doesn't necessarily mean she supplied the poison."

"If she lied about knowing what thallium is, because she fears one of her associates or servants supplied it in her stead."

"Possibly. Her confusion seemed real, though. The more likely link would be if one or more of these women asked her for poison and she refused, and someone else—possibly a rival—got word of it and offered their services. In short, I don't think Queen Mab provided the poison, but I do think she has very good reason to worry about being blamed."

TWENTY-THREE

I know we should go directly to the town house. It's late, and we barely got two hours of sleep last night. But I don't want to go back yet. I really don't. The New Town streets are deserted, and it's a gorgeous night, clear and warm. Gray is relaxed and open, and I don't want to break this spell. I want to tread every empty street and talk, just talk.

When the silence is broken by the sound of a distant quarrel, I pause, but it's just two drunken men arguing about a horse race.

Gray touches my shoulder. "Let us take another route and avoid that unpleasantness."

We look around. My gaze catches on the Scott Monument, rising above buildings to our left.

Gray follows my gaze. "Does that still stand in your time?"

I smile. "It does, and I've gone up a couple of times. What I really wanted was to sneak up at night, but it's too locked down for that."

"Would you like to sneak up now?"

When I hesitate, his gaze empties as that portcullis starts to fall.

"I'd love to," I blurt. "I just know how late it is and how little sleep you got last night, so I don't want to impose."

"It is hardly an imposition if I asked you, Mallory," he says, his voice cool, as if suspecting this is an excuse.

I want to curse at him for being so damn prickly. Instead, I find myself saying, "I really would love to, if it's okay with you. I was just thinking what a gorgeous night it is, and how much I'd like to stay out longer."

He relaxes. "All right then. Let us climb the monument."

We are at the top platform of the monument, with panoramic views of the city. I lean out and look over Edinburgh, my eyes slitted against the breeze, a little sharper up here. After a moment, Gray moves up beside me. He comes as close as he can without actually touching me as he looks out, and we stand there for a few minutes in silence, taking in the view.

"It's beautiful," I say.

"Different from your time?"

"Some of it. I would still see the castle and Calton Hill. The Old Town is still separated from the New by the Mound, but there's not the economic demarcation—there are good and not-so-good areas on both sides. Most of the nearby buildings look the same. They're heritage buildings, so they can't be torn down, although that one there on Princes"—I point—"is just a shell in my day. An American technology billionaire got around the rules by gutting it and raising a modern building inside. Then there's a hotel being built over there in the shape of a yellow coil. People are already calling it the golden turd."

He laughs softly at that.

"Most modern buildings are off in the distance. During the day, the biggest difference you'd see here is that the streets are full of cars. At night, the biggest difference would be the illumination. Even at this time, you'd look out on a sea of lights."

"That must be very pretty."

"It is . . . if you're looking down. But lights mean light pollution, and you lose the night sky. You still have that here." I gaze up, smiling at the constellations. "As pretty as lights can be, I prefer the stars. Your view is definitely the better one."

He says nothing, but in that silence, I feel the weight of questions. When I glance over, he's looking out, his gaze on the treetops below.

"What is it like?" he says. "Being in another place? Earlier this evening, we talked about what it is like to be in another body, but I presume this is much the same. Uncomfortable and foreign."

"Foreign, yes. Uncomfortable . . . ? There's a saying, and I don't know if you have it, but in my time, we'd say that I'm a fish out of water. Out of my natural environment. That's not exactly true. A fish can't breathe out of water. I can breathe here just fine. I can survive just fine."

"Survive," he says. "Life at the most basic level. As one might survive very difficult circumstances."

I shake my head. "It's not like that. It can be a difficult situation, because I'm lost, in so many ways, my brain overloading trying to figure it out. Like being in another country where I don't know the customs and I know just enough language to get by."

"Also difficult because it's not your home. You cannot take an ocean liner back to your family and friends."

Here is the elephant in the room. The part about me being here that makes others uncomfortable—the knowledge that I'd rather be somewhere else.

Does he want me to say that isn't so bad? Does he want me to lie?

Time to get this conversation over with.

I turn to face him. He's still looking out.

"Dr. Gray?"

It takes him a moment to pull back from the view and meet my gaze, and even then, his eyes are hooded and unreadable.

"I know this is difficult," I say.

He opens his mouth, as if to protest.

I hurry on. "I'm asking you to train me as your assistant. I'm asking to be considered part of your investigations with Detective McCreadie. Yet if I saw the way home, I'd take it, and leave you in the lurch. Like an employee who pretends they're in for the long haul just to get training they can use somewhere else. Which is why I need to be honest and admit that, if I get the chance to leave, I'm taking it."

He starts to turn away, but I zip into his path, making him bump into me and back up fast.

"I won't leave without saying goodbye," I say. "I won't leave without finishing whatever I have to finish. I know it's still shitty, and you're not only concerned that you'll be left in the lurch but that others will be hurt. I'm spending a lot of time with Isla, and then I'm going to disappear from her life, and that feels shitty, too, and I start to think maybe I should keep my distance from everyone."

"No," he says. "Isla would not want that. She understands the situation."

I turn back to look out at Calton Hill, rising to my right. "I know it's inconvenient for you. It would be easier if I were happy to leave that life behind. If I didn't have the sort of family or friends or career or home that I wanted to return to."

"I would hardly call having a good life there 'inconvenient,' Mallory."

There's a warmth in his voice, and when I look over, a faint smile plays on his lips.

"You know what I mean," I say.

"I would not ever want for you to have had a worse life," he says softly.

Heat rises in my cheeks. I don't know why, only that I pull my gaze away and busy myself gazing on the night city.

After a moment, I say, "My life wasn't perfect. I worked too hard. I let everything else slide. Hobbies. Friends. Even my family. I tucked it all aside, temporarily, until I hit my goal. But the goalpost kept moving. Finish my degree. Get a job. Rise to detective. Earn a spot on major crimes. And each new goal was harder to reach, needing more of my time and concentration, everything else falling by the wayside. I'd tell myself I'd start dating again next year. I'll go camping with my friends next year. I won't skip every other Sunday dinner with my parents next year. I'll visit Nan longer next year."

My voice cracks on the last, and I lean farther over the railing as if that will hide it.

Gray says nothing, and my cheeks heat more as I realize I've overshared.

I straighten and clear my throat. "I'm sorry. I'm tired, and I didn't mean to vent."

"While I am not certain what 'vent' means, I believe I can decipher it in context. I'm quiet because I'm listening, Mallory. I'm listening because I want to understand, and perhaps, because I am uncomfortably seeing myself in what you're saying."

"I think you've struck the balance better."

A one-shouldered shrug. "Perhaps somewhat better, but there is so much to do, so much to learn, so much to accomplish, and the clock seems to be ever ticking, reminding me that time is running out. Only it is also running out on everything else."

I turn away to blink back tears as I nod. "I don't want to be retiring from the police force in thirty years, realizing I've achieved everything I want there . . . and having nothing to retire *to*." I straighten. "But I'll figure that out. The point is that I know it would be easier for everyone if I wasn't in such a hurry to get home. It feels rude."

He chuckles at that.

"It does," I say, facing him. "Like a guest who can't wait to leave. It makes everyone uncomfortable. I'm not unhappy here. If someone said my visit would last another month, I'd throw myself into that month and love every minute of it."

"The problem is not knowing."

"Yes. Not knowing when—or if—I can get back. I do have a life I need to return to. If I didn't, I'd stay. I've been so lucky. I can't imagine landing in a better place."

He glances over. Our eyes meet, and his mouth opens. He starts to say something, but the words are drowned out by a sudden scream from below.

"Murder!"

TWENTY-FOUR

The scream rips through the quiet night air, as distinct as if the woman who shouted it stood right beside me, but I still look at Gray.

"Did she say—?" I begin.

"Murder!" The scream comes again. "Help! My master has been murdered! Poisoned!"

We look at each other. Then we both take off for the stairs so fast we crash into each other. Gray steps back, tipping his hat to tell me to go first, and it's wonderfully gallant, but when I demur, he's off with an obvious exhale of relief.

There are times when chivalry is terribly inconvenient, and this is one of them—when someone is in dire need of assistance and custom dictates that you rush to her aid behind a woman in long skirts. Also, the slower Gray goes, the longer it takes for him to find out what's happening.

I take the endless stairs as fast as I can, and I still nearly fall twice. I'm wearing my maid skirts, which only reach the top of my boots and that helps, but I'm still moving slower than I'd like. Gray doesn't notice, but in his defense, that's only because he's long gone.

I get outside to see him running in the direction of the woman, whose screaming has fallen to babbling. When he reaches the street, he glances back. I wave, and he takes off.

I would love to say I can move faster now that I'm on solid ground, but these boots aren't made for running.

The woman's voice comes from a street near the monument, and at first my heart clenches, thinking of Queen Mab. But I soon realize the voice comes from even closer, just over by St. Andrew Square. I can see the Melville Monument from here and run toward it. I find the right street and reach the end of it to see Gray giving orders to a man while anxiously glancing down the street. When he spots me, he nods and turns his full attention to the man.

Gray is outside a narrow town house. It's on a street even finer than his, though this particular town house is smaller, as if two sets of builders had started from opposite ends of the road and didn't have quite enough room when they reached the middle. A woman stands on the doorstep. White-haired and pale-faced, she's kneading the skirt of a lopsided dress, one that looks as if it was hastily pulled on in the night.

The man Gray is talking to seems to be staff from a neighboring town house. Gray is trying to tell him to fetch the police. It's a simple—and obvious—request, but the man's face is set in a way that says he's not taking orders from Gray.

"My master," the woman on the doorstep whimpers. "He's dead. Murdered in his bed."

Two other people stand on doorsteps, one looking like a housekeeper, the other a homeowner. Gray wheels toward the housekeeper.

"You there—"

She shuts the door before he can finish. I walk up to the guy on the sidewalk.

"You heard the gentleman," I say. "Get the police. Do you want to be arrested for obstruction of justice?"

The man gapes at me.

I wave a hand at him. "Did you hear me? Get the police. Now. And if you try hiding behind a door like that woman over there, I'll be sure the police know where you live. If there has truly been a murder, she's a suspect for sure."

"What?" a voice says as the door reopens.

"Oh, there you are. Accidentally shut the door on yourself, did you?" I turn back to the man. "Go now. The address is . . ."

Gray rattles it off. I repeat it and say, "Now fetch the police." As the man staggers off, I turn to the distraught woman and soften my tone. "You said your master is dead. Can you take us to him, please, ma'am?"

She only stares at me.

"She's not letting me inside," Gray murmurs under his breath. "That was my first request, obviously. I have told her that I am a doctor."

"Bloody hell," I mutter. I march to the woman. "This man is a doctor. He also works with the police. What if your master isn't dead? What if he is dying, poisoned as you say, and you refused to allow medical treatment that could have saved him? How do you think that's going to look?"

She stares at me. I try not to sigh. I've leaned too hard into Detective Mallory mode, but I can't say I'd have done anything different if I'd paused to think about it. We have a presumably murdered man inside these walls, and I'm not going to stand out here and beg people to do the obvious.

I walk up the steps and past the woman, who makes a mewling noise but doesn't try to stop me. The door is ajar. I push on it and call over my shoulder, "To everyone who wants to listen in but not get involved, this is Dr. Gray, who has come following this woman's shouts of murder. She claims her employer is dead within, and so we are seeing whether he may be in need of medical assistance. I would appreciate it if someone could accompany us inside, to confirm that we don't steal the silver."

"I will," says a soft voice. It's a young woman on a neighboring doorstep, one who looks like a maid. "I do not think you will steal the silver, miss, but I would not wish you to be blamed for such a thing."

As she hurries over, she shoots a look at the distraught woman, a look that might call her out for behaving poorly . . . or might say she *is* likely to claim we stole the silver.

The maid is a couple of years younger than me, red haired with an Irish accent. She dips her head to Gray and says, "Sir," and I decide she'll do very well indeed. Gray walks past the housekeeper, who makes no move to stop him. After we are inside, the housekeeper closes the door and calls after us, "He is in his bedroom. On the second floor. First room on the left."

I think she's going to leave us to go up alone, but when we reach the next level, her footsteps sound on the stairs below. By the time we're walking to the bedroom, she's already climbing the next flight to us.

We enter the room. It's huge, as if it had once been two rooms. The bed is high, with four posters and a curtain. Gray pushes back the curtain. The stink of vomit and emptied bowels rushes out, but it is not until we see the figure on the bed that the maid gives a little cry, hands flying to her mouth.

"Mr. Ware," she says. "Oh, poor Mr. Ware."

On the bed lies a man about the same age as the woman at the door. The man is almost bald, with smooth plump cheeks and wild iron-gray eyebrows. His eyes are open, staring into nothing, and there is no doubt the man is dead, but Gray still checks before pronouncing that he has passed.

"I found him like that," says the older woman, who hovers in the doorway.

"And you are?" I say, and then add a polite "Ma'am?"

"Mrs. Hamilton. The housekeeper. Mr. Ware had been poorly, but he often was—he liked his rich foods—and I intended to call the doctor in the morning."

As Gray examines Ware's eyes, Mrs. Hamilton steps in, past what looks like a cane oddly lying beside the wall. There's a mark on the wall above it.

Before I can investigate that, I notice something in the man's hand. A cord. From the curtains? I draw them back and then notice a brass object on the floor, partly hidden in the curtain folds. I bend and lift the curtain to see it's a bell. I lift my gaze to a hanger beside the man's bed. I glance at the cord clutched in the dead man's hand.

"That is from the bell, is it not?" I say.

"Y-yes," Mrs. Hamilton says. "It might have been loose."

"Or no one was answering, and in his distress, he pulled hard enough to yank it from the wall."

"He was often poorly," she says, a whine touching her voice. "The doctor told him to watch his diet, and I cooked exactly what the doctor prescribed, but he would sneak in cheeses and creams and pastries, and then he would be up all night, sick to his stomach."

"Which was his own fault, and you tired of him summoning you for nighttime stomach upsets."

"'Twas his own fault, and he could be most disagreeable when his stomach was off. Like a child who sneaks sweets."

"Is there no one else in the house to hear him?"

"The maids live out. Mr. Ware never married, and there was no one to rein in his indulgences, so it fell on me, and I am his housekeeper, not his wife."

I glance at Gray. He murmurs, "Go on," under his breath, telling me to keep up the interview while he examines the body.

"You say he liked his treats," I say. "Did he receive any lately?"

"If they arrived at the door, I was sure to hide them."

"Eat them, you mean," the young maid mutters under her breath.

"What's that?" Mrs. Hamilton says.

The maid lowers her gaze. "I was agreeing, ma'am, that you would ensure he does not receive food that is delivered to the house. Mr. Ware knew that, as I heard it, and so if he did receive food, he would do so at his office."

I glance at the man. "He had not retired then?"

"He would not, despite his doctor's urging," the housekeeper grumbles. "He said he could find no one to take over the business, but there are many young men who would have been happy to do so."

"What was his profession?" I ask.

"He was a solicitor."

There's a moment where I link this to Mr. Burns. To me "solicit" means sales. Then I remember where I am. Mr. Ware was a lawyer, the sort who advises on the legal matters that won't land you on the gallows . . . at least not without a great deal of creative ingenuity.

"Was he in the office today?" I ask.

"He was in the office every day," she mutters. "Even Sunday, if he can manage to sneak there while I am at church."

"His office is here in the New Town, I presume?" I say. That's a reasonable guess given the luxury of his surroundings.

"It is here in the house, miss," the young maid says.

I must look confused, because she continues with, "Mr. Ware's office is on the third floor, and there is a separate staircase. It lies . . . outside Mrs. Hamilton's domain. He hires me to clean it weekly."

Mrs. Hamilton resumes her grumbling at that. So Mr. Ware keeps his offices right here in his town house, but off-limits to his housekeeper, which may explain why he spends so much time in there.

I suspect when I get access to that office, I'll find he's built himself a cozy little bachelor pad, complete with forbidden foods.

Forbidden foods that may be poisoned.

Unless Mrs. Hamilton is lying and poisoned him herself. While she isn't his wife, I'm getting the sense of something close to a longtime marriage, one held together more by necessity than love. Two organisms dependent upon each other for survival. In that situation, would Mrs. Hamilton rid herself of her boss? Only if doing so would win her a sizable inheritance, and something tells me that won't be the case. If I had Mrs. Hamilton making *my* food, I wouldn't give her any reason to hurry my demise.

I walk over to Gray. He's busy checking Mr. Ware's legs, which has Mrs. Hamilton yelping at the sight of her employer's bare skin. I notice redness on his lower legs, and his big toes are bright red.

When I frown and move toward Mr. Ware, Mrs. Hamilton sputters and says, "Cover the poor man up," but Gray ignores her.

"The redness and swelling," I whisper when I am beside Gray. "I didn't see that with the others."

"It is gout."

"Ah, a preexisting condition."

Gray nods toward the cane and asks Mrs. Hamilton, "He has difficulty walking from the gout, I presume, but had it grown any worse lately?"

"The gout is always growing worse," she snaps. "On account of his poor eating." Then she says, grudgingly, "But, yes, it was much worse yesterday. He came down from the office early and went straight to bed. He said his gout was something fierce. I brought him a plain dinner, but he could not eat it, complaining of pain in his stomach and his legs. He asked for the doctor." She quickly adds, "In the morning. He asked that he be sent for in the morning."

I glance down at that cord, still clutched in Ware's hand. I picture him asking Mrs. Hamilton to send for the doctor right away. Had she refused? Or claimed she would and then didn't?

With only the two of them in the house, there's no one to dispute her version of events. Just that cord and that cane, and the vision of a violently ill man, pulling on the bell until it broke, hurling his cane into the wall in his frustration. A man who died alone, his housekeeper finally investigating only after his room went quiet.

The neighbors will have heard something. That is where her story will fall apart. These town houses are solidly built, but I still hear Gray's neighbors. Normal talking will go unnoticed. Shouting will not.

I look at Ware's bald pate, but Gray shakes his head. Like the swollen legs, that's not a symptom. As I'd recalled, it's rare for thallium to cause hair loss quite so quickly anyway. Also, I presume Mrs. Hamilton or the maid would have commented if this was a new development.

"Otherwise, the symptoms seem quite the same, though more acute in this case," Gray murmurs under his breath. "We will need Isla to confirm poison."

Before I can say more, there's a knock at the door. Mrs. Hamilton goes down and admits two officers, who join us in the bedroom. One is in his thirties, and when he sees Gray, his gaze shutters. The younger man smiles and greets him with an accent that I'm coming to learn means one is from the Highlands.

There are a lot of former Highlanders in Edinburgh, victims of the clearances. Nan used to talk about them—her own family having been pushed from their croft—and I'd always figured it happened eons ago. That's how it felt, hearing her talk, but this young officer's family could have been driven off their homestead when he was a child.

Gray explains the situation as succinctly as possible, and then asks if one of the officers could bring Detective Crichton.

"At this hour?" the older man says, in a northern English accent. "Not bloody likely."

"He doesn't like to be disturbed in the night, sir," the younger constable says. "Been with the police office nearly from the start and says he's earned his sleep."

"I have heard that," Gray murmurs. "Would you say Detective Crichton would prefer if I were to rouse Detective McCreadie?"

The younger officer gives a knowing grin. "Oh, I would say he would much prefer it, sir." He turns to his partner. "What say you?"

I brace for the other officer to protest, but he only shrugs and says, "McCreadie's a good fellow. You can run and fetch him."

"You will pass Dr. Addington's home on the way," Gray says. "Would you please inform him that there has been a murder, and ask what he wishes you to do?"

"Yes, sir."

"Please speak to Dr. Addington directly. He may prefer to convey a message through his butler, but messages are easily misunderstood, and it is best to be clear."

"Yes, sir." The young man tips his hat to Gray, and then he's gone.

TWENTY-FIVE

By the time McCreadie arrives, I'm pacing the floor. He walks in, and I have to resist the urge to slump and say "Finally!" The detective in me has been foaming with frustration. The murder weapon could be right above us, in Ware's office, and each moment we waste is a moment when the killer might return to sneak off with it.

Every time Mrs. Hamilton made a move toward the door, I wanted to drag her back, lest she suddenly realize she really ought to hide the food that poisoned her boss. Even when the young maid left, I slipped to the window to be sure she actually went home, just in case.

Then McCreadie walks in, looking fresh and dapper, wide awake and, worst of all, cheerful.

"Fancy meeting you two at a murder scene in the middle of the night," he says. "We really ought not to make a habit of this."

"This is Mr. Ware," I say. "He died—"

"Mallory," he says, clapping me on the shoulder. "You poor girl. It is well past your bedtime. No need to worry about this unpleasantness. Run along home, and let us handle it."

"Tease her at your peril, Hugh," Gray murmurs under his breath. "It has taken you twenty-nine and a half minutes to arrive, and she has been counting every one of them."

"Missed me, did you? I am flattered, though I must warn that you are much too young for my tastes. Now, if you were thirty, it would be a vastly different thing but, alas, you are a mere child and, while adorable, I cannot think of you as more."

"Do you hear that little noise she's making?" Gray says. "It sounds suspiciously like a growl. I would heed the warning."

"It is the most adorable little noise, coming from the most adorable little maid."

"Have you been drinking?" I say.

"Why does everyone ask me that when I am in a good mood?"

"Because you are in a good mood at an ungodly hour."

He only smiles at me. "Not drinking, my bonny lass, but imbibing in a far more pleasant restorative. Sleep. You ought to try it."

"I need—" I glance at the officers and Mrs. Hamilton and then clear my throat as I raise my voice a little. "Detective McCreadie, sir, Dr. Gray has suggested I search the offices above for any sign of the food that might have poisoned poor Mr. Ware. Might I do that, perhaps accompanied by one of these fine officers of the law?"

"You may do so accompanied by me," he says, "and by Dr. Gray himself, if he is done here."

"Dr. Addington—" Gray says.

"—is unable to join us," McCreadie says. "He would like Mr. Ware's remains transported to your examination room, where he will tend to them at a more seemly hour. He is also quite displeased at being woken two nights in a row."

"And he'd like people to stop dying at unseemly hours?" I say.

"His own words almost precisely, miss," the younger officer says with a grin.

I shake my head. "All right. You two—" I cut myself off with a cough before I give orders.

McCreadie says, "If you two gentlemen would watch the body for us, we would greatly appreciate it. One of you can stand guard in here and the other at the front door, please."

"Dear God," I say as I open another drawer and pull out a wrapped piece of hard cheese. "The man is a squirrel. There are stashes of food everywhere."

I glance over to Gray, who is staring down into a desk drawer.

"More food?" I say with a sigh.

He slaps it shut. "No."

"But you did find something."

"Nothing that would have poisoned him."

"Ah. Porn?"

Across the room, McCreadie chokes.

"Sorry," I say. "Literature of a pornographic nature. Is that better?"

"Not really," Gray says. "But yes, that is what it is."

"Can I look?" I say. "I'm really quite curious about what constitutes pornography in this time. Pretty girls showing off their ankles?"

McCreadie chokes on another laugh. "You truly do have an interesting view of our world, Mallory. I am not certain whether to be amused or offended."

"You personally prefer porn that shows more than ankles. Got it."

His laugh turns to a horrified sputter as his cheeks redden.

"Adorable," I say. "You are utterly adorable, Detective McCreadie."

"Fine," he says. "I deserved that. Now, can we focus on gathering this food please? There is quite enough of it to keep us occupied."

"True, but on second thought, I actually am going to need to confiscate the porn. Remember what I said about Mrs. Young's secret profession?"

McCreadie's color rises again. "Er, yes. I suppose . . . That is to say, it could be a link, so we really ought to . . ." He clears his throat. "Duncan, would you say something, please?"

"I agree that we must take it," Gray says. "And do not worry, Hugh. I will not fight you for the right to examine it more closely. You may do so yourself, in the privacy of your own home, with my blessing."

More sputtering and blushing from McCreadie, which really *is* adorable.

"Do you guys want me to look at it?" I say. "I have a description of Mrs. Young, though it'd be better if I'd met her. We're working on that, right?"

McCreadie says, "If by 'we,' you mean 'me,' I am not only working on it but have secured an interview for tomorrow."

"Good lad."

I get a look for that, but I ignore it and open the drawer. Yep, that's porn, several chapbooks' worth. I take them out and leaf through the first, which seems to be a mix of text and images. The text is so shoddily printed it's almost unreadable, but as with modern porn, I suspect the story isn't the point.

The pictures are the main attraction, and they are particularly interesting in a world that predates easy photography. They *are* photographs, but grainy, with the women looking in the other direction, probably to disguise their expression, which after hours of posing, would not exactly be coquettish.

I'm turning the page when McCreadie clears his throat. "I believe you can do that later, Mallory."

"When you're not there to watch me reading it?"

When he sputters, I close the book and tuck the chapbooks into a box of food we are collecting. "There. Better? If it helps, half my modern-day male coworkers would have reacted the same way. Another quarter of them would have snickered and made lewd jokes."

"And the fourth quarter?" Gray asks.

"They'd have been like you. Said nothing and acted as if it was no different than leafing through financial records. At least we know Ware's infirmities weren't affecting *that* part of his anatomy."

More sputtering from McCreadie.

Gray shakes his head. "You are having far too much fun tormenting poor Hugh."

"Tormenting him by making accurate medical observations that may play a role in the investigation? As I believe we have established, we have two victims known for philandering and a third who recently abandoned his wife to marry his mistress. The working capacity of elderly Mr. Ware's nether regions may be significant. Now, stop distracting me. We need to find what poisoned the old guy."

"May I suggest a likely suspect up there, Mallory?"

I turn and find myself looking at a box perched atop a second cabinet. In my defense, the box is above my head, which is why I didn't see it. Also, there's clearly an address written on the side, which makes it seem like a simple piece of parcel post.

"Would someone send food through the mail?" I say as I pull down the box.

"That has been delivered. There is no postage mark on it."

He's right. I turn the box over in my hands to see it has only a delivery address and name. No postage marks and no return. Of course, that doesn't mean it came bearing gifts of an edible nature, like Leslie's figs.

I'm about to ask Gray what made him think that when I notice a red smear with a thumbprint in it. The purplish-red stain of smeared jam, right beside the delivery address.

I open the box. There's another smear of jam inside, as well as crumbs.

"Those are pastry flakes," Gray says, peering over my shoulder. "With sugar dust. You are looking for the remains of a jam-filled pastry, such as a tart."

"There's a sitting area in the next room," McCreadie says. "I'll check there."

I notice something on the inside of the lid and lift it to see a handwritten message.

In sincerest gratitude for both your work and your kindness.

There's a signature scrawled below. An indecipherable signature.

"Can you make that out?" I say, tapping it.

"No, it is worse than your penmanship."

"Yeah, yeah. I've seen plenty of unreadable signatures, but those are for business. Presumably, if you've sent a gift you'd want the recipient to know who sent it . . . unless that's exactly what you *don't* want."

Gray takes the box into the light and peers at it. "The signature doesn't seem to be composed of actual letters. It is simply a scrawl emulating a signature."

"In a box with such tasty treats that Ware isn't going to question who sent it. Presumably a client who appreciated his legal work. Good enough for him." I lean against the desk, deep in thought for a moment. Then I say, "Lord Leslie's figs came delivered, and he would not say from whom. He hid the entire box, which made Annis think there might have been a message written directly on it."

"As with this one."

"Right. And maybe it was equally indecipherable."

"A sentimental note, presumably from a past lover, but with an indistinguishable signature."

"I presume you'll be taking the box as potential evidence?" I call to McCreadie in the next room.

"I will."

"May I trace the handwriting first?"

"I'll do that," Gray says. "You still don't quite have the knack of using a pen without making an infernal mess."

I look pointedly at the spot of ink on Gray's shirt, from his note-taking earlier this evening. He follows my gaze, but only frowns, as if the stain is invisible to his eyes.

"Fine," I say. "You can trace it. And let's work on finding the one that the figs came in. We can compare the handwriting. If the same person sent both, then that helps clear Annis." I glance over at Ware's desk. "Unless Mr. Ware had any dealings with Lord Leslie, dealings that Annis might not want coming out after her husband's death. Please tell me this wasn't the lawyer he summoned last night to change his will."

"I certainly hope not."

McCreadie clears his throat from the doorway. When we turn, he lifts a tiny china plate. "I believe I have found the remains of the pastry."

He lowers the plate to show nothing but crumbs.

An hour later, I am gathering food. No, not still gathering it in Ware's office. After we found the pastry flakes—which are almost certainly too small for Isla to analyze, especially when poison would likely be in the jam—we took what we'd found and left the officers to guard the door. We'll come back in the morning to search further.

Right now, I'm gathering food in Gray's kitchen. The guys are hungry. Okay, it's not only the guys. I'm starving, so while they put Ware's body in the examination room, I offered to get snacks. Maybe handling a dead body doesn't make most people peckish—especially when the victim was almost certainly killed by poisoned food—but both men said a bite to eat seemed like a fine idea, so I'm running with it.

When the kitchen door opens behind me, it comes from the direction opposite the stairs, meaning it comes from Mrs. Wallace's quarters.

"I am fixing a plate for Dr. Gray and Detective McCreadie," I say, my head still in the icebox as I survey the options. "Might I have a bit of this cold ham?"

No answer. I turn to see Mrs. Wallace taking day-old bread from the counter and slicing it. She's nearly as tall as Isla, and her steel-gray hair suggests she's at the far end of middle age, but her face suggests she hasn't passed forty yet.

"I can do that," I say.

She keeps cutting and then takes the platter of ham from me and begins slicing it.

"I apologize if I disturbed you," I say.

She adds a small pot of mustard to the tray and then opens a tin of cookies.

"I know it's very early," I say.

"I was already getting up to start breakfast. As Dr. Gray has evidently had another night without sleep, he may not wish to dine at the usual time. Ask him that, and ask whether Detective McCreadie will be joining him."

"Yes, ma'am."

"You were out as well," she says.

"I was with them, ma'am. Working. There was another murder."

That gets a reaction. The barest flinch. "Not anyone else they know, I hope," she says as she sets jam on the tray.

"No. A solicitor by the name of Ware. Poison, it seems."

She nods, almost absently now that I've confirmed the deceased isn't another family member. She cuts off a pat of butter and puts it on a tiny plate. Then she glances at the stove, where I've set a kettle, shakes her head and gets the stove going properly.

"You're angry with me," I say. "Is it because I was out with Dr. Gray again at night? It really was work."

"I know."

"Is it because I've been up all night, and Alice will need to help cover some of my chores?"

"Not only Alice."

I wince. "You've been covering for me, too. I'm sorry. If Dr. Gray has no need of me, then I will only require a brief nap before I resume my duties. I know this is inconvenient. I'm supposed to be the housemaid, and if I don't do my chores, someone has to cover for me."

"I cannot blame you for preferring your work with Dr. Gray and Mrs. Ballantyne." She takes a tea canister from the cupboard. "My concern, Catriona, is that better employment might not be your goal."

Her tone is even and calm, but the use of Catriona's name isn't accidental.

"You think I'm still up to something," I say as I try to take down tea-cups, but she elbows me aside and does it herself.

"Oh, I *know* you're up to something, lassie. You are trying to better your position. The question is: How?"

"*How* I'm trying to better it? By becoming Dr. Gray's assistant, of course. You think that is only a strategy—that I am feigning interest so that I might do that instead of scrubbing chamber pots. I am not, but even if I were, the important thing is only whether I *am* helping. He would not keep me on otherwise, nor would Mrs. Ballantyne allow me to waste his time."

"I do not care whether you are interested in his studies or feigning it, Catriona. Most people in this life are not doing work they enjoy and no one expects them to. You are, as you said, actually helping him, and that is enough for me . . . unless that is not how you are trying to better yourself."

I lean against the counter. "I don't understand."

She meets my gaze. "Truly? You jump when Dr. Gray calls. You trip over yourself to prove your worth to him. You take an interest in his stud-ies to the point of reading his books in your spare time. And you spend the night chasing poisoners with him, never complaining once that you need to be abed. That is not the Catriona I know."

She lifts her hands. "Before you say that you aren't that Catriona, I do not believe your story that you have lost your memory. I would, however, be willing to forgive the lie if you only wish to reconsider your choices and do better. And if doing better means a position as Dr. Gray's assis-tant and nothing more."

"Nothing . . ." I slump back. "You think I want to marry him."

She snorts. "Marry him? If that is your plan, you had best return to being Catriona now and save yourself the trouble. Yes, I know you come from a family good enough that such a union would only be unusual. But if you have made the mistake of thinking Dr. Gray is in desperate need of a wife, on account of any qualities that might make decent women reject him . . ."

"I have no doubt Dr. Gray could get himself a respectable wife anytime he wanted."

She relaxes. "Good. Do not deceive yourself on that count."

"If you don't think I'm aiming to be his wife, then you think . . . ? Ah, his mistress. I suppose that's a more reasonable goal."

"It would be if you were ten years older," she says tartly. "And age is only one of the many qualities you lack in that regard. You are young and pretty, and you think that will be enough. It is not. Dr. Gray does not dally with mere girls."

"So I've been told, which is one reason I'm comfortable working with him. I know he doesn't want anything untoward from me."

She says nothing to that, only finishes fixing the tray, complete with two plates and two teacups. I meet her gaze and take down another plate and teacup for myself, all the while braced against her complaint.

"I will ask what time Dr. Gray would like breakfast," I say.

I pick up the tray and leave, feeling her gaze on me and all the judgment that it carries.

TWENTY-SIX

This time, Gray examines the body before Addington arrives . . . or he does so after McCreadie and I convince him that he doesn't aid the investigation by waiting. Gray can do his internal exam post-autopsy, but before that, he can help Addington by preparing the body. That means undressing Ware, which allows him to conduct a more thorough external examination. McCreadie stays long enough to have his bite to eat, and then he has to leave, and Gray and I examine the body together.

I ask questions about the gout. I've heard of it—it's still a condition in the twenty-first century—but I know nothing about it, and Mrs. Hamilton's comments led me to think it might be connected to food, which could be what killed Mr. Ware.

"It is believed that a rich diet contributes to it," Gray says as he examines Mr. Ware's perfectly manicured fingernails. "But it is an arthritic condition, not an intestinal one, and it would not have killed him. From what Mrs. Hamilton said, I believe it was a more acute poisoning than the others. That will be clearer in the autopsy."

"By examining the internal organs."

"Correct." He glances up. "Is it different in your time?"

"Not really. We have more methods for identifying poison, but you still start with the autopsy and then send tissue samples to the lab." I glance up at him. "How does that work here? You have Isla right upstairs. Do the police offices have a laboratory on site?"

"Hardly. In a case of poisoning, the tissues must be delivered to an expert. That may require sending the entire stomach through the mail."

"Through the . . . ?" I shake my head, unable to imagine packaging up organs and loading them onto a horse-drawn mail coach.

"As Isla has pointed out, criminal poison cases are much rarer than people seem to think. There are only a handful of experts in detecting it. Isla learned it . . . Well, you ought to ask her how she gained her expertise."

"I will. Thank you. Is it okay if I take a print from Ware's fingers? I want to compare it to the one on the box."

He jerks up from his work. "Of course. I had not thought of that. Yes, we must do that right away. What will you need?"

"The very thing you accused me of making such messes with earlier. Except now I get to make a mess with it on purpose."

His eyes glitter. "Ink."

We roll ink on Ware's finger and then onto paper. I show Gray what I'm looking for as identifiers.

"Not that we still need to do this back home," I say. "The tech takes the print and runs it through a computer that looks for a match. I actually learned fingerprinting as a kid. I had a kit and there was one summer where I fingerprinted everything."

His lips twitch in a smile. "Did you catch any criminals?"

"Hell, yeah. I proved it was my dad sneaking cookies instead of me." I pause, magnifying glass in hand. "Although now I have to wonder whether my parents didn't set that one up for me. Dad never was much for cookies."

I move to the papers we'd brought from Ware's office. One has the traced note. Another has my rough diagram of the fingerprint.

I show both to Gray, and I'm about to tell him what to look for when he says, "It is a match."

I nod. "The whorl there"—I tap with the forceps—"and the ridges over here"—another tap—"seem to match. Detective McCreadie will want to do a proper comparison with the actual box, but I think we can safely say that the fingerprint belongs to the victim."

"Sadly."

"Yep."

We finish the external exam and find nothing new. From what we can tell, Ware died of poison contained in an item he willingly ingested.

After that, it's time for breakfast, over which we bring Isla up to speed. Then Isla and I take the food samples up to her laboratory.

"I'll test the pastry flakes," she says, "although they really may be too small and, as you said, the poison was more likely in the jam."

"And all we have of that is a smear."

"Which I cannot test."

As she begins, I tell her what Gray and I had been discussing: chemical methods of poison detection.

"He told me to ask where you got your training," I say.

She pauses and smiles, as if at the memory. "That is a story. Let me get this started, and I'll tell you." She prepares the sample and then says, "It was before I married. I was interested in poison, and I had begun a correspondence with one of the up-and-coming chemists in the field—Thomas Scattergood. He invited me to come and train under him, and I was utterly delighted . . . until I realized he likely thought me a man, as I always corresponded with my initials. Obviously, I could not go and put him in such a spot. I was about to decline when Hugh found out."

Her smile returns, and I realize this aspect of the story holds a large share of the credit for that smile. "Hugh went to my mother. He wished to escort me to Yorkshire to at least meet with Mr. Scattergood. That, of course, was not possible. I could not be escorted by an unrelated man. So he offered . . ." She swallows and fusses with the experiment. "He offered to remedy that."

"By *marrying* you?"

"He was being foolish. Young and reckless. Of course my mother said no. She took me herself, as Duncan was in school and Lachlan abroad. She insisted I go and speak to Mr. Scattergood in person and see what he said. He was shocked to see I was a woman, but he recovered with aplomb and invited me to train under him for a few weeks. Mother remained with me—even staying in the laboratory when there were no other women present to act as chaperones." She starts the burner. "I am very fortunate, to have such good friends and family and mentors."

"All of which you deserve. So you learned poison detection from Mr. Scattergood."

"I did. We had one case of possible criminal poisoning while I was there. Suspected strychnine." She passes a sly smile my way. "Do you know one of the ways to test for that?"

I shake my head.

"It leaves a bitter taste."

"The poison tastes . . . Wait. You said *test*. Please tell me you don't mean tasting the tissue."

"Heavens, no. You taste the extract that comes from boiling the tissue."

I stare at her. "You drink a brew made from human tissue . . . that's been sent through the mail?"

"You sip it. Judiciously. My goodness, Mallory. The look on your face. You are not nearly dedicated enough to the pursuit of science."

"Yeah, that's why I'm a cop. I'll throw myself in the line of fire and wrestle the bad guy to the ground. You can sip tea made from moldering human organs."

"Such a lack of dedication." She adjusts the beaker under the flame. "What would my brother say?"

"That he'll stick with cutting off the tissues for *you* to drink."

She shakes her head with a smile. "That reminds me of a jest Lachlan and I played on poor Duncan, shortly after Duncan declared he wished to follow our grandfather into medicine. I found an old book on diagnosing illness by drinking a patient's urine, and we tried to convince Duncan that's what he'd need to do."

"What'd he say?"

"That any substance found in urine fell under the auspices of chemistry and therefore drinking it would be my job."

I grin. "Touché. How old was he?"

"Far too young to be so clever. Then Annis found out we were teasing him and gave us a proper dressing-down. If Duncan wished to be a doctor and we did anything to discourage him, we'd be dealing with her, which was threat enough." A fond smile lights her face, only to fall as she turns back to the experiment. "I miss that Annis."

I say nothing, just wait and listen, and after a moment, the smile returns, wistful now. "I remember another time, when she'd taken Duncan and me to the park. A couple of boys taunted Duncan for his skin color. Annis cursed them."

"She swore at them?"

"No." Her lips twitch. "She cursed them. She said a bunch of nonsensical words and claimed they would suffer her curse for their cruelty."

"What did she curse them with?"

"Oh, that was the best part. They asked, of course, and she only said that they would find out soon enough."

I laugh.

"That was our Annis," Isla says. "I catch glimpses of her now and then but . . ." She shrugs. "It is like glimpsing the sun between the clouds. Too fleeting by far."

She turns her attention to the experiment. After a moment, when I am sure there isn't more she wants to say, I return to her tutelage under Thomas Scattergood and she embraces the change of topic.

TWENTY-SEVEN

As expected, Isla can't find any trace of poison in the few flakes of pastry that remain. It's too small a sample, and it would make far more sense to put the poison in the jam filling. That is all gone, save for the smear, which is also too small to analyze.

We test a few other possible sources for the poisoned food, but we're mostly just killing time waiting for Addington to be finished with his autopsy so Isla can get a tissue sample. This time, Addington doesn't bother speculating on the type of poison. He concludes that it is poison and then decides he's going to outsource the testing to the "capable Mrs. Ballantyne." That would be far more gratifying if he didn't add "who has far more time for such things."

Whatever his excuse, we're just happy he surrenders that task to an actual chemist who will perform the correct tests. Isla does that, and the results are the same as they'd been for Leslie. Yes to heavy metal poisoning. No to arsenic.

While I privately examine the pornography, Isla confers with Gray and McCreadie, who had returned. We now know that two victim's corpses plus the gin and the pudding all contained a non-arsenic heavy metal. Gray and McCreadie will be taking this evidence to Detective Crichton to argue for access to the first two bodies. To do so, they'll need to explain that we suspect it's a rare poison, which means they need to fully understand that poison. Isla is coaching them. It would be far easier if she just went herself to explain, but no one suggests that. I have a feeling they won't even be saying who found these results, just that the tests were conducted by a trained chemist.

As for the porn, I've been given a good description of Mrs. Young, but it doesn't match any of the women in the chapbooks. Even if it did, I'm not sure what kind of link that would give us, but I had to check.

After Gray and McCreadie leave, Isla and I do the same. We've taken on the task of searching Ware's office for anything that could link him to the victims, most notably Lord Leslie.

My mother is a defense attorney, and as a kid, I'd pick up extra money working at her office, filing and copying mostly. It was enough to teach me that I didn't want a career in law, but it also gave me a basic understanding of the paperwork side, which should come in handy here.

There are no file cabinets. No file folders either. A filing system is one of those things that I presumed had been around forever. It hasn't. In this period, papers are either kept in pigeon holes or—in the case of someone like a lawyer, with lots of paperwork, they're bound or stored in pouches.

We start by searching both for an obvious "Lord Gordon Leslie" pouch of client files. Not finding that, we each take a stack of pouches and set to work.

"Oh," Isla says as we begin. "I have also sent a message to Annis, asking whether she knows Mr. Ware. Or, I should say, I have sent it to Sarah, which is wiser."

"Ah, right. Probably better not to ask her directly, in case the message is read by the messenger."

"No, no. I sent it with Simon, to be delivered after he is finished with Duncan and Hugh. My concern is simply that my sister may ignore it altogether. Sarah will ensure she does not."

I open a pouch on the massive desk. "I understand they parted ways after Annis's marriage."

"That is one way of putting it."

"Another being that Annis dumped Sarah because she objected to the marriage."

"Hmm." Isla starts riffling through papers. "If I were Sarah, I'd have never come back. But Sarah has always been a kind soul, quick to see the goodness in anyone."

"Dr. Gray certainly seemed surprised to see her back in Annis's life."

192 • KELLEY ARMSTRONG

"Hmm."

I should leave it at that, but this case involves Annis and so it involves Sarah, and therefore I must fully understand the situation. Or that makes an excellent excuse for what I am about to ask.

"There was a history there?" I say.

She looks up in surprise. "History?"

"Between Dr. Gray and Sarah? His reaction suggested as much."

I wait for her to laugh it off and tell me I am overdetecting. Instead, a look passes over her face, one of clear discomfort, and she shakes her head.

"There was some unpleasantness, which I am certain he would prefer to forget."

"Let me guess. He would have been in his midteens when he last saw her, and she's very pretty. An infatuation? He said or did something he's embarrassed by now? Or was it more than an unrequited attraction?"

Isla's lips press together in obvious annoyance.

"I'm overstepping," I say. "Sorry."

"No, it is not you. It is my sister, as usual. I do not know whether Duncan had an infatuation. I do not think so—he gave no sign of it—but I would not presume to know his mind on such matters, and Sarah was pretty and kind. The situation occurred when he was twelve or thirteen. Annis accused him of spying on Sarah while she was dressing."

"Oh."

"He did not. Yes, I realize boys of such an age may do such a thing. They are curious, and they may not consider how disrespectful it is. That isn't my brother, which only made matters worse, because he was horrified and humiliated. Our father insisted he apologize or be punished."

"What did he do?" I ask as I get out a new pouch.

"He apologized for accidentally stumbling on a scene he ought not to have witnessed."

I set down the pouch. "So he accidentally saw Sarah dressing?"

"I do not know what he saw, only that he avoided both Sarah and Annis until the furor died down, and even then, he was cautious around them."

"Around *them*. Not just Sarah."

"It was Annis who was angry. Sarah said it was a mistake and tried to downplay the matter, but Annis would not let her."

I consider that as I flip through the new file pouch. When I'm done, I say, "Exactly how close were Annis and Sarah?"

"Very close," Isla says as she skims through the contents of a pouch. "Mother often joked that she had three daughters. Annis met Sarah at school, and they became inseparable."

"And Dr. Gray 'accidentally stumbled on a scene he ought not to have witnessed.' That was his phrasing."

"As close to it as I recall."

I open my mouth to ask more. Then I shut it. This is a question for Gray, and I'll ask it as soon as I can, because it could have a bearing on the case, if my suspicion is correct.

We continue reading through the client files. I'm making a list of client names along with the case type. I'm also skimming for any mention of Leslie.

"Mr. Ware certainly had a wide breadth of specialities," Isla says. "I have set aside papers from several clients that are members of the gentry, in case they are associates of my brother-in-law. I shall have to make a list, as I do not know many of his circle."

"The Leslies didn't socialize with your side of the family."

Her mouth tightens again. "My sister scaled the social ladder and would prefer not to be reminded of the climb."

"How did she hook up with Leslie?"

"By *hook*, I presume you mean *ensnare*."

"No, I'm just wondering how they got together. Was there ensnaring involved?"

"Mutual ensnaring."

"His title for her dowry?"

"Yes, and while I hate to pity my sister, I must say he got the better end of the bargain. Being shortsighted, he cared only for the dowry and the debts it would pay, but what truly saved him financially was Annis herself. We Grays all have a talent. Hers is business."

I bring over several more pouches. "I heard she was in London conducting business for her husband when he got sick. I figured he was otherwise engaged?"

She snorts. "Otherwise engaged with his hunts and his women. Gordon was not a fool. Once he realized my sister's talents, he employed them. She has been his proxy for over a decade now. At first, he made excuses. Eventually, he stopped bothering. She was the face of his financial interests, while he was presumed to make the decisions."

194 • KELLEY ARMSTRONG

"Which he did not."

"Were they living in the poorhouse? No? Then he did not."

I set down the pouches. "Sarah said that Annis didn't care about inheriting the estate. That she'd be glad to be rid of it. That suggested she expected to inherit money instead. But Annis didn't seem worried about the will being changed. Has anyone seen it yet?"

"No, and Annis seems in no rush to do so. Hugh says the officer in charge of the investigation has requested it. Annis is also apparently unconcerned with that."

I have an idea why, but I'll wait to see the will.

"So how did they meet?" I ask. "Annis and Lord Leslie?"

"Through our father. Lord Leslie was a business associate. I do not recall who introduced *them*, but Lord Leslie—being forever short of ready money—was eager to speculate, and my father had the touch there. He helped Gordon make a bit of money through burial societies . . . and then Gordon saw a quicker source of capital."

"Annis's dowry."

"It was a match made in . . . well, someplace."

I chuckle. "Someplace warm." I stop, pages in hand. "Wait."

"Burial societies," she blurts, before I can speak. "Was not one of our victims a gravedigger?"

I'm at the desk, digging through the stacks. "Young was, which might not be significant in itself—one gravedigger and one burial-society investor—but then there's this."

I hand her four client files. All show Ware representing clients involved in the funerary business—one owning a cemetery, one investing in cemeteries, and two managing burial societies.

"That didn't immediately seem significant," I say. "Ware handled all kinds of clients, like you said. But I haven't found four clients in any other shared area of business."

"And I have two more," she says. "Mr. Ware assisting them in various areas of the funerary trade."

"Did Lord Leslie still invest in it?" I ask.

"He did. That is one reason Annis is particularly suited to handle his business affairs. She may turn up her nose at our family trade, but growing up, she knew more about it than any of us." She pauses. "I think, at one time, she had hoped to inherit it."

"Damn."

Isla plucks out two client files from her own stack. "I do not like my sister, Mallory. That may be obvious. I love her, but I do not like her, if that makes sense."

"It does."

"I do not like the way she has treated Sarah and our mother, and I will never forgive her for how she has treated Duncan. She was not always like that toward him, and somehow, that makes it worse."

She scans pages as she continues, "When Duncan came to live with us, Annis delighted in him. He was so solemn and so quick-witted. Some girls would like a giggling baby to play with. Annis was different. She longed for a younger sibling to teach. Lachlan and I had quite enough of that from her, but then along came Duncan, who wanted nothing more than to learn. He *adored* her."

"What happened?"

Isla checks a cabinet, yanking open another drawer. "She grew up. She developed aspirations, and she learned that Duncan stood in the way of those. I will never forgive her for rejecting him as she did, but if I am to give her even the barest iota of sympathy, I will admit that, at the time she turned her back on him, she had also suffered a disappointment, one that made her . . ." She sucks in a breath. "It made her hard, and it made her cold."

"She found out your father was leaving the business to Lachlan. Despite the fact Lachlan had no interest in it. Annis was the oldest child and, being Scottish, she *could* actually inherit it."

"Yes. I will not bore you with the drama, but a drama it was. Annis went away with Sarah for two years, and when she returned, she had set her sights on a wealthy husband and decided we all stood in the way of that goal, especially Duncan. That is inexcusable. Punish my father, yes. But not us, and certainly not Duncan."

"Is it worse now that Dr. Gray inherited the business she wanted?"

"I would need more than passing contact with Annis to answer that."

I flip through a few more client files. "Does Dr. Gray know Annis wanted the business?"

"He knows that she initially wanted it. When our father died, Lachlan *did* attempt to give it to her, at our mother's urging, both because Annis wanted it and because Duncan—like Lachlan—did not. Annis had no idea what we were talking about. Running a funerary parlor? Why on earth would she want to do that?" Isla takes out more client file pouches. "I am certain Lord Leslie is still involved in such businesses, at least as a speculator, and that seems a potential link."

"Though not necessarily one that clears Annis of suspicion."

Isla is about to answer when voices waft up from below.

"You do not understand," a man is saying. "Mr. Ware is representing me in a very urgent matter."

"Mr. Ware is not representing anyone in anything," one of the officers says. "He is dead."

"I know, which is why I must obtain my papers. They are due today. I realize that seems ghoulish—the poor man is scarcely cold—but it truly is urgent. If I do not deliver the papers by the end of the day, I shall lose my business before it can begin."

Isla walks to the stairs and calls down. "Let him up, please. We shall supervise him."

A moment later, a man crests the stairs. He's in his late twenties, with sideburns to rival McCreadie's, though that is the only fashionable thing about him. His dark hair is unkempt and his suit looks like a secondhand one that has been tailored—badly—to fit his lean frame.

"Thank you, ma'am," he says to Isla, panting slightly. "I do apologize for this. I am most frantic."

"Yes, we heard."

His gaze cuts to me, and he dips his head. "My apologies to you as well, miss. I will not interrupt your work. I only wish to retrieve my papers."

"Yes, of—" Isla begins.

I clear my throat to cut her off. "I am afraid that will not be as easy as it seems. All Mr. Ware's papers are part of his estate. They will be held until the lawyers have cleared them."

The poor man's eyes bug. "What?"

"But as your matter is urgent, I can find the papers you require, though you may not take your *entire* client pouch at this time."

He exhales. "Thank you. Those specific pages are fine."

"Your name?"

"Morris. Cyrus Morris."

I start to ask for ID, and then remember that's not a thing in this world.

Isla had been quite horrified by the idea that, in the future, people must carry proof of their identity.

I find the file, which is on the desk. "I do not mean to be rude . . ."

"It is I who am being rude, miss, interrupting your work in light of such a tragedy."

"You have cause. However, I am going to need to ask you the nature of your business, to ascertain that I am providing the pages to the correct person."

"Of course. The pages I am looking for are an agreement to rent an office. I am a clocksmith, setting out on my own after a lengthy apprenticeship, and I have finally found office space I can afford." He rattles off the address of the property, and I take the agreement from his files and hand it to him.

"Thank you," he says, bobbing his head and wiping his damp brow. "Again, I am sorry. Mr. Ware was a fine gentleman. Very fine indeed. May I ask what happened to him?"

"Something he ate," I say.

"Ah. He *was* fond of his rich foods. I remember him saying that his housekeeper swore they'd be the end of him." He makes a face. "That sounds very flippant. I do not mean that. She was always after him to repair his diet, but he said that if the food did not kill him, the gout would, and he would rather it was the food."

"Personally, I would agree."

He smiles at me. "As would I." He shuffles his papers. "Might I have something to affix these together?"

He motions toward a length of string on the opposite side of the desk. I wave for him to go ahead. Isla has returned to searching the room for more client pouches. As Morris takes the string, his elbow hits a stack of papers I'd been sorting. They cascade to the floor. He dives to pick them up.

"I have it," I say, as I bend to collect the fallen papers while he blurts apologies. Then I pause. "When was the last time you saw Mr. Ware, sir?"

"Three days ago."

I try not to sag in disappointment. Then he adds, "Oh, and I dropped off these papers yesterday."

Bingo.

"You didn't happen to see whether Mr. Ware was eating anything at the time?"

Morris smiles. "He was always eating something. Yesterday, there was a tray of lunch from his housekeeper, which he was ignoring in favor of a pastry."

That has Isla stopping her work. "What sort of pastry?"

"A jam tart. I do not blame him. It looked quite delicious, with cherry jam and a bit of clotted cream on top."

"Did he say where it came from?" I ask.

The young man shakes his head. "He was not in the mood for conversation when I arrived, having just dealt with a most unpleasant woman."

"A woman?"

Morris backs against the desk, half sitting against the edge. "A client, presumably. They were arguing when I came in. Something about an investment her husband was making through Mr. Ware. It does not signify, I suppose, except that you may also need to deal with her." He shudders. "I would be prepared."

I ask what they'd been arguing about—so we can "be prepared"—but Morris had retreated quickly when he heard the raised voices. Nor can he provide any information about the woman herself, who stormed past him.

"Nearly knocked me flying, she did. Strode straight to her carriage, waiting in the mews. Oh, I can tell you that the carriage had a crest on the door. A lion under a mountain peak." He straightens. "I hope you do not encounter her. She is quite the virago." He taps his pages. "Thank you again for this. I shall return in a few days to see about obtaining the rest of my papers."

He leaves, and I wait until the door shuts behind him.

"Please tell me the Leslie family crest does not have a lion under a mountain peak."

"It has a lion under two chevrons," she says grimly. "Which could look like a mountain peak."

"Shit."

TWENTY-EIGHT

After that, we reboot our search with a new goal: get through the client pouches as fast as we can—looking for any mention of Lord Leslie or Annis—and separate out all the ones related to the funerary business. We're finishing up that when the clock strikes ten . . . and I remember that Jack had promised to give us the broadsheet writer's response by ten.

I leave Isla to search the last bunch of pouches as I fly down the stairs and take off as quickly as I can without attracting undue attention. At least in the modern day, I can always quicken my walk to a jog and no one thinks much of it, even if I'm not wearing jogging attire. Here, walking fast nearly gets me stopped by two gentlemen who clearly suspect I'm absconding with my employer's silver.

I make it to the town house slightly out of breath. In a world where women rarely exceed a brisk walk, Catriona's lungs aren't made for sprints. The corset doesn't help. I've been getting better at learning to breath Victorian-style, which is actually the proper way—from my diaphragm—but in my hurry, I forgot and returned to my more modern breathing.

Gray hasn't returned yet, and I don't see Alice, so I swing into the kitchen with, "Did anyone come calling?"

Mrs. Wallace doesn't look up from her bread kneading. "No."

I hesitate.

"Yes, I am certain," she says. "The front doorbell rings in the kitchen, and I have been here since you left."

Damn it. That's what I get for taking Jack at her word. At least we have another lead to pursue. I just don't like where that one is heading. I might not be fond of Annis, but I really don't want Gray and Isla dragged into a scandal.

I start to say that I'll go do some of my chores, but that sounds as if I expect a pat on the head for doing my damn job. I'll just do it.

I head off in search of Alice, to be sure she isn't covering my chores, but she's in her room, working on her lessons. The Victorian era has a reputation for dumping kids into the workforce before they're old enough to attend school. That's not entirely inaccurate. The poorer the family, the more likely they'll need those kids pulling in a few pence as soon as possible. But Victorians value literacy more than I expected and Victorian Scotland values it more than Victorian England. Literacy rates here are high enough that I have to wonder whether there's a reason Catriona couldn't read and write, possibly a learning disability. I'm not sure what Alice's level of literacy was when she came to work here, but she's at what I'd consider a middle-school level now, under Isla's tutelage, Alice's afternoons being almost exclusively for lessons.

To someone from my world, the very fact that Alice needs to earn her keep at all is repugnant. At first, did I judge Isla and Gray for employing a twelve-year-old child? Hell, yes. But as Isla confessed, she'd actually wanted to adopt Alice. McCreadie stopped her, and she'd been outraged . . . until she realized he was right. To her, for a ten-year-old pickpocket to be adopted by a wealthy family would be a dream. The musical *Annie* come to life. But that's fiction, and the reality is that Alice doesn't want what she'd consider charity. She wants to earn her keep, and the best Isla can do is make sure she's housed and fed and paid as well as she'll accept—again, too much would feel like charity—and to insist on these lessons in hopes Alice won't be "in service" her entire life.

I pop in on Alice and give her a break under the guise of helping with her lessons—she's doing math, and honestly, the kid is far better at it than I was at her age. Then I hear Isla come in, and I zip down to tell her that Jack hasn't stopped by and Gray is still out.

"Then you shall teach me to use a knife," she says as she pulls off her gloves.

"I'll . . . what?"

"Teach me to use a knife," she says. "That is what we discussed, yes?

To alleviate my brother's concerns over my safety, I must learn to defend myself. We'll start with knife work."

"Somehow I don't think that'll make him feel better. How about we start with defensive walking?"

She pauses, fingers on her boot buttons. "I hope that is a joke, Mallory."

"Nope. If you're going to walk around the Old Town, there's a right and a wrong way to do it. Well, I shouldn't say 'wrong'—that implies if you're attacked, it was your own fault—but there's a better way to do it. You need to act as if you belong there while also being aware of your surroundings at all times. We'll—"

"I am a Victorian widow who travels alone. I am well aware of the posture to strike and the need to remain alert to all dangers, whether they be pickpockets or gentlemen who wish to keep me company, for my own safety."

"Okay, then we'll move to physical self-defense. I'll show you a few ways you can grab someone, even throwing a man twice your size."

"That sounds delightful. And how well does it work in a corset and long skirts?"

"Er . . ."

She shakes her head. "I would certainly like to learn such things, but for now, I have obtained this." She pulls a four-inch blade from her boot. "And I believe I ought to know how to use it."

"Where did you get . . . ? Jesus, Isla. Seriously? That is—"

"A knife. Like yours."

"Uh, no." I take out mine and show her. "That is twice the size of mine, and you're lucky you didn't slice off your foot. How did it even fit into your boot?"

"With difficulty."

I shake my head.

"So you will show me how to use it?" she asks.

"I . . ."

"Good. Let us take this lesson out-of-doors."

Here's the thing. I don't actually know how to fight with a knife. I studied martial arts as a kid—judo, karate, and aikido—and that's my go-to form of self-defense, along with some basic pugilism I picked up in middle school when a friend and I decided to challenge the fact that the boxing team was for boys only. I actually really enjoyed boxing . . . until I reached the age where the boys were so much bigger that I gave it up.

As a cop, I also know how to shoot, but thankfully that's not a skill I've ever had to employ. My experience is all on the range, and I enjoy that, too, as a sport.

Now here I am in a world where my attire means I can't kick, and I can barely punch. I've joked about a gun, and I wouldn't turn one down, but I'm hardly going to pull it in a street fight.

My only option is knives. Okay, fine, the other option would be: Don't get into street fights.

Had someone ever suggested I'd one day find myself in Victorian Scotland, I might have envisioned all the things I would do there. Nowhere on that list would I expect to find "bare-knuckle brawling," but little about this world is what I expected.

Catriona had a knife—a little switchblade that I've become rather fond of. But I'm painfully aware of how badly I use it. Knife fighting just wasn't a thing in my suburban Vancouver neighborhoods.

I have been practicing, though, and I show Isla a few basic moves, which mostly consist of "keep the pointy end away from you" and "don't let go." As a cop, I know that the biggest danger of carrying a weapon is that someone with a whole lot more experience will get it away from you and use it *on* you.

I'm demonstrating a thrust when laughter burbles up from the direction of the stables. I look over to see Simon leaning on a shovel, watching us.

"You truly have forgotten much, haven't you?" he says as he walks over.

"Yes, I'm not as good at this as I once was."

He laughs again. "No, you have forgotten that you do not know how to use it at all. It is merely a theatrical prop, to wave about at any who are not frightened off by your sharp tongue."

I click my knife back into its handle. "I suppose you could do better?"

"I think Mrs. Ballantyne could do better without any training at all."

I scowl at Simon, but he only laughs and puts out his hand for the knife. I hand it over. He takes it, flicks it out, and then turns to Isla.

"The first thing to remember, ma'am, is that you are not actually going to use the knife. You only wish for your opponent to think you will."

"And if they call your bluff?" I say.

"Run."

I glare at him.

"What?" he says. "Running is an excellent strategy."

"It is, and so I would like you to demonstrate . . . after putting on a corset and five layers of long skirts."

He taps the knife in my direction. "You forget, Miss Mallory, that I have worn both."

"And run?"

"Like the devil himself was on my tail. When one's very existence is considered an offense to man and God, one learns to run fast, in any outfit . . . or none at all." He pauses and then blushes as he turns to Isla. "My apologies, ma'am. I did not mean to speak quite so freely."

"You never need apologize to me," she says. "But I do believe Mallory has a point. Even if I do not find my dress as encumbering as she does, I am not much of a runner. I would certainly hope that showing my knife would be enough, but if it is not, then I do need to be able to use it."

He waves at us. "Carry on then."

I glance over. "You're going to watch, aren't you?"

"Absolutely. I have not had such entertainment in days."

I ignore him and resume the lesson. We've barely been at it five minutes before the door bursts open, Mrs. Wallace striding out, Alice following.

"What is going *on* here?" Mrs. Wallace bears down on me.

I lift the knife over my head. "It was a lesson, ma'am."

"One I requested," Isla says.

The housekeeper doesn't seem to hear her, just keeps coming at me. "Are you trying to kill the mistress? Or *get* her killed? No one else is going to put up with your shenanigans if Mrs. Ballantyne bleeds to death in a ditch."

"That is a colorful picture," Isla murmurs.

Mrs. Wallace turns to her. "Oh, I can make it far more colorful, ma'am. Your fine self lying dead in a pool of blood because your housemaid decided to teach you how to wield a knife." Her gaze drops to the blade in Isla's hand. "Good lord. Where did you get that?"

Isla's jaw sets. "It was Father's. I have had it for years in a drawer, and now I wish to use it."

"To do what? Kill wild beasts in the jungle? That is a hunting knife." She plucks Catriona's switchblade from my hand. "This is the sort of knife you want, not that monstrosity."

Isla blinks. "I . . . Yes, I suppose that would be—"

"We shall go tomorrow to buy you a proper knife, ma'am. And then I will teach you how to use it. This one"—she jabs the blade at me—"will get you killed with that lunging and stabbing nonsense. She looks like a player on the stage."

Simon snickers, and she wheels on him.

"And you, lad, watching this fiasco and not saying a word. Please tell me *you* know how to use a knife."

"He employs a different defense strategy," I say. "Running for his life."

"And yet Dr. Gray sends you to watch over his sister in his stead? How are you supposed to manage that?"

"I am quite strong," Simon says. "I could probably carry Mrs. Ballantyne as I flee."

Mrs. Wallace waves the knife at him. "You will learn to use one of these, in case the mistress ever requires you to do so. She will also learn. And you, too, Mallory, if I can manage to undo whatever damage has already been done by whoever trained you."

"And me?" Alice pipes up from behind the housekeeper.

"That is up to Mrs. Ballantyne." Mrs. Wallace puts her hand out for Isla's knife. "Now give me that." She pauses and modulates her tone. "Please, ma'am."

Isla mutely hands it over.

"Okay, I've gotta ask," I say, "since no one else is going to. *You* know how to use a knife?"

"Of course," she snaps. "One does not carve a roast ham with one's bare fingers." She catches my look. Then she turns toward the barn, twenty feet away. "The tree there, with the knot in its side. Do you see that?"

I nod.

She draws back her hand and before I can blink, she whips our knives, one after the other. Both embed themselves squarely in the knot.

Then she turns to me. "Do I know how to use a knife, Mallory?"

"Holy—" I cut myself off before I finish the curse.

Alice claps. "Where did you learn to do that?"

"The circus." Mrs. Wallace strides to the door as we all stare after her.

"Wait," I say. "The circus? You were in—"

The door slaps shut behind her. I continue staring. Then I turn to Isla. "Is she serious?"

"I have no idea. There is much I know about Mrs. Wallace, and I have long suspected there is even more that I do not. Now, Alice, are you done with your lessons?"

TWENTY-NINE

Alice *is* finished with her lessons and has gone to help Simon with the horses. Isla and I have retrieved our knives, and we're heading inside when I notice the little gated garden and stop.

"This garden," I say. "Is it . . . ? Er, that is to say, I have heard about such things as . . ."

"Poison gardens," Isla says. "You may say the word, Mallory. I will not take offense. It does grow toxic plants. Not all are dangerous, and none would kill you with a single touch. That is melodrama for works of fiction, where some spinster lady tends her poison garden, purely as a hobby, you know."

"As one does."

I touch the wrought-iron gate around the tiny plot. Isla comes up beside me and starts naming off the contents. Some I know from my macabre interests. Deadly nightshade. Opium poppies. Castor plants. There are a few I'm surprised to see because I recognize them from my dad's garden at home, like hellebore, which Isla says is a purgative and, yep, too much is deadly. Then there's laurel . . .

"It is used for making killing jars," she says.

My brows shoot up. "Killing jars?"

"You put it into a jar with a beetle or butterfly, and it will die. It's very popular with children."

"That's . . . concerning."

"Duncan was particularly fond of them."

"Even more concerning."

She laughs. "I suspect some children might have a disturbing fascination with killing insects, but for Duncan, it was about studying them. Laurel allows them to perish intact."

"Ah, that makes sense. So all these plants also have uses in chemistry, I presume?"

The corners of her mouth twitch. "Not all. While some are for my work, there are several selected purely for interest. Also, it is possible that a few were planted after my marriage, when it behooved me to discreetly remind my husband of my particular skills."

I snort a laugh. "I'll bet."

"Not that I would have ever made him seriously ill. But a tiny pinch of laburnum in his soup did help when I felt particularly helpless in my situation. Even the discomfort of a bad oyster had him thinking I'd found him out on something or other. With Lawrence, there was always something or other."

"I'm sorry."

She shrugs. "Had I been the sort to suffer his infidelities and insults in silence, I suspect there would have been fewer of them. The more I objected, the more he was determined to prove his right to both. I had not been raised to accept either, and so I would not."

"Rightly."

"I thought so. Others disagreed. Annis . . ."

She inhales deeply, and seems about to stop but then plunges forward. "Annis counseled me to turn a blind eye. She did so in her usual imperious manner, but it was not . . . unkindly meant. Let Lawrence do as he would and take full advantage of my position as a married woman, as if it were a business arrangement that was not entirely satisfactory but sufficient to my purposes."

"Like *her* marriage."

"Yes. I wanted more. I wanted what my grandparents had. A love match and a true partnership. Annis could not understand that."

I think I might know why, though I say nothing.

"Communing with my pretty plants?" says a voice behind us.

Even when I look, it takes a moment to realize I'm seeing Annis. She's dressed in what I've come to realize are called widow's weeds. It's a form of mourning modeled after Queen Victoria, and it's only expected of women. Annis's dress is black and heavy enough to conceal her figure. Everything on her—from her shoes to her umbrella—is black, and she has no jewelry. She's expected to wear all this for at least a year, after which she can don more fashionable black dresses and black jewelry. Next comes the stage Isla is at—a full two years after losing her husband—where she can wear shades of gray and other muted colors. It's fine for a woman like Queen Victoria, who chooses such a path, but for women like Annis and Isla, coming out of horrible marriages, it seems like a punishment.

Isla and I both turn as Annis walks over, lifting the heavy veil from her black hat. Sarah lingers behind to speak to the coachman before hurrying to catch up.

"Mallory and I were discussing my garden," Isla says.

"You mean *my* garden. Or it was, before I gifted it to you, my interests having moved on." She glances my way, her eyes glittering. "Or did they?"

Sarah closes her eyes and shakes her head.

"*Annis,*" Isla says sharply. "This is not a game."

"No, it is a matter of life and death. First my husband's and now mine. Your little housemaid is investigating Gordon's murder, along with our brother and his friend. While I appreciate your concern, Isla, it only takes one disgruntled former employee to recall that this garden used to be mine, and then it will seem a sure sign of my guilt."

"Fine." Isla turns to me. "This garden was, as my sister says, hers."

"A very long time ago," Sarah says. "And Annis's interest was purely theatrical."

Annis's brows rise. "Theatrical?"

"You took immense pleasure in tending a garden of poisonous plants because you are a perverse creature who loves to shock the good people of polite society."

"I believe you have mistaken me for someone else, dear Sarah," Annis murmurs. "I am the very model *of* polite society."

Sarah rolls her eyes at that.

Annis turns to Isla. "You wished to speak to me? Something about a Mr. Ware and whether he was involved in my husband's business affairs?"

"Yes."

"I have heard of the man, but only in passing, and not through Gordon. And, yes, I hardly needed to deliver that answer in person, but if I stayed in that house a moment longer, I feared I might indeed murder someone."

"We ought to take lodgings at a hotel, Annis," Sarah says.

"And let Helen toss my belongings into the rubbish heap? No. It is still my house, and I will stay there and graciously allow her to do the same, until I have removed everything that is indisputably mine."

I glance at Isla.

"What is that look for, girl?" Annis says. "You have something to say. Speak. I know you are quite capable of it. Too capable."

"We have a witness who reports seeing you at Mr. Ware's office yesterday, arguing with him about your husband's business dealings."

Her brows rise. "My husband was murdered yesterday. I would hardly go off chasing business matters under such circumstances."

"No?"

She pauses. "All right. I would. But I did not. When did this witness purport to see me?"

I hesitate as I realize I should have pressed Morris for more details. No matter—I know his business address. "I will obtain that information, ma'am."

"Then do so, because I was not at Mr. Ware's offices. As far as I know, I have never met him. If he does have business with my husband, I know nothing of it."

"I was under the impression you *ran* your husband's business."

She gives me a thin smile. "My husband allowed me to 'play' businesswoman—as he put it—because such a thing is for people like me, born to the middle class. I have a natural ability for it. In the genes, apparently, and men like him lack it because they have evolved—as Mr. Darwin would put it—to a higher level of being."

"One would think that survival of the fittest means having the skills to make money. So that one might actually survive."

"Why do they need to make money, my dear, when they get it from the poor? And from those of us in the middle class who happily labor for them in recognition of their superior qualities? Yes, I ran his business, but that does not mean I know *all* his business. I gave Gordon money to play with. It kept him happy."

"Play with?"

"Investments and such."

"Would they have anything to do with the funerary business?"

"Oh, I am certain they did. My husband had early success with such speculation—thanks to my father and later to me—and he is not a man to stray from what worked once, even if it did not seem to *keep* working quite as well."

"Without you or your father to advise him."

"Yes, but Gordon made enough to keep him occupied. Between that and his mistresses and his hunting, I hardly ever saw him. This is why I did not kill my husband, child. I had no reason to do so. We had reached a point where we quite happily pursued our own lives, rarely intersecting."

"You have your own money."

"I do. When I took over the business, I made Gordon promise that I could keep five percent as a managerial fee, for ribbons and whatnots. I invested much better than he did."

"So Helen inherits the house and the title."

"Yes."

"And the money and business?"

Here she sighs and leans a hip against the poison-garden fence. "His money, yes. The business, however, goes to me, and without the income it generates—or the ability to sell it—I daresay she will not be able to keep the house."

"That's what your husband wanted to change before he died. To give her the business as well as the money."

"Yes. But I hardly cared. The business is not truly mine. I will sell it, and I will appreciate the proceeds, but I do not need them. I have enough to live very comfortably."

"You mean start your own business," Sarah murmurs.

"Certainly not. I am going to retire to a house in the country, where I shall put on grand dinner parties and rarely rise from my very comfortable divan."

Sarah looks at me. "That is a joke. She will start her own business. She would go mad otherwise."

"If the police investigate, they'll want to see the will and your investment portfolio," I say.

"Investment portfolio? What a fancy name for it." She waves a hand. "They shall have what they require. My papers are at the ready. Now, Isla? Are you going to provide your sister with a cup of tea? Or must I go begging for refuge elsewhere?"

"Come in. I'll ask Mrs. Wallace to fix us something."

THIRTY

I don't go with Annis and Isla for tea. I am still the maid, and I can't raise Annis's suspicions higher. Also, I need time to think things through. I stay in the courtyard, leaning on the wrought-iron fence, staring into the poison garden. I barely have time to focus my thoughts before a soft voice says, "Miss Mitchell?"

I glance to see Sarah with the back door open. I think she's inviting me in, but then she steps out and shuts the door behind her.

"May I speak to you?" she says.

I nod, and she comes to stand beside me.

"I can only imagine what you must think of Annis," she says after a moment.

I make a noncommittal noise.

Sarah continues, "She would hate to hear me saying this, but she is not as terrible as she seems. Not as terrible as she wishes to be seen. Perhaps not even as terrible as she wishes to *be*."

Another noncommittal noise.

"Annis is many things, most of them making her difficult and even unlikable."

"I do not think she wants to be likable."

Sarah sighs. "That is the problem, Miss Mitchell. I do not merely tease when I call her a perverse creature. She delights in being difficult, in doing and saying the unexpected and the ill-advised, and I fear it will . . ."

She swallows. "I fear it will take her to the gallows, and she will not see it coming until the noose is around her neck."

"It's easy to be difficult when one never has to suffer the consequences."

Sarah lowers her gaze. "That is true. I did not grow up in the same circumstances as Annis. My family was respectable but poor, and it is quite a different thing. Annis never understood that. She would chide me for accepting a tutor's harsh words, while I was only happy to have a tutor, which I only did by the grace of her dear mother. If Annis balked or skipped lessons, the tutor didn't dare even tell her mother. If I had done the same, he'd have refused to teach me. There were so many things she could do that I could not, and she would grow very cross with me for not defying convention more . . ."

Sarah shakes it off. "That has nothing to do with the current situation."

"Which is that you fear Lady Leslie will tie her own noose by doing things like telling me this used to be her garden when there was no need to do so."

"Yes."

"She was still correct that it would have looked suspicious if it came out later. Also, it was a secret she otherwise needed Mrs. Ballantyne and Dr. Gray to keep, as they knew it was her garden. That wouldn't be fair, though I doubt that was her primary concern."

"Do not be so certain. Annis would find it difficult to admit she is concerned for her siblings. For some women, sentimentality can feel like weakness."

"Because we are told we are emotional creatures, sentimental and silly, and to be taken seriously we must disown those parts of ourselves. I am not certain how attachment to one's family is sentimentality, though. Disengagement feels more like distancing, which is understandable if those family members have done something to deserve it. If they have not?" I shrug.

Sarah drops her gaze more and fidgets. "I spent my youth making apologies for Annis, to those who could not understand my attachment. I told myself that if I ever returned to her favor, I would no longer do that. But it is no less difficult now than it was before."

I'm about to say something when the coach appears in the mews, Gray swinging out of it before it has fully stopped.

"Mallory," he says, bearing down. "Good. You are here. We must—"

He slows as he notices Sarah on my other side. "Oh. I . . . did not see you there, Sarah." He straightens and pulls at his cravat. "I apologize for my outburst."

She smiles. "Never apologize for your enthusiasm, Duncan. It is delightful to see that you have not lost it. I remember I first thought you such a quiet and studious lad. Then something would seize your interest and you were quite transformed."

Gray makes a noise, as if he isn't quite certain what to say to that.

Sarah touches his arm with her fingertips. "I am glad to see you well, Duncan. You and Isla both. I will leave you and Miss Mitchell to your investigation and join your sisters in their tea."

She heads inside, and Gray stands there, looking momentarily adrift, his burst of enthusiasm evaporated.

"Dr. Gray?" I say.

He snaps back. "Yes, we must talk."

"We must. But before that, I have a question that is going to seem very personal, and I apologize in advance, but I assure you, it's pertinent to the case."

He frowns. "Personal? About me?"

"About Sarah."

The confusion only grows, which means my first guess—that he'd had a crush on Sarah or even a youthful entanglement—was indeed wrong, as Isla said. Yes, Gray is flustered by Sarah, and a past attachment seems the obvious answer, but it is not. Which leads to my second guess.

"Your sister and Sarah," I say. "Did they have a, uh, Sapphic relationship?"

He blinks.

"I'll put it more plainly. Were they lovers?"

"I know what 'Sapphic' means, Mallory, and you did not need to be quite so circumspect with me. I am only trying to figure out where that guess came from."

"I'm a detective, and as you said, I'm better at observing people than things. The clues are there, and when I hedged around it with Isla, she mentioned that, as a boy, you accidentally saw something involving Sarah, which Annis misrepresented. I'm going to guess you saw them together, and to keep you from telling anyone, Annis claimed you'd spied—indiscreetly—on Sarah."

He hesitates. Then says, "I would not have told anyone what I saw."

"I know," I say softly.

As soon as the words leave my mouth, I realize that's presumptuous of me, but Gray only nods.

"Thank you," he says. "I would like to think that it is obvious I am not such a person. I was not at that age either. I believe Annis panicked and lashed out, as she is wont to do."

"Which doesn't make it okay. I'm sorry. That must have been . . . difficult."

"Humiliating," he says abruptly. "Humiliating and shaming, and even then I did not tell her secret. I only admit it now because you guessed it, and you believe it might be an issue for her case."

"Motivation."

He frowns.

"Let's back up," I say. "Annis and Sarah had a romantic relationship, presumably until Annis married. Sarah objected to the marriage, understandably. Annis went through with it and severed ties with Sarah. If Annis was determined to deny that part of herself, even keeping Sarah as a friend might have undermined that. Especially when Annis's marriage was not exactly a loving one." I consider. "Though if she was visiting Queen Mab, she was still having marital relations with her husband, at least sporadically."

"A man like Gordon would have insisted on it." He pauses. "Though it may be indelicate of me to say so."

"There's no need for delicacy with me. Lord Leslie struck me as a man who likes to conquer. No matter how many mistresses he had, he'd have expected to exercise his conjugal rights. The visits to Queen Mab were likely to ensure Annis didn't have children. But the real problem here is that it could provide motivation for murder. Annis didn't seem to have any. She might not get along with her husband, but she gains little from his death. But what if she has reunited with the love of her life? She could discreetly resume their relationship, I suppose . . ."

"Does my sister strike you at the discreet sort? She might have been careful at one time, but she has grown far bolder with age, and far more accustomed to doing as she likes. No, I think I see your meaning now. Even if she attempted discretion and Gordon found out?" He shakes his head. "He might be relentlessly unfaithful himself, but he would not abide it from his wife, particularly if the person cuckolding him is a mere woman."

"If Annis kills Gordon, where does that leave her and Sarah? Could they be together? A widow living with her dear friend? I don't know what it's like for lesbians in this time, but I had a great-aunt who spent her adult life living with her best friend."

His lips quirk a little. "Two spinsters, sadly unable to find husbands, forced to live out their lives, just the two of them. Yes, that is quite how it is in this time. It is one of the few things women have easier than men. If two bachelor friends live together, everyone suspects they are homosexuals, even if they are not. Two women?"

"The poor old dears. At least they have each other."

"Precisely, and to answer your question, yes, that is what Annis and Sarah could do, particularly now that Annis is widowed. It does not mean I think she *has* murdered Gordon, but it provides motivation."

Gray and I stand in silence at the poison-garden fence. Then his head jerks up.

"Oh!" he says. "I quite forgot why I came in such a rush. Bloody hell. Hugh will be waiting and . . ." He shakes it off. "Come. Simon has watered Folly, and the coach is the fastest way there."

"The fastest way where?"

"To the police office. A woman was caught sneaking into the Burns house this morning to fetch clothing."

"Ah. Mrs. Burns, I presume."

"Yes." A dramatic pause. "The *first* Mrs. Burns."

THIRTY-ONE

We're at McCreadie's police office. It's in the higher-income end of the district where the Burnses live—which is why it caught the case. The lead detective—Crichton—is also the asshole who took the lead on the raven killer case after McCreadie worked the first murder.

Okay, I can't say for sure that the lead detective is an asshole. I've never met him. I have seen him speak, though, pompously addressing the press, and I've certainly heard Gray's opinion of him. McCreadie is more circumspect, and I give him full credit for that.

I won't say McCreadie only cares about solving the case. That'd be disingenuous. Like me, McCreadie is ambitious. But like me, he's decided that the best way to get ahead is to do the work and prove himself. While it's not the fastest ladder up, it is the steadiest.

McCreadie is the kind of guy that senior officers love to bring on their team, because he works hard and lets them take the credit. That means he's the first to be pulled onto a high-profile case, which suits him just fine.

When we enter the station, Crichton is nowhere to be found. Thankfully, he's off doing actual case work. While I'd offered to try convincing Addington to let us exhume Burns, Detective Crichton has taken on the task. He has acknowledged that Addington is wrong about it being arsenic, and while he's not certain about this "thallium nonsense," the arsenic error should be enough to get the body exhumed. Whether Addington agrees is a whole other matter, and it will likely need to go over his head, which will be awkward. If Detective Crichton is handling that, then he's doing exactly what I'd want from my superior officer—to tackle the political wrangling while I pursue leads.

On the way to the police office, I explained what we found at Ware's office. Simon has dropped us off outside the back door, and Gray ushers me into a room where McCreadie is waiting. I quickly bring him up to date.

"So of our four victims," McCreadie says, "we have a gravedigger, a solicitor who worked with funerary clients, and an earl who invested in the funerary business. I like that a lot better than the 'murderous wives' theory."

"Agreed," Gray says. "Though if this Cyrus Morris fellow saw Annis at Mr. Ware's office, a new theory may not clear her of suspicion."

"It will shift the motive from personal to professional, while making her responsible for more than her husband's death." McCreadie glances at me. "Do you see something there that I am missing? A reason Annis would murder a gravedigger and a salesman?"

"No," I say. "But we'd need to link Burns to the other three to know what *anyone's* motive could be. I know he got himself in hot water with some shady deals, and I know the funerary business can be shady, apologies to Dr. Gray."

"None needed," Gray murmurs. "I am well aware of the problems in my profession. It is too easy to take advantage of the grieving."

"Do you have copies of the legal cases against Burns?" I ask McCreadie.

"They were delivered this morning. I was already going to suggest that you speak to the first Mrs. Burns alone, as you seem to put women at ease. Why don't you do that while Duncan and I read through the legal cases?"

"Sounds like a plan."

The first Mrs. Burns still goes by that name. The marriage might have been illegal, but her children deserve their father's surname as a shield of legitimacy in a world that requires it.

Gray said Mrs. Burns was discovered sneaking into her former spouse's apartment. More accurately, she had not "snuck" but walked straight in, under the guise of being a neighbor fetching a pot that the second Mrs.

Burns had borrowed. She'd been caught gathering clothing and then claimed it was hers, stolen by her former husband for his new wife.

The first Mrs. Burns—Clara—is being held in a tiny room, not unlike the sort where I've interviewed witnesses and suspects. I enter carrying a tray with a teapot.

"Mrs. Burns, ma'am?" I say.

The woman at the table looks about forty, which I've come to realize for the Victorian poor means she's probably closer to thirty. She's trim and pleasant looking with gray-streaked dark hair and a smile that is both kind and wry, as if she's nothing more than a wee bit embarrassed at being taken into police custody.

"I'm Mallory," I say. "I have been asked to bring you tea and sit with you until Detective McCreadie is finished with his business."

"Is Detective McCreadie the braw one with the whiskers?" Braw means handsome. While she has a thick brogue, there's also a careful choice of words that suggests an above-average education.

"He is, and I am a poor substitute, I know."

She laughs at that, a soft and genuine laugh. I serve the tea and then sit.

"Is that sugar?" she says, pointing at the tiny pot.

I pass it to her, and she stirs in three spoonfuls and then sips it, sighing with pleasure.

"Perhaps I will not mind going to prison after all," she says. "My eldest is old enough to care for the wee ones a day or two."

"Having been in a prison cell, I don't think there's sugar," I say. "Possibly tea, but I certainly wouldn't drink it."

"You do not look the sort of lass who ends up in prison."

"It was a single night, for a mistake." I sip my own tea. "As I suspect this is also a mistake."

"It is. The clothing is mine."

"Hmm." Another sip. "Bad enough your husband left you for another woman. To take your clothing, too?"

"Oh, it is only the clothing that I miss."

I laugh under my breath. "Still, it would grate something terrible, knowing his new wife is wearing your dresses."

She sets down her teacup. "Let me settle a misunderstanding, which I hope you can pass along to the handsome Detective McCreadie. I bear my successor no ill will. In fact, I pity her. My burden has been shifted to her shoulders, and the lass deserves better."

"Your burden being your late husband."

"My late *supposed* husband, yes. I fear you will find my story falls far short of the melodrama one might expect from my tale of woe. Cast off for a younger woman. Discovering I was never wed, and my children are bastards, their wretched father refusing to pay a hap'ney for their care, because how does he truly know they are his, when I am so wanton as to bear children out of wedlock?"

"Your *children* are not the bastards," I mutter.

She smiles thinly. "I have heard that. I have said that, too. When he first left, I was as frantic as one might imagine. But then a miracle occurred. Once I was left in charge of the family purse, even without his contributions it grew fatter. It is amazing how much money a family can save when they are not also supporting a husband's mistress. My children and I are fine, miss. Better without him than we'd been with him. It is only the shame we must escape, and I intend to do so once I have the money saved to join my sister's family in the country. She has a little empty cottage on her farm, and while she is offering for free, I want to be able to pay proper rent, and it may take time to settle on new work there."

"I am glad you are finding your way, ma'am, and free of your husband. I do not blame the new Mrs. Burns for what she did to escape such a man."

I try not to hold my breath awaiting the response. I don't need to. It comes quickly.

"She did no such thing," Clara says, in a tone more exasperated than offended. "Only a fool poisons her husband these days and thinks to get away with it. The moment a man falls ill with a stomach complaint, all eyes fall on his wife. The girl is no fool. Fool*ish* to have wed him, but I did the same at her age, and I would like to think I was not a fool—only a girl with an empty place in her heart that a clever tongue could fill."

"You do not think she killed him?"

"I know she did not."

"Because you have spoken to her. You know where she is. You were taking that clothing to her."

She flinches and then quickly sips her tea before giving a thin smile. "That would be a poor tale, would it not? The abandoned wife aiding the lass who stole her husband? It is a very unsatisfying sort of melodrama."

I shrug. "Two women recognizing they have both fallen prey to the same man? The first wife recognizing that *he* is the villain rather than the other woman? That is the best sort of story."

"I am not harboring my husband's former mistress."

No, just stealing clothing that McCreadie says would be several sizes too large for you, the second Mrs. Burns being a plump and buxom young woman.

I sip my own tea. "That is unfortunate. If you were, I would ask you to take a message to her. There is a certain pudding we found in the icebox that she made for him—"

She cuts me off with a sharp laugh. "*Made* for him? Did he actually believe such a tale? The girl toasts bread into charcoal."

"Which you know because . . . ?"

"Because he would come by to see the children, or so he said, but it was always at suppertime. When I said *she* could make his supper, he'd tell me terrible tales of her cooking. No, she did not make any pudding. She may have said so, but she did not." A moment's pause. Then she says, "Was the pudding poisoned?"

"If you see her, could you ask her where it came from?"

She doesn't answer.

"I have another question," I say. "One for you."

"You seem to have a lot of them, for a wee lass who only brings the tea."

I shrug. "Curiosity is my utmost failing."

She shakes her head but says, "Ask your question."

I'm about to when the door opens, and McCreadie strides in, papers in hand.

"Mrs. Burns," he says.

"I prefer Clara."

A quick nod. Then he sets the papers down. "I have been investigating your former husband's business dealings, as we consider other motives for his murder."

"*That* is where you should start," she murmurs. "Women were not the only victims of his lies and his charm."

"So we have discovered. I wish to discuss these." He pushes them forward. "I can read them to you if—"

"I know my letters, sir. I always thought that was why Andrew Burns married me. He could scarcely decipher a newspaper. He would bring all his business papers home for me to read to him. I even wrote his replies."

She skims the papers on the table and pokes one with a finger. "I remember this one. The man found our apartment and came right inside, shouting at me while Andrew was away."

"That must have been difficult," I say.

She shrugs. "I didn't blame the poor fellow. He had lost his wife, and he thought he was getting a proper burial for her. He had paid Andrew to make sure she was six feet under, and then he went and saw the gravediggers at work only to discover they were removing other bodies to make room for her."

"They were . . ." I stare at McCreadie. "They were taking out bodies to put in new ones?"

"There is a limited amount of burial space in the kirkyards," he says.

I gape before reading the page myself. "And the case was *dismissed*?"

Clara's brow furrows, likely at my choice of words, and McCreadie says, "The court did not pursue it."

I scowl. "Because the poor man paid to have his wife buried six feet down and he got it. What he did *not* get was a promise that she would stay there."

"Yes, it is a common enough practice," McCreadie says to me. "Bodies are buried on top of one another in full kirkyards, and if you wish to be buried deeper, you pay for that, and others—who have no such assurances—are moved."

"Moved *where*?" I wave off my own question. I don't want to know. "I know the church—*kirk*yards are overcrowded, as you said. That is where private cemeteries come in."

"But it is not always easy to convince people that such burials will still permit entry to heaven." He looks at Clara. "Excuse our digression, ma'am. Miss Mitchell is new to Edinburgh, and some things require explanation."

"You provide it very kindly, sir," she says. "My mother used to say one can judge a man's character by how he treats animals. I have learned she was wrong. A man can be very kind to animals and terrible to people. A better measure is how he treats women." Her gaze drops to his hand. "You will make some woman a fine husband someday."

"Oh, I do not know about that, but you are very kind to say so. As for this case, was the selling of such burial plots common for your husband?"

"At one time. He had quite the swindle going."

"His alone?" McCreadie asks. "Or did he work with anyone?"

The answer hits me then, my gaze lifting to McCreadie's as he holds himself calm awaiting the answer.

"He worked with a couple of men," she says. "They dug the graves."

"Would you happen to know the names of any of them?"

Now she's the one going still. She looks up at McCreadie. "That man who died before my former husband. He was a gravedigger, was he not?"

McCreadie says nothing, but Clara hurries on. "I do not recall their names. It was years ago. But I do know where Andrew kept his papers, if that helps."

McCreadie smiles. "It would help immensely, ma'am."

Under that smile, she flushes, and then fidgets, as if embarrassed by her reaction. It is quite a smile, and McCreadie uses it to full advantage.

"Do you know whether he was still involved in any funerary business?" I ask.

At her frown, McCreadie interprets. "Any form of business that touches upon matters of death, whether it is burial plots or friendly societies or even renting coaches for funerals. If his current business is remotely related to that, it could prove helpful."

She shakes her head. "I have not known his business since he left. The new Mrs. Burns is also well educated. She was a governess before she . . . Well, she had a bit of trouble with the master of the household. She reads and writes even better than I do." She touches her fingers to her teacup. "Or so I have heard."

"I understand," I say. "But as you *did* have recent contact with him— perhaps when he came around hoping for supper—he might have mentioned his current business. If that is something you could think upon after you leave . . ."

"I could certainly do that. You are right, miss. I might recall some bit of useful information later, either about that or the pudding."

McCreadie cocks a brow my way, but I ignore it. "That would be wonderful. Then I believe Detective McCreadie might have a few more questions for you?"

"I do not," he says. "If you can promise me that you will be at home— and that you will send me anything more you recall—I see no reason to hold you further."

"Thank you, sir." She glances at the teapot and sugar bowl. "Might I have another cup?"

"You may," I say as I lift it. "And if you do remember anything of use, I am quite certain I could find a packet of sugar to send home with whoever brings us the message."

She smiles. "You do know the way to a woman's heart, miss."

Clara is gone, and we're in the other room, with Gray anxiously awaiting an update, which I provide.

"She is almost certainly harboring the second Mrs. Burns," Gray says. "From whom you hope to gain information on the origins of the pudding and whether any of Burns's current business involves things that might also have interested Lord Leslie and Mr. Ware."

"That's the idea," I say. "I bribed her with sugar."

McCreadie says, "She is also going to supply us with the whereabouts of Burns's business papers, which might lead to a connection with Mr. Young."

"Will that require more sugar?" Gray asks.

"Do you have a shortage?"

"Oh, it is *my* sugar you are bargaining with, is it?"

McCreadie pulls out a chair and sits. "It is certainly not the sugar of a police office, paid for by the people."

"Do the people want this poisoner caught or not?" Gray says.

"Depends," I say. "If they keep targeting guys like Young, Burns, and Leslie, maybe not."

Gray shakes his head. "I am teasing about the sugar. You may have a pound if it helps. You simply need to sneak it past Mrs. Wallace."

"You're kidding, right? Did you know she was a circus knife thrower?"

McCreadie laughs. "Best not let Mrs. Wallace hear you making such jests."

"Oh, I don't think it's a—"

The door opens, a young man bursting in, panting slightly, and I make a mental note not to push the circus connection. That doesn't mean I'm dropping it, though, I will get an answer to this . . . eventually.

McCreadie rises. "Samuel . . . ?"

The young man—not much more than a boy—grips the back of his chair as he catches his breath. "I went to speak to that fellow. The clerk who bought the new office."

"Cyrus Morris, yes. What—?" McCreadie stops, his face paling. "Is he all right?"

"Y-yes, sir. I mean, he is in good health. Cyrus Morris, that is. He is in fine health."

"All right . . ."

"But he does not know anything about a visit to Mr. Ware's office this morning."

McCreadie frowns. "He claims not to have been there?"

"He *was* not there, sir. He said he did not know what I meant about an urgent signing of the rental, as it was already signed and delivered yesterday. He was most confused, and also very distraught to learn that Mr. Ware has passed."

"Would you describe Mr. Morris?" I ask.

The young constable looks from me to McCreadie.

"Please, Samuel," McCreadie says. "Miss Mitchell was the one who met him at the office while she was going through Mr. Ware's papers."

Samuel nods and glances my way before his gaze settles on my forehead. "Yes, miss. He was about thirty, with brown hair."

"Sideburns?" I quickly amend to, "Whiskers?"

"I did not notice any."

"And his size, his build?"

"He was somewhat portly, miss."

I look at McCreadie. "That wasn't the man who came to the office."

THIRTY-TWO

So the guy who came to Ware's office was an imposter. An imposter who knew the name of one of Ware's clients and happened to know that same person was closing a deal for an office rental. That's going to seriously limit the suspects, and McCreadie and I have a few ideas. One is that the fake Mr. Morris knows the real one. McCreadie is going to follow up on that by returning with Samuel. Meanwhile, Gray and I will chase down another possibility.

We walk to Ware's house. News of his death hasn't hit the papers yet. Which means his town house is quiet save for a neighboring staff member with the housekeeper, Mrs. Hamilton, who is in the parlor, sitting there, staring into nothing.

"Mrs. Hamilton?" the neighbor says. "The police would like to speak to you."

She braces, then looks up and sees us. I won't say she seems relieved, but she pulls herself together briskly as she rises.

"Come in, Dr. Gray," she says. She glances over our shoulders.

"It is only us," Gray says. "We told your neighbor we worked with the police, and she misconstrued. We are, however, here on a police matter."

"Of course." She waves us toward the chairs. "May I bring tea?"

"No need," Gray says. "We are only stopping in briefly."

She settles into a chair.

"As you may recall, my assistant here, Miss Mitchell, was assisting the police by conducting the search of Mr. Ware's rooms."

"Yes."

"A gentleman came to retrieve an urgent document, and upon his providing details to prove the document was his, she gave it to him. We have since discovered he was an imposter."

Her eyes round, and her gaze shoots to me.

Gray continues, "It was not Miss Mitchell's fault. My sister was also there, and the young man did provide the name of the client and information from his papers. That leads us to hope you might be able to identify him as a colleague of Mr. Ware's. Perhaps a fellow solicitor."

"Oh, I do not know Mr. Ware's colleagues, sir. My business was the house."

"May we provide you with his particulars? In hopes Mr. Ware may have entertained him in the house?"

"He did not entertain here," she says. "Not guests nor friends nor colleagues. It was very much the two of us. He went out, to be sure, but he rarely brought anyone in."

"Let us hope this was an exception."

When Gray nods my way, I describe the young man.

"Oh!" Mrs. Hamilton says. "I most certainly do know him, and that makes quite a lot of sense. He would know Mr. Ware's business quite intimately. It is his clerk, Mr. Fischer."

I try not to wince. Ware's clerk. Of course. No one knows my mother's cases better than her clerks. For a matter like a rental contract, Ware would likely have given that over entirely to the young man. The paperwork had been completed yesterday, and Mr. Fischer knew there was a copy in the file.

"Thank you," I say. "Where would I find this Mr. Fischer?"

"I wouldn't know, miss. As I said, I know nothing about Mr. Ware's business."

Gray pushes harder. Can she give us anything, be it a street name or a neighborhood or even a public house the two might have frequented after hours? Mrs. Hamilton has only a name: John Fischer.

"He's only been working for Mr. Ware for a few months now," she says. "I've scarcely met him more than a half-dozen times. He popped in downstairs here now and then to fetch lunch for the master."

"A few months?" I say.

"Perhaps four or five? His former clerk retired."

"Might we take another look upstairs in the office?" I ask. "In case Mr. Fischer's address is there?"

"Certainly."

"So the clerk pretended to be a client," Gray says as we enter the office.

"Hmm."

"If he merely wanted information, he could have introduced himself properly. Which suggests he was after something else and that taking Mr. Morris's documents was a distraction."

"Hmm."

We enter the office proper, and Gray looks about at the stacks of papers.

"Yes," I say. "It was like this when Fischer entered. You're being very circumspect, circling around the obvious question of how closely I watched him. Whether he'd have had the opportunity to steal anything. The answer is that I didn't leave him alone in the room, but I wasn't exactly keeping an eagle eye on him."

I walk to the desk. "When I handed him the rental papers, he asked for string to bind them. Taking the string put him at the desk covered in stacks of paper. He 'accidentally' knocked a stack off. He tried to clean it up, but I wasn't about to let a client rifle through legal papers. However . . ."

"While you were cleaning them up, he had access to the desk and the pages stacked there."

"Yes. Isla had moved into the next room. Fischer wouldn't have had a lot of time, but if he'd already seen what he wanted on the desk, he could have grabbed it and added it to his own papers in his satchel."

Gray splays a few client files on the desk. "There is a lot of paper here. I do not expect you would know what is missing."

"Actually, I might. I made a list of the client names and their business as I was going through their files. The list is back at the house."

Gray volunteers to retrieve my notes while I do my work, which is pretty much just standing and staring at the desk and trying to remember both how it looked when Fischer arrived and exactly what he'd done. I'd arranged client files—pages from their pouches—in stacks. How many pages could he have been holding before I'd have noticed it was more than his own supposed documents? I hadn't been paying that much attention, and as soon as I'd risen with the dropped pages, he'd put his papers into his satchel. I'd have noticed an inch-thick stack, but it could have been anything smaller.

Whatever he wanted had to be openly visible on the desk. And it wouldn't be in the stack he knocked on the floor. Nor, as I think of it, any close enough to his goal that he'd get in my way when I picked up the scattered pages.

"I have it," I say when Gray returns. "He definitely took pages from this stack, and possibly also from this one." I tap a second stack.

"That is remarkable memory work," Gray says as he hands over my notes.

"The process of deduction. Elementary, my dear doctor."

He arches one brow.

I point to the stacks on the desk. "I narrowed it down to the likely area on the desk he accessed. Then I cheated a bit and speculated that it has something to do with a funerary connection. Unfortunately, there were a number of client files in that quadrant. However, I am absolutely certain pages are missing from these two stacks, because the remaining ones were askew, and I left everything tidy."

"That is an excellent deduction."

"Right? I'm a freaking genius." I take my notes, skim for the name on the file, and crow in success. "We have a winner! This was a new client who had invested in a cemetery, which suggests we are on the right track with our theory."

"And the other one?"

"Slow your roll, Doctor. I need to consult my notes, and this is a much bigger stack." I find the entry and skim it. "Okay, looks like Ware handled a lot for this Primrose fellow. My notes say Primrose had invested in burial societies and cemeteries among other things. I see pages for both still in here, so I can't tell exactly what's missing. There were multiple investments in funeral businesses, and some are still here."

"Primrose, you said?"

I check the file. "Neil Primrose."

"*Lord* Primrose?"

"Uh . . ." I flip through. "His address is one of those fancy house names."

"Fancy . . . ?"

"Where you can write Rosehip House on the envelope and expect the post office to know where to send it."

"Rosehip House is Lord Primrose's Edinburgh home. Lord Primrose . . . who is also a school friend and hunting companion to the late Lord Leslie."

"And *that's* a lead."

Back at the house, we send word to McCreadie via Simon. Annis's coach is there, having apparently returned to pick her up, and I slow to see the crest on the door.

"Yes," Gray says. "It is, as you reported, a lion under two chevrons."

"Only I didn't report that. I *relayed* the report . . ."

"Which came from Mr. Morris, who is not Mr. Morris at all, but Mr. Ware's clerk, rather desperate to cover a few of his master's business dealings."

"And if he's desperate to throw us off the trail, what better way than to toss us a scapegoat, in the form of a woman already suspected of murdering her husband in the same manner as his boss died."

Gray exhales. "Yes." He straightens again. "Which is not to say that he absolutely couldn't have seen Annis there."

I resist the urge to lay my fingers on his arm, but I do soften my voice. "I think you can safely say that is *not* the case, Dr. Gray. Remember that Annis honestly seemed not to know Ware. We were trying to find out when 'Morris' saw her so that she could provide an alibi. But Morris is Fischer, who lied. Fischer knew she was suspected of killing her husband, and so it was easy to pretend he'd heard her arguing with Mr. Ware the day before he died, and he heard nothing useful except that the alleged argument was about her husband. He didn't see her, conveniently, and only caught sight of the carriage. It wasn't even a clever lie. Like Annis said, why would she be running about the city the day after her husband's death?"

"He saw an opportunity with you there, and so he quickly formulated a story."

"Yep. But Lord Leslie is still dead, and papers belonging to one of his good friends were stolen by the next victim's clerk. So there's a connection, and we need to talk to Annis about that."

He nods and pushes open the back door. We go inside to hear voices from the next level up, where we find Annis, Sarah, and Isla finishing a late lunch.

"And here is Duncan," Sarah says with a smile. "In time for dessert, as always." She glances at Isla. "Does he still do that? Find himself much too busy for the meal but suddenly appear once it is time for dessert?"

Isla returns the smile. "On occasion, yes."

Discomfort crosses Gray's face. I understand that look better now. It's partly because Sarah reminds him of an awkward secret he holds, but it's also the discomfort of having an old family friend reminisce about your childhood antics when you are well past being a child.

Sarah is only being kind, and I personally appreciate the insight into a young Duncan Gray, but it's like having an elderly aunt pull out your baby pictures.

"Duncan is not here for dessert," Annis says as she cuts into a coconut cake. "He is here to ask something, as is that girl of his."

Isla makes a noise in her throat.

"Fine," Annis says. "That *assistant* of his."

"Her name is Miss Mitchell. Or Mallory, if you prefer."

Annis only shakes her head and says, "Speak, Duncan. Before you burst."

His eyes narrow slightly, and he pulls out a chair, motioning for me to do the same.

"Oh, now he is being contrary," Annis says. "I have accused him of something as insulting as enthusiasm, and so he will prove me mistaken. Cutting off his nose to spite his face."

"Do you know a Lord Primrose?" I say, as I pass a slice of cake to Gray. "Lord Neil Primrose of Rosehip House."

"Unfortunately."

"We need to speak to him. This afternoon if possible."

"Well, unless you can fly, that will prove difficult. He is on safari in Africa."

"How about Mr. Bailey?" I say, naming the client whose file had missing pages. "Do you know him?"

Annis takes another bite of cake and then says, "I believe he is a confederate of Lord Primrose. A banker perhaps? Or a factory owner? Someone in trade, but rather well off."

I turn to Gray, who is already eating his cake. "How would we find him?"

Annis sighs. "You would ask me to help. My brother is going to be quite useless in such social matters unless Mr. Bailey is a man of science or a comely widow."

Gray's gaze shoots to Annis, but she only takes another bite of her cake. "I will find what you need, Miss Mallory." She glances at Isla. "Is that better?"

A knock at the door sounds before Isla can comment—if she planned to. I push back my chair. "I'll get that."

"Of course you will," Annis murmurs. "You conveniently remember your role when it behooves you to do so." When I hesitate, she waves toward the door. "Go on, girl. Satisfy your curiosity. I'm sure my brother will follow once he has finished his cake."

THIRTY-THREE

I throw open the front door, hoping to see Jack. Instead, my gaze drops to the head of a girl younger than Alice.

Her face tilts up to mine. "Miss Mallory?"

"Yes?"

"My mother sent me to pass along a message to you."

"Oh." I see the resemblance between the girl and the woman I spoke to only hours ago. "You must be Clara Burns's daughter."

She nods. "Edwina, ma'am."

"Come in then. Come in."

She hesitates, but I usher her inside, saying, "I have something for your mother, in return for the message."

She frowns. "But I have not delivered the message yet."

"You have come all this way, and that alone deserves something."

She steps in and then stops there, staring down at the gleaming floor. I have to urge her every step of the way. Now, in my time, a child would—rightfully—be wary following a stranger into a house. This doesn't seem like that. It's the house itself that makes her nervous, as if the housekeeper or butler will appear at any moment, shouting at her to take her "dirty" self back into the streets.

I manage to get her up the next floor and to the dining room door.

"This is Edwina," I say. "She has news from her mother, Clara Burns."

I turn to Edwina. "I believe there's a slice of cake left that I really hate to toss out, if you would like it."

The girl stares at me.

"The child is terrified, girl," Annis snaps. "Take her to the kitchen where she can eat in comfort."

I'm about to snap something back when I catch both Isla and Sarah looking at me, Isla subtly nodding and Sarah's pained look telling me she wishes Annis were not right, but she is.

I see the girl then, and she does indeed look terrified. I'm trying to give her a treat, but to her, I'm forcing her into the lion's den, with the sort of people she has been taught to avoid, lest she say or do something untoward.

"My apologies, Edwina," I say. "Yes, let us take the rest of this cake to the kitchen, and you can deliver your message there."

The scrape of chair legs as Gray rises. "I shall join you." He catches Isla's look. "In a moment. Once I have finished my tea."

I escort Edwina down two levels to the kitchen, where Mrs. Wallace is folding sheets fresh from the laundress. I quickly explain and add, "I promised Edwina's mother some sugar if she could help. Dr. Gray said it would be all right."

I tense, praying Mrs. Wallace isn't going to balk. Sugar is far from the cheap commodity it is in the modern world. The housekeeper seems to consider and then nods at the girl, her gaze softening as she says, "Certainly. I will package up some sugar."

I take Edwina into the room where the staff eats. As I set the cake plate down with a fork, I settle into the seat opposite.

"Your mother sent you with news?"

Edwina eats a bite as she nods. "She says the pudding was delivered. It came in a box addressed to my father, but his new wife couldn't make out the name of the person who sent it. The message said it was a gift for work he had done. The box has been burned." She looks up from her cake. "Mama said you would ask after it."

I smile. "I would have. Thank you."

So someone sent the pudding, and the new Mrs. Burns decided to pretend she made it by destroying the box. She may have suspected it came from a mistress, in which case she'd have no qualms about the subterfuge.

"Mama said you also asked about work my father was doing, and I am to give you this."

She passes over a tiny folded piece of paper. On it is an address.

"Mama does not know what it is for. She said you would ask that, too. All she has is that."

"Which I appreciate, and I will certainly be sending you home with some sugar."

"Thank you, miss." She eyes her half-eaten slice of cake and, with great reluctance, pushes it toward me. "Might I have this wrapped, miss? I have a little brother and sister at home, and Mama says we ought to share when we can."

"I think you can finish that, and I will find a treat for them."

"There is half of the cake left in the cupboard," Gray says as he walks in. "Mrs. Wallace cuts them in two, part for lunch and part for tea. You may take the other half."

I smile over at him. "You'll survive?"

"I will send Alice to the baker's for cream pastries. It is a sacrifice I am willing to make."

"As you prefer cream pastries anyway." I turn to Edwina. "This is Dr. Gray."

The girl eyes him. "You are the gentleman who owns this house?"

"I am."

"And you are a doctor?"

"I am."

Edwina takes a moment to assimilate this before diving back into her cake. "I have a friend who looks like you. His name is Harry. He says when he grows up, he will be a highwayman."

"A noble profession," Gray says with all seriousness.

"I will tell him he could be a doctor and live in a grand house with cake, but I think he will still want to be a highwayman."

"I do not blame him."

The girl continues eating her cake as I tell Gray about the pudding and give him the address.

He fingers the piece of paper and then nods. "That is our afternoon squared then. Will you join me?"

Edwina doesn't look up from her cake as she says, mouth full, "You will want to leave through the front door, sir. My mother said I should come around the back, but I did not like the looks of the man lurking about the gardens."

Gray and I exchange a look. The part-time gardener, Mr. Tull, is Jamaican.

Gray clears his throat. "You mean the man working in the gardens?"

"No, sir. I didn't see anyone working. This fellow was playing the hiding game that Harry likes. Where you hide and watch people. Harry says it is what a highwayman must do. Lurking. That is the word. You lurk behind trees and bushes until a fine coach comes."

"There is a man lurking in my garden?"

"Near it. He was watching the back door, and so I decided to come around the front."

"I think I should—" Gray and I say in unison.

We look at each other for a moment. Then he says, "Your next words were 'Let Dr. Gray investigate,' yes?"

I snort and turn to Edwina. "Mrs. Wallace will bring you the sugar and package the other half of the cake for you. Please thank your mother for us and tell her, if she remembers anything else, we would very much appreciate it."

"We need a plan," I say as I pause at the back door.

"Stride out there, apprehend the prowler, and demand to know what he is about?"

I sigh. "You aren't very good at this, are you?"

"I am quite good at this. You have seen me apprehend brigands. Would you disagree?"

"Let's try a new tactic," I say. "We're going to stroll out, as if nothing is amiss. We'll continue on to the stables, talking. I'm going to suggest we discuss the case. That'll keep him from running. We'll pretend—"

Heels clack down the stairs, and Annis says, "What are you two whispering about?"

"There is a prowler," I say. "The Burns girl spotted him. We are coming up with a plan to flush him out and—"

"Oh, for heaven's sake."

Annis strides past and throws open the rear door before I can stop her. "You there!" she calls.

Though I can see no one in sight, the bushes erupt as a man wheels to flee.

"Go on, Duncan," she says. "Apprehend the fellow."

Gray takes off after the prowler.

"Oh, stop grumbling, girl," Annis says to me. "You are only peeved because your skirts prevent *you* from chasing him."

"Annis . . ." Sarah says, coming up to us with a sigh.

"Tell me I am wrong," Annis says to me.

"You are wrong," I say. "It is not merely the skirts, but also the corset and boots."

"Which you have worn all your adult life, have you not?" Annis gives me a look far too intense for comfort.

"Doesn't mean I have to like them," I mutter.

"Miss Mitchell has not been wearing them nearly as long as we have," Sarah says. "Being young, she has come comparatively recently to such encumbrances. Oh, it looks as if Duncan has caught the fellow."

I hike up my skirts and take off out the door. Sarah's right. Gray is holding a man up against the stable wall.

I zip out to join them as Gray demands to know what the man was doing. The man sputters some excuse and then another until Annis walks by, heading to the coach with Sarah. Once she's past, she calls over her shoulder.

"He is a member of the press, dear brother."

"I know that," Gray says. "The ink stains give it away. As does the printer dust on his trousers. I did not ask who he was, but what he was doing."

"Spying on you, obviously," Annis says.

"On me?" Gray glances over at her.

"Hmm, no. You are correct. He could be spying on me." She walks back and uses her umbrella to chuck the man under the chin. "Am I your prey, dear boy? If so, I might suggest that is a dangerous game to play with an alleged murderess."

"Annis!" Sarah says.

"I did not murder my husband, boy. I would have too little to gain and too much to lose. Simple common sense, really. Duncan, please put the man down, though you have my permission to grab him again if he tries to run. He has gone to great lengths to win an interview, and so I shall grant it."

"Actually . . ." the man says as Gray lowers him to the ground. "I was . . ." His gaze shunts to the house. "Your sister is a chemist, is she not? A chemist whose sister has been accused of using poison?"

Gray stiffens, but Annis only laughs. "A chemist? She is a woman. How ever would she be a chemist? That is nearly as poor an excuse as saying you are here for me. Obviously you have come to spy on my brother here, Dr. Duncan Gray, who is investigating the murder of my husband."

Gray clears his throat. "I am not—"

"He is humble," Annis says. "It is his worst failing. One of them at least. He is also stubborn and overly curious." She looks at the reporter and snaps, "Are you writing this down?"

"Er, yes." He pulls out a notebook and pencil.

"No, Annis," Gray says. "He is not writing anything down. Lady Leslie is joking, of course. The police are the ones investigating—"

"That would be Detective McCreadie, who is my brother's childhood friend. A most winning fellow. Quite clever for one so handsome. The two rarely coincide, sadly. Detective McCreadie is very good at his job. Good enough to enlist the services of my brilliant brother."

Gray clears his throat. "Annis—"

"Did I mention he is overly humble? My brother is a master of detection, who quietly aids the police through his scientific investigation. Have you heard of the Duke Street case? That was Duncan's work. As was the—"

"Annis," Gray says more sharply. "Those cases were solved by the good men of the Edinburgh police."

"With your scientific help, and the city deserves to know that." She looks at the reporter. "I am blessed to have such a team working on my behalf. A brilliant scientist, a clever detective and . . ." She peers at me. "What are you again?"

"A housemaid."

She waves at me. "Speaking of clever, does she not easily pass for a pretty housemaid? You would hardly guess her true identity, would you?"

"Wonder Woman, I hope," I mutter under my breath. "Or at least Nancy Drew."

"She is my brother's assistant," she says. "A budding scientist and detective, who would play the role of housemaid far better if she learned not to mutter under her breath and glare daggers at her social betters."

"Annis . . ." Sarah whispers.

"I am done," Annis declares. She sweeps up her skirts and turns on her heel. "I have said all I need to say. My brother knows I am innocent, and he will find the devil who murdered my husband."

The reporter starts after Annis, shouting questions like she's twenty feet away.

"Did she just save Isla's ass?" I murmur. "Or her own?"

"I have no idea," Gray says, and we hightail it back into the house before the reporter comes after us.

THIRTY-FOUR

I put together a sandwich to go, and then we leave out the front door. Simon is off on errands, and we don't want to wait for the coach, so we take a hansom cab to follow up on the address.

I'm not sure what to think about what Annis did. I want to be furious with her. She distracted that reporter from herself and any suspicions that might fall on her for being at the home of the brother who's helping investigate the murder. Instead of downplaying that, she overplayed it, because *that* is Annis, as I'm coming to learn—theatrical and grandstanding. The press thinks she killed her husband? Oh, look over here at her brother— did you not know the role he's played in solving Edinburgh crime? She might as well have played a one-woman band, marching around him and tossing confetti.

I understand that the reporter seemed to be interested in Isla and Annis was protecting her, and I appreciate that, but if so, why not divert attention her own way instead of Gray's? She shielded her sister—and herself—by throwing her brother to the wolves instead, and that pisses me off.

We knew our mysterious broadsheet writer had suggested Gray played a role in the current investigation, and it was only a matter of time before the press showed up at his doorstep, but when they did, Gray would have ducked and diverted and downplayed. He likes his place in the shadows, quietly helping McCreadie and the police.

I suppose I should be impressed that Annis knows the cases he's investigated, but it only confuses me more. She's embarrassed by her family and yet somehow follows her brother's secret exploits? Maybe she keeps tabs on him so she isn't caught off guard if he's ever shoved into the limelight. Or if it ever benefits her to do the shoving.

"Is this . . . going to be a problem?" I say in the cab.

"For Isla? Hugh and I are already aware of the concern, and he is taking steps to protect her."

Of course he is.

"Which is a different sort of protection, yes?" Gray says. "She would not object to that."

"She would not, although I would strongly suggest he talk to her about it, rather than attempt to shield her completely. She's aware it's an issue, and she was going to speak to him."

"I'll make sure she does."

I glance over. "And what about what Annis did back there? Is it going to be a problem?"

"No," he says firmly. "It is a bit of tittle-tattle. Nothing more. No one cares about science. As for me supposedly solving crimes, it will be seen as mere sibling pride." A thin smile. "Which will amuse anyone who knows Annis."

"I still want to throttle her."

He lifts his shoulders in an elegant shrug. "If I am to give her any credit, she did manage to provide the fellow with scraps he mistook for a meal. Nothing will come of it, and no one will question why she was at the house, as she was obviously the doting sister enlisting the aid of her younger sibling."

I hope so. I really do.

I look out the window. "We're leaving the city?"

"Barely," he says. "The address is on the outskirts. I am not familiar with it myself, but the driver says he'll find it."

The driver may have exaggerated slightly. He makes a few wrong turns and circles around before coming to a stop at the end of a dirt road.

"This is it, sir," the driver calls.

Gray opens the door and frowns.

"Yes, I'm certain," the man says before Gray can ask. "I'm guessing you'd like me to wait."

"Please."

Gray helps me out. Then he gives the man payment for the first half of the trip, so he won't worry if we disappear from sight.

A small marker indicates this is indeed the address on the paper. We look around. It's vacant land and the smell is . . . ripe.

"Bog," Gray says. "Or so I hope, though this *is* downhill from the city."

I shudder. "Prime land then."

"Indeed."

We can pretend it's just a bog, but yes, chances are it's not fresh spring water creating the swampy land. I try not to think too much about Victorian sanitation. Try really, really hard. Oh, it's better than it was, as Isla has explained. At least they're now aware that overcrowded cities mean polluted waterways, which mean disease and death. London has its first proper sewer system, and Edinburgh diverted sewage away from the Water of Leith in a major project a few years ago.

We follow a narrow road. At first, there's nothing to see. It's scrubby, wet, stinking wasteland. After about fifty feet, the road forks. I'm looking both ways when Gray points out deep grooves at the end of the left fork, as if a coach has parked there more than once.

We walk along an ever-narrowing path until we reach the ruins of several rustic stone buildings.

"Diverted water flow," Gray says as he circles it. "It could be natural in nature, but more likely from the city."

"The city installs something that changes the water flow, for their own benefit, and it causes flooding down here, which collapsed the farmhouse and rendered the farmland unfarmable."

"That would be my presumption."

It'd be easy to blame the city for that, but as an urban center grows, its need to bring in fresh water and get rid of wastewater increases. I can only hope the city compensated the farmer for his lost land.

"How long ago do you think it happened?" I ask, gesturing at the ruined buildings.

"A decade or so."

I shade my eyes against a rare burst of sunshine. "And someone has now bought the land and is using it for . . . ?" I frown as I keep looking. "Nothing. Between the smell and the damp ground, it would take twenty-first-century engineers to turn this into usable land. For now, the only thing it's good for is a con job."

Gray's brows lift, as if he doesn't recognize the word.

"Fraud," I say. "Someone is trying to pass this land off as something it isn't. Getting people to invest in a proposed project. But anyone who comes out here will know it's bullshit."

"Yet someone *has* been here, according to those coach tracks."

We walk past a crumbling barn and make it maybe twenty feet, around a small forest, before I say, "Oh!"

Gray shades his eyes. "It appears this piece of land has *one* excellent feature."

"This view," I say.

Edinburgh rises before us over a field of verdant green. A picture-perfect view. Is this how someone is selling the property? Bring prospective investors here, keep them preoccupied—and keep their noses plugged—until they can see this view?

"And here is our answer," Gray says.

I think he means the view. Then I notice the mausoleum. Kind of hard to miss in this wasteland, but it's tucked to the side of the forest we just passed, and I'd been so entranced by the view that I had indeed missed it.

"There's . . . a mausoleum in the middle of nowhere," I say.

"There is indeed," Gray says as he picks his way over.

"Little small, isn't it?"

"It is."

Gray circles the building, which is barely big enough to hold four tightly packed caskets. Something about the perspective seems off, and it takes a moment—

"Samples!" I say.

When he looks over, I explain, "You have sample coffins in your showroom. When I first saw them, I thought they were for babies, given the infant mortality rate. But that's what this looks like. A model mausoleum. Like what you'd show prospective buyers. A scale model that lets them see the proposed outside and *inside*."

I tug open the door to find the interior dark and empty. "Or not."

Gray prowls about the site, viewing the mausoleum from all angles. I'm doing the same when my gaze falls on marks in the dirt. Divots at perfectly distanced intervals. Also footprints. When I notice a spot of silver under a tangle of undergrowth, I bend to lift a leaf.

"Is that mercury?" I ask, pointing at the droplet of liquid metal.

He crouches. "It is indeed." A moment's pause and then he nods. "From a camera. Excellent work, my girl."

"Woof."

His lips twitch in a smile. "I would offer to scratch behind your ears, but I suspect you'd prefer a treat."

"No, *you'd* prefer a treat. I'd like cold, hard cash."

He flips a thruppence my way.

I catch it. "Why thank you, sir. I find I have grown most fond of money."

"Odd. That seems a common condition among those who do not have it." He sobers. "In all seriousness, any time that you require money, Mallory—"

"I'm good." I pocket the coin. "What would I do with more anyway?"

That faint smile returns. "Run off and start your own consulting-detective business?"

"Then go broke and hungry because it's still fifty years before anyone would hire a woman detective. I like being your eager apprentice. Takes the pressure off. If we screw up, it's your fault, 'cause I'm just a girl. It's a wonder I can tie my own bootlaces."

I peer at the mercury spot. From a camera? Why would . . . ?

I laugh as the answer hits me.

"You've figured it out?" Gray says.

"Five minutes after you, I bet."

"Five seconds, at most."

I move into position, over by those divots, which I realize come from a camera tripod. Photography isn't exactly new, but it's not as if every family has a camera or knows how to use one. When we see photos of Victorians, they seem a dour lot, which influences our vision of them as staid and rigid. Believe me, if it took an hour to snap a selfie, you wouldn't be grinning either.

Photos *are* possible, though, and that's what someone has done here. They built a miniature mausoleum and then shot photos of it with the city rising in the backdrop, and it would look amazing. It's the Victorian equivalent of a deepfake. It would seem like a gorgeous full-scale marble mausoleum on an equally gorgeous piece of land.

Picture this for your loved one's afterlife.

"They're selling this land as a cemetery," I say.

"Possibly," Gray says. "More likely, though, they are selling plots. Or, even more likely, groups of plots to speculators who are relatively new to investing."

"People who want in on hot opportunities, but don't have a lot of money to invest and aren't savvy enough to come out for an in-person look."

"They may be focusing on investors from outside Edinburgh, in which case the photographs would suffice. After all, it is a photograph. What other proof is needed?" He stands in the spot, bending slightly for the angle. "It is rather genius."

"Agreed. That's the scheme then. They had Young—the gravedigger—help set this up and possibly even find potential clients. Then Burns, having plenty of experience with fraudulent investments."

"Mr. Ware to handle the legal aspects and give it an air of respectability, as he is renowned for his fairness."

"Mmm. Would it be Ware, though? Or his clerk, Fischer? Fischer gets a job with a respected but elderly lawyer and processes the legal work under the auspices of his office, even luring in some of Ware's own clients, like Primrose."

"True. That seems more plausible. Mr. Fischer did join the firm only a few months ago. Then there is Lord Leslie. We cannot directly connect him to this scheme yet, but it is plausible that he is connected, given that he had an interest in funeral-related investments and Mr. Fischer stole client papers from one of his close friends and one of his business associates."

"Would Leslie allow a close friend to invest in a fraudulent scheme?" I peer out at the landscape before answering my own question. "Likely not, but he may not have known Lord Primrose invested . . . or Lord Primrose did *not* invest and played another role, such as bringing in investors."

"As Lord Leslie may also have done." Gray runs his fingers over the fake mausoleum, the roof peak barely coming up to his forehead. "That is the thing about being a member of the gentry. I do not know whether it is different in your time, but here, people who are not part of those circles have a very skewed view of them."

"They presume they're all fabulously wealthy and terrifically clever, particularly when it comes to money."

"Indeed. If an ordinary tradesman with a bit of money to invest caught wind of a scheme that had the attention of men like Lord Leslie and Lord Primrose?"

"Insider-trading tip."

"I am not certain what that means, but in context, yes. They would only need to hear that such men had taken an interest—or invested a bit of money—and they would see a ripe opportunity."

"Especially if the nobility seemed to be trying to keep it a secret. Blocking the middle classes from enjoying the opportunities that might elevate their own status."

Gray lifts a finger. "Elevate their *fortunes*. Not their status. That is quite another thing."

"Damned British class system. Still, having money is a generational step up the ladder. It would help get their sons noticed by the gentry."

"Better yet, their daughters."

"Like Annis." I pause. "I can't imagine her getting mixed up in a scheme like this. If she did, the scam would be a lot less obvious."

"Scam? I presume that is another word for fraud. Yes, if Annis was behind this, we would not have puzzled it out quite so readily."

"*If* we've puzzled it out," I say. "It's a theory. We need more."

"Then let us speak to Hugh and see whether we can find this Mr. Fischer."

THIRTY-FIVE

An hour later, I'm scrubbing Gray's fireplace. It's my own fault really. Okay, fine, it's my own *choice*. I've sidelined myself from the next part of the investigation to get caught up on some of my chores, because there wasn't enough detective work for four people and this next bit didn't require my particular skills. In fact, as a visitor to this world, I was the least useful.

When we'd returned, we'd learned that Detective Crichton had managed to obtain a sample from Young's cadaver, and Isla has already tested it. As expected, the results match those of Leslie and Ware. While Crichton is still arguing to exhume Burns, I'm not sure how much that will matter until we have a suspect. At some point, we'll need to confirm Burns died the same way, to charge a suspect, but until then, we can proceed with the assumption he's part of the scheme, pending evidence that he's not.

The next step is forensic in nature. Forensic accounting, that is. Clara Burns provided the location of her former husband's secret business papers. McCreadie found them and had them transported to the police office for reading. That's what he's doing, along with Gray and Isla, both having volunteered. Yes, literacy rates are good in Scotland, particularly in Edinburgh, but that doesn't mean the average police constable can decipher business documents, especially when the documents might be written in a way that'll obscure their true nature.

I managed to handle the search at Ware's office, but it hadn't been as easy as I expected. I don't have the grounding in this world to understand everything I'm reading when it gets into the complexities of the law or of business. Part of it is the time period and part of it is the locale. Even in the modern world, there'd be plenty of Scottish or British terminology that'd fly straight over my head.

So I opted to catch up on some chores, even when the others tried to convince me to nap instead. Not only did I graciously step aside from the investigation, but I gave up the chance to take a well-deserved rest. Impressive work ethic, huh? Well, no. It's not as if I gave up the chance to track down or even interview a suspect. As for resting, I'd only lie in bed thinking, and I think better while my hands are busy.

I scrub and I think, and I pull together the pieces while resisting the urge to leap to conclusions. Leave all my options open and don't get too heavily invested in any theory. Yes, I think we're right about the fake cemetery, but we're going to need a whole lot more to connect that to the other victims.

It's past teatime when the others return with exactly the "more" we need. Proof that James Young, gravedigger, had indeed been involved with Andrew Burns's burial plot scheme from a few years back. As a gravedigger, Young would have the inside track on people who were desperate for a "proper" kirkyard burial. Burns would get in touch and offer them a plot guaranteed six feet below ground in one of two kirkyards where Young worked. Young would clear the way to put the bodies in the promised spot . . . and then move them again when they needed to sell that spot to someone else.

We also get a lead on Fischer. Isla found his name in several of the files, as a young law clerk who'd started working with Burns a few years ago on what seems to be legitimate business. Well, legitimate as far as they can tell, but none of us is an expert in Victorian fraud. Isla knows someone who is, though she's not saying more. She'll talk to her contact for further information. I suspect it's a former employee, one she took in and launched on a more respectable road. Meanwhile, McCreadie has dug up enough clues to start a proper search for Fischer.

"Any suggestions for me?" I say.

"For both of us," Gray adds. "We can certainly find avenues of inquiry to pursue, but if you have anything in particular, Hugh, say the word."

"The word is 'sleep,'" Isla says. "You both desperately require it."

Gray glances at me. "I was thinking of something somewhat more active, that Mallory and I could jointly pursue."

"If you wish to jointly pursue sleep and make it more active, that is no concern of mine," Isla says calmly as she bites into her scone.

McCreadie chokes on his tea.

Gray only shakes his head. "I see Mallory's sense of humor is contagious."

"Get some rest," Isla says. "In your own beds. I will tell Mrs. Wallace we shall dine quite late this evening."

A half hour later, Gray and I are in the stairwell together, as Isla goes down to speak to Mrs. Wallace before heading out to meet her former-con-artist contact.

I look at Gray. "Am I the only one who feels like a kid sent to bed early while the grown-ups do something interesting?"

"I am not certain how 'interesting' Hugh's and Isla's tasks are, but yes, I do feel as if I have been trundled off to bed when I am not at all tired."

"You shouldn't put up with that, you know. You're the man of the house."

His lips twitch. "If that is intended to goad me into disobeying my sister, I hardly need the incentive, as I have been doing it all my life."

"What do you suggest we do instead?"

"Find Jack. She has blocked your request for an audience, and *you* should not accept such treatment."

I laugh softly. "Yeah, that doesn't work with me either. I'm annoyed with Jack blowing me off, but we're well on our way to a resolution here, and I see nothing her broadsheet-writing friend can add."

"But do we *know* there isn't anything the writer can add? If we have nothing else to do, and we are not tired enough to sleep, should we not pursue this potential avenue, in case it proves fruitful?"

"You have a point."

"An excellent point. Unless you would rather rest?"

"Absolutely not."

I don't realize the problem until we set out. I only have one way of contacting Jack—talking to Elspeth at Halton House.

I'm taking Gray to a fight club.

I'm overreacting. It'll be fine. Gray is an intelligent and levelheaded adult, who may be fascinated by the concept of a fight club, but knows such "entertainment" is off-limits to men like him, at least if his idea of fun is to be found in the ring rather than the spectator stands.

The British class system works both ways, and while it definitely benefits Gray, it restricts him, too. Also, there's no reason for him to realize Halton House is a fight club, right? It won't be active this early in the evening. I'll make it clear to Elspeth that Gray is "with the police," and she'll take that as her cue to keep quiet.

Just an ordinary rooming house. That's all. Nothing more interesting than that. Nope, nope, nope.

We arrive at the rooming house to find the front door open. A sign at the desk informs visitors that they have no rooms to let. I guess Elspeth doesn't spend her entire day sitting here turning people away. She's only at her post in the late evening, when she can let the right people in.

Gray stands in the foyer while I poke about. There's not much to see. You aren't going to leave the front door unlocked with anything of value at the desk. I pull out the sign-in book and flip through. Just pages of faded ink with more recent entries to keep up the illusion that it's an active rooming house.

When Gray still says nothing, I glance over. Incuriosity is hardly his defining feature, yet he's standing there, head tilted, as if he's lost interest in his surroundings and retreated into his thoughts.

"Bare-knuckle boxing!" Gray exclaims, suddenly enough to have me wheeling.

He smiles, and it might be the closest thing to a grin I have ever seen from him. His eyes light up and his entire face animates in a way that makes my heart do a little pitter-patter. Then I realize what he's said.

"W-what?" I say.

"It is a boxing club," he says. "Of the wagering sort. Quite illegal." He walks past me into the rear hall. "Do you not smell that?"

"Smell what?" I say carefully.

"Blood and sawdust. I have been to such an establishment in London with my brother. We did not stay overlong. The fighters were . . ." He makes a face, the smile fading. "I have no issue with the sport, of course, but they were bringing fighters from Africa. While Britain may have outlawed slavery, it still engages in practices that seem akin to it in all but name." He glances over. "I hope they do better in your time."

"Umm . . ."

He shakes his head. "In any event, when Lachlan and I realized that the fighters were not there entirely of their own free will, it quite changed our mind about staying." He pauses. "I do hope this is not the same sort of establishment." Another pause. "No, I doubt it is. That one was a good deal more genteel, serving a clientele who would not venture here."

"A wealthy clientele being less likely to notice mistreated fighters."

"Notice or care."

I remember myself and say, "Whatever the smell, this is a rooming house, sir. Look, there is a book for guests to sign in."

"A book filled with ink so faded that unless they serve ghosts, this is not a rooming house. The outside basement windows are blackened, and the buildings on either side house businesses that seem permanently closed, suggesting they are owned by the same people as this building."

When I say nothing, he meets my gaze. "Are you telling me this is not a fighting establishment, Mallory?"

"You do throw some low blows," I grumble.

His brows rise.

I continue, "If I say yes, this isn't a fighting establishment, then I'm lying, and if I'm lying, you can't trust me."

"I do not believe I said anything of the sort," he says mildly.

"It was in the look. Fine, it's a fight club. No, there isn't any information we might require that you could obtain by getting into the ring."

His brows shoot higher.

"If you aren't thinking that already, you will soon," I say. "The answer is no."

"Of course it is. I could hardly step into the ring as a man of quality. Nor, as a man of color, could I hope to do so in disguise. It is impossible."

"I'm sorry."

"And I appreciate that you sound as if you actually mean that."

"I do. Now, we need to speak to the woman who runs the club— Elspeth—when she arrives. If she picks up any hint that you might like to fight, she's going to use that to her advantage. She'll offer a trade— information for a fight. Or she'll suggest that you don't have what it takes to fight, hoping to goad you into proving her wrong."

"I believe we have already established that ploy does not work with me."

"It might if you're looking for an excuse."

"I will not be." He looks about. "When do you think we could expect her?"

"When do places like this usually open?"

"Not for a couple of hours yet." He steps further into the hall. "Might she be upstairs? This is posing as a rooming house, after all. Or, perhaps, she is downstairs, in the establishment. Yes, that is the most likely answer. She is downstairs."

"You just want an excuse to see the club." I wave off his mock-innocent look. "Fine. We'll look for her down there *if* the door is unlocked."

"Unlocked or easily unlocked?"

I shake my head and walk toward the basement door.

THIRTY-SIX

We try the door at the top of the stairs. It's locked, and it isn't the sort of lock opened with a hairpin.

"You cannot let the lock win," Gray says. "Conquer it. I have faith in you."

When I raise a middle finger, he says, "You do realize I have no idea what that means."

"Use your imagination." I check the lock and shake my head. "I need a skill upgrade for this one. If you want to get me a treat, bring me someone who can give me lessons in picking locks."

"Where might I find someone like that?"

"A locksmith."

"*They* certainly would not teach you how to illegally open a lock."

"Cross a palm with enough silver and you can learn pretty much anything. Also, how do you think they became locksmiths in the first place?" I straighten. "I can't open—"

A shadow passes behind Gray, and there is one unforgivable second where I think it's his own shadow, cast by the light filtering through grimy windows. When I realize my mistake, my mouth opens to shout a warning, but he's already sensed someone there, and he's spinning, fists rising.

The first blow hits Gray's jaw before he can swing. He staggers back as I leap forward, but a second attacker lunges between us and slams his fist into Gray's stomach with enough force that I scream in rage as I launch myself at him.

Gray smacks into the wall, his head snapping forward, and after I barrel into the man I hit, I claw past him to get to Gray, slumped on the floor. When the man tries to grab Gray, I slash his arm with my knife, and he pulls back, gasping, blood welling up on his white shirt.

"Stay away from him," I snarl.

"Like bloody hell—"

I wave the knife, cutting him short. "You've just attacked an unarmed visitor. A doctor."

"He doesn't look like a doctor."

"Does he look like a thief?" I snap. "He's clearly a gentleman. The front door was open, and we were looking for the proprietor. We've done nothing wrong."

I turn to Gray, slumped unconscious against the wall. I grip his shoulder, and he falls to the side.

"I need a doctor," I say to the two men.

"I thought he was one."

Gray is unconscious, *deeply* unconscious, and I'm trying not to freak out about that. Also trying not to freak out over that blow to his stomach.

I'm checking Gray's breathing, about to snap again at the men to bring help, when hands seize my shoulders. I swing my knife, but the other man grabs my arm and deftly plucks the blade from my hand. I punch and thrash. My blows make contact, but there's two of them—two very big men—and before I know it, I'm being shoved through a doorway.

I recover my footing and spring at them, but one shoves me backward into the darkness. As I fall, the floor disappears beneath me. At the last second, I realize I'm tumbling down stairs, and I manage to throw myself forward, landing hard across the risers and grabbing the edge of the landing.

I lie there, gripping the landing, and trying to get upright. Something hits me. Something heavy enough that my hold breaks and I slide down the stairs, and while the corset acts like armor for my stomach, each edge slams into my chin, as whatever hit me threatens to steamroll over me.

It's Gray. I realize that as I grapple to stop my fall and my hand touches warm skin. They threw Gray into the stairwell after me, and his unconscious body is propelling me down the stairs. I catch the edge of a step and manage to pause our fall, but Gray is no lightweight and I soon start to slide. I wedge one boot against the wall, grab his shirt in both hands and rise as best I can while steadying him.

I look down the stairs to see how much farther there is to go. It's pitch dark. All I can do is keep hold of Gray—or his clothing at least—and try to get him down without both of us falling the rest of the way.

I stretch my leg down as far as I can. When my foot taps a solid landing, I exhale in relief. Only two more stairs to the bottom.

I wedge my hands under Gray's torso and ease him down as best I can. He still hits each step, making me wince. At the bottom, I feel around until I find a wall. Then I prop him against it.

"Dr. Gray?" I say, and almost laugh at myself. The man didn't wake up being thrown down a stairwell. He's not going to wake to the sound of his name.

The half laugh catches in my throat.

The man didn't wake up being thrown down a stairwell.

My hands fly to his neck. Well, they try to fly to his neck, though in the darkness I poke him in the face. I quickly find the right spot and press my fingertip against it. Is that a pulse? Please let it be—

Yes, that's a pulse.

I check his breathing. It's shallow but steady, which means the blow to the stomach didn't crack ribs and pierce his lungs.

I awkwardly kneel beside him. "Dr. Gray?" I rub my hand against his cheek, which sounds very sweet, but it's a brusque "*please* wake up" rub rather than a gentle caress. "Dr. Gray?"

I shake his shoulder. No response. Panic licks through me. He's breathing. His heart is beating. That's the limit of what I know to check for.

"Dr. Gray?" I rub his cheek again. "Come on. Please wake up, Dr. Gray."

"Duncan." His voice is thick, almost a groan. "I will only respond to Duncan."

I exhale a profanity. "You're lucky you're hurt or I'd smack you for scaring the shit out of me."

"If you cannot call me Duncan to rouse me from death's door, at least you could shed a tear of relief at my waking, and then throw yourself into my arms, instead of cursing and threatening to hit me."

"Yeah, and the woman who'd have done that would have let those guys keep hitting you. Or let you fall all the way down the stairs."

"True." A whisper of fabric, as if he's shifting position. "Did you threaten them with your knife?"

"I cut the guy who hit you in the stomach."

"Thank you."

"Hmm. I'd deserve that more if he hadn't gotten the damn knife away from me."

"And I would sympathize more if I weren't smarting myself from the humiliation of being laid low without landing a single blow."

"There were two of them, they were very big, they ambushed us, and they didn't fight fair."

"Despicable. We *must* cultivate a better class of assailants, Mallory."

I sputter a laugh. "We really must, Dr. Gray."

"Duncan. We really must, *Duncan*."

I sigh. "I can't. I'm already afraid of calling Isla by her given name in public, and that would be far less scandalous."

"What do you call me in your head? Dr. Gray?"

I hesitate. Then I say, "Just Gray. Which sounds disrespectful. It's not, but yes, it's also a bit overly familiar."

"No, it is a common form of address among male colleagues, and so I will take it as a compliment that you see me as such. You may call me that aloud as well."

I sigh again.

"Still no?" he says, and the word comes lightly, but I hear the thread of disappointment.

"Maybe," I say. "In private. If I slip up, people would presume they missed the 'Dr.'"

"Excellent. And if you successfully manage to do that without slipping up, we can move on to Duncan." A sudden movement as if he's straightening. "How are you? I have not asked that."

"I'll be battered and bruised," I say, "but I'm fine. How's your stomach?"

"I am attempting not to vomit, which would quite ruin this little moment of ours. It is rather nice, don't you think, sitting here in the dark?"

"How hard was that bump on your head, Gray?"

"Hard enough that I am thinking I rather like the sound of 'Gray.' It makes me feel less like your employer and more like your partner in these investigative endeavors. Come over here." He reaches out, touches me, and then withdraws fast. "My apologies. I ought not to blindly grab you in the dark."

I laugh softly. "It was my elbow, which is significantly bonier than whatever you thought you grabbed."

"Good." He catches my elbow again and tugs me over until I am sitting beside him, leaning against each other in the dark. "You're certain you're all right?"

"All things considered, I am."

There's a long pause. "And beyond the scope of our current circumstances? How are you doing?"

I'm quiet for a moment. Then I say, "It's good being busy."

"I can imagine it is." A long pause. "Last night, I don't believe I properly expressed my sympathy for what you're going through. That must make me seem very selfish. The man who considers only that he might lose his new assistant."

"It's not selfish. What happened to me isn't your fault, and you can't fix it. I wouldn't particularly want to throw myself into training a rookie knowing she could vanish at any moment."

"I am quite certain any of us could 'vanish' at any moment."

"Like being hit by a bus? Or thrown down a stairwell for reasons unknown?"

"Omnibus drivers are a reckless lot. I suspect stairwell-throwing is a less common form of sudden demise, although, speaking as a physician, I can confirm that stairs are terribly dangerous." He shifts behind me. "I am not as concerned about losing my new assistant as I am about losing someone whose company I enjoy."

I lean back against him. "Ditto."

"Ditto?"

"It means 'the same.' I like your company, too."

Silence. Then, "You make it seem very easy to say such things."

"I know, right? Tell someone you think they're cool, and the universe doesn't collapse around you. Weird."

"Cool? I presume that's a compliment."

"It is. And—" I stop as something squeaks near us. "Is that a rat?"

"Probably."

I scramble up. "We need to get out of here."

"We could check the door. See whether it's locked."

"The—? Goddamn it. We haven't even checked the door."

"Don't look at me. I've suffered a head injury and cannot be held responsible for any mental oversights. Also, you could turn on the light."

"*What?*"

"Using my superior powers of detection, I believe I catch the faint smell of gas lighting."

"We've been sitting in the dark—"

"Head injury. Not responsible. Also, I could be wrong. It does happen."

I start feeling along the wall, only to remember I'm not going to find a switch. The gas needs to be lit at a source. I do, however, nearly stumble over a table, and on it is a match box. That tells me there's a light nearby, and I soon find it.

The lamp flickers, faint, as if it isn't the main source of illumination, but I can make out the stairs and the door at the top. I march up the stairs, turn the knob and—

Locked.

I examine the knob, but the key works from the other side. I march back down.

"I suppose that would have been too easy," Gray says. He's pushing to his feet now, and while he's wobbly, there's also an unguarded look about him that makes me forget how annoyed I am about him not mentioning the lights and the door.

I help him find his balance. "Are you sure you should be standing?"

"I believe so." He tilts his head one way and then the other. "I have quite the ringing in my skull, and my stomach hurts enough that I might not even be tempted by cream pastries. Also, I do believe . . ."

He unbuttons his jacket. I yelp, seeing blood soaking through his shirt.

He only sighs. "Yes, the stitching has come undone. Likely in the tumble down the stairs." He does up the jacket again. "It will be fine. The question now is *why* were we pushed down here?"

"I don't care about why. I care about whether there's a way *out* of down here. You saw windows from the outside, right?"

Before he can answer, there's a click upstairs, metal on metal. The sound of a door being unlocked. It creaks open, and I back in front of Gray, shielding him, but he steps up beside me. Light floods the open doorway, and I squint and blink against it until a figure appears.

Gray's hand tightens on my upper arm, and he tugs me back. To his credit, he steps back with me. He's injured, and he acknowledges that, and he doesn't leap in front of me to fight.

As boots thump down the stairs, Gray backs us away. He stops when he sees it's a woman, but he keeps his grip on me.

"Elspeth," I say. "Good. We came looking for Jack, and a couple of—"

I stop as I see the two hulking figures to her rear, one behind the other. "Your bouncers, I presume."

"My . . . ?" She shakes off the question and continues descending the steps. "Came looking for Jack, you said?"

"We did." I glance at the two guys, not sure which pronoun I should use for Jack in front of them. "Jack was supposed to stop by Dr. Gray's house this morning." I glance at Gray. "This is Dr. Gray—the person your men punched and shoved down the stairs."

I expect a look of horror—or at least chagrin—but her gaze stays stony. "You take me for a fool, don't you, lass?"

"No, this is really Dr.—"

"I know who it is," she says. "My concern is for the part where you pretend to be looking for Jack. Where is he? That is my question to *you*. And it is one you are going to answer. If you do not . . ." She glances back at her two goons.

"Are you saying Jack's missing?" I ask.

"You have until the count of five to tell me what you have done with—"

"Nothing," I say. "Jack was supposed to come by Dr. Gray's at ten. He never showed up."

"Five," she says. "Four."

"We've been investigating a murder all damn day," I say. "The murder of Mr. Ware, a solicitor who was poisoned, like Lord Leslie and the others. I'm sure it's in the evening papers, but we haven't had time to check, being a little busy solving the case."

"Three," she says.

Now Gray does step in front of me. "You do realize we are working with the police, yes?" he says. "And that Detective McCreadie knows exactly where we are, having sent us here to chase down this lead with Jack?

I understand you are upset about the disappearance of your young friend, but to think we kidnapped him is quite the leap of logic."

"Leap of logic?" She advances on Gray and waves a piece of paper. "Explain this then, *sir.*"

Gray unfolds the note as I look around him.

Mallory Mitchell and Dr. Duncan Gray
12 Robert Street

Below that is what looks like random letters, and I presume it's just illegible handwriting, but as much as I squint, I can't make the groupings form proper words.

"You did not expect Jack to be so clever, did you?" Elspeth says. "He does not go snooping about on his own. He had young Bob, and he sent him back with this note, telling me you had taken him. We were determining what to do about it when you saved us the trouble."

"What's that part say?" I ask, pointing to the last line.

Elspeth hesitates. "I was working on that. Jack loves his secrets and ciphers. I have no patience with them."

"Then how does he expect you to know what it says?"

"He doesn't," Gray says. "Jack meant for the note to be delivered to one of us at the town house. That is what this means. It is *addressed* to us, not *accusing* us."

"Of course you would say that," Elspeth says, but there's the briefest hesitation before she speaks.

"It's a modified Caesar cipher," Gray explains. "It says to meet him at the address given."

One of the goons snatches the letter from Gray and hands it to Elspeth as Gray says, mildly, "It is clear that Jack intended that note for us and is doubtless waiting at the address given."

"Since ten this morning?" Elspeth sniffs. "You really do think me a fool."

"If he has been gone since ten, then he is in trouble, and we must speak to 'young Bob' as quickly as possible."

THIRTY-SEVEN

The boy is upstairs, having been ordered to stay out of this bit of business. Gray questions him. Bob dissembles—clearly uncomfortable with revealing what Jack had been up to—until Elspeth snaps at him to tell the truth or Jack's death will be on his conscience. After that, he admits Jack heard about Mr. Ware's murder and went to his house to investigate on behalf of her writer friend.

While there, Jack overheard enough conversation to realize Isla and I were upstairs searching the office. She was trying to figure out how to weasel her way in—on some pretense of needing to speak to us—when the clerk, Fischer, arrived. She eavesdropped on that conversation and waited until he came out and then tried to speak to him, hoping for insight into the murder.

Fischer blew her off and was clearly rattled. That piqued her interest, so she followed him. She saw where he was going and gave Bob the note. A smart thing to do . . . except she was so distracted over Fischer that she hadn't explained it was to go to the people listed, at the address listed. I guess she thought he'd figure that out.

Instead, Bob delivered the note to the same place he took all her notes: Elspeth. The Victorian equivalent of texting a friend before you head into a guy's apartment. Smart. It works better when the messenger knows what he's supposed to do.

The obvious next step is for Gray and me to go to the address given.

Elspeth won't hear of it. She's going herself, with her two heavies, and we aren't invited. Gray argues but not nearly strenuously enough. I keep my mouth shut until we've left Halton House.

"You mis-deciphered the address, didn't you?" I say.

"I may have. Quite accidentally, of course."

I shake my head. "Where did you send them?"

"To the general area where the boy left Jack. I am only fortunate he did not see her to the specified address."

"So where are *we* going?"

"To a butcher's shop."

"Tell me you mean that literally, and you don't suspect Fischer has body parts strewn about his lodgings."

"One can only hope."

I could ask *which* outcome one can only hope for, but I decide—with Gray—it's best not to know.

Yep, it's a butcher's shop, and I'd need to be starving to buy food there. The smell makes me consider vegetarianism, and that's before we get close enough to see the flies on the meat. Meat that hangs a few feet above a street awash in excrement from horses and not-horses.

"It's like something out of a horror movie," I whisper to Gray.

"I presume that is not a good thing?"

My retching noises set the corners of his mouth twitching.

"It's not even the worst part of the Old Town," I whisper. "Do I want to see a butcher shop there?"

"It is likely no worse. Food adulteration is a never-ending concern in all areas, starting with convincing physicians that feeding chalk-whitened milk to babies is a health risk."

I stare at him.

"I believe you have mentioned our infant mortality rate," he murmurs. "We are an unhealthy lot."

"Hell, no. If babies survive drinking that, you guys are freaking *invincible*."

"It is getting better," he says. "Various food laws have been passed in recent years. But, as always, the pace of change is slow."

Gray surveys the shop.

"Jack could have seen Fischer go inside," I say. "But she's not going to summon us to meet her here if he only popped in for a leg of lamb. That's an apartment over the shop, right?"

His gaze rises to it. "Several, I would presume."

"Then one of them will belong to Fischer."

Gray was wrong. Like he said, it happens. While there are multiple rooms over the butcher's shop, only one is an apartment. The others are storage, as evidenced by the thick doors and heavy locks. Over the shop are two levels of storage, with the apartment at the top.

There's only one way in—the rickety back stairs.

"I'll go up and knock," I say.

Gray opens his mouth to argue.

"Fischer has met me," I say. "And he knows I was going through Ware's office. While we didn't find any sign of Fischer's address there, he won't know that. I just say that I came across it and followed up to be sure the poor man knew of his employer's demise and—Oh, my goodness, aren't you Mr. Morris?"

"At which point he grabs you and drags you into his apartment before you can raise the alarm."

"Excellent. That's exactly where I want to be." I lift a hand against Gray's scowl. "There's a landing on the second floor. You can wait there, and if I am apprehended, you may fly to my rescue."

"And try not to get knocked down the stairs again?"

"I didn't say that. It would be rude. But yes, please, no more knocks to the head. I like your brain just the way it is."

He opens his mouth. Pauses. Then says, "That is oddly flattering."

"As it should be. I've never said that to anyone else."

I head up the stairs. He follows to the second level. We aren't too concerned about Fischer looking out back and seeing us, given the blackout-blind level of soot on the outside of the window. I was also not concerned he'd hear us chatting below over the din of shoppers.

I rap on Fischer's door. When no one answers, I knock again and call, "Mr. Fischer? I must speak to you. It is about Mr. Ware's bequeathments."

Now, that should get the attention even of a spooked law clerk who may have murdered his employer. When I press my ear to the door, though, I hear nothing. I motion for Gray over the landing, and then I pop the lock with my hairpin.

I ease open the door. Inside, with those grimy windows, it's nearly pitch black. This time, I do look for gas lighting. That's when Gray walks in.

"He will not have gas," he says as he walks to a lantern.

A box of matches rests below it, and Gray lights the lantern and shines it around.

"Damn," I say. "Someone's a bit of a hoarder."

The place is jammed with furniture and odds and ends, many of them broken. There's a workbench with a few tools, but the bench is dusty.

"The kind of guy who can't walk past a trash heap without rescuing something," I say. "Has every intention of fixing it, but never quite gets around to it."

From deep in the sea of rubbish comes a dull thump.

"And rats," I say. "He's also collecting rats." I survey the mess. "Want to wager on how many of these things have rodent nests?" I shake my head. "First order of business: confirm this is Fischer's apartment."

Gray lifts an envelope from a stack of papers. On it is Fischer's name and this address.

"You are a genius," I say.

Another thump. I peer into the mountains and molehills of furniture.

"The rats will scatter when you draw close," Gray says. "As we search, I would suggest banging on each object."

I move aside an upended chair and then skirt around two stacked tables. Another thump. I follow it to an old steamer trunk at the bottom of a pile. I crouch and knock on the side. A muffled thump from within follows.

"Duncan!" I say, glancing over to see him rifling through the mail.

I climb onto an old desk to clear furniture off the pile. It's been stacked almost to the ceiling with small bookcases. The top one is heavier than I expect, and when I heft it, my boot slips on the desk. Gray grabs me before I fall. Then he heaves the bookcase off, and we keep clearing until we're down to the steamer trunk.

It's locked. When I see that padlock, I let out a stream of profanities. It wasn't enough to bury the trunk—Fischer had to stick a massive padlock on it.

Gray grabs the lock and twists hard, and the clasp holding it on snaps. It's a travel trunk, the clasp only meant to keep out casual thieves.

I yank open the lid, and there is Jack, bound and gagged.

I let out a few more profanities as I pull out my knife—returned by Elspeth—and cut off the gag.

"Thank you," Jack croaks. "Also, I do appreciate the very colorful words of outrage on my behalf."

"Oh, I can find a few more," I grumble as I cut her bindings. "Including a few for the person who decided she should confront a potential killer without waiting for the backup she summoned."

"I did wait. You took your time coming."

"Because you weren't clear in your damned message." I yank off the bindings as Gray helps her out of the trunk. "It went to Elspeth, who thought you were saying we were the ones *responsible* for your disappearance."

"I am fine," she says. "Thank you for asking."

"Yeah? Ask Dr. Gray how he is, after being hit in the face, sucker-punched in the gut, and then tossed down Elspeth's basement stairs while unconscious."

"Are you all right, sir?" she says, peering up at him.

"Reasonably. And you?"

"Also reasonably."

"Good," I say. "Do you need a reassuring post-trauma hug?"

Jack hesitates, as if confused. Then she says, "Gods, no." She considers. "Well, perhaps, yes. A small one."

I embrace her, and she falls into it, allowing a fierce hug before moving back.

"It was rather traumatic," she says. "I thought I might die."

"I'm sorry. We came as soon as we could."

She rubs her arms. She's dressed in her male-passing outfit, but she's lost her cap, and the loose mop of curls makes it hard to imagine Fischer mistook her for a boy.

"I thought I was being clever," she says. "I also did not think he was a killer. At most, I presumed he was an unwitting accomplice, who might be eager to confess in the hope of redemption."

"That's not what happened?"

"It is not . . . and yet it is," she says. "He didn't transform into some demon. He overpowered me, yes, but he never stopped apologizing, never stopped trying to convince me *he* was the victim. Even when I was in that truck, he talked for what seemed like hours."

Gray murmurs to me, "I will stand watch at the door."

I nod my thanks. "We ought to take this conversation elsewhere, but I also want the opportunity to search."

"I agree," Gray says. "Talk and search, and if he comes back, he is certainly not putting the three of us into trunks."

"He might," Jack says. "There are enough of them." She tries for a smile, but her eyes tear. She blinks it back, looking mortified.

"Did he confess to the murders?" I ask.

She shakes her head. "He said 'it' was not his idea. I presumed he meant the murders, but then he seemed to be talking about something else that involved the dead men. He said it was Mr. Burns's idea, and he was pulled into it, and then when Lord Leslie came in, he was expelled from the group. That is when people started to die, and he thought he was safe until he heard of Mr. Ware's death. He said Mr. Ware was *not* involved, and so the killer murdered him either by accident or mistake. He feared he would be the next to die." She pauses. "I did not understand most of what he was saying. Does it make sense to you?"

"It does."

She shivers. I resist the urge to ask if she'd like another hug. She's suffered a trauma, one that will later strike in nightmares and fears of confined places. We can talk about that later, though I'm not certain she'll take the advice of a teenage housemaid.

"Dr. Gray?" I say.

"Yes, I heard all that," he says. "And it makes sense to me as well. At least insofar as understanding the references. Mr. Fischer seemed to be practicing his defense strategy."

"Hmm."

"You think he is not the killer?" Gray says.

"I think we need to finish searching his apartment before he returns." I look at Jack. "Did he give any indication where he was going?"

"To resolve this, he said. That was all."

"Then you should head home."

She squares her thin shoulders. "No, I shall help. There is a lot to search, and you may not have long to search it."

THIRTY-EIGHT

There is indeed a lot to search. Every piece of stacked furniture could have a clue taped under it or stuffed into a drawer. Gray and Jack handle that while I search Fischer's personal belongings. There's not much of the latter. He has a drawer of clothing, all of it similar to what I saw him wearing—well made but clearly secondhand. I find a bit of hidden money, less than Catriona had squirreled away. A pocket watch. A couple of pieces of hair jewelry—mourning souvenirs from dead relatives?

Then, between two shirts, I find folded pieces of paper. On the first is a half-written note.

> You cannot do this to me. I have been a loyal partner for five years. Without me, you would be in prison now. I have done nothing to earn your mistrust nor Lord Leslie's. He does not even know me. He has only decided I cannot be trusted and—

The note ends there. I flip to the next page. The same handwriting.

> You owe me. I demand a hundred pounds, or I shall tell your pretty new wife that you are a liar and a cheat, and I shall tell all your investors that there is no cemetery, only a bog—

Again, it ends. On the third and last page:

Please, Andy. Do not do this to me. I beg of you. Tell Lord Leslie I can be trusted. Tell him that he is mistaken, and Mr. Ware suspects nothing. Do you truly believe Lord Leslie's promises? He cheated me of my share, and now he will cheat you and James of yours. That witch plays him like a puppet. Do you not see that?

I flip through the three notes. Then I step out of the tiny area Fischer uses for his bedchamber.

"Dr. Gray?"

"Hmm?"

"Have you seen a sample of Fischer's handwriting anywhere?"

"Yes, over here."

Gray walks to the pile of mail at the door and hands me a piece that is clearly written by Fischer. It matches the handwriting on the letters, which I expected, but I needed to be certain.

I hand the unfinished notes to Gray.

He skims through them. "They seem to be practice letters, unsent. Mr. Fischer had been excised from the cemetery scheme. Gordon thought Mr. Ware was suspicious and did not trust Mr. Fischer to maintain his composure. From what both you and Jack said, he is a nervous sort."

"He is. This also gives our link to Lord Leslie. He came into the scheme late, probably through Lord Primrose, and then muscled his way into a position of authority. Enough to get Fischer dropped. Does that sound like Leslie?"

"It sounds precisely like him." Gray flips to the last letter. "This mention of a woman—"

"Mallory?" Jack says from the other side of the apartment, hidden by piles of furniture.

We both hurry to where she's standing beside a wardrobe with one missing door. "I thought this was empty, but when I shut the bottom drawer, it caught, and in attempting to close it, I discovered a false back."

She points to the half-open drawer. I crouch to pull it open and see what she means. What seems to be the back has come free, revealing a hidden compartment. I tug the drawer all the way out. Inside is a locked box.

"I did not touch it," Jack says.

"Thank you."

The box is small. A snuffbox? I have no idea what a snuffbox looks like, only that it's a historical object—maybe from this time period, maybe not—and when I see this, that's what springs to mind. It's ornamental enough that I'd presume it's a woman's piece, but I've learned that Victorian men are just as likely to have pretty things. This box is indeed pretty, made of tortoiseshell with an inlaid painting of a Greek ruin. There's a clasp with a tiny lock for a tiny key.

I turn the box over. On the bottom are the initials JTF.

"A very nice piece for someone in Fischer's circumstances," I say.

"The plate has been added later," Gray says. "Likely there was another one, with other initials."

"Ah. Buy it secondhand, remove the initials and add your own. Now let's see if I can get it open."

I take out a hairpin, but it's too large. Before I can say a word, Gray passes over a stickpin. I hesitate to use it. Like the box, the pin is very pretty—gold with royal-blue enamel around a pearl.

"I wouldn't want to break your pin," I say.

"It is old. Use it."

It takes a bit of poking and prodding, but then the lid snaps open. Inside are two vials. One contains a chunk of gray metal that looks like lead. The other holds pale powder.

"Is that arsenic?" Jack says, pointing to the powder.

"Something like that," I say.

Gray catches my eye, and I nod. This certainly looks like thallium—the metal—and thallium sulfate—the powder.

"Then he did it," Jack says. "He murdered those people."

Gray takes the box and starts to pick up the vials. Then he murmurs "Fingerprints" and leaves them where they are, nestled in velvet in the small box. He sets the box aside and takes a pair of gloves out of his pocket.

Footsteps clatter on the stairs.

"Down!" I say, waving for everyone to duck.

Jack hides behind an upturned table, while Gray and I zip behind the wardrobe.

"Is it a problem that we found the poison?" I whisper.

His brows knit. "You are concerned that we will be blamed?"

My concern was the chain of evidence, but now that he says this, I see a new problem. Gray is brother to the prime suspect in Lord Leslie's death. He's also brother to the chemist who may have supplied the poison. What happens if he's found in the new suspect's apartment with the evidence?

It shouldn't be a problem unless someone is hell-bent on blaming Annis. That's exactly what Fischer's lawyer might do, but we have a valid reason for being here, even for breaking in. We followed Jack's note, which Elspeth and others have seen, and we found Jack held captive.

A key scrapes in the lock. Fischer doesn't realize it's already open. He's distracted and, I suspect, running on autopilot.

"He'll bolt," I whisper.

"I'll catch him," Gray says.

I shake my head as I picture those three flights of rickety stairs. "Slip over behind him, and cut off his escape."

Gray nods. The door is opening, but Fischer is on the other side of it, giving Gray time to duck and dart past a few piles of furniture. By the time Fischer is closing the door, Gray is by the wall, crouched and hidden.

I watch in a broken mirror as Fischer steps inside. He throws down his key by the stack of mail.

"I am returned," he says, as if calling a weary greeting to his wife. He continues inside and unbuttons his jacket. "I did not find what I needed. My partner had a place where he kept his business papers, and the police have discovered it."

He walks farther into the apartment. "I had hoped I could burn the papers. I ought to have done so after Andy's death, but I feared I would be caught sneaking in and they seemed safe where they were. Now I am . . ." He rubs his mouth. "I will not say I am undone. I still hope to fix this, and when I do, I can release you. I only hope it is soon. If it is not . . ."

He runs a hand through his hair. "You ought not to have come here. That was your own doing, and if it is your *un*doing, then you have no one to blame but yourself. Whatever your reporter friend pays you, it is not enough to take such chances. It is your own fault, working for such a person, getting involved in murders, dressing like a boy. If I had known you were a girl, I would not have done this. I am sorry if this is to be your fate, but you—"

He stops short, seeing the open steamer trunk. Then he leaps forward and nearly dives into it, as if Jack could somehow be hiding in its depths. He picks up the cut ropes and runs them through his hands.

"No," he whispers. "No, no, no. How—?"

He stops, and I think he's seen me in the mirror. But he's staring at a spot just out of my sight.

"What . . . ?" he whispers.

Footsteps as he strides toward the spot. I inch to angle myself and see what he's noticed. A heartbeat before I see it, I know what it is. The snuffbox. Gray had put it down to don his gloves, and then we heard footsteps.

Before I can swing out, Fischer snatches up the open box in his ungloved hands. I inwardly wince while reminding myself that no judge or jury would have accepted fingerprint evidence anyway. I keep swinging out, though, and he startles back.

"You!" he says, fumbling the box.

I tense, ready to grab the box, but he recovers and holds it out.

"What is this?" he says.

"You tell us," Jack says as she steps from her hiding place. "It has your initials on it."

"My what? Where?"

"On the bottom."

"No!" I say.

I lunge before he dumps out the poison, but when he tips the box, he grabs the vials before they fall. Then he stares at the bottom of the box.

"No, this is not—"

"Not your initials?" Jack says.

I throw her a look that asks her to stop. I do it as nicely as I can. This guy locked her in a trunk. He was willing to let her die in there—he just said as much. I understand how much she is enjoying uncovering his scheme. I just don't want her doing or saying anything that could help his case.

"Put the box down," I say.

"Is this—is this *poison*?" His voice rises as he holds up the vial of powder.

"Just give me the—"

"She planted this," he says. "I swear it. She did this. She came in here and planted it and then led you here."

"Me?" Jack squawks.

"No. Her. *She* sent you here."

"Who sent her here?" I ask carefully.

His gaze meets mine. "You know who I mean, and I'll not condemn myself by uttering the accusation, or she will murder me as she did the others."

"Fine. Then you can tell the police when you are safely in prison."

"Prison?" His eyes bug.

"Where did you think you were going?" Jack says. "Out for tea?"

"N-no. The police will not believe me. They will say I killed the others. That is her plan. She had already set me up, and it was not enough. She had to be sure."

He shakes the box at me. "A locked snuffbox with my initials on it. Containing poison. Where was it hidden? Someplace I would never stumble upon it? She sent this girl pretending to work for Edinburgh's secret criminal reporter, and when that did not work, she sent you."

"No one sent us. We came looking for our friend here."

"Who was sent by *her*. Do you not see that?"

"No one sent me either," Jack says. "I was on a story. Following you was part of that story, and you stuffed me into a box and left me to die. We all heard you say you would leave me there if you had to. Now you will tell the police you are not a murderer?"

Fischer bolts, box in hand. He gets three strides before he sees Gray blocking the doorway.

"You aren't leaving," I say. "Not without a police escort."

He backs up slowly, but there's no place else for him to go. When he hits the wall, I start toward him. Gray stays at the door, blocking his exit.

"I did nothing," Fischer whines. "Nothing. That witch sent the girl, and I had to put her into that chest. I had no choice. Do you not see? I—"

He whips the snuffbox at me. I dive and catch it.

"Mallory!" Gray says.

I think Gray is shouting a warning to catch the box. Then I see Fischer with the vial of powder. The uncapped vial.

Shit.

"Hey," I say, pulling Fischer's attention my way as Gray takes a step toward him. "If you didn't do this, you need to explain that. Tell the police—"

Fischer's arm flies up, slamming the contents of the open vial into his mouth. Gray catches his arm, but it's too late. Fischer is coughing and hacking, choking on the thallium sulfate powder.

Gray grabs Fischer and thumps him hard between the shoulder blades. I snatch up the vial. It's empty but for a smattering of powder on the sides.

Gray has Fischer around the waist, gripping him from the back and hefting him, trying to forcibly expel what he's swallowed.

"We need an emetic." His gaze shoots to the small kitchen. "See if there is any syrup of ipecac in his medicine cabinet. Or mustard powder. Even salt will do."

My first-aid training tells me none of that is used anymore, but if it makes Fischer vomit up the poison, I don't care what damage it might cause.

"Jack?" I say. "We need . . ."

We need what?

A doctor? We have one.

An ambulance? That isn't even a thing.

"The police," I say. "Or a cab. We need . . . Jack?"

The door stands open, and there is no sign of Jack.

THIRTY-NINE

Jack has gone for help. I tell myself that is the answer, but I don't believe it. She fled before the police could arrive. Before she could be pulled into this.

Or did she flee for another reason?

She planted this. I swear it. She did this. She came in here and planted it and then led you here.

I push that aside and focus on getting Gray what he needs. He's trying to manually force Fischer to vomit, but only gets thin strings of bile and saliva.

"Can we pump his stomach?" I say. "At a hospital? Is that a thing? Stomach pumping?"

His brows knit. Then he says, "Gastric lavage. Yes, that would be my next step, but we do not have time to get him to a hospital."

Gray tells me what to look for—any kind of tubing, any kind of pump or suction device. There's nothing to be had in this apartment, and while I'm searching, he's doing his best to get Fischer to vomit. The man has passed out, and that makes it easier . . . until he starts to convulse. That's when Gray sends me to get a cab. I race out, hoping to see Jack returning with help, but there is no sign of her.

I hail a hansom cab. Gray pays extravagantly for the driver's assistance carrying Fischer down all those flights of stairs. Then he sends me in search of McCreadie.

I find the detective by the sheer luck of him being at the police office as I arrive, and we get to the Royal Infirmary, where Gray had convinced them to take Fischer in for urgent care.

At that point, with Gray not being a practicing doctor, he has to leave. McCreadie sets a constable at the door and informs the hospital that the man in their care is wanted for the murders of four people. After that, all we can do is wait.

I haven't said a word since we left the hospital. I'm too deep in my thoughts. The doctors don't know whether Fischer will pull through, and while I understand that McCreadie had to tell them Fischer is a murder suspect, I'm afraid that might affect their care.

By the time we got him admitted, it was too late for a stomach pumping—and I'm not sure how much good it would have done—so they're using other methods that may at least slow the poison. Are those the right methods? I think Prussian blue is used for thallium in our day, but I'm not certain enough about that to do more than mention it . . . and back down after I get blank looks. The lack of a treatment doesn't mean thallium is automatically lethal—just that the victim will survive or not, and that is largely out of the hands of the medical profession.

Fischer is unconscious and may never wake up. That bugs the hell out of me. Is it because I want him to face justice? Maybe, but my gut says there's more to my unease. I want him to wake up so I can question him properly. Was he really shocked at finding that poison? Or was he faking it? Even if he was shocked, that doesn't mean he isn't the killer—someone who knew the truth could have planted the vials. Still, it raises a whisper of doubt, and I want to question him and be completely certain he is responsible for those deaths. That's a sort of closure we don't always get, and I might just need to deal with that.

McCreadie takes us to a pub. We're in the New Town, and we should go home for the late dinner Mrs. Wallace made, but no one can face that. McCreadie sends a message to Isla inviting her to join us, and we take a tiny room in the back. A private room, I realize, as I catch Gray tipping one of the staff, who closes the door behind us.

We settle into chairs and say nothing. When the door opens, I expect to see a server coming for our order, but instead she carries a tray with glasses, a bottle, and steaming meat pies. She sets it down on the table and retreats with only a nod as the men thank her. Belatedly, I turn to add my own thanks, but the door is already shut.

Gray serves the pies and pours the whisky and, again, I belatedly realize I should at least have offered to do that. Each thought needs to shove past the gloom, and turning those thoughts into action seems like more work than it's worth.

"You do not think Fischer is the killer," Gray says to me.

I sip my whisky, feeling the burn of it and saying nothing.

"You think he is telling the truth that he was framed," Gray presses.

I try to answer. I don't want to be rude and ignore Gray's questions. But the words won't come. No, the *lie* won't come.

Do I think it wasn't Fischer? I don't know. Do I think he was framed? I don't know.

What I *do* know is that he kept talking about a woman, one who played Leslie like a puppet. When I asked who he meant, he said I knew who he meant.

And I do, don't I?

Annis.

If Fischer doesn't wake up to defend himself and indict her, should I keep my mouth shut? I wouldn't if I knew Annis murdered four men and framed Fischer. But I'm not convinced that's the story. He already tried to frame her by suggesting—as Morris—that he'd heard her arguing with Ware.

"It's fine," I mumble. "I'm just in shock."

"Is there anything you want to talk about?" Gray asks.

Damn it, Gray. Don't push. Just don't push. Not in front of McCreadie.

"Maybe later," I say, as I gulp my whisky. "When I feel more myself."

"You mean when Hugh isn't here, and you can discuss what Mr. Fischer said about Annis without putting anyone in a difficult position."

I glare at him.

Gray turns to McCreadie. "Mr. Fischer blamed Annis for the deaths."

"He blamed a woman," I cut in. "He just said 'she.'"

"He said you knew who he meant. He called the woman a witch, which is obviously Annis."

"That isn't funny," I say.

"It is not meant to be." Gray turns to McCreadie again. "Mallory is uncomfortable with mentioning this to you and equally uncomfortable with *not* mentioning it."

"Tell me exactly what he said," McCreadie says.

We do that. McCreadie considers as he drinks his whisky.

"Fischer already knew Annis was a suspect, yes?" he says.

"Yes," I say.

"And he tried to throw suspicion her way by suggesting she'd been at Mr. Ware's offices, when we know she wasn't there."

"Yes. Which means he may be continuing the same tactic. I didn't want to put you in a tough spot by mentioning it."

McCreadie shrugs. "It is not a difficult spot. If Fischer recovers, he may continue his accusation, and we will be prepared for that tactic. If he does not, then—insofar as I can see—the evidence all points to him and none to Annis. Correct?"

"Correct."

"You have the snuffbox?" McCreadie asks.

Gray produces it, and while it's wrapped in paper, I still cringe at the thought of him carrying around key evidence in his pockets.

"We can check for prints," I say, "but we know Fischer touched it. Both the box and the vials."

"It would not stand in court regardless," McCreadie says. "Though it would have made us rest easier in our judgment."

"Any chance Fischer is telling the truth? That, yes, he was involved in the scheme, but the killer is framing him and planted that?" I finger my whisky glass. "I don't like the initials."

"Too obvious," Gray murmurs as he takes a bite of his pie.

"Victorians *don't* just randomly engrave their initials on all their belongings?" I say with a strained smile.

"We *do* like our engravings. To have such a box initialed would not be unusual. But to then use it to hide the very poison with which you have murdered four people?"

"It's a long shot."

"Very long," Gray says. "Which does not mean Fischer definitely *didn't* kill them."

McCreadie nods. "Someone who knows he did it may have hidden the evidence to prove it. The only problem with that is the poison itself being so rare."

"Presuming that's thallium in the vials," I say. "Which Isla can probably tell us. But if it is, and someone did plant it, they had to know what Fischer was using. That would mean an accomplice. Possibly even the person who supplied him with the thallium."

"Supplied him with it," McCreadie muses, "and did not understand what he was using it for until people began to die."

Gray pours a finger of whisky into my glass. "We have not heard from Jack again after she fled."

"He says, apropos of nothing," I mutter.

Gray arches his brows.

I turn to McCreadie. "Jack took off, like we said."

"Because she did not wish to risk being implicated in the man's death," McCreadie says.

"That's what I'm hoping, but also . . ." I glance at Gray, who keeps his expression neutral. He doesn't need to say anything. I understand what he's hinting at here. He revealed his sister's connection, and now I must throw Jack under that same bus.

"Jack found the poison," I say. "Dr. Gray and I were in the next room, out of sight. She found the box. Which means Fischer could be right that she planted it. He thought she was working for the killer. Maybe she is . . . or maybe she's the killer."

"Did she touch it?" McCreadie asks.

"No, she was careful not to do that. If we can get her fingerprints, we could compare them to any found on the box. I'm sure we can get an exemplar from the scene, particularly that trunk she was in."

"I will have the trunk transported to the police office to make that easier. It can be examined in the morning. Does that help?"

"It does . . ." I say. "However, since she was careful not to touch it, that suggests she knows we might be able to link her to the box that way. And if she knew that . . . ? Well, one thing about my world is that it's difficult to wander around wearing gloves unless it's winter. Victorians do it all the time."

"Meaning she could have only handled it wearing gloves," McCreadie says. "That complicates matters."

It does.

FORTY

I've retired to my room to do what everyone has been encouraging me to do for the past twelve hours—get some rest. When we returned from the pub, I declared I'd had enough to eat and would retire as soon as I'd served the late meal. Isla shooed me off directly to bed, which I would have appreciated if I thought I could actually sleep.

I'm not tired enough to take off my dress and lie down. I'm not revving to go, either, as I had been when Gray and I slipped out to find Jack. I'm conflicted, and our chat at the pub was supposed to help that, but it didn't. Worse, when something brings my mood down—like this—I start to mentally poke all the tender spots that I try so hard to avoid, chief among them being my situation.

Isla keeps saying we'll find a way for me to go home, and I know she means well, but how exactly does she expect to do that? Oh, she's had a few ideas, but they're like the ones I had when I first arrived. Return to the spot where I crossed. Return at the same time of day. Mentally will myself to cross over. It's magical thinking, and that's all I have because this is as incurable as thallium poisoning. We can try this and that to ease my discomfort, but ultimately, whether I return or not seems out of our control.

No, that's not true. From what I saw last month, I can cross back if I die. I'll have a moment or two, as I pass from this life, to catch a glimpse of my old world before I'm dead. How do I get back there *without* dying two seconds later? I have no idea, and I'm sure as hell not going to die to find out.

These are the thoughts that intrude as I try to relax, and I struggle to banish them and focus on the case, but that is another sore spot, and I can't bring myself to poke this one even when I know I should.

I'm propped up in my bed, weighing the likelihood that I am in for the night and can undress, because it's not like in the modern world, where I can just yank my clothing back on. Nor can I comfortably lie flat in a corset. So I'm propped there, watching the night creep from the window, when a tap comes at the door. I consider ignoring it. I'm supposed to be asleep, after all. But that's not Mrs. Wallace's brisk knock or even Gray's polite but confident rap.

"Come in," I say.

While I expect Alice, I'm not surprised when Isla steps in. She shuts the door behind her.

"You are not sleeping," she says.

"Hmm."

"Duncan's worried."

"Did he send you up to check on me?"

Her brows shoot up. "Send me up? That would require admitting he is concerned. It might even require admitting to *himself* that he is concerned. That would not do at all. Surely the world would end if anyone realized he is actually . . ."

"A really sweet guy?"

She shudders. "The horror. No one must know. It is a secret. A very poorly kept secret, to be sure, but a secret nonetheless, and we must allow him to maintain the illusion."

I manage a smile and shake my head. "I'm fine."

She motions to the bed, and I wave for her to take a seat as I pull myself upright.

"You are not fine," she says. "You are upset about the case, particularly the potential connection to Annis and Jack, which is making you uncomfortable to the point of melancholia."

"Were you able to examine the residue?"

"You do not wish to speak of Annis and Jack. All right then. Yes, I have examined the metal in the one vial and the powder residue in the other.

Based on the physical properties and microscopic examination, I would say it is indeed thallium."

I nod. Then I say, "Can we set Annis and Jack aside and talk through the case?"

"I am not certain we *can* talk through it properly without mentioning them, but I understand what you mean. Focus on this Fischer person."

I fuss and tug at my dress until Isla says, "Make yourself comfortable, Mallory, as you would at home. You hardly need be concerned about propriety with me here."

I tug at the skirts and get my legs crossed under them.

She laughs. "And that does not look comfortable at all. To each their own, I suppose."

"Yep, it's better in sweatpants, but this will have to do."

"Sweaty pants? Yes, we have very different ideas of comfort."

I stop myself from explaining and grab my paper and pen.

"You are writing while in bed?" Isla says. "Please do not let Mrs. Wallace see that, or I fear I will be unable to stop her from tossing you out the door."

"Nah, if I get ink on the bedding, she'll toss me out the window."

"You do know we have pencils, yes? Remind me to bring you a few tomorrow."

I dip the pen into the well and make sure it's drip-free before bringing it to the book. "Start with the cemetery scheme. From what we understand, Burns and Fischer came up with it. They brought Young in because they'd worked with him before and he would have a line on less affluent investors."

Isla nods. "They need an affluent investor, though, to initially buy the property, and that would have been Lord Primrose. I confirmed as much while you were out with Duncan, which is why I did not join you at the public house. I discussed the issue with someone knowledgeable in matters of fraud, and they suggested I discover who owned the property. It is Lord Primrose. Whether he knew it was truly a scheme or not is uncertain. My contact said either is possible. Lord Primrose's only true concern would be obtaining a decent return on his investment."

"Which he would get. No need to con him, but no need to tell him the whole scheme anyway. He buys the cemetery land, and Burns and Fischer bring investors to buy plots. At some point, Lord Leslie gets wind of it, and he wants in."

"He sees the fraud for what it is and bullies his way to the forefront. That was Gordon through and through."

"Cunning enough to see the con job. Unethical enough to want in. Belligerent enough to get what he wants . . . at the expense of Fischer, whom he—correctly—viewed as the weak link. From the letters, it seems Leslie was concerned that Ware was onto the plot. Either Ware really was or that was an excuse Leslie used for jettisoning Fischer."

"Then Fischer takes his revenge by killing the three who cut him from what he saw as *his* scheme. He also poisons his employer, fearing the man *did* suspect something. Is that the motive then? Enraged vengeance against those who wronged him?"

"Seems a bit harsh. I'd say the motive is money. Fischer was cut out, and so he killed the other three, and either continues the scheme alone or—more likely—empties the coffers and runs. Killing Ware was about covering his tracks."

"Did he plan to have the wives take the blame? It would seem so, given his rantings about Annis. It did not work for the bachelor Mr. Ware, but by that point, Mr. Fischer would no longer care about shifting blame. The city is in a panic, four people poisoned, and he has time to collect his money and flee before anyone connects him to Mr. Ware."

"If they even would connect him. He's a recent employee and there was no trace of him in the office. The housekeeper didn't even know where he lived."

Isla leans over to read my notes. "Is that it then? The murders are all solved if Mr. Fischer is indeed the killer?"

"I think so."

"And if it is Jack?"

"If it's Jack, we'd be back at square one. We know next to nothing about her, which means I couldn't even guess at a motive. We'd need to start digging into her as a suspect."

"Which does not make sense yet, when you have two better ones. Mr. Fischer and my sister."

I say nothing.

"And if the killer is Annis?" Isla presses. "How does that work?"

I set my pen back in the holder with a decisive click. "If it is Annis, then I don't see any motive for her to kill her husband."

That isn't true. There's her relationship with Sarah, but that isn't my secret to share. I can't, however, pretend Annis is motive-free.

"Strike that," I say. "She likely has motives for killing her husband that aren't readily apparent. But the other men? I don't see any motive for her killing them. Which means we stick with the simple solution. The one that fits."

"Mr. Fischer. Unless he is correct, and it was Annis pulling Gordon's strings. What if Annis is behind Gordon bullying his way into the scheme? That would make sense. Gordon brings her the investment opportunity. She sees through it. She uses Gordon to infiltrate—and eventually take over—the scheme. Then she sees a bigger opportunity. Kill Mr. Young and Mr. Burns, blaming their wives and using the fiction of a poisoning ring to her advantage."

"Then kill her husband, knowing she'll be the prime suspect?"

"It is perverse and unexpected, which is precisely my sister's style."

I say nothing. She has a point, one I have already made to myself. Annis was conveniently out of town. Yes, she'll be blamed, but if she did this, she'll have made sure she can't be connected to it.

"If the two wives fail to be convicted," Isla continues, "Annis has Mr. Fischer waiting in the wings to be framed. Then Mr. Ware must die because Gordon may have legitimately worried the solicitor had caught wind of the scheme. Annis efficiently ended all potential threats to her plan."

"Which ultimately is what? Fischer's motive would be revenge or money. Annis wouldn't need revenge and doesn't need money."

I know what would drive her to want to get rid of her husband. Sarah. As long as Annis was married to Leslie, any relationship they had would be risky. Instead, she could be a wealthy widow, unencumbered by obligations—business or marital. Free to be with the forbidden love of her life.

Free to be happy. To *finally* be happy.

I would be cheering her on . . . if it weren't for four dead bodies and three innocents framed in their deaths.

"That is the sticking point," Isla says. "I do not see Annis's motive."

Is love motive enough for such crimes? Is Annis capable of such crimes in pursuit of it? She is difficult and complicated and not a very nice woman, and I don't mean that in the positive sense, where a woman can be "not nice" and still be good and admirable. In her way, Annis is as much a bully as her husband. She mistreats her family, especially Gray, and I cannot forgive her for that.

Does that make her a woman who would murder four people and frame three others to secure her own happiness? There's cruel, and then there's downright evil.

Is Annis evil?

I don't want her to be. Whatever she has done to Isla and Gray, they still care about her, still long to believe she isn't capable of this, and I desperately want them to be right.

"I do not think her capable of this," Isla says, as if reading my mind. "Yet I fear saying so and being proven wrong, and then I am shamed by that fear, because it proves I am not as firmly on her side as I ought to be."

"No, it means you're human. I can count on one hand the people I'm one hundred percent certain couldn't commit murder. As for Annis, yes, some things bother me, but they don't ultimately lead anywhere. For example, the poison garden. Is it concerning that it used to be hers when she's a suspect in her husband's death? Damn right it is. But that's herbal poisons, and we're talking a rare chemical element. Not the same thing. She wasn't interested in chemistry."

When Isla says nothing, I look over at her.

"She . . . did take an interest in chemistry," Isla says. "It was not the same as my own, but we shared equipment and . . ."

"Still means nothing," I say, a little too quickly.

"But now that I have mentioned it, you will be unable to forget it. I do recall that she had a different interest than I did, which is why we shared little more than the equipment." She rises. "Her notes are still in my laboratory. Let us take a look, and with any luck, set our minds at ease."

FORTY-ONE

We find the notes. Three books of them right in the middle of the shelf, as if awaiting Annis's return.

Did *Isla* await her return? Hoping someday Annis would once again take an interest in the poison garden? In the laboratory? The younger sister keeping these books exactly as they were, as if her older sister might need them at any moment?

We take down the books and begin with the earliest one. It's soon apparent exactly how Isla's and Annis's interests differed. For Isla, chemistry is all about hard science, with practical applications in medicine. Annis's interest, at least in her early teens, is . . . unexpected. Or maybe, considering this is the girl who started a poison garden, not so unexpected.

Annis was all about alchemy. The woo-woo side of chemistry. While Isla says that most alchemy in the Victorian period, as in earlier eras, aimed at turning base metals into gold, Annis's experimentation was a little more eclectic. Turning metal into gold, sure, and if that sounds laughably naïve, remember that chemistry *is* often turning item x into item y, where item y usually has a more valuable use, like medicine. But while Annis dabbled in gold alchemy, she was more interested in things like finding the secret of life. How could you use chemicals to prolong life? Or prolong health? What if there was an elixir that would cure all diseases?

That is what Annis—circa early teens—was interested in. Her notes betrayed a brilliance beyond her years but also both an ambition that I recognize in the adult Annis and an enthusiasm I do not. In some ways, reading those entries, I'm reminded of Gray, and I'm saddened to think this is an Annis lost to time. I suspect I would have liked her very much.

While I'm saddened, I'm also relieved, because there's nothing about poison in these journals. Quite the opposite. Annis's interest, like her sister's, looks to herbalism and chemistry for health benefits. Keeping people alive, rather than killing them.

It gets even more fascinating—and more of a relief—in the third book, where her poison garden becomes obviously related to her alchemy. She wasn't growing plants to kill people or to harm those who'd wronged her. There's no sign of her even slipping a little into someone's soup, as Isla had done with Lawrence.

Instead, Annis was investigating whether the route to a cure-all could lie in poison. And if *that* sounds odd, I have to remember that most poisons either also have curative powers or were once believed to have them. Just look at radium—the ultimate cure-all until people realized it's freaking radioactive.

"Annis was very young," Isla says with a smile. "That is not a vantage point I have ever had on my sister. Here, she is young and passionate and naïve in the sweetest of ways."

That's true. For all Annis's brilliance and enthusiasm, she wasn't exactly on the verge of creating an actual cure-all. She was exercising her creative and scientific mind. A hobby that yielded little in the way of useful results, though she did make a few accidental discoveries, like a poultice that made cheeks rosy without cosmetics.

We're about a third of the way through the last book when something stops us both short. A change in handwriting. Entire chunks of notes written in a very different hand and also written in the third person.

"Annis acquired an assistant," I say.

"Evidently." Isla shines the lantern on the page. "I recognize this handwriting, but I cannot place it."

"A friend pulled into playing secretary?" I say. "Or a maid coerced into making notes?"

"Either is possible. If Annis decided she didn't need to take her own notes, she'd certainly find someone else to do it."

"Leaving her to the higher—and more interesting—role of scientist."

"Yes. But the handwriting seems more than vaguely familiar. I feel as if I have seen its like— Oh!"

She pushes her stool back and hurries from the room. When I hesitate, she calls "Mallory?" from the hall, and I follow. We take the stairs down a level to where she has her bedchamber, as does Gray.

Isla swings into her room and crosses to a dresser. Both siblings have larger-than-usual rooms for this period, which I strongly suspect once belonged to their parents. While neither room is twenty-first-century-sized, they've each chosen one significant extra to turn it into more than just a bedchamber. For Gray, it's a desk, so he can burn the midnight oil *and* the predawn oil.

For Isla, it's a chaise longue in the most adorable reading nook. That means she doesn't have a writing desk, and so she stuffs her papers into the dresser. And I do mean "stuffs." One trait the siblings have in common is that they both, to put it kindly, lack my personal sense of tidiness. Isla only has to tug a drawer on her dresser and papers fly out as if they were rammed in on a spring-loaded base.

"I need a bigger dresser," she mutters as she bends to pick up pages from the floor.

"Or I could help you organize your things."

"They *are* organized," she says. "There is simply too *much* of them."

Yep, exactly like her brother.

I don't offer to help. I learned that lesson with Gray.

"Here!" She waves a folded letter in an opened envelope. "It is from yesterday."

She hands me the letter. It's addressed to Isla and as soon as I see the handwriting . . .

Oh no.

I dowse the flare of dismay and focus on the letter. The envelope is addressed to Isla, but hand-delivered. I open it and skim the letter as any hope that I'm mistaken evaporates.

Dearest Isla,

I know it has been many years since we spoke, but I must say how good it was to see you and Duncan again. I only wish the circumstances could be different. Still, I wanted to thank you for your kindness today. Your sister does not deserve it. I know that, as much as it pains me. I can only hope

that the rift can still be mended, if that is what you want. If it is not, I understand, and I am indebted to you for your kindness in Annis's time of need.
All my love, always,
Sarah

"There," Isla says. "That mystery is solved. The person who assisted Annis with her notes was Sarah, which makes complete sense. They were written around the time Sarah came into her life."

I nod, gaze fixed on that handwriting.

"I am correct, am I not?" Isla says. "It is not precisely the same, but it is close enough to be clearly Sarah, writing twenty years later." She pushes pages back into the drawer. "Not that it matters. It was a minor and inconsequential mystery."

Her mood is lighter now. We've read Annis's notes and see nothing concerning there. One fewer thing to implicate her sister. It takes Isla a few moments to realize I'm just standing there, silently holding the note.

"Mallory?"

"I . . . have seen this writing before," I say. "Or, at least, the printed version, as on this envelope."

"Hmm?"

"The box in Ware's office," I say. "The box we think the poisoned treats came in."

Her gaze drops to the letter, and the color falls from her face. I motion for her to wait. Then I bring the traced note from the box and hand it to her.

"Am I wrong?" I say quietly.

She lays out the envelope, the traced note and the letter. Looks from it to the handwriting. She's trying to tell herself that it is not the same hand. That someone in Annis's household addressed the envelope and must be the person who wrote that note on the box.

Yet that is not the answer, because the writing is unmistakably the same hand, whether written or printed. That hand is Sarah's.

"Maybe the writing in the box was only similar," I say.

She shakes her head. "It is the same. Or close enough that if it is at all different, it is the writer attempting to disguise their hand." She grips the letter. "The writer being Sarah."

She shakes her head vehemently and turns to me. "I cannot believe it, Mallory. Perhaps it makes me a monstrous sister, but I could sooner see Annis behind this than Sarah. I know it has been many years since I knew Sarah, and not well even then, but I cannot imagine . . ."

She inhales. "I just cannot imagine. That is all. It makes me wonder . . ." She trails off.

"Wonder what?" I ask.

Another sharp shake of her head. "Not yet. I am sorry. I just . . . I cannot yet. We need to see Annis. Tonight. I must . . . I must get this straight in my head."

I want to ask more. So much more. But her expression says she's resolute—both in her determination to see Annis and her determination not to pull me into her confidence yet.

"All right," I say. "Let us go see Annis."

FORTY-TWO

When we leave, Gray is in the funerary parlor. I want to speak to him, but Isla is too distressed. She insists we leave a note and go quickly. It's already past nine, and any delay will make it less likely that Annis will admit us.

We arrive at the Leslie house to find a battlefield, an army camped on either side of the front line. The maid who escorts us in quietly explains that Annis and Sarah are in Annis's rooms, with access to roughly half of the house, while Leslie's sister Helen has claimed the other half. The two sides are actively avoiding one another.

"Even Miss Sarah," the girl whispers. "She is so terribly sweet, and always tries to make peace—particularly between Lord Leslie and his wife—but even she does not dare get involved in this."

When shoes tap along a nearby hall, both Isla and I tense, knowing who it is and arranging our features into twin masks of impassivity as Sarah rounds the corner.

"Isla," she says with a smile. "Miss Mitchell."

"I apologize for the lateness of our visit," Isla says.

"Not at all. We shall be up for hours yet. Packing, packing, endlessly packing." She pauses, her hand touching Isla's arm as she lowers her voice. "Is it true?"

"True . . . ?"

She lowers her voice more. "One of the maids is courting a policeman, and he says a man has been arrested for the poisoning murders, including Gordon's."

"There has been progress in the case," I say.

Relief washes over Sarah's face. "In other words, yes, although you are not permitted to say so. If this nightmare is anywhere near an end, we shall owe an endless debt of gratitude to you both, as well as Duncan and Detective McCreadie." She glances toward a lit room down the hall. "I have not told Annis the news, in case it is untrue. May I . . . hint?"

"Best not yet," I say. "We'll know more tomorrow."

Disappointment fills Sarah's eyes. "I understand. Another sleepless night, then." She steers us down the hall and into the room where Annis is packing books.

"Isla," Annis says. "Miss Mallory. I do hope you came to help me pack."

"I need to talk to you, Annis," Isla says.

Annis's gaze shoots to me.

"I'm going to look for that fig box," I say. "I know it's probably long gone, but I'd like to try."

Annis waves at the hall. "Feel free. If you go past the trophy room, though, you trespass on Helen's domain. I won't say you may *not* go there without her permission, only that if you do, tread lightly. The lioness has excellent hearing and is fond of prowling her territory, lest I abscond with anything that is not mine."

"Come," Sarah says, beckoning me back to the hall. "I will show you about and then fetch tea for Annis and Isla."

Sarah shuts the door behind us. As we head down the hall, she points at doors, naming the room beyond.

"That is Annis's bedchamber, which you may search, of course, but I cannot imagine Gordon would put the fig box in there. His own bedroom is in the next wing, which is in Helen's territory, but if you decide to search it, I would agree with Annis. Do not ask Helen's permission. Simply be cautious, and Annis will handle the situation if you are discovered."

Sarah continues on, "This is Annis's sitting room and then her office is—" She turns sharply to me. "Office! Yes. When the figs came for Gordon, I was in the trophy room with him. Afterward, he went to his office and took the box. I searched in there myself, after he claimed it was missing, but I did not find it."

"I will check his office then. I presume it is in Helen's territory."

Her lips twitch in a humorless smile. "Disputed territory. It is in Annis's side of the house, but Helen has forbidden her to enter and, in turn, Annis has forbidden *her* to enter. They have declared it no-man's-land, pending the reading of the will, when the contents must be examined."

"Where would I find his office?"

She starts to give me directions. Then a voice says "Miss Sarah?" from down another hall.

"Coming!" she calls. She quickly gives me the directions to Leslie's office and adds, "I will see what is the matter and then I will keep the way clear for you. Helen ought to have retired by now."

I thank her. As she hurries off, I watch her go. Could that really be the person who murdered four people? I don't think so. Other than with Leslie, Sarah lacks motive. What I fear is that Annis is setting Sarah up. And not just Sarah. If I'm right, there are three levels of blame here. Three ways for Annis to get away with murder.

First, the wives. That's a half-hearted scheme, mostly relying on public opinion to blame the wives for poison. Annis herself, of course, will have an alibi. If the women are not blamed, then there is Fischer. And if all else fails, who does she toss onto the gallows?

Her long-lost love. The woman she sent packing when she married.

Is it coincidence that Sarah came back into her life now?

Maybe not.

I hope this isn't the answer. I really do.

Once Sarah is gone, I hurry along the halls, following the route she gave me, until I reach a closed door.

I check both ways and turn the knob—

Locked. Naturally.

I bend to the lock, which is thankfully no more difficult than the one on the trophy room. I pop it open, slip in, and quietly close and lock the door behind me. Then I look around the room.

Huh. Well, this is not what I expected. Lord Leslie struck me as the sort who'd have a grandiose office that he never used. Like people who have a grandiose library when they never read.

This is more utilitarian than I expected, but he's clearly making a show of working, which makes sense from what I know of the man. There are papers and binders everywhere. It's not the paper tornado I'd see in Isla's and Gray's rooms. It's a more organized chaos, everything obviously arranged.

I walk over to the desk, expecting to see dust on the stacked papers, as if this show of busyness had been staged long ago. There isn't a speck of dust. Okay, well, just because Annis runs the business doesn't mean Leslie plays no role in it. The cemetery scheme says he has his own projects.

The cemetery scheme.

I am in Leslie's office, where I can further investigate the fraud and his role in it.

Where I might find evidence that Annis was also involved.

Yes, yes, I'm supposed to be looking for the fig box, but that was just an excuse to let me nose about while Isla talks to Annis.

I start working as quickly as I can, going through the papers on the desk. They all seem to be for legitimate business. I'm shifting the stack aside when I knock the blotter, and a piece of paper peeks out from under it.

I lift the blotter. Under it are a key and a piece of folded paper. I examine the key. Then I go to the door, open it, and put the key into the keyhole. It fits, but it doesn't turn. Not a key for this room then.

I take out the paper and unfold it. I read it. Reread it to be certain I'm not misunderstanding.

It's what seems to be a record of transfer from one account to another. A transfer into an account managed by Andrew Burns. And the person transferring the money?

Annis Leslie.

I stare at the signature. Something about it . . .

I rifle through the papers on the desk. I'd seen business pages with her signature. I pull one out and compare it.

The one on the money transfer is not Annis's signature. It only superficially resembles it.

Leslie was forging his wife's signature to give money to Burns.

I dig through the rest of the papers as fast as I can, but there's nothing else like this. That's why it was hidden.

Yet why would Leslie keep it? Why not burn it?

I glance at the fireplace to see bits of paper in the hearth. I hurry over and drop to my knees. Most of the remaining paper is scraps, and I can see only a letter or two on the tiny blackened pieces. I peer into the dark hearth and notice something pale. Moving a log, I find a sheet of paper that is only half burned.

I take it out. Then I rock back on my heels.

It's a sheet of paper with the same line written over and over again.

With gratitude for both your assistance and your kindness.

It's the line from the box we found in Ware's office. A variation on it, at least. And with each iteration, the writing changes.

With each iteration, it gets closer to Sarah's handwriting.

Someone was trying to copy Sarah's hand.

Lord Leslie? He forged his wife's signature on the bank withdrawals, and then forged Sarah's hand?

No. Annis's signature was poorly done. A haphazard effort by someone who didn't care to do better. This is meticulous. Practiced and precise.

My gut sinks as I look around the office. What had I thought when I first came in? That it wasn't what I expected from Leslie. It was less ostentatious. It was more obviously used. A practical, working space. A space that had reminded me a bit of Gray's and Isla's work areas, though this was better organized.

I'm not in Leslie's office.

I'm in Annis's.

FORTY-THREE

I spend the next few minutes double-checking my suspicion. I open drawers. I scan books on the shelf. I examine the papers more carefully. There is soon no doubt that I am in Annis's office.

I'm holding the handwriting practice in one hand and the forged money transfer in the other when a board creaks in the hall. I freeze. Steps sound, as soft as if they were from slippered feet.

I dowse the lantern and hold my breath. Moonlight filters through the half-open blind, and I watch the doorknob turn one way and then the other. I creep over.

Someone is there. Someone stands right outside the door.

I swear I hear breathing.

I wait for the sound of a key in the lock. When it doesn't come, I lower myself to one knee and peer out the keyhole. My line of sight is blocked by dark fabric. The black of mourning.

Annis?

I hold my breath. Two seconds tick past. Then those soft slippered steps, and the black wall of fabric moves from my line of sight. The steps continue down the hall, heading opposite the direction of Annis's wing. I can see nothing from my narrow vantage.

I unlock the door and crack it open, ever so carefully. I catch sight of the retreating figure.

A slender brunette in mourning black gliding down the hall.

Gliding to *her* territory.

Helen.

I consider. Then, once she's gone, I slip out and start after her, rolling my footfalls to move as quietly as I can.

I've made it to the end of the hall when footsteps come from the opposite direction, and I turn to see Sarah hurrying my way. On seeing me, she smiles. I head back to her, still moving slowly and quietly, which has her arching her brows.

"I was avoiding Helen," I whisper.

"She's prowling so late?" Sarah shakes her head. "Let me peek in the office, and make sure it looks as it did or she will surely notice."

She stops at a closed door and puts her hand to the knob.

"That's not where I was," I say.

I point at the cracked-open door two down.

She frowns. "That isn't Gordon's office. It is Annis's."

"Yep, apparently, I misheard your directions."

"No matter. I shall stand guard while you search—"

A commotion sounds, deep in the bowels of this monstrosity of a house. The butler's voice booms that it's nearly midnight, and they cannot simply barge in at such an hour.

I wince. "Dr. Gray has arrived, I presume. We left a note to tell him where we were going."

"Let me handle this, and then we shall search Gordon's office together."

I follow Sarah, but with every step, it becomes clearer that the new arrival isn't Gray. Another man is arguing with the butler, and I don't recognize his voice. Then footsteps thump, at least three pairs of them, the butler still trying to stop the intruders.

I pick up my pace.

"Where is she?" a man says.

"If you mean Lady Leslie, she is abed, and you shall not—"

"It's all right," Annis's voice replies. "I am right here. If you would be so kind as to introduce yourself, gentlemen?"

"Detective Crichton," the man says. "Here to arrest you for the murder of your husband."

* * *

By the time we reach the scene, it's a clamor of voices—Annis seeming more aggrieved than concerned, the butler sputtering that the police have no right to intrude so late, and Isla arguing that this is preposterous as she demands to speak to Detective McCreadie.

"McCreadie isn't in charge of this case," Crichton says as Sarah and I round the last corner. "He is enjoying a much-deserved rest while I handle this unpleasantness."

In other words, Crichton is swooping in for the glory of the sensational arrest.

"But—but—" Sarah says. "Has not someone else been arrested? A clerk for the deceased lawyer?"

"There is a suspect for the other murders," Crichton says. "He is currently in hospital, having attempted to take his own life."

"Did he name Lady Leslie as her husband's killer?" Sarah says. "Is that not an obvious ploy?"

"He is as yet unresponsive. This arrest arises from new information."

"What new information?" Isla cuts in.

His cheek twitches. He's going to refuse to tell her. I see it in his eyes.

"Please, sir," I say, dipping in a half curtsy. "I know you are only doing your job, and I do not envy you for it. My lady and Lady Leslie's friend here are understandably confused and distraught. I believe you can settle their concerns by answering their question, if you are able."

In other words, tell them what this new evidence is, so they'll know it exists and stop their caterwauling.

"Fine," he says. "Since the young maid asked so prettily. Let this be a lesson to you ladies. Good manners are not the sole province of the well-to-do." He turns to me. "I apologize, miss, that the evidence may be a little difficult for you to understand, but I know you work for Dr. Gray, and I am certain he can better explain it."

"Thank you, sir. I'm sure he can."

"Lady Leslie? Your husband was drawn into a scheme to defraud speculators. He was convinced to invest heavily, and we have just obtained evidence that the money he used was your own personal funds, which he took—quite unlawfully—from your accounts."

"What?" Annis says.

"Come now, my lady. This is no surprise to you. It is your motive for murder. You discovered he was set on bankrupting you, and so you killed him."

"Bankrupting me? I do not understand."

"You are mistaken, sir," Sarah says. "Lord Leslie would not have done such a thing to his wife. He would not have dared."

"He *should* not have dared," Crichton says. "That mistake was his un-doing."

"But this makes no sense," Isla says. "The fellow in the hospital was part of the scheme you speak of, was he not? Now you believe he has murdered his co-conspirators . . . but *not* Lord Leslie?"

"We believe Lady Leslie took advantage of the first two deaths to mur-der her husband and have him seem one of the victims. Otherwise . . ." He shrugs. "We are not ruling out the possibility she was responsible for all four."

"What?" Isla says. "No. It is this other gentleman. He had thallium in his rooms. I tested it myself."

Crichton had been turning away. Now he slowly pivots to face Isla. "Mrs. Ballantyne?"

"Yes."

"The chemist?"

"Yes, I am—"

"An obvious source for that poison, no?" Crichton steps toward her. "Why has this connection not been made?"

It has. By multiple people. The fact that Crichton has only realized it proves he's a shitty detective. It also proves that McCreadie has been keeping this connection from him, and that is a very dangerous place for McCreadie to be.

Before anyone can speak, Annis says, "The connection has not been made because I have little to do with my sister. A woman chemist? It is nearly as big a disgrace as a bastard brown-skinned brother inheriting my family home, which I have not stepped inside in nearly a year." Her chin jerks up, as if remembering something. Then she spins on Isla. "This is your doing."

"What?"

"You have always hated me, Isla. Envied and hated me, and now you have reported me for murder and come to gloat as I am arrested. You will not get away with this. Mark my words. I will have my revenge."

Isla stares in confusion. Sarah only gapes. And me? I have to resist the urge not to applaud.

Annis doesn't actually think Isla reported her. She's blaming her to clear up any misconception that they get along well enough to co-conspire.

With those words, Annis turns and puts out her hands. "Arrest me. Take me to prison. I shall fight when I am prepared to fight, and not a moment sooner."

Annis leaves without another word. We follow, and by the time we reach the door, McCreadie is there with Gray, having heard the news. There's a brief exchange, but they don't stand in Crichton's way. He has the right to make the arrest.

Only McCreadie is allowed to accompany Annis. Gray may visit in the morning. Again, there's no point in arguing. At least we have McCreadie to see that Annis is processed properly and that Gray is allowed to see her tomorrow.

Once Isla and I are in the coach with Gray, Isla asks her brother what he knows. As for how they heard about the arrest, McCreadie is popular with the constables, and when several on night duty learned that Lady Leslie was about to be arrested, one went to his apartment to warn him. According to Gray, McCreadie knows only what we heard—there is evidence that Leslie stole from his wife to invest in the cemetery scheme.

"Any idea where the evidence came from?" I ask.

"It was dropped off by a boy who ran before anyone realized what he had," Gray says. "A street lad hired to deliver it, likely with no connection to whoever sent it. I obtained a description, to be sure it was not Elspeth or Queen Mab's errand boys. It was not."

I nod.

"And you two?" Gray says. "You were investigating a lead, I presume?"

I glance at Isla.

Grief flickers over her face before she says, "I fear the culprit is indeed Annis, at least for Gordon's murder. And, worse, I fear she has taken steps to frame Sarah."

"What?" Gray says.

Isla explains about the handwriting match between the letter clearly from Sarah and the box found in Ware's office.

"Does that not implicate *Sarah*?" Gray says.

Isla says, "Beyond not being able to imagine such a thing, I remember when we were younger and I overheard Mother once speaking to Annis. There had been an incident at school. Annis had added a herb with a laxative effect to another girl's tea, yet she had Sarah brew the tea, making it seem as if Sarah was responsible. Wanting to believe the best of Annis, Mother suggested that it was a mistake and Annis did not intend for Sarah to be blamed, should anyone realize the tea had been tampered with. Annis admitted to adulterating the tea and agreed, yes, she did not intend for Sarah to take any blame."

"You did not believe Annis," Gray says.

"At the time, I wanted to. I still want to. I hope that she did not intend for Sarah to be blamed, but only that implicating her would weaken any case against Annis."

"Because no one would think Sarah actually responsible. It would show how easy it is for someone—like Annis herself—to be framed."

"Perhaps."

Gray gazes out the window. "At the risk of underestimating Annis, I still find it hard to believe she would do such a thing. Either the murders or the blaming of her dearest friend. The handwriting may have seemed *like* Sarah's, but perhaps that is accidental. The killer utilized a feigned hand that happens to resemble Sarah's. As proof that Annis framed Sarah, it is—I mean no disrespect, Isla—rather weak."

"There's more," I say, grudgingly.

They both turn to me.

I hesitate, not for Annis's sake but for theirs. I don't want to be the one to lay more proof at their sister's feet. Yet, if she did it, I can't let her go free. That has been the guiding principle from the start, for all of us.

I tell them what I found, the key and the handwriting practice and the forged money transfer.

"It was most definitely Annis's office?" Isla asks.

I describe how it looked and what I found inside.

"Yes, that is Annis's," Isla says.

"Sarah confirmed it," I say. "I went to the wrong room."

"And the key," Gray says. "It is for the trophy room, I presume."

"I couldn't check, but it definitely wasn't for the office."

He clears his throat. "While I have hated to mention it, that part has bothered me. The locked trophy room. I fear we lost sight of it."

I wince. "No, I lost sight of it. You didn't remind me of it because it works against Fischer—or anyone outside the house—as a suspect in Lord Leslie's death. It's further evidence against Annis. Particularly if that key in her office is for the trophy room."

"We shall need to check tomorrow," Isla says.

We lapse into troubled silence for the rest of the ride.

Once we're at the town house, there is no late-night snack, no lazing around with a glass of whisky. Gray and Isla declare they're too tired to stay up. I follow suit. *Yes, so terribly tired. I'll see you in the morning.*

Gray heads off first, and I start for my room, but then divert to slip back to where Isla is heading to her chambers.

"Are you all right?" I ask quietly.

"I have to be, don't I?" she says, managing a wan smile.

"I'm sorry."

She squeezes my arm. "I know, and I can see this is difficult for you, which I presume is on our behalf."

"I know you didn't get along with Annis, but she's still your sister."

She nods, almost absently. Then she motions me to follow her into her chambers and closes the door before speaking. "What Annis said, about me informing the police on her and being there to see her arrested, what is your interpretation of that?"

"She was shielding you. Crichton's attention had turned in your direction, and the surest way to divert it was to prove you two aren't close enough to conspire. To do that, she had to mock you. Mock Dr. Gray. Pretend to think you hate her enough to turn her in to the police."

"That is what I was thinking. I just didn't want . . ."

"To credit Annis if credit wasn't due? It is. The performance was a little ham-handed, but Crichton doesn't seem to require subtlety."

"No, subtlety would be quite lost on him." She goes quiet. "Hugh has made a mistake here, hasn't he? One that could endanger his career."

"I don't know."

A wry half smile. "You don't know whether it will endanger his career, but you do know it was a mistake. He should have been forthright about the connection between my work and Annis being accused of procuring poison. He ought to have ordered a search of our house immediately. With the delay, a search now is almost pointless, as I will have had time to prepare."

"He thought he was doing the right thing, protecting you."

"But it may end up causing more trouble . . . for him and for me."

"I think it can still be fixed. We just need to speak to him."

"We'll do that tomorrow. Thank you. You are a very good friend. To all of us." She puts out her arms.

I embrace her for a moment before I say, "Get some sleep. Dr. Gray and I are going to the jail tomorrow, and I don't know whether you'll want to join us."

"I absolutely want to. Whether I am allowed is quite another thing, and I fear I will not be."

"Detective McCreadie will make sure you are."

"I hope so. Whatever Annis has done, she is still my sister, and I am concerned for her."

"I know." I give her another quick hug. "We will speak in the morning."

FORTY-FOUR

I'm up early to get a few chores done, which sounds like such dedication to my job . . . until I admit that I won't get back to sleep and house-cleaning lets me accomplish something while my brain works through the case. I head down to the funeral parlor first. Cleaning it is my job, and it's been neglected since all this started.

I'm halfway down the stairs when I smell booze. My first thought is that a bottle broke in Gray's office. We must not have put it back securely the night we had a few drinks in there. Then I hear the sound of move-ment in the lab. I do not for one second think that Gray is down there getting loaded. Yes, his sister has been arrested for multiple murders. Yes, if convicted, Annis could drag the whole family down with her, Victorian morals being what they are. But anytime I've seen Gray reach for the bottle, it's social—a drink with me or Isla or McCreadie.

If I smell booze and hear movement, it's because Gray is working, alco-hol being used as a fixative for corpses.

Still, I do check the front door, just to be sure there's no chance I'll walk in on an intruder. After all, it isn't even light out, meaning it can't be past five in the morning. The door is bolted and the floor is clear of footprints, which in this era is the simplest way to tell whether someone has broken in.

I head to the lab door, rap on it, and only get a grunt.

"May I enter, sir?" I ask.

"That depends." Gray's voice is almost a warning growl. "Are you going to keep calling me 'sir' even when we are alone?"

"Sorry," I say as I open the door. "Habit."

"Habits can be broken."

His tone is snappish, meaning that growl really was a warning—telling me he's in a foul mood. As the smell suggested, he's working on a preserved body. Or part of one. It's a lower leg with a wicked gash.

I don't ask what this has to do with the case. Nothing, and everything. Nothing in the sense that it's unrelated to the poisoning deaths. Everything in the sense that Gray is up before five studying an unrelated bit of forensics for the same reason I'm up cleaning. His brain is buzzing, and he can't stay asleep.

"I came down to clean the parlor," I say. "I can sweep quietly out here or I can go upstairs and polish the dining room table."

"Or you can take this." He thrusts out a ruler. "Measure this wound. Unless you'd rather hold the leg, but I know you do not like handling dead bodies. Germs and such."

Yep, he's definitely in a mood. I bite my tongue and answer by striding forward and taking hold of the leg. He grunts and starts his measurements.

"Is the wound what killed him?" I ask when I can't stay silent any longer.

"I did not steal part of a corpse to study it, Mallory."

I bite my tongue harder before I say, evenly, "If you're going to keep snapping at me, Duncan, I'm going to walk out and let you handle this yourself."

He looks over, eyes narrowing. "That is a poor trick."

"What trick?"

"Calling me Duncan, so that I will be pleased enough to forget my ire."

"Is that ire caused by me?" I say.

"No."

"Then I don't give a shit whether you drop it, *Gray*. Just stop aiming it my way or I'm leaving."

A grunt. Then, "You are correct. I apologize."

When he looks over, expectantly, I say, "Don't expect a pat on the head for apologizing. You *were* being an ass, and I deserved that apology. Now, I didn't accuse you of *stealing* anything. I thought you'd been given this post-mortem to study, but I know people like their loved ones to be buried whole, for religious reasons. It wasn't removed post-mortem. I can see that now. It was amputated."

He nods, finally mollified. "Yes, it was amputated, and I requested the limb, which I have been storing for later study. The fellow claimed the cut came on the shop room floor—an accident with a blade—but I believe it was an ax. I am trying to determine that, as well as determine whether it was accidental or intentional. There is a small cut." He points at it. "This could indicate intention."

I examine the cut, which is ragged. "Someone hit him with an ax, and he managed to evade it, but then was hit again."

"He was in some trouble with moneylenders. He insists the injury was accidental, and so my interest is purely academic, although, if I conclude it was an ax and possibly intentional, Hugh could take that information to the man and see whether he wishes to alter his story."

Gray keeps working, explaining as he goes, relaxing, too, until he's finished. Then he says, "I fear Annis's chances are not good."

"I know," I say softly.

He goes quiet again as he replaces the limb in its jar. Then he says, "There are times I remember a very different Annis, from when I was quite young. And then there are times I think I am misremembering and confusing her with our mother."

"Isla says Annis was very different toward you when you were little."

"That is what I thought, although then it makes me wonder what I did to change her treatment of me."

"Nothing. She seems to be the one who changed."

"Perhaps, but . . ."

I follow as he takes the jar to a closet. It's the storage cupboard for such things, and he doesn't turn on the light, leaving only the shadowed illumination through the doorway as he places the jar on a shelf.

"I did not like Sarah when they first became friends," he says. "That is when Annis began to change, and I blamed Sarah, as her new friend. Annis found out and was quite peeved. That leads me to wonder whether I am misremembering the sequence of events. Whether I was jealous of Sarah, and my behavior turned Annis against me, particularly if her interest in Sarah was more than friendship. She could have feared I'd drive Sarah away."

"If she did, then that was something for her to discuss with you. It was no excuse for how she came to treat you."

He fingers another jar, his gaze on it. "I could not sleep tonight. I kept thinking . . . No, I kept *feeling*. It was as if I were a child again, losing my sister to a dark shadow that *is* my sister." He shakes his head. "That makes no sense, does it?"

I step into the closet. "No, it's exactly right. There is something dark in Annis. Something troubled. It stole her from you once, and now, if she did this, it's stolen her again."

"Yes. Even if the gallows takes her, I feel as if the gallows is not to blame. Nor the police. Nor the lawyers. Just Annis herself, some demon inside her." He finally looks over, his nose wrinkling. "I should be careful how I word that, or someone may think I blame demonic possession."

"I know what you mean. There's a shadow inside her, and while it's still part of her, it's not the whole of her. That makes all this so much harder to accept."

"It does."

I take another tentative step closer. When I am near him, he puts an arm around my shoulders, and I let myself lean against him, and we stand like that, taking shelter together in the darkness before the day begins.

By seven, McCreadie has come to escort us to the prison. He's obviously been up all night, and it's the most rumpled I've seen him, which is to say that he looks like the average person at seven in the morning. The strain shows on his face, though, and in the endless worried glances he shoots Isla's way.

While I prepare to serve breakfast, I leave the three of them alone, knowing Isla needs to talk to McCreadie . . . and both McCreadie and Gray need to hear what Crichton said last night about Isla.

I join them for breakfast to discuss that. It turns out that McCreadie's only professional sin is that of omission. I say "only," but for a cop it's still a serious one. He can't decide not to pursue an uncomfortable lead. While Gray and Isla are quick to absolve him, I can tell McCreadie realizes what he did and regrets it. Not, I think, that he wishes he'd set Crichton on Isla, but that he'd raised the possibility and then done the work to absolve her.

He'll have to do that now, and he vows to make sure she is both investigated and absolved as expediently as possible.

As for the case, McCreadie has little more to give us. In digging through Burns's papers, he found two more money-transfer notes, and he's confirmed that the money for the scheme wasn't coming from the business. It was financed from Annis's personal accounts—money stolen by her husband. With that, I finally see a satisfactory motive for Annis.

Lord Leslie was stealing his wife's money. That would be horrible enough in my day, but here it would be so much worse. Having her own money put Annis in a rare position, with rare freedom. Her husband stole that from her . . . after she saved him financially.

Annis had spent her adult life earning money that Leslie spent on hunting trips and mistresses, and still that wasn't enough. He started draining her personal accounts. I can imagine the rage and impotence that might lead Annis to murder.

I could even understand it . . . if she weren't framing her lover and closest friend.

Is this why Annis let Sarah back into her life? Was it all a setup? The idea makes me feel sick, but the timing cannot be denied. How did the reunion come about? Did Annis reach out first? Did Sarah joyfully return, thinking she'd finally been allowed back into her old lover's life? This is a question we need answered, as soon as possible.

We take the coach to the jail. It's below Calton Hill. In my time, it's gone—except for the Governor's House—but in its day, it was considered the worst prison in Scotland. In this period, it's also where executions are held, after the public hangings ended. The jail looks like a small city itself—or a castle keep, castellated towers soaring above a high stone wall.

McCreadie is hoping to get us all in, but the chances of that are slight. Gray will be permitted, as a gentleman and Annis's brother. I might, as his assistant. Men of privilege are afforded extra accommodations, and if their "assistant" is a young woman, well, the rich are different.

In Isla's case, though, the fact that she is a gentle*woman* acts against her. A sister of lower class might be permitted in. Someone like Isla? Heavens, no.

And that is exactly the reception we get. Yes, Gray can go in. Isla, absolutely not. Me? Well, the guard in charge of visitors is considering that, having already accepted Gray's healthy bribe.

McCreadie is arguing for Isla, while she whispers for him to let it go, not to upset the guard and impede *my* chances. As McCreadie is dialing back his protests, a man strides in. He's about fifty and florid faced, and his gaze goes straight to Gray.

"You," he says.

The look Gray turns on him is perfectly placid, even as the rest of us bristle at the man's tone.

"Yes?" Gray says.

"You're a medical man, aren't you?"

When Gray hesitates, McCreadie cuts in. "Dr. Gray is fully trained in both medicine and surgery, though he does not currently follow either profession."

"Can you set an arm?" the man says. "Stitch a gash?"

"Certainly," Gray says. "I will do that if you will—"

"Yes, yes," the man says. "I heard what you want. Your sister and your assistant can go in with Detective McCreadie here. I need you to patch up one of my guards. There was a fight this morning, and I'll not have that butcher of a prison doctor treating my men. You can do better, I've heard?"

"I believe I can. Thank you."

Isla opens her mouth, likely to protest Gray being commandeered when he wanted to see Annis, but he shakes his head.

"Show me to your man, sir," he says. "Hugh, would you escort Isla and Mallory to my sister? I will meet you there when I am finished."

We're moving along a narrow corridor when we pass a constable heading the other way. He greets McCreadie and nods to us. Then he stops, boots squeaking.

"You're the ladies that wanted to speak to Mrs. Young, aren't you?"

It takes a moment for me to figure out what he means. A moment for *all* of us to figure it out, our brains so focused on Annis.

Mrs. Young. Shit! Yes. The gravedigger's wife. The woman in prison for his murder.

"Is she still here?" I ask.

The constable looks confused by the question. "Yes, ma'am."

His confusion tells me that, despite two more viable suspects in cus-tody, no one is rushing to free Mrs. Young. She's going to need someone to advocate on her behalf and hurry that process along. I'm sure Isla would take the reins there, but she's distracted and doesn't seem to make the connection herself.

"I do not believe we shall need to speak to her," Isla says. "The investi-gation is past that point."

I remember the night I spent in an Edinburgh jail. The horror of it. Gray had come as soon as he could, but that wait had seemed endless.

"May I speak to her?" I murmur to McCreadie. "I know that until there is a formal arrest made for her husband's murder, I cannot say anything about that, but perhaps I might offer some reassurances."

"Of course," he says.

"Yes," Isla says. "Of course. I did not even think of that. The poor woman. I could go with you."

"No, you speak to Annis. I will be along in a moment."

I glance at McCreadie, who nods to the constable. "Would you escort Miss Mitchell to Mrs. Young and then bring her to see Lady Leslie with us?"

"Certainly, sir."

FORTY-FIVE

My sojourn in an Edinburgh jail had actually taken place in a holding cell at a police office. I'd been thrown in with other women either sleeping it off or awaiting a charge. This is different only in the sense that I find Mrs. Young in a cell by herself. Otherwise, it's as dismal as the subterranean holding cell at the police office. She's in a cramped little cell with only a pot to piss in. Fine, she also has a wooden bench and a moth-eaten blanket, but otherwise, it's her and the bucket . . . and the rats and the shouts of the other inmates and the sickening smell of unwashed bodies and bodily fluids.

I'm hoping for a room where we can talk, but that's not happening. I'm left at the door to her cell as the constable steps aside.

"Mrs. Young," I say.

She's sitting on the bench and, God, she's young. I should have expected that after speaking to her stepdaughter, but Mrs. Young looks like a girl herself, a pretty, dark-haired pixie drowning in her prison dress. Her stepdaughter said she was an art model, and I can see why. There's an ethereal beauty to her. When she looks up, her eyes meet mine, big blue eyes with the wariness of some forest creature.

"Mrs. Young?" I say again. "I'm Mallory Mitchell. I spoke to your"—do they use stepdaughter yet?—"husband's daughter and your boys the other day."

With that, the wariness vanishes, and she's off the bench in a blink, gathering the too-long skirt as she rushes to the bars.

"Eliza and the boys?" she says. "Are they well?"

"They are," I say. "Very worried about you, but Eliza is taking care of everything."

Her face lights up in genuine affection. "She is such a good girl."

"I'm sorry this happened to you," I say. "I know it's horrible, but I wanted to assure you that the police are continuing to investigate other suspects for your husband's murder. They haven't stopped now that you've been arrested. I know both of the criminal officers and an outside investigator, and they are working on theories that do not involve you, and they're making progress on those theories."

It takes her a moment to parse out what I've said, and I'm about to reword it when she nods.

"They do not presume it is me," she says. "They are making progress, as you say?"

"They are."

"Will the police come to speak to me? I am not certain how I can help, but no one seems to be interested in asking questions, nor listening to my story."

I want to get back to Isla. I want to speak to Annis. But I cannot dash off on this poor woman in these wretched circumstances. I've suggested that the investigation is currently focused on the possibility of another suspect . . . and now I can't spend five minutes hearing her side of the story? It'll sound like false assurances, when it only means that we're beyond the stage where anything she can add will help.

Five minutes. I can and will give her five minutes.

"I work with the investigator who is assisting the police," I say. "Anything you can tell me, I will pass on to him, and then I can promise he'll return for more if he needs it."

Which I'm sure he won't, because by then someone else—Fischer or Annis—will have been charged with Young's murder and Mrs. Young will be freed.

I continue, "Tell me what you remember. We already know you were not at home. Eliza explained."

Mrs. Young's cheeks flush bright red. "I—I knew I should tell the police where I'd been, but I feared what might happen to my children if I did."

"We have proof you were not home, which helps, but the poison was already in the house when you left."

"The poison was in the house?" Sudden horror, and she chokes out the next words. "Where the boys could have eaten it? Or Eliza? Or her grand-parents? Are they all right? Could they have consumed any?"

"No," I say. "It was in something that belonged solely to your husband, and it was hidden."

One moment's pause. Then she sinks onto the end of her bench. "It was in the gin. Oh, thank the lord." Another flush of scarlet as she levers up. "I only mean . . ."

"That the rest of your family could not have been poisoned."

"Yes." Her gaze goes distant as she whispers, "I almost—I almost threw that bottle out. I knew it was there, and I thought of making it disappear, because how could he admit it was gone if he wasn't supposed to have it? He'd promised us he would not drink. Yet I feared if he discovered it missing, he'd blame Eliza. I should . . . I should have . . ."

She trails off and continues staring into nothing. Then her head jerks up.

"The gin," she breathes, hand flying to her mouth. "The poison was in the gin?"

"It was."

"I saw who gave it to him."

"What?" I say.

She grips the bars. "I saw the woman who gave it to him."

My gut drops to my boots. "A woman gave it to him?"

"Yes. He was at home, by himself, because it was a Sunday, and the rest of us had gone to church, but the walk was quite chilly, so I slipped home to fetch a shawl for Mrs. McKay—that is Eliza's grandmother. As I came around the corner, I saw a woman on our steps, knocking at the door. It looked as if she was going to set the basket down and leave after she knocked, but my husband opened it before she could go and then—"

She takes a deep breath and presses her hands to her chest, as if slowing her story. "I hurried closer to the stairs. I know my husband had—that he had other women, and to have one at our home, where our children might have seen her? It was too much. I planned to confront her and tell her to stay away from my home, so I drew closer. I heard their con-versation, which was very brief. She had a soft voice, and it was hard to hear her but she seemed to be thanking him for some past kindness. He invited her in, but she said no, she had to go to church, and she left the basket and hurried down the steps."

"Where you were waiting."

Mrs. Young drops her gaze. "Where I *intended* to be waiting, but on hearing her, I realized this was only someone he had helped, perhaps because he hoped for something in return." Her mouth twists with a pained smile. "Instead, he got a bottle of gin."

"So you didn't confront her?"

"I retreated into the shadows. You will ask whether I saw her, and I wish— how I wish—I could say that I saw her face and can describe it in detail."

"But you cannot."

She shakes her head. "I caught only a glimpse, and even then, it was hidden by a widow's veil, which seemed to prove he had indeed done her a kindness. He is a gravedigger, you see, and so it made sense."

"She was repaying the kindness of someone who'd helped with her husband's burial."

"Yes. So I did not see her face. I can only say that she had a very sweet and soft voice, and that she is about my own size."

"Your own height?"

"My height and my size. Perhaps a little taller, but not much."

"Shorter than average, then, and slender."

"Quite. Oh, and she spoke very well. A genteel lady, much reduced in her circumstances, given her attire."

When I must look uncertain, she adds, "I have done seamstress work, and her widow's weeds were not new and hadn't been well made even when they were. Not quite as ill-fitting as this dress." She lifts her skirt with a twist of a smile. "But not well fitted either."

"Her accent and her words suggested a high birth and good education, but her dress was not out of place in your neighborhood."

"Yes."

Because she needed to fit in. The widow's weeds gave her an excuse for a veil, but a fine dress would have still stood out. She didn't hide her upper-crust speech—she didn't expect to be speaking at all—but she could hide the rest.

I ask again about the woman's size, and Mrs. Young is certain she was shorter than me and very slight of stature. Which means it was definitely not tall and full-figured Annis. And I think I know who it was.

* * *

I try not to hurry off, distracted, and I take my proper leave of Mrs. Young. As the constable leads me to Isla and Annis, my brain works furiously. Little pieces that had been nudging at me—not quite fitting the Annis theory—now fall into place. This was not what I expected. Not what anyone expected. But that's the idea, isn't it?

We walk into another area of the prison, one that looks much cleaner, almost administrative. A door opens, and Isla walks out, looking distraught. McCreadie reaches for her elbow and she brusquely brushes him off, only to stop herself and turn. I don't catch what she says, but he goes to squeeze her shoulders in reassurance, and she falls into his arms, clearly catching him off guard.

I slow as McCreadie hugs Isla. I want to give them that moment, for her grief and his support, but of course the constable barrels right along, making Isla jump back when she hears his boot steps. She straightens and wipes away a tear with a gloved hand. Then she sees me.

"Annis will not speak to us," she says.

"She won't meet with you?" I say.

An angry shake of Isla's head. "No, they made her come. She is in there. She just will not speak. Will not respond. I want to shake her. I *would* shake her. But . . ." She crosses her arms, the defensive gesture not quite hiding a shiver. "She is not being her usual imperious self. She is not being obstinate and high-handed, acting as if this is all a mistake easily resolved. That I could understand. This is . . ." Another shiver as she grips her arms and McCreadie lays a hand on her shoulder, squeezing it.

"Annis is not herself," McCreadie says. "I think she is in shock."

"May I speak to her?" I ask.

"We can try," McCreadie says. "But I do not think it will help."

"Just me. Alone." I meet his gaze and then Isla's. "Please. I have something I need to say to her, and I think it would be better coming from a stranger."

"I understand, but I fear it will not work. It is like talking to a stone maiden."

"That's fine. She might not answer me, but I need her to hear me."

McCreadie opens the door. "We shall be out here."

FORTY-SIX

Earlier, I'd expected to meet with Mrs. Young in a visitors' room. Not quite the sort where I might meet a prisoner in the modern world, but certainly not "standing outside her cell." Now I am indeed stepping into such a room—and it's the luxury-hotel version of it.

Somehow, Annis has earned the privilege of not only speaking to her visitors in private, but doing so in what I can only guess is the office of some high-level prison employee.

It's a small room with a fireplace, a table, and two comfortable chairs before the fire. Annis sits in one of them. She's also been granted the privilege of wearing her own clothing, though her widow's weeds look a little worse for wear. There's a carpetbag beside her. Things Isla brought. It hasn't been touched. Nor has the teacup by her elbow.

Annis sits and stares into the fire, and she does not even glance over when I enter.

I don't take the other chair. I stand in the middle of the room, letting her continue to ignore me. I count to three. Then I speak.

"Sarah killed your husband," I say. "But I think you already figured that out."

A flinch. Oh, she tries to hide it. Overdoes the effort, which turns it into almost a convulsion as she finds her composure. She keeps her gaze on the fire, and she says nothing.

"Sarah killed Lord Leslie," I say. "She may have also killed the others. And she's framing you."

No response there. No response because this is not news to her. None of it is news—she'd only reacted the first time because she hadn't expected anyone else to figure it out.

I continue, "I just spoke to Mrs. Young. She saw who dropped off the poisoned gin that killed her husband. She hadn't realized that's what killed him, of course, so she didn't mention it before. She saw a woman in widow's weeds and a veil over her face. Tiny and soft-spoken. Not you."

No reaction. I step closer. "While the description matches Sarah, one could argue that you sent her. You tricked her into writing the notes that came with the gifts—very generic notes—and then you sent her to deliver them, and she had no idea the gifts were poisoned. Except the evidence suggests you wrote the notes faking her handwriting."

No response.

"I found a burned paper in your office fireplace. I found the key for the trophy room." I haven't confirmed that, but I run with it here. "I also found a receipt for a money transfer hidden on your desk, which is odd, because you seemed genuinely confused to hear the police say your husband was forging your name to take out money."

Still nothing. I move until I'm right at her shoulder, close enough to hear her breathing.

"It was convenient, wasn't it? That I found those things? Evidence of the money theft, in case you tried to argue you didn't know about it. Evidence of the handwriting practice, in case you tried to say Sarah had actually written those notes. The missing key for the room where your husband died." I lay my hand on the back of her chair. "Any guess who led me to your office?"

Her breathing hitches.

"Sarah told me Lord Leslie took the figs into his office. Then she gave me directions, which led me to *your* office instead. I figured I'd misunderstood. But I've thought it through, and I know I followed her directions correctly. She led me there, knowing I could open the lock—as I did on the trophy room—and that I should find at least one of her clues. If I didn't, well, none of that evidence was going anywhere, and you were going to prison that night—she'd made sure of that. The police would find the rest of the planted evidence eventually."

Silence.

I move closer and look down at her. "If you're framing Sarah, you're doing a shitty job of it, and I don't think you do a shitty job of anything."

"Perhaps you don't know me that well. A shocking thought given our lengthy acquaintance."

I snort. "I knew you well enough to know you'd respond to that. I also think I know you well enough to know that if you're not defending yourself to the police, you have a helluva good reason. Whether you did it or not, you'd be talking. Or you'd be sitting there like the queen herself, waiting for these fools to finish chasing their tails before you deigned to respond."

She only shakes her head.

I continue. "You've unsettled Isla. Do you know that? You two might not be close, but she knows her Annis, and you are not her right now. You are something she's never seen her big sister be. Scared."

"Did you not point out that I face the gallows?"

"Except you don't, do you? You're not afraid of what happens if you don't get out of this alive." I step in front of her. "You're afraid of what happens if you do."

Her gaze jumps to mine, an involuntary reaction before she jerks it away. "You are a foolish girl. You talk and you talk when you should think and be silent lest you speak nonsense."

"So I'm right. Good. Sarah isn't who she seems to be, but you've always known that. I'm not sure I could be friends with someone who plays the good girl . . . and blames me for her misdeeds. But it's not just friendship, is it? You love her."

A twitch, the dart hitting.

"I heard a story about you two in school, where you allegedly set Sarah up to take the blame for making a girl sick. Later, that gave me pause. I read your journals from the poison garden. You never experimented with them as poison, even to wreak a little justifiable revenge. But someone else had access to that garden, someone who'd worked with you on it. Sarah."

She scoffs, "You draw that conclusion because I didn't write 'I shall use this concoction to make my enemies pay'?"

"No, I draw it because you were meticulous in your notes, and you showed no interest in brewing poisons. Your goals were too lofty for that nonsense. Sarah brewed that tea and made the girl ill. Everyone presumed it was you, and you fell on your sword for her. You do that a lot, I think.

After all, you're Annis Gray and then Lady Annis Leslie—you don't give a damn what anyone thinks about you. You do as you please, even to your family. You turned your back on Duncan, and left him to figure out what he'd done wrong. Did you know he thinks it was because he didn't care for Sarah at first, because he was rude to her?"

"He *was* rude."

"Because he was jealous of you paying attention to her? Or because something about her—or about how she treated you—bothered him, even if he wasn't quite sure why? Which sounds more like the brother you know?"

She doesn't answer.

"You turned your back on him," I say again. "Was that Sarah's suggestion? Distance yourself from your inconvenient half brother? Or was that bit of pure evil all you?"

Another flinch.

"I don't care," I say. "Well, yes, I do care, which is why I won't cut you any slack if you did it because of Sarah. Same as I won't cut you slack if she's the one who claimed Duncan watched her undressing when he saw you two together. You still went along for it. Chose your lover over your family."

"I was . . . very young."

"You're not now, and you're still shitty to him. The point is that Sarah is an evil witch, and you tried to escape her by marrying Lord Leslie. Only you never stopped caring, so when she came back, you let her. Now she's murdered four people, including your husband, and she's set you up to take the fall. You're not defending yourself, which means this is a power play. She has you squarely under her thumb, and you'd damn well better realize it. Keep your mouth shut, and she'll trot out the evidence to exonerate you and falsely convict Fischer. Say anything, though—blame her in any way—and you're going down."

A five-second pause, before she finds her composure enough to say, "You really are a foolish child."

"And you really aren't as good at this manipulation stuff as you think. Weird, because you've learned from a master. Every time you insult me, Annis, I know I've guessed right. So now you only have to wait for Sarah to free you . . . into another kind of prison, one where she holds the keys. She lets you out, and you owe her everything, and you know what she's capable of."

Annis glances to the side, away from me.

"Look me in the eye and tell me I'm wrong," I say. "Maybe I've misunderstood a few things. I'm sure I have. But look at me and say I am fundamentally incorrect that Sarah did this and that she will set you free if you keep your mouth shut."

She lifts her gaze to mine. "Leave this alone, Miss Mitchell. It doesn't concern you."

"It concerns Isla and Duncan—"

She cuts me off, and I think she's going to give me shit for calling them by their first names, but instead she says. "I will not let it concern them. They are safe. Their sister will be freed, and any shadow on their names will be lifted, and they will be safe. In every way."

The way she says those last three words—her inflection and the look in her eyes—rocks me back on my heels. "Sarah has threatened them, hasn't she? This isn't just about you. You're afraid for them."

"I am Annis Gray," she says, lifting her chin. "I do not care about anyone but myself."

Bullshit. I've seen her defend and shield Isla, and even Gray. I think of all the things I could say. All the questions I could ask. But I've got all she's giving, and it's enough.

"All right," I say, dipping my chin. "As long as they're safe . . ."

"They will be."

"Then you've made your choice."

"And I am the only one who has to live with it." She looks me in the eye again. "Goodbye, Miss Mitchell."

When I come out of Annis's visiting room, Isla and McCreadie are gone.

"They took Mrs. Ballantyne in for questioning," says the constable who'd escorted me.

"What?"

He shrugs. "She's a herbalist, and Detective Crichton thinks she might have given her sister the poison. Makes sense, doesn't it?"

"I need . . ." I trail off before saying I need to go to her. I am not a cop. I have no authority as one and even less as a woman. Instead, I say, "And Detective McCreadie?"

"He went along with them."

Good. McCreadie is with her. He'll handle this, and I need to trust he'll do it right this time.

"I should speak to Dr. Gray," I say. "Would you take me to him?"

"Certainly."

We head down to the infirmary, only to discover that the guard's injuries required additional supplies, which Gray has gone to fetch. He left for home only moments ago.

"I will catch a hansom and meet him there," I say to the constable. "Thank you for your help."

FORTY-SEVEN

That damned coach ride seems to last forever. We hit a traffic snarl on Princes Street. Yep, they have rush hour in Victorian Scotland, too. I pay the driver and tell him I'll walk. Then I fairly fly along the sidewalk, while worrying that the delay will mean I miss Gray and should have waited at the prison.

I make it to the house. There's no sign of Simon or the coach. Damn it, I've missed them.

I still head to the back door. It's unlocked, and I stride in, ready to call for Mrs. Wallace when I realize how still and silent the town house is. That's not natural. There is always noise, even if it's just Mrs. Wallace clattering in her kitchen. But the lights are all out, and there's a chill in the air, as if no one lit the coal stoves.

Something is wrong. Something is—

A memory twitches. Mrs. Young saying just this morning how the gin had been dropped off when everyone was supposedly at church. In other words, Sarah had picked the one time many Scottish homes are guaranteed to be empty.

Is it Sunday? I actually need to pause and think about that before I recall us hurrying off this morning and Isla saying something to Mrs. Wallace about not joining her and Alice. She must have been saying she wouldn't join them at church. That's why the house is empty.

And without Mrs. Wallace here, how the hell am I supposed to know whether Gray stopped in?

Um, detective, right?

I check the rear door for the telltale clumps of dirt that Gray would have tracked in. Nothing. He could have come through the front, having Simon wait at the curb. No dirt there either, which means Gray hasn't arrived yet.

I pace back to the rear door. That's where he'll enter, because Mrs. Wallace locked the front, leaving the rear open in case Gray and Isla were too distracted to find the key.

As I walk to the door, I turn on the hall lighting. Another step, and I pause. There are footprints coming in the rear door. No clumps of dirt, but the distinct outline of prints on the clean floor. Small prints. Like a woman's boots.

Uh, because I just walked through there. In women's boots.

True, but I'd come down the middle, and these are off to the side.

Alice's footprints? Mrs. Wallace's? They'd have been in their Sunday best, walking out after the floor had been cleaned. Yes, these prints head inside, but maybe they came back for something?

I take off my own boots and follow the prints. They head straight up the stairs. That would mean Alice, heading up to her room to fetch something. I bend. The prints look a little large to be Alice's. Also, the heel is small. A woman's fancy boot rather than a preteen's Sunday best shoe.

I head up to the first floor, with the main rooms. A dusty print on the steps says the person kept climbing. Up to Gray and Isla's bedroom level? No, the footprints continue past that. It must be Alice then. There's nothing on the fourth floor but our rooms and . . .

And Isla's laboratory.

I remember Annis's face when I mentioned her siblings. Her firm promise they'd be fine. Which meant Sarah has threatened them.

Last night, Crichton might have suggested Isla was involved, but he'd done nothing about it. Then, this morning, she'd been taken for questioning.

I follow the boot prints, and they lead right to Isla's laboratory. I throw open the door, my knife at the ready, but the room is empty. I still stride in, stockinged feet silent as I check behind the lab table. Nothing. I snatch up the lantern, light it, and hunker down. The prints are harder to see now, as the dirt wears off the soles, but I pick up one over by the bookcase.

I find the right book easily. There's a smudge in the light layer of shelf dust. Thank God for Isla's insistence on cleaning in here herself . . . which means it hasn't been dusted in weeks.

I open the book. The inside pages have been hacked away in the middle to make a hiding place. And in that hiding place? A vial of thallium.

I drop the vial into the bottomless pit of my pocket and head back into the hall. I've missed Sarah, but I've found the thallium she planted. Now I just need to wait for Gray—

A drawer shuts in my bedroom. The clack of it has me freezing mid-step. I turn on my heels. My door is ajar. I hadn't noticed that because I don't care if Alice sneaks in. I've actually shown her my hiding spots, and I know she'd never steal from me. As for Mrs. Wallace, I doubt she'd steal and the unlocked door proves I have nothing to hide. I'm not exactly keeping a diary of my experiences as a time traveler.

I walk to the door and press my hand against the wood. The door opens a quarter inch. The click of someone rifling through my toiletries drawer.

I peek through. A figure stands with her back to me, as she paws through Catriona's belongings. She is slight of build, but her hair is dark.

Jack?

Is Jack the one who planted the thallium?

My stomach clenches. We did wonder if she could have hidden the thallium in Fischer's room, but we'd gotten caught up in our whirlwind of more likely suspects: Fischer and then Annis and now Sarah.

I know Sarah is the killer. That doesn't mean she's working alone.

I step in and clear my throat. "Hello, Jack."

She spins, and I blink. It's Sarah, wearing a dark wig.

"Oh!" she says, her hands flying to her mouth. "Oh, Miss Mallory. I am so embarrassed. I can only wonder how this must appear."

"As if you're searching my room for any notes on the case?"

"I . . ." She leans one hand against the dresser, as if needing the support. "I am sorry. I simply had to know what you and Dr. Gray had uncovered against poor Annis. His room is locked, and I do not share your skill with prizing them open, so I checked your room, as you are his assistant."

"I am."

She ducks her head, and I recognize the gesture. Earlier, I'd seen it as embarrassment. Ducking to hide a blush. But there's no blush. You can't fake one, and she knows it.

"You must think me such a foolish woman." She touches the wig. "Trying to disguise myself, as if I am a detective. I just . . . I do not know what to do, now that Annis is in prison. I feel so helpless."

"You could try hiding thallium in Isla's lab."

Her brows crease in a perfect impression of bewilderment. "Hide what?"

"I know you're framing Annis, Sarah. Don't worry. She didn't tell me anything. She won't because she's afraid of you."

A burst of soft laughter. "Afraid of *me*? *Annis*? I will admit there are times when I have been frightened of her, but she has nothing to fear from me."

"Yeah, I'm not playing this game. You've finally found an unreceptive audience, Sarah. That's the problem when you meet people who haven't known you long enough to be horrified by the very thought that you'd commit murder."

She stares at me. Then her bottom lip trembles. "I . . ." She staggers to my bed and sinks onto it, her head dropping. "I have done a horrible thing. The most horrible thing. You are correct. I committed murder. I did not mean to. I only wished to frighten Gordon. I wanted him to think Annis poisoned him and stop stealing from her, but I did not know what I was doing, and I gave him too much."

"And Mr. Young?" I say. "You were spotted giving him the gin bottle. The widow's weeds were a nice touch, though."

When I say "widow's weeds," I get the first genuine reaction out of her. The barest hint of worry chased by rage, both quickly dismissed as she finds a more suitable expression of wide-eyed horror. "Widow's weeds? Do not tell me Annis murdered—"

"Pause. Think. That doesn't work, timing-wise. She was in London on business. You're panicking, Sarah. If you don't want to truly embarrass yourself, slow down and think. Annis is the clever one. Yours is an animal cunning hidden behind a vapid face."

She launches herself at me. It's "vapid" that does it, surprisingly. I only meant to goad her and instead I hit a launch-sequence button.

Sarah flies at me, and I back up fast, smacking into the corner of the dresser. Pain courses through my back. She grabs for my knife, but I have the sense to slash at her. The blade cuts into her arm, and she howls like a banshee and springs at me with a ferocity that—as much as I hate to admit this—I do not expect.

I know what she has done, and yet I've still bought enough of her act that when naked rage contorts her beautiful face, I stagger back. She smacks my arm, and the knife goes flying. I dive at her, and she grabs my hair and wrenches, and the sudden pain has me gasping. I twist to punch. Her gloved hand slaps over my mouth, the fabric stinking of some chemical.

No, it's not her gloved *hand*. It's a rag. When she'd been hunched over on the bed, feigning distress, she hadn't been playing on my sympathies. She'd been preparing the cloth, and now it's covering my mouth and nose, and the smell of it makes my head throb and my gorge rise.

Not chloroform. Something else.

Something poisonous.

Sarah shoves me. I stumble, the nausea so intense that I gag. I try to right myself, but she trips me and the next thing I know, I'm on the floor beside the bed and she's on my back, pinning me.

My brain screams for me to vomit, instinct insisting I need to puke this poison from my gut. It's not in my gut, though. It's in my lungs. But the panic wipes away any thought except survival.

I have been poisoned.

"Do you want to survive, Miss Mallory?" she whispers. "The poison will kill you in less than an hour, but I have the antidote. Would you like it?"

I retch. She slams the heel of her hand into my back, pressing my diaphragm into the floor until I can barely breathe.

"I am going to make a deal with you, Miss Mallory. I will give you the antidote in exchange for Duncan's notes. I presume he knows nothing of your conclusions? If he did, you'd hardly be here alone, would you? You came looking for him, I bet. You went to the prison and saw Annis, and she told you something and you raced home to tell your master."

"She told me nothing," I wheeze. "Dr. Gray's the one who figured it out."

She laughs. "I would caution against such lies, or I might decide your darling Duncan has to die. You wouldn't want that. I see the way you look at him."

"The same way Annis looks at you."

It's a game try, but she only snorts. "Is it? Silly Annis. She thinks she is a sphinx, but I have always seen through the façade. Even as a girl, I saw how she looked at me, understood what it meant. Does that shock you, Miss Mallory? My admission of Sapphic love?"

"*Her* Sapphic love. Not yours."

"True. I prefer men, but I can be what Annis needs, in return for what she is willing to give."

"Her lifestyle. Her money and position. The things you lack."

"The things *she* would have lacked, too. She'd have lost it all if her idiot husband had gotten away with his nonsense."

"You knew about his scheme. You knew he was stealing from her."

"He confided in me."

A terrible thought hits. "You were sleeping with him. That's why you had the trophy room key. That's why he wouldn't have said anything if you snuck in after we left. You weren't in the hallway with the rest of us. You went back inside to hurry his death along before he signed those papers to stop Annis from getting the business. A business she didn't much care about . . . because she still thought her own funds were intact. You knew better. You knew everything because you were sleeping with—"

She slams my face into the floor. Blood fills my nose, and I wheeze, gasping.

"Your hour is wasting, Miss Mallory. Suffice to say that I saved Annis from that idiot and from bankruptcy, and if it had gone correctly, there'd have been no one to blackmail her or besmirch her name. That sniveling clerk would have gone to prison and—after I made a charitable visit to his prison cell—she'd have been free of him, too. I saved Annis's fortune and her good name, and if I expected to share in that, it is because she owed me. You needn't be concerned about Annis. I have always taken good care of her, and I will continue to—"

"Mallory!"

The voice booms from downstairs, and it is undeniably Gray.

Sarah and I both freeze.

"Seems the fascination runs both ways, doesn't it?" she says.

I say nothing. I focus everything on Gray's voice and the distant clomp of his boots. I suppose I should be holding my breath, praying he will come to my rescue. That's the proper romantic fantasy, isn't it? And it's the last thing I want. He needs to leave before he gets hurt.

"Call to him, and I will kill you," she whispers in my ear. "He will find you in a pool of your own vomit, clutching a vial of thallium powder. Perhaps you will even pen a quick note, confessing to the murders. Everyone will like this solution. The only thing better than a murderous woman is a murderous servant—it sends the nobility into such a delicious tizzy. You are an odd one, after all, and that is what Duncan and Isla get for taking you into their confidence."

I only half hear her. I'm focused on Gray. He's stopped calling, and his footsteps are receding.

Good. Keep going. Decide you are mistaken. I am not here after all.

A distant door clacks shut, and I relax.

"There," Sarah says. "He has gone to seek his pretty little maid elsewhere. Now, as to the terms of my—"

Another door clacks, and I realize I wasn't hearing the one leading outside; I was hearing the one in the stairwell. Gray left and has now returned.

The thump of boots on the stairs. Boots that climb past the second level, past the third . . .

Don't come up, Duncan. Please. Decide I'm not here and—

I wince as I mentally curse. He's not going to decide I'm not here. He *knows* I am. Because I left my damn boots at the back door.

I start to speak to Sarah, but she slaps a hand over my mouth.

"Have I not warned you?" she says. "If you wish to live, you'd best hope he leaves."

I peel back her fingers. "Then let me get rid of him," I whisper. "You no longer have time to kill me and escape."

"Would you like to test that?"

"Mallory?" Gray calls.

"I am in my room, sir!" I call back before Sarah can stop me. "I am indisposed. I had to rush from the prison. It is my monthlies, and I feel very poorly."

Do I expect Gray to buy that? Not really. If he does, great. But if he doesn't, then he's going to know something is wrong and won't barge in.

Sarah might say she'll kill me, but she really *can't* escape that fast, meaning her only option would be to attack him. Even as I think that, her gaze goes to my knife, five feet from us.

"Please, sir," I say, when silence comes from the hall. "This is most embarrassing, and I ought not to even mention it. Would you make my excuses to Mrs. Ballantyne?"

"Certainly." He coughs, as if in discomfort. "Might I bring you something for the pain?"

"I have that, thank you, sir. I only need to rest. It has been a most trying few days."

"It has been," he says. "I will tell Isla and Mrs. Wallace that you are not to be bothered, except to bring your meals."

The thought of food has my stomach lurching.

"Thank you," I say.

"I will leave you to your rest, then."

He walks, a little too heavy footed, down the hall. Equally heavy footsteps tromp down the stairs.

"There," I whisper as I glance at her. "He is gone."

She reaches into her pocket and pulls out a vial. Then she opens it.

"Drink this antidote," she says as she passes it over. "Quickly."

I take the vial, rise to my knees and lift it to my lips. Before I can drink any, I cough, doubling over. When I've recovered, I lift the vial again and tip it into my mouth. Then I start to sputter and choke.

"Th-th-that—" I say. "That was not an an—an—"

"You accuse me of such terrible crimes," she whispers at my ear, "yet you do not truly think I am your equal in wits. I have heard you speak to Duncan when you think you are alone with him, and you do not use such pretty manners as you did just now. You might as well have shouted that you were not alone in here. How long will it take him to sneak back to your rescue?"

I collapse, eyes rolling as I convulse on the floor.

"Too long to save you," she says with a smile. "I've decided I rather like this plan, even if I do not have time to write your death confession. Duncan will find you and realize that is why you were so quick to get rid of him—you were ending your wretched murderess life."

I'm on my back, sputtering and writhing. She glances once at the door, and then, pulls her skirts tight and slides under the bed, as effortlessly as if she's a child playing hide-and-seek, as if there's not a woman she poisoned, dying on the floor beside her.

Once she's hidden under the bed, she adjusts herself into the shadows.

"Sweet dreams, Miss Mallory," she says, as my eyes stutter closed.

I shut my eyes. There's a moment of silence. Then the swish of fabric and fingers on my chin—Sarah's fingers, turning my face away from the bed so I don't give away her hiding spot.

The barest creak of the door. Another creak of the hinges. Gray looking in and then slipping inside, trying to figure out where I am. I wait for the first step into the room, eyes shut as I play dead, the "antidote" having been dumped on the floor when I faked the coughing fit.

When Gray's footsteps enter the room, I roll, my stomach lurching, my vision clouding at the sudden movement. For a moment, I'm blinded, and I imagine Sarah flying from under the bed and launching herself at Gray.

But the blindness lasts only a second. Then I can see enough to grab the knife.

"She's under the bed!" I shout. "Block the door!"

Gray stands frozen inside the door, staring at me in confusion. I can only imagine what I look like, my eyes watery from retching, hair yanked from its pins.

"Duncan!" cries a muffled voice from under the bed. Sarah appears, pulling herself up on the other side of it. "Oh, Duncan, thank the heavens you have come. Your maid—she tried to murder me. Poison me." She gestures wildly at me. "She has the empty vial. I tricked her into thinking I had drunk it. She is mad. Utterly mad. I came to see how you and Isla were, and I caught her hiding poison in Isla's laboratory."

Gray is silent a moment. Then he says, "I presume she killed Lord Leslie and framed my sister?"

"Yes." Sarah feigns a sob. "She is a monster."

"I was not speaking to you," he says.

Sarah's shoulders convulse. She hovers there, as if suspended by strings. Then she charges. And here Gray makes the same mistake I did. He knows what she's done, but the residue of her charade lingers, and he doesn't expect this sudden transformation from sweet and gentle woman to howling beast.

She falls on him, and I'm there in a flash, pulling her off him as she kicks and screams. She tries to turn on me, but by then Gray has her, one forearm held in each hand as he restrains her.

"The antidote," she spits, trying to look at him. "I have poisoned your sweet Mallory, and if I do not give her the antidote, she will die."

His eyes widen, head snapping my way.

"Yeah, ignore that," I say. "I already heard the antidote bullshit. She's going to say she'll give it to you if you let her go. She slapped a dosed cloth over my mouth. An inhalant, which you can't cure by *drinking* an antidote. All I needed was a bit of fresh air. The real poison was that so-called antidote, which I dumped."

She snarls and throws herself at me, but Gray only tightens his grip.

"I'll be fine," I say. "It's time to bring in the police."

FORTY-EIGHT

Sarah is arrested for the murders. All of them. Isla is free from any charges or suspicion, and Annis and Mrs. Young are released from prison. Fischer survives his self-poisoning, and we discover the real reason she tried to frame him: he knew about her affair with Lord Leslie. He realized Sarah knew about the cemetery scheme, and she was the woman he feared, not Annis. Even in that clumsy lie about seeing a woman arguing with Mr. Ware, he'd intended to set up Sarah.

Sarah doesn't confess to anything, of course. She just cries, a lot, never breaking character even when she is tried for murder. She is the victim here. The victim of Annis and Fischer, who are clearly in cahoots. In a jury trial, she might have gotten away with it, but we're lucky enough to have a judge who puts his trust in the evidence.

The most damning evidence comes in the form of a paper trail. Bank records, to be precise. It was Sarah who forged the withdrawals in Annis's name, allegedly for the cemetery investment, but they'd really gone toward a nest egg of her own that would also give Annis a motive for murder.

The plan was to murder Lord Leslie and frame Annis. Then, Sarah would swoop in to save her lady love with evidence proving Annis was innocent . . . and putting Annis forever in Sarah's debt. Sarah would enjoy the lifestyle Annis could provide, which she had sorely missed, her own fortunes having plummeted until dire straits brought her back to Annis.

That was the plan. But Sarah got greedy. It happens. You come up with the so-called perfect crime, and you have to reach just a little farther. She stuck her fingers into the cemetery scheme with those withdrawals that allegedly went to Burns. Burns found out about it . . . and knew that money didn't end up in his account. Being partners with Young, he'd shared his suspicions, so they both had to die.

As I'd learned from Fischer's unsent letters, Fischer had been kicked out of the scheme when Leslie came in. Lord Leslie was a big fish, and if he didn't like Fischer, he was gone. Of course, the one who really didn't trust Fischer was Sarah. But then Leslie thought that Mr. Ware had gotten a whiff of the scheme, and Sarah decided the solicitor had to die.

Not only did that clear away all the threats, but it gave Sarah the idea to frame Fischer. Sure, if the police arrested him, Sarah wouldn't have the same power to hold over Annis, but this was a tidier solution . . . until things went wrong and it was time to throw Annis—temporarily—to the wolves.

Four people died, and four more were accused of the crimes—the three wives and Fischer. All that so Sarah could get the cushy life she'd envisioned when she first met Annis. That is horrifying on a level I don't think I'd have understood if I hadn't met Sarah—the real Sarah, the one who'd seen me "dying" in agony and only turned my face the other way so I wouldn't reveal her hiding spot.

There are monsters in this world, and now I have met one.

While awaiting the trial, I get a note from Jack finally.

Well, you solved the case. Clever girl! I should have stuck around to catch some of the glory, but I knew you could handle it. Come by Halton House if you have exclusive updates you want to share with my writerly friend. He'll make it worth your while.

At least the note makes me laugh. Cheeky as hell, considering she'd taken off and left us in the lurch. I'll excuse it based on the trauma of her kidnapping and, possibly, a desire not to get involved with the police. As for exclusive updates, the only person who'd benefit from those is Jack herself, so I think I'll ignore the invitation. Oh, she might say they're for her "writerly friend" but I'm enough of a detective to have realized there is no friend. I'd bet Catriona's nest egg that the broadsheet writer is Jack herself. I'm sure I'll meet her again, but I'm not going to rush to give her any exclusives until she can be of help to *us*.

The day after I get Jack's note, I slip into the Old Town to check on Mrs. Burns and Mrs. Young. Mrs. Burns's landlady tells me she is gone. Apparently, Andrew Burns bequeathed them a hundred pounds, out of guilt. The Young family is preparing to move as well. An anonymous citizen—outraged at Mrs. Young's wrongful arrest—found them better lodgings and paid the first year's rent.

Burns didn't leave his first family any money. And that "anonymous citizen" isn't anonymous to me. While Isla would gladly be their benefactor, she doesn't have that sort of money. Gray does. He has quietly found ways to get both families what they need to start over.

The wheels of justice turn swiftly in this world, and soon we have a trial and verdict—guilty. With it comes the sentence: Sarah will hang for her crimes.

A day after the sentence is passed, I'm in the town house library, dusting and working through my feelings, knowing I'm partially responsible for sending a woman to the gallows.

"I am going," Annis announces as she walks in, and I look around. There's no one in the room except us.

"You're going to . . . ?" I say slowly.

"The execution." Her chin lifts. "I could say that I wish to see her hang, but that would be a lie. I do not wish her to die alone, whatever she has done. I am going. You may accompany me."

"I may . . . accompany you? To the hanging?"

"Or not," Annis says with a flutter of her hand. "Suit yourself. I only thought it might interest you, as you were instrumental in solving the crime. It would be too much for Isla. Duncan, too."

It takes a moment for me to realize the truth. Annis doesn't want Sarah to be alone when she dies . . . and *she* doesn't want to be alone when she watches it.

For Annis, I'm still a stranger, and yet I'm a stranger she's come to know over the last few weeks—between the investigation and her current stay in the guest room. This isn't something she can ask of a friend or a relative, but she can ask it of me, and she *is* asking, however she words it.

"I'll come," I say.

"Good." She starts to leave and then turns. "Not a word to Isla or Duncan.

I will make sure you are properly attired, and we shall devise an excuse for you to be out of the house."

A week later, I am climbing into Annis's coach, after slipping out and walking a mile to meet up with her. I sit beside her, and she says nothing. We start toward the prison, and she says nothing. Then, when we slow for traffic congestion, she says, "You must think me a fool."

"No," I say carefully. "You fell in love. The sort of love you never expected to be reciprocated, and when it was . . ." I shrug. "It was overwhelming."

"Overwhelming," she murmurs. "Yes, that is the word. Sarah arrived in my life at precisely the right time, as I was realizing I had no interest in men. We became friends. Unlikely friends, to most, but I was not only dazzled by her beauty but utterly fascinated by what lay beneath it. Her cunning. Her ferocity. Even her cruelty. I had my own capacity for callousness, but hers was another thing altogether, and even when I was the victim of it, I was bedazzled. And it is not as if I saw it often. To me, she was what you saw—sweet and considerate and caring . . . unless I crossed her."

"So you learned not to cross her."

She nods and finally turns my way. "When we were young, we had a dream. A dream where I would inherit the family business, and we would live together as spinster friends."

"But you didn't inherit the business."

Her mouth twists. "I did not. That was made abundantly clear to me years before our father died. I knew Lachlan would refuse it, and so I had presumed I would be next in line. Isla had no interest and the circumstances of Duncan's birth would surely make such a thing impossible. An intelligent woman who understood the business and *wanted* it had to be a better choice than the bastard, half-caste son who did neither."

I tense.

She makes a face. "I offend you with my language. I do not think of Duncan that way, whatever you may believe. I only parrot how the world sees him, and so surely I would be a better heir than that."

"Your father disagreed."

"I found out that it would pass to Duncan if Lachlan refused. Still, I had a plan. I would go into business for myself. Sarah and I would be as any middle-class couple, with me playing the role of the man, working to support a household led by her."

"So what happened?"

Her mouth twists. "I discovered that Sarah did not share the dream the way I thought she did, as least not if it didn't come with my family's money. When Gordon took an interest in me, she played matchmaker behind my back. She begged me to marry him. If I played the role of wife, she would stay on as my companion and all would be well. I hated the idea, but I loved her, and so I agreed." Her mouth tightens. "Then I found them in bed together."

I make a noise under my breath.

"Yes," she says. "I do not know how much you understand Sapphic women, but there are some who are only attracted to other women and some who are attracted to both men and women. On first seeing them together, I thought Sarah must be the latter, and I felt terrible for not recognizing she might have other needs. But in the few moments I dared watch, I realized something else, too. I realized . . ." Her voice cracks, just a little. "Her reciprocation of my desire was simply a mirror reflecting back what I wanted to see. She wished me to feign carnal attraction to Gordon, in order to win us an improved position in life, and that was exactly what she had done with me."

"I'm sorry."

She continues as if she didn't hear me. "Rather than confront her, I tested her by saying that I did not think we should continue as lovers after my marriage, as it would be unsafe. She expressed two heartbeats of regret before embracing the idea." A twist of her lips. "She even offered to perform my marital duties for me—as repugnant as that would be to her—if it helped my situation."

I shake my head.

"That had been her plan all along, I think," she says. "Convince me to marry a wealthy lord and then take my place in his bed while convincing me it was best if we remained platonic friends. All the benefits of a highborn marriage with none of the responsibilities. I might have been foolish, but I was not a fool, and I would not let her treat me as one. I informed her that once I married, she would require her own lodgings and her own income. She threatened to leave. I did not stop her."

"And you were blamed for driving her off."

"She is very good at manipulating blame in my direction while pretending to be staunchly at my side."

"Yet you allowed her back into your life."

"That is the most humiliating part. Sarah has tried to reconcile with me for years. Every time her fortunes took a tumble, I would get a very pretty letter, begging for reprieve. I would respond with a check, no note attached. A couple of months ago, when I was having difficulties of my own and much in need of a friend, she showed up at my doorstep. I had long ago forgiven her for seducing me. After all, women feign interest in men all the time to better their positions. I kept her away because I feared what other damage she might do, but she returned so cowed and contrite that I decided I would allow a renewed friendship. Only friendship. Then Gordon fell ill and . . ."

"You needed someone, and she was there."

Another twist of her lips. "My staunchest supporter."

We've reached the prison gates. Annis's lawyer is there to greet us. He doesn't try to dissuade her. He obviously knows better. As we walk, he only explains what will happen, and Annis nods absently.

The night I passed through time, I'd jogged by the "shadow of the gibbet" in the modern-day Grassmarket district, and I'd reflected on that haunting reminder. It's only been a handful of years since executions became private. Now they're held here, at Calton Jail, in a cell constructed for the purpose. That's where Annis's lawyer takes us.

There are maybe a half-dozen people clustered there, and everyone except us seems to be attending in some official capacity.

"Does Sarah not have family?" I whisper.

"She severed herself from them long ago," Annis says. "They were shopkeepers. Decent people, who spent every shilling they had sending her to a good school, and she did not so much as thank them."

They were a step on the ladder upward, and once she'd passed that step, she didn't look back. Oh, she might have, at her most destitute, as she did with Annis, but the fact that they aren't here says everything.

The fact that *no one* else is here for Sarah says everything.

Those who knew her only socially—as Isla and Gray had—bought her act. So did every journalist who covered the trial, and every broadsheet and pamphlet writer who spun the story of the sweet and pretty lady deceived and trampled by her upper-crust friends. Yet the emptiness of this courtyard says that there *were* people who saw her true nature . . . and they were the ones she should have treated best—her family, her friends, her lovers.

I don't notice when the door opens to bring Sarah out. There is no fanfare. Not even a murmur in the sparse gathering. Annis turns, and that is the only way I realize Sarah is here.

I have tucked myself into shadows, in hopes Sarah doesn't see me. Annis came to be here for her, the one person who did, and I won't ruin that by attracting Sarah's attention.

Sarah doesn't seem to see Annis at first. She climbs to the gallows. Someone in religious attire says a few words. I expect Sarah to weep. To fall to her knees. To continue the act of the innocent. And there's where I misunderstand her. There's no audience for a performance, so she doesn't bother to give one.

"Do you have anything to say?" the minister asks.

She turns to those assembled. Her gaze sweeps them. Then it lands on Annis, and there is no doubt she noticed her the moment she walked in. "Only that I am indeed guilty of an unforgivable crime. The crime of naïveté. I loved a woman, the best friend I could have had. Loved her even when she cast me out. When she let me back into her life, I thought myself blessed, only to realize I had been tricked again. She simply wanted me to take the blame for her terrible crimes. Now I see you've come to gloat, Annis. To watch me—"

I step out. I move right beside Annis, where Sarah cannot fail to see me. She stops midsentence. Her mouth works, unable to find words as the fury rises, her cheeks flaming scarlet with it.

She opens her mouth to speak again, but the minister is already tugging her back, using her pause as an excuse to end her speech. She seems ready to fight, but a guard steps out to restrain her, and she decides not to bother. I may have cut her diatribe short, but those around us heard and understood, and they may be officials, but that won't keep them from selling those final words.

Even on the gallows, Miss Sarah blamed Lady Annis Leslie. Beautiful, sweet Miss Sarah forced to stand and receive the noose while the icy Lady Leslie looked on, the woman so cruel she could not even grant her friend a peaceful end.

That will be the story, and Annis will never escape it, because it's such a good story, with the delicate damsel and brutal bitch firmly occupying their proper roles.

The hangman steps forward, and the hairs on my neck rise, as I remember words of the woman we'd followed at the beginning of this case.

It seems I am not the one who needs to worry about paying a visit to Calcraft's toilet.

Is this the man behind the gallows moniker? William Calcraft? I can't see him. He's hooded and silent as he moves forward to do his job.

Before Sarah's hands are tied, before the hood goes over her head, she looks out at Annis one last time, blows her a kiss, and says, "I hope you never meet my equal, dear Annis."

"I pray I do not," Annis whispers.

And then the rope is placed, the hatch is opened, and Sarah drops through.

FORTY-NINE

Annis wanted me to come back to the town house alongside her. No need to hide where I'd been, now that it's over. Instead, I ask to be let out as soon as we enter the New Town, and I walk the rest of the way.

I come in the back door. Voices drift down. Isla and Gray, up in the drawing room, comforting their sister, as best Annis will allow.

I stand there, and I listen to them, and I hope Annis does allow it. I hope she understands what a treasure she has in her family. She might have turned her back on them, and they have every reason not to allow her into their lives again. Just as she had every reason not to go to Sarah's execution today. But there are times when we are able to put aside our own pain and do what we think is right. Annis did that today. Isla and Gray have done it for Annis since the beginning of this investigation, and I hope to hell she recognizes that and does what Sarah could not: prove herself worthy of the love she threw away.

I consider going up to my room, but I want to be someplace else. As much as I've learned to love my cozy little attic room, right now it's only a reminder of where I am. Of who I am.

Seeing Sarah die had been . . .

I hesitate to say traumatic. After all, I've seen people die before. People who deserved it so much less. Only weeks ago, I held a man as he passed from this life and begged forgiveness for his crimes. Compared to that, seeing Sarah—her face covered—drop from a gallows should quickly fade into an uncomfortable memory.

It won't. I know that. I watched a state-sanctioned murder, and I cannot get it out of my head. When I try, I find myself instead thinking of my grandmother on her deathbed.

I so desperately hadn't wanted to watch Nan die, yet I'd steeled myself to be there for her. But I hadn't been there. I was here, and I'm still here, and she must be gone by now. Did she die alone? She'd been so close to the end, and if my parents hadn't been able to make it in time, she'd have been alone, and even Sarah had someone at her death, and she was a million times less deserving than Nan, and that is not fair. It is so god*damned* unfair.

I'm down in the funeral parlor, sitting on Gray's office floor, knees pulled up as I try to cry. I *want* to cry. No bullshit about how I'm not that kind of woman. Tears aren't weakness. They're release, and I want desperately to find that, and I can't. I sit dry-eyed, thinking about Sarah and Annis and my grandmother and my parents and my old life. I grieve for all of them, the pressure building until I want to scream.

I don't hear the door open. I hear nothing until I see black-clad legs, and then I scramble up as fast as I can manage.

"Dr. Gray," I say.

I tense for him to give me shit for calling him that, but he only says, softly, "I thought I might find you down here. I went out to look for you and saw your boots at the rear door."

"I did not wish to disturb you."

"You accompanied Annis to the hanging, did you not?"

I hesitate. Then I nod.

"And . . . ?" he says.

"It was—" My voice catches. "It was awful. I knew—I knew it wouldn't be easy, but I didn't expect . . . It was awful."

"Yes."

I lift my gaze to his. "You've . . ."

"Twice. Hugh had to be there, and I did not wish him to go alone. If I'd had any idea Annis would go, I would have insisted on joining her, but she fooled me, as usual."

He motions for me to sit again, and I slide down the wall. He lowers himself beside me.

"Thank you for being there for her," he says.

I nod.

His voice softens. "I am sorry you had to endure that."

I nod.

"I am sorry you have had to endure all of this," he says.

When I open my mouth, he puts one gentle finger to my lips. "Do not say it isn't so terrible. I will no longer take umbrage at the suggestion that you miss your home, Mallory. I understand you can be content here and still miss it."

I nod, and feel the first prickle of tears.

He sits back against the wall, and his hand finds mine, entwining our fingers.

"I will miss you when you are gone," he says. "If I respond poorly to the reminder that you wish to return, that is all I am thinking. That I will miss you." He pauses, and then says, his voice barely audible, "Terribly."

I squeeze his hand, and the tears finally come, rolling down my cheeks as we sit there, hand in hand.

I will miss you, too, Duncan. Terribly.

ACKNOWLEDGMENTS

Thank you to my editor at Minotaur, Kelley Ragland, and my agent, Lucienne Diver, for all their help with this one. You're both awesome, as usual.

Thanks to Elizabeth Williamson and Allison MacGregor, for once again providing local reads and flagging things I got wrong about their city. Hey, at least with the pandemic behind us I actually got to do on-site research in Edinburgh. Didn't keep me from still making mistakes, of course.

Also, this time around I had some much-needed help with the nuances of period fashion, particularly how Mallory would have moved in her corset and endless layers. Big thanks to Elli F & Amanda KM for all their advice with that as well as some bits about Victorian living that I didn't quite get right the first time around.

JUNGLE OF STEEL & STONE

By George C. Chesbro

KING'S GAMBIT (1976)

SHADOW OF A BROKEN MAN (1977)

CITY OF WHISPERING STONE (1978)

AN AFFAIR OF SORCERERS (1979)

TURN LOOSE THE DRAGON (1982)

THE BEASTS OF VALHALLA (1985)

TWO SONGS THIS ARCHANGEL SINGS (1986)

VEIL (1986)

THE GOLDEN CHILD (1986)

JUNGLE OF STEEL & STONE

GEORGE C. CHESBRO

THE MYSTERIOUS PRESS

New York • London • Tokyo

The Mysterious Press, 129 West 56th Street, New York, N.Y. 10019

Printed in the United States of America

First Printing: February 1988

10 9 8 7 6 5 4 3 2 1

Library of Congress Cataloging in Publication Data

Chesbro, George C.
    Jungle of steel and stone/George C. Chesbro.
    p.   cm.
    ISBN 0-89296-204-6
    I. Title
  P53553.H359J8   1988
  813'.54—dc19   87-21873
                                                          CIP

for Mark and Michaele

JUNGLE OF STEEL & STONE

CHAPTER ONE

Veil dreams.

Vivid dreaming is his gift and affliction, the lash of memory and a guide to justice, a mystery and sometimes the key to mystery, prod to violence and maker of peace, an invitation to madness and the fountainhead of his power as an artist.

Now vivid dreaming is also his passport to the land where his love is lost.

"Come to me," Sharon whispers. "Love me, Veil. Tango with me on the edge of time."

"Yes," he replies, and begins his dream journey through no time and across no space to the place beyond the Lazarus Gate, a perilous state of consciousness a sigh from death that only Veil can reach and return from safely. Sharon had gone beyond the Lazarus Gate to be with him at his time of greatest danger, and now she is trapped there.

As he approaches death he becomes pure blue flight, an electric pulse with no differentiation between body and mind. There are no fixed reference points, no sound, only

1

the conviction that he is traveling at great speed. Then light arcs through him, flashing like lightning down his spine. He explodes and is reassembled, floating weightless, before the shimmering white radiance of the Lazarus Gate. As he unhesitatingly passes through there is another flash of blinding light and a great, booming chime sound that he feels in his head, heart, stomach, and groin.

Sharon Solow, naked like Veil, waits for him in an infinitely long corridor bounded on both sides by walls of swirling gray where ominous, toothed shapes lurk, melting away and re-forming, sighing, beckoning. Although there is no wind here, Sharon's waist-length, wheat-colored hair billows behind her as she comes toward him, and her glacial-blue, silver-streaked eyes gleam with love and desire. Her laughter, like their voices, is a chime scale that bounces off the deadly surface of the surrounding walls and falls around them in a cascade of fluorescent sparks.

"How am I doing down there?" Sharon chimes as she touches his mind and blends her dream-body with his.

Veil laughs. "Down where?"

"Down, around, over, under, between—whatever. What's happening to the rest of me?"

"You're as beautiful as ever," Veil says, reacting to the anxiety in her voice, gently caressing her mind.

"Really?"

"Yes, Sharon. Obviously you're being fed intravenously, but you're breathing on your own. You're bathed every day, massaged and moved into a different position every six hours."

"Am I still at the Institute for Human Studies?"

"No."

"Where, then?"

"You're being cared for in a CIA clinic in Langley, Virginia—it's the best."

"You've never mentioned that before."

"You've never asked before."

Sharon frowns. "But the CIA is your enemy."

"Not the CIA—just a man by the name of Orville Madison."

"He's the 'fat fortune-teller' you once mentioned to me, the man who wants you dead, isn't he?"

"Yes. He was my controller twenty years ago, but he's moved up in the world since then; now he's the CIA's Director of Operations."

"I don't understand. If this man hates you so much, why would he allow me to be cared for in a CIA clinic?"

Veil does not reply. He tries to draw Sharon even closer to him, but she resists, moving back slightly in the endless corridor. In the wall to Veil's left, something moans.

"Tell me, Veil."

"It's not important."

"Please tell me."

"He's the man I made the arrangements with. Madison supervises your care."

"But he wants to kill you!"

"Yes, but in his own time and in a place of his choosing. For now it gives him pleasure to have power over me."

"And he has that power over you because of me, doesn't he?"

"Sharon—"

"What have you given him, Veil?"

My soul, Veil thinks. He says, "I've agreed to carry out certain special assignments for him when he asks—and if I approve of the assignments."

"I'm sorry, Veil."

"For what?"

"You've delivered yourself to a man who hates you in order to save me."

Veil shrugs. "I consider it a small price to pay for the woman I love. Besides, if not for what happened at the Institute, he might have put a bullet in my brain by now."

"But he intends to do that anyway!"

"One day, yes. But not now."

"You won't be free from him until I'm . . . well, will you?"

He would never be free, Veil thinks as he glances to his

right at the gray, chiming wall beyond which he had seen Sharon's flesh begin to glow and melt from her bones. His soul would belong to Orville Madison for as long as the CIA Operations Director allowed him to live.

"Madison is keeping his part of the bargain," Veil replies easily. "You're being kept in good health, and a team of specialists is constantly trying to work out ways to bring you back to consciousness."

"One day, maybe, I'll just be able to follow you back through the Lazarus Gate."

"Maybe."

"Does this Orville Madison know that you can contact me?"

"No."

"Does he know anything about this thing you can do?"

"Not really."

"Not really?"

"He knows about my brain damage and vivid dreaming, but not the rest of it."

Sharon laughs. "Wouldn't he be surprised!"

"I imagine so."

"But what does he think happened to me?"

"He just thinks you're in a coma."

"But he must have seen my EEG. Nobody in a simple coma spikes like that."

"He knows about the Lazarus Gate, but he thinks it's nothing more than a fleeting state of consciousness a very few people pass through just before death. He's right, of course."

"Except for you and me, Veil."

"Except for you and me." He could come and go at will; Sharon's mind was trapped there.

"If he ever found out that you can do this, he'd try to make you use it for him, wouldn't he?"

"Of course. Fortunately for me, Orville Madison's main interest is in controlling everybody around him and screwing his enemies. He loses interest quickly in things for which he can't see a practical application to his primary goals."

"Could you actually spy for him with your dreaming?"

"No. My dreams are just that—dreams. They're projections of my own mind, not an entry into anyone else's."

"But what is this?"

"This is an exception. Yours is the only mind I can actually touch; that's because you're here and because I'm able to reach this place in dreams. I always dream vividly and often imagine myself living other lives, experiencing things with somebody else's perceptions. But those dreams are nothing more than extensions of my imagination—a kind of sorting-out of things I know, or believe to be true. Except for what happens here beyond the Lazarus Gate, I can never be certain that what I experience in dreams has any basis in reality."

"You can be anyone you want to be."

"I can *imagine* myself as anyone."

Sharon is silent for a long time. "I want to be with you, Veil," she says at last. "I want to be with you back there—wherever 'back there' is. The other reality."

"You will be."

"I love you, Veil."

"And I love you," Veil says as he embraces Sharon, then rolls away from the dream into deep sleep.

CHAPTER TWO

The short, stocky black running up East Sixty-ninth Street toward Fifth Avenue was holding Victor Raskolnikov's statue under his right arm and carrying one of the art dealer's African spears in his right hand. His white shirt was stained red over the area of his left shoulder, and that arm flopped limply as he ran.

Pushing aside his thoughts of Sharon Solow, Veil Kendry took the wrapped painting he was carrying from under his arm and set it down against a fire hydrant. He was about to angle across the street to intercept the runner when he heard a car door open and slam shut close by. He glanced to his right in time to see a gaunt, pock-marked man in a purple T-shirt and grease-stained chinos skip around a late-model black Pontiac and start across the street. Then he saw Veil watching him—and froze. He licked his lips as fear moved across his face like a ripple in water, then abruptly turned around and got back into his car. He turned on the engine and backed down the street in a screech of burning rubber.

Veil sprinted across the street and was loping easily ten

yards behind the injured, burdened man when he suddenly realized that the black did not intend to turn at the corner. "Jesus Christ," Veil muttered as he surged forward in a renewed burst of speed. He was only a step or two behind the runner, reaching out for the man's collar, when the black, without hesitation, sped under the red traffic signal and leapt off the curb into the alley of steel death that was Fifth Avenue at 8:50 on a summer Friday evening.

Veil almost stumbled into the traffic, but he broke his momentum by grabbing the pole supporting the traffic signal. He swung out over the pavement, then just managed to pull himself in toward the sidewalk as the side of a taxi brushed against his spine and a loose sliver of chrome caught and tore his shirt. An instant later there was a deafening cacophony of blaring horns and skidding tires, and then, like a discordant echo, the screeching of locked brakes and the crashing of colliding, crumpling metal. Headlights popped, glass shattered. The din slammed against Veil's senses like a physical blow as he spun away from the pole, then watched and waited for almost two minutes before the mammoth chain collision finally ground to a halt.

Now Veil stepped out into the street, carefully picking his way across what resembled a lava flow of broken machinery, vaulting locked bumpers and rolling over crumpled hoods as he searched for what he assumed must be the crushed, lifeless body of the black. But there was no body; somehow the man had made it safely across the street and into the dark green forest-gloom of Central Park.

Veil turned back and immediately went to the aid of an injured motorist in a nearby car. The woman had banged her head on the windshield and twisted her ankle, but did not appear to be seriously injured. Veil wrapped her in his light jacket, then moved on to look for others who might need help. Sirens wailed as police and ambulances converged on the scene from all directions. On Sixty-ninth, a police car's siren died with a loud *whoop* as two patrolmen jumped out. Veil knew both of the men; one glared at him with open hostility, while the other offered a barely perceptible smile and nod, which Veil returned.

Openly displaying a friendly attitude toward Veil Kendry was not something a policeman in any of the five boroughs of New York City could afford to do without risk of career damage, Veil thought with vague amusement.

"Excuse me, sir."

Veil turned in the direction of the rich baritone voice and found himself looking into the dark brown eyes of an olive-complexioned, heavily muscled man dressed in a brown gabardine suit. "Yes?"

"Detective Vahanian," the man said, flashing a gold detective's shield. "What's your name, sir?"

"Veil Kendry."

The detective uttered a soft, almost imperceptible grunt of surprise. Shadows of uncertainty moved in the man's eyes, then were blinked away. "Did you see what happened here?"

"A man ran across the street against the light."

Vahanian looked out over the wreckage clogging the street and shook his head in disbelief. "How long ago?"

"Maybe twenty, twenty-five minutes," Veil replied as he glanced at his watch. "If you're also investigating a theft from the Raskolnikov Gallery, he's your man. He was carrying the idol they call the Nal-toon, and a spear he must have snatched off the wall."

"Obviously you read the papers."

"On occasion. Also, Victor Raskolnikov handles my work. I'm a painter. I know about the Nal-toon; it's been the bane of Victor's existence for the past two months. I don't think he'll ever handle another piece of primitive art."

"I wouldn't blame him. Where did this man go?"

"Into the park," Veil said, pointing across the street. "He was short, maybe five-five or six. Mid-twenties, black—but I don't think he was an American black. He had an Oriental cast to his features."

"It was almost dark twenty minutes ago."

8

"The streetlights were on."

"Just a minute," Vahanian said curtly, then turned and walked back to his unmarked car, which was parked up on the sidewalk. He spoke for a few moments into the car's two-way radio, then returned to Veil. By now, dozens of police cars, ambulances, and tow trucks had arrived at the scene. "Where do you live?" Vahanian continued as he removed a cheap ballpoint pen and small notepad from his inside breast pocket.

"Three eighty-five Grand. It's a loft on the Lower East side."

"How close were you to this man?"

"He was across the street, but I got a pretty good look at him. He was wearing a white shirt without a collar and dark slacks a size or two too big for him. He'd been injured—maybe shot—in the left shoulder, and it looked like he couldn't use the arm."

"Anything else?"

"No. It happened pretty quickly."

The detective replaced the pen and pad in his pocket, then studied Veil for a few moments. "You're very observant," he said, raising his eyebrows slightly. "It looks like you've earned your reputation."

"What reputation?" Veil asked carefully.

Vahanian shook his head. "It's not important."

"Victor Raskolnikov is a friend as well as my dealer. If there's a police line outside the gallery, I'd appreciate it if you'd take me past. I'd like to see if he's all right."

The detective nodded in the direction of his car. "I was going to ask you to come along, anyway. My partner may want to ask you some questions."

"Give me a minute. There's something—" Veil glanced down the sidewalk toward the fire hydrant where he had left his painting, and sighed with resignation.

"What's the matter?"

"Nothing," Veil said, walking toward the detective's car.

Vahanian got in, turned on the engine. He backed off the sidewalk, made a tight turn, then made his way slowly back down Sixty-ninth, weaving through an obstacle course of police cars and emergency vehicles. He pulled up on the sidewalk around the corner from the gallery, and Veil followed him through the throng that was gathered at the front and struggling for position in order to see in through the huge display window. There were audible gasps from some of the men and women. As they entered the building a helicoper flew overhead, heading for Central Park.

The long and narrow room inside the entrance—one of four display areas comprising the gallery—was filled with an eclectic mix of primitive art and modern paintings, including three of Veil's. At the end of the room, to the left of a vaulted archway leading to another area, the pedestal on which the Nal-toon had been displayed stood empty, like some wooden creature that had been decapitated. Victor Raskolnikov, impeccably dressed in a dark blue suit and gray silk vest, was standing in a pile of broken glass, steadying himself by leaning on the pedestal. Ashen-faced, obviously badly shaken, the portly Russian was trying hard not to look across the room to where the sagging corpse of a young, uniformed security guard was pinned to the wall by the long, razor-sharp head of an African ceremonial spear that had skewered the man's chest almost in the exact center; blood had spattered over one of Veil's paintings, hung to the left and slightly above the guard's head.

To Veil's right, a few yards inside the entrance, a huge, hulking man who he assumed was a detective was questioning a frail, trembling woman whom Veil judged to be in her mid- or late twenties. The man's back was to him, but he could see the woman's face—and she was clearly terrified. Her face was virtually bloodless, made to seem even whiter by the shimmering blue-black of her long hair and her large black eyes. She kept shaking her head, as if she were denying something. Occasionally a thin, tapered hand would brush away a strand of hair or pluck at her thin lower lip in a curiously birdlike motion.

The woman saw Vahanian, reached a trembling hand

out toward him. "Is Toby all right?" she asked in a quavering voice.

Vahanian turned to her, but before he could answer, the huge man took a step to his left and, like some tropical moon, eclipsed the woman from sight. The man's voice came across the room to Veil's ears as a low, slightly menacing rumble.

"Veil!" The Russian who was his friend and mentor lumbered like some circus bear down the length of the room, threw his thick arms around Veil, and kissed him on both cheeks. "God, I'm glad to see you here. This is a terrible, terrible thing."

Veil once again glanced over to where the hulking detective was questioning the woman. Something was wrong, he thought; he was becoming increasingly certain that the woman was terrified of the man, not the situation.

Vahanian walked over to the other man, and both detectives stepped aside and huddled for a whispered conference while the woman stared down at her feet and hugged herself, as if she were broken inside. Once, the big man looked back over his shoulder, and Veil found himself looking into a round, doughy face with small eyes that reminded him of two raisins lost in a pie; there seemed to be no light, no life, in them. Huge, gnarled hands closed into fists, then relaxed again. Veil held the man's gaze for a few moments, then abruptly turned to his friend.

"What happened, Victor?"

Raskolnikov spread his arms out to his sides in a gesture of helplessness. "I couldn't stop it, Veil. Everything just happened too quickly. Now this man I hired to guard the statue is dead."

"How did it happen?"

"The young woman over there came in with a young man. The man, he had a very strange look in his eyes—and he was looking at the statue from the moment he came in the door. He never said a word, just started walking straight toward the statue. The woman screamed and tried to stop him; she grabbed his arm and shouted at him in this funny language, like nothing I've ever heard

11

before—click! click! click! Very strange. The man just pushed her away, grabbed one of the spears off the wall, and used it to smash the glass case over the statue. He moved so fast that he caught Frank—the guard—by surprise. Frank yelled at the man to stop, and when he didn't, Frank kind of panicked, I guess. He drew his gun and fired—hit the man in the shoulder, I think. Then the man threw the spear at Frank. Veil, I've never seen anyone move that fast. One moment Frank was aiming and getting ready to fire again, and the next moment he was dead." The Russian paused, swallowed hard, then gestured toward the opposite wall without looking at it. "Like that."

"Your guard did hit the man, Victor. I saw him. He escaped into Central Park after causing the damnedest chain collision you've ever seen on Fifth. But they should have him soon. By now there'll be an army of cops beating the bushes for him, and they're using a helicopter. I just hope your statue isn't damaged."

"I don't give a damn about that statue!" Tears suddenly glistened in the art dealer's eyes. "I paid a lousy three thousand dollars for it. What's three thousand dollars— what's anything?—compared to a man's life? The newspapers sure as hell made a big stink about it, but they couldn't tell me what I should do with the damn thing. The police wouldn't take it off my hands because they said it was legally mine. The United Nations made a stink, too, but *they* wouldn't take it. If they took it, then they wouldn't have anything to make a stink about. I didn't want to sell it to just anyone, Veil, because I felt very deeply in my heart for that tribe. All I wanted was my money back, and that didn't seem unreasonable. Then this gangster business came up and the courts said I couldn't sell it to *anyone* until a complete investigation had been made, but the judges wouldn't take it off my hands, either. Hell, I figured I might as well keep the statue on display for the publicity value. But I didn't want the tribe to lose it to some thief, so I hired a guard to make certain it stayed safe until *somebody* told me what I was allowed to do with it. I simply should have sent it back to the tribe in the beginning. Then I wouldn't be responsible for this man's death."

"Take it easy, Victor," Veil said evenly. "You aren't responsible for anything but being a very decent man caught in a bind and trying to find the right thing to do. You didn't fire a gun to protect a piece of wood, and you didn't throw the spear."

"Are you Veil Kendry?"

Veil turned to find the big man with the doughy face and dead, raisin eyes standing very close behind him. "I'm Kendry," he replied evenly.

"You've met Detective Vahanian," the big man said in a rumbling, phlegmy voice as he jerked a thumb in the general direction of the dark-complexioned man who was standing off to one side, trying not to look embarrassed. "I'm Detective Nagle. I understand you witnessed what went on up the street."

"Yes. As I told your partner—"

"I know what you told my partner, and I don't need to hear it again. You're the one who needs to be told something."

"You sound like a man with heavy things on his mind," Veil said in a neutral, flat tone. "Why don't you unload them?"

Nagle leaned even closer, to the point where his face was only inches from Veil's, and Veil could smell beer and garlic on the man's breath. "You've got a bad rep, Kendry," Nagle rumbled, planting the thick index finger of his right hand in the center of Veil's chest.

"Do I?"

"You do. For one thing, I hear that you have a habit of sticking your nose in police business. I hear you think you're a hotshot private investigator."

Veil considered pushing the finger away from his chest but instead stepped back. Nagle grunted with satisfaction.

"You'd better back off from me, pal."

"Am I to take it that you're feeling a bit cranky this evening, Detective Nagle?"

Nagle frowned. "I'm in a good mood, Kendry. You'd better hope you never see me in a bad one."

Veil glanced across the room to where the woman was staring at him, the expression on her face frozen somewhere between fear and amazement. "Look, Nagle," Veil said easily, "I don't know what your personal problems are, and I don't care."

"You watch how you talk to me, chief."

"You picked up wrong information somewhere. I'm not an investigator, private or otherwise. I'm a painter."

"You bet your smart ass you're not a PI. You've got no license. If you had, it would have been pulled long ago. The point is that you act as if you were a PI. You've had run-ins with cops all over this goddamn city, and cops most definitely do not like amateurs stepping on their toes. We've got more than enough bag ladies, bums, street jugglers, and street musicians; we don't need a street detective."

"From time to time I do a favor for a friend."

"You seem to have a lot of friends."

"Yeah. I make friends easily."

"I've even heard it said that you have friends in very high places in Washington, like in the CIA."

Veil resisted the impulse to laugh. "Well, you couldn't be more wrong about that. But you'd be surprised how many of those street people you mentioned need a friend to take care of business for them. Sometimes I take money; more often I accept goods or services. But I'm not a private investigator, and I've never pretended to be."

"Are you a bad-ass, Kendry? Some people say you're a bad-ass."

"I can't help what people say," Veil replied, casually turning his head to watch as a police photographer began snapping pictures of the corpse hanging on the wall.

"Let's cut through the bullshit, chief. The message I have for you is short and sweet: I'm a much bigger bad-ass than you are. I'm telling you to stay the fuck out of my way. I don't know what you're doing in the neighborhood, or if you have any connection with these other people. If you do have a connection, it doesn't mean diddly-squat. If you're even *thinking* about poking your nose into this idol business, you think again. If you don't, it's possible you could lose whatever it is you do your thinking with. I don't want to see your face again. Got it, chief?"

"I hear what you're saying," Veil replied flatly, his face impassive as he stared back at the police detective.

"You carrying a gun?"

"I don't have a permit to carry a gun."

"That isn't what I asked you, chief," Nagle said tightly. "You just made a mistake. Turn your ass around and lean against that wall."

Veil did not move. "Are you trying to harass me, Nagle? I'm not a lawyer, but I can't think of any reasonable cause I've given you for searching me. I'd hate to see a lawsuit or a review board hearing keep you from your diligent pursuit of this case."

"You long-haired bastard!" Nagle reached for Veil, and suddenly lost all feeling in his right arm, below the elbow. Amazed, he looked down and saw that the other man, moving so quickly that the motion had been imperceptible, had gripped his arm and was pressing a thumb into a nerve inside the elbow.

"Excuse me, Detective Nagle," Veil said as he released the arm. "Are you all right? I thought you were going to fall."

Feeling slowly came back into Nagle's arm. The detective glanced down at his elbow, then back up at the man with the long blond hair and pale blue, gold-flecked eyes who stood before him. The man's face wore an expression of genuine concern—an act, for the eyes were absolutely cold and appraising.

Nagle roared with rage and swung a wild, roundhouse right fist at a head that was suddenly no longer there. An instant later he felt arms wrap themselves around his waist, fingers that felt like steel rods pressed into his solar plexus, and he doubled over with a gasp. But he did not fall; he could not fall. The powerful arms held him up while the fingers, hidden from view, continued to press

15

and knead, jab and squeeze, until sickness began to burn at the back of his throat. Veil's voice, soothing and solicitous, came from somewhere behind his right ear.

"Just relax, Nagle," Veil continued. "You'll be all right. Vahanian, you want to give me a hand here? I think your partner's just a little drunk; I smell booze on his breath. I hope he's not going to be sick."

Then the fingers were abruptly gone from his belly, the arms from around his waist. As if on cue and conspiring against him, his stomach churned and its contents splattered over the front of his jacket, slacks, and shoes. Then he fell forward. He tried to twist around, slipped, and sat down in the pool of vomit.

Veil stood over the soiled detective, waiting calmly. All activity in the gallery had stopped, and there was silence, broken only by Nagle's gasps, retching, and coughing. The police photographer, two morgue attendants, a patrolman, Vahanian, the woman, and the spectators beyond the plate-glass display window all gaped in astonishment. Raskolnikov kept shaking his head, as if the muscles in his neck had gone into spasm.

Finally Nagle stopped retching. He took a deep, shuddering breath, wiped away a trail of spittle that hung from his mouth, then unzipped his blue windbreaker and reached for his gun.

Raskolnikov grunted with alarm and started to step forward. Veil stopped his friend by planting a hand firmly on his chest, and by then Vahanian had stepped between Veil and Nagle. The stocky detective reached down and hauled his partner to his feet by the front of his jacket. Nagle's face was brick-red, the small eyes aflame now with rage, hatred, and humiliation. He lunged for Veil, but Vahanian—displaying amazing strength for a man at least seventy-five pounds lighter than his partner—managed to shove Nagle back against the wall, where he held him.

"Stop it, Carl!" Vahanian shouted. "You're losing it!"

Vahanian dropped his voice and, still holding the other man firmly against the wall, put his mouth close to Nagle's ear and spoke in a low murmur. Veil, his ears trained two decades before to pick out sounds of life and death from a cacophony of jungle noises, could make out just a few words and phrases.

"... *witnesses* ... *got you on the drinking* ... *not worth the trouble* ..."

Gradually Nagle stopped struggling, although his face remained the color of flame. Vahanian, careful to keep his right hand pressed against Nagle's chest, turned to face Veil. For a fleeting moment something that might have been respect flickered in his dark eyes, then was gone, replaced by the cold, hostile glint of a cop staring at an outlaw.

"I hope you appreciate the size of the pass you're getting on this one, Kendry."

"Oh, I certainly do. I certainly hope Detective Nagle is feeling better soon."

"Shut up!" Vahanian snapped. "Now you're pressing your luck with me! What I'm saying is that this is a once-in-a-lifetime pass you'll never get again." He took a deep breath, continued in a calmer voice, "We've got your statements, names, and addresses. If we have more questions, we'll know where to get in touch with you."

Nagle had gotten his second wind. Suddenly he bellowed and tried to run through Vahanian to get at Veil. Like an outweighed but fiercely determined offensive lineman, Vahanian blocked Nagle with his forearms, put his head down, and drove with his legs, pushing the bigger man toward the exit. A uniformed officer, barely able to suppress a grin, hurriedly opened the door. The crowd that had gathered outside quickly split, and Vahanian pushed Nagle out and into a car parked on the sidewalk. A few moments later Vahanian was behind the wheel, and the car shot out of sight with a squeal of spinning rubber.

Inside the gallery, the photographer finished his work. The morgue attendants removed the body from the wall, slid it into a plastic bag.

"My God, Veil," Raskolnikov breathed in a quavering voice. "What did you do to him?"

17

Veil looked at his friend, smiled. "Just helping a police officer—"

"You are crazy, my friend. You know that."

"—who became ill while performing his duty."

"What are you doing here, anyway?"

"I was on my way to get your opinion on one of my latest pieces."

"You have a painting with you?"

"I did have; somebody stole it. Just a minute, Victor."

Veil walked across the room to the woman who was standing absolutely still and looking profoundly forlorn, like some fragile piece of living sculpture that had been abandoned to the elements of confusion, fear, and panic and was in danger of shattering. She was a wounded woman, Veil thought. A man crucified on a wall by a spear was not the first horrible scene she had witnessed.

"I'm Veil Kendry," he said softly, looking directly into the large, liquid eyes and smiling gently. "The man who stole the idol is a friend of yours, isn't he?"

The woman swallowed and blinked; her eyes slowly came into focus on Veil's face, and the spare movement of her head was in direct contrast to the desperate, naked plea in her eyes.

"He's all right, at least for the time being," Veil continued. "The last time I saw him, he was disappearing into Central Park."

"But he'd been shot. . . ." The woman's voice was faint and breathy, as frail as her body.

"A shoulder wound and, judging by the way he was moving, not too serious. The cops probably have him by now, so he may already be on the way to a hospital."

The woman's eyes were the most expressive Veil had ever seen, and what they flashed now was relief. Her lips managed to form a shaky, tentative smile, and then she abruptly turned her head away, as if to hide whatever else might show in her eyes.

"I'm Reyna Alexander," the woman said, her voice muffled slightly by the thick strand of hair that had fallen across the side of her face. "Thank you for telling me that."

18

"You're welcome. I'd say you need a drink."

The woman shook her head. "I don't drink."

"Tea, then. Victor brews the strongest pot of tea this side of the Urals." Veil paused, then continued seriously. "You need something strong in you, Reyna. You need time to wind down."

"No. I just want to go home."

"Is anyone there?"

"No."

"Then I don't think that's a good idea—not for a while, anyway. You're suffering from shock."

"I want to go home."

"Where do you live?"

"Wesley Missionary College."

"How did you get here?"

"I have a car."

"Then I'll drive you. I know where the college is; I only live a few blocks from there. You don't have to be afraid. I'm quite harmless."

Now the woman looked at him again; there was a new emotion reflected in her eyes that Veil could not read. "That's not true. You're a very dangerous man; I could feel that all the way across the room. And you must be insane to talk that way, and do whatever it was you did, to Carl Nagle."

"That seems to be the consensus of opinion. You sound as though you speak from experience."

Fear shimmered across the surface of the black eyes. The woman pressed her lips tightly together and shook her head. "I don't know what you mean."

"I'm not dangerous to you."

Reyna Alexander studied him for a few moments, then nodded her head. "I know that, Mr. Kendry. And I would appreciate it if you'd take me home. Thank you."

CHAPTER THREE

Because of the chain collision on Fifth Avenue, most of the avenues and cross streets around midtown were jammed. Veil drove east on Sixty-eighth to the FDR Drive, then turned south and headed downtown toward the tip of Manhattan. A full moon was rising over the East River.

Reyna Alexander had turned on the radio the moment they'd gotten into the '79 brown Buick, then tuned it to one of the city's all-news stations. The theft of the Naltoon, the killing of the security guard, and the traffic tie-up were the lead items, but there were no details on who had stolen the idol or why. Nor was there any indication that the thief had been captured, despite the helicopter and the large numbers of policemen dispatched to the scene.

"He's K'ung, isn't he?" Veil asked casually as he maneuvered around a car that had stalled in the center lane.

Reyna glanced over at Veil and was obviously surprised. "You pronounce that remarkably well."

"I heard it pronounced that way on television a few

weeks ago, when the story first started to break. I have a fairly good ear for languages."

"So do a lot of other people, but I'm the only person in the northeast I know of who speaks K'ung—and you're the first person I've heard even come close to pronouncing the tribe's name correctly. Where did you learn to make the glottal sound?"

Veil thought about it, then decided that mentioning work with tribes in Southeast Asia would only lead to questions he could not—was not permitted to—answer. There were men in Washington who were extremely displeased by what they considered the high profile he had developed in New York. Orville Madison in particular was displeased, Veil thought, and that was dangerous. It did not matter what he did for this man or how often he did it; he was still under sentence of death. That had been made clear to him at the time when he had bartered his soul for Sharon's life.

"It doesn't matter," Veil replied evenly. "Am I right about him being K'ung?"

Reyna abruptly turned off the radio, looked at Veil, and nodded. "Yes. His name's Tobal'ak. I call him Toby. He's the chief's son—a prince." She paused, smiled wryly. "He's also the toughest kid in the rather large block known as the Kalahari Desert. The fools!"

Veil glanced sideways at the woman. There was sorrow and anxiety reflected in her eyes, but the rest of her face was clenched in anger. "Who are fools?" he asked quietly.

Reyna shook her head. "I shouldn't have said that. It's not their fault; all they could see was need, not consequences. I don't want to talk about it."

Veil waited a few minutes. He eased right in order to exit on Houston Street, then gently pressed the woman. "What was this Toby doing here? And why the secrecy? After all the publicity about the Nal-toon and the plight of the tribe it was stolen from, I would have thought that the arrival of a K'ung prince in New York City would have rated headlines. I never heard or read anything about him coming here."

21

Reyna made a sound that was somewhere between a laugh and a sob. "Toby's only been here two hours, and I only found out he was coming a little over three hours ago. I'm afraid I didn't have much time to call a press conference."

Again, sensing that the woman badly wanted to talk but could not be pressed further, Veil drove in silence. Finally Reyna sighed, leaned back in the passenger's seat, and rested her head against the window. When she spoke, her voice, muffled by the glass, was so faint that Veil had to strain to hear her over the hum of the engine.

"Obviously you've been following the story."

"Yes. Also, Victor Raskolnikov is a friend. I don't have to tell you how much trouble that idol has caused for him, which means that I took a rather personal interest."

"Still . . . Are you religious, Mr. Kendry?"

"No, but I think I appreciate the importance of religion in a lot of people's lives."

Reyna shook her head. "This is different. No matter how much you've read, and no matter how sensitive you may be, there's just no way you can appreciate how important the Nal-toon is to the K'ung. I spent years with that tribe—my parents were the first missionaries to make contact with that particular group, which is probably the most reclusive, isolated tribe in the Kalahari. Then I went back later as a missionary student working for my degree in anthropology. If any outsider could truly understand what the Nal-toon means to that tribe, you'd think it would be me. Wrong. I thought I did, but it wasn't until the Nal-toon was stolen and the entire social fabric of the tribe began to unravel that I fully began to sense the real depths of that meaning. To say that an idol *is* God to a people is one thing; to understand it in one's heart and mind is another. The Nal-toon isn't a symbol to the K'ung. The Nal-toon, the wood itself, *is* God, the only God, and He is their personal guest. God lives with them, watches over them, and He has given them the desert and everything in it.

"The Nal-toon is—was—their peace and happiness, and

their reason for living. They couldn't understand how God could be stolen; before the Nal-toon was taken, the K'ung had no concept of thievery. Now they're robbing each other blind—food, water, weapons, women. There's no longer any reason not to. After all, how could God allow Himself to be stolen? To the K'ung, God had abandoned them. The foundation of their daily lives had been blown away, and so they fell into a bottomless hole of hopelessness and meaninglessness—and they're still falling; they'll keep falling until finally the tribe destroys itself or the Nal-toon is returned to them. It's as if, in this country, God had been officially pronounced dead on the same day that all laws were repealed and all the police went home. Anarchy."

"I may not appreciate the full impact of their loss," Veil replied quietly, "but I think I understand something about hopelessness and suffering. The tribe's pain was made very clear in Berg's series of articles."

"God bless Alan Berg," Reyna said with feeling. "To think that a Jew would go to all that trouble for a tribe of primitive bushmen . . ."

Veil smiled wryly. "Why is that any more surprising than the fact that a bunch of conservative Christian missionaries would traipse around the desert for more than twenty years with the same group of absolutely recalcitrant idol-worshipers? Isn't compassion what religion—any religion—should be all about?"

Reyna raised her head from the window, turned, and looked at him. "Of course," she said tightly. "That was a stupid thing for me to say. Forgive me."

Veil shrugged as he exited from the FDR and turned right onto Houston Street. Here there was heavy Friday night traffic, and he purposely slowed. He was afraid that Reyna would stop talking once they reached the missionary college, and he wanted to hear what else she had to say about the warrior-prince who was—apparently—holed up somewhere in Central Park.

"Berg's a very good man," Veil said in a low monotone intended not to disturb the anthropologist's distant,

23

thoughtful mood. "He's also a great reporter—and incredibly lucky. He picked up the missionaries' pleas over the shortwave at *The Times*'s bureau in Johannesburg. He must have smelled a good story, because he hired a helicopter and went out into the desert himself to look into it. What he found was a special kind of horror—what had once been a proud tribe of hunter-gatherers had been reduced to squatting around in their own filth, stealing from each other, and subsisting entirely on emergency helicopter drops of food and medical supplies from South Africa and Botswana.

"Then Berg went to work. He hit every trading center on the perimeter of the Kalahari; the Nal-toon is a pretty distinctive piece of sculpture, so he reasoned that anyone who'd seen it would remember. Somebody did. He found a white hunter in Molepolole who'd bought it from a Bantu for the equivalent of a few dollars. The hunter, in turn, had sold it to a wholesaler who specialized in supplying primitive art for the markets in Europe and the United States.

"Then the trail disappeared when the wholesaler absolutely refused to say who he'd sold the statue to. But Berg kept digging and asking questions, and he picked up the trail again; it led straight underground into a smuggling pipeline used by organized crime. Nobody knows how, or why, the Nal-toon got into that pipeline, but once it did, its uniqueness made it relatively easy for Berg to track. And he tracked it right into Victor's gallery; Victor had bought it for three thousand dollars at a wholesalers' auction, and it came complete with a legal import certificate. Then Berg began writing his articles. He'd done an astonishing piece of investigative reporting, and he's bound to win a Pulitzer for it."

"While the K'ung starve and die," Reyna responded bitterly. "And they'll keep dying, one by one, unless they get their god back."

"I haven't forgotten that," Veil said evenly as he approached one of the two entrance gates leading onto the campus of Wesley Missionary College, a peaceful enclave comprised of several wooden buildings and well-manicured lawns spread out over a small, fenced-in area just south of Washington Square. "I'm sorry if I sounded insensitive."

The guard at the gate recognized Reyna and waved Veil through. Following Reyna's directions, he drove slowly through a network of narrow streets that were brightly illuminated by mercury-vapor lamps. He pulled over to the curb in front of a dormitory-style building, turned off the engine, and handed the car keys to Reyna.

"I should drive you home," Reyna said softly. She made no move to get out of the car.

"Not necessary. I told you that I only live a few blocks from here, down on Grand. With this traffic I'll probably get there faster if I walk."

"Thank you again."

"You're welcome." Veil opened the door on his side and started to get out. When he felt the woman's soft touch on his arm, he slid back in and closed the door.

"Toby was sent here as a goofy publicity stunt," Reyna said with a sigh. She hesitated, shook her head. "No! It's just not fair to say that. Floyd and Wilbur were desperate, and they thought they were doing the right thing."

"I take it that Floyd and Wilbur are the fools you mentioned."

Reyna nodded. "Floyd Rogers and Wilbur Mead. They're not fools, Mr. Kendry, but they are old—and they're senile. They also happen to be homosexual; that's neither here nor there, except to the Missionary Society, of course, but it does explain why the Missionary Society chose to leave two old men whose judgment is faltering buried in the desert for twelve years. They were an embarrassment.

"Anyway, while we were reading about the plight of the K'ung, Floyd and Wilbur were living it. When the Naltoon became a political football in the United Nations and was tied up legally because of the organized-crime connection, Floyd and Wilbur panicked. They came up with a scheme for arousing public outrage and bringing pressure to bear for the return of the idol; they would send a spokesman from the tribe to make a kind of personal appeal. They knew that the Missionary Society would never approve, so they never bothered to ask for approval; and they never bothered to tell anyone over here. As I understand it, they went to Alan Berg and got his cooperation. It was Berg who arranged to get travel documents for Toby. Together they took this twenty-five-year-old man who had never been out of the Kalahari to Molepolole, outfitted him in a suit of clothes, got a flight attendant to agree to keep an eye on him until they landed at Kennedy Airport, and put him on the plane. *Then* they called me at the college."

"You wouldn't have approved, either?"

"Are you kidding?"

"Maybe if there'd been more time to arrange—"

"No way. But I was an absolutely essential part of their plan because I know Toby, and I'm the only one around who speaks K'ung. Floyd and Wilbur knew I'd hide out on a mountaintop in Alaska before I'd ever agree to this insanity, assuming I was given a choice. So they made sure I wasn't given a choice. Once Toby was in the air, the plan had become a *fait accompli*. They knew I wouldn't abandon him."

"Why didn't you take someone with you to the airport?"

"Who?" Reyna asked with a sharp, bitter laugh. "I knew that Toby was going to be spooked enough without having to deal with a stranger. Also, I was very pressed for time. The overseas trunk lines were jammed, and I only got the call barely an hour before Toby's plane was due to land. I figured that the best way to handle the situation was to pick up Toby alone, reassure him that everything was going to be fine, put him up at the college overnight, then pack him off on the first Africa-bound plane leaving in the morning."

"Forgive me for asking, Miss Alexander—"

"My name's Reyna."

"And I'm Veil. Reyna, why did you take him to the gallery? You must have known it would be dangerous."

"I knew," Reyna replied, bowing her head slightly. "I felt I had no choice. The moment Toby got off the plane, I could see that he was full of shilluk."

"Shilluk?"

"It's a kind of combination narcotic-hallucinogenic drug. The K'ung make it by boiling down the sap of a certain cactus. Anyway, Toby had dosed himself to the eyeballs, which was going to make him even harder to handle. We no sooner got in the car than he demanded to see the Nal-toon. With all of the thousands of sights, sounds, and smells that he was experiencing for the first time, the only thing that interested him was seeing his god—immediately. And he wouldn't be put off until the morning. He wanted to see it at once, and when I said that we couldn't, he opened the car door and started to get out. We were on the Van Wyck Expressway, going fifty-five, at the time. The only way I could control him was to agree to take him to see the Nal-toon."

"Did you explain to him that the Nal-toon had to stay where it was?"

"Of course. I even lied to him—something I'd never done—and told him that we might be able to get the Nal-toon the next day. I was in a no-win situation, and I decided that the only way to keep him from hurting himself, or someone else, was to take him to the gallery so he could see for himself that his god was safe. It was a terrible mistake, obviously, and one I'll pay for, for the rest of my life. Because of me, a man is dead."

"No, not because of you. A properly trained guard never would have fired his gun in that situation. It seems clear that all your friend wanted was the idol; he threw the spear only after he was attacked."

"Still . . ."

"It's not difficult to understand why you felt you had to do what you did. I can also understand Toby's feelings, if not his behavior. Doped-up or not, he must have had some realization of how futile it would be to try to steal the statue and run away like he did. He got incredibly lucky twice; he wasn't squashed on Fifth Avenue, and Central

27

Park happened to be across the street. What on earth did he think he was going to accomplish?"

Reyna was silent for some time. When she did speak, it was not to respond to Veil's question. "There are no villains in this, only victims."

"Reyna, I know that you're physically and emotionally exhausted. I don't want to butt into your business, but I'd think that you'd want to be around when they bring your friend out of the park. I know the police would certainly appreciate it. Toby will be terrified and terribly alone without you; you, at least, can talk to him. Indeed, you're the *only* person in the city who can talk to him."

"There's no need, Veil," Reyna said distantly. "Not tonight."

"I don't understand."

Reyna put the keys in the ignition and turned it on. Then she turned on the radio. It took a few minutes for the news sequence about the stolen idol to be repeated, but when it was, there was nothing new to report: The K'ung warrior-prince had not yet been captured.

"Nobody goes to ground like a K'ung," Reyna said simply as she turned off the radio, removed the keys from the ignition, and put them in her purse. Then she got out of the car.

Veil got out, walked around the car, and started up the sidewalk after the woman. Reyna turned and waited for him. She was trembling slightly, but her voice was steady.

"Thank you again, Veil—for the ride, and for your understanding."

"Are you sure you're all right?"

Reyna nodded, then dropped her gaze and suddenly began to tremble. "Veil, there's something I have to say to you."

Veil reached out to grip Reyna's shoulders, but the woman shook her head and moved back a step.

"What is it, Reyna?"

"That . . . man . . ."

"What man? The detective? Nagle?"

Reyna nodded. "I don't know what you did to him, or how you did it. I've never seen anyone . . ."

"You know this creep, don't you? What happened between you and him?"

"He'll never forget what you did," Reyna said quickly, still refusing to meet Veil's gaze. "You have to watch out for him. He's more dangerous than you can ever know. He'll kill you if you get in his way, Veil; he may decide to kill you, anyway. You may not believe that a policeman would do that—or that he could do it and get away with it. Carl Nagle can. Nobody can stop him. I'm telling you this because I know you're a kind man, and I don't want that man to hurt you."

"Reyna, I want you to tell me about Carl Nagle."

But Reyna had already spun around and was running up the sidewalk toward the three-story, wood-framed dormitory. Veil waited until she was safely inside, then turned and walked back the way he had come. A light rain had begun to fall.

•   •   •

Veil found Victor Raskolnikov's black, chauffeured limousine outside the brick building where his loft was located. Veil opened the back door and slid into the luxurious, leather-scented interior.

"You're wet." The Russian's voice was steady, but his face was still ashen.

"Yeah."

Raskolnikov used the ivory handle of his walking cane to press a button on the ceiling; a bar revolved out of the seat back. "Scotch, of course."

"A big one, Victor. No ice. Thanks."

The art dealer poured the drink, handed the tumbler to Veil. "How's the girl?"

"Upset, of course, but she'll be all right."

"Well, she's not the only one who's upset. How do you feel about the possibility of crossing that detective's path again?"

"Why?"

"I'd like you to do some work for me. Nobody in the city has the range of contacts and sources of information that you do. I've been slandered by the United Nations, jerked around by the courts and police, and generally hassled since the beginning of this damn idol business. Because the freedom to make my own decisions was taken away from me, I find I am responsible for a young man's death."

"Victor—"

"I'm sorry, Veil, but I do feel responsible. Now I am thinking that I want to do something about it, although I'm not sure what. I do know that I would like to be kept informed of what is happening."

"You'll be able to read about it in the papers."

"Not everything gets into the papers. In any case, I have a strong feeling about this idol and the young man who stole it."

"The idol was originally stolen from his tribe, Victor," Veil said quietly. "He was just trying to get it back."

"You are right, of course, and that is why I have a strong feeling. I just want you to keep your ear to the ground. If you hear nothing special, so be it."

"I was going to keep an eye on things, anyway, Victor, and I'll certainly keep you informed. I have a strong feeling too."

"Well, now you'll be paid for your trouble."

"Victor, I can never repay you for what you've done for me."

"Nonsense. I make money off your talents. You are a fine artist and getting better. The Raskolnikov Galleries are not exactly a philanthropic organization. I have done very well with your dream-paintings, and I will do even better in the future as you become better known. In fact, I take great pride in the fact that I discovered you. Now I am asking you to use your, uh, darker skills on my behalf. Do you need money?"

"No. I'm still living off what you got for me on my last two paintings."

"Then I will at least pay you for the painting that was

stolen. After all, it was stolen while you were trying to get back the idol."

"No."

"All right, my friend," Raskolnikov said resignedly, tapping his cane on the floor. "I know better than to argue with you. We will decide later what payment you will take. Cash or barter—either is fine with me."

Veil drained his glass, then set it down on the mahogany bar shelf. "Thanks again for the drink, Victor," he said as he opened the door and got out.

"You will be careful!"

"Sure. I'll be in touch. Right now I'm going to get some sleep."

"Veil! You watch out for this Nagle fellow, huh? I have a very strong feeling about him, too, and it's a bad one. I know that you'd eat him for breakfast one-on-one, but he's a cop and he has friends. They have guns."

"Good night, Victor."

CHAPTER FOUR

Veil dreams.

Floating in a bodiless dream state through the Kalahari night, he watches as a tall Bantu crawls slowly and silently, like some great black desert lizard, to the crest of a steep star dune and peers over its spine. Below, in the dune's trough, the huge fire that had painted the sky an hour before is dying, reduced to a broad grid of glowing embers that pulse like a breathing creature in the desert wind just beginning to rise from the north.

The man can tell from the layout of this camp that it is K'ung, not Bantu, and he knows that not even the presence of Christian missionaries—indicated by the Land-Rover parked on the lee side of a smaller dune to the west—will guarantee him a welcome. Missionaries or no, the man knows that he may be killed if he hails the camp; at the least he will probably be beaten, then stripped of the precious medicinal herbs he has spent the last six days gathering in the open desert.

The man inches backward, then abruptly freezes as a strong puff of wind causes the bed of coals below him to flare briefly. In that instant the man glimpses something a short distance from the fire that causes him to grunt softly with surprise and intense interest.

A wooden statue, perhaps half-a-man high, rests on a flat, hard-packed bed of sand.

This is not just any K'ung tribe, the Bantu thinks as darkness once again washes over the statue in the wake of the passing wind. It has to be the small band of which stories are told, the Lonely Ones of the deep desert with their strange, unshakable beliefs—and strange missionaries that other missionaries make jokes about. The statue must be the Nal-toon, the idol this tribe believes to be the Maker and Protector of all things.

Theirs is a silly faith, the man thinks. For almost three years he has been a Christian, a believer in the Jesus-God, Who is invisible. Unlike the Nal-toon, the Jesus-God cannot be stolen, burned, or harmed in any way. The Jesus-God is the mightiest warrior of all and does not have to be guarded by anyone who might fall asleep—as the K'ung warrior the man has glimpsed sprawled on the sand near the idol has done.

The man's lips draw back in a sly smile. Obviously, he thinks, the sleeping man is not the legendary Tobal'ak, about whom so many fantastic stories are told. Tobal'ak, it is said, does not require sleep like ordinary men, and he is never far from the Nal-toon.

The Bantu rests his forehead on the night-cool sand, breathing deeply and regularly as he tries to weigh the risks and consequences of a failed attempt to steal the idol against the certain rewards that success will bring. He knows he will be killed if he is caught. But who will catch him? Tobal'ak? The man does not believe all the stories that are told about the K'ung warrior—indeed, he is not even sure he believes there is such a warrior as Tobal'ak, any more than he believes that the Nal-toon is anything but an ugly piece of carved wood.

On the other hand, the man knows that the idol will be worth a great deal to the white hunters who regularly pass through the Bantu camps at the edge of the jungle looking for such objects, which, it is said, are sold to other tribes in faraway places. An object as large as the Nal-toon should be worth many steel knives, the man thinks, as well as a large pouch of matches. He may even ask for the most precious gift of all—a radio like the missionaries carry.

The Bantu makes his decision. He rises, picks up his bundle of herbs, and moves stealthily along the spine of the dune until he is directly above the Nal-toon and its sleeping guard, upwind of any dogs that may be in the camp. He puts his bundle down, then slides silently down the inner face of one of the radiating arms of the dune. He puts his hands out to his sides and brakes to a stop as he comes abreast of the idol. He waits for a time, pressing back against the sand and listening in the darkness. However, there are no sounds of alarm, and the guard continues to sleep.

Then, in an unbroken series of smooth and silent movements, the man reaches over the spine of the radiating arm, seizes the idol with both hands, then starts back up the face of the dune. The Nal-toon is much heavier than the man thought it would be, and he finds himself clumsily plowing in the sand, driving with his legs and gasping for breath. But he makes it back to the top of the dune safely.

Standing on top of the dune, the Bantu's lips curl back from his teeth in a contemptuous sneer as he looks down on the sleeping camp. The K'ung—at least this tribe of K'ung—are like children, he thinks. If this piece of wood is their only god, as he has been told it is, they should have taken more care in guarding it.

Suddenly he feels the curious, empty feeling in his stomach, which the missionaries have told him is guilt. The man knows that, as a Christian, he is not supposed to steal—not even from his enemies. But he reminds himself that he has not been a Christian for very long and thus cannot be expected to follow all the many rules which have been laid down for him by the missionaries. Also, he has been told that the Jesus-God will always forgive him, as long as he is sorry.

And he is truly sorry, the Bantu thinks; he would not have stolen this tribal god were it not for the fact that he wants knives, matches—and maybe a radio.

The Bantu hefts the idol under his arm, slides his carrying sling over his shoulder, and starts toward the north, leaning into the wind that swirls around him and quickly erases the evidence of his passage.

Veil leaves the man's mind and rolls away from the dream to another, to be with Sharon.

CHAPTER FIVE

Veil was up before dawn. He ate a breakfast of black coffee, cheese, and bread as he listened to the news. Toby had not been found, and the police dragnet had now shifted to a systematic search of abandoned buildings, alleys, and unused storefronts on both the East and West Sides. By six-thirty, Veil was entering Central Park at Sixty-ninth Street, retracing the steps of the K'ung warrior-prince.

Nobody goes to ground like a K'ung warrior.

He did not bother looking for signs where Toby had gone in, for he knew that any spoor would have been obliterated—first by the feet of police officers—and later by reporters and the curious. Instead he walked straight ahead, glancing to his left and right, studying the general terrain and looking for the most likely escape route for a fleeing bushman to take.

Veil smiled thinly and shook his head at the thought of how preposterous was the thing he was trying to do. He hadn't done any tracking in more than seventeen years, and in the jungles of Vietnam, Laos, and Cambodia he had

36

been tracking Viet Cong and Pathet Lao, whose sandals left the distinct imprint of tire tread. Here he was in Central Park—an area larger than some countries, used every day by thousands of people wearing everything from sneakers to combat boots. Toby, Veil thought, could be anywhere; he could even be where the police thought he was, cowering in some rat-infested basement. But Veil did not think so.

Nobody goes to ground like a K'ung warrior.

He kept walking in a straight line, down into a grassy bowl ringed by trees. Despite the early hour, lovers on their blankets were already—or maybe still—at each other, and joggers of every shape glided or huffed along. Veil ducked when someone shouted a warning and a purple Frisbee sailed just over his head.

Tracking the K'ung had been a great idea, Veil thought as he climbed halfway up the opposite face of the bowl, turned, and sat down on the grass. It was just impossible to execute.

Then he saw Reyna Alexander come crawling on her hands and knees out of the trees directly across the way. The anthropologist wore jeans, sneakers, and a long-sleeved cotton blouse. Her long, blue-black hair was tied back in a ponytail that flowed like an ink stain across her back as, oblivious to the startled and curious stares of lovers, joggers, and Frisbee players, she slowly crawled fifteen feet out onto the grass, then stopped before a small patch of bare ground. After almost a minute of staring at the ground she rose, brushed grass and dirt off her jeans, then headed back into the wooded area.

Anyone who even presumed to track someone else through Central Park had to be good, Veil thought, and he sensed that the frail woman was, indeed, very good. He was about to rise and follow her when he realized that he was not the only one with that idea. He caught a movement out of the corner of his eye, looked across the bowl to his right, and saw a man in tan chinos and a red tank top appear to wave at him. Then the man passed the edge of his hand across his throat. A moment later a man rushed past from behind, brushing Veil's shoulder. The man—squat, balding, and wearing a pair of plaid Bermuda shorts with matching shirt—was clumsily trying to stuff a pair of binoculars back into a leather case as he ran. The men joined up on the sidewalk, then entered the wooded area. Veil rose and ran down the hill.

Like a brother to the night that had just passed, Veil slipped silently into the trees, perhaps twenty yards from where Reyna, and then the men, had entered. He had no trouble following the sound trail of cracking branches and muttered curses of the men ahead of him, and Veil followed, gliding from tree to tree through the shadows.

The two men stopped for a few moments to have a whispered conference, then moved to their left. Veil did the same, moving parallel to the men, and was twenty-five yards behind them when they emerged from the trees and onto a large expanse of rolling lawn.

Reyna's ebony-crowned head was just disappearing over the crest of another knoll. The two men hurried after Reyna, and Veil followed them.

Strung out over almost a quarter mile, the procession crossed the East Drive. Reyna angled in the direction of the zoo, walked another hundred yards, then once again dropped to her hands and knees on the perimeter of a large patch of bare ground. The two men stopped. Veil stopped, lay down on his back, and watched over the top of his crossed ankles.

Reyna raised little clouds of dust as she slowly crawled forward on the dirt, head very close to the ground. She rose when she reached the other side, cupped her hands to her mouth, and uttered a strange, guttural cry that carried clearly across the meadow, startling a flock of pigeons at the same time as it caused a jogger to glance up sharply, stumble, and fall.

Then Reyna began walking quickly to her left, disappearing into another wooded area. The two men exchanged a few words, then hurried after her. Veil, remembering the throat-cutting gesture the thinner man had made, sprang to his feet and ran after them.

He found Reyna and the two men thirty yards inside the

line of trees, behind the thick trunk of an ancient oak. Any concern Veil might have had about the men being police was instantly dispelled: the man in the Bermuda shorts was trying to drag a struggling Reyna to the ground, while the man in the tank top waited, switchblade in hand. Veil took the man with the knife first, hitting him with a powerful side kick in the solar plexus that sat him down hard on the ground, knife still in his hand. His face turned purple, and his eyes bulged as his mouth gaped open and his chest heaved in a desperate, silent plea for air that simply would not enter his lungs. In a continuation of the same motion Veil spun around and smashed the flat of his hand into the other man's face with enough force to crush the man's nose and snap off his front teeth. The squat man keeled over backward, unconscious.

"Excuse me," Veil said with a wink to the white-faced, astonished Reyna as he grabbed the man in the tank top by the hair and pulled him behind a clump of brush. "I'll be right back."

Veil took the switchblade from the gasping man's hand, pushed him on his back, then straddled him. "Let's chat," he said in a flat voice as he tested the sharpness of the blade against the thickness of the hairs on the man's bare left shoulder.

"Gaa . . . gaa . . ."

Dissatisfied with the switchblade, Veil sank its tip into the trunk of a tree just behind the man's head and snapped off the blade. Then he reached down inside his boot and withdrew one of his most prized possessions—a short dagger with a blade made of the rarest Damascus steel, a gift taken in barter from a knife maker on Staten Island for whom Veil had performed a service three years before.

"Are . . . you a . . . cop?" the man managed to say.

"You should be so lucky." Veil pulled up the edge of the man's T-shirt and slit it from waist to neck; there was virtually no tug at all on the blade, and the cotton parted with a soft whisper. "That was to get your attention. If you don't give me the right answers, I cut you next. Who hired you to follow the girl?"

The man, still struggling to draw a full breath, stared

39

wide-eyed at the man with the long yellow hair and glacial-blue, gold-flecked eyes who was holding the tip of his knife just above the man's sternum. "A guy by the name of Picker Crabbe," he muttered hoarsely, licking his lips. "He's—"

"I know Picker. How much is he paying you?"

"A grand each if we brought him the statue the guy stole last night. Picker said that the girl was a friend of this guy, and she might lead us to him."

"She couldn't lead you to anybody after you jumped her. Why the hell did you do that?"

"Who the hell are you?"

Without hesitation Veil flicked his wrist, opening a three-inch gash just below the man's right nipple. Blood welled in the slit, rolled down the man's side. The man started to yell, but Veil clapped his hand over the open mouth, then held the tip of the knife against the man's throat. The man rolled his eyes and shook his head. Veil took his hand away and repeated the question. His voice was flat—absolutely devoid of emotion, implacable.

"She moves like a ghost," the man answered in a voice quivering with terror. Ignoring the knife now, he stared up at Veil as if he were looking at an angel of death. "We lost her for almost twenty minutes a while back. We didn't want to take a chance on losing her for good, so we decided to grab her and force her to tell us what she knew."

"You're idiots twice over. Picker's got a hole in his nose; every cent he can get his hands on goes for coke. Where in hell did you think he was going to get two thousand dollars to pay you?"

"He swore he could get the money. I think he was taking orders from someone else."

"Who?"

"I don't know."

"Take a guess."

"I really don't *know*, man! Hey, my partner and me just do odd jobs—things we pick up on the streets. Nothing else was happening, so we took this. Besides, if we had

40

gotten our hands on the statue, we wouldn't have given it to Picker until he gave us the money. We ain't that stupid."

"Why shouldn't Picker do the job himself and pocket the two grand if he got lucky?"

The man laughed nervously. "Hey, man, I don't know. Maybe Picker was afraid you'd be around."

The man was joking, Veil thought, but what he'd said could well be the truth. It was also true that the two men were nothing but low-level street thugs, "odd-job men." No one else would be working for Picker Crabbe. Veil clipped the man on the jaw with the heel of his left hand, then rose and walked from behind the brush to where Reyna waited. Her mouth was still slightly open, and she was staring at him dumbfounded.

"Good morning," Veil said, taking the woman by the hand and leading her out of the copse of trees. "Let's go get some coffee."

• • •

"Who were they, Veil?"

"Munchkins. Two very stupid street thugs working for another very stupid street thug. The man, or men, pulling their strings may not be so stupid, though. There are some nasty criminal types in the city who are definitely not art collectors but who want the Nal-toon. Do you have any idea why?"

Reyna sipped at her black coffee and grimaced. "Maybe they want to sell it?"

"No. Victor told me that the idol is worth only a few thousand dollars at most, and then only to a select clientele that collects primitive art. The people who control the smuggling route used to bring in the Nal-toon wouldn't cross the street for anything worth much less than a hundred thousand. Of course, the idol could have been hollowed out and stuffed with something—drugs, microfilm, gold, whatever. The problem is that nothing contraband that could have been stuffed in the idol *would* have been, not by these guys. The Nal-toon is just too ungainly and obvious, which is why Alan Berg was able to trace it in the first place. We're still left with the question of why a gang of mafiosi are looking to pick up a three-foot-high piece of carved hardwood."

"Oh, Veil," Reyna whispered. There was a slight tremor in her voice.

Veil glanced up from his coffee. Reyna, sitting across from him in the booth at the rear of the diner on Seventy-second Street, had her head bowed and her hands clasped in front of her, as if in prayer. Although she was just a few years shy of thirty, Veil thought, her appearance was that of a troubled child. He reached out and stroked her hair. "Easy, Reyna," he said gently.

"You sound so cold when you talk about it."

"I don't mean to. I was just trying to figure out what the bad guys' interests are. I *do* care."

Reyna looked up, smiled wanly, and squeezed his hand. "I know you do," she said, wiping tears from her eyes. "You came to the park to look for Toby, didn't you?"

"Well, I had the notion. I remembered what you'd said about 'going to ground'—hiding. I've had some experience with tribal hunter-gatherers, and I've done some tracking."

"It was in the Army, wasn't it?"

Veil said nothing.

"How old are you, Veil?"

"Pushing forty."

"Vietnam?"

"Somewhere in the vicinity," Veil replied with a thin smile. "Anyway, the minute I walked into the park, I knew I'd been suffering from delusions of grandeur. If an army of police who knew the territory hadn't been able to find him, then I wasn't going to be able to. Then I saw you at work. You're good."

For the first time since Veil had met her, the woman's face broke into a warm smile that was free of anxiety. "Why do you say that? I didn't find him, either."

"But you obviously knew what you were doing—whatever it was you were doing. What could you hope to find after all that traffic had been through there last night?"

"Oh, what I was doing isn't really all that mysterious.

The first thing Toby would have done when he got into the park was kick off his shoes and socks. K'ung have big splayed toes, so they leave distinctive footprints."

Veil shrugged. "Then we'll go back together and look for K'ung footprints."

Reyna shook her head. "I don't think we'll find any. Even at night, and even on strange terrain, Toby would have instinctively looked for and found hard or grassy ground to run on. He has jungle lore; the tribe occasionally hunts in the jungle along the edge of the desert."

"You do know one hell of a lot about this tribe, don't you?"

"I grew up with them, Veil. As a matter of fact, Toby was my best friend as a child; I learned to hunt and track with all the K'ung boy-children. I was a 'missionary kid.' "

"You told me that. Your parents were the first to make contact with this particular tribe."

"Yes. Anyway, after my parents were killed by a Bantu raiding party—"

"I'm sorry."

"Thank you. I was twelve. I became a ward of the Missionary Society, and it assumed responsibility for my support and education. I was sent to school in France and the United States, did some of my own missionary work with the K'ung, and now I teach at Wesley while I work on my dissertation. End of story. My background may seem a bit exotic, but it's really quite simple. I'm betting that *your* background is exotic. I've never seen anyone fight like you do."

Her story had not included any mention of Carl Nagle, Veil thought, but he did not want to press her further. "You're sure your friend is still in the park?"

"Oh, yes. Toby's recuperating, resting and waiting."

"Waiting for what?"

"To leave."

"Where would he go?"

Reyna studied Veil's face for a few moments, then abruptly dropped her gaze. "We'll just have to wait and see, I guess."

"Then the police may pick him up yet."

"No," Reyna said, her voice and limpid, black eyes once again filled with sadness. "He'll never allow himself to be captured alive, Veil. Never."

"Everything in Berg's articles indicated that the tribe was on its last legs—defeated, without hope, totally lethargic. I don't believe those are words I'd use to describe this Toby."

Reyna smiled grimly, shook her head. "Indeed not. Toby was always different—the toughest and meanest member of the tribe. He and I became friends, but he always resented my parents because they were Christian missionaries; in Toby's eyes they were enemies of the Nal-toon. No member of that tribe has ever been converted to Christianity, of course, but the attitude of the others was always rather mellow, if a bit condescending; after all, they could make good use of the knives, medicine, and other things we brought them. Toby, on the other hand, was always belligerent. Everyone always felt that he had a special relationship, if you will, with the Nal-toon. If there had been an official keeper of that idol, Toby would have been it."

"He's a zealot."

"Mmm. A zealot and a half. I strongly suspect that he doesn't view the loss of the Nal-toon in the way the others do. He may not see it as abandonment by their god but as a test of the tribe's worthiness. The use of shilluk has some religious overtones for the K'ung, which could mean that Toby perceives this journey as a kind of mystical rite to regain the Nal-toon's favor. If that's the case, Toby will also perceive virtually everything that happens to him as a test of his courage and faith; he will absolutely abandon himself to the belief that the Nal-toon will protect him from harm as long as he acts like a warrior."

"That would explain his dash across Fifth Avenue. It wasn't just panic."

"No. He believed he was protected."

"Hey, he may be on to something," Veil said, smiling. "After all, he did make it across the street—and they haven't found him yet. I may get myself a Nal-toon."

"Toby coming to New York City could be very bad news, Veil," Reyna said seriously. "You've seen what's happened already. He's dangerous."

"I know."

"All the time I was searching, I kept calling out to him. I wanted him to know he was in danger and that he could come to me. If he heard, he didn't respond." Reyna paused and sighed. "He probably doesn't trust me. He may not even think I'm real."

"Not real?"

"Veil, in New York, Toby might as well be a visitor from another galaxy; everything here is totally alien to him. Also, depending upon how much shilluk he brought with him, he'll view everything as part of some netherworld constructed by the Nal-toon to challenge him. He'll perceive the people here as a tribe of ghost-demons whom he can't trust but who can hurt him if he's not brave and true to his faith."

"Then we'd better find him before the police or Mafia do. I want to help, Reyna."

"I know. Thank you."

"If you can get me to him, I may be able to stop Toby from hurting himself or others."

"Yes."

"What do you suggest we do?"

"For now, wait."

Again, Reyna had averted her gaze, and Veil had the definite impression that she was hiding something—holding something back. "Would you like more coffee? Something to eat?"

Reyna shook her head, then looked at him and offered what seemed to Veil a slightly forced smile. "No, thank you. I guess what I'd really like is a little more information about you. You already know everything important there is to know about me."

"I strongly doubt that."

"It's true. But I know next to nothing about you—except that you're an artist, fight like nobody I've ever seen, and seem to be my guardian angel. Even your name is mysterious. Is Veil a family name?"

45

"More like a family prayer."

Reyna smiled warmly and cocked her head. "Please tell me about it."

"I was born with a very high fever, and a caul, and the doctors gave me about two hours to live. My parents had a metaphysical streak in them, so they immediately named me Veil. Who knows? Maybe my name saved my life."

Reyna laughed softly. "Then you do have your Nal-toon: your name."

"Why not?"

"You said you weren't religious."

"I'm not. I believe in gravity and mathematics. But I also, most definitely, believe in mystery. To me there's more mystery in one ordinary day in the life of any ordinary human being than there is in all of the religious fables ever told or written."

"Well, obviously I think differently. To me Our Lord Jesus is mankind's Savior and the Son of God." Suddenly Reyna put her hand over her mouth in a strikingly child-like gesture and giggled. "But I won't try to convert you."

"I'm relieved."

"I like you, Veil."

"Thank you. And I like you."

"Wow," Reyna said with a grin as she studied the solidly built man with the broad shoulders and thickly muscled arms sitting across from her. As solid as he was, she had never seen anyone as quick and lithe. "You certainly survived, all right."

Veil considered his reply carefully. Secretive by nature, the bizarre residue of his fever was something he almost never discussed, an affliction that was known only to a very few friends, like Victor Raskolnikov and a certain dwarf. And Sharon. Now, however, he decided that he would share this part of himself with Reyna Alexander, in the hope that she might come to appreciate the gift and share her own secrets—secrets he was certain she held and which he suspected could involve the Nal-toon, Toby, and his own new and powerful enemy, Carl Nagle.

"The fever left me with some permanent brain damage," Veil said at last.

Reyna's smile faltered, as if she were uncertain as to whether or not he might be joking. "Well, you certainly could have fooled me."

"If there's such a thing as a kind of psychic membrane separating the conscious from the unconscious, then the fever I was born with burned it away. It left me vulnerable, you might say, to my dreams. I'm what's known in the literature as a vivid dreamer; my dreams are every bit as real to me as what's happening at this moment."

"You mean, you can't tell when you're dreaming?"

"Now I can. For most of my life I couldn't, though."

Reyna thought about it, then suddenly frowned. "Nightmares . . . ?"

"Oh, as a kid, I not only was chased by the usual ogres and dragons, I was usually caught and eaten."

"Lord, Veil, I know you're minimizing it. The *terror* you must have felt!"

Veil shrugged, smiled easily. "It caused me some problems. For one thing, it made me into a very cranky kid, adolescent, and—for a good many years—adult. But that's another story or two."

"I'd like to hear all your stories."

"We'll see. Anyway, painting proved to be a kind of therapy. By more or less painting my dreams, I got to the point where I could recognize dreams and even control them. Now, when I start to have a nightmare, I just go away—unless I feel it could have some value."

"What possible value could a nightmare have?"

"Oh, you never know. We resolve a lot of things in dreams. In any case, that approach to painting lent my work a certain style, and it's been my good fortune to have people pay for it occasionally."

"I'm sorry to say that I've never seen any of your work, but you must be very good if you're shown in the Raskolnikov Galleries."

"Victor's kind. He thinks I'm *going* to be good."

"Nonsense. I know you're good now."

"Reyna, I'd like to know more about you."

This time Reyna did not look away, but her eyes

clouded, and she quickly shook her head as she plucked nervously at the sleeve of her blouse. "You know all there is to know."

"Are you all right?"

"Yes, thanks to you."

"Those two are gone from the park by now, and I strongly doubt that they'll be back. Are you sure you wouldn't like to go back and look for Toby's footprints together?"

The dark-haired woman with the troubled, dark eyes thought about it as she slowly folded her napkin, then set it down beside her empty cup. "No," she said at last. "He'll never show himself if you're with me. I think it's best just to let things sit for a while."

"Reyna, I keep getting the feeling that you're keeping something from me—something important. What is it?"

"Please don't, Veil," Reyna whispered.

"You can trust me."

"I think so."

"Know so."

"Veil, everything's happened so quickly. I . . . have a lot of thinking to do. By myself."

"All right," Veil said, reaching across the table and pressing her hand. "Then I'll take you home."

"It's not necessary, unless you're going that way."

"To tell the truth, I wasn't planning on it. There's somebody I'd like to talk to."

Reyna patted Veil's arm as she rose. "Then you go ahead and take care of your business. I really am all right. I'll take a cab home."

Veil paid the bill, then walked Reyna out to the curb and hailed a cab. When the taxi pulled away, he crossed the street and headed for the subway.

CHAPTER SIX

Veil searched the streets around Columbia University, then headed into Morningside Park. Fifteen minutes later he found Picker Crabbe. The tall, gaunt man was seated on a park bench near West 120th Street, casually leafing through the latest issue of *Hustler* while he waited for customers. The man glanced up and saw Veil approaching. He flung the magazine to one side, jumped up, and started running down the sidewalk in the opposite direction. Veil easily caught up with him, grabbed him by the arm, and spun him around.

"What the hell's the matter with you, Picker? This is the second time you've run away when you saw me."

"You're a crazy man," Crabbe said, wincing and raising his arms in front of his face as if to ward off a blow. It was just past ten in the morning, but the man's pupils were already dilated from the effects of cocaine.

Veil laughed as he released Picker Crabbe's thin arm. "If you ran every time you saw a crazy man in New York, you'd die of exhaustion before noon."

Crabbe sniffed, then pushed a strand of greasy gray-brown hair away from his eyes. He looked as if he wanted to run, but he stayed where he was. "You beat up on me pretty good."

"That was a year and a half ago."

"It was the kind of beating a man don't forget. You *thought* about what you were doing to me. Man, I ain't never been beat on like that."

"I don't see any lasting damage."

"Damage ain't the point, man. It hurt."

"It was supposed to hurt, and you were supposed to remember it the next time you were tempted to get into the child pornography and prostitution game. One of the kids you were pimping for had been kidnapped three months before, beat on, and drugged."

"I didn't do no kidnapping, and I didn't do none of that other stuff. I was just working for a piece of the action."

"I know. The man who did do the kidnapping is dead. You are out of that business now, aren't you?"

"Yes!"

"Good. Maybe you deserved to die, Picker. At the time I did give some thought to killing you. I didn't, so I figure you owe me something."

"What do you want?"

"Information. What were you doing parked on Sixty-ninth last night? I know you were supposed to be watching the art gallery, so give me the condensed version of the story."

Crabbe blinked slowly. "What art gallery?"

Veil sighed. "Picker, I just had a talk with those two jerks you got to tail the woman. Incidentally, they asked me to tell you that they resign."

"Oh, Jesus."

"So let's cut through the bullshit, okay? What were you doing there?"

"You're right. I was supposed to keep an eye on the place. There were other guys too. It was my bad luck to have you come along on my shift."

"Why were you supposed to watch the place?"

"To make sure that idol wasn't stolen. If it was, to try to

50

stop the guy; if I couldn't, to get a good look at who it was doing the stealing."

"Somehow I find that funny, Picker. You're telling me a thief was sent out to make certain the statue wasn't stolen by another thief?"

"It's the truth."

"Who hired you?"

"I can't tell you that, man."

"Now, Picker . . ."

To Veil's astonishment, tears welled in Crabbe's eyes, then picked up grime like mascara as they rolled down his cheeks. "I'm being straight with you, man," Crabbe said in a near whimper. "I don't mind telling you most of what I know, because I don't know that much. But I can't give you that name. I know you can bust me up, and God knows I don't want you to, but I can't give you the name. He's as crazy as you are, man; you're two sides of the same coin— except that you'll hurt me for this but you won't kill me. This guy'll hurt me worse than you did, and *then* he'll kill me. For sure. He likes it."

"How would he know you told me?"

"I ain't takin' no chances, man. I don't want to be tortured, and I don't want to die."

Veil looked at the trembling man before him, saw the tears in his eyes and the defeated sag of his shoulders. Suddenly he was disgusted with the terror in the world and ashamed of that part of it he had, with whatever justification, helped nurture. Picker Crabbe made him feel profoundly sad. There were too many Picker Crabbes in the world, he thought; victims who victimized, producing victims who victimized.

"Forget it, Picker," Veil said quietly. "I don't want the name of the man who put you on the job. But tell me this: If your man is so interested in the statue, why didn't he just have you steal it?"

"I'm not sure. He may have been afraid there was a police stakeout."

"So you and the others were put in place just to make certain that the police did their job?"

51

"I'm just guessing. He moved so fast, nobody could have stopped him."

"Why do these people want the statue?"

"I don't know."

"The two men you sent out told me you were going to give them a grand each if they brought you back the idol. Is that true?"

"Yeah."

"Do you have the money?"

"I could've got it."

"From the man whose name you won't give me?"

"Him or others. It was a street contract. The word was out that the statue was worth five grand to certain people." Crabbe paused, put a dirty index finger beside his nose. "I'd heard about the contract, but I knew those other two hadn't. I figured I had nothing to lose by promising those two guys a thousand each to follow the girl, then grab the idol from that guy if she found him. I'd still clear three grand."

"All right, then there's a general street contract out on the statue; anyone who brings it in and hands it over to certain people can collect the reward. Was it your idea to follow the woman?"

"Nah. The same guy who put me on the street to watch the gallery gave me the woman's address and suggested that I keep an eye on her."

•   •   •

Veil sat in the cool shadows at the rear of the church sanctuary throughout the afternoon. At four-thirty, a door to the left of the altar opened and a priest stepped through. The man was around six feet, Veil's height, and in his mid- to late fifties. His hair was thick and black, with a few pronounced streaks of gray. A solid man with broad shoulders, he walked with a severe limp that caused his body to roll from side to side as he moved to the center of the altar rail, kissed his purple vestment, then knelt and prayed for a few minutes. Finally he rose and entered the confessional to the far left. Veil looked around, determined that he was alone, then walked quickly to the confessional, went in, and sat down on the narrow wooden bench inside.

"I've come to talk about sin, Father," Veil said softly as a small door opened in the partition separating the two men.

There was a long pause, then, "Veil?" The priest's voice was hoarse and gravelly, as if something had been broken in his throat.

"Yes."

There was another equally long pause. When the priest finally spoke, there was a note of dry humor in his voice. "Am I to assume that you've found your way to God?"

"No, Father. I'm afraid I'll have to seek salvation in other ways."

"There are no other ways."

"For now I'll settle for having found my way to you."

"What do you want with me, Veil?"

"I need information that you may have, Father."

"Veil, this is a confessional."

"I'm aware of that, Father, and I don't mean to be disrespectful—but this is Little Italy, and I don't want to risk having anyone see you talking to me. I've attracted quite a following since yesterday, and I haven't quite figured out who's watching whom."

"God protects me, Veil."

"I need to get plugged in on some family business, Father."

"It isn't proper for you to come to me with such a request, Veil. I can't help you."

"I think you can. This isn't a matter anyone would have spoken to you about in the confessional. No disrespect meant here, either, Father—you happen to be one of the most truly religious and good men I know, but you also happen to be the closest thing to a 'house priest' the mob has."

There was a sudden, palpable increase in tension inside the confessional. "It is because I am not judgmental."

"It's because three generations of your family have been

Cosa Nostra; you're the only male who didn't go into the business—everyone around you did. As far as being judgmental is concerned, I don't recall that I was too judgmental when you came to me for help in finding out where your mistress had taken your illegitimate son; you couldn't go to anyone else. I was the one who negotiated what you might call a reconciliation agreement. Now I'm asking for your help."

The priest heaved a deep sigh. "What are you looking for, Veil?"

"Somebody else's god. You've heard about the idol they call the Nal-toon?"

"Yes."

"What have you heard?"

"I read the newspapers, listen to the news reports."

"What else do you hear?"

"Notwithstanding the great favor you did for me, Veil, I don't think it's right for you to come to me on a fishing expedition."

"This is a bit more than a fishing expedition, Father. The Mafia wants the idol, don't they?"

"Yes."

"Do you know why?"

"No."

"'Father . . . ?"

"It's the truth, Veil. The fact that it's wanted by the capos is common knowledge on the street; indeed, there's a bounty for anyone who brings the idol in and hands it over to any of the top people in the five families. However, the reason for their wanting it is a carefully guarded secret."

"They could be worried about the possibility that it wouldn't be turned in if people knew why they wanted it."

"Perhaps. I don't care to speculate."

"You mentioned five families. What happened to the sixth?"

There was a prolonged silence, and Veil could sense the conflict and indecision in the other man on the opposite side of the partition. "Vito Ricci is dead," the priest said at last. "His operations are being absorbed by the other families, along with those people who are deemed worthy. The Ricci family no longer exists."

Veil suppressed a whistle. "That's some bit of news."

"It's no news at all yet. The police and the FBI know that Vito is missing, of course, but that is all they know. It hasn't made the papers. Nobody will ever find his body, and the authorities will eventually just naturally assume he is dead."

"Execution?"

"Yes. It was Vito who was responsible for trying to squeeze the idol through that smuggling pipeline. Apparently he wanted it for personal reasons. It was an insane act, Veil, and it was not even properly executed at this end. If things had been properly planned, the idol never would have ended up on an auction block, and it certainly wouldn't have surfaced in some art gallery on the East Side in the same week that the first article appeared in *The Times*. The whole thing was an unmitigated disaster, and Vito paid for his mistake with his life." The priest paused, added dryly, "He must have been getting senile."

"Maybe. Is there a contract out on the K'ung?"

"The what?"

"The black who stole back the idol. Are there specific orders to kill him?"

"No, but I don't suppose that will prevent his death. The easiest way to obtain the idol, of course, is to kill the man carrying it."

"If they find him."

From the darkness on the other side of the filigreed partition came a hoarse chuckle laced with sadness. "Find him? How long can a bushman who's lived all his life in the desert hide in New York City?"

"He's doing pretty well so far, isn't he?"

"I believe he's dead, Veil. I am sorry if this is so, but I believe it's just a matter of finding his corpse and taking the idol from beside it."

"Could be."

"What was done against him and his tribe is very sad."

"Yeah. What do you think will happen to the idol if the police find him first?"

"Oh, I think it's safe to assume that the idol will eventually find its way into the hands of the capos."

"Why, Father? Is it because Carl Nagle is in charge of the police investigation?"

The question brought a sharp intake of breath; the partition vibrated, as if the priest had moved suddenly and inadvertently brushed against it. "What do you know about Carl Nagle?"

"Virtually nothing, except that he comes on pretty cranky. Within hours after the black ran off with the idol, someone gave a two-bit hood by the name of Picker Crabbe the name and address of the woman who'd brought the black to the gallery. The short time span makes me think that it was either Nagle or his partner—or both—who supplied the information. I'm thinking that detectives Nagle and Vahanian may be on the mob payroll. What do you think, Father?"

Veil waited almost a full minute, but the only sound from the other side of the partition was hoarse breathing. Finally it was Veil who spoke. "Thank you, Father," he said evenly. "I hadn't come to you before this, and I won't come again. I consider any debt there might have been between us paid."

Veil stepped out of the confessional booth, ducked through the heavy curtain, and walked in the cool, oddly comforting gloom of the sanctuary toward a side exit.

"Veil, please wait."

Veil turned and was alarmed to see the priest out of the booth and rolling toward him. Veil quickly glanced around but was engulfed in the priest's arms before he had a chance to see whether or not they were being observed. The priest kissed Veil on both cheeks, then hobbled back a step. His gray eyes gleamed in the semidarkness.

"I have not asked you why you want this information because I know it is for a good cause," the priest said in his broken voice. "You may not believe in God, Veil Kendry, but you are nonetheless a man of God. God's existence

56

does not depend upon your belief in Him, nor does He exact faith in return for His mercy, benevolence, and protection. You are a strange man, and there are strange— often conflicting—stories told about you. But there is no doubt in my mind that you walk with God, and God watches over and works through you. No doubt at all.

"My debt is not paid. As far as you are concerned, my debt will never be paid. You may come to me anytime someone is in need of help and you feel that information I can supply may be useful."

"Thank you, Father."

"I can never repay you for what you did with my . . . woman and my son. God forgive me for saying so, but not' even He could fill the hole left in my life when they were gone. For many years I have prayed to resolve this conflict. Sometimes I have—literally—prayed until my knees bled. But it seems I am all too human, too much of the flesh. The conflict cannot be resolved, and so I am reduced to prayers for the salvation of my soul despite the continual breaking of my solemn vows."

"You don't have to tell me these things, Father."

"Those were things I wanted to tell you. But there is also something I *must* tell you. It is Carl Nagle whom you must watch out for; I cannot stress this point strongly enough. Vahanian knows nothing, and he would be in great danger if Nagle even suspected that he did. Nagle is more than just one more crooked cop on the take, Veil. He's an enforcer. And he is quite mad. I've heard it said—often— that he enjoys inflicting physical pain. I don't know. Certainly he has no feelings that you and I would be familiar with. I have never known, or heard of, anyone so able to instill pure terror into anyone he chooses to intimidate. The measure of this is the fact that he is an Honors cop, one of the most decorated in the department. He is so successful in solving cases precisely because he can terrorize information out of anyone. He could have been promoted many times, but, of course, he cannot leave the streets because that is where he earns by far the greatest part of his income, for the Mafia. And, of course, he is at home there."

"Nobody's ever blown the whistle on this guy?"

"Three times his victims have tried. You must remember that the families have strong connections in the police department."

"Nobody, and no organization, has that much control over the police in this city; I know too many decent, honest cops at all levels of command."

"Nevertheless, Carl Nagle has always been exonerated. His three accusers ended up . . . broken. Word gets around. He is an unbelievably dangerous man, Veil, totally ruthless, without scruples or mercy. He is probably the man who was sent to kill Vito Ricci. He is truly a monster, and it is said that only those who have seen his true face can know just how terrible he is."

"To tell you the truth, Father, I didn't much care for his everyday face. I'll keep an eye out for him."

"There's more. I hear that the responsibility for finding the idol has been given to Nagle personally by the family heads. In fact, influence was brought to bear inside the police department to have Nagle transferred from his own precinct to the East Side after the idol turned up in the gallery; the families hoped that merely being in his jurisdiction would deter petty thieves. The fact is that Nagle has been skating on thin ice for some time, and so he's under particular pressure to see that the capos get the idol."

"Why has he been skating on thin ice?"

"Detective Nagle has always had a difficult time keeping his pecker in his pants. It seems he has a penchant for raping and sodomizing young women unfortunate enough to fall into his orbit—hookers, junkies, sometimes teenage runaways."

"Oh, Jesus."

"Yes—oh, Jesus. Anyway, even his outside employers have been finding Nagle a bit difficult to stomach lately. As you know, it's not easy to survive the disapproval of these people. Nagle knows that. He won't be raping any kids for a while, but he knows that he needs to get the idol for the capos in order to get back into their good graces. He's under pressure, which means that his low flash point is going to be even lower while he hunts for the bushman and the idol. Since you appear to be involving yourself in this matter, I wanted you to know the nature of one of your enemies. Carl Nagle is perhaps the cruelest and most dangerous man you've ever met."

"Well, those are two titles he'll have to earn," Veil said as he embraced the priest. "Thank you again, Father. You've been a great help."

"Go with God, Veil."

• • •

Twenty years before, in jungle ooze and rot, Veil had learned from the Viet Cong and Pathet Lao how to wait. And so he waited; for almost two weeks he waited, but there was no word of the missing K'ung warrior-prince or of the idol he carried. It was, Veil thought, as if Toby's god had somehow moved them both through time and space and returned them to the Kalahari. Which, of course, Veil knew had not happened.

He began to have the odd but persistent feeling that he knew something important, but he could not determine what it was.

In his quest to do what he could to save the K'ung's life and see the idol returned to its rightful owners, Veil viewed himself as a kind of lone guerrilla, without any natural constituency. To Toby, should Veil find him, he would be nothing but a hostile ghost, something to run a spear through. Also, he was certain that Reyna Alexander did not trust him completely. He did not return to Central Park, reasoning that if Reyna could not find Toby, he could not, either—and would not know what to do with the K'ung if he did.

The feeling that he knew something important persisted.

During the first week he'd called Reyna frequently but had found her gone at odd hours; when finally he had reached her, she had sounded sleepy—as though she were catching up on sleep whenever she could. Twice he had waited outside the missionary college, then tried to follow her when she had come out. Each time he had lost her; as good as he was at trailing and tracking, Reyna was better. Obviously wary, she started off each time in a different direction; then, in what had seemed a wink of an eye, she had vanished—into a crowd or store or around a corner. It had occurred to Veil that Reyna had found Toby and was hiding and ministering to him—but he had rejected the idea. If she had found the K'ung, Veil reasoned, she eventually would have convinced him to allow her to take him to a hospital, a police station, or perhaps even a foreign consulate to ask for asylum.

Veil concluded that Reyna was still searching for Toby—in Central Park, perhaps, but also beyond. She knew something.

They both knew the same thing, Veil thought. The crucial difference was that Reyna realized exactly what it was she knew.

The attention of the media had begun to flag in the second week, and there was only an occasional news update—using file footage—on the tribe itself, which was being kept informed of events by the two Wesley missionaries and had paused in its self-inflicted moral and physical genocide to await the outcome of Toby's strange odyssey.

In Southern California, a Church of the Black Messiah had been formed; emissaries from the mother church were en route to New York in order to consecrate Victor's gallery as holy ground.

Toby emerged from his cover on a Friday night, close to midnight. Veil had been painting at his easel since dawn, working on a new series of canvases, monitoring—as always—the news on both radio and cable television. When the bulletin was announced, Veil turned off the radio and concentrated on the CNN coverage. He tried to call Reyna, but she was not home.

After an hour of watching live coverage, interspersed

with reporters' speculations on where Toby had been hiding and where he was heading, Veil cleaned his brushes, washed up, and prepared to go out. Then he thought better of it. First, he knew he was exhausted; second, he saw no point in going to Central Park to join the crowd that was already there—police, reporters, and, undoubtedly, Carl Nagle. There was simply nothing he could do. Also, he strongly suspected that wherever Reyna Alexander was, she was not in Central Park.

Veil downed a stiff drink, then went to bed in order to rest his body and search his mind for the important thing that he knew.

CHAPTER SEVEN

Veil dreams.

He sees Toby running up the street toward Central Park and imagines himself entering the bushman's body, mind, and soul. In the process he wills himself to lose his language, to remember only those few English words Toby would have learned from Reyna and the missionaries. He will see through Toby's eyes, feel with Toby's body, think with Toby's mind, filter sensations through Toby's consciousness.

Veil will be Toby.

He has never seen such a weapon before, one that attacks hearing at the same time as it hurls an invisible spear to pierce the flesh and cause terrible pain. However, at the moment he'd heard the crash of the bang-stick and felt the hot pain in his left shoulder, he'd made a number of split-second decisions. Even as he'd hurled the spear at the man wielding the magic weapon, he'd been planning ahead, aware that he would have to run and seek sanctuary.

Now, as he runs on the *street* toward the jungle Reyna

has called *Centralpark*, Veil feels weighed down by the *clothes* the missionaries have forced him to wear. However, there is no time now to remove the *clothes*; his acute hearing and warrior instincts combine to warn him that a *Newyorkcity* warrior is close behind him and gaining. His shoulder burns with pain; he cannot stop and fight, so he must reach the safe, green darkness of *Centralpark*.

The muscles in his back reflexively tense in anticipation of the agonizing sting of a bang-stick spear, but he does not slow his pace as he approaches the *street* with its speeding *cars*. Buoyed by the feel of the Nal-toon under his arm, knowing that to stop or slow down will mean certain death or capture, Veil leaps out onto the *street* and races for the other side, rhythmically driving the shaft of the second spear he has taken to the smooth stone at his feet in an effort to maintain his momentum.

He is immediately assailed by blinding lights and sharp, blasting cries of hurting sounds that swirl around him like a great desert wind. Then he is across the *street*. He leaps over a low stone wall, trips, gets up, and stumbles into the protective, dark shroud of *Centralpark*. He trips again as he goes down a stone embankment and twists onto his wounded shoulder in order to protect the Nal-toon and his spear.

Ignoring the fresh stabs of pain in his shoulder, Veil removes his *shoes* and *socks*, then struggles to his feet. Without the *shoes* he feels lighter—just as the Nal-toon somehow feels lighter than it did in memory. He races through a stand of trees and around the perimeter of a huge clearing; bushes and tree limbs tear at his *clothes*, slowing him down, but he remains inside the line of trees in order to avoid the white glow of moonlight on the meadow to his right.

He stops on the side of a rocky hillside, starts to remove his *clothes*, then hesitates. The night is growing cold, he thinks, and he doubts that he will be able to build a fire. The *clothes* will afford him some protection from the night-cold, and he decides to keep them on.

Veil searches until he finds a large outcropping of rock at the northwest end of a large body of water that is surrounded by a number of the curious, winding paths of smooth stone which the *Newyorkcities* seem to build everywhere. He sets down his spear and the Nal-toon, then takes a piece of *clothes* from his body and uses it to soak up the blood running down his left arm. When he is satisfied that he will leave no blood-spoor to follow, he picks up the spear and Nal-toon and clambers up the long, sloping rock face before him.

After a time he finds a cleft in the rock just wide enough to allow his body to pass through. He eases himself down and finds himself on a narrow, sandy patch of ground that spreads out beneath the cleft—which he can now see is the lip of an overhanging ledge. He pulls the Nal-toon and spear after him, then lies down in the darkness and listens carefully, trying to distinguish those night sounds that could signal danger from the overall din that *Newyorkcity* emits like the never-ending howl of some great wounded beast.

The relative quiet of *Centralpark* is suddenly broken by distant, wailing sounds that seem to come from the direction of the place where he found the Nal-toon. Without knowing why, Veil is convinced that the shrieking, ululating sounds have something to do with him; he fears they are the sounds of magic machines the *Newyorkcities* can use to track him. Clenching his teeth against the pain in his shoulder, Veil stretches up on his toes in order to see over the lip of the ledge.

What Veil sees startles him, and truly frightens him for the first time. A flying machine that is not an *airplane,* one which he has seen before only in the desert, suddenly comes scudding low, like a giant insect, across the trees at the southern end of the meadow before him. He has seen how these flying machines can soar and sweep and even hover in the air for a long period of time. He had always assumed that these magic machines were used by the white tribes only to drop bundles of food to the K'ung in times of need, but now one of them is searching for him, lighting the ground with its fire-eyes.

The *Newyorkcity* hunters have very powerful magic, Veil thinks, and it occurs to him that they may be able to find him, no matter where, or how well, he hides. If that is the case, he wants to die fighting as a warrior, not like some wounded animal cowering at the back of a cave.

He starts to pull himself up through the cleft, then remembers with a sharp jolt that he is under the Nal-toon's protection. He has been a fool, Veil thinks, for the Nal-toon has given these things to the *Newyorkcities*, just as He gave the desert, and everything in it, to the K'ung. The Nal-toon sees and controls everything, and there would be no point to this trial if the *Newyorkcities'* magic machines and weapons were all-powerful. No. He will be safe for as long as he displays courage and keeps faith in the Nal-toon.

Veil eases himself down into the darkness beneath the overhang. He touches the face of the Nal-toon and immediately feels better.

When he again peers over the lip of the ledge, Veil can see that the first flying machine has been joined by a second. Both are hovering, lighting the meadow around the water. *Newyorkcity* warriors, all wearing identical blue *clothes*, swarm over the meadow and through the trees where he had been only a short time before. All of the warriors carry what appear to be bang-sticks of different sizes.

He has killed one of their tribesmen, Veil thinks, and the *Newyorkcity* warriors will surely kill him if he is caught. He will have failed the trial set by the Nal-toon, and the Nal-toon will never be returned to his people.

However, Veil thinks, the fact that the warriors are so earnestly searching for him seems to mean, as he'd suspected, that their magic is not all-powerful. He decides it is a very good sign.

He quickly ducks when he hears footsteps clatter on the rocks near him. Gathering the Nal-toon and spear against his chest, Veil presses back beneath the overhang as a cone of light flashes down through the narrow opening and sweeps the sandy area where he had been a moment before. Then the light goes out and the sound of *shoes* on stone moves away.

Veil sighs with relief, then rolls over on his right side in an effort to ease the pain in his left shoulder. He knows that the bang-stick has left its small, hurting spear deep in the muscle; he can feel it there, grinding against the bone every time he moves. He knows he must take it out, for the slightest movement of his arm sends jagged flashes of pain down through the muscles to his fingertips. He can only hope that the bang-stick spear is not poisoned. However, poisoned or not, he cannot attempt to remove the spear before morning; he needs a fire, and a night-fire would be certain to attract the *Newyorkcity* warriors.

He wishes he had more shilluk to ease his pain, but he does not; he consumed all of it during his terrifying journey on the *airplane*.

But the Nal-toon is with him, Veil thinks as he gently strokes God's wooden surface, and that is enough for any K'ung warrior. The Nal-toon's face conjures up images of the desert. Home. He will survive this great trial with the Nal-toon's help—and, indeed, that help is already apparent, for God has made Himself noticeably easier to carry. When he returns with the Nal-toon to his people, things will be as they were before; there will be joy, laughter, and dancing in the camp, and for the rest of his life the Nal-toon will look upon him with special favor.

Veil's pain begins to ease as he continues to stroke the Nal-toon's rough surface. Finally he rests his head on God, closes his eyes, and drifts off to sleep within sleep.

•   •   •

Still imagining himself as Toby, Veil dreams he awakens to find himself sick to his stomach and feverish. The pain in his left shoulder has become a constant, searing ball of agony that sends flickering tongues of flame out into his neck, down through his arm, and into his fingers.

He is being poisoned by the bang-stick spear. The spear must be cut out.

The thought of cutting into his own flesh without the numbing embrace of shilluk fills him with a cold fear, but he knows that he must begin immediately; if he waits any longer, he will soon be too weak to make the effort.

He picks up a dry stick and clenches it between his teeth to keep from crying out as he drags himself from beneath the ledge and struggles to his feet; thunderbolts of pain crash through his arm.

"Nal-toon, help me," Veil whispers around the stick in his teeth. "Make me strong; make this warrior worthy of you."

Using his right arm, Veil pulls himself up to the lip of the overhang. He peers out over the rock formation—and freezes. His sanctuary is surrounded by *Newyorkcities*. There are runners dressed in strange, brightly colored *clothes* loping along the stone paths; other *Newyorkcities* throw discs that float in arcs through the air; women push babies in machines that roll along the ground like *Land-Rovers* but are silent.

Newyorkcity warriors in blue *clothes* walk in pairs. Their eyes are searching, and they occasionally touch the bang-sticks they carry in hiding pouches at their sides.

Struggling against the draining effects of his fever, Veil lets himself back down, then lies under the ledge and waits until nightfall, when he can no longer hear the *Newyorkcities* in *Centralpark* laughing and shouting as they carry on their frenzied, apparently meaningless, activities. As the moon rises, Veil once again drags himself out from beneath the ledge onto the narrow strip of sand. He drags the Nal-toon after him.

Despite the great risk of attracting enemy warriors, Veil knows that he must build a fire. He uses a piece of flint from the small medicine pouch he wears around his neck to fire sparks into a pile of dry leaves and twigs he has swept up from the sand and placed against a vertical face of the rock. The leaves catch first, and Veil carefully feeds the delicate wisps of flame with increasingly larger sticks and clumps of dried brush, which he pulls from cracks in the rock.

When he is satisfied with the fire's heat, he grasps the shaft of his spear and places the long, iron head into the heart of the flames. Then he strips the *clothes* from the upper part of his body.

He is ready.

Gripping the spear's shaft just behind the head, Veil fixes his gaze on the face of the Nal-toon. In the flickering firelight, magnified by the fever-heat in Veil's brain, the gnarled face of God seems very much alive to him; God is breathing, gazing back kindly at His worshiper. Veil opens his eyes wide and continues to gaze into the carved eyeholes of the Nal-toon. Then he begins to take a series of deep, measured breaths until he feels a kind of misty, numbing warmth seeping into his mind and muscles. When he looks back into the fire, he imagines that he can see the desert in all its countless, shifting guises; when he glances back at God, the images of home continue to dance on the Nal-toon's face.

He slowly withdraws the iron spearhead from the fire, then holds it aloft for a few moments to allow it to cool. Then, still breathing deeply and clinging to the desert-images in his mind, Veil begins to probe the wound in his shoulder with the needle-sharp point of the spear.

Huge drops of sweat pop from his skin, glisten in the firelight, then roll off his flesh, to be sucked up by the sand. Sweat forms a stinging film over his eyes as Veil struggles to maintain the desert-images, his only shilluk, before him.

Then the small metal bang-stick spear is out. Veil reels from pain, but he knows that there is still one thing left he must do. He shoves the spearhead back into the flames and slowly counts to ten. Then, in one swift motion, he withdraws the iron and slaps its face against the torn, bleeding flesh of his left shoulder. There is a sharp hiss, accompanied by the sweetish smell of burning flesh.

The desert-images explode in a kaleidoscope of color and distant, wailing sound as Veil faints.

• • •

Veil's dream-body, his Toby, awakens to the feel of a cold rain falling on his face and an animal sniffing at his left ear. His instincts, born of survival in a narrow twilight zone separating life from death in the desert, tell him to remain still.

He parts his lips slightly to let raindrops fall on his parched and swollen tongue, but even this small movement brings a menacing growl from whatever animal crouches to his left, just beyond his field of vision. It does not sound like a leopard, Veil thinks, and a lone baboon or jackal would not come this close to a breathing man. It could be a *Newyorkcity* camp dog, but it sounds larger.

Still sniffing and growling, the animal moves forward until Veil can see it; it is a dog, but unlike any he had ever seen before. This animal is all black. Muscles ripple beneath its sleek, glistening hide, and its bare fangs are white and unchipped. The dog's tail appears to have been torn off in a fight, for it is no more than a lump on the animal's hindquarters.

Breathing evenly and staring directly into the dog's eyes, Veil gropes with his right hand for his spear. Suddenly the black dog snaps at his face, and Veil moves his head aside just in time to avoid the animal's sharp fangs. At the same moment his fingers touch the shaft of his spear. He grips the shaft and rolls hard to his left, lunging directly at the startled animal and driving the spearhead deep into its throat.

The dog coughs a thick spray of blood and saliva, then shudders and collapses without a sound across Veil's chest. Veil immediately presses his mouth to the animal's throat and drinks the nourishing blood that pulses from the severed jugular. The blood hits Veil's stomach with the force of a physical blow; its effects spread quickly throughout his body, warming him and lending him strength. He is still drinking in great, deep gulps when the animal's heart finally stops beating.

The Nal-toon is merciful, Veil thinks; evidently satisfied with the courage he has displayed up to this point, God has provided him with the food he needs to go on.

His strength replenished, Veil carefully wraps the Nal-toon in a piece of *clothes*, then places God under the overhang, out of the rain. He drags the dog's carcass under the ledge, then meticulously smooths out all signs of struggle and death from the sand. He builds a small fire, then dresses the cauterized wound in his left shoulder with herbs from his medicine pouch and strips of *clothes*.

Reasonably free of pain, with his belly full and his mind in peaceful communion with God, Veil once again lies down and drifts off to sleep within sleep.

•　•　•

In Veil's dream, his Toby has lost track of the time that has passed since he found sanctuary in *Centralpark*, but the wound in his shoulder is now almost completely healed. Also, there has been such an abundance of food in this jungle that his normally lean body has begun to show traces of fat.

While the first dog had been delivered to him by the Nal-toon, he has had to stalk the others he has eaten. The water in the large pool nearby is not as sweet as that in the desert, but Veil has never seen water in such quantity; here it is not necessary to quickly scoop it up and store it in eggs before it seeps into the ground. He has been free to drink his fill each night, and this has made the long, hot, and waterless days spent hiding under the ledge easily bearable.

Now he feels strong and rested, and he knows that it is time to begin his journey to the vast, smooth, stone fields where the *airplanes* stay. There, he thinks, the *airplane* that brought him to *Newyorkcity* will be waiting to take him home. The Nal-toon will make sure that it is so.

Veil made no attempt to remember the many bends and sharp turns in the *streets* Reyna used to bring him from the *airplane* fields to the Nal-toon; there had been no need, for Veil does not travel on *streets*. He had carefully noted the position of the setting sun—first at the *airplane* field and again at the place where he had found the Nal-toon. The two sightings are all he needs, and he knows the precise direction in which he must travel to reach the *airplane* fields. The sun, and the stars at night, will guide him there.

It is night now, and the full moon is partially obscured by clouds. With *Centralpark* free of *Newyorkcities*, he goes to the pool to drink and wash himself. Once again, as on other still nights, he hears the roar and cough of great hunting cats; the sounds seem close, to the east. Veil has become increasingly puzzled by the sounds, for they would seem to indicate that there are hunting cats in *Newyorkcity*; yet he has never found any spoor.

70

The *clothes* given to him by the missionaries have become shredded and filthy, an affront to his senses. He removes them, washes them as best he can, and, from the strips, fashions a loincloth, a cloak to ward off the night chill, and a carrying sling.

He walks to the crest of a hill and takes his bearings, using a tall *building* in the distance as his first landmark. He carries enough strips of dried dog meat in his sling to last many days; he wishes he had an egg in which to carry water but he does not, and he does not dwell on the problem. Water seems to be plentiful in *Newyorkcity*.

Drenched in moonlight, Veil stands perfectly still for a few minutes, closing his eyes as he offers thanks to the Nal-toon and prays for a safe journey home so that his people may survive. Then he hitches his sling with its precious contents over his shoulder, grips his spear in his right hand, and starts down the hill.

He retraces his original route, skirting the large, open meadow by moving, as silently as his moon-shadow, through the encircling trees. Finally he comes to a wide, stone path which he must cross. He crouches, listening, but can hear nothing but the intermittent whine of *cars* on the *street* a hundred or so running-steps to his right. He straightens up and steps out onto the stone path.

Suddenly two *Newyorkcities* leap out from behind a tree. *"Hold it, turkey!"*

Veil stops and assumes a fighting stance. He knows that he cannot hope to escape with the Nal-toon in the sling weighing him down, and so he will have to fight. He waits calmly, body half turned and spear arm cocked, as the warriors approach. Veil is relieved to see that the men carry only knives and not bang-sticks.

"Hey, Mason! Will you look at this turkey? He's gotta be stone crazy."

"Fuckin' loony, all right."

The taller of the two men approaches, waving his knife back and forth in front of his body, then stops a few paces away from Veil. *"What's in the sack, man?"*

Veil cannot understand the warrior's words, but their threatening tone is unmistakable. He considers his op-

71

tions, then decides that it would be better not to battle the
two *Newyorkcities* if there is any way to avoid it. To fight,
he must set down the Nal-toon, and he does not wish to do
this. Also, a wound—even if not fatal—could force him to
go to ground again in *Centralpark*, perhaps for many more
days. He wants to go home. Courage, he thinks, must
always be tempered by wisdom.

"Let me pass," Veil says evenly, using his free hand to
make the sign of truce used by both K'ung and Bantu.

The short man frowns. *"Christ, Blade, you ever hear
anyone talk like that?"*

The other man shakes his head. *"I ain't sure it's real talk
at all. I think he's just makin' crazy noises."*

"Hand over the sack, man!"

"Hey, watch out for that pig-sticker he's got."

*"Shit. I'm gonna hang that spear on my wall. You circle
around on his ass. First one with an open shot cuts out the
fucker's heart."*

Veil shifts his weight to his opposite foot and hefts his
spear as the short man begins circling to his left. The
Newyorkcities are leaving him no choice, he thinks. Their
intentions are clear, and he wastes no further time in
waiting. Suddenly he leaps forward, thrusting the spearhead through the taller man's throat.

Anticipating a knife thrust from his left flank, Veil spins
away from the expected direction of attack, freeing the
spearhead from the dead man's neck with a flick of his
wrist. He ends in a crouch, weight slightly forward on the
balls of his feet, spear held ready to impale the other
attacker.

But the second man makes no move of any kind. He
stands very still, hands shaking at his sides as he stares in
horror at the nearly decapitated body spouting blood over
the stone path.

"Shit, man, you killed him! You killed Mason!"

Veil takes two running-steps and thrusts with his spear.
The man screeches and tries to twist away, but the spearhead slices into his shoulder. Veil pulls back the spear, and
the man slumps to the ground. Veil leaps into position to
make a kill-thrust, but the pitiful helplessness and strange

72

behavior of the man cowering on the stone path makes him hesitate.

The *Newyorkcity* warrior is crying. His face is wet with tears.

"Holy shit. You gonna kill me too? Don't kill me, man. I'm really sorry."

At first Veil is confused by the tears in the man's eyes, then he is disgusted; never before has he seen a warrior weep. "I will not kill you," Veil says contemptuously as he picks up the knife the man has dropped and puts it into his sling. "Give thanks to the Nal-toon."

Immediately dismissing the battle with the two *Newyorkcities* from his mind, Veil moves across the stone path and into a thin line of trees. There he crouches and peers over the top of the stone wall that separates *Centralpark* from the rest of *Newyorkcity*. The *street*, filled with *cars* when he first ran across it, is now almost empty.

Veil climbs over the wall and races across the *street* to a dark area between two *buildings*. He presses back against one of the *buildings* and waits, watching and listening. There are no shouts or wailing sounds, no sign that anyone has seen him.

He goes on, sprinting from one shadow-area to another, until he eventually finds his way blocked by a *building* unlike any he has seen before. It is not as tall as many of the others he has passed, but it sprawls for a considerable distance to both the north and south, blocking his path. *Newyorkcities* in white *clothes* go in and out of its many openings.

He finds a way around the *building*, then turns east again. He walks across a stone field filled with empty *cars*, climbs over a metal barrier, and drops to the grassy earth on the other side. He crosses a very wide *street*, then crouches and stares in awe at the vast, swiftly moving body of water Reyna had called a *river*. He has never imagined there could be so much water in one place, water that seems to flow forever, with no beginning and no end.

In the middle of the *river*, directly in his path, is land with *buildings* on it. He must somehow reach that land, Veil thinks; the sky is beginning to glow, and he needs a place to go to ground during the day when the *Newyork-cities* come out.

He has no idea how deep this *river* is; the water is too murky to tell. However deep it is, it must be crossed. He will have to wade and trust in the Nal-toon to see him safely across. He is running out of time.

The *river* may well come up to his neck, Veil thinks, and he does not want the Nal-toon to get wet. He removes the sling from around his neck, wraps it tightly around the Nal-toon, the spear, and the knife. Holding the bundle above his head, he begins to walk down the steep incline leading to the *river*.

He has only gone a few steps when he slips on wet stones and plunges into the water. His mind screams in panic as foul-smelling water closes over his head, blinding him, filling his nose and mouth. He stretches his legs, frantically searching for a bottom that isn't there. Now he will die, Veil thinks; he will sink forever and be buried beneath this depthless *Newyorkcity river*.

However, despite his panic, Veil has never lost his grip on the Nal-toon. Now God slowly begins to carry him back to the surface.

Veil is choking, but he manages to control his cough reflex and hold his breath as he clings to the *clothes* in which he has wrapped the Nal-toon. After a few moments his head pops above the surface. Coughing and choking, swallowing water, he heaves his body across the Nal-toon, wraps his arms around God, and holds on. The choking spasms pass, and Veil frantically gulps air while he breathes a prayer of thanks to God, Who is now transporting him across the *river* on His back.

But then Veil realizes that a great effort on his part is still required; there is fantastic power in the movement of the *river*'s great, wet body, and that movement is carrying him to the south. If he does not fight that power, Veil thinks, he will be carried past the land and helplessly swept down the middle of the *river*, where the *Newyork-cities* will easily kill him with their bang-sticks.

Ignoring the pain in his left arm, Veil uses it alone to grip the Nal-toon. He lashes out with his feet and beats at the water with his free hand, struggling with all his might against the force of the *river*. The muscles in his arms and legs begin to burn, but he struggles even harder; he closes his eyes and increases the tempo of his thrashing. When he opens his eyes and glances up, he finds he is only a short distance from the land.

Suddenly he is caught in a small tidal whirlpool and spun around. He reaches out with his hand—and his fingers catch in a crevice between two large rocks. With his last strength he pulls himself in to the land. He clambers up over rocks, then falls, gasping for breath, on dewy grass.

He is cold and thirsty. He does not want to drink any more of the foul-smelling water, for he fears that it may be poisoned. However, he feels that he has no choice but to slake his thirst now, while he has the chance, for he has not passed a single spring and he has no idea where the *Newyorkcities* draw their water. Having caught his breath, he lies on his belly on the rocks and drinks; the water tastes terrible, but it dulls his thirst.

Veil rises, turns, and starts to walk toward the nearest *building*. He has gone only a few steps when he stops and tenses as a sleepy-looking *Newyorkcity* emerges from one of the *buildings* and begins walking almost directly toward him on one of the stone paths. Veil grips the shaft of his spear but does not draw the head from its wrapping of *clothes*.

The man barely glances at Veil. *"Good morning,"* he says, yawning and rubbing his eyes.

Veil senses no threat in the man's tone or bearing, and he allows him to pass by. "Go in peace," he says softly.

It is growing lighter. Veil puts his bundle under his arm and moves toward a space between two *buildings*.

"Hey, you! Where the hell do you think you're going?"

This voice, coming from Veil's left, is definitely threatening. Veil quickly places his bundle on the ground, pulls the spear free, and wheels to find a *Newyorkcity* warrior, dressed in blue *clothes* and carrying a bang-stick, running toward him. Knowing that his spear is useless against a bang-stick, Veil picks up the bundle and sprints in the opposite direction, along the side of the *building*.

"Stop, you son of a bitch, or I'll shoot your black ass!"

Veil rounds the *building*, races to the end, turns left, and runs down a lane of grass bounded by the *river* and the *building*. He sees a narrow opening, ducks into it. The passageway reeks of rotting, unburied scraps of food, but there are piles of battered metal objects behind which he can hide. He crouches down behind three of the objects and waits, spear held ready, certain that he can kill his attacker at close range.

The enemy warrior appears at the entrance to the passageway a few seconds later. The man's face is flushed, and Veil can hear the breath rasping in his lungs. The hand holding the bang-stick is shaking as the man moves slowly into the passageway.

Veil is about to leap out and hurl his spear when the warrior suddenly stops. He wipes a glistening sheen of sweat from his face, then begins to back away.

"Shit. I'm not about to risk my ass on a part-time job. Fuck him."

Veil smiles grimly and allows himself to relax as the *Newyorkcity* disappears from sight. He rearranges his bundle into a sling that he can once again carry around his neck, then looks up and squints into the bright sunlight at the end of the passageway. The light makes his head ache and his eyes burn. He is beginning to feel sick and dizzy, and he knows that he must quickly find a place to go to ground.

Directly above his head is a metal structure with small platforms that project from the side of the *building*. He might be able to go to ground on top of the *building*, he thinks. He leaps for the bottom of the metal structure, grips it, and is pleasantly surprised when a portion of the structure swings down, making it simple for him to climb; as he does so, the bottom portion of the structure swings back into its original position.

Veil lies down on the sticky, pebbled surface on top of the *building* and stares out over *Newyorkcity*. This land is so vast, he thinks, so strange. In all directions, *buildings* thrust toward the sky; countless *cars* speed along on countless *streets,* which crisscross and stretch into the distance as far as he can see. . . .

Suddenly, without warning, his entire body spews sweat, and he feels his insides begin to churn. Something is terribly wrong with him, Veil thinks, and he quickly removes his cloak and loincloth so as not to soil himself. Then he vomits, and he continues retching long after there is nothing left in his stomach. He collapses on his right side, gasping for breath—and then the process begins all over again.

At last, exhausted and barely able to see, Veil drags himself away from the soiled area, then collapses in a pool of his own sweat and passes out.

• • •

In Veil's dream, his Toby awakens groggy and disoriented. Then he remembers: The *Newyorkcities* are after him and he is sick—probably from poisoned water. But he must go on.

Veil tries to stand but cannot. He loses track of time as he lies sprawled on the hot surface, only half conscious. His flesh burns, and he cannot remember ever being so thirsty; he is so thirsty, Veil thinks, that he would even drink more of the poisoned water—if only he could get to it.

He must go on. If he remains where he is, the *Newyork-cities* will eventually find and kill him. He must go on. Suddenly it is night, although Veil's Toby does not remember sleeping. He does not know how much time has passed since he climbed to the top of the *building,* and his fever-thirst is now so great that his swollen tongue fills the back of his throat, making it difficult for him to swallow and breathe.

He stinks of sickness.

"Give me strength, Nal-toon," he murmurs.

He struggles to his knees, then laboriously rises to his feet. Sweat oozes in great drops from his pores, rolls and gathers into a shining film; his flesh steams in the cool night air. He sways, but manages to remain standing, leaning on his spear for support, he hitches the sling over his shoulder and staggers across the top of the *building* to the metal structure. Slowly he descends, concentrating intently on each hand- and foothold.

On the ground he moves unsteadily off to his left, then crosses a narrow *bridge* that spans this arm of the *river*. The sight and sound of the water playing against his jagged thirst is almost overwhelming, but Veil now has second thoughts about drinking it; the Nal-toon will not reward him for stupidity or weakness, he thinks, and he must search for sweet water to cool his fever and purge his body. He manages to align himself with a chosen landmark, staggers on.

Eventually he staggers into a small clearing surrounded by trees. However, the area is too small to offer sanctuary—most of it is open, in full view of *Newyorkcities* in *cars* on the *bridge* overhead.

Veil moves around the perimeter of the clearing, then stops and begins to tremble with hope and anticipation when he hears the sound of splashing water. He moves quickly toward the sound and discovers, near a tree, a strange structure of stone and metal. Water spouts from the center of the structure. He has no idea where the water comes from, for he can see no spring anywhere nearby. He assumes it is but another example of the *Newyorkcities'* magic, a place where *Newyorkcities* drink. This water will be sweet.

When he has looked around and satisfied himself that there are no *Newyorkcities* in the area, Veil moans and runs to the water. Supporting himself with his hands against the stone base, he thrusts his face into the cool, cascading water and drinks.

He drinks until he vomits, then repeats the process again and again; he knows that he must purge his body of as much of the poison *river* water as possible. Eventually he begins to drink more sparingly. When he has finally slaked his thirst, he uses handfuls of the clear water to wash his body.

For a few moments his head clears and his vision snaps

back into sharp focus—but then his vision again blurs, his head throbs, and his body breaks into a sweat. He leans against the stone-and-metal water structure until a spell of dizziness passes. He drinks again, then starts off on a line of march parallel to the *bridge* overhead. He knows that he must find sanctuary before the sun rises, or he will be finished.

Veil passes out of the clearing and finds himself in a maze of metal *buildings*, much smaller than those on the other side of the *river*. In agony, he struggles on, moving in a pain-blurred, staggering, slow-motion race against the glow of approaching dawn.

Finally he comes to a barrier of woven metal strands stretching north and south as far as he can see. On the other side of the barrier are long, rectangular, wooden objects that sit on metal *wheels* but are not *cars* or *Land-Rovers*; there are more of the objects than Veil can count, and all of them rest on twin strands of thick metal that weave and crisscross one another like the sand-tracks of many desert snakes.

He has found his sanctuary, Veil thinks. He can hide inside one of the wooden structures. But first he must find a way to get past the barrier, which has countless little knives running along its top.

If he cannot go around or climb over the barrier, Veil thinks, then he must dig his way under.

He waits for an attack of nausea and dizziness to pass, then moves slowly to his left, studying the ground. When he sees what appears to be a patch of soft ground, he drops to his knees and begins to dig with his knife and scoop with his hands. He frequently has to pause in order to catch his breath, but he eventually manages to dig a trench beneath the barrier; he slides under, dragging his spear and carrying sling after him.

As Toby walks unsteadily toward one of the railroad cars, Veil leaves the K'ung, rolling away from the dream and floating up through sleep toward his own dawn.

CHAPTER EIGHT

Veil, feeling emotionally drained and physically exhausted from his dream-trek, signed in with the security guard at the north entrance to the missionary college complex, then headed toward the faculty dormitory. He met Reyna, approaching from the opposite direction, on the sidewalk outside the building.

"Good morning," Veil said with a smile. "If you don't mind my saying so, you really look like hell."

The frail woman with the large, soulful eyes managed to smile back. "Hi. You don't look so hot yourself."

"I think we've both had a rough night, each in a different way."

"Toby . . ."

"I know. I listened to the news reports. He's been sighted in all five boroughs, as well as in Connecticut. A man in New Jersey swears that Toby materialized in his living room and stole his stamp collection. Obviously, Toby's been busy. He's also now a national celebrity, with offers from all three networks to foot his legal expenses in exchange for exclusive rights to his story. I'm sure if Toby knew about all the deals that were being cooked up on his behalf, he'd hurry right in."

"It's not funny, Veil."

"Toby's situation isn't funny at all," he replied evenly. "I think the reaction of the public and media is."

"There's mass hysteria, Veil. There are vigilante groups forming."

"That isn't funny, either. You've been out looking for him, haven't you?"

Reyna nodded wearily. "Veil, forgive me. I don't mean to be rude, but I'm very tired."

"Reyna, I think I have a pretty good idea where you've been looking." Veil removed a folded map from the back pocket of his jeans, held it up. "We should talk. I think it's time we started working together."

Reyna's eyes darted back and forth between Veil's face and the map in his hand. Her own face reflected consternation at first, then suspicion and fear. "How did you—?"

"Just a second," Veil said softly, quickly replacing the map in his pocket as he glanced over Reyna's shoulder and saw a black, unmarked police car pull up to the curb ten yards behind her. "We've got company. Just take it easy, Reyna, and stay cool. I'll handle Mr. Nagle. Trust me."

Reyna wheeled around and stiffened when she saw Carl Nagle and Vahanian emerge from the car. Her hand, cold and dry, reached out for Veil's, and he gripped it. Nagle's face flushed when he saw Veil. The big man started forward but stopped when his partner calmly stepped in front of him, blocking his way. There was a whispered but heated conversation, during which Vahanian's view appeared to prevail. Nagle threw up his hands in a gesture of frustration, but he stepped back and leaned against the rear fender of the car while Vahanian came down the sidewalk to Veil and Reyna.

"Good morning," the olive-skinned, husky detective said. His smile revealed even, white teeth.

"Good morning," Veil replied, his voice flat.

"Miss Alexander, may we talk?"

"If you'd like." Reyna's fingernails were digging into

81

Veil's flesh, but her tension was not immediately apparent in her voice.

"Perhaps we could go up to your apartment?"

Reyna quickly shook her head. "There's no need. I've already told you all I know."

Nagle, still extremely agitated, abruptly pushed off the fender and poked a thick index finger through the air in Veil's direction. "You can go, Kendry!"

Veil looked at Reyna and winked. "Do you want me to go?"

"Please don't go," Reyna said in a small voice. "Not while he's here."

"I'll stay," Veil announced to the huge detective.

Nagle started to come down the sidewalk but stopped when Vahanian wheeled around and vigorously shook his head. Nagle hesitated, then turned and went back to his previous position.

Vahanian turned back to Reyna. "Will you tell me where you've been?"

"I've been walking all night. When I heard the news about Toby, I got upset and couldn't sleep."

"Strange I didn't see you in Central Park."

"Why is it strange? By the time I heard the news, he was already gone from Central Park—at least, that was the report."

"Miss Alexander, I'm going to ask you the most important question up front. Are you now hiding, or did you ever hide, the African somewhere?"

"That's a ridiculous question."

"The man's a total stranger to this culture and environment. I don't understand how he could have remained free and survived this long without help."

"God is helping him."

Vahanian grimaced. "The idol? Don't tell me *you* believe—"

"God, Lieutenant, not the Nal-toon."

"Then God is going to be in trouble with the Criminal Justice System of the State of New York."

"In which case it's the State of New York that's in trouble."

"I find it unlikely that God would help a killer who's a fugitive from justice."

"Toby has killed twice—both times in self-defense. He and his people have been terribly wronged. I don't believe he's guilty in the eyes of Our Lord."

Veil gave Reyna's hand a reassuring squeeze, then released it and casually strolled down the sidewalk toward the police car. Nagle saw him coming, and the detective's doughy face creased in a puzzled frown—although the raisin eyes remained as dull as stone. Veil stepped into the street, walked around the car, and leaned on the trunk across from Nagle.

"It's a pain in the ass having to drag Vahanian around with you everywhere, isn't it?" Veil asked in a low voice.

Nagle's mouth was slightly open. He shook his head, blinked slowly. "What did you say?"

"Do you believe in mental telepathy?"

"Kendry, what the hell are you talking about?"

"I'm trying to read your mind. What I pick up is that you're thinking that it's a pain in the ass to have to drag Vahanian around. If you were alone, you'd just drag that girl into the car and beat whatever information you want out of her."

Suddenly the tiny eyes came alive, seemed to grow larger as they glittered like polished agates. The muscles in Carl Nagle's jaw contracted so quickly that his teeth came together with an audible click. He started to walk around the car, a movement that caught Vahanian's eye and caused the other detective to glance up sharply.

"Kendry, I'm warning you—!"

"No, I'm warning you," Veil said in the same low, even tone as he turned his head, smiled, and nodded at Vahanian. "If you come any closer, I'll do more than make you toss your cookies; I'll kill you. At my trial I'll bring up the fact that you killed Vito Ricci. I'll also mention the matter of you being on the Mafia payroll for years, acting as an enforcer. You're a rapist and sadist, Nagle, and my guess is that your victims will come forward in a flood once you're dead. Then, of course, I'll get off on self-

83

defense, since your partner and the woman can see that you're about to attack me. Do I have your attention, Carl?"

Veil waited for a response, but there was none. It was as if his words were a kind of sound-Medusa that had turned Carl Nagle to stone. The detective was standing perfectly still, rigid, and the life had once again gone out of his eyes; he seemed to be staring through, or somewhere beyond, Veil.

"Outstanding," Veil continued. "Even though you appear vaguely catatonic at the moment, I'll assume that your ears still work. That bushman is still on the loose— but you're not going to kill him, and you're not going to get your hands on the idol. Now, I know that you're in trouble with your Mafia bosses, and I know that they're counting on you to get that idol for them. Tough shit. The price for having me mind my own business is for you to take a walk from this case. I don't give a shit how it's done, but do it; have a heart attack or something. Now get in the car and wait there like a nice policeman."

Nagle's eyes went slowly out of focus as his hand slowly moved toward his gun. Vahanian had stopped talking, and both he and Reyna were staring anxiously at Nagle and Veil.

"Carl, you'll be dead before you can pull the trigger," Veil said easily. "You know it's true; you can feel it in your guts. Now get in the car."

Moving like an automaton, Nagle turned, walked back around the car, and got into the rear. He sat very straight, his back not touching the seat, and blankly stared ahead. His face was the color of rotten meat.

"All finished, Lieutenant?" Veil asked as Vahanian hurried up the street toward him.

Vahanian said nothing. He glanced through the windshield at his stricken partner, quickly looked up at Veil, then got into the car behind the wheel and rolled up the windows. Veil watched as Vahanian tried to talk to Nagle, but the other man remained trapped in his raging prison of silence. Again Vahanian, a puzzled expression on his face, glanced at Veil, who smiled, nodded, and waved.

Vahanian abruptly turned the key in the ignition and drove away.

"What on earth did you say to him?" Reyna asked as Veil walked over to her.

"Nothing, really, just trying to make friends." Veil removed the map from his pocket. "Will you invite me up to your apartment?"

"Yes," Reyna replied quietly. "Of course."

He followed Reyna into the faculty dormitory, up three flights of a narrow, wooden staircase, and into a small but brightly decorated one-bedroom apartment. There were a number of paintings, most of them reflecting religious themes. On one wall hung a huge crucifix. Another wall was covered by a montage of photographs of Reyna as a child, a man and woman Veil assumed were her parents, and a gathering of tribesmen he recognized as K'ung.

Reyna went into the kitchen to make coffee. When she returned, she found Veil leaning on a table; before him was a section of a map of New York City—Manhattan, with Central Park as its rectangular, emerald-green heart.

"Toby went into the park here," Veil said, pointing to Fifth Avenue and Sixty-ninth Street. "I think we can assume he also came out about the same place, since the mugger was killed near there. He stayed in the park, near water and living on, say, dog meat until his wound had healed sufficiently for him to travel. Now he knows where he wants to go—or he *thinks* he knows where he wants to go. There were reported sightings all over the city, but most of those are due to the mass hysteria you mentioned." Veil paused and moved his finger to the island in the middle of the East River. "One of the reports came from a security guard on Roosevelt Island. That, I believe, was the only accurate sighting. There's no way of knowing how he got across the river; he certainly didn't get swimming lessons in the Kalahari. He could have crossed hand over hand on the tramway cable or managed to float across on debris. He may even have floated across on the Nal-toon. What I am sure of is that he's heading southeast. He's clever and incredibly strong-willed; if he needed to get across the river, he'd have found a way.

85

"I know a few things about so-called 'primitive tribes-men,' Reyna. Toby may be a savage on the loose in the city, but he's not *lost*—at least not in the sense that he's forced to wander around aimlessly. This is a man who can hunt for days in open desert and still find his way back to his tribe's camp. The sun was low in the sky when you picked him up, and it didn't set until just after you'd reached Victor's gallery. The setting sun is the only point of reference Toby needed to orient himself."

Veil unfolded another section of the map, which showed the borough of Queens. With his index finger he traced along the red line he had drawn from Roosevelt Island through Queens to a large *X* in the middle of a purple patch of color next to Jamaica Bay.

John F. Kennedy International Airport.

Veil glanced up at Reyna, who slowly nodded. "You do know," Reyna said softly. "Poor Toby. He thinks that all he has to do is get back to the airport in order to be transported home."

"As in most primitive tribes, K'ung learning is probably almost entirely experiential and literal. Toby will use what he knows, just as he does in the desert. In Toby's mind a plane—something he probably thinks of as magi-cal, a device provided for his personal benefit by the Nal-toon—brought him here, so one will be waiting to take him home—if he can get to the place where it's kept. Getting there is the trial that you mentioned."

"Yes." Reyna sighed as she sat down on the floor and rested her head against a table leg. "I believe that's what Toby is thinking, and what he's trying to do. But then, I know the K'ung very well. You don't. How did you come up with this idea?"

"Dreams. Deduction. Knowledge flying on the wings of imagination. Just a bit of inspired guesswork. His route is thirteen miles as the crow flies, which is precisely the way he'll be going. We have to find him before someone else does, or before he shows up at JFK and tries to walk on a plane."

"He'll be very careful, Veil. He'll move slowly. During

these past weeks I've been back and forth over that route, trying to find Toby, but also to leave totems—signs, warnings—that he can read. I'm hoping he'll read the totems, have second thoughts about what he's trying to do, go to ground, and wait for me to come around. But I don't think he will."

"I wonder what shots he had before he left."

"Lord, Veil, that's been one of my biggest concerns. He's probably already sick. He knows absolutely nothing about this environment. He'll continue to kill dogs or cats for food, which is all right, but there's no telling what he's been drinking or what he *will* drink. He has no resistance to most of our diseases, and whatever inoculations he was given will give him only limited protection. When Toby's thirsty, he drinks; he knows nothing about typhus. He could have drunk from the East River, or even from some sewage outlet." Reyna paused, looked up at Veil. Tears welled in her eyes, flowed down her cheeks. "I'm afraid that if Toby gets sick, he'll go to ground until he gets better—or until he dies."

"Well, we'll just have to find him. Will you trust me now?"

"Yes."

"Will you let me help you?"

"Yes, Veil. Thank you."

"At least it's not all bad news. If we're right about his thinking and his plans, there couldn't possibly be a better route in all of New York City for him to follow. Look at it: He's got the railroad yards in which to hide, and then— assuming he can get through the Sunnyside section of Queens—he's going to run into hundreds of acres of cemetery. After that he's got the Long Island Expressway to cross, but then he's back into another cemetery—and a golf course after that. He's back in the open then, and probably finished, but six miles of good cover in the middle of New York City certainly isn't bad. I'll have to remember to congratulate Victor on having his gallery on Sixty-ninth Street; the angle of the setting sun from there is what gave Toby this route."

"It's a miracle, Veil."

"You'll get no argument from me." Veil reached down and stroked Reyna's hair. "You get some rest. I'll come back later this afternoon and we'll talk about the most efficient way to hunt for Toby. I'll pick up a portable tape recorder. You can tape a message. That way we can split up and cover more territory. I know he won't come to me, but at least he can hear you talking to him while I look for signs."

He turned and headed for the door.

"Veil?"

He turned with his hand on the knob. "Yes?"

Reyna got to her feet, then studied him in silence for a few moments. "I have a confession to make," she said at last.

He smiled. "I can't wait to hear what it is."

Reyna tugged at the sleeve of her blouse in a gesture that had by now become familiar to Veil. "Toby isn't the only man I've been looking for over the past weeks. I've also been searching for Veil Kendry."

Veil felt the muscles in his face stiffen, and his smile vanished. "I don't know what you mean, Reyna."

"For one thing, I've been back to the Raskolnikov Gallery to look at your work. You called them 'dream-paintings,' and now I see what you mean. They're haunting and beautiful, Veil—unlike anything else I've ever seen."

Veil began to relax. "Thank you."

"They're 'real,' but not quite real—like a dream. And you dream like that because of the brain damage you mentioned?"

"Yes."

"I've also been reading up on the war in Vietnam."

Veil felt his stomach muscles begin to flutter. "Why have you been reading up on the war?"

"I used to date a history professor at Columbia. His specialty is Southeast Asia, and he has a rather peculiar—at least, I used to think it was peculiar—obsession. He'd heard stories about a man—an American—fighting with the Hmong tribes in Laos as part of the CIA's secret war against the Pathet Lao. This man—he was said to have blond hair, incidentally—must have been a CIA agent, as well as a regular Army officer, because the CIA controlled everything that went on in Laos and Cambodia. My friend told me that this blond-haired man—if there ever was such a man, and my friend was never certain—had become a legend. None of the tribesmen my friend interviewed knew the man's name, but other research led my friend to believe that his code name may have been Archangel. As the legend goes, this man had won virtually every medal there was to win while he was fighting with the Special Forces in Vietnam. Then—"

Veil held up his right hand, palm out. It was at once a simple gesture yet complex, inasmuch as it involved a number of Zen teachings in the art of projecting mental force. It stopped Reyna cold. She closed her mouth in the middle of a sentence, then stared in bewilderment into the eyes, suddenly grown cold, of the man standing in the doorway of her apartment.

"I think we have enough to concern ourselves with, Reyna, without getting sidetracked into talking about Vietnam or half-baked war stories. I've heard dozens of stories like the one you're telling me. They're all non-sense."

"Veil, I feel very strange."

"You're tired. You need some rest."

"This was important. It was something I wanted to share with you, because you seem so much like this man. My friend says he's sure—"

Veil slowly moved his hand back and forth, and Reyna again fell silent. Veil was aware that at the moment he seemed a stranger—and, perhaps, a bit frightening—to Reyna. It was what he wanted. "Don't stalk me, Reyna. Please. No good will come of it."

CHAPTER NINE

"Veil, darling," the voice on the intercom intoned sweetly, "are you in the mood to receive a visitor?"

"It depends on who it is, Chuck."

"The sweet man says that his name is Gabriel Vahanian, and he has the *prettiest* detective's badge. He's a real hunk, Veil."

"Anybody with him?"

"Nope. He's alone."

"Send him up, Chuck. Thanks."

Veil slipped the tape recorder he had purchased under his platform bed, draped all of his canvases, then walked across the spacious loft and pulled open the sliding door. Vahanian, looking tired and anxious, emerged from the elevator. Veil stepped aside and motioned for the detective to enter.

"What's the story on the fag and the other four guys down there?" Vahanian asked as he looked around the sparsely furnished, paint-splattered loft.

"That 'fag' is a friend of mine who would have done you

very serious damage if you'd tried to come up here without permission or a warrant. He and the others are occasional students of mine."

"Karate?"

"Martial arts in general. Karate is just a name for a rather specific Japanese system."

"I'd heard you were pretty good at that stuff. I didn't know you were an instructor."

"I'm not. For every eight hours they stand guard, I give an hour to share some of the things I know."

"Eight hours for one; that's expensive time."

"They're not complaining."

"Who teaches you?"

"A barber, a tugboat captain, and a stockbroker. Sometimes, when I'm judged particularly worthy, there is a special session with a fifth-grade teacher who flies in from Seattle to teach me."

"What things make you particularly worthy?"

"I never know. When I do know, I'll join their ranks."

"Kendry, I don't understand what you're talking about."

"I'm talking about secret knowledge."

"Where did you learn your basic skills?"

Veil did not reply.

Vahanian stared hard at Veil. "You used what you know to do something funny to Nagle at the gallery, didn't you?"

"I don't know what you mean. The good detective had been drinking and he threw up. I was just trying to come to the aid of an officer of the law."

"Bullshit."

"Whatever you say."

"Do you always keep bodyguards outside your loft?"

"No."

"Why now?"

"I've been suffering from anxiety attacks. Why did you come to see me, Lieutenant?"

Vahanian took a deep breath, slowly let it out as he ran his fingers through his thick, black, wavy hair. "Sorry if I sound snappish, Kendry. I've been up twenty-four hours."

"It's okay."

"We're not enemies, are we?"

"I don't like the company you keep."

"Neither do I. Believe me, it's not by choice."

Veil shrugged. "As far as I'm concerned, we're not enemies."

"I came to ask you a question, which I hope you'll answer."

"Let's hear the question."

"I'd like to know what you said to my partner."

"Oh, that. I told Nagle I knew he was a Mafia enforcer, rapist, child molester, and all-around sadist. I also mentioned, in passing, that he had executed Vito Ricci, that he was on the Mafia's shit list for his somewhat excessive behavior, and that for an act of penance he's supposed to make sure that the Nal-toon is delivered safely to any one of the remaining five families. I very politely asked him to decline the Mafia assignment and request transfer to another case, since the K'ung obviously need the idol more than the Mafia does. That's about it. Is he still upset?"

Vahanian seemed stunned as he stared at Veil, his mouth slightly open, his breathing rapid and shallow. "You got anything here to drink?" he said at last.

"Scotch or bourbon?"

"Bourbon."

"Water? Ice?"

"Neat. A big one, if you don't mind."

Veil went into the kitchen, removed a bottle of bourbon from a cabinet, and poured a heavy tumbler half full. When he returned to the other room, he found Vahanian sitting on the floor, back braced against one of the support pillars that ran down the center of the loft.

"Cheers, Lieutenant," Veil said as he handed the drink to the detective. "You'll excuse me if I don't join you. It's still early, and I've got things to do."

Vahanian downed the drink in three quick swallows, then set the glass down on the polished hardwood floor. "I'm with the New York State Police, Kendry, on special assignment to the NYPD. I've been investigating Nagle for close to a year, and I only know maybe half of what you just told me."

"So the NYPD is on to Nagle?"

Vahanian nodded. "They've suspected for some time, especially since the last big problem he had. But it's tough to nail him down. He's very good at what he does, Kendry, and he covers his tracks well."

"Oh, he has great technique. It's called terror."

"Are you sure of your information?"

"Yes."

Vahanian studied Veil for a few moments, then nodded. "I can see that you are. Will you give me the name of your informant?"

"No. I won't even confirm that I got the information through an informant."

Vahanian sighed with resignation. "One of the biggest problems we've been having is getting anyone to testify against him. Terror isn't the word for what Nagle instills in his victims—and we suspect there are a lot of them. Do you know of anyone who might be willing to come forward?"

"I might. But I wouldn't even think of mentioning this person's name until you have Nagle nailed down tight. Sorry, Lieutenant, but Nagle's your problem."

Vahanian rose to his feet, straightened his sport jacket. "Judging from the presence of those bodyguards downstairs, I'd say he's also your problem."

"I don't think of Nagle as a problem."

"You know, the attitude of the police department in this city toward you is very ambivalent."

"I don't consider that a problem, either."

"May I ask what your interest in this matter is?"

"I don't really have an interest. I'm just a friend of Reyna Alexander's."

Vahanian grunted with disbelief, then headed toward the door. "Thanks for the drink."

"Lieutenant?"

The detective turned, raised his thick eyebrows slightly. "What is it, Kendry?"

"Information for information? Now I'd like to ask you a question."

"Let's hear the question," Vahanian replied with a thin smile.

"I know that Nagle was ordered to execute Vito Ricci, because it was Ricci who was responsible for trying to squeeze the Nal-toon through an otherwise secure smuggling pipeline. Do you know why Ricci did it?"

Vahanian shook his head. "Not really."

"Not really?"

"No. To tell you the truth, we—or I, at least—don't really care what Ricci was up to. My assignment is to help the NYPD get Nagle. As far as the city and state are concerned, we'd just as soon all those Mafia bastards shot each other out of existence. Still, for what it's worth, Intelligence did pick up rumors that the heads of the other five families were planning to shut him down—forcibly retire him, you might say. Hell, he was pushing ninety. Maybe he went senile."

"Thanks, Vahanian."

The detective hesitated a moment, then came back across the loft and extended his hand to Veil, who gripped it. "You watch your ass, Kendry."

"I have some very skilled friends watching my ass for me, Lieutenant. You're the one riding the back of the tiger. You watch *your* ass."

"I will. See you."

"See you."

•   •   •

"Veil!"

Veil turned off his flashlight, crossed the width of the empty boxcar in two long strides, and leapt through the open door. He hit the ground in full stride, darted between two uncoupled cars, and ran toward the sound of Reyna's voice. He rounded a car, slowed when he saw that Reyna was not in danger.

Reyna was thirty yards farther down a stretch of empty track, crouched down beside the rails and staring at something on the ground. Veil jogged down the tracks, squatted beside Reyna—and winced.

Two broken teeth jutted from the middle of a pool of dried vomit that was marbled with streaks of blood. More blood had stained the surrounding gravel a dull brown.

"Toby's sick," Reyna said, her voice catching. "And he's hurt."

"Take it easy," Veil whispered, taking Reyna into his arms. "We don't know for sure that it's Toby's."

"It's Toby's," Reyna said, her voice thick with grief and anxiety. "I know it's his. It's on the route." She drew a deep, shuddering breath. "The vomit isn't that old. Toby was here."

Veil led Reyna a few yards away from the spot, then held her until she stopped trembling. He gently sat her down on a rail, then slowly walked up and down the tracks, studying the ground. Fifteen yards to the right of the vomit he found wood splinters and a streak of white powder.

"Reyna," Veil said evenly, "please come here."

Reyna rose and walked unsteadily to Veil, who handed her a few of the wood splinters. "What do you think?" he continued. "Could these be from the Nal-toon?"

Reyna studied the splinters, turning them in her fingers, smelling them. "Three of them are," she said tightly. "You can still smell the campfire smoke, and they're bleached from heat, sand, and wind. The other two aren't."

Veil wet the tip of his index finger, touched it to the white powder, then put his finger to his tongue. Instantly the tip of his tongue went numb, and the back of his throat was filled with a bitter, medicinal taste. "Well, I'll tell you what this is," he said, spitting out the taste. "It's pure heroin—top-quality white stuff, not the Mexican brown." When Reyna didn't respond, Veil turned and looked up at her. The woman was standing very straight, eyes closed, hands curled into fists at her sides. "Reyna?"

"What?" the woman responded through clenched teeth.

"Are you all right?"

"Yes," she said, turning away.

Veil rose and brushed off his jeans. "Vito Ricci's old-age pension award to himself," he said absently. "This certainly shows the old man wasn't senile. He wasn't about to be dependent upon the kindness of strangers—or his former business partners. He was just a little bit stupid and a big bit unlucky."

"What are you talking about?" Reyna asked in a subdued voice.

"Vito Ricci is the man who tried to slip the Nal-toon through the Mafia's smuggling pipeline."

"Because of the heroin inside." Reyna's voice now sounded haunted.

"Of course. He cared nothing for the idol; in fact, he probably didn't even know what it was. What he did care about was the fact that he was being pushed out of the organization. These people eat their own. Ricci was justifiably afraid of not only losing everything he had, but also of being killed in the bargain. So he made a private deal—a huge one—on his own, enough in itself to get him killed if it were found out. Ironically, whoever was handling things for him on the other end must have thought that a statue like the Nal-toon was a perfect item in which to send the heroin to Ricci; after all, the Nal-toon was just another piece of primitive art. Who would even notice it, much less bother to try to trace it? Just hollow out the statue, fill the space with a few million dollars' worth of pure heroin, drop it in the pipeline as a 'personal' item for Ricci, and forget about it."

"Lord knows what Toby will think when he sees that stuff trickling out of the Nal-toon," Reyna said in the same haunted voice. She swallowed hard, rubbed her eyes. "He'll die if he eats it, won't he?"

"If he eats enough of it, yes—which might not be too much. It's incredibly pure." He watched as Reyna bowed her head and clasped her hands in prayer. He waited a few moments, then stepped close to her and touched her shoulder. "Reyna," Veil continued quietly, "I don't mean to be insensitive, but prayers aren't going to help Toby now."

"That isn't true, Veil," Reyna whispered without opening her eyes. "Toby is sick, he's badly injured, and the Naltoon is filled with death that Toby is almost certain to think is something else, some gift sent to him by the Naltoon. God's intervention is Toby's only hope now."

Veil gripped Reyna's wrist and gently but firmly pulled her back along the way they had come. "Pray on the way to the cemetery," he said curtly.

•   •   •

It was dark when Veil drove the rented car back over the Queensborough Bridge into Manhattan. He glanced sideways at Reyna and could see that she was barely able to hold back tears. "Tomorrow's another day," he said softly. "We'll go into the other cemeteries—New Lutheran and Zion. We'll just keep at it until we find him."

The tears finally came, and Reyna brushed them away with the back of her hand. "What haunts me is the possibility that we could have passed within a few feet of him, and Toby was passed out or too sick to respond."

"It's possible, sure—but it's just as possible that he's farther to the southeast, gone to ground in one of the other cemeteries. Or he's simply ignoring us because he's not ready to come out yet. The good news is that if we can't find him, it's not likely that anyone else will, either."

"Until he comes out below the golf course," Reyna replied hoarsely. "Somebody will be sure to spot him, and he'll be trapped. I told you he won't be taken alive, Veil."

They drove in silence for almost ten minutes before an accident in the center and outside lanes of the FDR Drive brought traffic to a crawl. Veil looked at Reyna, who was sitting bolt-upright in her seat, staring straight ahead. In her face was a terrible fear, and Veil suspected that it was more than fear for Toby. He said, "Let's talk about a gutsy friend of mine by the name of Reyna Alexander."

"Thank you for calling me your gutsy friend," Reyna mumbled in a flat monotone, "but let's not talk about me."

"I think it's time, and I think you want to. Let's you and I exorcise a few of your ghosts—and I'm thinking of a big, fat, ugly one in particular."

"I don't know what you're talking about."

Veil reached across the seat and plucked at the left sleeve of Reyna's beige, long-sleeved blouse. "There are needle tracks under there, right?"

Reyna's head snapped around, and her eyes were wide in terror before an old haunt. "Yes," she breathed, and in the sound of that one word was a universe of guilt, shame—and relief.

Veil edged over into the inside lane where traffic had slowly begun to move past a cordon of blinking lights from a patrol car and tow truck. "Jesus, Reyna, I hope they're not fresh."

Reyna shook her head. "They're not. It's been years."

"How did it happen?"

"Veil, I really don't want to talk about it."

"Yes, you do. Tell me about it."

There was a prolonged silence. Veil waited, certain that the words would eventually come—and they did.

"I told you I was twelve when my parents died," Reyna said in a low voice. "It was in the Kalahari, with the K'ung. A warrior party of Bantu attacked. It was . . . horrible. My parents went down in each other's arms while they were being . . . poked to death by Bantu spears. Poked to death. All over."

Veil reached out for Reyna's hand and squeezed it tightly.

"I escaped by running into the desert," Reyna continued. "By that age, I was at home almost everywhere in the desert. I had enough lore to find my way back—except that I didn't want to find my way back. I was out of my mind with terror and horror, and all I wanted to do was die. I almost did. I had no water, and after a while I just lay down in the trough of a dune. Toby came after me and found me. He'd brought a water-egg for me. They carry water in ostrich eggs, you know."

"I know," Veil replied softly. "It was in the newspaper articles."

"Toby half dragged, half carried me back to the camp. By then the battle was over. The Bantu had been driven off, and the K'ung—out of respect for my feelings—had already buried my parents. They'd even . . . even . . ."

"Reyna?"

Reyna sobbed once, then brought herself back under control. "They'd even made a cross out of firewood and put it up over my parents' grave. In all the time—the years—that my parents had spent with them, with all the subtle and not-so-subtle proselytizing they'd done about Jesus Christ, this was the first time the tribe had shown even the slightest interest in the meanings or symbols of Christianity. They'd loved my parents, Veil, even as my parents had loved them."

"Yes. It doesn't surprise me."

"The wireless in the Land-Rover was broken, so there was nothing to do but wait. After two call-ins were missed, the Missionary Society had the South Africans send out a helicopter to check on things. They found me and took me back to Johannesburg." Reyna paused, sniffed. "Toby saved my life, Veil. It's so terribly important to me that I save his."

"I understand. What happened to you after they took you out of the desert?"

"It's pretty much as I told you. I became a ward of the Missionary Society. I was given the best schooling, then brought back here to attend college. But I couldn't get those . . . images out of my mind. Always, night and day, I would have these flashes of memory, see my parents holding on to each other while they went down under the spear thrusts . . ."

"It's okay, Reyna. It's over now."

"Yes. Except . . . like you, I guess, I was an extremely troubled adolescent. I'm ashamed to say it, but God wasn't enough solace for me in those days. Nothing seemed to be able to block the memories—except drugs. Eventually I became hooked on heroin."

"And you were eventually arrested by Carl Nagle."

Reyna uttered a sharp cry, then doubled over in her seat

99

and clutched at her stomach, as if a knife had been plunged into her. "It was horrible, Veil. Horrible. He did things . . . I don't think I'll ever feel clean again."

"You're clean, Reyna," Veil said gently as he stroked her back. "The sin and the filth are his, not yours. Know that and accept it."

Veil continued to stroke Reyna's back, and finally she began to relax. She sighed, straightened up. Then she took Veil's hand, kissed it, held it up to breast. "I guess you could say that my experience with Nagle was almost therapeutic," she said with a quick, nervous giggle. "That . . . man was so terrible, fear of him became even stronger than my craving for drugs. The Society stood by me, of course. They put me in a rehabilitation program, supported me all through withdrawal. But I swear it was fear of *him* as much as any treatment program that kept me off drugs after that." Reyna let herself fall over onto Veil, who wrapped his arm around her. "I'm still so afraid," she added quietly.

The security guard at the gate recognized Reyna and waved Veil through. "Don't be," he said as he drove slowly through the narrow streets of the campus. "I have a strong feeling that Mr. Nagle's clock is about to be cleaned good for him. I wouldn't be surprised to see him put out of everybody else's misery permanently."

Reyna shuddered, the muscles in her body rippling like a physical prayer. "Why do you say that?"

"It's just a strong notion. Nagle's not going to bother you again, Reyna."

"Oh, Veil," Reyna breathed into his side. "Can you promise me that?"

"I promise you that."

Veil parked the car at the curb in front of Reyna's dormitory, got out, and walked around the car to open Reyna's door. Reyna stepped out, clasped both of his hands in hers. Suddenly she seemed older—no longer a frightened child but a beautiful woman who was still very anxious but far more in control of her fears. Even her face looked fuller, as if her body had gained weight with the unburdening of her soul. She was, Veil thought, quite lovely.

"Veil, thank you so much."

"For what?"

"For somehow understanding that I needed to talk about that—even now, in the midst of all this other terrible business."

"It's precisely because of all the other things going on that I knew you needed to talk. There were a lot of things pressing on you besides Toby's situation. It was time to ease some of that pressure and show you that you don't have to carry it alone."

Reyna grinned coquettishly. "Are you interested in sin?"

"Not nearly as much as I am in salvation."

"Would you stay with me tonight?"

"If that's what you want, it would be my distinct pleasure."

"We're between summer sessions, so there aren't too many people in there. Still, we'll have to be *very* quiet. Do you think that two skilled trackers like you and me can manage to make love in near silence?"

Veil smiled as he put a finger to his lips. Then he put his arm around Reyna's shoulders and led her up the walk toward her dormitory.

CHAPTER TEN

Veil dreams.

Veil is Toby.

He turns his head at the sound of barking and sees two large dogs bounding toward him from his left. Dazed, Veil clutches his sling and stumbles toward the opening in the wooden object. As he reaches it he drops his spear, braces his forearms on the raised wooden floor of the object, and makes a desperate attempt to heave himself up to safety. Suddenly he hears a man shouting somewhere above his head, and Veil cringes; but the unseen *Newyorkcity* seems to be shouting at the dogs, hurling things at them in an effort to scare them away.

Veil glances up at the *Newyorkcity* who has saved him, and he sees a short, heavy man dressed in ragged *clothes*. Without warning the man's foot shoots out and catches Veil on the jaw and the side of the head.

"Get out of here, you son of a bitch! You'll have every railroad cop in the yard down on us!"

"I'm sick," Veil whispers, still hanging on to the platform. He can see nothing now, and his head feels as if it is about to explode. "I need . . . help."

A second kick knocks Veil to the ground. Dimly, through a shimmering orange haze, Veil sees the blurred images of two men emerge from the hole of darkness above his head. The *Newyorkcities* have him now, he thinks. He is finished.

But they must not get the Nal-toon.

Veil rolls to his right. He pulls the sling from around his neck and uses the last of his strength to hurl the Nal-toon into the darkness beneath one of the wooden structures. Then he passes out.

• • •

There is too much pain in this dream, Veil thinks. Too much misery and loneliness in imagining himself as the K'ung warrior-prince. He does not want to suffer like this, and he starts to roll away from the dream of Toby, drifting off toward the Lazarus Gate and the woman he loves trapped beyond it. Then he stops. His suffering is only imaginary, while Toby's is real. Only by entering the mind of Toby can he hope to understand what the man is thinking and perhaps anticipate his actions.

"*. . . Veil, come to me. Love me. Tango with me on the edge of time. . . .*"

"*. . . Can't . . .*"

"*. . . You don't have to suffer like this . . .*"

"*. . . Dream is the key to finding him, must . . .*"

• • •

Veil returns to Toby, once again becomes Toby as a squealing blade of sound seems to slice through his brain. He senses movement all around him, and he shakes his head in an effort to clear it.

The Nal-toon! he thinks. Where is the Nal-toon?

He lifts his face from the gravel and turns his head in time to see that the wooden object under which he lies is moving over him; one of the metal *wheels* is rolling toward his stomach, and in a moment he will be cut in two. . . .

Veil pushes against the ground with his hands, rolls to

his right, and lies flat between the thick strips of metal. A moment later the heavy *wheel* grinds over the place where he had been.

The air is filled with nerve-shattering sound, but Veil is virtually oblivious to it; he feels the hard, familiar surface of the Nal-toon pressing against his ribs, and joy floods his being. Still keeping himself pressed flat to the ground as more objects roll over him, he reaches out and wraps his arm around God. As he does so, he feels a thin stream of powder trickling from His base.

The blood of the Nal-toon! Veil thinks, turning his head and gazing in awe at the white streak on the ground. It is a bad sign; he has failed, and his punishment will be death in this terrible, flickering tunnel of darkness, movement, and noise.

Then the darkness suddenly lifts, and the great roar dissipates, leaving Veil and chasing after the wooden objects as they move away. Bright, hot morning sunlight beats down on his back.

The Nal-toon has spared him!

Despite nausea and a hammering pain on the left side of his head where his eye is swollen shut, Veil manages to struggle to his feet. Cradling the Nal-toon in his arms, using the palm of his left hand to stem the flow of God's blood, he staggers toward the open, black maw of another wooden object. He knows there could be danger in the darkness, perhaps more *Newyorkcities* waiting to attack him, but he feels that he has no choice but to take the risk. He must find a place to hide.

He reaches the opening, sets the Nal-toon down inside, then pulls himself up over the lip of the floor. He lies on his back for some time, too weak to move, gasping for breath. Finally he manages to roll away from the light at the opening. He listens, but there is no other sound in the darkness; he is alone and safe. He is still under the protection of the Nal-toon.

He puts his hand to the left side of his face where the *Newyorkcity* kicked him. Pain stabs through his skull and flashes behind his eyes as his fingers touch the tender, puffy flesh. He is sick, Veil thinks, is missing teeth, and he cannot see out of his left eye. But he is alive, and besides, he has suffered worse. Long thirst in the desert is worse. This would not be a worthy trial if there were not some suffering demanded of him. The only important thing is that he continue to think and act as a warrior.

"Thank you, Nal-toon," he murmurs.

Now his thoughts turn to the strange, powdery blood of God. It is a good sign, not bad, Veil thinks with growing excitement. Since it is obvious that he still enjoys the Nal-toon's favor, it seems possible that the Nal-toon has provided His white blood as a gift to help him.

Gritting his teeth against the fierce pain that whipsaws back and forth behind his eyes, Veil rolls over on his side. He sits up and carefully, reverently, examines the Nal-toon and the white blood trickling from His base. God must be providing him with this blood for a reason, Veil thinks, but he does not know how it is meant to be used. However, it is certain that any gift flowing from the very heart of the Nal-toon will be far more powerful than anything he has ever known; it will have to be used with great care.

Veil tears off a piece of *clothes* from his sling and uses it to stop up the flow in the Nal-toon's base. Then he carefully sweeps the blood that has already flowed onto the wood into a small pile. Uttering a prayer, he pinches some of the powder between his thumb and forefinger and puts it on his tongue. The blood has a bitter taste, like a medicinal herb. He takes a slightly larger pinch, puts it to his nose, and sniffs.

Immediately a sensation of warmth sweeps up through his nostrils and flows like warm water behind his eyelids. A few seconds later, to Veil's amazement, the pain in his face dulls, receding to a tiny point somewhere inside his left ear.

The Nal-toon's blood acts like shilluk, Veil thinks, and his heart pounds with excitement. Except that the blood is many times more powerful than shilluk. Now he knows that the Nal-toon has given him His blood in order to ease

105

his pain, and it is meant to be sniffed in very small amounts.

As if to reaffirm his new knowledge, Veil takes a slightly larger pinch of the Nal-toon's blood-shilluk and breathes it into his nostrils. The residual pain in his left ear blinks out as a pleasing sun-warmth oozes down through his entire body. He hears a sound like the rustling of wind in the desert; the wind is filling him, lifting him off the ground. He is floating away . . .

Enough! Veil thinks. The Nal-toon's gift must be used with as much care as water in the open desert.

The pain has disappeared, and despite the odd sensation of floating, Veil is no longer nauseous. None of the magic machines the Nal-toon has given the *Newyorkcities* can compare with this wondrous gift, he thinks. He cannot remember ever feeling so at peace.

Veil eases himself down on his stomach, rests his head against the Nal-toon, and drifts off to sleep within sleep.

•   •   •

It is night when Veil awakens, as Toby, in his dream; once again he is nauseous and in excruciating pain. He vomits, and this causes new club-blows of pain to hammer against the left side of his skull.

Moaning in agony, he searches in the darkness until he finds a few grains of the Nal-toon's blood-shilluk. He hurriedly sniffs some from the palm of his hand and immediately begins to feel better. He starts to inhale more, then stops himself. He will take only as much as he needs to ease his pain and sickness, Veil thinks; to take more, to deliberately seek euphoria and the comfort of sleep, would be to abuse this most wondrous gift. Also, he must remain conscious now; it is night and he must move on.

Replacing the carrying sling around his neck, Veil eases himself to the ground. His stomach knots with anxiety when he looks up at the sky, for clouds obscure the stars. His sickness has disoriented him, causing him to lose track of the direction in which he must go in order to reach the *airplane* fields. He needs the stars.

The stars in the sky over *Newyorkcity* are different than in the sky over the desert, he thinks, and it is often difficult to see them through the background of lights and the haze of smoke that chokes the air of this strange land. But the configuration of the stars, though different from those at home, remains consistent, and that is all he needs in order to orient himself. But he must be able to see them.

He leans against the side of the wooden object and waits, trying to remain calm. He is certain that the Nal-toon will soon clear the sky for him, and his faith is rewarded; soon a wind rises from the north and begins to blow the clouds across the sky. Veil gains his bearings from a brief glimpse of the stars, and a short time later clouds blow back over the moon, shrouding him in darkness.

He retches again. When the spasms pass, Veil carefully removes the piece of *clothes* covering the base of the Nal-toon, then allows a small amount of the precious blood-shilluk to flow into his palm. He inhales the powder and, as before, his pain and nausea immediately disappear. It is a fine night, Veil thinks. It is good to be alive, under the Nal-toon's protection.

• • •

Time has lost meaning. Veil moves slowly, wearily, staggering from side to side. He constantly has to remind himself not to test the Nal-toon's mercy by being careless, and yet he is only dimly aware of entering an area of more *streets* and *buildings*.

He almost weeps with joy when he comes upon a wooded area that seems almost as densely forested as *Centralpark*.

He enters the jungle on a stone path, passes through a copse of trees, and finds himself at the edge of a clearing filled with stone totems. These totems are different from the one his people erected on the graves of Reyna's parents, Veil thinks, but he instinctively senses that they are death-totems. He is in a jungle where the *Newyork-cities* bury their dead.

His first reaction is fear, for in his feverish state he imagines that he can see the spirits of dead *Newyorkcities* hovering over their totems. Then he reminds himself that he is under the protection of the Nal-toon; no spirit will attack a warrior moving under the protection of God. His fear passes.

In a spirit of thanksgiving and respect, and to assure that the *Newyorkcity* spirits do not betray his presence, Veil sets about constructing his own small peace totems. When his closed left eye begins to throb, he sniffs more of the Nal-toon's blood-shilluk. He finishes his totems in a state of pain-free euphoria.

Within a short time he has found an area suitable for going to ground. There is a shallow stream nearby; Veil lies down in its clear waters, occasionally drinking as he allows the water to cool his burning flesh.

He uses a sharp-edged, flat rock to scoop out a shallow trench in the soft, cool earth on the stream's sloping bank. He anchors the surrounding soil with sticks and rocks, then devises a cover of leafy branches woven together with vines and supple twigs. Finally Veil settles down in the trench with the Nal-toon close to his belly. He pulls the woven cover over him and rests his head on a soft, leafy mat he has woven for that purpose. Feeling pain and nausea, he sniffs more blood-shilluk and closes his eyes, enjoying the feeling of sanctuary and the warm sense of well-being that the Nal-toon's gift brings him.

He realizes with some surprise that he is not hungry, despite the fact that he cannot remember when he last ate. Hungry or not, Veil thinks, he must eat to keep up his strength. He will stay in this jungle of the dead until he feels better. Here he can snare small game and fashion new weapons.

Veil allows himself the luxury of sniffing more of the precious blood-shilluk, and he drifts away like a leaf rolling in a gentle breeze.

• • •

Veil is no longer concerned with the passage of time. Far more important to him is the fact that the blood-shilluk seems to have dried up his insides, for he no longer suffers such severe bouts of vomiting and diarrhea. However, he remains very weak, and he finds it difficult to hunt for food. Despite his weakness, he does manage to snare a rabbit and a large rat.

Veil imagines that he can feel some of his strength returning—but very slowly. The swelling on the left side of his face has gone down, and his left eye has opened, although the vision in that eye is so blurred as to be useless. He manages to fashion new weapons: a bow, its wood flame-hardened and strung with thin, plaited vines; arrows with flame-hardened tips dipped in his own waste; a throwing stick.

But he is not recovering as quickly as he thinks he should. Every labor is an immense effort requiring deep concentration and exercise of will; he suffers terrible headaches, and the flesh on the left side of his face burns when he touches it. He begins to fear that his continuing sickness and pain are at least partially the result of some *Newyorkcity* magic spell that is draining his strength, and it is only the Nal-toon's blood-shilluk that is keeping him alive in this place.

He has confirmed his suspicion that the Nal-toon's gift is very dangerous if used in excess—it brings deep unconsciousness, which, however pleasant, could prove deadly to him, inasmuch as it renders him totally vulnerable to his enemies. Thus he is now constantly on guard to use the great gift sparingly, only on those occasions when his sickness and pain seem unbearable, or when his bowels loosen, or when the ache in his head threatens to blind him in both eyes.

He has also begun to notice another effect of the blood-shilluk: When he goes too long without using the gift, he experiences sharp stomach cramps.

At last he decides that he is simply not going to grow

stronger as long as he remains where he is, possibly being drained by a *Newyorkcity* magic spell. Despite his terrible weakness, Veil resolves to move on at nightfall.

• • •

Later in this dream-day Veil is aroused from his stupor by the sound of a voice. A woman is speaking his language.

Reyna.

He should trust her. He should go to her. She will help him.

No.

Overwhelmed by loneliness and longing at the sound of his own language, Veil begins to weep soundlessly. He has never been so sick or weak, and he comes very close to removing the woven cover over his head and revealing himself.

No.

If the *Newyorkcities* can cast a spell to drain his strength, Veil thinks, they may also be able to raise spirits from this jungle of the dead to try to trick him. Even if the voice is really Reyna's, there is always the possibility that she means to betray him. The voice could be but a part of the trial set by the Nal-toon, and Veil feels that he cannot afford to take a chance.

No.

Veil wriggles even deeper into his trench. He holds the Nal-toon tightly in an attempt to banish his loneliness. Faced with the possibility that he is being hunted by spirits, he is now firmly resolved to move at nightfall, no matter how weak he is. He must get to the *airplane* that will take him home.

CHAPTER ELEVEN

Veil waited, back braced against a tree trunk and hands thrust into the pockets of his jeans, as Reyna slowly approached through a field of small, uniform grave markers. She looked pensive, Veil thought, but not as distraught as she had appeared earlier. Throughout the morning they had walked, together and apart, through Calvary Cemetery, with Veil playing a recording of Reyna's voice while Reyna called out—and sometimes sang—in the K'ung tongue. They had made no attempt to track Toby, only to announce their presence. Then Reyna, fearing that Veil's presence would frighten Toby, had gone off alone.

She had been gone almost an hour and a half, and from the way she walked, Veil felt certain she had found something.

"He's been here," Reyna announced as she came up to Veil, wrapped her arms around his middle, and rested her head on his chest. In her voice was relief, mingling with anxiety and fatigue.

"You're sure?" Veil asked.

"Yes," she said, freeing one arm, turning and pointing to the north. "He came in around Fifty-first Street, just below Queens Boulevard. I found one of his footprints on some bare ground. He's sick, so I guess he can't help being careless."

"That's good news," Veil said quietly. "Just so long as he doesn't become too careless."

"Um-hmm." Reyna again wrapped both arms around Veil, and he eased them both down until they were sitting on the ground. For a few minutes Veil thought the woman might be sleeping, but then her voice came to him, muffled slightly by the material of his light jacket. "I don't know whether or not he's seen any of my totems, but I saw one of his. It's a spirit-totem erected to show respect for the spirits in a place of the dead. Toby recognized this as a cemetery."

"But no sign of Toby himself?"

Veil felt Reyna shake her head. "I found the place where he went to ground. There's a stream beyond the woods behind me."

"I know. I saw it."

"That's where he rested—near the bank." She paused and looked up at Veil. "There were feces and vomit around the site, as you would expect," she continued with a slightly puzzled frown. "What's surprising is that the feces aren't as loose as you'd think they would be in somebody suffering from typhus or dysentery—or both. We know he's very sick and badly injured. Lord, the very fact that he can still walk at all is amazing. He must have a very high fever and be in terrible pain."

"It could be the heroin," Veil said as he absently stroked Reyna's hair.

"What?"

"The heroin, Reyna. Toby may have accidentally found how to use it in a way that can benefit him. It's true that it wouldn't take much of it to kill him, but it's also true that if he, say, sniffs a small amount at a time, he'll get the benefit of its medicinal properties. Heroin is an unbelievably potent anesthetic, of course, but it also tends to dehydrate. It would tighten his bowels somewhat. In this

112

case, the crap inside that idol could be Toby's salvation—
at least for a time."

"But how could he know to sniff it?"

Veil shrugged. "It comes from the Nal-toon, right? It's a
divine gift, so he has to do *something* with it. It tastes like
hell, so he must have tried smelling it and gotten some
into his nose. Bingo."

"If that's true, Veil, then it's another miracle."

"Mmm. What do you think the chances are that he'll
come back there?"

"No chance. If Toby intended to use that place again,
he'd be there now—during the day. He was there last
night, but he's someplace else now. Sick or not, Toby feels
that he must keep moving as best he can." Reyna sighed,
rose to her feet, and brushed off her jeans. "Rest time is
over. I'm going ahead."

"Let me come with you," Veil said, rising. "I'm not the
tracker you are, but I'm not bad."

"Indeed," Reyna replied impishly, rising up on her toes
to kiss him. "You're not bad at anything. Still, you'd only
frighten him, and I don't want you getting a spear in the
belly button. Sick as he is, he probably hasn't gone far.
You wait here, I'll be back."

•   •   •

Veil glanced at his watch; it was almost six-thirty. He
cursed softly under his breath, then set off at a quick pace
through the field of grave markers. He passed through a
stand of trees, jumped over a stream, and hurried toward
the southeast end of the cemetery. He sighed with relief
when he saw Reyna sitting on the edge of a low stone wall
that marked the border of the cemetery. Behind her, traffic
moved by on Fifty-eighth Street. Stripped of the muffling
effect of the trees inside the cemetery, the air was filled
with the groaning hum of rush-hour traffic on the Queens
leg of the Long Island Expressway.

"I was worried about you," Veil said as he sat on the
wall next to Reyna. "You've been gone all afternoon."

"I'm sorry," Reyna replied, squeezing Veil's hand. "I've
been waiting. I think you passed Toby somewhere back

there. I wanted to come back and get you, but I was afraid to take a chance that he might get spooked and slip out ahead of us at this end."

Veil raised his eyebrows slightly, then shaded his eyes from the slanting rays of the setting sun and looked back the way he had come. "You're sure he's still back there?"

"Not a hundred percent, maybe ninety. After I left you I did a quick walk-through to this end. I figured that if I found sign here, it would mean that he was still ahead of us and we wouldn't waste time looking any longer in this cemetery. Anyway, as you can see, there's a lot of bare ground down here at this end. I couldn't find any tracks."

"Granted that he's sick, hurt, and moving very carefully, it's still only a mile, maybe less, from the stream to here. You'd think he would have come farther during the night."

Reyna twisted around to look at the expressway and the embankment beyond. "I know. Just because I couldn't find sign doesn't mean that he's still back there."

"We still have a couple of hours of daylight left. If you want to go into Mount Olive and look around, I'll stand guard here."

"It's a thought," Reyna said absently.

"It's your decision, Reyna."

"We'll both wait here," Reyna announced decisively. "By the time I get started over there, it will be dark, anyway. I still believe he's behind us. If we spread out a bit and stay through the night, we may at least keep him contained here—and tomorrow I'll go back in and really start looking. We'll keep the tape recorder running. Do you think the batteries will last?"

"I have spares in my pocket." Veil paused, turned to Reyna. "It may be time to start thinking about what we're going to do with Toby *after* we find him."

Reyna looked away. "I haven't even tried to think that far ahead."

"I'm not sure I believe you, Reyna. Even assuming that we nab him before anybody else does, we still have big problems, don't we?"

"Yes," Reyna answered softly.

"The obvious first step is to turn him in to the police

after we hide the idol somewhere. Then we mount the best possible legal defense, which I'm sure we can do considering the publicity Toby has generated."

"That's not the point, Veil."

"Prince Toby of the K'ung isn't going to fare too well when he comes up against our legal system, is he?"

"No." Reyna shuddered, then abruptly swept her hair back from her face in an almost defiant gesture. "There are two murder charges against him. The fact that Toby acted both times in self-defense and that there are extenuating circumstances won't help him escape a trial. The authorities will never allow him out on bail, which means that Toby could be required to spend months in a prison cell. And *then* he could get a prison sentence. He won't last a week in a cell, Veil. It will kill him. He'll be alone in a cage, in a place where nobody speaks his language. . . . Toby will simply refuse to eat or drink anything, and then the end will come very quickly. In his mind he will have failed, and the Nal-toon will be lost to his people forever. The will to live will drain out of him like water down a drain."

"And he could be right about the idol being lost to his people forever. Not a very happy ending."

Reyna heaved a deep sigh, then bowed her head. "Shit," she murmured dispassionately.

Veil put his hand under Reyna's chin and gently lifted her head. Her eyes were filled with tears. "We've looked at the problem and discussed it, as we had to," Veil said evenly. "We had to think a couple of steps ahead, but now it's only a waste of time to be distracted by future problems. You need to focus all your energy and concentration on finding Toby. You let *me* worry about what to do with him when you do, okay?"

Reyna stared into Veil's eyes for a few moments, then nodded and forced a smile. "Okay."

"Good!" Veil kissed Reyna on the forehead. "Now let's talk about important things. It could be a long night, and it's time to think about how to keep the members of this safari in good spirits."

This time Reyna's smile was genuine. "You're going for food?"

115

"Right."

"I wondered when somebody was going to think about feeding the chief tracker of this expedition."

"I propose to pick up provisions from the jungle deli, which I'm sure is only a block or two away. What will the chief tracker have?"

"Roast beef on a roll—make that two—with lettuce, tomato, and mayo. Black coffee. And watch out for unfriendly natives; since you'll be carrying the provisions, I don't want you to get mugged."

• • •

Veil ordered the sandwiches and coffee to go in a nearby delicatessen, then went to a pay phone in the corner. He dropped a quarter in the slot and dialed a number. Victor Raskolnikov answered on the third ring.

"Victor, it's Veil."

"Veil! I've been trying to get hold of you! Who's that *strange* man answering your phone?"

"A friend holding down the fort. Listen, Victor, I—"

"Have you found out anything?"

"Not over the phone, Victor. I have a strong suspicion there may be heavy ears slapped on to a few phones in the city. But I do have to talk to you."

"Okay," the Russian said evenly. "I understand. Say it the best way you can."

"Things are warming up, and they may come to a boil soon. I will have a few things to report to you."

"Excellent."

"You and I discussed the matter of compensation for my services, you may recall. I believe it will be barter, if that's agreeable to you."

"What do you need, my friend?"

"First let me give you some indication of what I want to do. I think you'd agree that even matters of vital importance can get tangled up in our legal system?"

"I agree."

"Assuming I can find the package we're mutually interested in, I'd like to dump the whole bundle in the sand—a direct drop. Anyone else interested in the package can go look for it there."

Raskolnikov's deep, booming laugh carried over the phone into the delicatessen, startling the man behind the counter, who had placed Veil's order on top of a glass display case. "I love it!" Raskolnikov barked.

"At the moment you might say I'm trapped in the bush, and I'm up to my ass in alligators. I need someone to man a control center and coordinate things. It's specialized work and time-consuming. Can you give me the time?"

"The time is yours," Raskolnikov answered uncertainly, "but I don't know much about these things."

"If you're agreeable, and if I get lucky with my quarters, a man with an ugly face, an ugly nickname, and a very beautiful heart will get in touch with you, perhaps as early as tonight. He'll know exactly what to do. You'll work together."

"It will be done, Veil."

"There's more. The ugly man will know how to take care of business, but the business may require some heavy financing. We're talking big bucks—cash—up front. I can see money down the road coming from the sale of exclusive rights to stories about the package, told by people who have been on the inside. It's exploitive, but I don't see any other way to buy all the sand we're going to need. In other words, I see no reason why you wouldn't be reimbursed, but the cash is going to be needed quickly."

"It will be done, Veil. You just concern yourself with the proper wrapping of the package. What you want is precisely what I want."

"I'll be in touch when I can, Victor. You'll stay by the phone?"

"I'm here."

"Thanks, Victor," Veil said, and hung up.

"Hey, pal!" the counterman called. "Your stuff's ready."

"In a minute," Veil said without turning, and dropped another quarter in the slot.

He spoke to his personal physician, then spent fifteen minutes on the phone talking to a friend he had not seen in six years. When he hung up, Veil was barely able to suppress laughter. The last number he dialed was his own.

"Veil Kendry's residence."

"It's me. Be careful what you say."

"Veil, darling! We've all been worried about you. Where *have* you been?"

"How are things?"

"No problems."

"Any calls? Be careful."

"A couple of miscellaneous items, Veil, but nothing you'd be interested in at the moment. Victor called."

"Got it."

"Also a couple of mystery guests—although it could have been the same person both times."

"Any clues?"

"The first mystery guest simply hung up. The phone rang again about five minutes later. There was music playing."

"Did you recognize it?"

"Verdi's *Requiem*."

• • •

Veil brought the food and coffee back to Reyna. A brief ripple of anxiety passed across her face when he told her that he had to leave for an hour or two and could not explain why, but she contented herself with asking him to return as quickly as possible.

Veil drove the rented car back into Manhattan, south to Little Italy. He parked six blocks away from the church, in an underground garage. He left the garage through a rear emergency exit and walked two blocks before ducking into an alley and waiting. When he was satisfied that he was not being followed, he walked around the block, then headed toward the church as it began to grow dark. He entered the darkened sanctuary, paused, and listened. When he heard nothing, he slipped silently into the confessional booth.

"It's me," Veil said as the wooden panel in the partition slid back.

"So you got my message," the gravelly, broken voice said. "I was hoping that you'd know it was me and realize that it was important enough for you to come down."

"Yes. I'm sorry I took so long to get here. You've been waiting a long time."

"It's all right. God and I are old friends, and we've been talking. You recall mentioning a man by the name of Gabriel Vahanian?"

"Yes," Veil said, feeling the hairs on the back of his neck begin to rise. "He's Nagle's partner."

"Not anymore. He's dead."

"Nagle?"

"Yes. Nagle shot him in the ear with a Magnum. There are a lot of rumors on the street. Somebody did or said something to Nagle that pushed him over the edge at about the same time he found out that Vahanian had been asigned to spy on him. Yesterday the families made a decision to execute him, and he may have found out about that too. Whatever; the point is that he's on the run and off the leash. There are no controls on him anymore."

"I hear you, Father."

"It's come out that the idol is filled with heroin."

"Mm-hmm."

"It's white and pure; there's talk of the package being worth six or seven million dollars, depending on how it's cut."

"Does Nagle know about the heroin?"

"Probably. The information is on the street. His former employers speculate that he'll go after it on his own, since that kind of money is the only chance he has to survive. Nagle makes even these people nervous. A mad dog is not to be taken lightly, and it's rumored that Nagle has a large collection of very powerful weapons. You must be very careful, Veil."

"I will. Thank you very much, Father."

"Go with God, Veil."

• • •

"It's me."

"Veil, darling!"

"Your watch is over, Chuck. You get out of there and take the other guys off the street. Just lock up and split."

"What's the matter, Veil?" All traces of femininity had

119

disappeared from the voice, replaced by the hard, tempered tone of a warrior.

"The guy I told you about is on the loose and over the edge. He doesn't have to play by any rules, and he's rumored to be carrying heavy artillery. He may well come gunning for me, and he'll blow up anybody or anything in his way. I won't be going back there until this thing is over, so I don't need you any longer."

"Do you want me to gather up your paintings and take them someplace safe?"

"No. Just get out of there. Tell the other guys I said thanks, and I'll be in touch."

"Veil, there must be something we can do to help."

"No, Chuck. I can handle it."

"Indeed you can. But be certain to take care, Veil."

"Thank you, friend."

● ● ●

"I've been worried about you," Reyna said, wrapping her arms around Veil and squeezing him hard. "A little scared, too, I guess."

"I'm sorry I had to leave you."

"Were you able to take care of your business?"

"It turned out to be a waste of time, nothing important. No sign of Toby, huh?"

"No."

"Why don't you sleep for a while, Reyna? I've got things covered now."

"I already took a nap." She reacted to Veil's look of surprise with a shrug. "If Toby can crawl and is determined to get past us, Veil, he will; he could make a shadow seem noisy, and we can't possibly cover everyplace down here he could slip through. We can only hope that he'll stay where he is and I'll find him, or that he'll react to my presence and come to me on his own. You sleep. I'll wake you if there's a need."

"Wake me in an hour. Tomorrow could be a long day. We'll take turns resting."

CHAPTER TWELVE

Veil dreams.

He is Toby.

He leaves his shallow trench soon after moonrise. He is naked; his *clothes*, filthy from his sickness, have been buried. He has constructed a new carrying sling from relatively clean pieces of *clothes*, and in it he carries the Nal-toon and his new weapons.

He has gone only a short distance when he realizes, with pangs of frustration and despair, that he will not be able to travel much farther. Perspiration runs in thick streams off his flesh, draining him of strength, as well as precious fluids and salt. His legs feel ready to collapse under him at any moment. The left side of his head throbs, each drum-pulse sending a blinding stab of pain down through his left eye into his neck. His bowels are constantly churning. Even the air seems to be dragging him down, like the water in the *river*, and he senses that the *airplane* fields are still very, very far away. . . .

He needs more of the Nal-toon's blood-shilluk, Veil thinks.

121

The amount of the Nal-toon's gift that he sniffs this time is considerably larger than what he has used in the past. However, the effect is the same; his pain abruptly vanishes. A warm, liquid sensation creeps down through his body and into his limbs, accompanied by an almost overwhelming desire to sleep.

Veil staggers and falls. A heavy, shapeless weight with wings flaps inside his skull, threatening to club him into unconsciousness. He knows that he will be in deadly peril if he loses consciousness on open ground, and he somehow manages to will himself back onto his feet.

He stumbles onto a stone path and staggers forward on its hard surface until he comes to a large meadow. By squinting, he is able to focus the vision in his right eye sufficiently to see in the moonlight a field filled with the *Newyorkcities'* spirit-totems. His knees sag, and he falls again. He sucks in a series of deep breaths to focus his energy, then somehow manages to crawl on his hands and knees through the totem field, dragging his precious bundle after him.

After what seems an agonizing eternity of dizziness and nausea, Veil reaches the jungle beyond the totem field. He feels a slight depression under his hands and collapses on his side into it. He tries to pull some leaves and branches over his body but can't seem to grasp anything with his fingers. He shifts his weight until he can feel the hard, comforting shape of God against his belly, then releases his terrible burden of will and passes out.

•   •   •

When Veil, as Toby, awakens, the sun is already well over the horizon and climbing rapidly into the sky. The ground under him is damp, and he is shaking with cold. His entire body throbs with pain and sickness. He cannot travel now, Veil thinks; it is day in this jungle of the dead, and there is a spirit moving around.

A voice is calling him.

The voice is Reyna's. For a long time she calls to him repeatedly, then abruptly falls silent. Then her voice comes to him again, this time from a greater distance. She is singing a camp song of love, fire, and water. Tears spring to Veil's eyes, and he stifles a sob as loneliness and soul-pain blow through him with the sudden ferocity of a sandstorm.

Reyna sings songs of children, and Veil weeps. Reyna's voice drifts away, then comes closer again. In between songs she calls out, asking him to come to her.

Yes! Veil thinks. Enough pain, sickness, and—most terrible burden of all—loneliness. He can trust Reyna; she will care for him until he is well; she will help him return with the Nal-toon to his people. His suffering will be over. Surely he has proven himself as a warrior. . . .

A chill ripples through his body. Veil starts to roll out of the depression—then freezes.

What if he is wrong? What if his trial is not over and the voice of Reyna is really that of a *Newyorkcity* spirit calling him to doom? How can he know? Only the Nal-toon decides such things.

Deciding that he cannot risk failure simply because of personal suffering, Veil settles back into the depression and finally manages to pull some leaves over his body. He closes his eyes and reminds himself that no personal suffering is beyond endurance as long as God is with him, and God is; the Nal-toon has repeatedly provided him with sanctuary and has even given him His precious blood to ease his suffering.

Veil shifts his position slightly until he can see out through a space in his covering of leaves. He tenses when he sees blurred movement on a knoll just beyond the field of spirit-totems. He squints and is finally able to make out the figure of Reyna. She stands very still for a long time, and Veil begins to fear that she has picked up his spoor and is about to descend on him. She slowly turns in a full circle, then drops to her hands and knees and begins to crawl along the edge of the field.

Veil's stomach knots with anxiety. If the figure is Reyna, or a spirit with Reyna's skills, she will certainly find his spoor. Perhaps.

She has found it, Veil thinks as adrenaline flows into his system, sharpening his senses and reflexes. He watches with growing tension as the Reyna-figure crawls slowly through the spirit-totems, following his spoor of wet, crushed grass and leaves. Surely she will find him now.

He must quickly decide what to do.

Should he kill the Reyna-figure?

Or does the Nal-toon mean for Reyna to find him, since he has not gone to her? Has the Nal-toon sent Reyna to end his suffering and take him home?

"Help me, Nal-toon," Veil whispers. "Help me to decide."

As if in immediate response to his prayer, the Reyna-figure abruptly crawls off in the wrong direction. She stops, looks around, then shakes her head in frustration. Veil begins to relax but then tenses again as the Reyna-figure stands, puts her hands on her hips, and appears to stare directly at his hiding place.

She has found him, Veil thinks.

He will attack if she comes for him, he thinks. He will let the Nal-toon guide his muscles and reflexes, will let the Nal-toon decide whether this Reyna-figure lives or dies and whether or not he must now prepare for his final battle with the *Newyorkcities*.

Then the Reyna-figure turns and stares off in another direction. And another. Then she shakes her head again and walks quickly back the way she came, disappearing over the knoll.

It certainly was a spirit, Veil thinks with satisfaction, but he was not tricked by it. He held firm, and the Nal-toon sent the spirit away.

His loneliness dissipates as Veil begins to feel a comforting sense of oneness with God. His heart fills with joy and thanksgiving as he sniffs a small portion of the Nal-toon's blood-shilluk and drifts off to sleep.

•　•　•

At nightfall Veil-in-Toby rises and moves on through the jungle of the dead. He abruptly stops and drops to the ground when he again hears Reyna's voice calling to him from somewhere in the darkness ahead of him.

He sniffs some blood-shilluk to focus his senses, then creeps soundlessly forward until he comes to the edge of a stand of trees. Before him, thirty running-steps away across an open expanse, Reyna and a man whose features are hidden by the night sit on a stone barrier. Between them is some kind of magic box that makes the sound of Reyna's voice. The box repeats the same message over and over, but Veil no longer even bothers to listen. It is silly magic, he thinks, and now that he knows it is magic, it has lost its stranglehold on his heart.

Veil moves laterally, inside the shrouding darkness of the line of trees. He fears the Reyna-figure most; if she does possess Reyna's skills, she might well see or hear him, no matter how stealthily he moves. But he goes on, moving silently past the position of the man-in-night until the sounds from the magic box can no longer be heard.

He waits, crouched behind the stone wall and peering over its edge until the *street* beyond is momentarily clear of *cars*. Then, gripping his carrying sling against his chest, he sluggishly climbs over the wall and runs as straight and fast as he can across the *street*. Fueled by anxiety, he makes it safely across the *street* and into the shadows cast by a *building*.

The effort is exhausting, and now he doubles over as his stomach muscles knot with pain. He waits for the spasms to pass, then turns and moves south along the face of the *building*, darting from moon shadow to moon shadow.

Suddenly he sees before him a great *street* that is even wider than the one he had to cross to get to the *river*. There are a great many fast-moving *cars* on this great *street*, their light-eyes cutting sharp, moving swaths in the darkness. Veil waits, but the great *street* never seems to be entirely empty of *cars*.

He could wait here forever for the *street* to empty, Veil thinks. Despite the *cars*, he must go on.

Veil eases the carrying sling to the ground, lifts the Naltoon, and allows some of the blood-shilluk to flow into his palm. He sniffs it, but this time the pain does not immediately vanish, as it usually does. He waits for the familiar, warm rush that will wash away his terrible hurt, but it does not come. There is some easing of the pain, but Veil still feels crippled. Recognizing the danger but feeling that he has no choice, he sniffs still more of the blood-shilluk. Finally the rush comes and the pain vanishes. He replaces the Nal-toon in his sling, lifts up the bundle, then walks forward a few steps and crouches down at the very edge of the great *street*.

A cluster of *cars* speed by, leaving in their wake a relatively long stretch of darkness. There are more light-eyes in the distance, bearing down on him, but Veil feels that he must move now, for there might not be another moment of darkness as long.

He straightens up and runs as fast as he can halfway across the great *street* to a stone barrier that separates the *cars* on his side from those on the other, which move in the opposite direction. His lungs ache and his chest heaves as he gasps for air; sweat pours off his naked body and his vision blurs badly, but he knows that he cannot stop to rest. It is too easy for the *Newyorkcities* to see him in the light-eyes of their *cars*.

Everything seems to be spinning around him, but Veil somehow manages to climb over the stone wall. He stumbles into the *street*, staggers and falls. Despite the fact that he is totally disoriented, he struggles to his feet. He sways, then sits down hard with a jolt that shoots up his spine and sends shock waves of pain through his head.

Suddenly he sees the light-eyes of a *car* bearing down on him very fast. Veil wills himself to his knees, then up on his feet as the *car* emits a wave of screeching, blaring sounds like those he heard when he crossed the *street* by *Centralpark*. The light-eyes shoot toward him, then suddenly begin to veer wildly back and forth as the screeching sounds build to a deafening, almost physical thing that batters at his ears. He smells something burning. Then the sound abruptly stops as the light-eyes stop, and Veil feels the cool touch of metal against his stomach.

Veil sways as he stares, mesmerized, into the right light-eye of the *car*. Then he falls forward onto the *car*'s metal skin.

"What the fuck's the matter with you, you crazy son of a bitch? You want to commit suicide, do it with someone else!"

There is a *Newyorkcity* warrior standing beside him. The man is shouting and waving his arms, obviously threatening him.

"Please help me, Nal-toon. I cannot see well enough to fight. I am too weak to fight."

"What the hell did you say?"

"Please, Nal-toon. Have mercy one more time."

"God damn, you smell like a fucking sewer! You're on drugs, aren't you?"

Yes, Veil thinks—the Nal-toon is causing the warrior to stay his hand. Now it is up to him to summon the necessary will and strength. . . .

Veil pushes off the *car*'s metal skin. Holding his bundle against his body with both hands, he staggers the rest of the way across the *street*, stumbles over an embankment, and falls into night on the other side.

CHAPTER THIRTEEN

Veil awoke with a start, momentarily disoriented by the close proximity of his dream-Toby to their present position and by the fact that his dream-Toby's actions had gone far beyond anything Reyna had told him or that he could reasonably assume to have happened.

He looked around for Reyna but could not see her. There was only the sound of the tape recorder playing its loop, and an occasional *whoosh* of night traffic on the expressway. Alarmed, he leapt to his feet, looked around again, then arbitrarily chose to go to his left—in the direction of the expressway.

He found Reyna standing just inside a copse of trees, staring out over an empty expressway.

"Don't be frightened, Reyna," Veil said as he came up behind her. "It's me. What's the matter?"

Reyna pointed out toward the expressway. "Nothing, I guess. Something happened out there a few minutes ago."

"What?"

"It must have been a near accident. There isn't that

much traffic, but a dog might have been crossing. All of a sudden there was a lot of honking and a screech of brakes. I was terrified that Toby had gone around us, tried to cross the expressway and been hit by a car. I ran over here, but now I can't see. . . . Veil, what's wrong?"

"Nothing," he replied tightly.

"You look very strange."

"I was just thinking that it could very well have been Toby who spooked that driver."

"Well, we really have no way of knowing," Reyna said after thinking about it for a few moments. "We can't look for spoor until it gets light, but he couldn't have come through this area without leaving tracks. If we find any, we'll know he's gone on to the next cemetery."

"He has a few city blocks to cross before he gets there."

"Yes, but it's dark. It will be dawn in a couple of hours. He knows that, so he'll go to ground at the first opportunity—when he reaches the cemetery. What concerns me is the fact that if Toby has crossed the expressway, it means he's not paying any attention to either me or the totems I left." She paused, shrugged. "There's nothing to be done about it now. You must be hungry."

"A little," Veil replied distantly, still distracted by the overlap between the near accident in his dream and its real-life counterpart.

They walked back to their original position. Veil took a sandwich out of the bag, uncapped a container of cold coffee, then sat on the wall and began to eat. He ate in silence for a few minutes, thinking, then slowly became aware that Reyna was staring at him.

"I talked to my friend again," Reyna said when Veil glanced over at her.

Veil sipped at his coffee. "What friend?"

"The one I told you about; the one who's writing a history of the Vietnam War."

"Oh, that friend. The one who half believes in fairy tales."

"He says he's now convinced that this story about Archangel—the yellow-haired soldier and CIA agent I told you about—is true, and he's really excited about it."

129

"I thought we weren't going to talk about this subject anymore."

"As I recall, you asked me not to stalk *you*. Unless you're Archangel, I can't see what harm it does to talk about him. Does it bother you to have me talk about him?"

She was getting cute, Veil thought as he took another bite of his sandwich, drank more coffee, and said nothing.

"Are you?"

"Am I what, Reyna?"

"Are you Archangel?"

"I'm a painter."

"*Were* you Archangel twenty years ago?"

"Now you're stalking me again, Reyna."

"My friend says this Archangel had developed a reputation as a real crazy man, willing to do anything. He also happened to be the U.S. Army's best martial-arts expert. It seems that the Pentagon wanted to—"

"Reyna, are you very attached to this friend of yours?"

"Yes," Reyna answered after a pause. The sly, coquettish tone she had been using was gone, replaced by a note of confusion brought on by the sudden coldness in Veil's voice and eyes. "I like him very much."

"I'm sorry to hear that."

"*Why*, Veil?"

"Because he's going to be dead very soon." Orville Madison would kill anyone he suspected of knowing about Archangel. And then the Director of Operations would kill him. And he would let Sharon die.

They stared at each other in silence broken only by the sound of the tape loop on the recorder and the faint drone of the small transistor radio in Reyna's pocket. When Reyna finally spoke, her tone was filled with reproach. "Oh, Veil, that's a terrible joke."

"I'm not joking," Veil responded curtly. From the moment Reyna had again brought up the subject of Archangel, Veil's mind had been working rapidly, sorting through options available to him. He'd decided that the researcher had to be stopped, if possible, and that Reyna was the most likely candidate to stop him. If Reyna were to perform this task, she first had to be convinced of its necessity; she had to be thoroughly shaken, and he could think of nothing more terrifying than the truth.

Reyna had involuntarily taken a step backward. "Veil," she said in a small voice, "after all you've done for Toby, I'm almost ashamed to tell you this—but I have to. Sometimes you frighten me. You can go through these sudden changes; when you do, something projects out from you that another person can almost *feel*. This is the second time you've frightened me."

Veil shifted his position slightly so that the light from a nearby street lamp fell across his face and eyes. He knew very well what was projected there, and he wanted Reyna to feel its full impact; he wanted her frightened. "You don't have to be frightened of me, Reyna," he said in a low, flat voice. "But the story *I* heard about this Archangel *is* pretty scary. If it's true, it explains why your friend doesn't have too much longer to live. Would you like to hear the story?"

"I'm not sure, Veil. I . . . don't think so."

"Oh, but I think you should. If the story is true, it could be that you're the only person who can save your friend's life. I don't have the slightest idea how you'd get him to stop his research on this Archangel story, because he's obviously hyper about it, but that's what you'd have to do if you want to save his life—and others'."

"Veil, please stop. Now you're frightening me very much."

"Once—and only once—this Archangel's company commander gave him what might be considered a compliment; actually it was a half compliment. The man called Archangel the finest warrior he'd ever met, and the worst soldier to ever make it out of boot camp; apparently, Archangel didn't like to take orders. I've heard those stories about him being mad. Who knows? He may have had emotional problems caused by a handicap no one knew about. The rumors were that he was hell on wheels in battle because he was too crazy to fear death, and he loved violence—probably because it freed him from the pain caused by this peculiar handicap. No matter. Because he didn't give a damn about anything but killing the enemy, he managed to amass more honors than any other man fighting in Vietnam. Since he was also CIA—and had been since his days in boot camp—as well as an Army captain, he was chosen by the agency to go into Laos and organize the Hmong tribes that were fighting against the Pathet Lao. Since Archangel's activities were strictly illegal, they were also, of necessity, top-secret; thus the need for a code name.

"Archangel continued his winning ways—if you can call them that—in Laos. He learned the language. He was very effective, not only as a combat fighter but also as a technician and planner. The people of the Hmong became fiercely, even obsessively, loyal to him, and he to them. In fact, he became so effective that the Pathet Lao put what amounted to a five-thousand-dollar bounty on Archangel's head—a small fortune to any Hmong, not to mention just about any native of Southeast Asia. It was never collected by anyone, although hundreds of people had opportunities. Now, that's how legends grow about madmen.

"In the meantime, Archangel was having a grand and glorious time. In fact, freed of virtually all constraints imposed by military discipline, free to do nothing but go around killing the enemy, he was—if you'll pardon the crudeness—happy as a pig in shit. And, of course, during the time all this was taking place, it was clear to everyone except a few generals and politicians that we were losing the war.

"Now, enter the villain of the piece: Archangel's CIA controller. As the story goes, this man could—if one wanted to be excessively charitable—be called a sadistic son of a bitch. He was a controller in every sense of the word; he not only wanted to control his operatives' actions, but he also wanted their souls. He enjoyed gutting people. He and Archangel didn't get on well.

"Back in the United States, a few generals and politicians had decided that all that was needed to boost public morale and rally support for the war was a bona fide hero—someone like Sergeant York in World War I, or Audie Murphy in World War II. This person's war record would be made public, a tremendous media blitz would be unleashed, and our hero would spend the rest of the war running back and forth across the country making public appearances, talking up the war effort, that sort of thing. Archangel was the man chosen to play this public-relations hero. Understand—he wasn't chosen because he was the best candidate. True, he had the best war record—if one reduces that to counting medals, which is what was done. Also, he was deemed photogenic. But he was indeed crazy and, for the most part, uncontrollable. Archangel was chosen because his controller had done a truly heroic job of lobbying. The controller did this because his own career would be enhanced if one of his men did the job, of course, but the most important reason for the lobbying effort was the controller's knowledge that Archangel would truly detest the part. Archangel belonged in the jungle, not on television, and the thought of putting Archangel on television and the lecture circuit pleased the controller immensely.

"Archangel wasn't in a position to refuse, so he had to accept the assignment. The controller brought in a South Vietnamese colonel to replace Archangel with the Hmong—a very strange choice, Archangel thought at the time—and Archangel was sent off to Hawaii for six weeks of rest, recreation, and intensive drilling on how to become a comic-book hero. In the United States everything was being geared up for our hero's entrance onstage. It was insane, by the way, because Archangel would have lasted about a week on this trip before he broke some talk-show host's neck. But that's neither here nor there."

"He was never put in place, was he?" Reyna asked, her voice breaking slightly. In the pale light cast by the street lamp her face looked as ashen as it had when Veil had first seen her.

"Obviously not," he replied dryly. "If he had been put in place, your friend wouldn't have anything to dig for, would he?"

"What happened, Veil?"

"The story goes that Archangel—who never slept well—was walking the streets of Saigon a few hours before his early-morning flight back to the United States was scheduled to take off. He was approached by a pimp who offered him a young boy and girl for his sexual pleasure. Archangel knew the children; they were from the Hmong tribe he'd fought with."

Reyna uttered a tiny gasp, but Veil spoke through it. "When that plane landed in Washington, the entire Washington press corps, the Joint Chiefs, dozens of politicians, and no less than the president of the United States were waiting to greet Archangel. The problem was that Archangel had never boarded the plane. At the time the plane had taken off, he was in a small office in the basement of the United States Embassy in Saigon breaking the bones of his controller.

"You see, it seems that, two months before, the controller had been approached by the South Vietnamese with a problem they wanted the controller to help them solve. There was this South Vietnamese colonel who'd just about cornered the Saigon markets in drug dealing, racketeering, and pornography. He'd become a considerable embarrassment to the government, but he was from an important family; they couldn't just put him in prison. The controller was asked to find someplace to put him, and the controller thought it would be a great idea to put the colonel in charge of Archangel's Hmong tribe."

"To gut Archangel," Reyna whispered hoarsely. "To snatch his soul."

"Ah, yes. The controller knew what would happen and didn't care. Within a week this colonel had begun selling Hmong children to pimps in Saigon; within a month the entire village had gone over to the Pathet Lao. Now, in a beautiful stroke of irony, the South Vietnamese—led by the colonel—were about to make their first commando foray over the border. They planned to wipe out the village.

"After busting up his controller, Archangel stole a

134

heavily armed helicopter and took off for Laos. He intended to warn the village; if necessary to save the village, he intended to fight with the Pathet Lao against the South Vietnamese. He'd turned traitor. Archangel stopped the raid and saved the Hmong, but his helicopter was shot down. Like any legend, he had more lives than a cat; he survived the crash, eluded capture, and a week later came crawling out of the jungle, crossed back over the border, and turned himself in to the Americans—who now had one very large problem. Archangel was thrown into the stockade while everyone put their heads together and tried to figure out what to do with him.

"You see the problem. Literally overnight, the war hero—for whom a tremendous publicity campaign has been planned—turns up a traitor, not to mention a potential source of considerable embarrassment to the United States if he ever tells what he knows. His real identity officially hasn't been made public, but there are enough people who know it to enable some ambitious reporter to track it down. Naturally Archangel could have been put in the stockade for the rest of his life—or even shot. But then, there would be the danger of some reporter—or some historian, like your friend—taking an interest and starting to ask questions. What everyone really wanted was for Archangel to disappear off the face of the earth. And be forgotten.

"It was the controller, obviously a man with a silver tongue, who finally came up with a solution that was acceptable to the Pentagon: Simply let Archangel go—with a few strings trailing behind him. All of his military records are drastically altered, and all of his honors taken away. Then he's given a medical discharge as a psycho. His end of the deal involves keeping his mouth shut and thus avoiding summary execution on some street corner. Needless to say, the whole public-relations idea was dropped."

"Oh, Veil." Reyna sighed.

"Oh, but there's more. As always, Archangel's controller has his own angle. Archangel has just about ruined this man's career, as well as put him in the hospital. The controller wants revenge, and—with the Pentagon's acceptance of his plan to set Archangel free—he thinks he has it. He knows just how crazy and violent Archangel is, and he thinks that the worst punishment that can be inflicted on Archangel is to set him free, to cut him loose from the armed forces. As a civilian, Archangel will have no franchise to wreak destruction. With no way to calm his demons, Archangel will self-destruct, end up killing himself with booze and drugs, or simply die in some alley. And to make certain that Archangel understands the name of the game, the controller imposes his own private penalty: Archangel is given an indeterminate sentence of death. He will be placed under constant surveillance by the controller's men, and he's informed that if the day ever comes when he finds peace of mind or true happiness, that will be the day he takes a bullet through the brain."

"Veil," Reyna whispered as she took a tentative step forward, "that's a terrible story."

Veil held up his hand, stopping her. "It's a story that can't be told, Reyna. After all that's come out since the end of the war, the story of Archangel wouldn't seem like such a big deal. But it's still a very big deal to the controller, who survived the damage to his career and now occupies a very high, and very sensitive, post in the CIA's Operations Division. He can't afford even to be identified, much less embarrassed. All the old rules, including Archangel's death sentence, still hold, even after all these years. Without realizing it, your friend has been busily tripping any number of invisible alarm signals. Believe me, the controller knows exactly what your friend is up to, and your friend is damn lucky he isn't dead already. In any case, he soon will be if he doesn't drop the project—and that includes burning his manuscript and any research records he's kept. The manuscript and records will be destroyed in the end, anyway; it's a question of whether he does it himself or lets his assassins do it for him."

Reyna drew in a deep breath, then threw her head back and defiantly brushed a strand of hair away from her face.

Then she pushed Veil's hand aside, stepped forward, and wrapped her arms tightly around his waist. "You *are* Archangel, aren't you?"

"If I were," Veil said quietly as he stroked the woman's raven-black hair, "it means that your friend can get me killed too. And you, since he's got such a big mouth—and these people hear everything. Do you understand?" He waited until he felt Reyna's head nod. "Good. We're going to have to find a way of convincing your friend to stop writing about Archangel if he wants to save his ass. And my name can't even be breathed."

"Yes, Veil. I do understand."

"Let me think about the problem. You'll do the groundwork, and I may follow up by scaring the shit out of him—without hurting him or letting him know who I am."

Reyna lifted her head and parted her lips slightly. Veil was about to lean over and kiss her when the shots rang out.

Veil immediately leapt to the ground and listened. There were more shots—rifle fire and what could have been the cough of a shotgun. The sounds were carrying on the night air from somewhere across the expressway, to the southeast.

"It's Toby!" Reyna screamed.

"Take it easy," Veil said, holding her tightly. "It may not be. The police wouldn't just start shooting like that unless they were returning fire, and Toby wouldn't know what to do with a gun if he had one."

"They're *vigilantes*, Veil! I *know* they've got Toby down there! They're killing him!"

"Not yet, they haven't," Veil said flatly as he started to lead Reyna out of the cemetery and toward the car. "If they'd killed him, they wouldn't still be shooting. Don't panic. If he's dead, there's nothing we can do about it. If he's alive but in trouble, it won't help him if we panic. We'll get in the car and head over there. Turn up that radio."

Veil quickly led Reyna the half block to where the car was parked. He eased Reyna into the passenger's seat, then slid in behind the wheel and started the engine. The firing had stopped abruptly—something Veil regretted, for he now had nothing to guide him to the site. He pulled out onto Fifty-third Street and turned right, heading for the overpass that would take him to the other side of the expressway. As he approached the intersection, an unmarked police car with a portable flasher on its roof sped through the intersection from Veil's left, barely missing the front of his car.

With his right hand Veil reached across the seat and braced Reyna as he floored the accelerator and twisted the wheel to the right. The well-tuned car responded instantly, screaming around the corner on two wheels. The car bounced down, fishtailed, then straightened out as Veil sped down the street after the police car.

"Good grief," Reyna murmured through clenched teeth.

Veil glanced at the speedometer; they were going sixty miles an hour and still gaining speed. "Brace your hands against the dashboard," he said evenly.

Reyna's face was bloodless, but her mouth was set in a determined line. "What will he do if he sees you chasing him?"

"Nothing, I hope. He'll probably assume I'm another cop. In any case, he's not going to stop for us."

The deadly popping of gunfire had resumed; it was closer now, somewhere in the streets off to their right. Veil kept the accelerator to the floor as he sped across a bridge. The car hit the peak of a shallow crown, soared through the air, then slammed back to the ground. The gap separating him from the police car had narrowed to a few yards, and the back of the driver's head was now clearly visible.

Suddenly Reyna clutched at Veil's arm with both hands, almost causing him to lose control of the car. "Oh, my God," she said with a gasp. "That's Carl Nagle!"

Veil, who had been focusing on the car's trunk, now shifted his gaze to the driver's head—and saw that Reyna was right. Questions flashed through his mind and were instantly dismissed. It seemed doubtful that Nagle would be riding around in a stolen police car, yet the flasher—and the police radio he undoubtedly had inside the car—could have been stolen, or purchased, some time before he'd fallen out of favor with all the various powers that had ruled his existence. For the first time Veil saw beneath the thuggish exterior of the man to what had to be a keen, if hopelessly twisted, mind; an outlaw, hunted by both the police and the Mafia, Carl Nagle had managed to wire himself into everything the police did. Veil debated whether or not to tell Reyna that Nagle was on his own, running from everyone, then decided that it would serve no purpose other than to frighten her even more than she already was. Gabriel Vahanian was dead, he thought, and now he was the one looking up the ass of the tiger.

"Lie down on the seat," Veil said calmly, gently squeezing Reyna's knee. "I won't let him hurt you. I promise."

Reyna did as she was told, ducking down and curling into a ball on the seat, but both hands continued to grip Veil's leg.

Nagle suddenly turned hard to the left. Veil stayed with him, narrowly missing a parked car. At the next block Nagle turned right; Veil followed, expertly keeping the car under control as the rear end fishtailed. In the block ahead he could see a milling knot of people and the flashing lights of police cars.

The brake lights on Nagle's car came on as he abruptly pulled over to the curb. Veil reacted instantly, again planting his hand on Reyna's chest and bracing her as he slammed on the brakes. He eased up to prevent the brakes from locking, slammed them on again, and brought the car under control, stopping it at the curb across the street from, and slightly behind, Nagle's car.

Veil immediately ducked down and peered over the dashboard at Nagle; the man was sitting rigidly in his car, radio microphone in his hand, staring down the street. Imprisoned in his own world of desperation and madness, apparently he had never even noticed the car pursuing him.

"Veil . . . ?"

"It's all right. Nagle doesn't know we're here. You stay right where you are."

Reyna's voice was a croaking whisper. "Toby?"

"No sign of him, but a lot of men are pointing toward a building under construction. He must be in there someplace."

"Thank God he's still alive," Reyna said in a small voice. "Are there police?"

"Yes."

"Veil, maybe we should talk to them now. This is getting pretty hairy."

"Hang in there, sweetheart. Remember, if Toby is taken into custody, the odds are overwhelming that he'll die—and his tribe along with him."

"I just don't want him to die now."

"There's still time. Nobody's gone into the building yet, and Nagle's still in his car. I want to see what he's up to."

Veil waited, and after another minute Nagle began speaking into his microphone. Down the street, a uniformed officer leaned into his car, obviously listening to his radio. Nagle released the transmit button on his microphone, waited a few seconds, then pressed it and spoke again. The patrolman suddenly began shouting orders to the other police on the scene as he pointed to his left.

"Veil . . . ?"

"Nagle's working on his own, Reyna. He's feeding phony information to the police down the street now."

Even as Veil spoke, there was a flurry of activity among the group of policemen by the building; they ran to their cars, got in, and drove off. The crowd that had been milling in the street and on the sidewalk gradually began to disperse. One man reached down into a garbage bin and retrieved a shotgun from where he had hurriedly thrown it at the approach of the police. He and six other men walked halfway up the block, then disappeared into a bar.

"Veil . . . ?"

"Shhh. Just stay there."

Almost ten minutes passed. Then the door of the car

across the street opened. Nagle stepped out and began walking casually down the middle of the street, toward the building skeleton. In one hand he carried a powerful flashlight, and in the other what appeared to be an Uzi submachine gun equipped with a custom-made silencer. He stepped up on the sidewalk and vanished through an opening in the fence surrounding the construction site.

"Nagle's gone into the building," Veil continued as he opened the door and got out. "You stay put. Lock the doors."

"Veil?" Reyna cried out as she sat up and reached for him. "What are you going to do?"

"I'm going to kill the son of a bitch," he replied evenly as he blew Reyna a kiss, then closed the door.

Veil, moving as silently as death, ran down the street and across the intersection to the construction site. He waited, pressed back against the fence next to the opening, listening. When he heard nothing, he darted through the opening, angling across to the opposite side. There he crouched low in the darkness, listening again. This time he heard the faint, shuffling sound of footsteps on wood scaffolding.

Suddenly a bright cone of light from Nagle's flashlight pierced the darkness on the second floor of the steel skeleton. There were more shuffling footsteps, then the clatter of loose boards. Veil thought he heard a faint, low rumble, as if Nagle were talking to himself.

Veil straightened up and moved off to his right. At the corner of the building he reached up and gripped a steel girder, then began to climb up the grid work. Suddenly he heard a can clatter, back near the entrance. He turned his head in time to see the unmistakable figure of Reyna—a master tracker undone and made careless by her terror of the monster that was Carl Nagle—trip and fall through the opening in the fence. A moment later she cried out in pain.

Veil immediately released his grip on the steel and dropped back to the ground. He landed, then sprinted through the rubble-strewn darkness toward where Reyna

141

lay at the bottom of a wedge of dim light cast by street lamps. Without slowing his pace he ran through the light, reaching down as he did so and grabbing a handful of Reyna's jacket, jerking her off the ground and carrying her to the other side of the opening just as a burst of fire, sounding like nothing so much as a person spitting watermelon seeds at an impossibly fast clip, raked across the fence just above Veil's head. He fell on top of Reyna to shield her with his body, holding her head down with his hand, burying his own head in her thick hair and waiting as the *pfft-pfft* sound of bullets striking wood slowed in tempo—then stopped.

Veil got up on his hands and knees and, pulling Reyna along with him by her belt, scurried forward to the shelter of a wide support girder.

"Shh, shh," Veil intoned to the whimpering Reyna as he held her tight. Her eyes were wide with horror, and her breath came in short, panting gasps. "You have to control it, Reyna. Shh."

Finally Reyna was able to control her sobbing, although she continued to breathe in gasps. "Wh-what in—God's name?"

"It's called a submachine gun, sweetheart," Veil said, peering around the girder and looking up. Nagle's light was out. "Unfortunately, that particular model fires up to three hundred rounds a minute."

"He plans to use that on *Toby*?"

"Obviously, he'll use it on anyone who gets in his way—he'd use a cannon if he had one. There's no time now for details, but Nagle's on the outs with both the cops and the crooks. He's out of his head but not so crazy that he isn't thinking. He needs the heroin in the Nal-toon to finance an escape out of the country. I didn't tell you before because I didn't want you more frightened than you already were. Now—what the *hell* are you doing here?"

Reyna clung to Veil as she shook her head in fear and frustration. "I got to thinking that Nagle had a gun and you didn't."

"I don't need a gun to kill Nagle, Reyna."

"But there's also Toby to consider. I'm not sure you fully appreciate how dangerous he is. The man can almost literally see in the dark; to him you're probably just another enemy. If you passed him in the dark, he might kill you. It was just you against both of them."

"Didn't it occur to you that I'd considered that?" Veil whispered angrily. He swallowed his irritation, took a deep breath. "Thank you, Reyna. I know how you feel about Nagle. Coming in here took a lot of guts."

"I wanted to call out to Toby, explain to him what was happening."

"Who's there?" Nagle's voice was right above them.

Veil signaled with his hand for Reyna to crawl along the foundation to the next girder. "Somebody who's going to take that toy away from you, Nagle, and shove it up your ass. Just be patient. I'll be up there in a few minutes."

"Kendry?! Is that you, you fucker?"

"Get out of here, Nagle," Veil said in a casual tone, his voice carrying easily in the steel-amplified darkness. "Unless all your brains have run out your ears, you have to know this play is over. Somebody's bound to hear that thing, even with a silencer, and you must have sprayed at least a hundred rounds into the street. Your ex-colleagues on the force are probably on their way back here right now. My advice is to split and try again another day."

He could almost feel Nagle straining to hear in the darkness, and Veil listened with him. There was no wail of police sirens.

Nagle's answer now came—a burst of fire. But the angle was wrong, and the bullets plowed harmlessly into the dirt a few feet from where Veil was standing. Veil moved in a crouch along the foundation to where Reyna was waiting.

"Veil," Reyna whispered urgently, "I have to talk to Toby. He has to understand what's happening."

"You're not going to talk to anyone," Veil whispered back in a firm voice. "Nagle may think it was me who stumbled in through the entrance. We're going to take our time and work our way very carefully around the building, and then you're going to scoot your cute ass right back out the way you came in."

"No," Reyna answered in a tone filled with quiet determination. "You don't know everything, Veil Kendry. Believe me, you need me to protect you from Toby. We're in this together, and I'm not leaving here without you."

"Reyna—"

Reyna suddenly released Veil, turned, cupped her hands to her mouth, and called out in the clicking language of the K'ung. Her lilting voice rose and fell, eerily beautiful as it echoed back and forth inside the steel shell.

"That you, Alexander?!" There was a burst of fire, fifteen yards wide of the mark. "Oh, kid, if you think what I did to you before was something, wait until I get my hands on you this time!"

"What did you say to Toby?" Veil whispered.

"I kind of introduced you, said that you were with me and trying to help him too. I asked him not to harm you and told him that the other man was his enemy and wanted to kill all of us. I asked him to trust us and to try to escape when he had the chance. I told him where we'd parked the car, then asked him to go there and wait for us."

"Do you think he'll do it?"

"No," Reyna answered after a pause. "But I didn't think it would hurt to try."

Suddenly a powerful beam of light cut through the darkness and swept across the fence in front of them. There was a clatter of loose scaffolding, and Veil peered around the edge of the girder to see the light descending a ramp.

Nagle's rumbling voice was stretched taut with madness. "You ain't carrying, Kendry. If you were, you'd have used your piece by now. I'm going to shoot you in half, you fucker, and then I'm going to fuck that girl's brains out—literally. I'm going to kill her with my cock."

Veil put his fingers to his lips to warn Reyna into silence. He motioned for her to lie flat on the ground, then reached down to his boot for his knife. Back against the steel, Veil again peered around the edge of the girder. Nagle was three quarters of the way down the ramp, flashing his light around the ground floor.

Suddenly there was a thud, then a clatter that sounded like wood against steel.

"What the fuck?!"

Veil watched as Nagle rubbed his forehead, then put his hand into the light. There was blood. He cursed again, then shined the light into the darkness above him. Something that looked like a line of night flashed down through the light, and Nagle cried out in pain as he shined the light on the inside of his right bicep, where a featherless arrow hung loosely from the flesh. He pulled out the arrow and flung it away, then fired a burst of gunfire up into the darkness.

"I'm gonna get you, you black bastard!" he shouted as he started back up the scaffolding.

"Now I'm going to take him," Veil said, starting to step out from behind the girder.

"Wait!" Reyna hissed as she grabbed hold of the back of his jacket.

Veil turned and was startled by the expression on Reyna's face. Her eyes gleamed, and her lips were set in a crooked grin that had no laughter in it. She was trembling all over, but Veil did not think it was from fear. "What's the matter?"

"Nagle isn't going to find Toby," Reyna answered through bloodless lips that barely moved. "I don't want you to go up there."

"I can take care of myself, Reyna. You know that. Nagle has to be killed."

"No," Reyna said, the word punctuated by gunfire from above. Bullets ricocheted off the steel girders, whining in the night and shooting off sparks. "If Nagle kills you, then he'll have me—and I can't describe the horrible things he'll do to me. You promised he'd never hurt me."

"He can't hurt you if he's dead, Reyna. The best way for me to protect you is to kill the bastard."

"No. I'm afraid. Toby will get out of here on his own.

145

He'll go into the next cemetery and go to ground to rest. I want you to take me out of here, Veil."

"Reyna—"

"You promised, Veil. I'm afraid."

He studied Reyna's face for a few moments, then abruptly took her by the hand and led her back the way they had come. He paused at the edge of the building, listening. Nagle had apparently forgotten all about them, for he was now up on the third floor, cursing and flashing his light around.

Veil pushed Reyna through the opening in the fence, then followed her as she walked quickly, body stiff and hands clenched into fists at her sides, to the car. She got into the car, slamming the door shut behind her.

Veil slid in behind the wheel, turned, and studied Reyna. Her face was still clenched into a grim mask that seemed ready to break at any moment, and Veil felt certain she was on the verge of hysterical laughter.

"Reyna?"

"Mmm. I'm all right."

"The safari's going to take a break for a few hours. You say Toby will rest; we need to rest, and I have to make a couple of phone calls. I'm going to check us into a hotel."

"Mmm."

"Reyna, what's the matter?" Veil asked as he started the engine and pulled away from the curb.

"Nothing," Reyna replied curtly.

Veil was approaching the intersection when Carl Nagle suddenly walked through the opening in the fence. Veil floored the accelerator and yanked the wheel hard to the left. The car shot forward, bumped up over the curb, and shot down the sidewalk only inches from the fence. Nagle glanced around. His mouth dropped open and he half fell, half stumbled back through the opening as Veil sped over the spot where he had been standing only a moment before.

"Win some, lose some," Veil said as he braked, bucked down off the curb, and turned left at the corner.

They drove in silence for a few minutes as Veil headed

toward the business section of Sunnyside. Reyna sat as rigidly as if she had been skewered with a metal rod.

"God forgive me," the woman said in a voice just above a whisper.

Veil reached over and gently stroked the back of her neck. "What was that business back there all about, Reyna?"

Reyna reached over her shoulder, found Veil's hand, and squeezed it. "I knew you could kill Nagle. I'm beginning to think that Archangel—"

"Don't call me that, Reyna—not ever. Don't even repeat the name, except to your friend. You told me you understood."

Reyna released Veil's hand, slowly leaned forward, and rested her head against the dashboard. "I'm sorry," she said quietly. "What I meant to say is that I'm beginning to believe that you can do just about anything."

"I certainly could have killed Nagle. Why did you stop me?"

"You really would have killed him, wouldn't you? Even in the dark, with just your knife against that terrible gun."

Veil said nothing.

"Then we would have had Toby trapped inside the building," Reyna continued after a pause. "I could have talked to him and known for sure that he was listening. Then the sun would have risen and we'd have been able to find him. Maybe he would have finally come to us."

"Those thoughts occurred to me," Veil said dryly.

"God forgive me."

"For what, Reyna?"

"You would have killed him."

"Yes."

Now Reyna turned to face Veil. The mask finally broke as tears welled in her eyes and flowed down her cheeks. "May God forgive me, Veil. May you and Toby forgive me if anything happens to the two of you. I didn't want Carl Nagle to die so easily."

CHAPTER FOURTEEN

Veil dreams.

He assumed he would be Toby, but he unexpectedly finds himself in the mind, looking through the eyes, of a sixteen-year-old boy. He is wondering if his mother might not be right. What if Toby *is* the Black Messiah? And what if Toby *does* take a special interest in *him*? Usually this thought makes the boy uneasy, but at other times it makes him feel good.

Sometimes, when the boy feels depressed or confused, he tentatively tries speaking to Toby's spirit, asking for the African's help or advice. The boy has often thought about the weeks Toby spent in Central Park and the pain He must have suffered from the bullet wound in His arm.

As a result of his thoughts, the boy has found that he no longer even wants to risk hurting people; he has turned from mugging as a chief source of income to robbing stores, stealing various items and selling them to a fence who lives in his neighborhood.

However, even robbing stores has begun to bother him. The boy has been having nightmares as a result of his worry that Toby *might* be watching him, judging him—perhaps waiting to kill him, as He killed the two muggers, if the boy does not stop stealing altogether.

The boy's problem is that he does not know any other way to obtain the money he is used to having in his pockets. Now he is broke; he needs money and has decided that he has no choice but to get it the fastest and easiest way he knows—mugging subway riders in Manhattan.

He'd boarded the subway bound for Manhattan but had almost immediately suffered from a shortness of breath and a fluttering heartbeat. He does not want to threaten anyone with a knife; he does not want to put himself into a situation where he might have to hurt—or even kill—someone.

His mother could be right. Toby could be watching him.

He gets off the subway while still in Queens, at a stop on a street running parallel to Mount Olive Cemetery. The boy walks nervously to the north end of the cemetery, then stops when he comes to an intersection where all the streetlights have been shot out by children with air rifles. The intersection is dark, and the store on the corner closest to him is a camera shop. The boy glances quickly around him. Seeing that the street and sidewalks are empty, he walks quickly to the store.

There is an old steel gate drawn across the entrance to the shop and an adjacent display window. The boy knows it will be a simple matter for him to break the window with a rock or his elbow, reach through two broken slats in the gate, and grab two or three of the cameras on display. The fence might give him as much as twenty dollars per camera. It isn't much, the boy thinks, but at least he won't be broke.

The boy searches at the curb until he finds a piece of broken pavement. He walks back to the window, raises the chunk of cement—and stiffens. He slowly lowers his hand as he feels his body break into a sweat.

This is ridiculous, the boy thinks. He has done this sort of thing countless times in the past and has never been caught. Yet he's never been so nervous. What terrifies him

149

is the thought that a Black Messiah might be around—a Black Messiah Who kills thieves.

To reassure himself that he is not being watched by anyone, much less Toby, the boy walks to the corner and again looks around. The block across the intersection is completely dark, and the boy marks that street as his escape route. To his left, halfway down the block, is a garishly lit bar, but there is no one standing outside on the sidewalk. All of the buildings on the block to his right have been razed to make room for a high rise; the steel skeleton of the building soars from behind a plywood fence into the night sky. He is alone, the boy thinks, absolutely alone.

He walks back to the camera shop, takes a deep breath, then smashes the stone through the window. A shrill alarm bell sounds, but the boy has expected that, and he does not panic. He reaches through the gate, through the broken pane of glass, grabs two Polaroids and a Nikon, then sprints across the intersection toward the night-black street beyond. He leaps up on the sidewalk, sprints twenty yards, then tries to stop with a suddenness that causes him to turn his ankle, stumble, and fall. He hurls the cameras away from him, scrambles to his feet, and stumbles backward until he bumps hard and painfully against the brick facade of the building behind him. His heart pounds wildly inside his chest, and his mouth has gone absolutely dry. He badly wants to scream, to howl his regret and sorrow at the sky, but no sound will come out of his throat. In this terror-filled moment the boy knows beyond any doubt that he is going to die.

Toby stands in the darkness no more than ten feet away from the spot where the boy cowers.

The figure is cloaked in darkness, but there is no doubt in the boy's mind that it is Toby. Toby is naked, slumped against a shop door, breathing hoarsely. Toby holds a ragged bundle in His arms, and from the cloth protrudes the head of a wooden statue.

His mother was right, the boy thinks. The Black Messiah has been watching him; Toby has seen, and now He will kill.

150

The boy's mouth opens and shuts a few times before he finally finds his voice. "*Sheeeit!*" he screams.

The sound of his own yell galvanizes the boy's muscles. Oblivious to the pain in his twisted ankle, he pushes off the brick wall and dashes out into the street, expecting at any moment to feel a spear tearing into his back, ripping through his heart and lungs.

He makes it down the street to the bar and goes crashing through the door. He runs into a table, spins around, and sprawls on the floor.

"Hey, kid—!"

"He's gonna kill me, man!" The boy sobs, squirming in pain on the floor and clawing at his twisted ankle. "He's gonna kill me!"

A big man with anchor tattoos on both hairy forearms laughs as he slides off his bar stool. He reaches down and hauls the boy to his feet by the shirt collar. "Who's gonna kill you, kid?"

The boy swallows hard, wipes tears from his eyes, and points a trembling finger in the direction of the street. "Toby," he croaks. "The Black Messiah."

The big man's eyes narrow as he shakes the boy. "You've seen the African?"

"Out *there*, man!" the boy says, his head bobbing up and down. "He's right down the street!"

Suddenly the bar is filled with excited shouts, the grating sounds of chairs scraping on the hardwood floor, then the ominous clanking of steel. The boy stares wide-eyed as men rush past him, over him, pushing at each other as they pour out the door. Most of the men carry weapons of some sort, and only now does the boy realize that the bar was filled with a vigilante group on the hunt for Toby. In a few moments he is alone; everyone, including the bartender, has rushed out into the street.

The boy gets to his feet and limps out of the bar in time to see a naked black figure carrying a bundle dart through a gap in the fence surrounding the half-finished building in the next block. The vigilantes have seen Him and are

151

shouting excitedly, waving their weapons in the air, as they run through the intersection.

By the time the boy reaches the construction site, a dozen men are clustered around the gap in the fence where Toby had disappeared. There is a great deal of shouting and confusion. One man, armed with a hunting rifle, steps through the gap into the darkness beyond, but he reappears after only a minute or two.

"It's dark as shit in there," the man says. "I ain't takin' no chance on gettin' a spear stuck up *my* ass."

The men back up into the middle of the street. One of the men grunts as he points to an area high up on the steel skeleton. He raises his rifle to his shoulder and squeezes off a shot. Another man shouts that he has seen Toby. More shots are fired. Bullets ricochet off the forest of steel girders, and a few of the men duck and run for cover from their own bullets.

Veil rolls away from the dream, but he does not awaken, and he does not enter into deep sleep. Instead he searches for Toby until he finds him and becomes him.

Veil is Toby.

He cannot remember ever feeling so tired or sick. The Nal-toon has set him a very great trial, he thinks, one which is perhaps greater than any K'ung warrior has been asked to endure. He prays that he will have the strength to continue.

But then he reminds himself that if the trial is great, so are the Nal-toon's gifts; food, sweet water, sanctuary in the *Newyorkcities'* jungles of the dead, and—most wondrous treasure of all—the Nal-toon's blood-shilluk. He must have courage.

He lies in a shallow trench he dug at the bottom of a shallow basin, near a stream, in a copse of trees surrounded by brush-covered knolls. He knows that it is not good cover, but he has simply been too exhausted and sick to search for better. He has to rest.

A short time before, he took an unusually large dose of the blood-shilluk, but it does not seem to be having the usual rapid effect; his bowels churn and he is still in great pain. Indeed he has found that he must continue to take increasingly larger doses of the God-medicine in order to function at all.

He wishes he could think clearly, for the behavior of some of the *Newyorkcities* is increasingly confusing to him. It is difficult for him to imagine any tribe that would not be totally united in their desire to possess the Nal-toon, Who is all.

Yet . . .

There was the young *Newyorkcity* warrior who had surprised him in the dark *street*. The warrior could have attacked him but had run away.

And there was Reyna, and the man-in-night.

Veil is now considering the possibility that it had been Reyna in the last jungle of the dead, not a spirit, and that she was trying to find him in order to give him aid. Perhaps Reyna and the man-in-night have been trying to help him all along. Obviously, Veil thinks, they seem to know where he is going, yet have not told any other *Newyorkcities*.

He remembers vividly how the *Newyorkcities* running after him in the *street* had strengthened his muscles and cleared his mind, enabling him to run and hide in the open *building*.

The problem had been that the *building* was a trap, not sanctuary, and when the huge warrior with the hand-light and big bang-stick had entered, Veil had assumed that this was the *Newyorkcities'* champion, their greatest warrior, sent to duel with him in a battle of honor. In his weakened condition, Veil had known that he had no real chance against this land's most powerful warrior, but he had resolved to fight with courage and die with honor.

From the moment the warrior had entered the *building*, Veil had stalked him from a higher level—and it had come as a shock to Veil to see how poorly the huge man tracked in the darkness; even with his powerful hand-light, his healthy body and two good eyes, it had seemed to Veil that the man could not see or move. With growing excitement at the thought that the Nal-toon might purposely be

153

weakening this champion, Veil had continued to stalk the man, squinting his good eye in order to focus his vision. He'd known that he would have to be very cautious, for even a good hit with a poisoned arrow would not prevent the man from using his deadly bang-stick.

Then, to Veil's amazement, the man-in-night and Reyna had come into the *building*. And the *Newyorkcity* champion had tried to kill them. Reyna and the man-in-night who traveled with her were willing to risk their lives for him, Veil had thought.

Perhaps. If it was not a trick to put him off-guard.

Veil had stalked the warrior as the warrior stalked Reyna and the man-in-night. He had ignored Reyna's pleas for him to run, for there had been the possibility that she was trying to force him out into the open, where other *Newyorkcities* would be waiting for him.

On the other hand, if it was not a trick, Veil would not abandon the two people who were risking their lives for him. That was not the way of the warrior. If Reyna and the man-in-night were his allies, then he would fight to help them—and he would trust the Nal-toon to see into his heart and watch over a K'ung warrior who was doing what he thought he must.

Then the warrior had started down after Reyna and the man-in-night, and Veil had attacked—first with his throwing stick, and then with a poisoned arrow that had found its mark. Reyna and the man-in-night had escaped.

Veil had watched with some amusement as the big warrior had continued to stumble around in the dark, looking for him. Veil had not been able to understand how a man who was facing death would waste a single heartbeat pursuing another warrior he obviously could not find.

He had waited patiently until he'd been absolutely certain that all the *Newyorkcities* were gone before he'd left the *building*. By then the excitement and activity had begun to take their toll; his stomach had begun to cramp severely, his legs wobbled under him, and he could barely see.

He'd been halfway down the *street* before he'd realized that he was being followed. A chill had gone through him, for in the time that his senses had deserted him, his pursuer could easily have killed him, especially if the *Newyorkcity* had a bang-stick.

Breathing a prayer of thanks to the Nal-toon for making him aware of his pursuer, Veil had hobbled as fast as he could down the *street*, then cried inwardly with joy when he had seen a gap in the stone wall to his right, which led into a jungle. He'd darted into the jungle, then ducked behind a tree and waited.

Veil had been surprised to find that his pursuer was the same young warrior who had confronted, then run away from him earlier. The boy had no weapons, and so Veil had merely put the tip of an arrow against the boy's throat.

"Holy shit!"

"Go away. I do not want to kill you. Just go away."

Although his entire body trembled with terror, the young warrior had stood his ground.

"Man, I can't understand a word you're saying, but I can see that you're hurt. I want to help you, and I promise I won't tell anyone where you are. Come home with me. My mom thinks you're like Jesus, and maybe I do too. She'll fix you up, and then you'll have a good place to hide."

"Go!" Veil had commanded, removing the arrow tip from the boy's throat and pointing toward the *street*. And the boy had run away.

Perhaps he should have killed the boy, Veil thinks—but the boy had not killed him when he'd had the chance. Veil finds everything confusing; life is clean and simple in the desert, and it is usually easy to tell friends from enemies. Not in *Newyorkcity*; this is a place that clouds a warrior's mind and drains his will.

He sniffs a large amount of the Nal-toon's blood-shilluk. Then, impatient with the increasing slowness of the effect, he sniffs still more. Finally, his head spinning, Veil passes out.

•　　•　　•

Night-chill awakens Veil-in-Toby. He lies still, listening, trying to probe the darkness with his hunter-warrior's senses in order to evaluate the surrounding area. When he is satisfied that there is no one near, he pushes aside the brush that covers him and sits up. The pain that shoots through his skull almost makes him keel over, and he quickly sniffs some blood-shilluk. It takes a long time for the blood-shilluk to take effect, but Veil waits, unwilling to risk passing out if he takes more. He must move on.

It occurs to him that he should eat, although he has not been hungry for a long time. He has no food but resolves to find the strength to hunt at the earliest opportunity. He drinks at a nearby stream, then moves on to the southeast.

A full moon lights the open ground. Under other circumstances he might not travel so quickly after the incident in the open *building*, but he feels that the Nal-toon now wants him to hurry. No matter how much he rests, Veil thinks, he seems to grow progressively weaker. He must get to the *airplane* fields soon. He is terribly lonely and he wants to go home.

He moves through the trees around the perimeter of a meadow. As he approaches the far end Veil stops and gazes suspiciously at an area where the meadow narrows. The whole jungle is growing smaller, he thinks, narrowing. Although he has been walking in a straight line through trees, he now finds that there is a stone wall close to his right, and beyond that a *street*. He is in danger.

His head pulses with pain, but he resists the impulse to take more blood-shilluk; while the God-medicine at one time cleared his senses and eased his pain, it now tends to confuse and disorient him even further. He is no longer sure of the proper amount to take, and so he decides to try to take none—at least not while he is traveling.

Veil slumps down, braces his back against a tree, and checks his weapons. He has lost his throwing stick, but he still has his bow, six poisoned arrows, and a hastily constructed spear with a sharp stone head, lashed to the

156

shaft with vines. He considers these adequate replace-
ments for the spear and knife lost in the place of the
rolling wooden objects.

He is so very, very tired, Veil thinks—yet he must make
a decision. He does not wish to go out into the lighted
street while there is still cover, but the narrowing of the
jungle before him makes him nervous; it is an area where
man-snares could be set, or where *Newyorkcities* could be
waiting to ambush him.

To go out into the *street* where he can be seen, Veil
thinks, or go on into the narrow jungle where he can be
trapped?

He knows he must make the decision, and it looms as an
unbearable, momentous hurdle. Suddenly he begins to
weep.

"Great Nal-toon, please help me," Veil whispers,
ashamed of his sobbing but unable any longer to control
his depthless sorrow and loneliness. "My will is leaving
me, and I do not think I can go on without strength, which
You must give me. When will I be judged to have passed
Your trial, great Nal-toon? Please have mercy on and
forgive me, Nal-toon, for this warrior is finished."

CHAPTER FIFTEEN

Veil rose to his feet and glanced around them, while Reyna continued crawling on her hands and knees along a bare patch of ground where there were many footprints. Throughout the day, mourners had cast hostile glances at the man and woman who acted strange and carried a noisy tape recorder. However, it was not annoyed mourners that concerned Veil; once, just before noon, he'd caught the glint of metal where the bright sunlight had shafted down through a gap in a heavily wooded area with no graves. He had the strong feeling that they were being watched, and it did not surprise him. After the incident at the construction site he knew that anyone with a map, ruler, and a modicum of intelligence could at least guess that the K'ung prince was heading southeast, even if his destination was unclear. Veil expected any number of hunters in the field before nightfall.

"Who were you talking with on the phone last night?" Reyna asked without looking up from the ground.

"Victor Raskolnikov and a couple of other friends," Veil

answered absently as he continued to study the surrounding woods and the small field of grave markers, which they were now searching. "One's a doctor, and the other's a pilot and a mercenary. They're going to deliver Toby and the Nal-toon back to the Kalahari. Victor's financing the operation."

"Oh, Veil," Reyna said, glancing up at him. She was crying but with joy. "Why didn't you tell me before?"

Veil shrugged. "We can't take Toby anywhere unless we find him."

"How will they do it?"

"In stages. First he'll be flown over the border into either Canada or Mexico—it hasn't been decided which yet, and that decision rests on a couple of other factors. If the doctor can patch him up, he'll be given false travel documents and put on a plane to Botswana. Otherwise, Walrus—the pilot—will deliver Toby himself. Your missionary friends have already been contacted, and they're taking care of business at the other end."

Reyna got to her feet, walked over to Veil, and hugged him. "Thank you," she said simply.

"Don't thank me yet. We have to get Toby to Flushing Airport. Right now that fifteen miles might as well be fifteen thousand. Have you found anything?"

"Not here. I'm pretty sure he's behind us."

"If you do find spoor, don't react. I think we've got company."

"I know. I saw a couple of them. They're waiting for us to deliver the goods, aren't they?"

"Of course. How did you read them? Cops or crooks?"

"I think crooks."

"Agreed. Cops would handle it differently." Veil held Reyna out at arm's length and smiled. "You're holding up beautifully."

Reyna grinned shyly. "What else is there to do?"

"Nothing. I'm just telling you that you're special."

"Thanks. My biggest concern right now is that Toby will try to circle around through the streets tonight."

"Because he'll see that this is a bottleneck?"

"Yes. And he'll sense the presence of the men—if they're still here tonight."

Veil glanced at his watch. "It will be dark in a couple of hours, so it's time for us to lose our observers. We'll walk back up to the other end of the cemetery, then go out and get something to eat. Keep talking to him. Lay it on the line, Reyna. Make it short and sweet. If he doesn't come to us tonight, it's all over."

•   •   •

Veil worked quickly in the darkness, stooping and opening the canvas sack he had brought back with him. Inside was a three-hundred-yard length of strong twine to which tiny bells had been attached at twenty-yard intervals. Twine and bells had been stained black.

Both Veil and Reyna had covered their exposed flesh with mud.

Avoiding the patches of bright moonlight that fell through the trees, Veil went to the far edge of the cemetery. He tied one end of the twine around a tree trunk, then worked his way back. Within twenty minutes he had strung the entire width of the bottleneck.

Veil took both of Reyna's hands in his. "Assuming Toby finally decides to do things the easy way, do you think he can find us?"

"I don't know, Veil."

"Well, we can't use the recorder or have you call out anymore, because we don't know who else might be listening. So we'll have to do it the hard way, if necessary. You stay here, and I'll go out along the line about a hundred yards. When and if he does come through here, he should hit that string. He's sick and weak, so I should be able to sit on him before he can stick me with anything."

"Veil, you have to be *so* careful. If he even nicks you with one of those arrows . . ."

"You let me worry about it. And I'm in charge now, so you'll do exactly as I say. No matter what you hear, you stay put. *I'm* the only one who reacts to anything. For one thing, somebody other than Toby might trip the line. I don't want you shot. And speaking of shots, if you hear any gunfire, you get the hell out of here. There'll be nothing more you can do, and I'll meet you at the car. You understand?"

"Veil, I can't just—"

"You'll do as I say, Reyna. End of discussion."

．　　●　　●

Veil knelt beside a tree and stared out over a moonlit expanse of grave markers, listening for the tinkle of bells and thinking of the other men who were undoubtedly close by, also watching and listening. He was going to have to be fast, Veil thought. And lucky.

Suddenly the line shook, and there was the sound of bells. To his left.

"Hey!" a man shouted. "There's some kind of line strung across here!"

Veil sprinted silently through the trees. He had gone fifty yards when a figure lurched out at him from behind a tree, to his right.

"I've got—" the man managed to shout before Veil broke his neck. The revolver in the man's hand went off, shattering the stillness.

"Reyna, it's over!" Veil shouted as he picked up the dead man's gun and shoved it into the waistband of his jeans. "They're all over the place! Get out of here!"

He was answered by a fusillade of bullets that ripped through the leaves and branches around him and thudded into the tree trunks.

"*Veil? Are you all right?*"

"Be quiet! Get out of here! Run!"

There were more shots. Veil ducked and cursed when he heard Reyna call out what he assumed was a warning in K'ung.

There was an answering cry—a distant, ululating, banshee howl that filled the void of night like a physical presence and seemed to come from all directions at once; it began as a low, quavering moan, then abruptly climbed the scale to a warbling, high-pitched scream broken by clicks.

The strange, chilling cry was repeated once, and in the

deep, prolonged silence that followed, it was as if time had been stopped.

That silence was broken by Reyna's startled scream of terror.

"Don't hurt her!" Veil shouted as he ran toward the sound of Reyna's voice. "I'm coming out!"

"Veil, stay away!"

Guns barked in the darkness, and bullets slapped through the leaves just above Veil's head, but he kept running. He shifted the gun in his waistband back against his spine, then slowed as he approached the open, moonlit area in front of the trees where he had left Reyna. He sucked in a deep breath, then slowly walked out into the cold, pale moonlight. He stepped up on a grave marker and raised his hands in the air.

"Here I am," Veil announced, tensing his stomach muscles in anticipation of a bullet he was certain was about to slam into him. "Don't hurt the woman."

A disembodied voice came from somewhere inside the wooded area. "Right this way, pal."

Veil, keeping his arms raised, stepped down from the grave marker and walked toward the sound of the voice. He sighted Reyna the moment he passed into the trees. She was standing in front of a large oak tree, flanked by two men with guns. The man to her left had the fingers of one hand wrapped in her hair and was holding Reyna's head back at a sharp angle. The second man had his gun pointed at Veil's chest.

"That's it," the short, swarthy man holding Reyna said as Veil came within a few paces of them. Veil stopped. The man turned his head slightly, shouted, "I've got Kendry and the woman! Any sign of the African?"

"No!" a man's voice called back. "Hey, that son of a bitch killed Richie!"

"What do we do with them now?" the swarthy man asked his partner.

"We know the nigger's out there; that had to be him doing the screeching. We gotta go out and get him."

"Maybe he'll come to us if he knows we're going to kill his friends."

"Nah. The guy's a fucking savage. He won't give a shit. We're wasting our time with these two. Let's kill 'em like Nagle said we should do in the first place, then we'll go help the other guys look."

"Right," the swarthy man said perfunctorily, tightening his grip on Reyna's hair as he leveled his gun at Veil's head.

Veil watched the man's finger begin to tighten on the trigger. He was about to dive and roll to the side when a dark, silent shape literally seemed to rise from the night behind the man holding Reyna. There was a strangled scream, and suddenly there was an arrow protruding from the man's neck. The dead man's finger twitched on the trigger, sending a bullet whining past Veil's left ear.

Startled, the second man had jumped, then started to turn around as his partner had screamed. What he saw was a black wraith hurtling through the air toward him. The gunman shrieked and fired wildly as a spear narrowly missed his head. Then the bushman was on him. The man pounded at Toby's shoulders with the butt of his gun. Finally Toby's body went limp, and his fingers slipped from the man's throat as he slumped to the ground and lay still.

There was no time for Veil to pull his gun from his belt, and no way to fire past Reyna if he could. He leapt forward and swung. The gunman, taking aim at Toby, caught Veil's movement out of the corner of his eye and turned just enough to take the full force of the blow over his left ear. Veil's fist smashed into the man's temple, crushing the thin layer of bone and the brain beneath.

Reyna dropped down beside the fallen Toby as Veil grabbed his gun, crouched and turned, ready to fire at any sound or movement.

"Hey!" a voice shouted somewhere out in the night. "What the hell's going on over there?"

Veil knelt down beside the sobbing Reyna and felt for Toby's pulse. "He's alive," Veil said, relieved to feel the faint but steady beat of the bushman's heart, "but barely. The wound on his head looks as if it may be infected, and I wouldn't be surprised if he has a concussion."

163

"Hey, Jimmy!" the voice called. "You guys still over there?" There was a pause, then a tense, "Okay, I'm going to get some help!"

"Let's go," Veil said, lifting Toby in his arms. "You take the Nal-toon."

"Go where?"

"Straight ahead, through the bottleneck and into the other section. We need a place to hide, and this certainly isn't it."

"I'm going ahead," Reyna said, picking up the Nal-toon and darting away, gliding over the ground like some huge moth in the moonlight.

Cradling Toby high on his chest, Veil trotted at a steady pace and, after a time, emerged from the bottleneck into a field of older graves marked by towering tombstones and an occasional mausoleum.

Suddenly Reyna, out of breath from the exertion of running with the Nal-toon, appeared beside him. "There's an old mausoleum off to the left," she said, panting. "A big one. It's hard to be certain with all the shadow, but it looks as if the seal might be broken and the door slightly open. The problem is that there's a high fence around the whole thing, and it's padlocked."

"Go," Veil said curtly.

For the past few minutes the night had been filled with the sound of sirens as the police, alerted by the gunfire, had converged on the cemetery from all directions. Now, as Veil jogged after Reyna, beams of light began carving the darkness around them, and the static-broken voices of men speaking through walkie-talkies could be heard.

Veil rounded a sculpted angel and found himself before a huge, fenced-in mausoleum. Reyna, shaking with panic, was punching at the ancient, rusted padlock on the gate.

"Get away from there," Veil said evenly as he gently lay Toby down on the ground.

Veil stood with his legs slightly apart before the lock, staring down at it, emptying his mind of all concern about the strength of the metal and the approaching police. He waited until he felt power manifest itself as a small, warm ball just behind his navel, then abruptly raised his right arm and chopped with the heel of his palm against the upper part of the lock. Nothing happened. Calmly, ignoring the walkie-talkie voices that now seemed to be all around them, Veil relaxed his muscles, then squared off again. He waited for his power to focus, then snapped his hand at the lock again. The lock snapped apart.

Reyna removed the lock and pushed the gate open. Veil lifted Toby in his arms, stepped into the mausoleum courtyard, turned, and waited. Reyna stepped through with the Nal-toon, then closed the gate behind her, wincing as it squeaked on its rusty hinges. She reached through the bars, put the lock back in place, and squeezed it shut. Rust and friction held it in place.

"You go ahead!" Reyna whispered urgently, placing the Nal-toon on top of Toby's still body. "I have to clean up behind us!"

Veil crossed the courtyard and squeezed through the narrow opening where the door was ajar and into the utter darkness of the crypt. He eased Toby and the Nal-toon to the floor, then turned and watched as Reyna, crabbing backward on her hands and knees, attempted to erase the evidence of their passage. Her hands flew as she straightened the tall grass and clumps of weeds that had been bent or crushed. She made it to the crypt and slipped through the opening just as two uniformed policemen appeared from behind the stone angel.

Veil and Reyna huddled together as one of the policemen tested the gate. There was the grating squeal of metal—but the lock stayed in place. The policemen moved on.

Veil and Reyna moved back and sat down on the dirt floor of the moldering crypt. Despite the fact that they were touching, they could not see each other. Except for the bar of moonlight at the opening, the heavy, dank darkness was total. Things scuttled around them on the floor. They sat without speaking, listening to Toby's rattling, hoarse breathing as they waited for the dawn.

165

CHAPTER SIXTEEN

Veil rested on his haunches, back braced against the rough, clammy stone of the crypt, staring out through the narrow gap at the entrance. He felt Reyna come up behind him, grunted with pleasure when she put her hands on his shoulders and began to knead the thick, stiff muscles around his neck and collarbone.

"How's Toby?" Veil asked quietly.

Reyna sighed as she rested her head on Veil's back. "He's conscious, but he's burning up with fever. The wound on his head looks terrible. It's very swollen, and there's a lot of pus."

Veil straightened up and went to the rear of the mausoleum where, two hours earlier, they had built a small fire to see by and to ease Toby's racking chills. Cracks in the stone provided some ventilation, and Reyna had carefully selected the wood to be burned, but there was still enough smoke to make Veil's eyes tear. Toby did not seem to mind. The warrior-prince sat propped up against the fungus-covered burial vault. His one good eye glowed like a cat's in the firelight as he stared back at Veil. Veil smiled, but Toby's face remained impassive.

"I'm looking at one tough man," Veil said thoughtfully. "I can't believe he got this far, much less had the will, strength, and guts to attack those two men. Please tell him for me that he is the finest warrior I have ever met, and I honor him."

Reyna translated Veil's remarks, but Toby remained silent. He took a large pinch of the heroin that had dribbled from the base of the Nal-toon, sniffed it. His eyelids fluttered.

"From the way he's been snorting that stuff," Veil continued, "I'd say he's on his way to becoming a full-blown addict."

"It's all right," Reyna replied in a firm voice. "It's a miracle that a substance which destroys countless lives helped to save Toby's. It kept him going. God provided it for him. When the time comes that Toby no longer needs it, God will take away the craving." She paused, bowed her head. "Damn, I could hang myself for losing that radio. Now we don't know what's happening or who could be out in the cemetery looking for us. Toby needs medicine and bandages, and we *all* need food and water."

"We can't move yet, Reyna. You'd better believe that the bad guys are still out there someplace." As well as Carl Nagle, Veil thought, but he didn't say so. "What were you two talking about before?"

Reyna shrugged her frail shoulders. "Nothing important. I was just trying to ease Toby's pain with talk—and reassure him. If and when we do get some medicine for Toby, I'm afraid that it may be a job to get him to take it. He thinks the heroin is the only medicine he needs."

"Well, that's understandable. It's all he's had to hold him up so far."

"Also, he still isn't sure he trusts us." She paused, smiled thinly. "When I picked him up at the airport, I told him we were in New York City. All this while he's been thinking that we're all one tribe called 'Newyorkcities.' Betrayal of the tribe is not something a K'ung can easily understand. Good grief."

Veil studied Toby, the filthy, festering wound on the bushman's face, and made a decision. "I know something about thirst," he said in a flat voice, "and this man is suffering. I'm going out to get some things. We can't wait until night. Without water, Toby may not last through the day."

"No!" Reyna cried as she grabbed at Veil's sleeve. Toby started at Reyna's sharp tone, but Reyna turned and spoke reassuringly to him. Toby eased himself back against the vault, and Reyna again spoke to Veil. "You can't go. What if something happens to you?"

"Nothing's going to happen to me."

Reyna emphatically shook her head. "Although I sometimes wonder, you are not Superman. You could be killed, or arrested by the police. Without you Toby is lost. I can't carry him, and I don't know what plans you've made. It won't make any difference if I'm caught. Besides, I move as well as you do—and there's a good deal less of me to spot."

"No," Veil said curtly. "I don't want to frighten you, but I also shouldn't have to remind you that Carl Nagle could be out there somewhere."

Reyna paled at the mention of the man's name, but her mouth remained set in a determined line. She raised her chin slightly. "Toby does need water to make it through the day, Veil. I'm going to get it, and you can't stop me." She turned to speak to Toby, but the bushman had lapsed into unconsciousness.

"Here," Veil said resignedly, handing Reyna a slip of paper. "If you can get to a phone, call this number. Either Victor Raskolnikov or a man named Walrus will be at the other end. It's a secure line, so you can talk freely. Both men know who you are. Let them know what's happening."

Reyna nodded as she put the paper into a pocket in her jeans. She kissed Veil quickly, then slipped out into the day.

. • •

Reyna had been gone almost an hour and a half. Veil was debating whether or not to go look for her when she suddenly appeared at the entrance. She was carrying two large bags of groceries.

"Hey, am I glad to see you!" Veil said as he took Reyna in his arms.

"Take it easy, Veil!" Reyna replied with a grin, her eyes gleaming. Relief at returning safely had made her euphoric. "You're squashing the sandwiches!"

"Anybody see you?"

"Are you kidding? Spot the chief tracker? No way." Reyna's smile slowly faded. "There are still men out there, though, and they're not cops."

"Were you able to talk to Victor or Walrus?"

"Walrus." Reyna paused, smiled. "He's a funny man."

"Mmm. His friends think so."

"I told him that we had Toby and that we were going to lie low for a while here."

"Is everything ready in Flushing?"

"Yes. He said to tell you that everything's in place and he's ready to go when you are. He gave me another number, and we're to call him as soon as we get out of here."

"Good." Veil took the bags from Reyna, set them on the floor, then took Reyna in his arms again and kissed her hard.

"I'm afraid I spent all the money you gave me, Veil," Reyna said when he had released her. "Do we have anything left?"

"Just change for phone calls," Veil replied as he began to empty the bags Reyna had brought. He set antiseptic, bandages, and bottled water off to one side. "But money's the least of our worries right now. Damn, you're lucky you didn't break your back carrying all this stuff. You are one hell of a lot stronger than you look."

"You and Toby give me strength, Veil," Reyna said seriously.

169

"No. The strength is all yours."

"Oh! You'll find a *New York Times* and *Daily News* at the bottom of one of those bags. Just in case you want to keep track of our press notices."

"Outstanding," Veil said as he took the newspapers from the bag and began scanning the leads.

Reyna went to Toby, spoke to him softly and at length before opening a bottle of water and giving it to him. He drank it without hurrying and gave no indication that he wanted more. She gave him three pears, which he wolfed down while Reyna used water from a second bottle to begin washing his face wound.

Veil finished with the papers, then went to help Reyna medicate and bandage Toby's wound. The K'ung warrior sat stoically, sucking on an orange, as the man and woman worked on him. The only sign of his discomfort was an occasional flickering of an eyelid. He finally agreed to swallow four aspirin, after what seemed to Veil a long and torturous debate. But he also sniffed a large amount of heroin.

"There were three other reported sightings of Toby last night," Veil said as he gently rubbed antiseptic salve over Toby's eye and the side of his face. "All in different sections of Queens. The police must be getting tired of it, which could explain why they aren't roaming all over the cemetery right now."

"But the police *must* know he's here," Reyna insisted. "What about the bodies of the men who were killed?"

"The police claim it was gang warfare."

"In a cemetery, in the middle of the night? Do you think they really believe it?"

"No," Veil replied after a pause. "The arrow through the one man's throat is a giveaway, but it's not even mentioned in the stories. The police may not want to create a panic in the neighborhood, or they don't want a mob tearing up the cemetery, which is exactly what would happen if the police told all they knew or suspected. You're right—they have to know we're here. They'll be waiting and watching."

170

"How did the men who attacked us last night know where to look for us?"

"Nagle. They were his men—probably street thugs too low on the totem pole to know he's a marked man."

Reyna's hands began to tremble as she finished bandaging Toby's head. "Besides us, he's the only one who knew for certain that Toby was in the building. He looked at a map and made the right guesses. He knows, doesn't he?"

"I think so."

"You know so," Reyna said in a hollow voice. "We're trapped."

"We'll see," Veil said evenly. "Nobody—cops or crooks—can be certain that we didn't get out of here last night. In any case, it would take an army to guard the entire perimeter of this cemetery. There'll be cracks, and we'll get through. Let's not waste mental energy worrying about anything until we see what it is we have to worry about. Is the car where we left it?"

"Yes, but it looks to me like somebody's watching it."

"Shit," Veil said without emotion. "It figures, though. Nagel saw it. It means we're going to need other transportation."

"Lord, Veil, won't anything go right for us?"

Veil raised his eyebrows slightly. "Toby's still alive, isn't he? And we're all together. Doesn't Wesley Missionary College teach you people about mustard seeds?"

"*Touché*," Reyna answered with a wry grin. "You're right, of course. Can Walrus or Mr. Raskolnikov pick us up somewhere?"

"Using Victor is a possibility; Walrus has to stay where he is. The problem is that I'd also like to keep Victor where he is, right up to the point where I'm certain I don't need him by a telephone any longer." He paused, absently began to peel an orange. "Let me think about it."

•   •   •

"I need the heroin in the Nal-toon."

Reyna, who had been sitting next to Toby and cradling the K'ung in her arms, glanced up at the spot where Veil

171

had been standing in silence for more than an hour while night fell. She could not see him. "Why, Veil?"

"Talk to Toby."

"I don't think he'll give it to you, Veil," Reyna said guardedly.

"He has to, Reyna. It's our ticket out of here, if there is one. I can't use Walrus, Victor, or John—the doctor. I need them where they are."

"But how—"

"Talk to him, Reyna. Tell him he has to give it to me if he wants to get home."

Reyna sighed, then hugged Toby even closer to her. "Toby?" Reyna said in K'ung. "We have to talk about something important."

Toby answered with a grunt.

"We need the Nal-toon's blood-shilluk."

Toby abruptly drew away from Reyna, then hugged the Nal-toon close to his body. "I don't understand," he said thickly. "The blood of the Nal-toon is mine; it is a gift to me from God. It is very powerful medicine."

"The Nal-toon provided you with blood when you needed it for pain," Reyna said after a long, thoughtful pause. "Now it is needed to help us escape the warriors who are hunting us. It is needed because the Nal-toon wishes to return with you to your people. For that to happen, we need the blood."

"Why?"

"Veil will tell us. He has a plan. He is our chief, and we must do as he says."

"No!" Toby cried, wrapping both arms around the Nal-toon. "My father is chief, not this man!"

Suddenly, close by, church bells began to peal; their sound, clanging and insistent, vibrated in the air.

Reyna could think of no reason why church bells would be rung after sundown. "They toll for thee," she whispered in K'ung.

"What?"

"Nothing, Toby."

"The voice of the Nal-toon speaks differently here."

Reyna felt a chill run through her, and she sat up straighter. "Yes," she said carefully. "What you say is true—the Nal-toon does speak differently here." She paused, took a deep breath. "Tonight, Toby, the Nal-toon's voice is for you alone. It means that you must decide what your god is saying. I tell you that I will never betray you. I tell you that I will die before I will allow you to be captured and the Nal-toon taken away. I also speak for Veil. You must trust Veil, as you must trust me. We want to take you home. Veil has said that he needs the blood-shilluk in order to accomplish this, but it is you who must listen to your heart, and the voice of the Nal-toon, and decide whether or not he is telling the truth and can be trusted."

Toby sat very still for a long time, staring vacantly at a point somewhere above Reyna's head. Finally Toby held the Nal-toon out to the woman. His hands were steady. Reyna bowed her head to Toby, then reverently handed the Nal-toon to Veil, who had stepped into the small circle of light cast by the fire's burning embers.

Veil set the idol down, knelt, bowed to the idol and then to Toby. "Tell him I have to crack open the bottom," he said quietly. "Only the bottom. I won't damage anything else."

"He's given up his god to you, Veil. It means you can do with it what you want."

"I want his permission."

"Toby," Reyna said in K'ung, "Veil and the Nal-toon wish to honor you by asking for your personal permission to open the base so as to remove all of the blood-shilluk. It must be done."

Toby nodded slightly in Veil's direction. "The Nal-toon has spoken to my heart and told me to trust this man."

"It's all right, Veil."

Veil sat down next to Toby on the floor of the crypt. He braced the Nal-toon across his knees with his left hand, then placed the fingers of his right against the false plywood bottom and began to apply steady pressure. The cracked wood squeaked. Veil stopped and glanced at Toby, but the bushman was staring straight ahead, his face impassive. Veil applied sudden, intense pressure, and the plywood cracked apart. Toby shuddered slightly, but otherwise did not react.

Veil quickly pulled the jagged pieces of plywood from around the base, then reached inside the hollowed-out idol. He pulled out three plastic bags, each one slightly larger than his fist. Two of the bags were intact, but the heroin in the third was trickling from a small gash in the plastic, caused by a plywood splinter. Veil pinched the bag closed, then set it down on the floor next to the others. "There it is," he said quietly. "That's what all the shooting is about."

Reyna whistled softly. "Pure white heroin. There must be enough junk there to supply all the city's addicts for a year."

"Does it bother you, Reyna?"

"No," Reyna answered evenly. "There's no craving. All that happened to me . . . it's like it happened to another person, in another lifetime."

Veil took out his handkerchief and poured some of the heroin from the broken bag into it. "You'd better save this for Toby," he said, holding the handkerchief out to Reyna. "He'll need it."

Reyna studied Toby's face for a few moments, finally shook her head. "No," she said. "He won't need it."

"He's in a lot of pain, Reyna, and we may have to move fast. He's an addict now, and he'll start suffering from withdrawal symptoms if he doesn't get it. This doesn't seem like the time to expect him to kick the habit cold turkey."

Reyna turned to Toby, spoke in K'ung. "Veil has said that you are a great warrior—but he does not yet fully understand how great. He thinks that you still need the Nal-toon's blood-shilluk, but I know you do not. You are with us now, and you no longer have need of the blood-shilluk. Your pain and sickness will still be great, but now the Nal-toon asks you to bear the pain without the great gift. Can you do this?"

"Why do you insult me?" Toby replied, looking away.

"He'll do without the heroin, Veil."

"Reyna—"

"He'll do without it," Reyna repeated in a firm voice. "He has to get off it sometime, so he may as well start now. Besides, I assume you don't want him spaced-out."

"I don't want him in pain," Veil said, folding the handkerchief and placing it next to the plastic bags.

"He'll be all right, Veil. What happens now?"

"First I want to say something," Veil said, reaching out and squeezing Reyna's hand. "You put up a good front, but I know what it cost you to go out there alone. Carl Nagle's out there someplace waiting for us—and you know it. I just want to say that I think you're one hell of a woman."

Reyna smiled. "Why, thank you, sir."

"I have to leave for a little while. I will be careful. I'll be back, and I'll try not to take too long."

"All right," Reyna answered in a small voice.

"Just in case, you have the telephone numbers for—"

"I don't want to know about any 'just in case,' Veil. You make sure you come back."

Veil picked up the broken plastic bag and put it in his jacket pocket. "See you later," he said, and slipped out into the night.

CHAPTER SEVENTEEN

"**H**ey, you."

Veil watched as the man started, then quickly turned and nervously peered into the darkness.

"That's right, you!"

This time the man drew a gun from a shoulder holster and pointed it over the stone wall separating the sidewalk from the cemetery. "Who's there?!"

"Just stand still and listen," Veil said softly. "Do what I say, and you could end up with more money than you'll know how to spend."

The man grunted angrily, put one hand on top of the stone wall, and vaulted over it into the darkness beyond. He landed on an incline and cursed as he fell. However, he was a lithe, agile man and was almost immediately up on his feet, running toward the spot from where he thought the voice had come. There was no one there. He searched the surrounding area as best he could in the moonlight but still found no one. He listened, gun held ready, but could hear only the sound of his own, slightly nasal breathing.

"Okay," the man said through clenched teeth as he slowly turned. "I'm listening."

Veil let the man wait. Ten minutes went by before the man cursed under his breath, turned, and walked back the way he had come. He was back at his post on the sidewalk when Veil spoke again.

"Hey, you, dummy. You almost blew it, pal. I picked you because you looked fairly bright. It just goes to show that looks can be deceiving. I want you to stand still and listen. A few minutes of your time could be worth millions to you. If you're not interested, I'll go talk to somebody with more brains. I know there are at least a half dozen of you guys hanging around."

"I'm listening. What's this about millions?"

"What's your name?"

"Sloane," the man said after some hesitation.

"All right, Sloane—"

"You Kendry?"

"First go up the block and tell your buddy that you have to take a crap or something. You have to come with me for a few minutes, and everything will be explained to you. If you try to tip off your buddy—if anyone tries to follow us in—you've blown it. Just keep thinking of what you could do with a few million dollars."

"Okay," Sloane mumbled. "Don't go away."

"Just remember to do exactly as I said."

As Sloane walked away, Veil moved silently through the trees and underbrush on a parallel course. He listened to the exchange between the two gunmen, then moved back with Sloane.

"I did it," Sloane said to the darkness beyond the wall. "What now?"

"Throw your gun over the wall."

"Hey, now, hold on a second!"

"You don't want to do it, don't. I'm gone."

"Okay!"

"Keep your voice down. And move slowly. You're going to be a rich man if you keep your cool, Sloane, but you'd

177

better make up your mind. You told your buddy you'd be back in ten minutes."

Sloane withdrew his gun from its holster, tossed it over the wall.

"Now you come over. Easy does it. Move off to your left."

Sloane did as he was told. He'd gone about fifteen yards into the cemetery when Veil suddenly appeared in front of him. Sloane stopped walking and stared at the muzzle of his own gun, which was pointing at his chest.

"You are Veil Kendry, aren't you?"

"Yes."

"Nagle talks a lot about you," Sloane said with a crooked smile. "I'm waiting to hear what you have to say, Kendry."

"Don't be impatient. Keep moving to your left, but stay inside the trees. Watch how you walk. You attract any attention with those big feet of yours, and I disappear."

•   •   •

Sloane squinted in the smoky air and grunted. In the dim, flickering light of the small fire he could just make out the objects of Nagle's hunt. The woman and the African. The idol.

"Here, catch," Veil said as he perfunctorily tossed the torn plastic bag at Sloane. Startled, the man juggled the bag in the semidarkness. White powder floated in the air, then slowly drifted down to the ground. "That's pure heroin. Check it out for yourself."

Sloane's hand trembled as he put a thumb and forefinger through the tear in the plastic, pinched some powder, tasted it. "Jesus H. Christ," he murmured. "I can't believe you're throwing this shit around."

"Good stuff?"

"Good?" Sloane wore a slightly dazed expression on his face. "What's left in this bag is worth a fortune. I'd heard rumors that this guy was carrying around something big . . ."

"I assume you'd know how to get rid of it?" Veil asked wryly.

Sloane had begun to sweat. His eyes were teary from the smoke and he rubbed them. "A little bit at a time, over the years," he said in a dry, cracking voice. "Maybe. It's suicide to cross the big guys on something like this."

"So? Like you said, you can spend the rest of your life selling it off in small bits. It sounds to me like a great way to beat inflation. On the other hand, they tell me that money is power. With the money you could get from the sale of that heroin, you might grow pretty big yourself."

The man could not take his eyes off the bag in his hand. "If they caught me, they'd take me apart with a chain saw," he said distantly.

"Getting big money means taking big risks, Sloane. You can always turn us in and collect a few thousand from your boss, can't you? You'll sleep better—but you'll also be making peanuts for the rest of your life while those 'big guys' jerk you around. Sooner or later small potatoes like you end up in jail, anyway. When you get canned for some penny-ante crime, you'll have plenty of opportunity to think about this opportunity you pissed away."

Sloane finally looked up from the bag. His eyes were round and bright in the firelight. "What am I supposed to do for this?"

"You've already earned what you're holding in your hand; you can walk out of here with it. Think of it as a down payment. There are two more bags like that one—bigger, because they're not torn. That bag's been dribbling for days."

"Jesus."

"Do as I ask and they're both yours."

Sloane's eyes went back to the bag in his hand, then to the fine powder strewn on the ground around the glowing embers of the fire. "What do you want me to do?" he asked hoarsely.

"What time do you get off?"

"I was supposed to be relieved an hour and a half ago."

"Then somebody may be there when you get back, so you'd better come up with a good story. First, we need a car. *Rent* one, don't steal it. Leave the car parked at the curb, on this side of the street, at the place where I spoke to you—or as close as you can without being spotted. Bring the keys and the rental slip to me, here."

Sloane glanced at Toby, who had been partially hidden in shadow. The fire suddenly flared, and the gunman could see the K'ung's bandaged head. Toby's good eye, glowing red and yellow in the firelight, stared balefully back at Sloane, who shuddered.

"Where are you going?" Sloane asked, still transfixed by Toby's unrelenting gaze.

"That's not your concern."

Sloane hefted the bag in his hand. "Dropping off a rented car doesn't seem like much to do for the fortune you're offering me," he said carefully.

"I knew you were bright. There's more—and this is the exciting part. I don't want anyone to see the car, but I do want you to be seen. You find someone you know on watch, go up to him. Tell him you're all worked up and can't sleep. Say you want to hang around because you don't want to miss anything if it happens. Say whatever you please, but be sure you make it sound convincing."

The man shook his head. "That's going to be tough to pull off."

"Ah, but think of all the money you're going to get for a single performance," Veil said evenly. "After you've set that business up, you bring me the keys and the rental slip. You wander off maybe a half mile up the cemetery, then you start yelling and shooting. You've seen us. You keep it up until you've got everyone running to you. That will give us time to get to the car."

"What am I supposed to say when they see you're not there?"

"Use your imagination," Veil said coldly. "That's what you're getting paid for. Just tell them we ran up the cemetery."

Sloane thought about it for a few moments, then nodded. His hands were shaking. "I'll do it. How will I get the rest of the heroin?"

"I'll be carrying it with me when we leave. I'll leave the bags behind the wall at the precise place where you jumped over. When I'm certain you've done your job, I drop the bags. That's it. After we're gone, you can pick up the heroin anytime you like."

"How do I know there are two other bags?" Sloane asked suspiciously.

Veil took two steps to his left, reached down into the darkness, held up the bags.

"How do I know you'll leave them like you say?"

"You don't, but that bag you're holding in your hand should buy us a little good faith. You were happy with the one; I didn't even have to tell you about the other two. We have no use for the heroin, so there's no reason why we shouldn't leave it—assuming you do your job. On the other hand, we have to trust *you* completely, and you might well decide that a bag in the hand is worth two behind the wall. Ours is the greater risk."

"All right," Sloane said sullenly.

"Remember this, Sloan: If you try crossing us, I'll make sure you never keep the bag you've got. You'll be killed. The point is that we have to trust each other if all of us are going to get what we want. It's a straight deal. You set it up so that we can get away, and you become an instant millionaire; try to screw us, and there's no way you can get away with it."

"I said I'd do it."

Veil glanced at his watch. "I'll see you back here in a couple of hours."

"I don't know if I can find a car-rental place open at this time of night."

"If you can't, it will be the most expensive car you never rented."

"You have to give me back my gun. I need it in case someone decides to check."

Veil took out his own gun and covered Sloane while he handed over the other man's revolver. Sloane slipped it back into his shoulder holster.

"Where's Nagle keeping himself?"

"I don't know," the gunman replied. "I've talked to him a couple of times on the phone, but I haven't seen him. One of the other guys said he thought he saw him cruising

181

around in a car, but he couldn't be sure. Hell, we're all working with no money up front."

"Then you're lucky I found you, aren't you?"

"I'll be back as soon as I can."

"Just keep thinking of those other two bags of heroin, Sloane."

The gunman carefully placed the bag of heroin in the pocket of his jacket, then slipped out of the crypt. Reyna followed him, replacing the lock on the gate and again straightening out the grass as she retreated.

• • •

Veil heard Reyna's low whistle from the far end of the field of tombstones. It meant that Sloane was on his way back. Alone.

Veil was standing just inside a dense stand of fir trees, fifty yards west of the mausoleum. Toby, the Nal-toon wrapped in his arms, lay unconscious at Veil's feet.

Sloane came into view in the moonlight, walking quickly along the line of trees, heading toward the mausoleum. Reyna suddenly appeared from the shadows, stuck the gun Veil had given her into Sloane's ribs, then grabbed his arm and pulled him into the trees. A minute later they both emerged from the darkness of the fir stand.

"Here are the keys," Sloane said nervously as he handed Veil a plastic key ring and a yellow rental slip. The night was cool, but the man's face glistened with sweat. "It's a new white Pontiac, and it's parked at the curb right where you told me."

"You look jumpy," Veil said evenly. "Relax. Remember that the show's only half over. You have to go up the cemetery and make a lot of noise."

Sloane blinked slowly, and his lips drew back to reveal broken, yellow teeth. "I need to have another bag before I do that."

"No. That wasn't the agreement. With two bags you might feel that you're far enough ahead of the game to walk away. Do your job and you'll get the bags. They'll be where I said they'd be."

"You got them with you?"

"They're in a safe place. When I hear you start shooting and yelling, I'll get them and take them to the wall."

"*You'll get them now, Kendry!*" Carl Nagle's voice, strangely hollow and tortured, washed over them like acid from the deep well of night.

"Holy Mother of God," Sloane croaked as he clawed frantically for the gun in his shoulder holster.

The explosive chatter of the submachine gun was deafening as the individual rounds blended into one jagged torrent of sound that reverberated off the massive tombstones and echoed in the darkness. Sloane's body was blown backward against a tree and momentarily pinned there by bullets; it jerked like a broken puppet, spouting blood from a dozen different places.

Then the firing stopped, leaving only faint echoes as a counterpoint to the rasping sound of Sloane's pulped corpse sliding down the tree trunk to the ground.

Carl Nagle walked unsteadily out from the trees, and suddenly the air was filled with the putrid, gagging odor of rotting flesh. As the huge man moved into the moonlight, Veil and Reyna could see that he held the Uzi braced in the crook of his left arm. There was thick, caked spittle on his cracked lips, and his eyes gleamed like lumps of banked coals in the puffed, waxy flesh of his face.

Nagle's right arm had ballooned out of the sling that supported it; it jutted grotesquely from his body, like a deformed, rotting gourd that had somehow taken root in his shoulder. Suppurating, swollen to almost twice its normal size, the flesh of the arm was a flaking, blackish green. Streaks of crimson radiated from the bicep to the hand, and up through the neck.

"Gas gangrene," Reyna murmured in horror.

Nagle's eyes had turned mud-black with fever and madness. He chuckled insanely as he leaned back, aimed the muzzle of the gun just over their heads, and fired off a burst into the trees. Leaves and broken branches rained down on Reyna and Veil, who had taken the woman in his arms and was trying to shield her with his body.

"The Lord is my shepherd," Reyna prayed. "I shall not want . . ."

183

Reyna flowed out of Veil's arms, crumpling to the ground. There were confused shouts all around them as men tried to determine from which direction the shooting had come. Pistol shots cracked as men stumbled in the darkness, firing at shadows and each other. Sirens wailed.

". . . He maketh me to lie down in green pastures, He restoreth my soul . . ."

"Listen to me, Nagle," Veil said carefully, his eyes fixed on the ribbed, black muzzle of the submachine gun pointed at his chest. "The cops are going to be here any minute."

Nagle's laughter was high-pitched and chilling. "I *am* the cops!" he howled. "I'm already here!"

Veil tensed slightly, but did not move. Nagle was six feet away, and Veil knew that it would take only a twitch of the man's finger to cut him in half.

". . . He prepareth a table before me . . ."

Nagle coughed hard, then glanced over at Sloane's bloody corpse. "Stupid shit," he mumbled, his words blurred by pain and insanity. "You're all stupid shits. Didn't you think this idiot would be *missed*? I've had men watching the cemetery, but I've been watching them. Sloane was so nervous when he came out of here that I thought he was going to have a heart attack. Then he brings back a rented car. Stupid shit."

"You're a dead man, Nagle," Veil said quietly. "You know it. This may be your last chance to do something decent. Stop the killing. If you believe you have a soul, take this opportunity to save it."

"Fuck my soul," Nagle slurred, spittle dribbling from the corners of his mouth. "I'm gonna be all right, Kendry. You can't kill Carl Nagle with a lousy toy arrow. Where's the rest of the heroin?"

"I'll give it to you if you put the gun down."

". . . Yea, though I walk through the valley of the shadow of death, I will fear no evil . . ."

The muzzle of the gun swung down toward Reyna, held steady. "You give it to me *now*, Kendry, or I make the girl a few ounces heavier."

". . . Thy rod and Thy staff, they comfort me . . ."

"Don't do it, Nagle!"

Nagle's eyes and the gun barrel swung back toward Veil, and Reyna suddenly sprang to her feet. Shrieking, she leapt at Nagle, startling the man and causing the burst of fire from his gun to miss Veil. Then Reyna was on him, using both hands to pummel and claw at his gangrenous arm. Blood and pus spurted from the swollen, drumhead-tight flesh. Nagle's mouth dropped open, and he uttered a guttural, soaring, animal howl; the gun dropped to the ground, and he slowly toppled backward, his left arm groping in the air as if searching for some invisible rope that would hold him up. He ended up on his back, still howling and clawing at the air, as Reyna, screaming with mindless rage, methodically kicked at the rotting arm, bursting and shredding the putrefied flesh from the bone.

With her screams wed to Nagle's in a horrible duet of insane rage and death, Reyna wheeled and picked up the submachine gun. She pointed the muzzle at Nagle's head and pulled the trigger. The gun chattered and kicked wildly, but Reyna kept her finger pressed on the trigger until the clip was empty and Nagle's head had been transformed into a pulpy mass that was spread over the ground, glistening in the moonlight.

Veil tore the gun from Reyna's hands and threw it into the woods. "He's dead, Reyna!" he shouted, grabbing Reyna's arms and shaking her. "It's over! Stop it!"

Reyna's mindless screeching gradually died down to a drawn-out moan. Her shoulders sagged, and she slumped against Veil's chest as a helicopter swooped overhead, bathing the field of tombstones in a white light that glittered off specks of marble and polished granite in the stone. The panicked gunfire in the night had stopped, but there were thrashing sounds all around them.

"I'd say it's just about time to move on, lady," Veil said quietly.

"Oh, Veil, how can we?" Reyna sighed, her voice barely audible. "It's finished, but at least we tried the best we could."

"It's not over till the fat lady sings, Reyna. Do you hear her?"

185

Reyna stepped back and looked at Veil. Slowly her face broke into a crooked grin. "She may not be singing yet, but I surely do hear her clearing her throat."

"Let's go," Veil said, lifting Toby in his arms. "You take the lead."

Reyna picked up the Nal-toon. "Straight down the cemetery?"

"It's too late to make it back to the mausoleum, so that seems as good a direction as any."

With Reyna leading the way, Veil trotted through the stand of fir trees. Men moved in the darkness around them. Suddenly Reyna stopped, turned back, and frantically waved at him before diving into some underbrush. Veil stepped behind a tree just as two uniformed policemen, shining powerful flashlights, emerged from the trees to his right and walked over the spot where he had been. Their walkie-talkies crackled in the darkness.

Veil hurried forward until he came abreast of Reyna. Both stepped behind another large tree as a portly policeman, red-faced and gasping for breath, ran past with his gun drawn. Reyna darted ahead, and Veil followed.

Then they reached the end of the cemetery.

Reyna, running a few paces ahead, abruptly stopped and stifled a cry. "Oh, no," she moaned as Veil came up beside her.

Before them was the rolling, manicured expanse of a golf course on which scores of heavily armed police trotted forward like a phalanx of Roman legionnaires; flashlights bobbed up and down, boring holes in the night. There was no place left to run.

Veil caught a movement out of the corner of his eye. He turned, saw Reyna place the Nal-toon on the ground. She pulled her T-shirt over her head, then slipped out of her jeans, underpants, and sneakers.

"Put the sneakers on Toby," Reyna said breathlessly as she scooped up a handful of the loamy soil and began to darken her body. "Your jacket is big enough to cover the rest of him."

Veil watched as Reyna wrapped her clothes around the Nal-toon and clutched the idol to her breast. "Reyna, you can't—"

"Oh, yes I can! *Go*, Veil! I'll get the cops off your back. Just keep going! I'll find you!"

"Reyna!"

But Reyna was already gone, sprinting out from the line of trees and across the moonlit expanse of the golf course. Immediately there were shouts. A helicopter rose from behind a banked sand trap, its air wash blowing sand that swirled and eddied in the glare of the craft's searchlights.

Veil waited, staring anxiously after Reyna's racing figure. Then the helicopter and police moved off after her, and the area directly in front of him was suddenly shrouded in darkness, providing him with a long, deserted corridor of night.

Toby was now semiconscious. Veil set the K'ung warrior on his feet. He wrapped his jacket around Toby, then pushed Reyna's sneakers on his feet. Deciding that they now had as good a chance in the streets as on the golf course, Veil steered Toby to the right, along the line of trees.

Toby tried to walk but could not. Again Veil swept the man up in his arms and hurried forward. There were no signs of any police.

He emerged from the line of trees at the point where the cemetery, the golf course, and the sidewalk intersected. Dozens of people were milling around in the street and on the sidewalk. Veil feared he might immediately be surrounded, but hardly anyone even bothered to glance at him or his burden; people were maneuvering for position in order to see out over the golf course, and everyone seemed to be talking at once, asking for or volunteering information.

"Get out of the way," Veil said, shouldering people aside. "I've got an injured person here."

A man called, "What's happening?"

"It looks as though they may have the African trapped in the cemetery," Veil replied. "Let me through, please."

And then he was through the crowd. He slipped through

a line of police cars parked at the curb with their motors running and lights flashing, then hurried across the street. He trotted into the next block, then stepped back into the night-shadows and waited. Ten minutes later Reyna, dressed and carrying the Nal-toon, emerged from an alleyway between two buildings near the intersection. Veil stepped out from the shadows. Reyna saw him, hurried down the street.

"*Voilà!*" Reyna said with a broad, triumphant grin. "Surprised?"

"*Surprised* isn't quite the word for it, but I can't think of what is," Veil replied, sighing with relief and gently touching his forehead to Reyna's. "How the hell did you get out of there?"

"A piece of cake. I made it into a stand of trees, hid the Nal-toon behind one, sat down, and started screaming. When the cops came, I just pointed and said that my boyfriend was chasing some crazy, naked black man who'd tripped over us. They ogled me for a while, then ran on. And here I am."

"I'm suitably impressed."

Reyna touched the unconscious Toby's forehead. "Lord, Veil, he's burning up."

"I know. We're running out of time. Check the parked cars and see if there are keys in any of them."

Reyna ran up and down the block, trying the doors and looking into the windows of the parked cars. She darted across the street, repeated the procedure, then ran back to Veil. "Nothing," she said, panting. "Do you want me to steal a police car?"

"No. They'd have us in five minutes. I could break into one and try jumping it, but the cops could be coming out of there anytime now. I'm afraid that carrying around Toby and the Nal-toon makes us a bit conspicuous." He paused, thinking, finally continued, "We're too close to what we want to risk losing it all by rushing things. The whole area's probably crawling with cops. After all that shooting in the cemetery, there could be roadblocks. What we need is a place to hole up, at least for a couple of hours."

"Veil, the racetrack! Aqueduct's only a few blocks away. If we could get in, there'd be water to cool Toby, and telephones! Do you think—"

"I certainly do," Veil said. "Let's go."

"Toby must be getting awfully heavy."

"No. Keep a steady pace. We're exposed now, and looking like we're in a big hurry will only draw more attention. Stay close and try to keep the Nal-toon between us."

They walked on, Reyna keeping close to Veil and using the Nal-toon and her shoulder to help support Toby's weight as best she could. People stopped and stared at them, but they continued walking at an even pace, their eyes straight ahead.

"I can see the parking lot!" Reyna cried as they turned a corner. "Veil, we're going to make it!"

Suddenly Toby stirred, opened his eye, spoke.

"Veil? Toby says that he can walk."

Veil set Toby on his feet. The K'ung swayed unsteadily, but remained on his feet. Reyna pressed the Nal-toon against his chest. Toby's arms came up, wrapped themselves tightly around his god. Veil and Reyna gripped Toby's arms, and they hurried forward until finally they stepped over a chain into the darkness of one of the racetrack's vast, empty parking lots.

"I'll run around," Reyna said. "There *has* to be some way for us to get in."

"No time," Veil said, taking the gun from the waistband of his jeans. "Too many people saw us, and I don't want to be wandering around if a police car comes cruising into this lot."

Using rags from a trash can to muffle the pistol's report, Veil fired two shots at the lock on one of the gates; the bullets served only to jam the locking mechanism. He was successful at a second gate; the first bullet pierced the lock pins cleanly and forced them apart. Reyna opened the gate, closed it behind them, and they moved into the racetrack.

CHAPTER EIGHTEEN

The enormous clock on the wall over the bank of pay phones read eleven o'clock. A few of the trainers and jockeys who had arrived before dawn were still working their horses on the track, but the stands were empty—at least for the time being. There had been a few policemen wandering through the complex, but fewer than Veil had expected.

The phones were in the open, at the junction of a long concourse and an exit ramp. Hunched down behind a row of seats just behind the ramp, Veil scanned the area around him. Satisfied that there was no one around, he vaulted over a steel railing to the ramp, then hurried to the nearest phone. He dropped a quarter in the slot and dialed the number Walrus had given Reyna. The phone was answered in the middle of the first ring.

"Yeah."

"Walrus, we have a problem."

"Where are you?"

"Aqueduct. It looks pretty quiet around here at the

moment, but the police must be watching the neighbor-hood."

"Oh, you bet your ass they are. Besides the police, you've got what must be half the population of New York City wandering around Queens looking for the three of you. You'll have to wait until after dark."

"That's a long time to wait, Walrus. Toby's living on borrowed time. Is John there?"

"He's on another line talking to my documents people in Canada. You want me to get him?"

"No. There's nothing he could really tell me from there, anyway. I'm not a doctor, but I'm pretty sure that every hour counts with Toby."

"I hear what you're saying, Veil." There was a long pause, and then the mercenary on the other end of the line continued, "If you want, I'll bring a car over right now and take you out. What worries me is the possibility that a car going into an empty parking lot will attract attention; then we have to get the three of you and the idol out and into the car. If there are eyes on the place, we'll be fucked. If you can hold things together until tonight, at least it will be dark."

"We'll still have a problem, Walrus. They've got night racing here again."

"Shit. I thought they'd given up trying to compete with the Meadowlands."

"The city needs the tax revenues, so they decided to give it another shot. They refurbished the place and opened up for night racing about a month ago. They're getting good crowds."

There was a prolonged silence on the other end of the line, then, "Maybe the fact that the place will be open for business could work to our advantage. Horse players don't give a shit about anything but the tickets in their hands and what's happening on the track. The parking lot will be jammed with cars, and you should be able to move with the crowds. But you're there and I'm here; you have to make the decision."

There was no real decision to make, Veil thought. If they

191

were captured, Toby would die, anyway. "Tonight," he said.

"Okay. I'll leave John near a gate with the engine running, and I'll come in for you. Where will you be?"

"It'll be better if we stay with the crowds until it's time to split. Make it near the rail at the west end of the track."

"Nine-thirty?"

"Nine-thirty."

"How's the girl holding up?"

"She's all right."

"Tough cookie."

"Yeah. I hope to hell John thought to put a bottle of Scotch in that black bag of his."

"Would you believe he didn't?"

"But there's always the Walrus to think of these things, right?"

"Do sharks shit in the ocean? A quart of Chivas, gently filed between analgesics and antibiotics."

"See you later."

"Yup."

• • •

Veil and Reyna, with Toby propped up between them, stood near the outer restraining wall as the fourth race began. The K'ung, his bandaged head covered by one of the three hats Veil had taken from a maintenance equipment room, was conscious but leaning heavily on Reyna. Reyna stood with both arms wrapped around him, fingers tightly gripping his blue coveralls, trying to make it appear that they were lovers. Veil carried the Nal-toon, wrapped in a plastic trash bag.

As Walrus had suggested, no one in the crowd pressing around them paid the slightest bit of attention to anything but the details of their own special world, dominated by running horses and pari-mutuel tickets.

"Veil," Reyna whispered, "I'm afraid."

"We're almost home free."

"I'm still afraid. What you say is going to happen just seems too easy."

Veil glanced at Toby. The bushman's open eye was glassy, and he was bent forward with both hands pressed to his stomach. Sweat ran off his face in steady, glistening rivulets. Still, despite his obvious pain, Toby seemed to Veil strangely serene—as if the K'ung had given himself up totally to their care and was no longer concerned with what happened.

"You're just hooked on excitement and having to do things the hard way," Veil replied softly, reaching around Toby and gently squeezing Reyna's shoulder. "Don't worry. Walrus will walk us out of here to the car, and everything's going to be fine."

Reyna did not reply, and Veil glanced at his watch; it was nine twenty-five. He resisted the impulse to turn and try to see if Walrus was making his way down through the crowd toward them, for he did not want the people behind him to glimpse his face before it was necessary.

The roar of the crowd subsided at the finish of the race—only to be supplanted by a curious beating sound that came from somewhere in the darkness high above the racetrack. Veil cocked his head, listening intently.

"Holy shit."

"Veil, what's the matter?"

"Let's go," Veil said, gripping Toby's arm by the elbow and pulling the K'ung under the rail. "I do believe our ride is here."

"Wh—"

"Our chauffeur's decided on an alternate mode of transportation. Damn it, Reyna, *come!*"

The beating sound came closer, falling out of the sky just above the harsh glow cast by the floodlights circling the central oval. Two jockeys cooling out their mounts sharply reined in their horses at the sight of the three people crossing the dirt track in front of them; one horse bridled, throwing its rider.

A low murmur came from the crowd, quickly rose to an excited roar that had nothing to do with racehorses.

Veil and Reyna, dragging Toby between them, were already halfway to the center of the grass oval when the

Jet Ranger helicopter, its running lights out and its identification numbers masked, dropped into the brilliant sea of light, bounced once, then came to rest on the grass.

As had often happened to him in combat, Veil now experienced the strange sensation that he existed in a world apart from everything that was happening around him. Despite the din of the crowd and the beat of the helicopter blades, Veil had a peculiar sense of quiet inside his mind in which particular sounds were amplified—his own breathing, their muffled footsteps on the grass, Toby's hoarse, tortured gasps as he tried to run, stumbled, and was dragged forward.

And then they were at the helicopter. Walrus, a hulking man with massive, sloping shoulders and a face that was a map of scar tissue, was seated at the controls of the Jet Ranger, casually holding out a tumbler half filled with Scotch. A young man with smooth, handsome features and prematurely gray hair was leaning out of the open cargo bay, his hand extended. Dr. John Schneider grabbed Toby's hand and pulled him into the helicopter while Reyna jumped up and rolled inside.

Veil handed the Nal-toon to Schneider, then planted his palms on the metal edge and prepared to leap into the cargo bay.

Someone was tugging at his leg. Without turning, Veil swung his fist behind him. His knuckles hit bone, and the hands came off his leg. With Schneider pulling on his collar, Veil leapt into the cargo bay and grabbed the glass from Walrus's hand as the scar-faced man pulled back on the control stick and the craft rose into the air.

"Cheers," Veil said with a laugh as he braced himself against a strut and downed a Scotch.

"What was the order of finish in that last race?" Walrus asked as he banked to the left and just cleared the tops of the flags on the track's grandstand. "I couldn't see the board from up there."

"Sorry, I missed it too," Veil replied. "I was looking at my watch."

Walrus grunted, then turned his attention to the craft's

small radar screen, on which three blips had suddenly appeared. Reyna, who had been shrieking with exultant laughter and pounding the floor, abruptly sobered when she saw that Toby had passed out. John Schneider, who had been examining Toby's head wound, checked the K'ung's pulse, then quickly administered an injection.

"I think he'll be all right," Schneider announced calmly.

"Reyna," Veil said, "meet Dr. John Schneider, our on-board medico."

"Thank you so much, Doctor," Reyna said, tears springing to her eyes.

"My name's John," Schneider said easily, without looking up from Toby, "and you're quite welcome. Who could turn down a free trip to Africa?"

"Walrus," Veil said as he poured himself another drink, "you were always a showboat, but this is ridiculous."

"Yeah," Walrus replied absently as he continued to study the blips on the radar screen. "Sorry about the change of plan. I sent Raskolnikov out on the point a couple of hours ago, and he reported an inordinate number of policemen taking an inordinate interest in every car leaving the track. All things considered, an airlift seemed like the best idea. Raskolnikov couldn't come in and tell you, because we were afraid he'd be spotted."

"How the hell did you come up with a Jet Ranger in two hours?"

"Ah, my friend, you wound me. You don't think I make contingency plans?"

"Sorry I asked."

"Reyna?" Walrus said, reaching back with his right hand. "As you may have guessed, I'm the Walrus. Come up here and let me kiss the hand of a gutsy lady."

Reyna, helped by Veil, walked forward, grasped Walrus's hand in both of hers, and kissed it. "Walrus, what can I say? How can I ever thank you?"

"Listen, m'dear, if you knew what a grand time Kendry, Schneider, and I are having, you'd realize that you don't have to say anything. Incidentally, open the brown envelope under my seat. That's for Toby. I figured he might want a souvenir to show his buddies."

Reyna opened the envelope and giggled when she saw the *Tourist Guide to New York City*. She stepped forward to kiss Walrus's cheek, then tensed when she saw his face. "What's the matter?"

"Lie flat on the floor," Walrus said curtly. "Wrap your fingers around the ridges and hang on. John, is that bay door secure?"

"Roger."

Reyna dropped to the floor, braced herself by grabbing hold of Veil's forearm. "Walrus . . . ?"

Walrus banked ninety degrees to his left and dropped still lower. "Those are cop 'copters," he said, nodding toward the radar screen, "or maybe Coast Guard. Unlighted, unidentified aircraft flying through city airspace makes them nervous and cranky."

"Oh, God," Reyna said, squeezing Veil's leg. "What are we going to do?"

"Lose them, of course."

"*How?*"

"Not to worry," Walrus said as he banked right and the helicopter scudded over the roof of a high rise. A white smudge had appeared at the top of the radar screen; Walrus flipped a switch beneath the screen, switching to a different mode, and the smudge became dozens of small blips. "We'll cut across JFK. That's a radar jungle. They won't follow us through there."

"Why not?"

"Because they'd be crazy to," Schneider answered dryly from the rear of the bay where he was lying across Toby and the Nal-toon. "They know they'd be killed."

Reyna glanced up, saw that the radar screen was now aglow with what seemed hundreds of tiny lights. Still holding tightly to Veil, she eased herself up into a sitting position beside him just in time to see brightly lit buildings and runways flashing by beneath and on either side of them. Shouting voices crackled in the air, and

Walrus abruptly turned the radio off. A 747 emerged from the darkness ahead of them, slanted across, and landed no more than two hundred yards to their right.

"Reyna?" Veil said quietly.

"Huh?"

"Do you believe in happy endings?"

Reyna was staring wide-eyed, mouth open, at the frenzy of activity all around them. The helicopter swooped over a building Reyna recognized as the International Arrivals Building. "What . . . huh?"

"I asked if you believe in happy endings."

"*What?*"

"Reyna," Walrus said, "tell him he'll get his answer *after* I land this thing."

And then they were beyond the airport. The lights on the radarscope dimmed as Walrus switched back to a mode with a tighter focus. There was no one following them.

Thirteen minutes later Walrus brought the helicopter down in a remote, dark corner of Flushing Airport. A two-engine jet was tied down off to one side of the weed-covered field, and Walrus taxied to within a few yards of it. Veil was the first out, and he took Toby's unconscious body from Schneider. Schneider jumped down, took Toby from Veil, and carried the K'ung to the plane. He strapped Toby onto a cot, then started the plane's engines.

Walrus was already out and busy ripping tape from the helicopter's identification numbers. Reyna, the *Tourist Guide to New York City* clenched tightly in her fist, jumped down from the cargo bay and threw her arms around Veil.

"Yes!" Reyna shouted, kissing Veil hard on the mouth.

"Yes?"

"Yes, I do believe in happy endings!"

Then Walrus was standing beside them, his huge arms draped around their shoulders. "No time for chitchat, folks. You two want to come along? I'm betting the cops are really pissed, if you'll pardon the understatement, and I'm betting they have a pretty good idea who they're pissed at."

Veil and Reyna smiled at each other. "I don't think so,"

Veil said to Walrus. "What the police think and what they can prove are two different things. Don't forget to write."

"I'll call whenever I can and keep you posted on progress. Try to stay out of the can."

"Yeah."

Walrus took the *Tourist Guide* from Reyna, kissed her. "Raskolnikov is probably out cruising on the highway looking for you two," Walrus shouted over his shoulder as he ran toward the plane. "I'll be in touch!"

"Be safe, my friend," Veil said quietly.

Veil and Reyna stood with their arms around each other, staring into the empty sky, long after the plane's lights had disappeared. Then they turned and, hand in hand, walked toward the lights of the city.

CHAPTER NINETEEN

Veil dreams.

Vivid dreaming is his gift and affliction, the lash of memory and a guide to justice, a mystery and sometimes the key to mystery, prod to violence and maker of peace, an invitation to madness, and the fountainhead of his power as an artist.

Once again, for the last time, Veil is Toby.

He has never felt quite this way before. There is a lightness in his chest and inside his mind that is new, and he understands that these feelings are gifts from the Naltoon. Only as a small child did he ever laugh or cry, yet now he feels like laughing and crying at the same time; he does and is not ashamed. He suspects that these new feelings will stay with him for the rest of his life.

He is different now than when he left, Veil thinks. He is filled with love. He thinks of Reyna and the man-in-night with love.

He even thinks of the two silly, old missionaries with love; they had kissed him when he had come down with the two *Newyorkcities* in their flying machine, and he had kissed the missionaries back.

He had stripped off his *clothes* and sat stiffly in the back of the *Landrover*, Nal-toon and Reyna's *paper* in his lap, as they had set off across the desert. However, despite his eagerness to reach his people, he had insisted during the night that they stop and rest. While the missionaries slept, Veil had stood watch over them.

It is the first time Veil has ever really cared about anyone who was not K'ung.

But the missionaries had also been anxious to reach the camp, and they had only slept a short while. Now, with a luminous dawn glowing in the sky behind them, Veil smells a campfire. He asks the missionaries to stop, which they do. Once again he kisses both of them, then gets out.

He walks up a dune and stands looking down on his people who have heard the approaching *Landrover* and are waiting expectantly. They see him, rise to their feet. With the sun burning behind him, Veil lifts the Nal-toon and Reyna's *paper* over his head, draws air deep into the light place in his heart, and screams with joy and triumph before rolling away to another dream that is more than a dream.

"*Veil, come to me. Love me. Tango with me on the edge of time.*"

Electric-blue flight, Veil speeds toward love and promises to be kept.